Vorkosigan's
Game

Lois McMaster Bujold

Vorkosigan's Game

THE VOR GAME
BORDERS OF INFINITY

Contents

The Vor Game   1

Borders of Infinity   267

THE VOR GAME

For Mom.

*And with thanks to
Charles Marshall
for firsthand accounts
of arctic engineering, and
William Melgaard
for comments on war and wargames.*

A MATTER OF PRINCIPLE . . .

Metzov smiled, a gloss over rage, and, in a horribly cordial voice, confided to Miles, "You know Ensign, back on Old Earth, in the event of a mutiny you could always persuade the army to shoot the navy, or vice versa, when they could no longer discipline themselves."

"Mutiny!" said Miles, startled out of his resolve to speak only when spoken to. "I thought the issue was poison exposure."

"It *was*. Unfortunately, due to Bonn's mishandling, it's now a matter of principle." A muscle jumped in Metzov's jaw.

"Principle, sir, what principle? It's *waste disposal,*" Miles choked.

"It's a mass refusal to obey a direct order, Ensign." The sergeant lined the grubs up in a crossfire array around the stiff-standing techs, and barked an order. They aimed their weapons at the techs.

"Strip," Metzov ordered through set teeth. "When you are again ready to obey your orders," Metzov continued in a parade-pitched voice, "you may dress and go to work."

. . . . Fifteen naked men started to shiver violently as the dry snow whispered around their ankles. Fifteen bewildered faces began to look terrified and their eyes shifted toward the nerve-disruptors trained on them.

Metzov's eye fell on Miles. "Vorkosigan, you can either take up a weapon and be useful, or consider yourself dismissed."

When Miles made no move, the sergeant walked over and thrust a nerve disruptor into Miles's hand. *This isn't going to be a mutiny. It's going to be a massacre . . .*

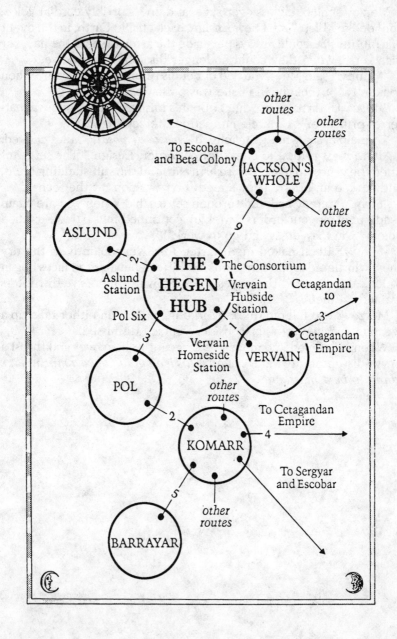

1

"Ship duty!" chortled the ensign four ahead of Miles in line. Glee lit his face as his eyes sped down his orders, the plastic flimsy rattling slightly in his hands. "I'm to be junior weaponry officer on the Imperial Cruiser *Commodore Vorhalas*. Reporting at once to Tanery Base Shuttleport for orbital transfer." At a pointed prod he removed himself with an unmilitary skip from the way of the next man in line, still hissing delight under his breath.

"Ensign Plause." The aging sergeant manning the desk managed to look bored and superior at the same time, holding the next packet up with deliberation between thumb and forefinger. How long had he been holding down this post at the Imperial Military Academy? Miles wondered. How many hundreds—thousands—of young officers had passed under his bland eye at this first supreme moment of their careers? Did they all start to look alike after a few years? The same fresh green uniforms. The same shiny blue plastic rectangles of shiny new-won rank armoring the high collars. The same hungry eyes, the go-to-hell graduates of the Imperial Services' most elite school with visions of military destiny dancing in their heads. *We don't just march on the future, we charge it.*

Plause stepped aside, touched his thumbprint to the lock-pad, and unzipped his envelope in turn.

"Well?" said Ivan Vorpatril, just ahead of Miles in line. "Don't keep us in suspense."

"Language school," said Plause, still reading.

Plause spoke all four of Barrayar's native languages perfectly already. "As student or instructor?" Miles inquired.

"Student."

"Ah, ha. It'll be galactic languages, then. Intelligence will be wanting you, after. You're bound off-planet for sure," said Miles.

"Not necessarily," said Plause. "They could just sit me in a concrete box somewhere, programming translating computers till I go blind." But hope gleamed in his eyes.

Miles charitably did not point out the major drawback of Intelligence, the fact that you ended up working for Chief of Imperial Security Simon Illyan, the man who remembered *everything*. But perhaps on Plause's level he would not encounter the acerb Illyan.

"Ensign Lobachik."

Lobachik was the second most painfully earnest man Miles had ever met; Miles was therefore unsurprised when Lobachik zipped open his envelope and choked, "ImpSec. The advanced course in Security and Counter-assassination."

"Ah, palace guard school," said Ivan with interest, kibbitzing over Lobachik's shoulder.

"That's quite an honor," Miles observed. "Illyan usually pulls his students from the twenty-year men with rows of medals."

"Maybe Emperor Gregor asked Illyan for someone nearer his own age," suggested Ivan, "to brighten the landscape. Those prune-faced fossils Illyan usually surrounds him with would give *me* depressive fits. Don't let on you have a sense of humor, Lubachik, I think it's an automatic disqualification."

Lubachik was in no danger of losing the posting if that were so, Miles reflected.

"Will I really meet the emperor?" Lubachik asked. He turned nervous eyes on Miles and Ivan.

"You'll probably get to watch him eat breakfast every day," said Ivan. "Poor sod." Did he mean Lubachik, or Gregor? Gregor, definitely.

"You Vorish types know him—what's he like?"

Miles cut in before the glint in Ivan's eye could materialize into some practical joke. "He's very straightforward. You'll get along fine."

Lubachik moved off, looking faintly reassured, rereading his flimsy.

"Ensign Vorpatril," intoned the sergeant. "Ensign Vorkosigan."

Tall Ivan collected his packet and Miles his, and they moved out of the way with their two comrades.

Ivan unzipped his envelope. "Ha. Imperial HQ in Vorbarr Sultana for me. I am to be, I'll have you know, aide-de-camp to Commodore Jollif, Operations." He bowed and turned the flimsy over. "Starting tomorrow, in fact."

"Ooh," said the ensign who'd drawn ship duty, still bouncing slightly. "Ivan gets to be a *secretary*. Just watch out if General Lamitz asks you to sit on his lap, I hear he—"

Ivan flipped him an amiable rude gesture. "Envy, sheer envy. I'll get to live like a civilian. Work seven to five, have my own apartment in town—no girls on that ship of yours up there, I might point out." Ivan's voice was even and cheerful, only his eyes failing to totally conceal his disappointment. Ivan had wanted ship duty too. They all did.

Miles did. *Ship duty. Eventually, command, like my father, his father, his, his . . .* A wish, a prayer, a dream . . . He hesitated for self-discipline, for fear, for a last lingering moment of high hope. He thumbed the lock pad and unzipped the envelope with deliberate precision. A single plastic flimsy, a handful of travel passes. . . . His deliberation lasted only for the brief moment it took him to absorb the short paragraph before his eyes. He stood frozen in disbelief, began reading again from the top.

"So what's up, coz?" Ivan glanced down over Miles's shoulder.

"Ivan," said Miles in a choked voice, "have I got a touch of amnesia, or did we indeed never have a meteorology course on our sciences track?"

"Five-space math, yes. Xenobotany, yes." Ivan absently scratched a remembered itch. "Geology and terrain evaluation, yes. Well, there was aviation weather, back in our first year."

"Yes, but . . ."

"So what have they done to you this time?" asked Plause, clearly prepared to offer congratulations or sympathy as indicated.

"I'm assigned as Chief Meteorology Officer, Lazkowski Base. Where the hell is Lazkowski Base? I've never even heard of it!"

The sergeant at the desk looked up with a sudden evil grin. "I have, sir," he offered. "It's on a place called Kyril Island, up near the arctic circle. Winter training base for infantry. The grubs call it Camp Permafrost."

"Infantry?" said Miles.

Ivan's brows rose, and he frowned down at Miles. "Infantry? You? That doesn't seem right."

"No, it doesn't," said Miles faintly. Cold consciousness of his physical handicaps washed over him.

Years of arcane medical tortures had almost managed to correct the severe deformities from which Miles had nearly died at birth. Almost. Curled like a frog in infancy, he now stood almost straight. Chalk-stick bones, friable as talc, now were almost strong. Wizened as an infant homunculus, he now stood almost four-foot-nine. It had been a trade-off toward the end, between the length of his bones and their strength, and his doctor still opined that the last six inches of height had been a mistake. Miles had finally broken his legs enough times to agree with him, but by then it was too late. But not a mutant, not . . . it scarcely mattered any more. If only they would let him place his strengths in the Emperor's service, he would make them forget his weaknesses. The deal was understood.

There had to be a thousand jobs in the Service to which his strange appearance and hidden fragility would make not one whit of difference. Like aide-de-camp, or Intelligence translator. Or even a ship's weaponry officer, monitoring his computers. It had been understood, surely it had been understood. But infantry? Someone was not playing fair. Or a mistake had been made. That wouldn't be a first. He hesitated a long moment, his fist tightening on the flimsy, then headed toward the door.

"Where are you going?" asked Ivan.

"To see Major Cecil."

Ivan exhaled through pursed lips. "Oh? Good luck."

Did the desk sergeant hide a small smile, bending his head to sort through the next stack of packets? "Ensign Draut," he called. The line moved up one more.

Major Cecil was leaning with one hip on his clerk's desk, consulting about something on the vid, as Miles entered his office and saluted.

Major Cecil glanced up at Miles and then at his chrono. "Ah, less than ten minutes. I win the bet." The major returned Miles's salute as the clerk, smiling sourly, pulled a small wad of currency from his pocket, peeled off a one-mark note, and handed it across wordlessly to his superior. The major's face was only amused on the surface; he nodded toward the door, and the clerk tore off the plastic flimsy his machine had just produced and exited the room.

Major Cecil was a man of about fifty, lean, even-tempered, watchful. Very watchful. Though he was not the titular head of Personnel, that administrative job belonging to a higher-ranking officer, Miles had spotted Cecil long ago as the final-decision man. Through Cecil's hands passed at the last every assignment for every Academy graduate. Miles had always found him an accessible man, the teacher and scholar in him ascendant over the officer. His wit was dry and rare, his dedication to his duty intense. Miles had always trusted him. Till now.

"Sir," he began. He held out his orders in a frustrated gesture. "What *is* this?"

Cecil's eyes were still bright with his private amusement as he pocketed the mark-note. "Are you asking me to read them to you, Vorkosigan?"

"Sir, I question—" Miles stopped, bit his tongue, began again. "I have a few questions about my assignment."

"Meteorology Officer, Lazkowski Base," Major Cecil recited.

"It's . . . not a mistake, then? I got the right packet?"

"If that's what that says, you did."

"Are . . . you aware the only meteorology course I had was aviation weather?"

"I am." The major wasn't giving away a thing.

Miles paused. Cecil's sending his clerk out was a clear signal that this discussion was to be frank. "Is this some kind of punishment?" *What have I ever done to you?*

"Why, Ensign," Cecil's voice was smooth, "it's a perfectly normal assignment. Were you expecting an extraordinary one? My job is to match personnel requests with available candidates. Every request must be filled by someone."

"Any tech school grad could have filled this one." With an effort, Miles kept the snarl out of his voice, uncurled his fingers. "Better. It doesn't require an Academy cadet."

"That's right," agreed the major.

"Why, then?" Miles burst out. His voice came out louder than he'd meant it to.

Cecil sighed, straightened. "Because I have noticed, Vorkosigan, watching you—and you know very well you were the most closely-watched cadet ever to pass through these halls barring Emperor Gregor himself—"

Miles nodded shortly.

"That despite your demonstrated brilliance in some areas, you have also demonstrated some chronic weaknesses. And I'm not referring to your physical problems, which everybody but me thought

were going to take you out before your first year was up—you've
been surprisingly sensible about those—"

Miles shrugged. "Pain hurts, sir. I don't court it."

"Very good. But your most insidious chronic problem is in the area
of . . . how shall I put this precisely . . . subordination. You argue
too much."

"No, I don't," Miles began indignantly, then shut his mouth.

Cecil flashed a grin. "Quite. Plus your rather irritating habit of
treating your superior officers as your, ah . . ." Cecil paused, apparently groping again for just the right word.

"Equals?" Miles hazarded.

"Cattle," Cecil corrected judiciously. "To be driven to your will.
You're a manipulator *par excellence*, Vorkosigan. I've been studying
you for three years now, and your group dynamics are fascinating.
Whether you were in charge or not, somehow it was always your idea
that ended up getting carried out."

"Have I been . . . that disrespectful, sir?" Miles's stomach felt
cold.

"On the contrary. Given your background, the marvel is that you
conceal that, ah, little arrogant streak so well. But Vorkosigan," Cecil
dropped at last into perfect seriousness, "the Imperial Academy is
not the whole of the Imperial Service. You've made your comrades
here appreciate you because here, brains are held at a premium. You
were picked first for any strategic team for the same reason you were
picked last for any purely physical contest—these young hotshots
wanted to win. All the time. Whatever it took."

"I can't be ordinary and survive, sir!"

Cecil tilted his head. "I agree. And yet, sometime, you must also
learn how to command ordinary men. And be commanded by them!

"This isn't a punishment, Vorkosigan, and it isn't my idea of a joke.
Upon my choices may depend not only our fledgling officers' lives,
but also those of the innocents I inflict 'em on. If I seriously miscalcu-
late, overmatch or mismatch a man with a job, I not only risk him, but
also those around him. Now, in six months (plus unscheduled over-
runs), the Imperial Orbital Shipyard is going to finish commissioning
the *Prince Serg*."

Miles's breath caught.

"You've got it," Cecil nodded. "The newest, fastest, deadliest thing
His Imperial Majesty has ever put into space. And with the longest
range. It will go out, and stay out, for longer periods than anything
we've ever had before. It follows that everyone on board will be in
each other's hair for longer unbroken periods than ever before. High

Command is actually paying some attention to the psych profiles on this one. For a change.

"Listen, now," Cecil leaned forward. So did Miles, reflexively. "If you can keep your nose clean for just six months on an isolated downside post—bluntly, if you prove you can handle Camp Permafrost, I'll allow as how you can handle anything the Service might throw at you. And I'll support your request for a transfer to the *Prince.* But if you screw up, there will be nothing I or anybody else can do for you. Sink or swim, Ensign."

Fly, thought Miles. *I want to fly.* "Sir . . . just how much of a pit is this place?"

"I wouldn't want to prejudice you, Ensign Vorkosigan," said Cecil piously.

And I love you too, sir. "But . . . infantry? My physical limits . . . won't prevent my serving if they're taken into account, but I can't pretend they're not there. Or I might as well jump off a wall, destroy myself immediately, and save everybody time." *Dammit, why did they let me occupy some of Barrayar's most expensive classroom space for three years if they meant to kill me outright?* "I'd always assumed they were going to be taken into account."

"Meteorology Officer is a technical speciality, Ensign," the major reassured him. "Nobody's going to try and drop a full field pack on you and smash you flat. I doubt there's an officer in the Service who would choose to explain your dead body to the Admiral." His voice cooled slightly. "Your saving grace. Mutant."

Cecil was without prejudice, merely testing. Always testing. Miles ducked his head. "As I may be, for the mutants who come after me."

"You've figured that out, have you?" Cecil's eye was suddenly speculative, faintly approving.

"Years ago, sir."

"Hm." Cecil smiled slightly, pushed himself off the desk, came forward and extended his hand. "Good luck, then. Lord Vorkosigan."

Miles shook it. "Thank you, sir." He shuffled through the stack of travel passes, ordering them.

"What's your first stop?" asked Cecil.

Testing again. Must be a bloody reflex. Miles answered unexpectedly. "The Academy archives."

"Ah!"

"For a downloading of the Service meteorology manual. And supplementary material."

"Very good. By the way, your predecessor in the post will be staying on a few weeks to complete your orientation."

"I'm extremely glad to hear that, sir," said Miles sincerely.

"We're not trying to make it impossible, Ensign."

Merely very difficult. "I'm glad to know that too, Sir." Miles's parting salute was almost subordinate.

Miles rode the last leg to Kyril Island in a big automated air-freight shuttle with a bored backup pilot and eighty tons of supplies. He spent most of the solitary journey frantically swotting up on weather. Since the flight schedule went rapidly awry due to hours-long delays at the last two loading stops, he found himself reassuringly further along in his studies than he'd expected by the time the air-shuttle rumbled to a halt at Lazkowski Base.

The cargo bay doors opened to let in watery light from a sun skulking along near the horizon. The high-summer breeze was about five degrees above freezing. The first soldiers Miles saw were a crew of black-coveralled men with loaders under the direction of a tired-looking corporal, who met the shuttle. No one appeared to be specially detailed to meet a new weather officer. Miles shrugged on his parka and approached them.

A couple of the black-clad men, watching him as he hopped down from the ramp, made remarks to each other in Barrayaran Greek, a minority dialect of Earth origin, thoroughly debased in the centuries of the Time of Isolation. Miles, weary from his journey and cued by the all-too-familiar expressions on their faces, made a snap decision to ignore whatever they had to say by simply pretending not to understand their language. Plause had told him often enough that his accent in Greek was execrable anyway.

"Look at that, will you? Is it a kid?"

"I knew they were sending us baby officers, but this is a new low."

"Hey, that's no kid. It's a damn dwarf of some sort. The midwife sure missed her stroke on that one. Look at it, it's a mutant!"

With an effort, Miles kept his eyes from turning toward the commentators. Increasingly confident of their privacy, their voices rose from whispers to ordinary tones.

"So what's it doing in uniform, ha?"

"Maybe it's our new mascot."

The old genetic fears were so subtly ingrained, so pervasive even now, you could get beaten to death by people who didn't even know quite why they hated you but simply got carried away in the excitement of a group feedback loop. Miles knew very well he had always been protected by his father's rank, but ugly things could happen to less socially fortunate odd ones. There had been a ghastly incident in the Old Town section of Vorbarr Sultana just two years ago, a destitute crippled man found castrated with a broken wine bottle by a gang of drunks. It was considered Progress that it was a scandal, and not simply taken for granted. A recent infanticide in the Vorkosigan's own district had cut even closer to the bone. Yes, rank, social or military, had its uses. Miles meant to acquire all he could before he was done.

Miles twitched his parka back so that his officer's collar tabs showed clearly. "Hello, Corporal. I have orders to report in to a Lieutenant Ahn, the base Meteorology Officer. Where can I find him?"

Miles waited a beat for his proper salute. It was slow in coming, the corporal was still goggling down at him. It dawned on him at last that Miles might really be an officer.

Belatedly, he saluted. "Excuse me, uh, what did you say, sir?"

Miles returned the salute blandly and repeated himself in level tones.

"Uh, Lieutenant Ahn, right. He usually hides out—that is, he's usually in his office. In the main administration building." The corporal swung his arm around to point toward a two-story pre-fab sticking up beyond a rank of half-buried warehouses at the edge of the tarmac, maybe a kilometer off. "You can't miss it, it's the tallest building on the base."

Also, Miles noted, well-marked by the assortment of comm equipment sticking out of the roof. Very good.

Now, should he turn his pack over to these goons and pray that it would follow him to his eventual destination, whatever it was? Or interrupt their work and commandeer a loader for transport? He had a brief vision of himself stuck up on the prow of the thing like a sailing ship's figurehead, being trundled toward his meeting with destiny along with half a ton of Underwear, Thermal, Long, 2 doz per unit crate, Style #6774932. He decided to shoulder his duffle and walk.

"Thank you, Corporal." He marched off in the indicated direction, too-conscious of his limp and the leg-braces concealed beneath his trouser legs taking up their share of the extra weight. The distance turned out to be farther than it looked, but he was careful not to pause or falter till he'd turned out of sight beyond the first warehouse-unit.

The base seemed nearly deserted. Of course. The bulk of its population was the infantry trainees who came and went in two batches per winter. Only the permanent crew was here now, and Miles bet most of them took their long leaves during this brief summer breathing space. Miles wheezed to a halt inside the Admin building without having passed another man.

The Directory and Map Display, according to a hand-lettered sign taped across its vid plate, was down. Miles wandered up the first and only hallway to his right, searching for an occupied office, any occupied office. Most doors were closed, but not locked, lights out. An office labeled Gen. Accounting held a man in black fatigues with red lieutenant's tabs on the collar, totally absorbed in his holovid which was displaying long columns of data. He was swearing under his breath.

"Meteorology Office. Where?" Miles called in the door.

"Two." The lieutenant pointed upward without turning around, crouched more tightly, and resumed swearing. Miles tiptoed away without disturbing him further.

He found it at last on the second floor, a closed door labeled in faded letters. He paused outside, set down his duffle, and folded his parka atop it. He checked himself over. Fourteen hours travel had rumpled his initial crispness. Still, he'd managed to keep his green undress uniform and half-boots free of foodstains, mud, and other unbecoming accretions. He flattened his cap and positioned it precisely in his belt. He'd crossed half a planet, half a lifetime, to achieve this moment. Three years training to a fever pitch of readiness lay behind him. Yet the Academy years had always had a faint air of pretense, We-are-only-practicing; now, at last, he was face to face with the real thing, his first real commanding officer. First impressions could be vital, especially in his case. He took a breath and knocked.

A gravelly muffled voice came through the door, words unrecognizable. Invitation? Miles opened it and strode in.

He had a glimpse of computer interfaces and vid displays gleaming and glowing along one wall. He rocked back at the heat that hit his face. The air within was blood-temperature. Except for the vid displays, the room was dim. At a movement to his left, Miles turned and saluted. "Ensign Miles Vorkosigan, reporting for duty as ordered, sir," he snapped out, looked up, and saw no one.

The movement had come from lower down. An unshaven man of about forty dressed only in his skivvies sat on the floor, his back against the comconsole desk. He smiled up at Miles, raised a bottle half-full of amber liquid, mumbled, "Salu', boy. Love ya," and fell slowly over.

Miles gazed down on him for a long, long, thoughtful moment.

The man began to snore.

* * *

After turning down the heat, shedding his tunic, and tossing a blanket over Lieutenant Ahn (for such he was), Miles took a contemplative half-hour and thoroughly examined his new domain. There was no doubt, he was going to require instruction in the office's operations. Besides the satellite real-time images, automated data seemed to be coming in from a dozen micro-climate survey rigs spotted around the island. If procedural manuals had ever existed, they weren't around now, not even on the computers. After an honorable hesitation, bemusedly studying the snoring, twitching form on the floor, Miles also took the opportunity to go through Ahn's desk and comconsole files.

Discovery of a few pertinent facts helped put the human spectacle before Miles into a more understandable perspective. Lieutenant Ahn, it seemed, was a twenty-year man within weeks of retirement. It had been a very, very long time since his last promotion. It had been an even longer time since his last transfer; he'd been Kyril Island's only weather officer for the last fifteen years.

This poor sod has been stuck on this iceberg since I was six years old, Miles calculated, and shuddered inwardly. Hard to tell, at this late date, if Ahn's drinking problem were cause or effect. Well, if he sobered up enough within the next day to show Miles how to go on, well and good. If he didn't, Miles could think of half a dozen ways, ranging from the cruel to the unusual, to bring him around whether he wanted to be conscious or not. If Ahn could just be made to disgorge a technical orientation, he could return to his coma till they came to roll him onto outgoing transport, for all Miles cared.

Ahn's fate decided, Miles donned his tunic, stowed his gear behind the desk, and went exploring. Somewhere in the chain of command there must be a conscious, sober and sane human being who was actually doing his job, or the place couldn't even function on this level. Or maybe it was run by corporals, who knew? In that case, Miles supposed, his next task must be to find and take control of the most effective corporal available.

In the downstairs foyer a human form approached Miles, silhouetted at first against the light from the front doors. Jogging in precise double time, the shape resolved into a tall, hard-bodied man in sweat pants, T-shirt, and running shoes. He had clearly just come in off some condition-maintaining five-kilometer run, with maybe a few hundred push-ups thrown in for dessert. Iron-grey hair, iron-hard eyes; he might have been a particularly dyspeptic drill sergeant. He stopped short to stare down at Miles, startlement compressing to a thin-lipped frown.

Miles stood with his legs slightly apart, threw back his head, and stared up with equal force. The man seemed totally oblivious to Miles's collar tabs. Exasperated, Miles snapped, "Are all the keepers on vacation, or is anybody actually running this bloody zoo?"

The man's eyes sparked, as if their iron had struck flint; they ignited a little warning light in Miles's brain, one mouthy moment too late. *Hi, there, sir!* cried the hysterical commenter in the back of Miles's mind, with a skip, bow, and flourish. *I'm your newest exhibit!* Miles suppressed the voice ruthlessly. There wasn't a trace of humor in any line of that seamed countenance looming over him.

With a cold flare of his carved nostril, the Base Commander glared down at Miles and growled, "*I* run it, Ensign."

Dense fog was rolling in off the distant, muttering sea by the time Miles finally found his way to his new quarters. The officers' barracks and all around it were plunged into a grey, frost-scummed obscurity. Miles decided it was an omen.

Oh, God, it was going to be a long winter.

2

Rather to Miles's surprise, when he arrived at Ahn's office next morning at an hour he guessed might represent beginning-of-shift, he found the lieutenant awake, sober, and in uniform. Not that the man looked precisely well; pasty-faced, breathing stertoriously, he sat huddled, staring slit-eyed at a computer-colorized weather vid. The holo zoomed and shifted dizzyingly at signals from the remote controller he clutched in one damp and trembling palm.

"Good morning, sir." Miles softened his voice out of mercy, and closed the door behind himself without slamming it.

"Ha?" Ahn looked up, and returned his salute automatically. "What the devil are you, ah . . . ensign?"

"I'm your replacement, sir. Didn't anyone tell you I was coming?"

"Oh, yes!" Ahn brightened right up. "Very good, come in." Miles, already in, smiled briefly instead. "I meant to meet you on the shuttlepad," Ahn went on. "You're early. But you seem to have found your way all right."

"I came in yesterday, sir."

"Oh. You should have reported in."

"I did, sir."

"Oh." Ahn squinted at Miles in worry. "You did?"

"You promised you'd give me a complete technical orientation to the office this morning, sir," Miles added, seizing the opportunity.

"Oh," Ahn blinked. "Good." The worried look faded slightly. "Well, ah . . ." Ahn rubbed his face, looking around. He confined his reaction to Miles's physical appearance to one covert glance, and, perhaps deciding they must have gotten the social duties of introduction out of the way yesterday, plunged at once into a description of the equipment lining the wall, in order from left to right.

Literally an introduction, all the computers had women's names. Except for a tendency to talk about his machines as though they were human, Ahn seemed coherent enough as he detailed his job, only drifting into randomness, then hung-over silence, when he accidentally strayed from the topic. Miles steered him gently back to weather with pertinent questions, and took notes. After a bewildered brownian trip around the room, Ahn rediscovered his office procedural disks at last, stuck to the undersides of their respective pieces of equipment. He made fresh coffee on a non-regulation brewer—named "Georgette"—parked discreetly in a corner cupboard, then took Miles up to the roof of the building to show him the data-collection center there.

Ahn went over the assorted meters, collectors, and samplers rather perfunctorily. His headache seemed to be growing worse with the morning's exertions. He leaned heavily on the corrosion-proof railing surrounding the automated station and squinted out at the distant horizon. Miles followed him around dutifully as he appeared to meditate deeply for a few minutes on each of the cardinal compass points. Or maybe that introspective look just meant he was getting ready to throw up.

It was pale and clear this morning, the sun up—the sun had been up since two hours after midnight, Miles reminded himself. They were just past the shortest nights of the year for this latitude. From this rare high vantage point, Miles gazed out with interest at Lazkowski Base and the flat landscape beyond.

Kyril Island was an egg-shaped lump about seventy kilometers wide and 160 kilometers long, and over five hundred kilometers from the next land of any description. *Lumpy and brown* described most of it, both base and island. The majority of the nearby buildings, including Miles's officers' barracks, were dug in, topped with native turf. Nobody had bothered with agricultural terraforming here. The island retained its original Barrayaran ecology, scarred by use and abuse. Long fat rolls of turf covered the barracks for the winter infantry trainees, now empty and silent. Muddy water-filled ruts fanned out to deserted marksmanship ranges, obstacle courses, and pocked live-ammo practice areas.

To the near-south, the leaden sea heaved, muting the sun's best efforts at sparkle. To the far north a grey line marked the border of the tundra at a chain of dead volcanic mountains.

Miles had taken his own officers' short course in winter maneuvers in the Black Escarpment, mountain country deep in Barrayar's second continent; plenty of snow, to be sure, and murderous terrain, but the air had been dry and crisp and stimulating. Even today, at high summer, the sea dampness seemed to creep up under his loose parka and gnaw his bones at every old break. Miles shrugged against it, without effect.

Ahn, still draped over the railing, glanced sideways at Miles at this movement. "So tell me, ah, ensign, are you any relation to *the* Vorkosigan? I wondered, when I saw the name on the orders the other day."

"My father," said Miles shortly.

"Good God." Ahn blinked and straightened, then sagged self-consciously back onto his elbows as before. "Good God," he repeated. He chewed his lip in fascination, dulled eyes briefly alight with honest curiosity. "What's he really like?"

What an impossible question, Miles thought in exasperation. Admiral Count Aral Vorkosigan. The colossus of Barrayaran history in this half-century. Conqueror of Komarr, hero of the ghastly retreat from Escobar. For sixteen years Lord Regent of Barrayar during Emperor Gregor's troubled minority; the Emperor's trusted Prime Minister in the four years since. Destroyer of Vordarian's Pretendership, engineer of the peculiar victory of the third Cetagandan war, unshaken tiger-rider of Barrayar's murderous internecine politics for the past two decades. *The* Vorkosigan.

I have seen him laugh in pure delight, standing on the dock at Vorkosigan Surleau and yelling instructions over the water, the morning I first sailed, dumped, and righted the skimmer by myself. I have seen him weep till his nose ran, more dead drunk than you were yesterday, Ahn, the night we got the word Major Duvallier was executed for espionage. I have seen him rage, so brick-red we feared for his heart, when reports came in fully detailing the stupidities that led to the last riots in Solstice. I have seen him wandering around Vorkosigan House at dawn in his underwear, yawning and prodding my sleepy mother into helping him find two matching socks. He's not like anything, Ahn. He's the original.

"He cares about Barrayar," Miles said aloud at last, as the silence grew awkward. "He's . . . a hard act to follow." *And, oh yes, his only child is a deformed mutant. That, too.*

"I should think so." Ahn blew out his breath in sympathy, or maybe it was nausea.

Miles decided he could tolerate Ahn's sympathy. There seemed no hint in it of the damned patronizing pity, nor, interestingly, of the more common repugnance. *It's because I'm his replacement here,* Miles decided. *I could have two heads and he'd still be overjoyed to meet me.*

"That what you're doing, following in the old man's footsteps?" said Ahn equably. And more dubiously, looking around, "Here?"

"I'm Vor," said Miles impatiently. "I serve. Or at any rate, I try to. Wherever I'm put. That was the deal."

Ahn shrugged bafflement, whether at Miles or at the vagaries of the Service that had sent him to Kyril Island Miles could not tell. "Well." He pushed himself up off the rail with a grunt. "No wah-wah warnings today."

"No what warnings?"

Ahn yawned, and tapped an array of figures—pulled out of thin air, as far as Miles could tell—into his report panel representing hour-by-hour predictions for today's weather. "Wah-wah. Didn't anybody tell you about the wah-wah?"

"No. . . ."

"They should have, first thing. Bloody dangerous, the wah-wah."

Miles began to wonder if Ahn was trying to diddle his head. Practical jokes could be a subtle enough form of victimization to penetrate even the defenses of rank, Miles had found. The honest hatred of a beating inflicted only physical pain.

Ahn leaned across the railing again to point. "You notice all those ropes, strung from door to door between buildings? That's for when the wah-wah comes up. You hang onto 'em to keep from being blown away. If you lose your grip, don't fling out your arms to try and stop yourself. I've seen more guys break their wrists that way. Go into a ball and roll."

"What the hell's a wah-wah? Sir."

"Big wind. Sudden. I've seen it go from dead calm to 160 kilometers, with a temperature drop from ten degrees cee above freezing to twenty below, in seven minutes. It can last from ten minutes to two days. They almost always blow up from the northwest, here, when conditions are right. The remote station on the coast gives us about a twenty-minute warning. We blow a siren. That means you must never let yourself get caught without your cold gear, or less than fifteen minutes away from a bunker. There's bunkers all around the grubs' practice fields out there." Ahn waved his arm in that direction. He seemed quite serious, even earnest. "You hear that siren, you run like hell for cover. The size you are, if you ever got picked up and blown into the sea, they'd never find you again."

"All right," said Miles, silently resolving to check out these alleged facts in the base's weather records at the first opportunity. He craned his neck for a look at Ahn's report panel. "Where did you read off those numbers from, that you just entered on there?"

Ahn stared at his report panel in surprise. "Well—they're the right figures."

"I wasn't questioning their accuracy," said Miles patiently. "I want to know how you came up with them. So I can do it tomorrow, while you're still here to correct me."

Ahn waved his free hand in an abortive, frustrated gesture. "Well. . . ."

"You're not just making them up, are you?" said Miles in suspicion.

"No!" said Ahn. "I hadn't thought about it, but . . . it's the way the day smells, I guess." He inhaled deeply, by way of demonstration.

Miles wrinkled his nose and sniffed experimentally. Cold, sea salt, shore slime, damp and mildew. Hot circuits in some of the blinking, twirling array of instruments beside him. The mean temperature, barometric pressure, and humidity of the present moment, let alone that of eighteen hours into the future, was not to be found in the olfactory information pressing on *his* nostrils. He jerked his thumb at the meteorological array. "Does this thing have any sort of a smell-o-meter to duplicate whatever it is you're doing?"

Ahn looked genuinely nonplussed, as if his internal system, whatever it was, had been dislocated by his sudden self-consciousness of it. "Sorry, Ensign Vorkosigan. We have the standard computerized projections, of course, but to tell you the truth I haven't used 'em in years. They're not accurate enough."

Miles stared at Ahn, and came to a horrid realization. Ahn wasn't lying, joking, or making this up. It was the fifteen years experience, gone subliminal, that was carrying out these subtle functions. A backlog of experience Miles could not duplicate. *Nor would I wish to,* he admitted to himself.

Later in the day, while explaining with perfect truth that he was orienting himself to the systems, Miles covertly checked out all of Ahn's startling assertions in the base meteorological archives. Ahn hadn't been kidding about the wah-wah. Worse, he hadn't been kidding about the computerized projections. The automated system produced local predictions of 86% accuracy, dropping to 73% at a week's long-range forecast. Ahn and his magical nose ran an accuracy of 96%, dropping to 94% at a week's range. *When Ahn leaves, this island is going to experience an 11 to 21% drop in forecast accuracy. They're going to notice.*

Weather Officer, Camp Permafrost, was clearly a more responsible position than Miles had at first realized. The weather here could be deadly.

And this guy is going to leave me alone on this island with six thousand armed men, and tell me to go sniff for wah-wahs?

On the fifth day, when Miles had just about decided that his first impression had been too harsh, Ahn relapsed. Miles waited an hour for Ahn and his nose to show up at the weather office to begin the day's duties. At last he pulled the routine readings from the substandard computerized system, entered them anyway, and went hunting.

He ran Ahn down at last still in his bunk, in his quarters in the officers' barracks, sodden and snoring, stinking of stale . . . fruit brandy? Miles shuddered. Shaking, prodding, and yelling in Ahn's ear failed to rouse him. He only burrowed deeper into his bedclothes and noxious miasma, moaning. Miles regretfully set aside visions of violence, and prepared to carry on by himself. He'd be on his own soon enough anyway.

He limp-marched off to the motor pool. Yesterday Ahn had taken him on a scheduled maintenance patrol of the five remote-sensor weather stations nearest the base. The outlying six had been planned for today. Routine travel around Kyril Island was accomplished in an all-terrain vehicle called a scat-cat, which had turned out to be almost as much fun to drive as an anti-grav sled. Scat-cats were ground-hugging iridescent teardrops that tore up the tundra, but were guaranteed not to blow away in the wah-wah winds. Base personnel, Miles had been given to understand, had grown extremely tired of picking lost anti-grav sleds out of the frigid sea.

The motor pool was another half-buried bunker like most of the rest of Lazkowski Base, only bigger. Miles routed out the corporal, what's his name, Olney, who'd signed Ahn and himself out the previous day. The tech who assisted him, driving the scat-cat up from the underground storage to the entrance, also looked faintly familiar. Tall, black fatigues, dark hair—that described eighty percent of the men on the base—it wasn't until he spoke that his heavy accent cued

Miles. He was one of the sotto voce commenters Miles had overheard on the shuttlepad. Miles schooled himself not to react.

Miles went over the vehicle's supply check-list carefully before signing for it, as Ahn had taught him. All scat-cats were required to carry a complete cold-survival kit at all times. Corporal Olney watched with faint contempt as Miles fumbled around finding everything. *All right, so I'm slow,* Miles thought irritably. *New and green. This is the only way I'm gonna get less new and green. Step by step.* He controlled his self-consciousness with an effort. Previous painful experience had taught him it was a most dangerous frame of mind. *Concentrate on the task, not the bloody audience. You've always had an audience. Probably always will.*

Miles spread out the map flimsy across the scat-cat's shell, and pointed out his projected itinerary to the corporal. Such a briefing was also safety SOP, according to Ahn. Olney grunted acknowledgment with a finely-tuned look of long-suffering boredom, palpable but just short of something Miles would be forced to notice.

The black-clad tech, Pattas, watching over Miles's uneven shoulder, pursed his lips and spoke. "Oh, Ensign *sir.*" Again, the emphasis fell just short of irony. "You going up to Station Nine?"

"Yes?"

"You might want to be sure and park your scat-cat, uh, out of the wind, in that hollow just below the station." A thick finger touched the map flimsy on an area marked in blue. "You'll see it. That way your scat-cat'll be sure of re-starting."

"The power pack in these engines is rated for space," said Miles. "How could it not re-start?"

Olney's eye lit, then went suddenly very neutral. "Yes, but in case of a sudden wah-wah, you wouldn't want it to blow away."

I'd blow away before it would. "I thought these scat-cats were heavy enough not to."

"Well, not *away,* but they have been known to blow *over,*" murmured Pattas.

"Oh. Well, thank you."

Corporal Olney coughed. Pattas waved cheerfully as Miles drove out.

Miles's chin jerked up in the old nervous tic. He took a deep breath and let his hackles settle, as he turned the scat-cat away from the base and headed cross-country. He powered up to a more satisfying speed, lashing through the brown bracken-like growth. He had been what, a year and a half? two years? at the Imperial Academy proving and re-proving his competence to every bloody man he crossed every time he did anything. The third year had perhaps spoiled him, he was out of practice. Was it going to be like this every time he took up a new post? Probably, he reflected bitterly, and powered up a bit more. But he'd known that would be part of the game when he'd demanded to play.

The weather was almost warm today, the pale sun almost bright, and Miles almost cheerful by the time he reached Station Six, on the eastern shore of the island. It was a pleasure to be alone for a change, just him and his job. No audience. Time to take his time and get it right. He worked carefully, checking power packs, emptying samplers, looking for signs of corrosion, damage, or loose connections in the equipment. And if he dropped a tool, there was no one about to make comments about spastic mutants. With the fading tension, he made fewer fumbles, and the tic vanished. He finished, stretched, and inhaled the damp air benignly, reveling in the unaccustomed luxury of solitude. He even took a few minutes to walk along the shoreline, and notice the intricacies of the small sea-life washed up there.

One of the samplers in Station Eight was damaged, a humidity-meter shattered. By the time he'd replaced it he realized his itinerary timetable had been overly optimistic. The sun was slanting down toward green twilight as he left Station Eight. By the time he reached Station Nine, in an area of mixed tundra and rocky outcrops near the northern shore, it was almost dark.

Station Ten, Miles reconfirmed by checking his map flimsy by penlight, was up in the volcanic mountains among the glaciers. Best not try to go hunting it in the dark. He would wait out the brief four hours till dawn. He reported his change-of-plan via comm-link to the base, 160 kilometers to the south. The man on duty did not sound terribly interested. Good.

With no watchers, Miles happily seized the opportunity to try out all that fascinating gear packed in the back of the scat-cat. Far better to practice now, when conditions were good, than in the middle of some later blizzard. The little two-man bubble shelter, when set up, seemed almost palatial for Miles's short and lonely splendor. In winter it was meant to be insulated with packed snow. He positioned it downwind of the scat-cat, parked in the recommended low spot a few hundred meters from the weather station, which was perched on a rocky outcrop.

Miles reflected on the relative weight of the shelter versus the scat-cat. A vid that Ahn had shown him of a typical wah-wah remained vivid in his mind. The portable latrine traveling sideways in the air at a hundred kilometers an hour had been particularly impressive. Ahn hadn't been able to tell him if there'd been anyone in it at the time the vid was shot. Miles took the added precaution of attaching the shelter to the scat-cat with a short chain. Satisfied, he crawled inside.

The equipment was first-rate. He hung a heat-tube from the roof and touched it on, and basked in its glow, sitting cross-legged. Rations were of the better grade. A pull tab heated a compartmentalized tray of stew with vegetables and rice. He mixed an acceptable fruit drink from the powder supplied. After eating and stowing the remains, he settled on a comfortable pad, shoved a book-disk into his viewer, and prepared to read away the short night.

He had been rather tense these last few weeks. These last few years. The book-disk, a Betan novel of manners which the Countess had recommended to him, had nothing whatsoever to do with Barrayar, military maneuvers, mutation, politics, or the weather. He didn't even notice what time he dozed off.

He woke with a start, blinking in the thick darkness gilded only with the faint copper light from the heat-tube. He felt he had slept long, yet the transparent sectors of the bubble-shelter were pitchy black. An unreasoning panic clogged his throat. Dammit, it didn't matter if he overslept, it wasn't like he would be late for an exam, here. He glanced at the glowing readout on his wrist chrono.

It ought to be broad daylight.

The flexible walls of the shelter were pressing inward. Not one-third of the original volume remained, and the floor was wrinkled. Miles shoved one finger against the thin cold plastic. It yielded slowly, like soft butter, and retained the dented impression. What the *hell . . . ?*

His head was pounding, his throat constricted; the air was stuffy and wet. It felt just like . . . like oxygen depletion and CO_2 excess in a space emergency. Here? The vertigo of his disorientation seemed to tilt the floor.

The floor *was* tilted, he realized indignantly, pulled deeply downward on one side, pinching one of his legs. He convulsed from its grip. Fighting the CO_2-induced panic, he lay back, trying to breathe slower and think faster.

I'm underground. Sunk in some kind of quicksand. Quick-mud. Had those two bloody bastards at the motor-pool set him up for this? He'd fallen for it, fallen right in it.

Slow-mud, maybe. The scat-cat hadn't settled noticeably in the time it had taken him to set up this shelter. Or he would have twigged to the trap. Of course, it had been dark. But if he'd been settling for hours, asleep . . .

Relax, he told himself frantically. The tundra surface, the free air, might be a mere ten centimeters overhead. Or ten meters . . . *relax!* He felt about the shelter for something to use as a probe. There'd been a long, telescoping, knife-bitted tube for sampling glacier ice. Packed in the scat-cat. Along with the comm link. Now located, Miles gauged by the angle of the floor, about two-and-a-half meters down and to the west of his present location. It was the scat-cat that was dragging him down. The bubble-shelter alone might well have floated in the tundra-camouflaged mud-pond. If he could detach the chain, might it rise? Not fast enough. His chest felt stuffed with cotton. He had to break through to air soon, or asphyxiate. Womb, tomb. Would his parents be there to watch, when he was found at last, when this grave was opened, scat-cat and shelter winched out of the bog by heavy hovercab . . . his body frozen rictus-mouthed in this hideous parody of an amniotic sac . . . *relax.*

He stood, and shoved upward against the heavy roof. His feet sank in the pulpy floor, but he was able to jerk loose one of the bubble's interior ribs, now bent in an overstrained curve. He almost passed out from the effort, in the thick air. He found the top edge of the shelter's opening, and slid his finger down the burr-catch just a few centimeters. Just enough for the pole to pass through. He'd feared the black mud would pour in, drowning him at once, but it only crept in extrusive blobs, to fall with oozing plops. The comparison was obvious and repulsive. *God, and I thought I'd been in deep shit before.*

He shoved the rib upward. It resisted, slipping in his sweating palms. Not ten centimeters. Not twenty. A meter, a meter and a third, and he was running short on probe. He paused, took a new grip, shoved again. Was the resistance lessening? Had he broken through to the surface? He heaved it back and forth, but the sucking slime sealed it still.

Maybe, maybe a little less than his own height between the top of the shelter and breath. Breath, death. How long to claw through it? How fast did a hole in this stuff close? His vision was darkening, and it wasn't because the light was going dim. He turned the heat tube off and stuck it in the front pocket of his jacket. The uncanny dark shook him with horror. Or perhaps it was the CO_2. Now or never.

On an impulse, he bent and loosened his boot-catches and belt buckle, then zipped open the burr by feel. He began to dig like a dog, heaving big globs of mud down into the little space left in the bubble.

He squeezed through the opening, braced himself, took his last breath, and pressed upward.

His chest was pulsing, his vision a red blur, when his head broke the surface. Air! He spat black muck and bracken bits, and blinked, trying with little success to clear his eyes and nose. He fought one hand up, then the other, and tried to pull himself up horizontal, flat like a frog. The cold confounded him. He could feel the muck closing around his legs, numbing like a witch's embrace. His toes pressed at full extension on the shelter's roof. It sank and he rose a centimeter. The last of the leverage he could get by pushing. Now he must pull. His hands closed over bracken. It gave. More. More. He was making a little progress, the cold air raking his grateful throat. The witch's grip tightened. He wriggled his legs, futilely, one last time. All right, now. Heave!

His legs slid out of his boots and pants, his hips sucked free, and he rolled away. He lay spread-eagled for maximum support on the treacherous surface, face up to the grey swirling sky. His uniform jacket and long underwear were soaked with slime, and he'd lost one thermal sock, as well as both boots and his trousers.

It was sleeting.

They found him hours later, curled around the dimming heat-tube, crammed into an eviscerated equipment bay in the automated weather station. His eye-sockets were hollow in his black-streaked face, his toes and ears white. His numb purple fingers jerked two wires across each other in a steady, hypnotic tattoo, the Service emergency code. To be read out in bursts of static in the barometric pressure meter in base's weather room. If and when anybody bothered to look at the suddenly-defective reading from this station, or noticed the pattern in the white noise.

His fingers kept twitching in this rhythm for minutes after they pulled him free of his little box. Ice cracked off the back of his uniform jacket as they tried to straighten his body. For a long time they could get no words from him at all, only a shivering hiss. Only his eyes burned.

3

Floating in the heat tank in the base infirmary, Miles considered crucifixion for the two saboteurs from the motor pool from several angles. Such as upside-down. Dangling over the sea at low altitude from an anti-grav sled. Better still, staked out face-up in a bog in a blizzard. . . . But by the time his body had warmed up, and the corpsman had pulled him out of the tank to dry, be reexamined, and eat a supervised meal, his head had cooled.

It hadn't been an assassination attempt. And therefore, not a matter he was compelled to turn over to Simon Illyan, dread Chief of Imperial Security and Miles's father's left-hand man. The vision of the sinister officers from ImpSec coming to take those two jokers away, far away, was lovely, but impractical, like shooting mice with a maser cannon. Anyway, where could ImpSec possibly send them that was worse than here?

They'd meant his scat-cat to bog, to be sure, while he serviced the weather station, and for Miles to have the embarrassment of calling the base for heavy equipment to pull it out. Embarrassing, not lethal. They could not have—no one could have—forseen Miles's inspired safety-conscious precaution with the chain, which was in the final analysis what had almost killed him. At most it was a matter for Service Security, bad enough, or for normal discipline.

He dangled his toes over the side of his bed, one of a row in the empty infirmary, and pushed the last of his food around on his tray. The corpsman wandered in, and glanced at the remains.

"You feeling all right now, sir?"

"Fine," said Miles morosely.

"You, uh, didn't finish your tray."

"I often don't. They always give me too much."

"Yeah, I guess you are pretty, um . . ." The corpsman made a note on his report panel, leaned over to examine Miles's ears, and bent to inspect his toes, rolling them between practiced fingers. "It doesn't look like you're going to lose any pieces, here. Lucky."

"Do you treat a lot of frostbite?" *Or am I the only idiot?* Present evidence would suggest it.

"Oh, once the grubs arrive, this place'll be crammed. Frostbite, pneumonia, broken bones, contusions, concussions . . . gets real lively, come winter. Wall-to-wall moro—unlucky trainees. And a few unlucky instructors, that they take down with 'em." The corpsman stood, and tapped a few more entries on his panel. "I'm afraid I have to mark you as recovered now, sir."

"Afraid?" Miles raised his brows inquiringly.

The corpsman straightened, in the unconscious posture of a man transmitting official bad news. That old they-told-me-to-say-this-it's-not-my-fault look. "You are ordered to report to the base commander's office as soon as I release you, sir."

Miles considered an immediate relapse. No. Better to get the messy parts over with. "Tell me, corpsman, has anyone else ever sunk a scat-cat?"

"Oh, sure. The grubs lose about five or six a season. Plus minor bog-downs. The engineers get real pissed about it. The commandant promised them next time he'd . . . ahem!" The corpsman lost his voice.

Wonderful, thought Miles. Just great. He could see it coming. It wasn't like he couldn't see it coming.

Miles dashed back to his quarters for a quick change of clothing, guessing a hospital robe might be inappropriate for the coming interview. He immediately found he had a minor quandry. His black fatigues seemed too relaxed, his dress greens too formal for office wear anywhere outside Imperial HQ at Vorbarr Sultana. His undress greens' trousers and half-boots were still at the bottom of the bog. He had only brought one of each uniform style with him; his spares, supposedly in transit, had not yet arrived.

He was hardly in a position to borrow from a neighbor. His uniforms were privately made to his own fit, at approximately four times the cost of Imperial issue. Part of that cost was for the effort of making them indistinguishable on the surface from the machine cut, while at the same time partially masking the oddities of his body through subtleties of hand-tailoring. He cursed under his breath, and shucked on his dress greens, complete with mirror-polished boots to the knees. At least the boots obviated the leg braces.

General Stanis Metzov, read the sign on the door, *Base Commander.* Miles had been assiduously avoiding the base commander ever since their first unfortunate encounter. This had not been hard to do in Ahn's company, despite the pared population of Kyril Island this month; Ahn avoided everybody. Miles now wished he'd tried harder to strike up conversations with brother officers in mess. Permitting himself to stay isolated, even to concentrate on his new tasks, had been a mistake. In five days of even the most random conversation, someone must surely have mentioned Kyril Island's voracious killer mud.

A corporal manning the comconsole in an antechamber ushered Miles through to the inner office. He must now try to work himself back round to Metzov's good side, assuming the general had one. Miles needed allies. General Metzov looked across his desk unsmiling as Miles saluted and stood waiting.

Today, the general was aggressively dressed in black fatigues. At Metzov's altitude in the hierarchy, this stylistic choice usually indicated a deliberate indentification with The Fighting Man. The only concession to his rank was their pressed neatness. His decorations were stripped down to a mere modest three, all high combat commendations. Pseudo-modest; pruned of the surrounding foliage, they leapt to the eye. Mentally, Miles applauded, even envied, the effect. Metzov looked his part, the combat commander, absolutely, unconsciously natural.

A fifty-fifty chance with the uniform, and I had to guess wrong, Miles fumed as Metzov's eye traveled sarcastically down, and back up, the subdued glitter of his dress greens. All right, so Metzov's eyebrows signaled, Miles now looked like some kind of Vorish headquarters twit. Not that that wasn't another familiar type. Miles decided to decline the roasting and cut Metzov's inspection short by forcing the opening. "Yes, sir?"

Metzov leaned back in his chair, lips twisting. "I see you found some pants, Ensign Vorkosigan. And, ah . . . riding boots, too. You know, there are no horses on this island."

None at Imperial Headquarters, either, Miles thought irritably. *I didn't design the damn boots.* His father had once suggested his staff officers must need them for riding hobbyhorses, high horses, and nightmares. Unable to think of a useful reply to the general's sally, Miles stood in dignified silence, chin lifted, parade rest. "Sir."

Metzov leaned forward, clasping his hands, abandoning his heavy humor, eyes gone hard again. "You lost a valuable, fully-equipped scat-cat as a result of leaving it parked in an area clearly marked as a Permafrost Inversion Zone. Don't they teach map-reading at the Imperial Academy any more, or is it to be all diplomacy in the New Service—how to drink tea with the ladies?"

Miles called up the map in his mind. He could see it clearly. "The blue areas were labelled P.I.Z. Those initials were not defined. Not in the key or anywhere."

"Then I take it you also failed to read your manual."

He'd been buried in manuals ever since he'd arrived. Weather office procedurals, equipment tech-specs . . . "Which one, sir?"

"Lazkowski Base Regulations."

Miles tried frantically to remember if he'd ever seen such a disk. "I . . . think Lieutenant Ahn may have given me a copy . . . night before last." Ahn had in fact dumped an entire carton of disks out on Miles's bed in officers' quarters. He was doing some preliminary packing, he'd said, and was willing Miles his library. Miles had read two weather disks before going to sleep that night. Ahn, clearly, had returned to his own cubicle to do a little preliminary celebrating. The next morning Miles had taken the scat-cat out. . . .

"And you haven't read it yet?"

"No, sir."

"Why not?"

I was set up, Miles's thought wailed. He could feel the highly-interested presence of Metzov's clerk, undismissed, standing witness by the door behind him. Making this a public, not a private, dressing-down. And if only he'd read the damn manual, would those two bastards from the motor pool even have been able to set him up? Will or nill, he was going to get down-checked for this one. "No excuse, sir."

"Well, Ensign, in Chapter Three of Lazkowski Base Regulations you will find a complete description of all the permafrost zones, together with the rules for avoiding them. You might look into it, when you can spare a little leisure from . . . drinking tea."

"Yes, sir." Miles's face was set like glass. The general had a right to skin him with a vibra-knife, if he chose—in private. The authority lent Miles by his uniform barely balanced the deformities that made him a target of Barrayar's historically-grounded, intense genetic prejudices. A public humiliation that sapped that authority before men he must also command came very close to an act of sabotage. Deliberate, or unconscious?

The general was only warming up. "The Service may still provide warehousing for excess Vor lordlings at Imperial Headquarters, but out here in the real world, where there's fighting to be done, we have no use for drones. Now, I fought my way up through the ranks. I saw casualties in Vordarian's Pretendership before you were born—"

I WAS a casualty in Vordarian's Pretendership before I was born, thought Miles, his irritation growing wilder. The soltoxin gas that had almost killed his pregnant mother and made Miles what he was, had been a purely military poison.

"—and I fought the Komarr Revolt. You infants who've come up in the past decade and more have no concept of combat. These long periods of unbroken peace weaken the Service. If they go on much longer, when a crisis comes there'll be no one left who's had any real practice in a crunch."

Miles's eyes crossed slightly, from internal pressure. *Then should His Imperial Majesty provide a war every five years, as a convenience for the advancement of his officers' careers?* His mind boggled slightly over the concept of "real practice." Had Miles maybe acquired his first clue why this superb-looking officer had washed up on Kyril Island?

Metzov was still expanding, self-stimulated. "In a real combat situation, a soldier's equipment is vital. It can be the difference between victory and defeat. A man who loses his equipment loses his effectiveness as a soldier. A man disarmed in a technological war might as well be a woman, useless! And you disarmed yourself!"

Miles wondered sourly if the general would then agree that a woman armed in a technological war might as well be a man . . . no, probably not. Not a Barrayaran of his generation.

Metzov's voice descended again, dropping from military philosophy to the immediately practical. Miles was relieved. "The usual punishment for a man bogging a scat-cat is to dig it out himself. By hand. I understand that won't be feasible, since the depth to which you sank yours is a new camp record. Nevertheless, you will report at 1400 to Lieutenant Bonn of Engineering, to assist him as he sees fit."

Well, that was certainly fair. And would probably be educational, too. Miles prayed this interview was winding down. *Dismissed, now?* But the general fell silent, squinty-eyed and thoughtful.

"For the damage you did to the weather station," Metzov began slowly, then sat up more decisively—his eyes, Miles could almost swear, lighting with a faint red glow, the corner of that seamed mouth twitching upward, "you will supervise basic-labor detail for one week. Four hours a day. That's in addition to your other duties. Report to Sergeant Neuve, in Maintenance, at 0500 daily."

A slight choked inhalation sounded from the corporal still standing behind Miles, which Miles could not interpret. Laughter? Horror?

But . . . *unjust!* And he would lose a significant fraction of the precious time remaining to decant technical expertise from Ahn. . . . "The damage I did to the weather station was not a stupid accident like the scat-cat, sir! It was necessary to my survival."

General Metzov fixed him with a very cold eye. "Make that six hours a day, Ensign Vorkosigan."

Miles spoke through his teeth, words jerked out as though by pliers. "Would you have preferred the interview you'd be having right now if I'd permitted myself to freeze, sir?"

Silence fell, very dead. Swelling, like a road-killed animal in the summer sun.

"You are dismissed, Ensign," General Metzov hissed at last. His eyes were glittering slits.

Miles saluted, about-faced, and marched, stiff as any ancient ramrod. Or board. Or corpse. His blood beat in his ears; his chin jerked upward. Past the corporal, who was standing at attention doing a fair imitation of a waxwork. Out the door, out the outer door. Alone at last in the Administration Building's lower corridor.

Miles cursed himself silently, then out loud. He really had to try to cultivate a more normal attitude toward senior officers. It was his bloody upbringing that lay at the root of the problem, he was sure. Too many years of tripping over herds of generals, admirals, and senior staff at Vorkosigan House, at lunch, dinner, all hours. Too much time sitting quiet as a mouse, cultivating invisibility, permitted to listen to their extremely blunt argument and debate on a hundred topics. He saw them as they saw each other, maybe. When a normal ensign looked at his commander, he ought to see a god-like being, not a, a . . . future subordinate. New ensigns were supposed to be a sub-human species anyway.

And yet . . . *What is it about this guy Metzov?* He'd met others of the type before, of assorted political stripes. Many of them were cheerful and effective soldiers, as long as they stayed out of politics. As a party, the military conservatives had been eclipsed ever since the bloody fall of the cabal of officers responsible for the disastrous

Escobar invasion, over two decades ago. But the danger of revolution from the far right, some would-be junta assembling to save the Emperor from his own government, remained quite real in Miles's father's mind, he knew.

So, was it some subtle political odor emanating from Metzov that had raised the hairs on the back of Miles's neck? Surely not. A man of real political subtlety would seek to use Miles, not abuse him. *Or are you just pissed because he stuck you on some humiliating garbage detail?* A man didn't have to be politically extreme to take a certain sadistic joy in sticking it to a representative of the Vor class. Could be Metzov had been diddled in the past himself by some arrogant Vor lord. Political, social, genetic . . . the possibilities were endless.

Miles shook the static from his head, and limped off to change to his black fatigues and locate Base Engineering. No help for it now, he was sunk deeper than his scat-cat. He'd simply have to avoid Metzov as much as possible for the next six months. Anything Ahn could do so well, Miles could surely do too.

Lieutenant Bonn prepared to probe for the scat-cat. The engineering lieutenant was a slight man, maybe twenty-eight or thirty years old, with a craggy face surfaced with pocked sallow skin, reddened by the climate. Calculating brown eyes, competent-looking hands, and a sardonic air which, Miles sensed, might be permanent and not merely directed at himself. Bonn and Miles squished about atop the bog, while two engineering techs in black insulated coveralls sat perched on their heavy hovercab, safely parked on a nearby rocky outcrop. The sun was pale, the endless wind cold and damp.

"Try about there, sir," Miles suggested, pointing, trying to estimate angles and distances in a place he had only seen at dusk. "I think you'll have to go down at least two meters."

Lieutenant Bonn gave him a joyless look, raised his long metal probe to the vertical, and shoved it into the bog. It jammed almost immediately. Miles frowned puzzlement. Surely the scat-cat couldn't have floated upward. . . .

Bonn, looking unexcited, leaned his weight into the rod and twisted. It began to grind downward.

"What did you run into?" Miles asked.

"Ice," Bonn grunted. " 'Bout three centimeters thick right now. We're standing on a layer of ice, underneath this surface crud, just like a frozen lake except it's frozen mud."

Miles stamped experimentally. Wet, but solid. Much as it had felt when he had camped on it.

Bonn, watching him, added, "The ice thickness varies with the weather. From a few centimeters to solid-to-the-bottom. Midwinter, you could park a freight shuttle on this bog. Come summer, it thins out. It can thaw from seeming-solid to liquid in a few hours, when the temperature is just right, and back again."

"I . . . think I found that out."

"Lean," ordered Bonn laconically, and Miles wrapped his hands around the rod and helped shove. He could feel the scrunch as it scraped past the ice layer. And if the temperature had dropped a little more, the night he'd sunk himself, and the mud re-frozen, would he have been able to punch up through the icy seal? He shuddered inwardly, and zipped his parka half-up, over his black fatigues.

"Cold?" said Bonn.

"Thinking."

"Good. Make it a habit." Bonn touched a control, and the rod's sonic probe beeped at a teeth-aching frequency. The readout displayed a bright teardrop shape a few meters over. "There it is." Bonn eyed the numbers on the readout. "It's really down in there, isn't it? I'd let you dig it out with a teaspoon, ensign, but I suppose winter would set in before you were done." He sighed, and stared down at Miles as though picturing the scene.

Miles could picture it too. "Yes, sir," he said carefully.

They pulled the probe back out. Cold mud slicked the surface under their gloved hands. Bonn marked the spot and waved to his techs. "Here, boys!" They waved back, hopped down off the hovercab, and swung within. Bonn and Miles scrambled well out of the way, onto the rocks toward the weather station.

The hovercab whined into the air and positioned itself over the bog. Its heavy-duty space-rated tractor beam punched downward. Mud, plant matter, and ice geysered out in all directions with a roar. In a couple of minutes, the beam had created an oozing crater, with a glimmering pearl at the bottom. The crater's sides began to slump inward at once, but the hovercab operator narrowed and reversed his beam, and the scat-cat rose, noisily sucking free from its matrix. The limp bubble shelter dangled repellently from its chain. The hovercab set its load down delicately in the rocky area, and landed beside it.

Bonn and Miles trooped over to view the sodden remains. "You weren't in that bubble-shelter, were you, ensign?" said Bonn, prodding it with his toe.

"Yes, sir, I was. Waiting for daylight. I . . . fell asleep."

"But you got out before it sank."

"Well, no. When I woke up, it was all the way under."

Bonn's crooked eyebrows rose. "How far?"

Miles's flat hand found the level of his chin.

Bonn looked startled. "How'd you get out of the suction?"

"With difficulty. And adrenalin, I think. I slipped out of my boots and pants. Which reminds me, may I take a minute and look for my boots, sir?"

Bonn waved a hand, and Miles trudged back out onto the bog, circling the ring of muck spewed from the tractor beam, keeping a safe distance from the now water-filling crater. He found one mud-coated boot, but not the other. Should he save it, on the off-chance he might have one leg amputated someday? It would probably be the wrong leg. He sighed, and climbed back up to Bonn.

Bonn frowned down at the ruined boot dangling from Miles's hand. "You could have been killed," he said in a tone of realization.

"Three times over. Smothered in the bubble shelter, trapped in the bog, or frozen waiting for rescue."

Bonn gave him a penetrating stare. "Really." He walked away from the deflated shelter, idly, as if seeking a wider view. Miles followed. When they were out of earshot of the techs, Bonn stopped and scanned the bog. Conversationally, he remarked, "I heard—unofficially—that a certain motor-pool tech named Pattas was bragging to one of his mates that he'd set you up for this. And you were too stupid to even realize you'd been had. That bragging could have been . . . not too bright, if you'd been killed."

"If I'd been killed, it wouldn't have mattered if he'd bragged or not," Miles shrugged. "What a Service investigation missed, I flat guarantee the Imperial Security investigation would have found."

"You knew you'd been set up?" Bonn studied the horizon.

"Yes."

"I'm surprised you didn't call Imperial Security in, then."

"Oh? Think about it, sir."

Bonn's gaze returned to Miles, as if taking inventory of his distasteful deformities. "You don't add up for me, Vorkosigan. Why did they let you in the Service?"

"Why d'you think?"

"Vor privilege."

"Got it in one."

"Then why are you here? Vor privilege gets sent to HQ."

"Vorbarr Sultana is lovely this time of year," said Miles agreeably.

And how was his cousin Ivan enjoying it right now? "But I want ship duty."

"And you couldn't arrange it?" said Bonn sceptically.

"I was told to earn it. That's why I'm here. To prove I can handle the Service. Or . . . not. Calling in a wolf pack from ImpSec within a week of my arrival to turn the base and everyone on it inside-out looking for assassination conspiracies—where, I judge, none exist— would not advance me toward my goal. No matter how entertaining it might be." Messy charges, his word against their two words—even if Miles had pushed it to a formal investigation, with fast-penta to prove him right, the ruckus could hurt him far more in the long run than his two tormentors. No. No revenge was worth the *Prince Serg.*

"The motor pool is in Engineering's chain of command. If Imperial Security fell on it, they'd also fall on me." Bonn's brown eyes glinted.

"You're welcome to fall on anyone you please, sir. But if you have unofficial ways of receiving information, it follows you must have unofficial ways of sending it, too. And after all, you've only my word for what happened." Miles hefted his useless single boot, and heaved it back into the bog.

Thoughtfully, Bonn watched it arc and splash down in a pool of brown melt-water. "A Vor lord's word?"

"Means nothing, in these degenerate days." Miles bared his teeth in a smile of sorts. "Ask anyone."

"Huh." Bonn shook his head, and started back toward the hover-cab.

Next morning Miles reported to the maintenance shed for the second half of the scat-cat retrieval job, cleaning all the mud-caked equipment. The sun was bright today, and had been up for hours, but Miles's body knew it was only 0500. An hour into his task he'd begun to warm up, feel better, and get into the rhythm of the thing.

At 0630, the deadpan Lieutenant Bonn arrived, and delivered two helpers unto Miles.

"Why, Corporal Olney. Tech Pattas. We meet again." Miles smiled with acid cheer. The pair exchanged an uneasy look. Miles kept his demeanor absolutely even.

He then kept everyone, starting with himself, moving briskly. The conversation seemed to automatically limit itself to brief, wary technicalities. By the time Miles had to knock off and go report to Lieutenant Ahn, the scat-cat and most of the gear had been restored to better condition that Miles had received it.

He wished his two helpers, now driven to near-twitchiness by uncertainty, an earnest good-day. Well, if they hadn't figured it out by now, they were hopeless. Miles wondered bitterly why he seemed to have so much better luck establishing rapport with bright men like Bonn. Cecil had been right, if Miles couldn't figure out how to command the dull as well, he'd never make it as a Service officer. Not at Camp Permafrost, anyway.

The following morning, the third of his official punishment seven, Miles presented himself to Sergeant Neuve. The sergeant in turn presented Miles with a scat-cat full of equipment, a disk of the related equipment manuals, and the schedule for drain and culvert maintenance for Lazkowski Base. Clearly, it was to be another learning experience. Miles wondered if General Metzov had selected this task personally. He rather thought so.

On the bright side, he had his two helpers back again. This particular civil engineering task had apparently never fallen on Olney or Pattas before either, so they had no edge of superior knowledge with which to trip Miles. They had to stop and read the manuals first too. Miles swotted procedures and directed operations with a good cheer that edged toward manic as his helpers became glummer.

There was, after all, a certain fascination to the clever drain-cleaning devices. And excitement. Flushing pipes with high pressure could produce some surprising effects. There were chemical compounds that had some quite military properties, such as the ability to dissolve anything instantly including human flesh. In the following three days Miles learned more about the infrastructure of Lazkowski Base than he'd ever imagined wanting to know. He'd even calculated the point where one well-placed charge could bring the entire system down, if he ever decided he wanted to destroy the place.

On the sixth day, Miles and his team were sent to clear a blocked culvert out by the grubs' practice fields. It was easy to spot. A silver sheet of water lapped the raised roadway on one side; on the other only a feeble trickle emerged to creep away down the bottom of a deep ditch.

Miles took a long telescoping pole from the back of their scat-cat, and probed down into the water's opaque surface. Nothing seemed to be blocking the flooded end of the culvert. Whatever it was must be jammed farther in. Joy. He handed the pole back to Pattas and wandered over to the other side of the road, and stared down into the ditch. The culvert, he noted, was something over half a meter in diameter. "Give me a light," he said to Olney.

He shucked his parka and tossed it into the scat-cat, and scrambled down into the ditch. He aimed his light into the aperture. The culvert evidently curved slightly; he couldn't see a damned thing. He sighed, considering the relative width of Olney's shoulders, Pattas's, and his own.

Could there be anything further from ship duty than this? The closest he'd come to anything of a sort was spelunking in the Dendarii Mountains. Earth and water, versus fire and air. He seemed to be building up a helluva supply of yin, the balancing yang to come had better be stupendous.

He gripped the light tighter, dropped to hands and knees, and shinnied into the drain.

The icy water soaked the trouser knees of his black fatigues. The effect was numbing. Water leaked around the top of one of his gloves. It felt like a knife blade on his wrist.

Miles meditated briefly on Olney and Pattas. They had developed a cool, reasonably efficient working relationship over the last few days, based, Miles had no illusions, on a fear of God instilled in the two men by Miles's good angel Lieutenant Bonn. How did Bonn accomplish that quiet authority, anyway? He had to figure that one out. Bonn was good at his job, for starters, but what else?

Miles scraped round the curve, shone his light on the clot, and recoiled, swearing. He paused a moment to regain control of his breath, examined the blockage more closely, and backed out.

He stood up in the bottom of the ditch, straightening his spine vertebra by creaking vertebra. Corporal Olney stuck his head over the road's railing, above. "What's in there, ensign?"

Miles grinned up at him, still catching his breath. "Pair of boots."

"That's all?" said Olney.

"Their owner is still wearing 'em."

4

Miles called the base surgeon on the scat-cat's comm link, urgently requesting his presence with forensic kit, body bag, and medical transport. Miles and his crew then blocked the upper end of the drain with a plastic signboard forcibly borrowed from the empty practice field beyond. Now so thoroughly wet and cold that it made no difference, Miles crawled back into the culvert to attach a rope to the anonymous booted ankles. When he emerged, the surgeon and his corpsman had arrived.

The surgeon, a big, balding man, peered dubiously into the drainpipe. "What could you see in there, ensign? What happened?"

"I can't see anything from this end but legs, sir," Miles reported. "He's got himself wedged in there but good. Drain crud up above him, I'd guess. We'll have to see what spills out with him."

"What the hell was he doing in there?" The surgeon scratched his freckled scalp.

Miles spread his hands. "Seems a peculiar way to commit suicide. Slow and chancy, as far as drowning yourself goes."

The surgeon raised his eyebrows in agreement. Miles and the surgeon had to lend their weight on the rope to Olney, Pattas, and the corpsman before the stiff form wedged in the culvert began to scrape free.

"He's *stuck,*" observed the corpsman, grunting. The body jerked out at last with a gush of dirty water. Pattas and Olney stared from a distance; Miles glued himself to the surgeon's shoulder. The corpse, dressed in sodden black fatigues, was waxy and blue. His collar tabs and the contents of his pockets identified him as a private from Supply. His body bore no obvious wounds, but for bruised shoulders and scraped hands.

The surgeon spoke clipped, negative preliminaries into his recorder. No broken bones, no nerve disruptor blisters. Preliminary hypothesis, death from drowning or hypothermia or both, within the last twelve hours. He flipped off his recorder and added over his shoulder, "I'll be able to tell for sure when we get him laid out back at the infirmary."

"Does this sort of thing happen often around here?" Miles inquired mildly.

The surgeon shot him a sour look. "I slab a few idiots every year. What d'you expect, when you put five thousand kids between the ages of eighteen and twenty together on an island and tell 'em to go play war? I admit, this one seems to have discovered a completely new method of slabbing himself. I guess you never see it all."

"You think he did it to himself, then?" True, it would be real tricky to kill a man and *then* stuff him in there.

The surgeon wandered over to the culvert and squatted, and stared into it. "So it would seem. Ah, would you take one more look in there, ensign, just in case?"

"Very well, sir." Miles hoped it was the last trip. He'd never have guessed drain cleaning would turn out to be so . . . thrilling. He slithered all the way under the road to the leaky board, checking every centimeter, but found only the dead man's dropped hand light. So. The private had evidently entered the pipe on purpose. With intent. What intent? Why go culvert-crawling in the middle of the night in the middle of a heavy rainstorm? Miles skinned back out and turned the light over to the surgeon.

Miles helped the corpsman and surgeon bag and load the body, then had Olney and Pattas raise the blocking board and return it to its original location. Brown water gushed, roaring, from the bottom end of the culvert and roiled away down the ditch. The surgeon paused with Miles, leaning on the road railing and watching the water level drop in the little lake.

"Think there might be another one at the bottom?" Miles inquired morbidly.

"This guy was the only one listed as missing on the morning report," the surgeon replied, "so probably not." He didn't look like he was willing to bet on it, though.

The only thing that did turn up, as the water level fell, was the private's soggy parka. He'd clearly tossed it over the railing before entering the culvert, from which it had fallen or blown into the water. The surgeon took it away with him.

"You're pretty cool about that," Pattas noted, as Miles turned away from the back of the medical transport and the surgeon and corpsman drove off.

Pattas was not that much older than Miles himself. "Haven't you ever had to handle a corpse?"

"No. You?"

"Yes."

"Where?"

Miles hesitated. Events of three years ago flickered through his memory. The brief months he'd been caught in desperate combat far from home, having accidently fallen in with a space mercenary force, was not a secret to be mentioned or even hinted at here. Regular Imperial troops despised mercenaries anyway, alive or dead. But the Tau Verde campaign had surely taught him the difference between "practice" and "real," between war and war games, and that death had subtler vectors than direct touch. "Before," said Miles dampingly. "Couple of times."

Pattas shrugged, veering off. "Well," he allowed grudgingly over his shoulder, "at least you're not afraid to get your hands dirty. Sir."

Miles's brows crooked, bemused. *No. That's not what I'm afraid of.*

Miles marked the drain "cleared" on his report panel, turned the scat-cat, their equipment, and a very subdued Olney and Pattas back in to Sergeant Neuve in Maintenance, and headed for the officers' barracks. He'd never wanted a hot shower more in his entire life.

He was squelching down the corridor toward his quarters when another officer stuck his head out a door. "Ah, Ensign Vorkosigan?"

"Yes?"

"You got a vid call a while ago. I encoded the return for you."

"Call?" Miles stopped. "Where from?"

"Vorbarr Sultana."

Miles felt a chill in his belly. Some emergency at home? "Thanks." He reversed direction, and beelined for the end of the corridor and the vidconsole booth that the officers on this level shared.

He slid damply into the seat and punched up the message. The number was not one he recognized. He entered it, and his charge code, and waited. It chimed several times, then the vidplate hissed to life. His cousin Ivan's handsome face materialized over it, and grinned at him.

"Ah, Miles. There you are."

"Ivan! Where the devil are you? What is this?"

"Oh, I'm at home. And that doesn't mean my mother's. I thought you might like to see my new flat."

Miles had the vague, disoriented sensation that he'd somehow tapped a line into some parallel universe, or alternate astral plane. Vorbarr Sultana, yes. He'd lived in the capital himself, in a previous incarnation. Eons ago.

Ivan lifted his vid pick-up, and aimed it around, dizzyingly. "It's fully furnished. I took over the lease from an Ops captain who was being transferred to Komarr. A real bargain. I just got moved in yesterday. Can you see the balcony?"

Miles could see the balcony, drenched in late afternoon sunlight the color of warm honey. The Vorbarr Sultana skyline rose like a fairytale city, swimming in the summer haze beyond. Scarlet flowers swarmed over the railing, so red in the level light they almost hurt his eyes. Miles felt like drooling into his shirtpocket, or bursting into tears. "Nice flowers," he choked.

"Yeah, m'girlfriend brought 'em."

"Girlfriend?" Ah yes, human beings had come in two sexes, once upon a time. One smelled much better than the other. Much. "Which one?"

"Tatya."

"Have I met her?" Miles struggled to remember.

"Naw, she's new."

Ivan stopped waving the vid pick-up around, and reappeared over the vid-plate. Miles's exacerbated senses settled slightly. "So how's the weather up there?" Ivan peered at him more closely. "Are you wet? What have you been doing?"

"Forensic . . . plumbing," Miles offered after a pause.

"What?" Ivan's brow wrinkled.

"Never mind." Miles sneezed. "Look, I'm glad to see a familiar face and all that," he was, actually—a painful strange gladness, "but I'm in the middle of my duty day, here."

"I got off-shift a couple of hours ago," Ivan remarked. "I'm taking Tatya out for dinner in a bit. You just caught me. So just tell me quick, how's life in the infantry?"

"Oh, great. Lazkowski Base is the real thing, y'know." Miles did not define what real thing. "Not a . . . warehouse for excess Vor lordlings like Imperial Headquarters."

"I do my job!" said Ivan, sounding slightly stung. "Actually, you'd like my job. We process information. It's amazing, all the stuff Ops accesses in a day's time. It's like being on top of the world. It would be just your speed."

"Funny. I've thought that Lazkowski Base would be just yours, Ivan. Suppose they could have got our orders reversed?"

Ivan tapped the side of his nose and sniggered. "I wouldn't tell." His humor sobered in a glint of real concern. "You, ah, take care of yourself up there, eh? You really don't look so good."

"I've had an unusual morning. If you'd sod off, I could go get a shower."

"Oh, right. Well, take care."

"Enjoy your dinner."

"Right-oh. 'Bye."

Voices from another universe. At that, Vorbarr Sultana was only a couple of hours away by sub-orbital flight. In theory. Miles was obscurely comforted, to be reminded that the whole planet hadn't shrunk to the lead-grey horizons of Kyril Island, even if his part of it seemed to have.

Miles found it difficult to concentrate on the weather, the rest of that day. Fortunately his superior didn't much notice. Since the scatcat sinking Ahn had tended to maintain a guilty, nervous silence around Miles except when directly prodded for specific information. When his duty-day ended Miles headed straight for the infirmary.

The surgeon was still working, or at least sitting, at his desk console when Miles poked his head around the doorframe. "Good evening, sir."

The surgeon glanced up. "Yes, ensign? What is it?"

Miles took this as sufficient invitation despite the unencouraging tone of voice, and slipped within. "I was wondering what you'd found out about that fellow we pulled from the culvert this morning."

The surgeon shrugged. "Not that much to find out. His ID checked. He died of drowning. All the physical and metabolic evidence— stress, hypothermia, the hematomas—are consistent with his being stuck in there for a bit less than half an hour before death. I've ruled it death by misadventure."

"Yes, but why?"

"Why?" The surgeon's eyebrows rose. "He slabbed himself, you'll have to ask him, eh?"

"Don't you want to find out?"

"To what purpose?"

"Well . . . to know, I guess. To be sure you're right."

The surgeon gave him a dry stare.

"I'm not questioning your medical findings, sir," Miles added hastily. "But it was just so damn weird. Aren't you curious?"

"Not any more," said the surgeon. "I'm satisfied it wasn't suicide or foul play, so whatever the details, it comes down to death from stupidity in the end, doesn't it?"

Miles wondered if that would have been the surgeon's final epitaph on him, if he'd sunk himself with the scat-cat. "I suppose so, sir."

Standing outside the infirmary afterward in the damp wind, Miles hesitated. The corpse, after all, was not Miles's personal property. Not a case of finders-keepers. He'd turned the situation over to the proper authority. It was out of his hands now. And yet . . .

There were still several hours of daylight left. Miles was having trouble sleeping anyway, in these almost-endless days. He returned to his quarters, pulled on sweat pants and shirt and running shoes, and went jogging.

The road was lonely, out by the empty practice fields. The sun crawled crabwise toward the horizon. Miles broke from a jog back to a walk, then to a slower walk. His leg-braces chafed, beneath his pants. One of these days very soon he would take the time to get the brittle long bones in his legs replaced with synthetics. At that, elective surgery might be a quasi-legitimate way to lever himself off Kyril Island, if things got too desperate before his six months were up. It seemed like cheating, though.

He looked around, trying to imagine his present surroundings in the dark and heavy rain. If he had been the private, slogging along this road about midnight, what would he have seen? What could possibly have attracted the man's attention to the ditch? Why the hell had he come out here in the middle of the night in the first place? This road wasn't on the way to anything but an obstacle course and a firing range.

There was the ditch . . . no, his ditch was the next one, a little farther on. Four culverts pierced the raised roadway along this half-kilometer straight stretch. Miles found the correct ditch and leaned on the railing, staring down at the now-sluggish trickle of drain water. There was nothing attractive about it now, that was certain. Why, why, why . . . ?

Miles sloped along up the high side of the road, examining the road surface, the railing, the sodden brown bracken beyond. He came to the curve and turned back, studying the opposite side. He arrived back at the first ditch, on the baseward end of the straight stretch, without discovering any view of charm or interest.

Miles perched on the railing and meditated. All right, time to try a little logic. What overwhelming emotion had led the private to wedge himself in the drain, despite the obvious danger? Rage? What had he been pursuing? Fear? What could have been pursuing him? Error? Miles knew all about error. What if the man had picked the wrong culvert . . . ?

Impulsively, Miles slithered down into the first ditch. Either the man had been methodically working his way through all the culverts —if so, had he been working from the base out, or from the practice fields back?—or else he had missed his intended target in the dark and rain and got into the wrong one. Miles would give them all a crawl-through if he had to, but he preferred to be right the first time. Even if there wasn't anybody watching. This culvert was slightly wider in diameter than the second, lethal one. Miles pulled his hand light from his belt, ducked within, and began examining it centimeter by centimeter.

"Ah," he breathed in satisfaction, midway beneath the road. There was his prize, stuck to the upper side of the culvert's arc with sagging tape. A package, wrapped in waterproof plastic. How *interesting*. He slithered out and sat in the mouth of the culvert, careless of the damp but carefully out of view from the road above.

He placed the packet on his lap and studied it with pleasurable anticipation, as if it had been a birthday present. Could it be drugs, contraband, classified documents, criminal cash? Personally, Miles hoped for classified documents, though it was hard to imagine anyone classifying anything on Kyril Island except maybe the efficiency reports. Drugs would be all right, but a spy ring would be just wonderful. He'd be a Security hero—his mind raced ahead, already plotting the next move in his covert investigation. Following the dead man's trail through subtle clues to some ringleader, who knew how high up? The dramatic arrests, maybe a commendation from Simon Illyan himself. . . . The package was lumpy, but crackled slightly— plastic flimsies?

Heart hammering, he eased it open—and slumped in stunned disappointment. A pained breath, half-laugh, half-moan, puffed from his lips.

Pastries. A couple of dozen lisettes, a kind of miniature popover glazed and stuffed with candied fruit, made, traditionally, for the midsummer day celebration. Month and a half old stale pastries. What a cause to die for. . . .

Miles's imagination, fueled by knowledge of barracks life, sketched in the rest readily enough. The private had received this package from some sweetheart/mother/sister, and sought to protect it from his ravenous mates, who would have wolfed it all down in seconds. Perhaps the man, starved for home, had been rationing them out to himself morsel by morsel in a lingering masochistic ritual, pleasure and pain mixed with each bite. Or maybe he'd just been saving them for some special occasion.

Then came the two days of unusual heavy rain, and the man had begun to fear for his secret treasure's, ah, liquidity margin. He'd come out to rescue his cache, missed the first ditch in the dark, gone at the second in desperate determination as the waters rose, realized his mistake too late. . . .

Sad. A little sickening. But not *useful*. Miles sighed, and bundled the lisettes back up, and trotted off with the package under his arm, back to the base to turn it over to the surgeon.

The surgeon's only comment, when Miles caught up with him and explained his findings, was "Yep. Death from stupidity, all right." Absently he bit into a lisette and sniffed.

Miles's time on maintenance detail ended the next day without his finding anything in the sewers of greater interest than the drowned man. It was probably just as well. The following day Ahn's office corporal arrived back from his long leave. Miles discovered that the corporal, who'd been working the weather office for some two years, was a ready reservoir of the greater part of the information Miles had spent the last two weeks busting his brains to learn. He didn't have Ahn's nose, though.

Ahn actually left Camp Permafrost sober, walking up the transport's ramp under his own power. Miles went to the shuttle pad to see him off, not certain if he was glad or sorry to see the weatherman go. Ahn looked happy, though, his lugubrious face almost illuminated.

"So where are you headed, once you turn in your uniforms?" Miles asked him.

"The equator."

"Ah? Where on the equator?"

"*Anywhere* on the equator," Ahn replied with fervor.

Miles trusted he'd at least pick a spot with a suitable land mass under it.

Ahn hesitated on the ramp, looking down at Miles. "Watch out for Metzov," he advised at last.

This warning seemed remarkably late, not to mention maddeningly vague. Miles gave Ahn an exasperated look, up from under his raised eyebrows. "I doubt I'll be much featured on his social calendar."

Ahn shifted uncomfortably. "That's not what I meant."

"What do you mean?"

"Well . . . I don't know. I once saw . . ."

"What?"

Ahn shook his head. "Nothing. It was a long time ago. A lot of crazy things were happening, at the height of the Komarr revolt. But it's better that you should stay out of his way."

"I've had to deal with old martinets before."

"Oh, he's not exactly a martinet. But he's got a streak of . . . he can be a funny kind of dangerous. Don't ever really threaten him, huh?"

"Me, threaten Metzov?" Miles's face screwed up in bafflement. Maybe Ahn wasn't as sober as he smelled after all. "Come on, he can't be that bad, or they'd never put him in charge of trainees."

"He doesn't command the grubs. They have their own hierarchy comes in with 'em—the instructors report to their own commander. Metzov's just in charge of the base's permanent physical plant. You're a pushy little sod, Vorkosigan. Just don't . . . ever push him to the edge, or you'll be sorry. And that's all I'm going to say." Ahn shut his mouth determinedly, and headed up the ramp.

I'm already sorry, Miles thought of calling after him. Well, his punishment week was over now. Perhaps Metzov had meant the labor detail to humiliate Miles, but actually it had been quite interesting. Sinking his scat-cat, now, that had been humiliating. *That* he had done to himself. Miles waved one last time to Ahn as he disappeared into the transport shuttle, shrugged, and headed back across the tarmac toward the now-familiar admin building.

It took a full couple of minutes, after Miles's corporal had left the weather office for lunch, for Miles to yield to the temptation to scratch the itch Ahn had planted in his mind, and punch up Metzov's public record on the comconsole. The mere listing of the base commander's dates, assignments, and promotions was not terribly informative, though a little knowledge of history filled in between the lines.

Metzov had entered the Service some thirty-five years ago. His most rapid promotions had occurred, not surprisingly, during the conquest of the planet Komarr about twenty-five years ago. The wormhole-rich Komarr system was Barrayar's sole gate to the greater galactic wormhole route nexus. Komarr had proved its immense strategic importance to Barrayar earlier in the century, when its ruling oligarchy had accepted a bribe to let a Cetagandan invasion fleet pass through its wormholes and descend on Barrayar. Throwing the Cetagandans back out again had consumed a Barrayaran generation. Barrayar had turned its bloody lesson around in Miles's father's day. As an unavoidable side effect of securing Komarr's gates, Barrayar had been transformed from backwater cul-de-sac to a minor but significant galactic power, and was still wrestling with the consequences.

Metzov had somehow managed to end up on the correct side during Vordarian's Pretendership, a purely Barrayaran attempt to wrest power from then-five-year-old Emperor Gregor and his Regent, two decades past—picking the wrong side in that civil affray would have been Miles's first guess why such an apparently competent officer had ended up marking out his later years on ice on Kyril Island. But the dead halt to Metzov's career seemed to come during the Komarr Revolt, some sixteen years ago now. No hint in this file as to why, but for a cross-reference to another file. An Imperial Security code, Miles recognized. Dead end there.

Or maybe not. Lips compressed thoughtfully, Miles punched through another code on his comconsole.

"Operations, Commodore Jollif's office," Ivan began formally as his face materialized over the comconsole vid plate, then, "Oh, hello, Miles. What's up?"

"I'm doing a little research. Thought you might help me out."

"I should have known you wouldn't call me at HQ just to be sociable. So what d'you want?"

"Ah . . . do you have the office to yourself, just at present?"

"Yeah, the old man's stuck in committee. Nice little flap—a Barrayaran-registered freighter got itself impounded in the Hegen Hub—at Vervain Station—for suspicion of espionage."

"Can we get at it? Threaten rescue?"

"Not past Pol. No Barrayaran military vessels may jump through their wormholes, period."

"I thought we were sort of friends with Pol."

"Sort of. But the Vervani have been threatening to break off diplomatic relations with Pol, so the Polians are being extra-cautious. Funny thing about it, the freighter in question isn't even one of our real agents. Seems to be a completely manufactured accusation."

Wormhole route politics. Jumpship tactics. Just the sort of challenge his Imperial Academy courses had trained Miles to meet. Furthermore, it was probably warm on those spaceships and space stations. Miles sighed envy.

Ivan's eyes narrowed in belated suspicion. "Why do you ask if I'm alone?"

"I want you to pull a file for me. Ancient history, not current events," Miles reassured him, and reeled off the code-string.

"Ah." Ivan's hand started to tap it out, then stopped. "Are you crazy? That's an Imperial Security file. No can do!"

"Of course you can, you're right there, aren't you?"

Ivan shook his head smugly. "Not any more. The whole ImpSec file system's been made super-secure. You can't transfer data out of it except through a coded filter-cable, which you must physically attach. Which I would have to sign for. Which I would have to explain why I wanted it and produce authorization. You got an authorization for this? Ha. I thought not."

Miles frowned in frustration. "Surely you can call it up on the internal system."

"On the internal system, yes. What I can't do is connect the internal system to any external system for a data dump. So you're out of luck."

"You got an internal system comconsole in that office?"

"Sure."

"So," said Miles impatiently, "call up the file, turn your desk around, and let the two vids talk to each other. You can do that, can't you?"

Ivan scratched his head. "Would that work?"

"Try it!" Miles drummed his fingers while Ivan dragged his desk around and fiddled with focus. The signal was degraded but readable. "There, I thought so. Scroll it up for me, would you?"

Fascinating, utterly fascinating. The file was a collection of secret reports from an ImpSec investigation into the mysterious death of a prisoner in Metzov's charge, a Komarran rebel who had killed his guard and himself been killed while attempting to escape. When ImpSec had demanded the Komarran's body for an autopsy, Metzov had turned over cremated ashes and an apology; if only he had been told a few hours earlier the body was wanted, etc. The investigating officer hinted at charges of illegal torture—perhaps in revenge for the death of the guard?—but was unable to amass enough evidence to obtain authorization to fast-penta the Barrayaran witnesses, including a certain Tech-ensign Ahn. The investigating officer had lodged a formal protest of his superior officer's decision to close the case, and there it ended. Apparently. If there was any more to the story it existed only in Simon Illyan's remarkable head, a secret file Miles was not about to attempt to access. And yet Metzov's career had stopped, literally, cold.

"Miles," Ivan interrupted for the fourth time, "I really don't think we should be doing this. This is slit-your-throat-before-reading stuff, here."

"If we shouldn't do it, we shouldn't be *able* to do it. You'd still have to have the cable for flash-downloading. No real spy would be dumb enough to sit there inside Imperial HQ by the hour and scroll stuff through by hand, waiting to be caught and shot."

"That does it." Ivan killed the Security file with a swat of his hand. The vid image wavered wildly as Ivan dragged his desk back around, followed by scrubbing noises as he frantically rubbed out the tracks in his carpet with his boot. "I didn't do this, you hear?"

"I didn't mean you. *We're* not spies." Miles subsided glumly. "Still . . . I suppose somebody ought to tell Illyan about the little hole they overlooked in his Security arrangements."

"Not me!"

"Why not you? Put it in as a brilliant theoretical suggestion. Maybe you'll earn a commendation. Don't tell 'em we actually did it, of course. Or maybe we were just testing your theory, eh?"

"You," said Ivan severely, "are career-poison. Never darken my vid-plate again. Except at home, of course."

Miles grinned, and permitted his cousin to escape. He sat awhile in the office, watching the colorful weather holos flicker and change, and thinking about his base commander, and the kinds of accidents that could happen to defiant prisoners.

Well, it had all been very long ago. Metzov himself would probably be retiring in another five years, with his status as a double-twenty-years-man and a pension, to merge into the population of unpleasant old men. Not so much a problem to be solved as to be outlived, at least by Miles. His ultimate purpose at Lazkowski Base, Miles reminded himself, was to escape Lazkowski Base, silently as smoke. Metzov would be left behind in time.

In the next weeks Miles settled into a tolerable routine. For one thing, the grubs arrived. All five thousand of them. Miles's status rose on their shoulders, to that of almost-human. Lazkowski Base suffered its first real snow of the season, as the days shortened, plus a mild wah-wah lasting half a day, both of which Miles managed to predict accurately in advance.

Even more happily, Miles was completely displaced as the most famous idiot on the island (an unwelcome notoriety earned by the scat-cat sinking) by a group of grubs who managed one night to set their barracks on fire while lighting fart-flares. Miles's strategic suggestion at the officers' fire-safety meeting next day that they tackle the problem with a logistical assault on the enemy's fuel supply, i.e., eliminate red-bean stew from the menu, was shot down with one icy glower from General Metzov. Though in the hallway later, an earnest captain from Ordnance stopped Miles to thank him for trying.

So much for the glamour of the Imperial Service. Miles took to spending long hours alone in the weather office, studying chaos theory, his readouts, and the walls. Three months down, three to go. It was getting darker.

5

Miles was out of bed and half dressed before it penetrated his sleep-stunned brain that the galvanizing klaxon was not the wah-wah warning. He paused with a boot in his hand. Not fire or enemy attack, either. Not his department, then, whatever it was. The rhythmic blatting stopped. They were right, silence was golden.

He checked the glowing digital clock. It claimed midevening. He'd only been asleep about two hours, having fallen into bed exhausted after a long trip up-island in a snow storm to repair wind damage to Weather Station Eleven. The comm link by his bed was not blinking its red call light to inform him of any surprise duties he must carry out. He could go back to bed.

Silence was *baffling.*

He pulled on the second boot and stuck his head out his door. A couple of other officers had done the same, and were speculating to each other on the cause of the alarm. Lieutenant Bonn emerged from his quarters and strode down the hall, jerking on his parka. His face looked strained, half-worry, half-annoyance.

Miles grabbed his own parka and galloped after him. "You need a hand, Lieutenant?"

Bonn glanced down at him, and pursed his lips. "I might," he allowed.

Miles fell in beside him, secretly pleased by Bonn's implicit judgment that he might in fact be useful. "So what's up?"

"Some sort of accident in a toxic stores bunker. If it's the one I think, we could have a real problem."

They exited the double-doored heat-retaining vestibule from the officers' quarters into a night gone crystal cold. Fine snow squeaked under Miles's boots and swept along the ground in a faint east wind. The brightest stars overhead held their own against the base's lights. The two men slid into Bonn's scat-cat, their breath smoking until the canopy-defrost cut in. Bonn headed west out of the base at high acceleration.

A few kilometers past the last practice fields, a row of turf-topped barrows hunched in the snow. A cluster of vehicles was parked at the end of one bunker—a couple of scat-cats, including the one belonging to the base fire marshall, and medical transport. Hand-lights moved among them. Bonn slewed in and pulled up, and popped his door. Miles followed him, crunching rapidly across the packed ice.

The surgeon was directing a pair of corpsmen, who were loading a foil-blanketed shape and a second coverall-clad soldier who shivered and coughed onto the med transport. "All of you, put everything you're wearing into the destruct bin when you hit the door," he called after them. "Blankets, bedding, splints, everything. Full decontamination showers for you all before you even start to worry about that broken leg of his. The pain-killer will hold him through it, and if it doesn't, ignore him and keep scrubbing. I'll be right behind you." The surgeon shuddered, turning away, whistling dismay through his teeth.

Bonn headed for the bunker door. "Don't open that!" the surgeon and the fire marshall called together. "There's nobody left inside," the surgeon added. "All evacuated now."

"What exactly happened?" Bonn scrubbed with a gloved hand at the frosted window set in the door, in an effort to see inside.

"Couple of guys were moving stores, to make room for a new shipment coming in tomorrow," the fire marshall, a lieutenant named Yaski, filled him in rapidly. "They dumped their loader over, one got pinned underneath with a broken leg."

"That . . . took ingenuity," said Bonn, obviously picturing the mechanics of the loader in his mind.

"They had to have been horsing around," said the surgeon impatiently. "But that's not the worst of it. They took several barrels of fetaine over with them. And at least two broke open. The stuff's all over the place in there. We've sealed the bunker as best we could.

Clean-up," the surgeon exhaled, "is your problem. I'm gone." He looked like he wanted to crawl out of his own skin, as well as his clothes. He waved, making quickly for his scat-cat to follow his corpsmen and their patients through medical decontamination.

"Fetaine!" Miles exclaimed in startlement. Bonn had retreated hastily from the door. Fetaine was a mutagenic poison invented as a terror weapon but never, so far as Miles knew, used in combat. "I thought that stuff was obsolete. Off the menu." His academy course in Chemicals and Biologicals had barely mentioned it.

"It is obsolete," said Bonn grimly. "They haven't made any in twenty years. For all I know this is the last stockpile on Barrayar. Dammit, those storage barrels shouldn't have broken open even if you'd dropped 'em out a shuttle."

"Those storage barrels are at least twenty years old, then," the marshall pointed out. "Corrosion?"

"In that case," Bonn craned his neck, "what about the rest of them?"

"Exactly," nodded Yaski.

"Isn't fetaine destroyed by heat?" Miles asked nervously, checking to make sure they were standing around discussing this upwind of the bunker. "Chemically dissociated into harmless components, I heard."

"Well, not exactly harmless," said Lieutenant Yaski. "But at least they don't unravel all the DNA in your balls."

"Are there any explosives stored in there, Lieutenant Bonn?" Miles asked.

"No, only the fetaine."

"If you tossed a couple of plasma mines through the door, would the fetaine all be chemically cracked before the roof melted in?"

"You wouldn't want the roof to melt in. Or the floor. If that stuff ever got loose in the permafrost . . . But if you set the mines on slow heat release, and threw a few kilos of neutral plas-seal in with 'em, the bunker might be self-sealing." Bonn's lips moved in silent calculation. ". . . Yeah, that'd work. In fact, that could be the safest way to deal with that crap. Particularly if the rest of the barrels are starting to lose integrity too."

"Depending on which way the wind is blowing," put in Lieutenant Yaski, looking back toward the base and then at Miles.

"We're expecting a light east wind with dropping temperatures till about 0700 tomorrow morning," Miles answered his look. "Then it'll shift around to the north and blow harder. Potential wah-wah conditions starting around 1800 tomorrow night."

"If we're going to do it that way, we'd better do it tonight, then," said Yaski.

"All right," said Bonn decisively. "I'll round up my crew, you round up yours. I'll pull the plans for the bunker, calculate the charges' release-rate, and meet you and the ordnance chief in Admin in an hour."

Bonn posted the fire marshall's sergeant as guard to keep everyone well away from the bunker. An unenviable duty, but not unbearable in present conditions, and the guard could retreat inside his scat-cat when the temperature dropped, toward midnight. Miles rode back with Bonn to the base Administration building to double-check his promises about wind direction at the weather office.

Miles ran the latest data through the weather computers, that he might present Bonn with the most refined possible update on predicted wind vectors over the next 26.7-hour Barrayaran day. But before he had the printout in his hand, he saw Bonn and Yaski out the window, down below, hurrying away from the Admin building into the dark. Perhaps they were meeting with the ordnance chief elsewhere? Miles considered chasing after them, but the new prediction was not significantly different from the older one. Did he really need to go watch them cauterize the poison dump? It could be interesting —educational—on the other hand, he had no real function there now. As his parents' only child—as the father, perhaps, of some future Count Vorkosigan—it was arguable if he even had the right to expose himself to such a vile mutagenic hazard for mere curiosity. There seemed no immediate danger to the base, till the wind shifted anyway. Or was cowardice masquerading as logic? Prudence was a virtue, he had heard.

Now thoroughly awake, and too rattled to even imagine recapturing sleep, he pottered around the weather office, and caught up on all the routine files he had set aside that morning in favor of the repairs junket. An hour of steady plugging finished off everything that even remotely looked like work. When he found himself compulsively dusting equipment and shelves, he decided it was time to go back to bed, sleep or no sleep. But a shifting light from the window caught his eye, a scat-cat pulling up out front.

Ah, Bonn and Yaski, back. Already? That had been fast, or hadn't they started yet? Miles tore off the plastic flimsy with the new wind readout and headed downstairs to the Base Engineering office at the end of the corridor.

Bonn's office was dark. But light spilled into the corridor from the

Base Commander's office. Light, and angry voices rising and falling. Clutching the flimsy, Miles approached.

The door was open to the inner office. Metzov sat at his desk console, one clenched fist resting on the flickering colored surface. Bonn and Yaski stood tensely before him. Miles rattled the flimsy cautiously to announce his presence.

Yaski's head swivelled around, and his gaze caught Miles. "Send Vorkosigan, he's a mutant already, isn't he?"

Miles gave a vaguely-directed salute and said immediately, "Pardon me, sir, but no, I'm not. My last encounter with a military poison did teratogenic damage, not genetic. My future children should be as healthy as the next man's. Ah, send me where, sir?"

Metzov glowered across at Miles, but did not pursue Yaski's unsettling suggestion. Miles handed the flimsy wordlessly to Bonn, who glanced at it, grimaced, and stuffed it savagely into his trouser pocket.

"Of course I intended them to wear protective gear," continued Metzov to Bonn in irritation. "I'm not mad."

"I understood that, sir. But the men refuse to enter the bunker even with contamination gear," Bonn reported in a flat, steady voice. "I can't blame them. The standard precautions are inadequate for fetaine, in my estimation. The stuff has an incredibly high penetration value, for its molecular weight. Goes right through permeables."

"You can't *blame* them?" repeated Metzov in astonishment. "Lieutenant, you gave an order. Or you were supposed to."

"I did, sir, but—"

"But—you let them sense your own indecision. Your weakness. Dammit, when you give an order you have to give it, not dance around it."

"Why do we have to save this stuff?" said Yaski plaintively.

"We've been over that. It's our charge," Metzov grunted at him. "Our orders. You can't ask a man to give an obedience you don't give yourself."

What, blind? "Surely Research still has the recipe," Miles put in, feeling he was at last getting the alarming drift of this argument. "They can mix up more if they really want it. Fresh."

"Shut up, Vorkosigan," Bonn growled desperately out of the corner of his mouth, as General Metzov snapped, "Open your lip tonight with one more sample of your humor, Ensign, and I'll put you on charges."

Miles's lips closed over his teeth in a tight glassy smile. Subordination. The *Prince Serg*, he reminded himself. Metzov could go drink the fetaine, for all Miles cared, and it would be no skin off his nose. His clean nose, remember?

"Have you never heard of the fine old battlefield practice of shooting the man who disobeys your order, Lieutenant?" Metzov went on to Bonn.

"I . . . don't think I can make that threat, sir," said Bonn stiffly. *And besides*, thought Miles, *we're not on a battlefield. Are we?*

"Techs!" said Metzov in a tone of disgust. "I didn't say threaten, I said shoot. Make one example, the rest will fall in line."

Miles decided he didn't much care for Metzov's brand of humor, either. Or was the general speaking literally?

"Sir, fetaine is a violent mutagen," said Bonn doggedly. "I'm not at all sure the rest would fall into line, no matter what the threat. It's a pretty unreasonable topic. I'm . . . a little unreasonable about it myself."

"So I see." Metzov stared at him coldly. His glare passed on to Yaski, who swallowed and stood straighter, his spine offering no concession. Miles tried to cultivate invisibility.

"If you're going to go on pretending to be military officers, your techs need a lesson in how to extract obedience from your men," Metzov decided. "Both of you go and assemble your crew in front of Admin in twenty minutes. We're going to have a little old-fashioned discipline parade."

"You're not—seriously thinking of shooting anyone, are you?" said Lieutenant Yaski in alarm.

Metzov smiled sourly. "I doubt I'll have to." He regarded Miles. "What's the outside temperature right now, Weather Officer?"

"Five degrees of frost, sir," replied Miles, careful now to speak only when spoken to.

"And the wind?"

"Winds from the east at nine kilometers per hour, sir."

"Very good." Metzov's eye gleamed wolfishly. "Dismissed, *gentlemen*. See if you can carry out your orders, this time."

General Metzov stood, heavily gloved and parka-bundled, beside the empty metal bannerpole in front of Admin, and stared down the half-lit road. Looking for what? Miles wondered. It was pushing midnight now. Yaski and Bonn were lining up their tech crews in parade array, some fifteen thermal-coveralled and parka-clad men.

Miles shivered, and not just from the cold. Metzov's seamed face looked angry. And tired. And old. And scary. He reminded Miles a bit of his grandfather on a bad day. Though Metzov was in fact younger than Miles's father; Miles had been a child of his father's middle age, some generational skew there. His grandfather, the old General Count Piotr himself, had sometimes seemed a refugee from another century. Now, the really old-fashioned discipline parades had involved lead-lined rubber hoses. How far back in Barrayaran history was Metzov's mind rooted?

Metzov smiled, a gloss over rage, and turned his head at a movement down the road. In a horribly cordial voice he confided to Miles, "You know, Ensign, there was a secret behind that carefully-cultivated interservice rivalry they had back on Old Earth. In the event of a mutiny you could always persuade the army to shoot the navy, or vice versa, when they could no longer discipline themselves. A hidden disadvantage to a combined Service like ours."

"Mutiny!" said Miles, startled out of his resolve to speak only when spoken to. "I thought the issue was poison exposure."

"It *was*. Unfortunately, due to Bonn's mishandling, it's now a matter of principle." A muscle jumped in Metzov's jaw. "It had to happen sometime, in the New Service. The Soft Service."

Typical Old Service talk, that, old men bullshitting each other about how tough they'd had it in the old days. "Principle, sir, what principle? It's *waste disposal,*" Miles choked.

"It's a mass refusal to obey a direct order, Ensign. Mutiny by any barracks-lawyer's definition. Fortunately, this sort of thing is easy to dislocate, if you move quickly, while it's still small and confused."

The motion down the road resolved itself into a platoon of grubs in their winter-white camouflage gear, marching under the direction of a Base sergeant. Miles recognized the sergeant as part of Metzov's personal power-net, an old veteran who'd served under Metzov as far back as the Komarr Revolt, and who had moved on with his master.

The grubs, Miles saw, had been armed with lethal nerve-disruptors, which were purely anti-personnel hand weapons. For all the time they spent learning about such things, the opportunity for even advanced trainees such as these to lay hands on fully powered deadly weapons was rare, and Miles could sense their nervous excitement from here.

The sergeant lined the grubs up in a cross-fire array around the stiff-standing techs, and barked an order. They presented their weapons, and aimed them, the silver bell-muzzles gleaming in the scattered light from the Admin building. A twitchy ripple ran through Bonn's men. Bonn's face was ghastly white, his eyes glittering like jet.

"Strip," Metzov ordered through set teeth.

Disbelief, confusion; only one or two of the techs grasped what was being demanded, and began to undress. The others, with many uncertain glances around, belatedly followed suit.

"When you are again ready to obey your orders," Metzov continued in a parade-pitched voice that carried to every man, "you may dress and go to work. It's up to you." He stepped back, nodded to his sergeant, and took up a pose of parade rest. "That'll cool 'em off," he muttered to himself, barely loud enough for Miles to catch. Metzov looked like he fully expected to be out there no more than five minutes; he looked like he was already thinking of warm quarters and a hot drink.

Olney and Pattas were among the techs, Miles noted, along with most of the rest of the Greek-speaking cadre who had plagued Miles early on. Others Miles had seen around, or talked to during his private investigation into the background of the drowned man, or barely knew. Fifteen naked men starting to shiver violently as the dry snow whispered around their ankles. Fifteen bewildered faces beginning to look terrified. Eyes shifted toward the nerve-disruptors trained on them. *Give in,* Miles urged silently. *It's not worth it.* But more than one pair of eyes flickered at him, and squeezed shut in resolution.

Miles silently cursed the anonymous clever boffin who'd invented fetaine as a terror weapon, not for his chemistry, but for his insight into the Barrayaran psyche. Fetaine could surely never have been used, could never be used. Any faction trying to do so must rise up against itself and tear apart in moral convulsions.

Yaski, standing back from his men, looked thoroughly horrified. Bonn, his expression black and brittle as obsidian, began to strip off his gloves and parka.

No, no, no! Miles screamed inside his head. *If you join them they'll never back down. They'll know they're right.* Bad mistake, bad . . . Bonn dropped the rest of his clothes in a pile, marched forward, joined the line, wheeled, and locked eyes with Metzov. Metzov's eyes narrowed with new fury. "So," he hissed, "you convict yourself. Freeze, then."

How had things gone so bad, so fast? Now would be a good time to remember a duty in the weather office, and get the hell out of here. If only those shivering bastards would back down, Miles could get through this night without a ripple in his record. He had no duty, no function here. . . .

Metzov's eye fell on Miles. "Vorkosigan, you can either take up a weapon and be useful, or consider yourself dismissed."

He could leave. Could he leave? When he made no move, the sergeant walked over and thrust a nerve disruptor into Miles's hand. Miles took it up, still struggling to think with brains gone suddenly porridge. He did retain the wit to make sure the safety was "on" before pointing the disruptor vaguely in the direction of the freezing men.

This isn't going to be a mutiny. It's going to be a massacre.

One of the armed grubs giggled nervously. What had they been told they were doing? What did they *believe* they were doing? Eighteen-, nineteen-year-olds—could they even recognize a criminal order? Or know what to do about it if they did?

Could Miles?

The situation was ambiguous, that was the problem. It didn't quite fit. Miles knew about criminal orders, every academy man did. His father came down personally and gave a one-day seminar on the topic to the seniors at midyear. He'd made it a requirement to graduate, by Imperial fiat back when he'd been Regent. What exactly constituted a criminal order, when and how to disobey it. With vid evidence from various historical test cases and bad examples, including the politically disastrous Solstice Massacre, that had taken place under the Admiral's own command. Invariably one or more cadets had to leave the room to throw up during that part.

The other instructors hated Vorkosigan's Day. Their classes were subtly disrupted for weeks afterward. One reason Admiral Vorkosigan didn't wait till any later in the year; he almost always had to make a return trip a few weeks after, to talk some disturbed cadet out of dropping out at almost the finale of his schooling. Only the academy cadets got this live lecture, as far as Miles knew, though his father talked of canning it on holovid and making it a part of basic training Service-wide. Parts of the seminar had been a revelation even to Miles.

But this . . . If the techs had been civilians, Metzov would clearly be in the wrong. If this had been in wartime, while being harried by some enemy, Metzov might be within his rights, even duty. This was somewhere between. Soldiers disobeying, but passively. Not an enemy in sight. Not even a physical situation threatening, necessarily, lives on the base (except theirs), though when the wind shifted that could change. *I'm not ready for this, not yet, not so soon.* What was right?

My career . . . Claustrophobic panic rose in Miles's chest, like a man with his head caught in a drain. The nerve disruptor wavered just slightly in his hand. Over the parabolic reflector he could see

Bonn standing dumbly, too congealed now even to argue any more. Ears were turning white out there, and fingers and feet. One man crumpled into a shuddering ball, but made no move to surrender. Was there any softening of doubt yet, in Metzov's rigid neck?

For a lunatic moment Miles envisioned thumbing off the safety and shooting Metzov. And then what, shoot the grubs? He couldn't possibly get them all before they got him.

I could be the only soldier here under thirty who's ever killed an enemy before, in battle or out of it. The grubs might fire out of ignorance, or sheer curiosity. They didn't know enough *not* to. *What we do in the next half hour will replay in our heads as long as we breathe.*

He could try doing nothing. Only follow orders. How much trouble could he get into, only following orders? Every commander he'd ever had agreed, he needed to follow orders better. *Think you'll enjoy your ship duty, then, Ensign Vorkosigan, you and your pack of frozen ghosts? At least you'd never be lonely. . . .*

Miles, still holding up the nerve disruptor, faded backward, out of the grubs' line-of-sight, out of the corner of Metzov's eye. Tears stung and blurred his vision. From the cold, no doubt.

He sat on the ground. Pulled off his gloves and boots. Let his parka fall, and his shirts. Trousers and thermal underwear atop the pile, and the nerve-disruptor nested carefully on them. He stepped forward. His leg braces felt like icicles against his calves.

I hate passive resistance. I really, really hate it.

"What the hell do you think you're doing, Ensign?" Metzov snarled as Miles limped past him.

"Breaking this up, sir," Miles replied steadily. Even now some of the shivering techs flinched away from him, as if his deformities might be contagious. Pattas didn't draw away, though. Nor Bonn.

"Bonn tried that bluff. He's now regretting it. It won't work for you either, Vorkosigan." Metzov's voice shook too, though not from the cold.

You should have said "Ensign." What's in a name? Miles could see the ripple of dismay run through the grubs, that time. No, this hadn't worked for Bonn. Miles might be the only man here for whom this sort of individual intervention could work. Depending on how far gone Mad Metzov was by now.

Miles spoke now for both Metzov's benefit and the grubs'. "It's possible—barely—that Service Security wouldn't investigate the deaths of Lieutenant Bonn and his men, if you diddled the record, claimed some accident. I guarantee Imperial Security will investigate mine."

Metzov grinned strangely. "Suppose no witnesses survive to complain?"

Metzov's sergeant looked as rigid as his master. Miles thought of Ahn, drunken Ahn, silent Ahn. What had Ahn seen, once long ago, when crazy things were happening on Komarr? What kind of surviving witness had he been? A guilty one, perhaps? "S-s-sorry, sir, but I see at least ten witnesses, behind those nerve disruptors." Silver parabolas—they looked enormous, like serving dishes, from this new angle. The change in point of view was amazingly clarifying. No ambiguities now.

Miles continued, "Or do you propose to execute your firing squad and then shoot yourself? Imperial Security will fast-penta everyone in sight. You can't silence me. Living or dead, through my mouth or yours—or theirs—I will testify." Shivers racked Miles's body. Astonishing, the effect of just that little bit of east wind, at this temperature. He fought to keep the shakes out of his voice, lest cold be mistaken for fear.

"Small consolation, if you—ah—permit yourself to freeze, I'd say, Ensign." Metzov's heavy sarcasm grated on Miles's nerves. The man still thought he was winning. Insane.

Miles's bare feet felt strangely warm now. His eyelashes were crunchy with ice. He was catching up fast to the others, in terms of freezing to death, no doubt because of his smaller mass. His body was turning a blotchy purple-blue.

The snow-blanketed base was so silent. He could almost hear the individual snow grains skitter across the sheet ice. He could hear the vibrating bones of each man around him, pick out the hollow frightened breathing of the grubs. Time stretched.

He could threaten Metzov, break up his complacency with dark hints about Komarr, *the truth will out.* . . . He could call on his father's rank and position. He could . . . dammit, Metzov must realize he was overextended, no matter how mad he was. His discipline parade bluff hadn't worked and now he was stuck with it, stonily defending his authority unto death. *He can be a funny kind of dangerous, if you really threaten him.* . . . It was hard, to see through the sadism to the underlying fear. But it had to be there, underneath. . . . Pushing wasn't working. Metzov was practically petrified with resistance. What about pulling . . . ?

"But consider, sir," Miles's words stuttered out persuasively, "the advantages to yourself of stopping now. You now have clear evidence of a mutinous, er, conspiracy. You can arrest us all, throw us in the stockade. It's a better revenge, 'cause you get it all and lose nothing. I lose my career, get a dishonorable discharge or maybe prison—do you think I wouldn't rather die? Service Security punishes the rest of us for you. You get it all."

Miles's words had hooked him; Miles could see it, in the red glow fading from the narrowed eyes, in the slight bending of that stiff, stiff neck. Miles had only to let the line out, refrain from jerking on it and renewing Metzov's fighting frenzy, *wait.* . . .

Metzov stepped nearer, bulking in the half-light, haloed by his freezing breath. His voice dropped, pitched to Miles's ear alone. "A typical soft Vorkosigan answer. Your father was soft on Komarran scum. Cost us lives. A court-martial for the Admiral's little boy—that might bring down that holier-than-thou buggerer, eh?"

Miles swallowed icy spit. *Those who do not know their history,* his thought careened, *are doomed to keep stepping in it.* Alas, so were those who did, it seemed. "Thermo the damned fetaine spill," he whispered hoarsely, "and see."

"You're all under arrest," Metzov bellowed out suddenly, his shoulders hunching. "Get dressed."

The others looked stunned with relief then. After a last uncertain glance at the nerve disruptors, they dove for their clothes, donning them with frantic cold-clumsy hands. But Miles had seen it complete in Metzov's eyes sixty seconds earlier. It reminded him of that definition of his father's. *A weapon is a device for making your enemy change his mind.* The mind was the first and final battleground, the stuff in between was just noise.

Lieutenant Yaski had taken the opportunity afforded by Miles's attention-arresting nude arrival on center stage to quietly disappear into the Admin building and make several frantic calls. As a result the trainee's commander, the base surgeon, and Metzov's second-in-command arrived, primed to persuade or perhaps sedate and confine Metzov. But by that time Miles, Bonn, and the techs were already dressed and being marched, stumbling, toward the stockade bunker under the argus-eyes of the nerve disruptors.

"Am I s-supposed to th-thank you for this?" Bonn asked Miles through chattering teeth. Their hands and feet swung like paralyzed lumps; he leaned on Miles, Miles hung on him, hobbling down the road together.

"We got what we wanted, eh? He's going to plasma the fetaine on-site before the wind shifts in the morning. Nobody dies. Nobody gets their nuts curdled. We win. I think." Miles emitted a deathly cackle through numb lips.

"I never thought," wheezed Bonn, "that I'd ever meet anybody crazier than Metzov."

"I didn't do anything you didn't," protested Miles. "Except I made it work. Sort of. It'll all look different in the morning, anyway."

"Yeah. Worse," Bonn predicted glumly.

Miles jerked up out of an uneasy doze on his cell cot when the door hissed open. They were bringing Bonn back.

Miles rubbed his unshaven face. "What time is it out there, Lieutenant?"

"Dawn." Bonn looked as pale, stubbled, and criminally low as Miles felt. He eased himself down on his cot with a pained grunt.

"What's happening?"

"Service Security's all over the place. They flew in a captain from the mainland, just arrived, who seems to be in charge. Metzov's been filling his ear, I think. They're just taking depositions, so far."

"They get the fetaine taken care of?"

"Yep." Bonn vented a grim snicker. "They just had me out to check it, and sign the job off. The bunker made a neat little oven, all right."

"Ensign Vorkosigan, you're wanted," said the security guard who'd delivered Bonn. "Come with me now."

Miles creaked to his feet and limped toward the cell door. "See you later, Lieutenant."

"Right. If you spot anybody out there with breakfast, why don't you use your political influence to send 'em my way, eh?"

Miles grinned bleakly. "I'll try."

Miles followed the guard up the stockade's short corridor. Lazkowski Base's stockade was not exactly what one would call a high-security facility, being scarcely more than a living quarters bunker with doors that only locked from the outside and no windows. The weather usually made a better guard than any force screen, not to mention the 500-kilometer-wide icewater moat surrounding the island.

The Base security office was busy this morning. Two grim strangers stood waiting by the door, a lieutenant and a big sergeant with the Horus-eye insignia of Imperial Security on their sleek uniforms. *Imperial* Security, not Service Security. Miles's very own Security, who had guarded his family all his father's political life. Miles regarded them with possessive delight.

The Base security clerk looked harried, his desk console lit up and blinking. "Ensign Vorkosigan, sir, I need your palm print on this."

"All right. What am I signing?"

"Just the travel orders, sir."

"What? Ah . . ." Miles paused, holding up his plastic-mitted hands. "Which one?"

"The right, I guess would do, sir."

With difficulty, Miles peeled off the right mitten with his awkward left. His hand glistened with the medical gel that was supposed to be healing the frostbite. His hand was swollen, red-blotched and mangled-looking, but the stuff must be working. All his fingers now wriggled. It took three tries, pressing down on the ID pad, before the computer recognized him.

"Now yours, sir," the clerk nodded to the Imperial Security lieutenant. The ImpSec man laid his hand on the pad and the computer bleeped approval. He lifted it and glanced dubiously at the sticky sheen, looked around futilely for some towel, and wiped it surreptitiously on his trouser seam just behind his stunner holster. The clerk dabbed nervously at the pad with his uniform sleeve, and touched his intercom.

"Am I glad to see you fellows," Miles told the ImpSec officer. "Wish you'd been here last night."

The lieutenant did not smile in return. "I'm just a courier, Ensign. I'm not supposed to discuss your case."

General Metzov ducked through the door from the inner office, a sheaf of plastic flimsies in one hand and a Service Security captain at his elbow, who nodded warily to his counterpart on the Imperial side.

The general was almost smiling. "Good morning, Ensign Vorkosigan." His glance took in Imperial Security without dismay. Dammit, ImpSec should be making that near-murderer shake in his combat boots. "It seems there's a wrinkle in this case even I hadn't realized. When a Vor lord involves himself in a military mutiny, a charge of high treason follows automatically."

"What?" Miles swallowed, to bring his voice back down. "Lieutenant, I'm not under arrest by *Imperial* Security, am I?"

The lieutenant produced a set of handcuffs and proceeded to attach Miles to the big sergeant. *Overholt,* read the name on the man's badge, which Miles mentally redubbed Overkill. He had only to lift his arm to dangle Miles like a kitten.

"You are being detained, pending further investigation," said the lieutenant formally.

"How long?"

"Indefinitely."

The lieutenant headed for the door, the sergeant and perforce Miles following. "Where?" Miles asked frantically.

"Imperial Security Headquarters."

Vorbarr Sultana! "I need to get my things—"

"Your quarters have already been cleared."

"Will I be coming back here?"

"I don't know, Ensign."

Late dawn was streaking Camp Permafrost with grey and yellow when the scat-cat deposited them at the shuttlepad. The Imperial Security sub-orbital courier shuttle sat on the icy concrete like a bird of prey accidently placed in a pigeon cote. Slick and black and deadly, it seemed to break the sound barrier just resting there. Its pilot was at the ready, engines primed for takeoff.

Miles shuffled awkwardly up the ramp after Sergeant Overkill, the handcuff jerking coldly on his wrist. Tiny ice crystals danced in the northeasterly wind. The temperature would be stabilizing this morning, he could tell by the particular dry bite of the relative humidity in his sinuses. Dear God, it was past time to get off this island.

Miles took one last sharp breath, then the shuttle door sealed behind them with a snaky hiss. Within was a thick, upholstered silence that even the howl of the engines scarcely penetrated.

At least it was warm.

6

Autumn in the city of Vorbarr Sultana was a beautiful time of year, and today was exemplary. The air was high and blue, the temperature cool and perfect, and even the tang of industrial haze smelled good. The autumn flowers were not yet frosted off, but the Earth-import trees had turned their colors. As he was hustled out of the Security lift van and into a back entrance to the big blocky building that was Imperial Security Headquarters, Miles glimpsed one such tree. An Earth maple, with carnelian leaves and a silver-grey trunk, across the street. Then the door closed. Miles held that tree before his mind's eye, trying to memorize it, just in case he never saw it again.

The Security lieutenant produced passes that sped Miles and Overholt through the door guards, and led them into a maze of corridors to a pair of lift tubes. They entered the up tube, not the down one. So, Miles was not being taken directly to the ultra-secure cell block beneath the building. He woke to what this meant, and wished wistfully for the down tube.

They were ushered into an office on an upper level, past a Security captain, then into an inner office. A man, slight, bland, civilian-clothed, with brown hair greying at the temples, sat at his very large comconsole desk, studying a vid. He glanced up at Miles's escort. "Thank you, Lieutenant, Sergeant. You may go."

Overholt detached Miles from his wrist as the lieutenant asked, "Uh, will you be safe, sir?"

"I expect so," said the man dryly.

Yeah, but what about me? Miles wailed inwardly. The two soldiers exited, and left Miles alone, standing literally on the carpet. Unwashed, unshaven, still wearing the faintly reeking black fatigues he'd flung on—only last night? Face weather-raked, with his swollen hands and feet still encased in their plastic medical mittens—his toes now wriggled in their squishy matrix. No boots. He had dozed, in a jerky intermittent exhaustion, on the two-hour shuttle flight, without being noticeably refreshed. His throat was raw, his sinuses felt stuffed with packing fiber, and his chest hurt when he breathed.

Simon Illyan, Chief of Barrayaran Imperial Security, crossed his arms and looked Miles over slowly, from head to toe and back again. It gave Miles a skewed sense of *déja vù.*

Practically everyone on Barrayar feared this man's name, though few knew his face. This effect was carefully cultivated by Illyan, building in part—but only in part—on the legacy of his formidable predecessor, the legendary Security Chief Negri. Illyan and his department, in turn, had provided security for Miles's father for the twenty years of his political career, and had slipped up only once, during the night of the infamous soltoxin attack. Offhand, Miles knew of no one Illyan feared except Miles's mother. He'd once asked his father if this was guilt, about the soltoxin, but Count Vorkosigan had replied, No, it was only the lasting effect of vivid first impressions. Miles had called Illyan "Uncle Simon" all his life until he'd entered the Service, "Sir" after that.

Looking at Illyan's face now, Miles thought he finally grasped the distinction between exasperation, and utter exasperation.

Illyan finished his inspection, shook his head, and groaned, "Wonderful. Just wonderful."

Miles cleared his throat. "Am I . . . really under arrest, sir?"

"That is what this interview will determine," Illyan sighed, leaning back in his chair. "I have been up since two hours after midnight over this escapade. Rumors are flying all over the Service, as fast as the vid net can carry them. The facts appear to be mutating every forty minutes, like bacteria. I don't suppose you could have picked some more public way to self-destruct? Attempted to assassinate the Emperor with your pocket-knife during the Birthday Review, say, or raped a sheep in the Great Square during rush hour?" The sarcasm melted to genuine pain. "He had so much hope of you. How could you betray him so?"

No need to ask who "he" was. *The* Vorkosigan. "I . . . don't think I did, sir. I don't know."

A light blinked on Illyan's comconsole. He exhaled, with a sharp glance at Miles, and touched a control. The second door to his office, camouflaged in the wall to the right of his desk, slid open, and two men in dress greens ducked through.

Prime Minister Admiral Count Aral Vorkosigan wore the uniform as naturally as an animal wears its fur. He was a man of no more than middle height, stocky, grey-haired, heavy-jawed, scarred, almost a thug's body and yet with the most penetrating grey eyes Miles had ever encountered. He was flanked by his aide, a tall blond lieutenant named Jole. Miles had met Jole on his last home leave. Now, there was a perfect officer, brave and brilliant—he'd served in space, been decorated for some courage and quick thinking during a horrendous on-board accident, been rotated through HQ while recovering from his injuries, and promptly been snabbled up as his military secretary by the Prime Minister, who had a sharp eye for hot new talent. Jaw-dropping gorgeous, to boot, he ought to be making recruiting vids. Miles sighed in hopeless jealousy every time he ran across him. Jole was even worse than Ivan, who while darkly handsome had never been accused of brilliance.

"Thanks, Jole," Count Vorkosigan murmured to his aide, as his eye found Miles. "I'll see you back at the office."

"Yes, sir." So dismissed, Jole ducked back out, glancing back at Miles and his superior with worried eyes, and the door hissed closed again.

Illyan still had his hand pressed to a control on his desk. "Are you officially here?" he asked Count Vorkosigan.

"No."

Illyan keyed something off—recording equipment, Miles realized. "Very well," he said, editorial doubt injected into his tone.

Miles saluted his father. His father ignored the salute and embraced him gravely, wordlessly, sat in the room's only other chair, crossed his arms and booted ankles, and said, "Continue, Simon."

Illyan, who had been cut off in the middle of what had been shaping up, in Miles's estimation, to a really classic reaming, chewed his lip in frustration. "Rumors aside," Illyan said to Miles, "what really happened last night out on that damned island?"

In the most neutral and succinct terms he could muster, Miles described the previous night's events, starting with the fetaine spill and ending with his arrest/detainment/to-be-determined by Imperial Security. His father said nothing during the whole recitation, but he had a light pen in his hand which he kept turning absently around and over, *tap* against his knee, around and over.

Silence fell when Miles finished. The light pen was driving Miles to distraction. He wished his father would put the damned thing away, or drop it, or anything.

His father slipped the light pen back into his breast pocket, thank God, leaned back, and steepled his fingers, frowning. "Let me get this straight. You say Metzov hopscotched the command chain and dragooned *trainees* for his firing squad?"

"Ten of them. I don't know if they were volunteers or not, I wasn't there for that part."

"Trainees." Count Vorkosigan's face was dark. "Boys."

"He was babbling something about it being like the army versus the navy, back on Old Earth."

"Huh?" said Illyan.

"I don't think Metzov was any too stable when he was exiled to Kyril Island after his troubles in the Komarr Revolt, and fifteen years of brooding about it didn't improve his grip." Miles hesitated. "Will . . . General Metzov be questioned about his actions at all, sir?"

"General Metzov, by your account," said Admiral Vorkosigan, "dragged a platoon of eighteen-year-olds into what came within a hair of being a mass torture-murder."

Miles nodded in memory. His body still twinged with assorted agonies.

"For that sin, there is no hole deep enough to hide him from my wrath. Metzov will be taken care of, all right." Count Vorkosigan was terrifyingly grim.

"What about Miles and the mutineers?" asked Illyan.

"Necessarily, I fear we will have to treat that as a separate matter."

"Or two separate matters," said Illyan suggestively.

"Mm. So, Miles, tell me about the men on the other end of the guns."

"Techs, sir, mostly. A lot of greekies."

Illyan winced. "Good God, had the man no political sense at all?"

"None that I ever saw. I thought it would be a problem." Well, later he'd thought of it, lying awake on his cell cot after the med squad left. The other political ramifications had spun through his mind. Over half the slowly freezing techs had been of the Greek-speaking minority. The language separatists would have been rioting in the streets, had it become a massacre, sure to claim the general had ordered the greekies into the clean-up as racial sabotage. More deaths, chaos reverberating down the timeline like the consequences of the Solstice Massacre? "It . . . occurred to me, that if I died with them, at least it would be crystal clear that it hadn't been some plot of your government or the Vor oligarchy. So that if I lived, I won, and if I died, I won too. Or at least served. Strategy, of sorts."

Barrayar's greatest strategist of this century rubbed his temples, as if they ached. "Well . . . of sorts, yes."

"So," Miles swallowed, "what happens now, sirs? Will I be charged with high treason?"

"For the second time in four years?" said Illyan. "Hell, no. I'm not going through that again. I will simply disappear you, until this blows over. Where to, I haven't quite figured yet. Kyril Island is out."

"Glad to hear it." Miles eyes narrowed. "What about the others?"

"The trainees?" said Illyan.

"The techs. My . . . fellow mutineers."

Illyan twitched at the term.

"It would be seriously unjust if I were to slither up some Vor-privileged line and leave them standing charges alone," Miles added.

"The public scandal of your trial would damage your father's Centrist coalition. Your moral scruples may be admirable, Miles, but I'm not sure I can afford them."

Miles stared steadily at Prime Minister Count Vorkosigan. "Sir?"

Count Vorkosigan sucked thoughtfully on his lower lip. "Yes, I could have the charges against them quashed, by Imperial fiat. That would involve another price, though." He leaned forward intently, eyes peeling Miles. "You could never serve again. Rumors will travel even without a trial. No commander would have you, after. None could trust you, trust you to be a real officer, not an artifact protected by special privilege. I can't ask anyone to command you with his head cranked over his shoulder all the time."

Miles exhaled, a long breath. "In a weird sense, they were my men. Do it. Kill the charges."

"Will you resign your commission, then?" demanded Illyan. He looked sick.

Miles felt sick, nauseous and cold. "I will." His voice was thin.

Illyan looked up suddenly from a blank brooding stare at his com-console. "Miles, how did you know about General Metzov's questionable actions during the Komarr Revolt? That case was Security-classified."

"Ah . . . didn't Ivan tell you about the little leak in the ImpSec files, sir?"

"*What?*"

Damn Ivan. "May I sit down, sir?" said Miles faintly. The room was wavering, his head thumping. Without waiting for permission, he sat cross-legged on the carpet, blinking. His father made a worried movement toward him, then restrained himself. "I'd been checking upon Metzov's background because of something Lieutenant Ahn said. By the way, when you go after Metzov, I strongly suggest you fast-penta Ahn first. He knows more than he's told. You'll find him somewhere on the equator, I expect."

"My *files*, Miles."

"Uh, yes, well, it turns out that if you face a secured console to an outgoing console, you can read off Security files from anywhere in the vid net. Of course, you have to have somebody inside HQ who can and will aim the consoles and call up the files for you. And you can't flash-download. But I, uh, thought you should know, sir."

"Perfect security," said Count Vorkosigan in a choked voice. Chortling, Miles realized in startlement.

Illyan looked like a man sucking on a lemon. "How did you," Illyan began, stopped to glare at the Count, started again, "how did you figure this out?"

"It was obvious."

"Airtight security, you said," murmured Count Vorkosigan, unsuccessfully suppressing a wheezing laugh. "The most expensive yet devised. Proof against the cleverest viruses, the most sophisticated eavesdropping equipment. And two ensigns waft right through it?"

Goaded, Illyan snapped, "I didn't promise it was idiot-proof!"

Count Vorkosigan wiped his eyes and sighed. "Ah, the human factor. We will correct the defect, Miles. Thank you."

"You're a bloody loose cannon, boy, firing in all directions," Illyan growled to Miles, craning his neck to see over his desk to where Miles sat in a slumping heap. "This, on top of your earlier escapade with those damned mercenaries, on top of it all—house arrest isn't enough. I won't sleep through the night till I have you locked in a cell with your hands tied behind your back."

Miles, who thought he might kill for a decent hour's sleep right now, could only shrug. Maybe Illyan could be persuaded to let him go to that nice quiet cell soon.

Count Vorkosigan had fallen silent, a strange thoughtful glow starting in his eye. Illyan noticed the expression too, and paused.

"Simon," said Count Vorkosigan, "there's no doubt ImpSec will have to go on watching Miles. For his sake, as well as mine."

"And the Emperor's" put in Illyan dourly. "And Barrayar's. And the innocent bystanders'."

"But what better, more direct and efficient way for security to watch him than if he is assigned *to* Imperial Security?"

"What?" said Illyan and Miles together, in the same sharp horrified tone. "You're not serious," Illyan went on, as Miles added, "Security was never on my top-ten list of assignment choices."

"Not choice. Aptitude. Major Cecil discussed it with me at one time, as I recall. But as Miles says, he didn't put it on his list."

He hadn't put Arctic Weatherman on his list either, Miles recalled.

"You had it right the first time," said Illyan. "No commander in the Service will want him now. Not excepting myself."

"Not that I could, in honor, lean on to take him. Excepting yourself. I have always," Count Vorkosigan flashed a peculiar grin, "leaned on you, Simon."

Illyan looked faintly stunned, as a top tactician beginning to see himself outmaneuvered.

"It works on several levels," Count Vorkosigan went on in that same mild persuasive voice. "We can put it about that it's an unofficial internal exile, demotion in disgrace. It will buy off my political enemies, who would otherwise try to stir profit from this mess. It will tone down the appearance of our condoning a mutiny, which no military service can afford."

"True exile," said Miles. "Even if unofficial and internal."

"Oh yes," Count Vorkosigan agreed softly. "But, ah—not true disgrace."

"Can he be trusted?" said Illyan doubtfully.

"Apparently." The count's smile was like the gleam off a knife blade. "Security can use his talents. Security more than any other department needs his talents."

"To see the obvious?"

"And the less obvious. Many officers may be trusted with the Emperor's life. Rather fewer with his honor."

Illyan, reluctantly, made a vague acquiescent gesture. Count Vorkosigan, perhaps prudently, did not troll for greater enthusiasm from his Security chief at this time, but turned to Miles and said, "You look like you need an infirmary."

"I need a bed."

"How about a bed in an infirmary?"

Miles coughed, and blinked blearily. "Yeah, that'd do."

"Come on, we'll find one."

He stood, and staggered out on his father's arm, his feet squishing in their plastic bags.

"Other than that, how was Kyril Island, Ensign Vorkosigan?" inquired the count. "You didn't vid home much, your mother noticed."

"I was busy. Lessee. The climate was ferocious, the terrain was lethal, a third of the population including my immediate superior was dead drunk most of the time. The average IQ equalled the mean temperature in degrees cee, there wasn't a woman for five hundred kilometers in any direction, and the base commander was a homicidal psychotic. Other than that, it was lovely."

"Doesn't sound like it's changed in the smallest detail in twenty-five years."

"You've been there?" Miles squinted. "And yet you let *me* get sent there?"

"I commanded Lazkowski Base for five months, once, while waiting for my captaincy of the cruiser *General Vorkraft*. During the period my career was, so to speak, in political eclipse."

So to speak. "How'd you like it?"

"I can't remember much. I was drunk most of the time. Everybody finds their own way of dealing with Camp Permafrost. I might say, you did rather better than I."

"I find your subsequent survival . . . encouraging, sir."

"I thought you might. That's why I mentioned it. It's not otherwise an experience I'd hold up as an example."

Miles looked up at his father. "Did . . . I do the right thing, sir? Last night?"

"Yes," said the count simply. "A right thing. Perhaps not the best of all possible right things. Three days from now you may think of a cleverer tactic, but you were the man on the ground at the time. I try not to second-guess my field commanders."

Miles's heart rose in his aching chest for the first time since he'd left Kyril Island.

Miles thought his father might take him to the great and familiar Imperial Military Hospital complex, a few kilometers away across town, but they found an infirmary closer than that, three floors down in ImpSec HQ. The facility was small but complete, with a couple of examining rooms, private rooms, cells for treating prisoners and guarded witnesses, a surgery, and a closed door labeled, chillingly, *Interrogation Chemistry Laboratory*. Illyan must have called down in advance, for a corpsman was hovering in attendance waiting to receive them. A Security surgeon arrived shortly, a little out of breath. He straighted his uniform and saluted Count Vorkosigan punctiliously before turning to Miles.

Miles fancied the surgeon was more used to making people nervous than being made nervous by them, and was awkward about the role reversal. Was it some aura of old violence, clinging to his father still after all these years? The power, the history? Some personal charisma, that made erstwhile forceful men flatten out like cowed dogs? Miles could sense that radiating heat perfectly clearly, and yet it didn't seem to affect him the same way.

Acclimatization, perhaps. The former Lord Regent was the man who used to take a two-hour lunch every day, regardless of any crisis short of war, and disappear into his Residence. Only Miles knew the interior view of those hours, how the big man in the green uniform would bolt a sandwich in five minutes and then spend the next hour and a half down on the floor with his son who could not walk, playing, talking, reading aloud. Sometimes, when Miles was locked in hysterical resistance to some painful new physical therapy, daunting his mother and even Sergeant Bothari, his father had been the only one with the firmness to *insist* on those ten extra agonizing leg stretches, the polite submission to the hypospray, to another round of surgery, to the icy chemicals searing his veins. "You are Vor. You must not frighten your liege people with this show of uncontrol, Lord Miles." The pungent smell of this infirmary, the tense doctor, brought back a flood of memories. No wonder, Miles reflected, he had failed to be afraid enough of Metzov. When Count Vorkosigan left, the infirmary seemed altogether empty.

There did not appear to be much going on in ImpSec HQ this week. The infirmary was numbingly quiet, except for a trickle of headquarters staff coming down to cadge headache or cold remedies or hangover-killers from the pliant corpsman. A couple of techs spent three hours rattling around the lab one evening on a rush job, and rushed off. The doctor arrested Miles's incipient pneumonia just before it turned into galloping pneumonia. Miles brooded, and waited for the six-day antibiotic therapy to run its course, and plotted details of a home leave in Vorbarr Sultana that must surely be forthcoming when the medics released him.

"Why can't I go home?" Miles complained to his mother on her next visit. "Nobody's telling me anything. If I'm not under arrest, why can't I take home leave? If I am under arrest, why aren't the doors locked? I feel like I'm in limbo."

Countess Cordelia Vorkosigan vented an unladylike snort. "You are in limbo, kiddo." Her flat Betan accent fell warmly on Miles's ears, despite her sardonic tone. She tossed her head—she wore her red-roan hair pinned back from her face and waving loose down her back today, gleaming against a rich autumn brown jacket picked out with silver embroidery, and the swinging skirts of a Vor-class woman. Grey-eyed, striking, her pale face seemed so alive with flickering thought one scarcely noticed she was not beautiful. For twenty-one years she'd passed as a Vor matron in the wake of her Great Man, yet still seemed as unimpressed by Barrayaran hierarchies as ever—though not, Miles thought, unmoved by Barrayaran wounds.

So why do I never think of my ambition as ship command like my mother *before me?* Captain Cordelia Naismith, Betan Astronomical Survey, had been in the risky business of expanding the wormhole nexus jump by blind jump, for humanity, for pure knowledge, for Beta Colony's economic advancement, for—what *had* driven her? She'd commanded a sixty-person survey vessel, far from home and help—there were certain enviable aspects to her former career, to be sure. Chain-of-command, for example, would have been a legal fiction out in the farbeyond, the wishes of Betan HQ a matter for speculation and side bets.

She moved now so wavelessly through Barrayaran society, only her most intimate observers realized how detached she was from it, fearing no one, not even the dread Illyan, controlled by no one, not even the Admiral himself. It was the casual fearlessness, Miles decided, that made his mother so unsettling. The Admiral's Captain. Following in her footsteps would be like firewalking.

"What's going on out there?" Miles asked. "This place is almost as much fun as solitary confinement, y'know? Have they decided I'm a mutineer after all?"

"I don't think so," said the Countess. "They're discharging the others—your Lieutenant Bonn and the rest—not precisely dishonorably, but without benefits or pensions or that Imperial Liegeman status that seems to mean so much to Barrayaran men—"

"Think of it as a funny sort of Reservist," Miles advised. "What about Metzov and the grubs?"

"He's being discharged the same way. He lost the most, I think."

"They're just turning him loose?" Miles frowned.

Countess Vorkosigan shrugged. "Because there were no deaths, Aral was persuaded he couldn't make a court martial with any harsher punishment stick. They decided not to involve the trainees with any charges."

"Hm. I'm glad, I think. And, ah . . . me?"

"You remain officially listed as detained by Imperial Security. Indefinitely."

"Limbo is supposed to be an indefinite sort of place." His hand picked at his sheet. His knuckles were still swollen. "How long?"

"However long it takes to have its calculated psychological effect."

"What, to drive me crazy? Another three days ought to do it."

Her lip quirked. "Long enough to convince the Barrayaran militarists that you are being properly punished for your, uh, crime. As long as you are confined in this rather sinister building, they can be encouraged to imagine you undergoing—whatever they imagine goes on in here. If you're allowed to run around town partying, it will be much harder to maintain the illusion that you've been hung upside down on the basement wall."

"It all seems so . . . unreal." He hunched back into his pillow. "I only wanted to serve."

A brief smile flicked her wide mouth up, and vanished. "Ready to reconsider another line of work, love?"

"Being Vor is more than just a job."

"Yes, it's a pathology. Obsessional delusion. It's a big galaxy out there, Miles. There are other ways to serve, larger . . . constituencies."

"So why do you stay here?" he shot back.

"Ah." She smiled bleakly at the touche. "Some people's needs are more compelling than guns."

"Speaking of Dad, is he coming back?"

"Hm. No. I'm to tell you, he's going to distance himself for a time. So as not to give the appearance of endorsing your mutiny, while in fact shuffling you out from under the avalanche. He's decided to be publicly angry with you."

"And is he?"

"Of course not. Yet . . . he was beginning to have some long-range plans for you, in his socio-political reform schemes, based on your completing a solid military career . . . he saw ways of making even your congenital injuries serve Barrayar."

"Yeah, I know."

"Well, don't worry. He'll doubtless think of some way to use this, too."

Miles sighed glumly. "I want something to *do*. I want my *clothes* back."

His mother pursed her lips, and shook her head.

* * *

He tried calling Ivan that evening.

"Where are you?" Ivan demanded suspiciously.

"Stuck in limbo."

"Well, I don't want any of it stuck to me," said Ivan roughly, and punched off-line.

7

The next morning Miles was moved to new quarters. His guide led him just one floor down, dashing Miles's hopes of seeing the sky again. The officer keyed open a door to one of the secured apartments usually used by protected witnesses. And, Miles reflected, certain political nonpersons. Was it possible life in limbo was having a chameleon effect, rendering him translucent?

"How long will I be staying here?" Miles asked the officer.

"I don't know, Ensign," the man replied, and left him.

His duffle, jammed with his clothes, and a hastily-packed box sat in the middle of the apartment's floor. All his worldly goods from Kyril Island, smelling moldy, a cold breath of arctic damp. Miles poked through them—everything seemed to be there, including his weather library—and prowled his new quarters. It was a one-room efficiency, shabbily furnished in the style of twenty years back, with a few comfortable chairs, a bed, a simple kitchenette, empty cupboards and shelves and closets. No abandoned garments or objects or leftovers to hint at the identity of any previous occupant.

There had to be bugs. Any shiny surface could conceal a vid pickup, and the ears were probably not even within the room. But were they switched on? Or, almost more of an insult, maybe Illyan wasn't even bothering to run them?

There was a guard in the outer corridor, and remote monitors, but Miles did not appear to have neighbors at present. He discovered he could leave the corridor, and walk about the few non-top-secured areas of the building, but the guards at the outside doors, briefed as to who he was, turned him back politely but firmly. He pictured himself attempting escape by rappelling down from the roof—he'd probably get himself shot, and ruin some poor guard's career.

A Security officer found him wandering aimlessly, conducted him back to his apartment, gave him a handful of chits for the building's cafeteria, and hinted strongly that it would be appreciated if he would stay in his quarters between meals. After he left Miles morbidly counted the chits, trying to guess the expected duration of his stay. There were an even hundred. Miles shuddered.

He unpacked his box and bag, ran everything that would go through the sonic laundry to eliminate the last lingering odor of Camp Permafrost, hung up his uniforms, cleaned his boots, arranged his possessions neatly on a few shelves, showered, and changed to fresh undress greens.

One hour down. How many to go?

He attempted to read, but could not concentrate, and ended sitting in the most comfortable chair with his eyes closed, pretending this windowless, hermetically-sealed chamber was a cabin aboard a spaceship. Outbound.

He was sitting in the same chair two nights later, digesting a leaden cafeteria dinner, when the door chimed.

Startled, Miles clambered up and limped to answer it personally. It was probably not a firing squad, though you never knew.

He almost changed his assumptions about the firing squad at the sight of the hard-faced Imperial Security officers in dress greens who stood waiting. "Excuse me, Ensign Vorkosigan," one muttered perfunctorily, and brushed past him to start running a scan over Miles's quarters. Miles blinked, then saw who stood behind them in the corridor, and breathed an "Ah" of understanding. At a mere look from the scanner man, Miles obediently held out his arms and turned to be scanned.

"Clear, sir," the scanner man reported, and Miles was sure it was. These fellows never, ever cut corners, not even in the heart of Imp-Sec itself.

"Thank you. Leave us, please. You may wait out here," said the third man. The ImpSec men nodded and took up parade rest flanking Miles's door.

Since they were both wearing officers' undress greens, Miles exchanged salutes with the third man, although the visitor's uniform bore neither rank nor department insignia. He was thin, of middle height, with dark hair and intense hazel eyes. A crooked smile winked in a serious young face that lacked laugh lines.

"Sire," Miles said formally.

Emperor Gregor Vorbarra jerked his head, and Miles keyed his door closed on the Security duo. The thin young man relaxed slightly. "Hi, Miles."

"Hello yourself. Uh . . ." Miles motioned toward the armchairs. "Welcome to my humble abode. Are the bugs running?"

"I asked not, but I wouldn't be surprised if Illyan disobeys me, for my own good." Gregor grimaced, and followed Miles. He swung a plastic bag from his left hand, from which came a muted clank. He flung himself into the larger chair, the one Miles had just vacated, leaned back, hooked a leg over one chair arm, and sighed wearily, as if all the air were being let out of him. He held out the bag. "Here. Elegant anesthesia."

Miles took it and peered in. Two bottles of wine, by God, already chilled. "Bless you, my son. I've been wishing I could get drunk for days, now. How did you guess? For that matter, how did you get in here? I thought I was in solitary confinement." Miles put the second bottle into the refrigerator, found two glasses, and blew the dust out of them.

Gregor shrugged. "They could scarcely keep me out. I'm getting better at insisting, you know. Though Illyan made sure my private visit was really private, you can wager. And I can only stay till 2500." Gregor's shoulders slumped, compressed by the minute-by-minute box of his schedule. "Besides, your mother's religion grants some kind of good karma for visiting the sick and prisoners, and I hear you've been the two in one."

Ah, so Mother had put Gregor up to this. He should have guessed by the Vorkosigan private label on the wine—heavens, she'd sent the *good* stuff. He stopped swinging the bottle by its neck and carried it with greater respect. Miles was lonely enough by now to be more grateful for than embarrassed by this maternal intervention. He opened the wine and poured, and by Barrayaran etiquette took the first sip. Ambrosia. He slung himself into another chair in a posture similar to Gregor's. "Glad to see you, anyway."

Miles contemplated his old playmate. If they'd been even a little closer in age, he and Gregor, they might have fallen more into the role of foster-brothers; Count and Countess Vorkosigan had been

Gregor's official guardians ever since the chaos and bloodshed of Vordarian's Pretendership. The child-cohort had been thrown together anyway as "safe" companions, Miles and Ivan and Elena near-age-mates, Gregor, solemn even then, tolerating games a little younger than he might have preferred.

Gregor picked up his wine and sipped. "Sorry things didn't work out for you," he said gruffly.

Miles tilted his head. "A short soldier, a short career." He took a bigger gulp. "I'd hoped to get off-planet. Ship duty."

Gregor had graduated from the Imperial Academy two years before Miles entered it. His brows rose in agreement. "Don't we all."

"You had a year on active space duty," Miles pointed out.

"Mostly in orbit. Pretend patrols, surrounded by Security shuttles. It got to be painful after a while, all the pretending. Pretending I was an officer, pretending I was doing a job instead of making everyone else's job harder just by being there . . . you at least were permitted real risk."

"Most of it was unplanned, I assure you."

"I'm increasingly convinced that's the trick of it," Gregor went on. "Your father, mine, both our grandfathers—all survived real military situations. That's how they became real officers, not this . . . study." His free hand made a downward chopping motion.

"Flung into situations," Miles disagreed. "My father's military career officially began the day Mad Yuri's death squad broke in and blew up most of his family—I think he was eleven, or something. I'd just as soon pass on that sort of initiation, thanks. It's not something anybody in their right mind would choose."

"Mm." Gregor subsided glumly. As oppressed tonight, Miles guessed, by his legendary father Prince Serg as Miles was by his live one Count Vorkosigan. Miles reflected briefly on what he had come to think of as "The Two Sergs." One—maybe the only version Gregor knew?—was the dead hero, bravely sacrificed on the field of battle or at least cleanly disintegrated in orbit. The other, the Suppressed Serg: the hysteriac commander and sadistic sodomite whose early death in the ill-fated Escobar invasion might have been the greatest stroke of political good fortune ever to befall Barrayar . . . had even a hint of this multi-faceted personality ever been permitted to filter back to Gregor? Nobody who knew Serg talked about him, Count Vorkosigan least of all. Miles had once met one of Serg's victims. Miles hoped Gregor never would.

Miles decided to change the subject. "So we all know what happened to me, what have you been up to for the last three months? I was sorry to miss your last birthday party. Up at Kyril Island they celebrated it by getting drunk, which made it virtually indistinguishable from any other day."

Gregor grinned, then sighed. "Too many ceremonies. Too much time standing up—I think I could be replaced at half my functions by a life-sized plastic model, and no one would notice. A lot of time spent ducking the broad marital hints of my assorted counsellors."

"Actually, they have a point," Miles had to allow. "If you got . . . run over by a teacart tomorrow, the succession question goes up for grabs in a big way. I can think offhand of at least six candidates with arguable stakes in the Imperium, and more would come out of the woodwork. Some without personal ambition would nevertheless kill to see that some of the others didn't get it, which is precisely why you still don't have a named heir."

Gregor cocked his head. "You're in that crowd yourself, you know."

"With this body?" Miles snorted. "They'd have to . . . really hate somebody, to tag me. At that point it really would be time to run away from home. Far and fast. Do me a favor. Get married, settle down, and have six little Vorbarras real quick."

Gregor looked even more depressed. "Now there's an idea. Running away from home. I wonder how far I'd get before Illyan caught up with me?"

They both glanced involuntarily upward, though in fact Miles was still not certain where the room's bugs were located. "Better hope Illyan caught up with you before anybody else did." God, this conversation was getting morbid.

"I don't know, wasn't there an emperor of China who ended up pushing a broom somewhere? And a thousand lesser emigrees— countesses running restaurants—escape *is* possible."

"From being Vor? More like . . . trying to run away from your own shadow." There would be moments, in the dark, when success would seem achieved, but then—Miles shook his head, and checked out the still-lumpy bag. "Ah! You brought a tacti-go set." He didn't in the least want to play tacti-go, it had bored him by age fourteen, but anything was better than this. He pulled it out and set it up between them with determined good cheer. "Brings back old times." Hideous thought.

Gregor bestirred himself, and made an opening move. Pretending to be interested to amuse Miles, who was simulating interest to cheer Gregor, who was feigning . . . Miles, distracted, beat Gregor too fast on the first round, and began to pay more attention. On the next round he kept it closer, and was rewarded by a spark of genuine interest—blessed self-forgetfulness—on Gregor's part. They opened the second bottle of wine. At that point Miles began to feel the effects, going tongue-thick and sleepy and stupid; it took hardly any effort to let Gregor almost win the next round.

"I don't think I've beaten you at this since you were fourteen," sighed Gregor, concealing secret satisfaction at the low point-spread of that last round. "You should be an officer, dammit."

"This isn't a good war game, Dad says," commented Miles. "Not enough random factors and uncontrolled surprises to simulate reality. I like it that way." It was almost soothing, a mindless routine of logic, check and counter, multiple chained moves with, always, perfectly objective options.

"You should know." Gregor glanced up. "I still don't understand why they sent you to Kyril Island. You've already commanded a real space fleet. Even if they were only a pack of grubby mercenaries."

"Shh. That episode is officially non-existent, in my military files. Fortunately. It wouldn't charm my superiors. I'd commanded, I hadn't obeyed. Anyway, I didn't so much command the Dendarii Mercenaries as hypnotize 'em. Without Captain Tung, who decided to prop up my pretensions for his own purposes, it would have all ended very unpleasantly. And much sooner."

"I always thought Illyan would do more with them, after," said Gregor. "However inadvertently, you brought a whole military organization secretly into the service of Barrayar."

"Yes, without them even knowing it themselves. Now, *that's* secret. Come on. Assigning them to Illyan's section was a legal fiction, everybody knew it." And would his own assignment to Illyan's section turn out to be a legal fiction too? "Illyan's too careful to get drawn into intergalactic military adventuring as a hobby. I'm afraid his main interest in the Dendarii Mercenaries is to keep them as far away from Barrayar as possible. Mercenaries thrive on other people's chaos.

"Plus, they're a funny size—less than a dozen ships, three or four thousand personnel—not your basic invisible six-man covert ops team, though they can field such, and yet they're too little to take on planetary situations. Space-based, not ground troops. Wormhole blockades were their specialty. Safe, easy on the equipment, mostly bullying unarmed civilians—which is how I first ran into them, when our freighter was stopped by their blockade, and the bullying went too far. I cringe to think of the risks I ran. Though I've often wondered if, knowing what I know now, I could have. . . ." Miles stopped, shook his head. "Or maybe it's like heights. Better not to look down. You freeze, and then you fall." Miles was not fond of heights.

"As a military experience, how did it compare with Lazkowski Base?" asked Gregor bemusedly.

"Oh, there were certain parallels," Miles admitted. "Both were jobs I wasn't trained for, both were potentially lethal, I got out of both by my skin—lost some skin. The Dendarii episode was . . . worse. I lost Sergeant Bothari. In a sense, I lost Elena. At least at Camp Permafrost I managed not to lose anyone."

"Maybe you're getting better," Gregor suggested.

Miles shook his head, and drank. He should have put on some music. The thick silence of this room was oppressive, when the conversation faltered. The ceiling was probably not hydraulically arranged to descend and crush him in his sleep; Security had far less messy ways of dealing with recalcitrant prisoners. It only seemed to lower at him. *Well, I'm short. Maybe it'd miss me.*

"I suppose it would be . . . improper," Miles began hesitantly, "to ask you to try and get me out of here. It's always seemed rather embarrassing, to ask for Imperial favors. Like cheating, or something."

"What, are you asking one prisoner of ImpSec to rescue another?" Gregor's hazel eyes were ironic under black brows. "It's a little embarrassing to me to come up against the limits of my absolute Imperial Rule. Your father and Illyan, like two parentheses around me." His cupped hands closed in a squeezing motion.

It was a subliminal effect of this room, Miles decided. Gregor was feeling it too.

"I would if I could," Gregor added more apologetically. "But Illyan's made it crystal clear he wants you kept out of sight. For a time, anyway."

"Time." Miles swallowed the last of his wine, and decided he'd better not pour himself any more. Alcohol was a depressant, it was said. "How much time? Dammit, if I don't get something to do soon, I'm going to be the first case of human spontaneous combustion recorded on vid." He jerked a rude finger at the ceiling. "I don't need to—don't even have to leave the building, but at least they could give me some *work*. Clerical, janitorial—I do terrific drains—anything. Dad talked with Illyan about assigning me to Security—as the only Section left that would take me—he must have had something more in mind than a m-, m-, mascot." He poured and drank again, to stop the spate of words. He'd said too much. Damn the wine. Damn the whine.

Gregor, who had built a little tower of tacti-go chips, toppled it with one finger. "Oh, being a mascot isn't bad work, if you can get it." He stirred the pile slowly. "I'll see what I can do. No promises."

Miles didn't know if it was the Emperor, the bugs, or wheels already in motion (grinding slowly), but two days afterwards he found himself assigned to the job of administrative assistant to the guard commander for the building. It was comconsole work; scheduling, payroll, updating computer files. The job was interesting for a week, while he was learning it, mind-numbing after that. By the end of a month, the boredom and banality were beginning to prey on his nerves. Was he loyal, or merely stupid? Guards, Miles now realized, had to stay in prison all day long too. Indeed, as a guard, one of his jobs was now to keep himself in. Damn clever of Illyan, nobody else could have held him, if he'd been determined on escape. He did find a window once, and looked out. It was sleeting.

Was he going to get out of this bloody box before Winterfair? How long did it take the world to forget him, anyway? If he committed suicide, could he be officially listed as shot by a guard while escaping? Was Illyan trying to drive him out of his mind, or just out of his Section?

Another month slipped by. As a spiritual exercise, he decided to fill his off-duty hours by watching every training vid in the military library, in strict alphabetical order. The assortment was truly astonishing. He was particularly bemused by the thirty-minute vid (under "H: Hygiene") explaining how to take a shower—well, yes, there probably were backcountry recruits who really needed the instruction. After some weeks he had worked his way down to "L: Laser-rifle Model D-67; power-pack circuitry, maintenance, and repair," when he was interrupted by a call ordering him to report to Illyan's office.

Illyan's office was almost unchanged from Miles's last excruciating visit—same spartan windowless inner chamber occupied mainly by a comconsole desk that looked like it could be used to pilot a jump ship —but now there were two chairs. One was promisingly empty. Maybe Miles wouldn't end up so literally on the carpet this round? The other was occupied by a man in undress greens with captain's tabs and the Horus-eye insignia of Imperial Security on the collar.

Interesting fellow, that captain. Miles summed him out of the corner of his eye as he exchanged formal salutes with Illyan. Maybe thirty-five years old, he had something of Illyan's unmemorable bland look about the face, but was more heavily built. Pale. He might easily pass for some minor bureaucrat, a sedentary indoorsman. But that particular look could also be acquired by spending a great deal of time cooped up on spaceships.

"Ensign Vorkosigan, this is Captain Ungari. Captain Ungari is one of my galactic operatives. He has ten years experience gathering information for this department. His specialty is military evaluation."

Ungari favored Miles with a polite nod by way of acknowledging the introduction. His level gaze summed Miles right back. Miles wondered what the spy's evaluation of the dwarfish soldier standing before him might be, and tried to stand straighter. There was nothing obvious about Ungari's reaction to Miles.

Illyan leaned back in his swivel chair. "So tell me, Ensign, what have you heard lately from the Dendarii Mercenaries?"

"Sir?" Miles rocked back. *Not* the curve he was expecting . . . "I . . . lately, nothing. I had a message about a year ago from Elena Bothari—Bothari-Jesek, that is. But it was only private, uh, birthday greetings."

"That one I have," Illyan nodded.

Do you, you bastard.

"—Nothing since?"

"No, sir."

"Hm." Illyan waved a hand at the spare chair. "Sit down, Miles." His voice grew quicker and more businesslike. Meat at last? "Let's go over a little astrography. Geography is the mother of strategy, they say." Illyan fiddled with a control on his comconsole.

A wormhole nexus route map formed in three bright dimensions over the holovid plate. It looked rather like a ball-and-stick model of some weird organic molecule done in colored light, balls representing local-space crossings, sticks the wormhole-space jumps between; schematic, compressing information, rather than to scale. Illyan zoomed in on a portion, red and blue sparks in the center of an otherwise empty ball, with four sticks leading out at crazy angles to more complex balls like some skewed Celtic cross. "Look familiar?"

"That in the center is the Hegen Hub, isn't it, sir?"

"Good." Illyan handed him his controller. "Give me a strategic summation of the Hegan Hub, Ensign."

Miles cleared his throat. "It's a double star system with no habitable planets, a few stations and powersats, and very little reason to linger in. Like many nexus connections, it's more route than place, taking its value by what's around it. In this case, four adjoining regions of local space with settled planets." Miles brightened each part of the image as he spoke, for emphasis.

"Aslund. Aslund is a cul-de-sac like Barrayar; the Hegen Hub is its sole gate to the greater galactic web. The Hegen Hub is as vital to Aslund as our gateway Komarr is to us.

"Jackson's Whole. The Hegen Hub is just one of five gates from Jacksonian local space; beyond Jackson's Whole lies half the explored galaxy.

"Vervain. Vervain has two exits; one to the Hub, the other into the nexus sectors controlled by the Cetagandan Empire.

"And fourth, of course, our, ah, good neighbor the Planet and Republic of Pol. Which in turn connects to our own multi-nexus Komarr. Also from Komarr is our one straight jump to the Cetagandan sector, which route has been either tightly controlled or outright barred to Cetagandan traffic ever since we conquered it." Miles glanced at Illyan for approval, hoping he was on the right track. Illyan glanced at Ungari, who allowed his brows to rise fractionally. Meaning what?

"Wormhole strategy. The devil's cat's cradle," Illyan muttered editorially. He squinted at his glowing schematic. "Four players, one game-board. It ought to be simple. . . .

"Anyway," Illyan stretched out his hand for the controller, and sat back with a sigh, "the Hegen Hub is more than a potential choke-point for the four adjoining systems. Twenty-five percent of our own commercial traffic passes through it, via Pol. And although Vervain is closed to Cetagandan military vessels just as Pol is closed to ours, the Cetas ship significant civilian exchange through the same slot and out past Jackson's Whole. Anything—like a war—that blocks the Hegen Hub would seem almost as damaging to Cetaganda as to us.

"And yet, after years of cooperative disinterest and dull neutrality, this empty region is suddenly alive with what I can only call an arms race. All four neighbors seem to be creating military interests. Pol has been beefing up the armament on all six of its jump point stations strung toward the Hub—even pulling forces from the side toward us, which I find a little startling, since Pol has been extremely wary of us ever since we took Komarr. The Jackson's Whole consortium is doing the same on its side. Vervain has hired a mercenary fleet called Randall's Rangers.

"All this activity is causing low-grade panic on Aslund, whose interest in the Hegen Hub is for obvious reasons most critical. They're throwing half this year's military budget into a major jumppoint station—hell, a floating fortress—and to cover the gap while they prepare, they too have hired guns. You may be familiar with them. They used to be called the Dendarii Free Mercenary Fleet." Illyan paused, and raised an eyebrow, watching for Miles's reaction.

Connections at last—or were there? Miles blew out his breath. "They were blockade specialists, at one time. Makes sense, I guess. Ah . . . used to be called the Dendarii? Have they changed lately?"

"They've recently reverted to their original title of Oseran Mercenaries, it seems."

"Strange. Why?"

"Why, indeed?" Illyan's lips compressed. "One of many questions, though hardly the most urgent. But it's the Cetagandan connection —or lack of it—that bothers me. General chaos in the region would be as damaging to Cetaganda as to us. But if, after the chaos passes, Cetaganda could somehow end up in control of the Hegen Hub—ah! Then they could block or control Barrayaran traffic as we do theirs through Komarr. Indeed, if you look at the other side of the Komarr-Cetaganda jump as being under their control, that would put them across two out of our four major galactic routes. Something labyrinthine, indirect—it smells of Cetaganda's methods. Or would, if I could spot their sticky hands pulling any of the strings. They must be there, even if I can't see them yet. . . ." Brooding, Illyan shook his head. "If the Jackson's Whole jump were cut, everyone would have to reroute through the Cetagandan Empire . . . profit, there. . . ."

"Or through us," Miles pointed out. "Why should Cetaganda do us that favor?"

"I have thought of one possibility. Actually, I've thought of nine, but this one's for you, Miles. What's the best way to capture a jump point?"

"From both ends at once," Miles recited automatically.

"Which is one reason Pol has been careful never to let us amass any military presence in the Hegen Hub. But let us suppose someone on Pol stumbles across that nasty rumor I had so much trouble scotching that the Dendarii Mercenaries are the private army of a certain Barrayaran Vor lordling? What will they think?"

"They'll think we're getting ready to jump them," said Miles. "They might go paranoid—panic—even seek a temporary alliance, with, say, Cetaganda?"

"Very good," nodded Illyan.

Captain Ungari, who had been listening with the attentive patience of a man who'd been over it all before, glanced at Miles as if faintly encouraged, and approved this hypothesis with a nod of his head.

"But even if perceived as an independent force," Illyan went on, "the Dendarii are one more destabilizing influence in the region. The whole situation is disturbing—growing tenser by the day, for no apparent reason. Only a little more force—one mistake, one lethal incident—could trigger turbulence, classic chaos, the real thing, unstoppable. Reasons, Miles! I want information."

Illyan, generally, wanted information with the same passion that a strung-out juba freak craved a spike. He turned now to Ungari. "So what do you think, Captain? Will he do?"

Ungari was slow to reply. "He's . . . more physically conspicuous than I'd realized."

"As camouflage, that's not necessarily a disadvantage. In his company you ought to be nearly invisible. The stalking goat and the hunter."

"Perhaps. But can he carry the load? I'm not going to have much time for babysitting." Ungari's voice was an urban baritone, evidently one of the modern educated officers, though he did not wear an Academy pin.

"The Admiral seems to think so. Am I to argue?"

Ungari glanced at Miles. "Are you sure the Admiral's judgment is not swayed by . . . personal hopes?"

You mean wishful thinking, Miles mentally translated that delicate hesitancy.

"If so, it's for the first time," Illyan shrugged. *And there's a first time for everything,* hung unspoken in the air. Illyan turned now to pin Miles with a gaze of grim intensity. "Miles, do you think you would—if required—be capable of playing the part of Admiral Naismith again, for a short time?"

He'd seen it coming, but the words spoken out loud were still a strange cold thrill. To activate that suppressed persona again. . . . *It wasn't just a part, Illyan.* "I could play Naismith again, sure. It's *stopping* playing Naismith that scares me."

Illyan allowed himself a wintry smile, taking this for a joke. Miles's smile was a little sicker. *You don't know, you don't know what it was like.* . . . Three parts fakery and flim-flam, and one part . . . something else. Zen, gestalt, delusion? Uncontrollable moments of alpha-state exaltation. . . . Could he do it again? Maybe he knew too much now. *First you freeze, and then you fall.* Perhaps it *would* only be play-acting this time.

Illyan leaned back, held up his hands palm to palm, and let them fall in a releasing gesture. "Very well, Captain Ungari. He's all yours. Use him as you see fit. Your mission, then, is to gather information on the current crisis in the Hegen Hub; secondly, if possible, to use Ensign Vorkosigan to remove the Dendarii Mercenaries from the stage. If you decide to use a bogus contract to pull them out of the Hub, you can draw on the covert ops account for a convincing downpayment. You know the results I want. I'm sorry I can't make my orders more specific in advance of the intelligence you yourself must obtain."

"I don't mind, sir," said Ungari, smiling slightly.

"Hm. Enjoy your independence while it lasts. It ends with your first mistake." Illyan's tone was sardonic, but his eyes were confident, until he turned them toward Miles. "Miles, you'll be traveling as 'Admiral Naismith,' himself traveling incognito, returning, possibly, to the Dendarii fleet. Should Captain Ungari decide for you to activate the Naismith role, he'll pose as your bodyguard, so as to be always in position to control the situation. It's a little too much to ask Ungari to be responsible for his mission and also your safety, so you'll also have a real bodyguard. This setup will give Captain Ungari unusual freedom of movement, because it will account for your possession of a personal ship—we have a jump pilot and a fast courier we obtained from—never mind where, but it has no connection with Barrayar. It's under Jacksonian registration at present, which fits in nicely with Admiral Naismith's mysterious background. It's so obviously bogus, no one will look for a second layer of, er, bogusity." Illyan paused. "You will, of course, obey Captain Ungari's orders. *That* goes without saying." Illyan's direct stare was chilly as a Kyril Island midnight.

Miles smiled dutifully, to show he took the hint. *I'll be good, sir— let me off planet!* From ghost to goat—was this a promotion?

8

Victor Rotha, Procurement Agent. Sounded like a pimp. Dubiously, Miles regarded his new persona twinned over the vid plate in his cabin. What was wrong with a simple spartan mirror, anyway? *Where* had Illyan gotten this *ship?* Of Betan manufacture, it was stuffed with Betan gimmickry of a luxurious order. Miles entertained himself with a gruesome vision of what could happen if the programming on the elaborate sonic tooth-cleaner ever went awry.

"Rotha" was vaguely dressed, with respect to his supposed point-of-origin. Miles had drawn the line at a Betan sarong, Pol Station Six was not nearly warm enough for it. He did wear his loose green trousers held up with a Betan sarong rope, though, and Betan style sandals. The green shirt was a cheap synthetic silk from Escobar, the baggy cream jacket an expensive one of like style. The eclectic wardrobe of someone originally from Beta Colony, who'd been knocking around the galaxy for a while, sometimes up, sometimes down. Good. He muttered to himself aloud, warming up his disused Betan accent, as he pottered about the elaborate Owner's Cabin.

They had docked here at Pol Six a day ago without incident. The whole three-week trip from Barrayar had passed without incident. Ungari seemed to like it that way. The ImpSec captain had spent most of the journey counting things, taking pictures and counting;

ships, troops, security guards both civil and military. They'd managed excuses to stop over at four of the six jump point stations on the route between Pol and the Hegen Hub, with Ungari counting, measuring, sectioning, computer-stuffing, and calculating the whole way. Now they had arrived at Pol's last (or first, depending on your direction of travel) outpost, its toehold in the Hegen Hub itself.

At one time, Pol Six had merely marked the jump point, no more than an emergency stop and communications transfer link. No one had yet solved the problem of getting messages through a wormhole jump except by physically transporting them on a jump ship. In the most developed regions of the nexus, comm ships jumped hourly or even more often, to emit a tight-beam burst that traveled at the speed of light to the next jump point in that region of local space, where messages were picked up and relayed out in turn, the fastest possible flow of information. In the less developed regions, one simply had to wait, sometimes for weeks or months, for a ship to happen by, and hope they'd remember to drop off your mail.

Now Pol Six didn't just mark, it frankly guarded. Ungari had clicked his tongue in excitement, identifying and adding up Pol Navy ships clustered in the area around the new construction. They'd managed a spiral flight path into dock that revealed every side of the station, and all ships both moored and moving.

"Your main job here," Ungari had told Miles, "will be to give anyone watching us something more interesting to watch than me. Circulate. I doubt you'll need to expend any special effort to be conspicuous. Develop your cover identity—with luck, you may even pick up a contact or two who'll be worthy of further study. Though I doubt you'll run across anything of great value immediately, it doesn't work that way."

Now, Miles laid his samples case open on his bed and rechecked it. *Just a traveling salesman, that's me.* A dozen hand weapons, powerpacks removed, gleamed wickedly back at him. A row of vid-disks described larger and more interesting weapons systems. An even more interesting—you might even say, "arresting"—collection of tiny disks nestled concealed in Miles's jacket. *Death. I can get it for you wholesale.*

Miles's bodyguard met him at the docking hatch. Why, oh God, had Illyan assigned Sergeant Overkill to this mission? Same reason he'd sent him to Kyril Island, because he was trusted, no doubt, but it embarrassed Miles to be working with a man who'd once arrested him. What did Overholt make of Miles, by now? Happily, the big man was the silent type.

Overholt was dressed as informally and eclectically as Miles himself, though with safety boots in place of sandals. He looked exactly like somebody's bodyguard trying to look like a tourist. Much the sort of man small-time arms dealer Victor Rotha would logically employ. *Both functional and decorative, he slices, dices, and chops. . . .* By themselves, either Miles or Overholt would be memorable. Together, well . . . Ungari was right. They needn't worry about being overlooked.

Miles led the way through that docking tube and into Pol Six. This docking spoke funneled into a Customs area, where Miles's sample case and person were carefully examined, and Overholt had to produce registration for his stunner. From there they had free run of the transfer station facilities, but for certain guarded corridors leading into the, as it were, militarized zones. Those areas, Ungari had made clear, were his business, not Miles's.

Miles, in good time for his first appointment, strolled slowly, enjoying the sensation of being on a space station. The place wasn't as free-wheeling as Beta Colony, but without question he moved in the midst of mainstream galactic technoculture. Not like poor half-backwards Barrayar. The brittle artificial environment emitted its own whiff of danger, a whiff that could balloon instantly into claustrophobic terror in the event of a sudden depressurization emergency. A concourse lined with shops, hostels, and eating facilities made a central meeting area.

A curious trio idled just across the busy concourse from Miles. A big man dressed in loose clothing ideal for concealing weapons scanned the area uneasily. A professional counterpart of Sergeant Overkill's, no doubt. He and Overholt spotted each other and exchanged grim glances, carefully ignored each other after that. The bland man he guarded faded into near-invisibility beside his woman.

She was short, but astonishingly intense, slight figure and white-blonde hair cropped close to her head giving her an odd elfin look. Her black jumpsuit seemed shot with electric sparks, flowing over her skin like water, evening-wear in the day-cycle. Thin-heeled black shoes boosted her a few futile centimeters. Her lips were colored blood-carmine to match the shimmering scarf that looped across alabaster collarbones to cascade from each shoulder, framing the bare white skin of her back. She looked . . . expensive.

Her eye caught Miles's fascinated stare. Her chin lifted, and she stared back coldly.

"Victor Rotha?" The voice at Miles's elbow made him jump.

"Ah . . . Mr. Liga?" Miles, wheeling, hazarded in return. Rabbit-like pale features, protruding lip, black hair; this was the man who claimed he wished to improve the armament of his security guards at his asteroid mining facility. Sure. How—and where—had Ungari scraped Liga up? Miles was not sure he wanted to know.

"I've arranged a private room for us to talk," Liga smiled, tilting his head toward a nearby hostel entrance. "Eh," Liga added, "looks like everybody's doing business this morning." He nodded toward the trio across the concourse, who were now a quartet and moving off. The scarves snapped along like banners, floating in the quick-stepping blonde's wake.

"Who was that woman?" asked Miles.

"I don't know," said Liga. "But the man they're following is your main competition here. The agent of House Fell, the Jacksonian armaments specialists."

He looked more like a middle-aged businessman type, at least from the back. "Pol lets the Jacksonians operate here?" Miles asked. "I thought tensions were high."

"Between Pol, Aslund, and Vervain, yes," said Liga. "The Jacksonian consortium is loudly claiming neutrality. They hope to profit from all sides. But this isn't the best place to talk politics. Let's go, eh?"

As Miles expected, Liga settled them in what was obviously an otherwise-unoccupied hostel room, rented for the purpose, Miles began his memorized pitch, working through the hand-weapons, baffle-gabbing about available inventory and delivery dates.

"I'd hoped," said Liga, "for something a little more . . . authoritative."

"I have another selection of samples aboard my ship," Miles explained. "I didn't want to trouble Pol customs with them. But I can give you an overview by vid."

Miles trotted out the heavy weapons manuals. "This vid is for educational purposes only, of course, as these weapons are of a grade illegal for a private person to own in Pol local space."

"In Pol space, yes," Liga agreed. "But Pol's law doesn't run in the Hegen Hub. Yet. All you have to do is cast off from Pol Six and take a little run out beyond the ten-thousand-kilometer traffic control limit to conduct any sort of business you want, perfectly legally. The problem comes in delivering the cargo back *in* to Pol local space."

"Difficult deliveries are one of my specialties," Miles assured him. "For a small surcharge, of course."

"Eh. Good . . ." Liga flicked fast-forward through the vid catalogue. "These heavy-duty plasma arcs, now . . . how do they compare with the cannon-grade nerve disruptors?"

Miles shrugged. "Depends entirely upon whether you want to blow away people alone, or people and property both. I can make you a very good price on the nerve disruptors." He named a figure in Pol credits.

"I got a better quote than that, on a device of the same kilowattage, lately," Liga mentioned disinterestedly.

"I'll bet you did," Miles grinned. "Poison, one credit. Antidote, one hundred credits."

"What's that supposed to mean, eh?" asked Liga suspiciously.

Miles unrolled his lapel and ran his thumb down the underside, and pulled out a tiny vid tab. "Take a look at this." He inserted it into the vid viewer. A figure sprang to life, and pirouetted. It was dressed from head to toe- and finger-tips in what appeared to be glittering skin-tight netting,

"A bit drafty for long underwear, eh?" said Liga sceptically.

Miles flashed him a pained smile. "What you're looking at is what every armed force in the galaxy would like to get their hands on. The perfected single-person nerve disruptor shield net. Beta Colony's latest technological card."

Liga's eyes widened. "First I'd heard they were on the market."

"The open market, no. These are, as it were, private advance sales." Beta Colony only advertised its second or third latest advantages; staying several steps ahead of everybody else in R&D had been the harsh world's stock-in-trade for a couple of generations. In time, Beta Colony would be marketing its new device galaxy-wide. In the meantime . . .

Liga licked his pouty lower lip. "We use nerve disruptors a lot."

For security guards? Right, sure. "I have a limited supply of shield nets. First come, first served."

"The price?"

Miles named a figure in Betan dollars.

"Outrageous!" Liga rocked back in his float chair.

Miles shrugged. "Think about it. It could put your . . . organization at a considerable disadvantage not to be the first to upgrade its defenses. I'm sure you can imagine."

"I'll . . . have to check it out. Eh . . . can I have that disk to show my, eh, supervisor?"

Miles pursed his lips. "Don't get caught with it."

"No way." Liga spun the demo vid through its paces one more

time, staring in fascination at the sparkling soldier-figure, before pocketing the disk.

There. The hook was baited, and cast upon dark waters. It was going to be very interesting to see what nibbled, whether minnows or monstrous leviathans. Liga was a fish of the ramora underclass, Miles judged. Well, he had to start somewhere.

Back out on the concourse, Miles muttered worriedly to Overholt, "Did I do all right?"

"Very smooth, sir," Overholt reassured him.

Well, maybe. It had felt good, running by plan. He could almost feel himself submerging into the smarmy personality of Victor Rotha.

For lunch, Miles led Overholt to a cafeteria with seating open to the concourse, the better for anyone not-watching Ungari to observe them. He munched a sandwich of vat-produced protein, and let his tight nerves unwind a little. This act could be all right. Not nearly as overstimulating as—

"Admiral Naismith!"

Miles nearly choked on a half-chewed bite, his head swivelling frantically to identify the source of the surprised voice. Overholt jerked to full-alert, though he managed to keep his hand from flying prematurely to his concealed stunner.

Two men had paused beside his table. One Miles did not recognize. The other . . . damn! He knew that face. Square-jawed, brown-skinned, too neat and fit for his age to pass as anything but a soldier despite his Polian civilian clothes. The name, the name . . . ! One of Tung's commandos, a combat-drop-shuttle squad commander. The last time Miles had seen him they'd been suiting up together in the *Triumph* 's armory, preparing for a boarding battle. Clive Chodak, that was his name.

"I'm sorry, you're mistaken," Miles's denial was pure spinal reflex. "My name is Victor Rotha."

Chodak blinked. "What? Oh! Sorry. That is—you look a lot like somebody I used to know." He took in Overholt. His eyes queried Miles urgently. "Uh, can we join you?"

"No!" said Miles sharply, panicked. No, wait. He shouldn't throw away a possible contact. This was a complication for which he should have been prepared. But to activate Naismith prematurely, without Ungari's orders. . . . "Anyway, not here," he amended hastily.

"I . . . see, sir." With a short nod, Chodak immediately withdrew, drawing his reluctant companion with him. He managed to glance back over his shoulder only once. Miles restrained the impulse to bite his napkin in half. The two men faded into the concourse. By their urgent gestures, they appeared to be arguing.

"Was that smooth?" Miles asked plaintively.

Overholt looked mildly dismayed. "Not very." He frowned down the concourse in the direction the two men had disappeared.

It didn't take Chodak more than an hour to track Miles down aboard his Betan ship in dock. Ungari was still out.

"He says he wants to talk to you," said Overholt. He and Miles studied the vid monitor of the hatchway, where Chodak shifted impatiently from foot to foot. "What do you think he really wants?"

"Probably, to talk to me," said Miles. "Damn me if I don't want to talk to him, too."

"How well did you know him?" asked Overholt suspiciously, staring at Chodak's image.

"Not well," Miles admitted. "He seemed a competent non-com. Knew his equipment, kept his people moving, stood his ground under fire." In truth, thinking back, Miles's actual contacts with the man had been brief, all in the course of business . . . but some of those minutes had been critical, in the wild uncertainty of shipboard combat. Was Miles's gut-feel really adequate security clearance for a man he hadn't seen for almost four years? "Scan him, sure. But let's let him in and see what he has to say."

"If you so order it, sir," said Overholt neutrally.

"I do."

Chodak did not seem to resent being scanned. He carried only a registered stunner. Though he had also been an expert at hand-to-hand combat, Miles recalled, a weapon no one could confiscate. Overholt escorted him to the small ship's wardroom/mess—the Betans would have called it the rec room.

"Mr. Rotha," Chodak nodded, "I, uh . . . hoped we could talk here privately." He looked doubtfully at Overholt. "Or have you replaced Sergeant Bothari?"

"Never." Miles motioned Overholt to follow him into the corridor, didn't speak till the doors sighed shut, "I think you are an inhibiting presence, Sergeant. Would you mind waiting outside?" Miles didn't specify whom Overholt inhibited. "You can monitor, of course."

"Bad idea," Overholt frowned. "Suppose he jumps you?"

Miles's fingers tapped nervously on his trouser seam. "It's a possibility. But we're heading for Aslund next, where the Dendarii are stationed, Ungari says. He may bear useful information."

"If he tells the truth."

"Even lies can be revealing." With this doubtful argument Miles squeezed back into the wardroom, shedding Overholt.

He nodded to his visitor, now seated at a table. "Corporal Chodak."

Chodak brightened. "You do remember."

"Oh, yes. And, ah . . . are you still with the Dendarii?"

"Yes, sir. It's Sergeant Chodak, now."

"Very good. I'm not surprised."

"And, um . . . the Oseran Mercenaries."

"So I understand. Whether it's good or not remains to be seen."

"What are you posing as, sir?"

"Victor Rotha is an arms dealer."

"That's a good cover," Chodak nodded, judiciously.

Miles tried to put a casual mask on his next words by punching up two coffees. "So what are you doing on Pol Six? I thought the Den— the fleet was hired out on Aslund."

"At Aslund Station, here in the Hub," Chodak corrected. "It's just a couple days' flight across-system. What there is of it, so far. Government contractors." He shook his head.

"Behind schedule and over cost?"

"You got it." He accepted the coffee without hesitation, holding it between lean hands, and took a preliminary slurp. "I can't stay long." He turned the cup, set it on the table. "Sir, I think I may have accidentally done you a bad turn. I was so startled to see you there. . . . Anyway, I wanted to . . . to warn you, I guess. Are you on the way back to the fleet?"

"I'm afraid I can't discuss my plans. Not even with you."

Chodak gave him a penetrating stare from black almond eyes. "You always were tricky."

"As an experienced combat soldier, do you prefer frontal assaults?"

"No, sir!" Chodak smiled slightly.

"Suppose you tell me. I take it you are—or are one—of the fleet intelligence agents scattered around the Hub. There had better be more than one of you, or the organization's fallen apart sadly in my absence." In fact, half the inhabitants of Pol Six at the moment were probably spies of some stripe, considering the number of potential players in this game. Not to mention double agents—ought they to be counted twice?

"Why have you been gone so *long*, sir?" Chodak's tone was almost accusative.

"It wasn't my intention," Miles temporized. "For a portion of the time I was a prisoner in a . . . place I'd rather not describe. I only escaped about three months back." Well, that was one way of describing Kyril Island.

"You, sir! We could have rescued—"

"No, you couldn't have," Miles said sharply. "The situation was one of extreme delicacy. It was resolved to my satisfaction. But I was then faced with . . . considerable clean-up in areas of my operations other than the Dendarii fleet. Far-flung areas. Sorry, but you people are not my only concern. Nevertheless, I'm worried. I should have heard more from Commodore Jesek." Indeed, he should have.

"Commodore Jesek no longer commands. There was a financial reorganization and command restructuring, about a year ago, through the committee of captain-owners and Admiral Oser. Spearheaded by Admiral Oser."

"Where is Jesek?"

"He was demoted to fleet engineer."

Disturbing, but Miles could see it. "Not necessarily a bad thing. Jesek was never as aggressive as, say, Tung. And Tung?"

Chodak shook his head. "He was demoted from chief-of-staff to personnel officer. A nothing-job."

"That seems . . . wasteful."

"Oser doesn't trust Tung. And Tung doesn't love Oser, either. Oser's been trying to force him out for a year, but he hangs on, despite the humiliation of . . . um. It's not easy to get rid of him. Oser can't afford—yet—to decimate his staff, and too may key people are personally loyal to Tung."

Miles's eyebrow rose. "Including yourself?"

Chodak said distantly, "He got things done. I considered him a superior officer."

"So did I."

Chodak nodded shortly. "Sir . . . the thing is . . . the man who was with me in the cafeteria is my senior here. And he's one of Oser's. I can't think of any way short of killing him to stop him reporting our encounter."

"I have no desire to start a civil war in my own command structure," said Miles mildly. *Yet.* "I think it's more important that he not suspect you spoke to me privately. Let him report. I've struck deals with Admiral Oser before, to our mutual benefit."

"I'm not sure Oser thinks so, sir. I think he thinks he was screwed."

Miles barked a realistic laugh. "What, I doubled the size of the fleet during the Tau Verde war. Even as third officer, he ended up commanding more than he had before, a smaller slice of a bigger pie."

"But the side he originally contracted us to lost."

"Not so. Both sides gained from that truce we forced. It was a win-win result, except for a little lost face. What, can't Oser feel he's won unless somebody else loses?"

Chodak looked grim. "I think that may be the case, sir. He says—I've heard him say—you ran a scam on us. You were never an admiral, never an officer of any kind. If Tung hadn't double-crossed him, he'd have kicked your ass to hell." Chodak's gaze on Miles was broodingly thoughtful. "What were you really?"

Miles smiled gently. "I was the winner. Remember?"

Chodak snorted, half-amused. "Yee-ah."

"Don't let poor Oser's revisionist history fog your mind. You were there."

Chodak shook his head ruefully. "You didn't really need my warning, did you." He moved to stand up.

"Never assume anything. And, ah . . . take care of yourself. That means, cover your ass. I'll remember you, later."

"Sir." Chodak nodded. Overholt, waiting in the corridor in a quasi-Imperial Guardsman pose, escorted him firmly to the shuttle hatch.

Miles sat in the wardroom, and nibbled gently on the rim of his coffee cup, considering certain surprising parallels between command restructuring in a free mercenary fleet and the internecine wars of the Barrayaran Vor. Might the mercenaries be thought of as a miniature, simplified, or laboratory version of the real thing? *Oser should have been around during the Vordarian's Pretendership, and seen how the big boys operate.* Still, Miles had best not underestimate the potential dangers and complexities of the situation. His death in a miniature conflict would be just as absolute as his death in a large one.

Hell, what death? What had he to do with the Dendarii, or the Oserans, after all? Oser was right, it had been a scam, and the only wonder was how long it had taken the man to wake to the fact. Miles could see no immediate need to reinvolve himself with the Dendarii at all. In fact, he could be well-rid of a dangerous political embarrassment. Let Oser have them, they'd been his in the first place anyway.

I have three sworn liege-people in that fleet. My own personal body politic.

How *easy* it had been to slip back into being Naismith. . . .

Anyway, activating Naismith wasn't Miles decision. It was Captain Ungari's.

Ungari was the first to point this out, when he returned later and Overholt briefed him. A controlled man, his fury showed by subtle signs, a sharpening of the voice, deeper lines of tension around the eyes and mouth. "You violated your cover. You *never* break cover. It's the first rule of survival in this business."

"Sir, may I respectfully submit, I didn't blow it," Miles replied steadily. "Chodak did. He seemed to realize it, too, he's not stupid. He apologized as best he could." Chodak indeed might be subtler than first glance would indicate, for at this point, he had an in with both sides in the putative Dendarii command schism, whoever came out on top. Calculation or chance? Chodak was either smart or lucky, in either case he could be a useful addition to Miles's side. . . .*What side, huh? Ungari isn't going to let me near the Dendarii after this.*

Ungari frowned at the vidplate, which had just replayed the recording of Miles's interview with the mercenary. "It sounds more and more like the Naismith cover may be too dangerous to activate at all. If your Oser's little palace coup is anything like what this fellow indicates, Illyan's fantasy of you simply ordering the Dendarii to get lost is straight out the airlock. I thought it sounded too easy." Ungari paced the wardroom, tapping his right fist into his left palm. "Well, we may still get some use out of Victor Rotha. Much as I'd like to confine you to quarters—"

Strange, how many of his superiors said that.

"—Liga wants to see Rotha again this evening. Maybe to place an order for some of our fictitious cargo. String it out—I want you to get past him to the next level of his organization. His boss, or his boss's boss."

"Who owns Liga, do you suspect?"

Ungari stopped pacing, and turned his hands palm-out. "The Cetagandans? Jackson's Whole? Any one of half-a-dozen others? ImpSec is spread thin out here. But if it were proved Liga's criminal organization are Cetagandan puppets, it could be worth sending a full-time agent to penetrate their ranks. So find out! Hint at more goodies in your bag. Take bribes. Blend in. And move it along. I'm almost finished here, and Illyan particularly wants to know when Aslund Station will be fully operational as a defensive base."

Miles punched the door chime of the hostel room. His chin tic'd up. He cleared his throat and straightened his shoulders. Overholt glanced up and down the empty corridor.

The door hissed open. Miles blinked in astonishment.

"Ah, Mr. Rotha." The light cool voice belonged to the brief blonde he'd seen in the concourse that morning. Her jumpsuit was now skin-fitting red silk with a downcurving neckline, a glittering red ruff rising from the back of the neck to frame her sculptured head, and high-heeled red suede boots. She favored him with a high-voltage smile.

"I'm sorry," said Miles automatically, "I must be in the wrong place."

"Not at all." A slim hand opened in an expansive, welcoming gesture. "You're right on time."

"I had an appointment with a Mr. Liga, here."

"Yes, and I've taken over the appointment. Do come in. My name is Livia Nu."

Well, she couldn't possibly be carrying any concealed weapons. Miles stepped within, and was unsurprised to see her bodyguard, idling in one corner of the hostel room. The man nodded to Overholt, who nodded back, both wary as two cats. And where was the third man? Not here, evidently.

She drifted to a liquid-filled settee, and arranged herself upon it.

"Are you, uh, Mr. Liga's supervisor?" Miles asked. No, Liga had denied knowing who she was. . . .

She hesitated fractionally. "In a sense, yes."

One of them was lying—no, not necessarily. If she were indeed high in Liga's organization, he would not have identified her to Rotha. Damn.

"—but you may think of me as a procurement agent."

God. Pol Six really was hip-deep in spies. "For whom?"

"Ah," she smiled. "One of the advantages of dealing with small suppliers is always their no-questions-asked policy. One of the few advantages."

"No-questions-asked is House Fell's slogan, I believe. They have the advantage of a fixed and secure base. I've learned to be cautious about selling arms to people who might be shooting at me in the near future."

Her blue eyes widened. "Who would want to shoot at you?"

"Misguided folk," Miles tossed off. Ye gods. He was not in control of this conversation. He exchanged a harried look with Overholt, who was being out-blanded by his counterpart.

"We must chat." She patted the cushion beside her invitingly. "Do sit down, Victor. Ah," she nodded to her bodyguard, "why don't you wait outside."

Miles seated himself on the edge of the settee, trying to guess the woman's age. Her complexion was smooth and white. Only the skin of her eyelids was soft and faintly puckered. Miles thought of Ungari's orders—take bribes, blend in. . . . "Perhaps you should wait outside also," he said to Overholt.

Overholt looked torn, but of the two, he clearly wanted more to keep an eye on the large armed man. He nodded, apparently in acquiescence, actually in approval, and followed her man out.

Miles smiled in what he hoped was a friendly way. She looked positively seductive. Miles eased cautiously back in the cushions, and tried to look seduceable. A veritable espionage fantasy encounter, of the sort Ungari had told him never happened. Maybe they just never happened to Ungari, eh? *My what sharp teeth you have, Miss.*

Her hand went to her cleavage—a riveting gesture—and withdrew a tiny, familiar vid disk. She leaned over to insert it in the vid player on the low table before them, and it took Miles a moment to shift his attention to the vid. The little glittering soldier-figure went through its stylized gestures once again. Ha. So, she really was Liga's supervisor. Very good, he was getting somewhere now.

"This is really remarkable, Victor. How did you come by it?"

"A happy accident."

"How many can you supply?"

"A strictly limited number. Say, fifty. I'm not a manufacturer. Liga did mention the price?"

"I thought it high."

"If you can find another supplier who offers these for less, I will be happy to match his price and knock off ten percent." Miles managed to bow sitting down.

She made a faint amused sound, down in her throat. "The volume offered is too low."

"There are several ways you could profit from even a small number of these, if you got into the trade early enough. Such as selling working models to interested governments. I mean to have a share of that profit, before the market is saturated and the price drops. You could too."

"Why don't you? Sell them directly to governments, that is."

"What makes you think I haven't?" Miles smiled. "But—consider my routes out of this area. I came in past Barrayar and Pol. I must exit via either Jackson's Whole or the Cetagandan Empire. Unfortunately, through either route I run a high risk of being relieved of this particular cargo without any compensation whatsoever." For that matter, where had Barrayar obtained its working model of the shield-suit? Was there a real Victor Rotha, and where was he now? Where *had* Illyan gotten their ship?

"So, you carry them with you?"

"I didn't say that."

"Hm." She smiled. "Can you deliver one tonight?"

"What size?"

"Small." One long-nailed finger traced a line down her body, from breast to thigh, to indicate exactly how small.

Miles sighed mournfully. "Unfortunately, these were sized for the average-to-large combat soldier. Cutting one down is a considerable technical challenge—one which I am in fact still working on myself."

"How thoughtless of the manufacturer."

"I entirely agree, Citizen Nu."

She looked at him more carefully. Did her smile grow slightly more genuine?

"Anyway, I prefer to sell them in wholesale lots. If your organization isn't financially up to it—"

"An arrangement might yet be made."

"Promptly, I trust. I'll be moving on soon."

She murmured absently, "Perhaps not . . ." then looked up with a quick frown. "What's your next stop?"

Ungari had to file a public flight plan anyway. "Aslund."

"Hm . . . yes, we must come to some arrangement. Absolutely."

Were those blue flickers what were called bedroom eyes? The effect was lulling, almost hypnotic. *I finally meet a woman who's barely taller than I am, and I don't even know which side she's on.* He of all men ought not to mistake short for weak or helpless.

"Can I meet your boss?"

"Who?" Her brows lowered.

"The man I saw you both with this morning."

". . . oh. So, you've already seen him."

"Set me up a meeting. Let's do serious business. Betan dollars, remember."

"Pleasure before business, surely." Her breath puffed against his ear, a faint spicy fog.

Was she trying to soften him up? What *for?* Ungari had said, don't break cover. Surely it would be in character for Victor Rotha to take all he could get. Plus ten percent. "You don't have to do this," he managed to choke out. His heart was beating entirely too fast.

"I don't do *everything* for business reasons," she purred.

Why, indeed, should she bother to seduce a sleazy little gun runner? What pleasure was in it for her? What was in it *besides* pleasure for her? *Maybe she likes me.* Miles winced, picturing himself offering that explanation to Ungari. Her arm circled his neck. His hand, unwilled, rose to stroke the fine pelt of her hair. A highly aesthetic tactile experience, just as he'd imagined. . . .

Her hand tightened. In pure nervous reflex, Miles leapt to his feet.

And stood there feeling like an idiot. It had been a caress, not incipient strangulation. The angle was all wrong for attack leverage.

She flung herself back in the seat, slim arm stretching along the top of the cushions. "Victor!" Her voice was amused, her brow arched. "I wasn't going to bite your neck."

His face was hot. "I-have-to-go-now." He cleared his throat to bring his voice back down to its lower register. His hand swooped to pluck the vid disk from the player. Her hand leapt toward it, then fell back languidly, pretending disinterest. Miles hit the door comm.

Overholt was there at once, in the sliding door aperture. Miles's gut eased. If his bodyguard had been gone, Miles would have known this at once for some kind of set-up. Too late, of course.

"Maybe later," Miles gabbled. "After you've taken delivery. We could get together." Delivery of a nonexistent cargo? What was he saying?

She shook her head in disbelief. Her laugh followed him down the corridor. It had a brittle edge.

Miles lurched awake when the lights snapped on in his cabin. Ungari, fully dressed, was in the doorway. Behind him their jump pilot, wearing only his underwear and a sleep-stunned expression, jittered uncertainly.

"Dress later," Ungari snarled to the pilot. "Just get us free of the dock and run us out beyond the ten-thousand-kilometer limit. I'll be up to help set course in a few minutes." He added half to himself, "As soon as I know where the devil we're going. *Move.*"

The pilot fled. Ungari strode to Miles's bedside. "Vorkosigan, what the hell happened in that hostel room?"

Miles squeezed his eyes against the glares of both the lights and Ungari, and suppressed an impulse to hide under the covers from both. "Ha?" His mouth was dry with sleep.

"I've just gotten an advance warning—bare minutes advance warning—of an arrest order being put out by Pol Six civil security for Victor Rotha."

"But I never touched the lady!" Miles protested, dizzied.

"Liga's body was found murdered in your meeting room."

"What!"

"The security lab has just finished timing it—to about when you met. Were to meet. The arrest order will be on the net in minutes, and we'll be locked in here."

"But I didn't. I never even saw Liga, only his boss, Livia Nu. I mean

—if I'd done any such thing, I'd have reported it to you immediately, sir!"

"Thank you," said Ungari dryly. "I'm glad to know that." His voice harshened. "You're being framed, of course."

"Who—" Yes. There could have been another, grimmer way for Livia Nu to have relieved Liga of that top secret vid disk. But if she wasn't Liga's superior, or even a member of his Polian criminal organization at all, who was she? "We need to know more, sir! This could be the start of something."

"This could be the *end* of our mission. Damn! And now we can't retreat back through Pol to Barrayar. Cut off. Where next?" Ungari paced, evidently thinking aloud. "I want to go to Aslund. Its extradition treaty with Pol has broken down at present, but . . . then there are your mercenary complications. Now that they've connected Rotha to Naismith. Thanks to your carelessness."

"From what Chodak said, I don't think Admiral Naismith would exactly be welcomed back with open arms," Miles agreed reluctantly.

"Jackson's Whole's consortium station has no extradition treaty with anyone. This cover's gone completely sour. Rotha and Naismith, both useless. It has to be the Consortium. I'll ditch this ship there, go underground, and double back to Aslund on my own."

"What about me, sir?"

"You and Overholt will have to split off and take the long way home."

Home. Home in disgrace. "Sir . . . running away looks bad. Suppose we sat tight, and cleared Rotha of the charges? We wouldn't be cut off any more, and Rotha would still be a viable cover. It's possible we're being hustled into doing just this, cutting and running."

"I don't see how anyone could have anticipated my information source in Polian civil security. I think we're meant to be locked up here in dock." Ungari tapped his right fist into his palm once, a gesture of decision this time. "The Consortium it is." He wheeled and exited, boots tromping down the deck. A change of vibration and air pressure, and a few muted clanks, told Miles their ship was now breaking from Pol Six.

Miles said aloud to the empty cabin. "But what if they have plans for both contingencies? *I* would." He shook his head doubtfully, and rose to dress and follow Ungari.

9

The Jacksonian Consortium's jump point station, Miles decided, differed from Pol's mainly in the assortment of things its merchants offered for sale. He stood before the book-disk dispenser in a concourse very like Pol Six's and flicked the vid fast-forward through a huge catalogue of pornography. Well, mostly fast-forward, his search was punctuated by a few pauses, from bemused to stunned. Nobly resisting curiosity, he reached the military history section only to find a disappointingly thin collection of titles.

He inserted his credit card and the machine dispensed three wafers. Not that he was all that interested in *The Adumbration of Trigonial Strategy in the Wars of Minos IV,* but it was going to be a long, dull ride home, and Sergeant Overholt did not promise to be the most sparkling of traveling companions. Miles pocketed the disks and sighed. What a waste of time, effort, and anticipation this mission had been.

Ungari had arranged for the "sale" of Victor Rotha's ship, pilot, and engineer to a front man who would deliver it, eventually, back to Barrayaran Imperial Security. Miles's pleading suggestions to his superior on how to make more use of Rotha, Naismith, or even Ensign Vorkosigan had then been interrupted by an ultra-coded message from ImpSec HQ, for Ungari's eyes only. Ungari had withdrawn to decode it, and emerged half an hour later, dead-white around the lips.

He had then moved his timetable up and departed within the hour on a commercial ship to Aslund Station. Alone. Refusing to impart the contents of the message to Miles, or even to Sergeant Overholt. Refusing to take Miles along. Refusing Miles permission to at least continue military observations independently on the Consortium.

Ungari left Overholt to Miles, or vice versa. It was a little hard to tell who had been left in charge of whom. Overholt seemed to be acting less like a subordinate and more like a nanny all the time, discouraging Miles's attempted explorations of the Consortium, insisting he keep safely to his hostel room. They waited now to board an Escobaran commercial liner slated for a nonstop run to Escobar, where they would report to the Barrayaran Embassy which would no doubt ship them home. Home, and with nothing to show for it.

Miles checked his chrono. Another twenty minutes to kill before boarding. They might as well go sit. With an irritable glance at his shadow Overholt, Miles trudged wearily down the concourse. Overholt followed, frowning general disapproval.

Miles brooded on Livia Nu. In fleeing from her erotic invitation he'd surely missed the adventure of his short lifetime. Yet that hadn't been the look of love on her face. Anyway, he'd worry about a woman who could fall madly in love at first sight with Victor Rotha. The light in her eyes had been more on the order of a gourmet contemplating an unusual hors d'oeuvre just presented by the waiter. He'd felt like he'd had parsley sticking out of his ears.

She might have been dressed like a courtesan, moved like a courtesan, but there'd been none of the courtesan's eagerness to please about her, nothing servile. The gestures of power in the garments of powerlessness. Unsettling.

So beautiful.

Courtesan, criminal, spy, what was she? Above all, who did she belong to? Was she Liga's boss, or Liga's opponent? Or Liga's fate? Had she killed the rabbity man herself? Whatever else she was, Miles was increasingly convinced, she was a key piece in the puzzle of the Hegen Hub. They should have followed her up, not fled from her. Sex wasn't the only opportunity he'd missed. The meeting with Livia Nu was going to bother him for a long time.

Miles looked up to find his way blocked by a pair of Consortium goons—civil security officers, he corrected his thought ironically. He stood, feet planted, and lifted his chin. What now? "Yes, gentlemen?"

The big one looked to the enormous one, who cleared his throat. "Mr. Victor Rotha?"

"If I am, then what?"

"An arrest order has been purchased for you. It charges you with the murder of one Sydney Liga. Do you wish to outbid?"

"Probably." Miles's lip curled in exasperation. What a development. "Who's bidding for my arrest?"

"The name is Cavilo."

Miles shook his head. "Don't even know him. Is he with Polian Civil Security, by chance?"

The officer checked his report panel. "No." He added chattily, "The Polians almost never do business with us. They think we ought to trade them criminals for free. As if we wanted any back!"

"Huh. That's supply and demand for you." Miles blew out his breath. Illyan was not going to be thrilled about *this* charge on his expense account. "How much did this Cavilo offer for me?"

The officer checked his panel again. His brows rose. "Twenty thousand Betan dollars. He must want you a lot."

Miles made a small leaky noise. "I don't have that much *on* me."

The officer pulled out his come-along stick. "Well, then."

"I'll have to make arrangements."

"You'll have to make arrangements from Detention, sir."

"But I'll miss my ship!"

"That's probably the idea," the officer agreed. "Considering the timing and all."

"Suppose—if that's all this Cavilo wants—he then withdraws his bid?"

"He'll lose a substantial deposit."

Jacksonian justice was truly blind. They'd sell it to anyone. "Uh, may I have a word with my assistant?"

The officer pursed his lips, and studied Overholt suspiciously. "Make it fast."

"What d'you think, Sergeant?" Miles turned to Overholt and asked lowly. "They don't seem to have an order for you. . . ."

Overholt looked tense, tight mouth annoyed and eyes almost panicked. "If we could make it to the ship. . . ."

The rest hung unspoken. The Escobarans shared the Polian disapproval of Jacksonian Consortium "law." Once aboard the liner, Miles would be on Escobaran "soil"; the captain would not voluntarily yield him up. Could, would, this Cavilo be able to bid enough to intern the whole Escobaran liner? The sum involved would be astronomical "Try."

Miles turned back toward the Consortium officers, smiling, wrists held out in surrender. Overholt exploded into action.

The sergeant's first kick sent the enormous goon's come-along stick flying. Overholt's momentum flowed into a whirl that brought his double hands up against the second goon's head with great force. Miles was already in motion. He dodged a wild grab, and sprinted as best he could up the concourse. At this point he spotted the third goon, in plainclothes. Miles could tell who he was by the glitter of the tangle-field he tossed in front of Miles's pistoning legs. The man snorted with laughter as Miles pitched forward, trying to roll and save his brittle bones. Miles hit the concourse floor with a whump that knocked the air from his lungs. He inhaled through clenched teeth, not crying out, as the pain in his chest competed with the burn of the tangle-net around his ankles. He wrenched himself around on the floor, looking back the way he had come.

The less enormous goon was standing bent over, hands to his head, dizzied. The other was retrieving his come-along stick from where it had skittered to a stop. By elimination, the stunned heap on the pavement must be Sergeant Overholt.

The goon with the stick stared at Overholt and shook his head, and stepped over him toward Miles. The dizzied goon pulled out his own stick and gave the downed man a shock to the head, and followed without a backward glance. Nobody, apparently, wanted to buy Overholt.

"There will be a ten percent surcharge for resisting arrest," the spokesman-goon remarked coldly down to Miles. Miles squinted up the shiny columns of his boots. The shock-stick came down like a club.

On the third blazing blow he began screaming. On the seventh, he passed out.

He came to consciousness altogether too soon, while still being dragged along between the two uniformed men. He was shivering uncontrollably. His breathing was messed up somehow, irregular shallow gasps that didn't give him enough air. Waves of pins-and-needles pulsed through his nervous system. He had a kaleidoscopic impression of lift tubes and corridors, and more bare functional corridors. They jerked to a halt at last. When the goons let his arms go he fell to hands and knees, then the cold floor.

Another civil security officer peered over a comconsole desk at him. A hand grasped Miles's head by the hair, and yanked it back; the red flicker of a retinal scan blinded him momentarily. His eyes seemed extraordinarily sensitive to light. His shaking hands were pressed hard against some sort of identification pad; released, he fell back into his huddle. His pockets were stripped out, stunner, IDs, tickets, cash, all dumped pell-mell into a plastic bag. Miles emitted a muffled squeak of dismay as they bundled the white jacket, with all its useful secrets, into the bag as well. The lock was keyed closed with his thumbprint, pinched against it.

The Detention officer craned his neck. "Does he want to outbid?"

"Unh . . ." Miles managed to respond, when his head was pulled back again.

"He said he did," the arresting goon said helpfully.

The Detention officer shook his head. "We're going to have to wait till the shock wears off. You guys overdid it, I think. He's only a little runt."

"Yeah, but he had a big guy with him who gave us trouble. The little mutant seemed to be in charge, so we let him take payment for both."

"That's fair," the Detention officer conceded. "Well, it'll be a while. Throw him in the cooler till he stops shaking enough to talk."

"Sure that's a good idea? Funny-looking as he is, the boy-ohs might want to play games. He might still ransom himself."

"Mm." The Detention officer looked Miles over judiciously. "Throw him in the waiting room with Marda's techies, then. They're a quiet bunch, they'll leave him alone. And they'll be gone soon."

Miles was dragged again—his legs didn't respond at all to his will, only jerking spasmodically. The leg braces seemed to have had some amplifying effect on the shocks administered there, or maybe it was the combination with the tangle-field. A long room like a barracks, with a row of cots down each wall, swam past his vision. The goons heaved him, not unkindly, onto an empty cot in the less-populated end of the room. The senior one made a dim sort of effort to straighten him out, tossed a light blanket across his still uncontrollably-twitching form, and they left him.

A little time passed, with nothing to distract him from the full enjoyment and appreciation of his new array of physical sensations. He'd thought he'd sampled every sort of agony in the catalogue, but the goons' shock-sticks had found out nerves and synapses and ganglial knots he'd never known he possessed. Nothing like pain, to concentrate the attention upon the self. Practically solipsistic, it was. But it seemed to be easing—if only his body would stop these quasi-epileptic seizures, which were exhausting him. . . .

A face wavered into view. A familiar face.

"Gregor! Am I glad to see you," Miles burbled inanely. He felt his burning eyes widen. His hands shot out to clench Gregor's shirt, a pale blue prisoner's smock. *"What the hell are you doing here?"*

"It's a long story."

"Ah! Ah!" Miles struggled up onto his elbow and stared around wildly for assassins, hallucinations, he knew not what. "God! Where's—"

Gregor pushed him back down with a hand on his chest. "Calm down." And under his breath. "And shut up! . . . You better rest a bit. You don't look very good right now."

Actually, Gregor didn't look so good himself, sitting on the edge of Miles's cot. His face was pale and tired, peppered with beard stubble. His normally military-cut and combed black hair was a tangle. His hazel eyes looked nervous. Miles choked back panic.

"My name is Greg Bleakman," the emperor informed Miles urgently.

"I can't remember what my name is right now," Miles stuttered. "Oh—yeah. Victor Rotha. I think. But how did you get from—"

Gregor looked around vaguely. "The walls have ears, I think?"

"Yes, maybe." Miles subsided slightly. The man on the next cot shook his head with a God-save-me-from-these-assholes look, turned over and put his pillow over his head. "But, uh . . . did you get here, like, under your own power?"

"Unfortunately, all my own doing. You remember that time we were joking about running away from home?"

"Yeah?"

"Well," Gregor took a breath, "it turned out to be a really bad idea."

"Couldn't you have figured that out in advance?"

"I—" Gregor broke off, to stare up the long room as a guard stuck his head in the door to bawl, "Five minutes!"

"Oh, hell."

"What? What?"

"They're coming for us."

"Who's coming for who, what the hell is going on, *Gregor*— Greg—"

"I had a berth on a freighter, I thought, but they dumped me off here. Without pay," Gregor explained rapidly. "Stiffed me. I didn't have so much as a half-mark on me. I tried to get something on an outbound ship, but before I could, I got arrested for vagrancy. Jacksonian law is insane," he added reflectively.

"I know. Then what?"

"They were apparently making a deliberate sweep, press-gang style. Seems some enterpreneur is selling tech-trained work gangs to the Aslunders, to work on their Hub station, which is running behind schedule."

Miles blinked. "Slave labor?"

"Of a sort. The carrot is, when the sentence is up, we're to be discharged on Aslund Station. Most of these techs don't seem to mind too much. No pay, but we—they—will be fed and housed, and escape Jacksonian security, so in the end they'll be no worse off than when they started, broke and unemployed. Most of them seem to think they'll find berths outbound from Aslund eventually. Being without funds is not such a heinous crime, there."

Miles's head pounded. "They're taking you away?"

Tension pooled in Gregor's eyes, contained, not permitted to seep over into the rest of his stiff face. "Right now, I think."

"God! I can't let—"

"But how did you find me here—" Gregor began in turn, then looked in frustration up the room, where blue-smocked men and women were grumbling to their feet. "Are you here to—"

Miles stared around frantically. The blue-clad man on the cot next to his now lay on his side, watching them with a bored glower. He wasn't over-tall. . . .

"You!" Miles scrambled overboard, and crouched at the man's side. "You want to get out of this trip?"

The man looked slightly less bored. "How?"

"Trade clothes. Trade ID's. You take my place, I take yours."

The man looked suspicious. "What's the catch?"

"No catch. I got a lot of credit. I was going to buy my way out of here in a while." Miles paused. "There's going to be a surcharge for my resisting arrest, though."

"Ah." A catch identified, the man looked slightly more interested.

"Please! I have to go with—with my friend. Right now." The babble was rising, as the techs assembled in the room's far end by the exit. Gregor wandered around behind the man's cot.

The man pursed his lips. "Naw," he decided. "If whatever you're in for is worse than this, I don't want anything to do with it." He swung to a sitting position, preparing to rise and join the line.

Miles, still crouched on the floor, raised his hands in supplication. "Please—"

Gregor, perfectly placed, pounced. He grabbed the man around the neck in a neat choke and flipped him over the side of his cot, out of sight. Thank God the Barrayaran aristocracy still insisted on military training for its scions. Miles staggered to his feet, the better to obscure the view from up the room. Some small thumping noises came from the floor. In a few moments, a prisoner's blue smock skidded under the cot to fetch up at Miles's sandaled feet. Miles squatted and pulled it on over his green silks—fortunately, it was a bit oversized—then struggled into the loose trousers that followed. Some shoving sounds, as the man's unconscious body was pushed out of sight under the cot, and Gregor stood, panting slightly, very white.

"I can't get these damn belt strings," Miles said. They skittered from his trembling hands.

Gregor tied up Miles's pants, and rolled up his overlong trouser legs. "You need his ID, or you can't get food or register your work-credits," Gregor hissed out of the corner of his mouth, and leaned artistically against the end of the cot in an idle pose.

Miles checked his pocket and found the standard computer card. "All right." He stood next to Gregor, teeth bared in a weird grin. "I'm about to pass out."

Gregor's hand locked his elbow. "Don't. It'll draw attention."

They walked up the room and slipped into the end of the shuffling, complaining, blue-clad line. A sleepy-looking guard at the door checked them out, running a scanner over the IDs.

". . . twenty-three, twenty-four, twenty-five. That's it. Take 'em away."

They were turned over to another set of guards, not in the uniform of the Consortium but some minor Jacksonian House livery, gold and black. Miles kept his face down as they were herded out of Detention. Only Gregor's hand kept him on his feet. They passed through a corridor, another corridor, down a lift tube—Miles nearly threw up during the drop—another corridor. *What if this damned ID has a locator?* Miles thought suddenly. At the next drop tube he shed it; the little card twinkled away into the dim distance, silent and unnoticed. A docking bay, a hatchway, the brief weightlessness of the flexible docking tube, and they boarded a ship. *Sergeant Overholt, where are you now?*

It was clearly an intra-system carrier, not a jump ship, and not very large. The men were separated from the women and directed down opposite ends of a corridor lined with cabin doors leading to four-bunk cubicles. The prisoners spread out, selecting their quarters without apparent interference from the guards.

Miles make a quick count and multiplication. "We can get one to ourselves, if we try," he whispered urgently to Gregor. He ducked into the nearest, and they hit the door control quickly. Another prisoner made to follow them in, to be met with a united snarl of "Back off!" He withdrew hastily. The door did not slide open again.

The cabin was dirty, and lacked such amenities as bedding for the mattresses, but the plumbing worked. As Miles got a drink of lukewarm water he heard and felt the hatch close, and the ship undock. They were safe for the moment. How long?

"When do you think that guy you choked is going to wake up?" Miles asked Gregor, who sat on the edge of one bunk.

"I'm not sure. I've never choked a man before." Gregor looked sick. "I . . . felt something strange, under my hand. I'm afraid I might have broken his neck."

"He was still breathing," Miles said. He walked to the opposite lower bunk and prodded it. No sign of vermin. He seated himself gingerly. The severe shakes were passing off, leaving only a tremula, but he still felt weak in the knees. "When he wakes up—as soon as they find him, whether he wakes up or not—it's not going to take them long to figure out where I went. I should have just waited, and followed you, and bought you back. Assuming I could bid myself free. This was a *stupid* idea. Why didn't you stop me?"

Gregor stared. "I thought you knew what you were doing. Isn't Illyan right behind you?"

"Not as far as I know."

"I thought you were in Illyan's department now. I thought you were sent to find me. This . . . isn't some kind of bizarre rescue?"

"No!" Miles shook his head, and immediately regretted the motion. "Maybe you'd better begin at the beginning."

"I'd been on Komarr for a week. Under the domes. High-level talks on wormhole route treaties—we're still trying to get the Escobarans to permit passage of our military vessels. There's some idea of letting their inspection teams seal our weapons during passage. Our general staff thinks it's too much, theirs thinks it's too little. I signed a couple of agreements—whatever the Council of Ministers shoved in front of me—"

"Dad makes you *read* them, surely."

"Oh, yes. Anyway, there was a military review that afternoon. And a state dinner in the evening, which broke up early, a couple of the negotiators had to catch ships. I went back to my quarters, some oligarch's old town house. Big place at the edge of the dome, near the shuttleport. My suite was high in this building. I went out on the balcony—it didn't help much. Still felt claustrophobic, under the dome."

"Komarrans don't like open air, either," Miles noted in fairness. "I

knew one who had breathing problems—like asthma—whenever he
had to go outside. Strictly psychosomatic."

Gregor shrugged, gazing at his shoes. "Anyway, I noticed . . .
there were no guards in sight. For a change. I don't know why the
hole, there'd been a man there earlier. They thought I was asleep, I
guess. It was after midnight. I couldn't sleep. I was leaning over the
balcony, and thinking, if I toppled off . . ." Gregor hesitated.

"It would be quick," Miles supplied dryly. He knew that state of
mind, oh yes.

Gregor glanced up at him, and smiled ironically. "Yes. I was a little
drunk."

You were a lot drunk.

"Quick, yes. Smash my skull. It would hurt a lot, but not for long.
Maybe even not a lot. Maybe just a flash of heat."

Miles shuddered, concealed in his shock-stick tremula.

"I went over—I caught these plants. Then I realized, I could climb
down as easily as up. More easily. I felt free, as if I *had* died. I started
walking. Nobody stopped me. All the time, I expected someone to
stop me.

"I ended up in the freightyard end of the shuttleport. At a bar. I
told this fellow, the free trader, I was a norm-space navigator. I'd
done that, on my ship duty. I'd lost my ID, and was afraid Barrayaran
Security would rough me up. He believed me—or believed something. Anyway, he gave me a berth. We probably broke orbit before
my batman went in to wake me that morning."

Miles chewed his knuckles. "So from ImpSec's point of view, you
evaporated from a fully guarded room. No note, no trace—and on
Komarr."

"The ship made a straight run through to Pol—I stayed aboard—
and then nonstop to the Consortium. I didn't get along too well at
first, on the freighter. I thought I was doing better. Guess not. But I
thought, Illyan was probably right behind me anyway."

"Komarr." Miles rubbed his temples. "Do you realize what has to
be happening back there? Illyan will be convinced it's some sort of
political kidnapping. I bet he's got every Security operative and half
the army tearing those domes apart bolt by bolt, looking for you.
You're way out ahead of them. They won't look beyond Komarr
till . . ." Miles counted out days on his fingers. "Still, Illyan should
have alerted all his outlying agents . . . almost a week ago. Ha! I bet
that was the message that put Ungari up in the air, just before he left
in such a hurry. Sent to Ungari, not to me." *Not to me. Nobody's even
counting me.* "But it should have been all over the news—"

"It was, sort of," Gregor offered. "There was a sententious announcement that I'd been ill and retired to rest in seclusion at Vorkosigan Surleau. They're suppressing."

Miles could just picture it. "Gregor, how could you do this! They'll be going insane back home!"

"I'm sorry," said Gregor stiffly. "I knew it was a mistake . . . almost immediately. Even before the hangover cut in."

"Why didn't you get off at Pol, then, and go to the Barrayaran embassy?"

"I thought I might still . . . dammit," he broke off, "why should these people *own* me?"

"Childish, stunt," Miles gritted through his teeth.

Gregor's head jerked up in anger, but he said nothing.

The full realization of his position was just beginning to sink in to Miles, like lead in his belly. *I'm the only man in the universe who knows where the Emperor of Barrayar is right now. If anything happens to Gregor, I could be his heir. In fact, if anything happens to Gregor, quite a lot of people will think I . . .*

And if the Hegen Hub found out who Gregor really was, a free-for-all of epic proportions could follow. The Jacksonians would take him for simple ransom. Aslund, Pol, Vervain, any or all might seek some power play. The Cetagandans most of all—if they could gain possession of Gregor in secret, who knew what subtle psychological programming they might attempt; if openly, what threats? And Miles and Gregor were both trapped on a ship they didn't control—Miles might be snatched away at any moment by Consortium goons or worse—

Miles was an ImpSec officer, now, however junior or disgraced. And ImpSec's sworn duty was the Emperor's safety. The Emperor, Barrayaran's unifying icon. Gregor, unwilling flesh pressed into the mold. Icon, flesh, which claimed Miles's allegiance? *Both. He's mine. A prisoner, on the run, trailed by God-knows-what enemies, suicidally depressed, and all mine.*

Miles choked down a lunatic cackle.

10

With a little reflection, possible now that the shock-stick reverbera-
tions were wearing off, Miles realized that he needed to hide. Gregor,
by his place as a contract slave, would be warm, fed, and safe all the
way to Aslund Station if Miles did not endanger him. Maybe. Miles
added it to his life's lessons list. Call it Rule 27B. Never make key
tactical decisions while having electro-convulsive seizures.

Miles began by examining the bunk cubicle. The vessel was not a
prison ship; the cabin had originally been designed as cheap transport, not a secured cell. Empty storage cupboards beneath the two
bunkstacks were too large and obvious. A floor panel lifted for access
to between-decks control, coolant and power lines, and the grav grid
—long, narrow, flat. . . . Rough voices in the corridor propelled
Miles's decision. He squeezed himself into the slice of space, face up,
arms tight to his sides, and exhaled.

"You always were good at hide-and-seek," said Gregor admiringly,
and pressed the panel down.

"I was smaller then," Miles mumbled through squashed cheeks.
Pipes and circuit boxes sank into his back and buttocks. Gregor refas-
tened the catches, and all was dark and silent for a few minutes. Like
a coffin. Like a pressed flower. Some kind of biological specimen,
anyway. Canned ensign.

The door hissed open; footsteps passed over Miles's body, compressing him still further. Would they notice the muffled echo from this strip of floor?

"On your feet, Techie." A guard's voice, directed to Gregor. Thumpings and bangings, as the mattresses were flipped and the cupboard doors flung open. Yes, he'd figured the cupboards for useless.

"Where is he, Techie?" From the directions of the shufflings, Miles placed Gregor as now near the wall, probably with an arm twisted up behind his back.

"Where is who?" said Gregor in a smeary tone. Face against the wall, all right.

"Your little mutant buddy."

"The weird little guy who followed me in? He's no buddy of mine. He left."

More shuffling—"Ow!" The Emperor's arm had just been lifted another five centimeters, Miles gauged.

"Where'd he go?"

"I don't know! He didn't look so good. Somebody'd worked him over with a shock stick. Recently. I wasn't about to get involved. He took off again a few minutes before we undocked."

Good Gregor; depressed maybe, stupid no. Miles's lips drew back. His head was turned, with one cheek against the floor above and the other pressing against something that resembled a cheese grater.

More thumps. "All right! He left! Don't hit me!"

Unintelligible guard growls, the crackle of a shock stick, a sharp intake of breath, a thump as of a body curling up on a lower bunk.

A second guard's voice, edged with uncertainty, "He must have doubled back onto the Consortium before we cast off."

"Their problem, good. But we'd better search the whole ship to be sure. Detention sounded ready to chew ass on this one."

"Chew or be chewed?"

"Hah. *I'm* taking no bets."

The booted feet—four of them, Miles estimated—stalked toward the cabin door. The door hissed closed. Silence.

He was going to have a truly remarkable collection of bruises on his backside, Miles decided, by the time Gregor got around to popping the lid. He could get about half a breath with each pulse of his lungs. He needed to pee. Come on, Gregor. . . .

He must certainly free Gregor from his slave labor contract as soon as possible after their arrival at Aslund Station. Contract laborers of this order were bound to be stuck with the dirtiest and most dangerous jobs, the most exposure to radiation, to dubious life-support systems, to long, exhausting, accident-prone hours. Though—true—it was also an incognito no enemy would quickly penetrate. Once free to move they must find Ungari, the man with the credit cards and the contacts; after that—well, after that Gregor would be Ungari's problem, eh? Yes, all simple, right and tight. No need to panic at all.

Had they taken Gregor away? Dare he release himself, and risk—

Shuffling footsteps; a widening line of light, as his lid was raised. "They're gone," Gregor whispered. Miles unmolded himself, centimeter by painful centimeter, and climbed onto the floor, a suitable staging area. He would attempt to stand up very soon now.

Gregor had one hand pressed to a red mark on his cheek. Self-consciously, he lowered his hand to his side. "They tapped me with a shock stick. It . . . wasn't as bad as I'd imagined." If anything, he looked faintly proud of himself.

"They were using low power," Miles growled up at him. Gregor's face grew more masked. He offered Miles a hand up. Miles took it and grunted to his feet, and sat heavily on a bunk. He told Gregor about his plans for finding Ungari.

Gregor shrugged, dully acquiescent. "Very well. It will be quicker than my plan."

"Your plan?"

"I was going to contact the Barrayaran Counsel on Aslund."

"Oh. Good." Miles subsided. "Guess you . . . didn't really need my rescue, at that."

"I could have made it on my own. I got this far. But . . . then there was my other plan."

"Oh?"

"*Not* to contact the Barrayaran Consul. . . . Maybe it's just as well you came along when you did." Gregor lay back on his bunk, staring blindly upward. "One thing is certain, an opportunity like this will never come again."

"To escape? And just how many would die, back home, to buy your freedom?"

Gregor pursed his lips. "Taking Vordarian's Pretendership as a benchmark for palace coups—say, seven or eight thousand."

"You're not counting in Komarr."

"Ah. Yes. Adding in Komarr would inflate the figure," Gregor conceded. His mouth twitched in an irony altogether devoid of humor. "Don't worry, I'm not serious. I just . . . wanted to know. I could have made it on my own, don't you think?"

"Of course! That's not the question."

"It was for me."

"Gregor," Miles's fingers tapped in frustration, against his knee. "You're doing this to yourself. You *have* real power. Dad fought through the whole Regency to preserve it. Just be more assertive!"

"And, Ensign, if I, your supreme commander, ordered you to leave this ship at Aslund Station and forget you ever saw me, would you?"

Miles swallowed. "Major Cecil said I had a problem with subordination."

Gregor almost grinned. "Good old Cecil. I remember him." His grin faded to nothing. He rolled up onto one elbow. "But if I can't even control one rather short ensign, how much less an army or a government? Power isn't the question. I've had all your Dad's lectures on power, its illusions and uses. It will come to me in time, whether I want it or not. But do I have the strength to handle it? Think about the bad showing I made during Vordrozda and Hessman's plot, four years ago."

"Will you make that mistake again? Trust a flatterer?"

"Not that one, no."

"Well, then."

"But I must do better, or I might be as bad for Barrayar as no emperor at all."

Just how unintentional had that topple off the balcony been? Miles gritted his teeth. "I didn't answer your question—about orders—as an ensign. I answered it as Lord Vorkosigan. And as a friend."

"Ah."

"Look, you don't need my rescue. Such as it is. Illyan's maybe, not mine. But it makes *me* feel better."

"It's always nice to feel useful," Gregor agreed. They mirrored edged smiles. Gregor's smile lost its bitter bite. "And . . . it's nice to have company."

Miles nodded. "That, truly."

Miles spent quite a lot of time over the next two days squashed under the deck or crouched in the cupboards, but their cabin was searched only once and that very early on. Twice other prisoners wandered in to chat with Gregor, and once, on Miles's suggestion, Gregor returned the visit. Gregor divided his rations with Miles automatically, without complaint or even comment, and would not accept a larger portion although Miles urged it on him.

Gregor was herded out with the rest of the labor crew soon after the ship docked at Aslund Station. Miles waited nervously, trying to give as long as possible for the ship to quiet down, for the crew to go off-guard, yet not so long as to risk the ship undocking and thrusting off with him still aboard.

The corridor, when Miles cautiously poked his head out, was dark and deserted. The docking hatch was unguarded, on this side. Miles still wore the blue smock and pants over his other clothes, on the calculated risk the work gangs were treated as trustys, with the run of the station, and he would at least blend in at a distance.

He stepped out firmly, and nearly panicked when he found a man in the gold and black House livery idling around the hatch's exit. His stunner was holstered; his hands cradled a steaming plastic cup. His squinting red eyes regarded Miles incuriously. Miles favored him with a brief smile, not breaking stride. The guard returned a sour grimace. Evidently his charge was to prevent strange people from entering, not leaving, the ship.

The station-side loading bay beyond the hatch proved to contain half a dozen coveralled maintenance personnel, working quietly down on one end. Miles took a deep breath, and walked casually across the bay without looking around, as if he knew just where he was going. Just an errand boy. No one hailed him.

Reassured, Miles marched off purposefully at random. A wide ramp led to a great chamber, raucous with new construction and busy work crews in all sorts of dress—a fighter-shuttle refueling and repairs bay, judging by the half-assembled equipment. Just the sort of thing to interest Ungari. Miles didn't suppose he'd be so lucky as to . . . no. No sign of Ungari camouflaged among these crews. There were a number of men and women in dark blue Aslunder military uniforms, but they appeared to be overworked and absorbed engineer-types, not suspicious guards. Miles kept walking briskly nonetheless, out another corridor.

He found a portal, its transparent plexi bellied out to offer passersby a wide-angle view. He put one foot on the lower edge and leaned out—casually—and bit back a few choice swear words. Glittering a few kilometers off was the commercial transfer station. A tiny glint of a ship was docking even now. The military station was apparently being designed as a separate facility, or at least not connected yet. No wonder blue-smocks could wander at will. Miles stared across the gap in mild frustration. Well, he'd search this place first for Ungari, the other later. Somehow. He turned and started—

"Hey, you! Little techie!"

Miles froze, controlling a reflexive urge to sprint—that tactic hadn't worked last time—and turned, trying for an expression of polite inquiry. The man who'd hailed him was big but unarmed, wearing tan supervisor's coveralls. He looked harried. "Yes, sir?" said Miles.

"You're just what I need." The man's hand fell heavily on Miles's shoulder. "Come with me."

Miles perforce followed, trying to stay calm, maybe project a little bored annoyance.

"What's your specialization?" the man asked.

"Drains," Miles intoned.

"Perfect!"

Dismayed, Miles followed the man to where two half-finished corridors intersected. An archway gaped raw and uncapped by molding, though the molding lay ready to install.

The super pointed to a narrow space between walls. "See this pipe?"

Sewage, by the grey color-coding, air and grav pumped. It disappeared in darkness. "Yeah?"

"There's a leak somewhere behind this corridor wall. Crawl in and find it, so's we don't have to tear out all the damn paneling we just put up."

"Got a light?"

The man fished in his pocketed coverall and produced a hand light.

"Right," sighed Miles. "Is it hooked up yet?"

"About to be. Damn thing failed the final pressure test."

Only air would be spewing out. Miles brightened slightly. Maybe his luck was changing.

He slid in and inched along the smooth round surface, listening and feeling. About seven meters in he found it, a rush of cool air from a crack under his hands, quite marked. He shook his head, attempted to turn in the constricted space, and put his foot through the paneling.

He stuck his head out the hole in astonishment, and glanced up and down the corridor. He wriggled a chunk of paneling from the edge and stared at it, turning it in his hands.

Two men putting up light fixtures, their tools sparking, turned to stare. "What the hell are you doing?" said the one in tan coveralls, sounding outraged.

"Quality control inspection," said Miles glibly, "and boy, do you have a problem."

Miles considered kicking the hole wider and just walking back to his starting point, but turned and inched instead. He emerged by the anxiously waiting super.

"Your leak's in section six," Miles reported. He handed the man his panel chunk. "If those corridor panels are supposed to be made of flammable fiberboard instead of spun silica on a military installation planned to withstand enemy fire, somebody's hired a real poor designer. If they're not—I suggest you take a couple of those big goons with the shock sticks and go pay a visit to your supplier."

The super swore. Lips compressed, he grasped the nearest panel edge fronting the wall and twisted hard. A fist-sized segment cracked and tore off. "Bitchen. How much of this stuff's been installed already?"

"Lots," Miles suggested cheerfully. He turned to escape before the super, worrying off fragments and muttering under his breath, thought of another chore. Flushed and sweating, Miles skittered off and didn't relax till he'd rounded the second corner.

He passed a pair of armed men in grey-and-white uniforms. One turned to stare. Miles kept walking, teeth clenching his lower lip, and did not look back.

Dendarii! or, Oserans! Here, aboard this station—how many, where? Those two were the first he'd seen. Shouldn't they be out on patrol somewhere? He wished he were back in the walls, like a rat in the wainscotting.

But if most of the mercenaries here were a danger to him, there was one—Dendarii truly, not Oseran—who might be a help. If he could make contact. If he dared make contact. Elena . . . he could seek out Elena. . . . His imagination outraced him.

Miles had left Elena four years ago as Baz Jesek's wife, as Tung's military apprentice, as much protection as he could get her at the time. But he hadn't had any messages from Baz since Oser's command coup—could Oser be intercepting them? Now Baz was demoted, Tung apparently disgraced—what position in the mercenary fleet did Elena hold now?

What position in his heart? He paused in grave doubt. He'd loved her passionately, once. Once, she'd known him better than any other human being. Yet her daily hold on his mind had passed, like his grief for her dead father Sergeant Bothari, fading in the rush of his new life. But for an occasional twinge, like an old bonebreak. He wanted/ did not want/ to see her again. To talk to her again. To touch her again. . . .

But more to the practical point, she would recognize Gregor; they'd all been playmates in their youth. A second line of defense for the Emperor? Reopening contact with Elena might be emotionally awkward—all right, emotionally searing. But it was better than this ineffectual and dangerous wandering around. Now that he'd scouted the layout, he must somehow get into position to bring his resources to bear. How much human credit did Admiral Naismith still have? Interesting question.

He needed to find a place to watch without being seen. There were all sorts of ways to be invisible while in plain sight, as his blue smock was presently demonstrating. But his unusual height—well, short-ness—made him reluctant to rely on clothes alone. He needed—ha! —tools, such as the case a tan-coveralled man had just set down in the corridor while he ducked into a lavatory. Miles had the case in hand and was around the corner in a blink.

A couple of levels away he found a corridor leading to a cafeteria. Hm. Everyone must eat; therefore, everyone must pass this way in time. The food smells excited his stomach, which protested half-rations or less for the past three days by gurgling. He ignored it. He pulled a panel off the wall, donned a pair of protective goggles from the tool case by way of a modest facial disguise, climbed into the wall to half-conceal his height, and began pretending to work on a control box and some pipes, diagnostic scanners placed decoratively to hand. His view up the corridor was excellent.

From the wafting odors, he judged they were serving an unusually good grade of vat-grown beef in there, though they were also doing something nasty to vegetables. He tried not to salivate into the beam of the tiny laser-solderer he manipulated while he studied passers-by. Very few were civilian-clothed, Rotha's wear would clearly have been more conspicuous than the blue smock. Lots of color-coded coveralls, blue smocks, some similar green smocks; not a few As-lunder military blues, mostly lower ranks. Did the Dendarii—Oser-ans—mercenaries—aboard eat elsewhere? He was considering aban-doning his outpost—he'd about repaired the control boxes to death by now—when a duo of grey-and-whites passed. Not faces he knew, he let them go by unhailed.

He contemplated the odds reluctantly. Of all the couple thousand mercenaries now present around the Aslunders' wormhole jump, he might know a few hundred by sight, fewer by name. Only some of the mercenary fleet's ships were now docked at this half-built mili-tary station. And of the portion of a portion, how many people could he trust absolutely? Five? He let another quartet of grey-and-whites pass, though he was certain that older blonde woman was an engi-neering tech from the *Triumph*, once loyal to Tung. Once. He was getting ravenous.

But the leather-colored face topping the next set of grey-and-whites to pass down the corridor made Miles forget his stomach. It was Sergeant Chodak. His luck had turned—maybe. For himself, he'd take the chance, but to risk Gregor . . . ? Too late to waffle now, Chodak had spotted Miles in turn. The Sergeant's eyes widened in astonishment before his face grew swiftly blank.

"Oh, Sergeant," Miles caroled, tapping a control box, "would you take a look at this, please?"

"I'll be along in a minute," Chodak waved on his companion, a man in the uniform of an Aslunder ranker.

When their heads were together and their backs to the corridor, Chodak hissed, "Are you insane? What are you *doing* here?" It was a mark of his agitation that he omitted his habitual "sir."

"It's a long story. For now, I need your help."

"But how did you get in here? Admiral Oser has guards all over the transfer station, on the lookout for you. You couldn't smuggle in a sand-flea."

Miles smirked convincingly. "I have my methods." And his next plan had been to scheme his way across to that very transfer station . . . Truly, God protected fools and madmen. "For now, I need to make contact with Commander Elena Bothari-Jesek. Urgently. Or, failing her, Engineering Commodore Jesek. Is she here?"

"She should be. The *Triumph*'s in dock. Commodore Jesek is out with the repairs tender, I know."

"Well, if not Elena, Tung. Or Arde Mayhew. Or Lieutenant Elli Quinn. But I prefer Elena. Tell her—but no one else—that I have our old friend Greg with me. Tell her to meet me in an hour in the contract-laborers quarters, Greg Bleakman's cubicle. Can do?"

"Can do, sir." Chodak hurried off, looking worried. Miles patched up his poor battered wall, replaced the panel, picked up his tool box, and marched casually away, trying not to feel like he had a flashing red light atop his head. He kept his goggles on and his face down, and chose the least-populated corridors he could find. His stomach growled. *Elena will feed you,* he told it firmly. *Later.* A rising population of blue and green smocks told Miles he was nearing the contract laborer's quarters.

There was a directory. He hesitated, then punched up "Bleakman, G." Module B., Cubicle 8. He found the module, checked his chrono —Gregor should be off-shift by now—and knocked. The door sighed open and Miles slipped within. Gregor was there, sitting up sleepily on his bunk. It was a one-man cubicle, offering privacy, though barely room to turn around. Privacy was a greater psychological luxury than space. Even slave-techs must be kept minimally happy, they had too much power for potential sabotage to risk driving them over the edge.

"We're saved," Miles announced. "I've just made contact with Elena." He sat down heavily on the end of the bunk, weak with the sudden release of tension in this safe pocket.

"Elena's here?" Gregor scrubbed a hand through his hair. "I thought you wanted your Captain Ungari."

"Elena's the first step to Ungari. Or, failing Ungari, to smuggling us out of here. If Ungari hadn't been so damn insistent on the left hand not knowing what the right was doing, it would be a lot easier. But this will do." He studied Gregor in worry. "Have you been all right?"

"A few hours putting up light fixtures isn't going to break my health, I assure you," said Gregor dryly.

"Is that what they had you doing? Not what I'd pictured, some-how . . ."

Gregor seemed all right, anyway. Indeed, the Emperor was acting almost cheerful about his stint as a slave laborer, as Gregor's morose standards of cheer went. *Maybe we ought to send him to the salt mines for two weeks every year, to keep him happy and content with his regular job.* Miles relaxed a little.

"It's hard to imagine Elena Bothari as a mercenary," Gregor added reflectively.

"Don't underestimate her." Miles concealed a moment of raw doubt. Almost four years. He knew how much he had changed in four years. What of Elena? Her years could have been hardly less hectic. *Times change. People change with them.* . . . No. As well doubt himself as Elena.

The half-hour wait for his chrono to creep to the appointed moment was a bad interval, enough to loosen Miles's driving tension and wash him in weariness but not enough to rest or refresh him. He was miserably conscious of losing his edge, of a crying need for alertness when alertness and straight-thinking escaped like sand between his fingers. He rechecked his chrono. *An hour* had been too vague. He should have named the minute. But who knew what difficulties or delays Elena must overcome from her end?

Miles blinked hard, realizing from his wavering and disconnected thoughts that he was falling asleep sitting up. The door hissed open without Gregor's having released the lock.

"Here he is, men!"

A half-squad of grey-and-white clad mercenaries filled the aperture and the corridor beyond. It hardly needed the stunners and shock-sticks in their hands, the purposive descent on his person, to tell Miles this hairy crew was not Elena's. The surge of adrenalin scarcely cleared the fatigue-fog from his head. *And what do I pretend to be now? A moving target?* He sagged against the wall, not even bothering, though Gregor lurched to his feet and made a valiant try in the constricted space, an accurate karate-kick sending a stunner flying from the hand of a closing mercenary. Two men smashed Gregor against the wall for his effort. Miles winced.

Then Miles himself was jerked from the bunk to be coiled, tripled-coiled, in a tangle-net. The field burned against him. They were using enough power to immobilize a plunging horse. *What do you think I am, boys?*

The excited squad leader cried into his wrist comm, "I got him, sir!"

Miles raised an ironic brow. The squad leader flushed and straightened, his hand twitching in the effort not to salute. Miles smiled slightly. The squad leader's lips tightened. *Ha. Almost got you going, didn't I?*

"Take them away," ordered the squad leader.

Miles was carried out the door between two men, his bound feet dangling ridiculous inches from the floor. A groaning Gregor was dragged in his wake. As they passed a cross-corridor, Miles saw Chodak's strained face from the corner of his eye, floating in the shadows.

He damned his own judgment then. *You thought you could read people. Your one demonstrable talent. Right. Sure. Should have, should have, should have,* mocked his mind, like the caw of some vile scavenging bird surprised at a carcass.

When they were dragged across a large docking bay and through a small personnel hatch, Miles knew at once where he was. The *Triumph,* the pocket dreadnought that had occasionally served as the fleet's flagship, was doing that duty again now. Tung of the dubious current status had been captain-owner of the *Triumph,* once, before Tau Verde. Oser had used to favor his own *Peregrine* as flag—was this some deliberate political statement? The corridors of the ship had a strange, painful, powerful familiarity. The odors of men, metal, and machinery. That crooked archway, legacy of the lunatic ramming that had captured her on Miles's first encounter, still not properly straightened out . . . *I thought I had forgotten more.*

They were hustled along swiftly and secretly, a pair of squadmen going ahead to clear the corridor of witnesses before them. This was going to be a very private chat, then. Fine, that suited Miles. He would have preferred to avoid Oser altogether, but if they must meet again, he would simply have to find some way of turning it to use. He ordered his persona as if adjusting his cuffs—Miles Naismith, space mercenary and mystery entrepreneur, come to the Hegen Hub for . . . what? And his glum if faithful sidekick Greg, of course—he would have to think of some particularly benign explanation for Gregor.

They clattered down the corridor past the tactics room, the *Triumph*'s combat nerve center, and fetched up at the smaller of the two briefing rooms across from it. The holovid plate in the center of the gleaming conference table was dark and silent. Admiral Oser sat equally dark and silent at the table's head, flanked by a pale blond man Miles presumed to be a loyal lieutenant; not anyone Miles knew from before. Miles and Gregor were forcibly seated in two chairs pulled back and distanced from the table, that their hands and feet might be unconcealed. Oser dismissed all but one guard to the corridor outside.

Oser's appearance hadn't changed much in four years, Miles decided. Still lean and hawk-faced, dark hair maybe a little greyer at the temples. Miles had remembered him as taller, but he was actually shorter than Metzov. Oser reminded Miles somehow of the general. Was it the age, the build? The hostile glower, the murderous pin-pricks of red light in the eye?

"Miles," Gregor muttered out of the corner of his mouth, "what did you do to piss this guy off?"

"Nothing!" Miles protested back, sotto voce. "Nothing on purpose, anyway."

Gregor looked less than reassured.

Oser placed his palms flat on the table before him and leaned forward, staring at Miles with predatory intensity. If Oser'd had a tail, Miles fancied, its end would be flicking back and forth. "What are you doing here?" Oser opened bluntly, without preamble.

You brought me, didn't you know? Not the time to get cute, no. Miles was highly conscious of the fact that he did not precisely look his best. But Admiral Naismith wouldn't care, he was too goal-directed; Naismith would carry on painted blue, if he had to. He answered equally bluntly. "I was hired to do a military evaluation of the Hegen Hub for an interested non-combatant who ships through here." There, the truth up front, where it was sure to be disbelieved. "Since they don't care for mounting rescue expeditions, they wanted enough warning to clear the hub of their citizens before hostilities break out. I'm doing a little arms dealing on the side. A cover that pays for itself."

Oser's eyes narrowed. "Not Barrayar . . ."

"Barrayar has its own operatives."

"So does Cetaganda . . . Aslund fears Cetagandan ambitions."

"As well they should."

"Barrayar is equidistant."

"In my professional opinion," fighting the tangle-field, Miles favored Oser with a small bow, sitting down—Oser almost nodded back, but caught himself—"Barrayar is no threat to Aslund in this generation. To control the Hegen Hub, Barrayar must control Pol. With the terraforming of their own second continent plus the opening of the planet Sergyar, Barrayar is rather oversupplied with frontiers at present. And then there is the problem of holding restive Komarr. A military adventure toward Pol would be a serious overextension of Barrayar's human resources just now. Cheaper to be friends, or at least neutral."

"Aslund also fears Pol."

"They are unlikely to fight unless attacked first. Keeping peace with Pol is cheap and easy. Just do nothing."

"Any Vervain?"

"I haven't evaluated Vervain yet. It's next on my list."

"Is it?" Oser leaned back in his chair, crossing his arms. It was not a relaxed gesture. "As a spy, I could have you executed."

"But I'm not an *enemy* spy," Miles answered, simulating easiness. "A friendly neutral or—who knows?—potential ally."

"And what is your interest in my fleet?"

"My interest in the Denda—in the mercenaries is purely academic, I assure you. You are simply part of the picture. Tell me, what's your contract with Aslund like?" Miles cocked his head, talking shop.

Oser almost answered, then his lips thinned in annoyance. If Miles had been a ticking bomb he could not have more thoroughly commanded the mercenary's attention.

"Oh, come on," Miles scoffed in the lengthening silence. "What could I do, by myself with one man?"

"I remember the last time. You entered Tau Verde local space with a staff of four. Four months later you were dictating terms. So what are you planning now?"

"You overestimate my impact. I merely helped people along in the direction they wished to go. An expediter, so to speak."

"Not for me. I spent three years recovering the ground I lost. In my own fleet!"

"It's hard to please everyone." Miles intercepted Gregor's look of mute horror, and toned himself down. Come to think, Gregor had never met Admiral Naismith, had he? "Even you were not seriously damaged."

Oser's jaw compressed further. "And who's he?" He jerked a thumb at Gregor.

"Greg? He's just my batman," Miles cut across Gregor's opening mouth.

"He doesn't look like a batman. He looks like an officer."

Gregor looked insensibly cheered at this unbiased encomium.

"You can't go by looks. Commodore Tung looks like a wrestler."

Oser's eyes were suddenly freezing. "Indeed. And how long have you been in correspondence with *Captain* Tung?"

By the sick lurch in his belly, Miles realized mentioning Tung has been a major mistake. He tried to keep his features cooly ironic, not reflecting his unease. "If I'd been in correspondence with Tung, I should not have been troubled with making this personal evaluation of Aslund Station."

Oser, elbows on table, hands clasped, studied Miles in silence for a full minute. At last one hand fell open, to point at the guard, who straightened attentively. "Space them," Oser ordered.

"What?!" yelped Miles.

"You," the pointing finger collected Oser's silent lieutenant, "go with them. See that it's done. Use the portside access lock, it's closest. If *he,*" pointing to Miles, "starts to talk, stop his tongue. It's his most dangerous organ."

The guard released the tangle field from Miles's legs and pulled him to his feet.

"Aren't you even going to have me chemically interrogated?" asked Miles, dizzied by this sudden downturn.

"And contaminate my interrogators? The last thing I want is to give you rein to talk, to anyone. I can think of nothing more fatal than for the rot of disloyalty to start in my own Intelligence section. Whatever your planned speech, removing your air will neutralize it. You nearly convince *me.*" Oser almost shuddered.

We were getting on so well, yes. . . . "But I—" they were hoisting Gregor to his feet too. "But you don't need to—"

Two waiting members of the half-squad fell in as they were bundled out the door, frog-marching Miles and Gregor rapidly down the corridor. "But—!" The conference room door hissed closed.

"This is not going well, Miles," Gregor observed, his pale face a weird compound of detachment, exasperation, and dismay. "Any more bright ideas?"

"You're the man who was experimenting with wingless flight. Is this any worse than, say, plummeting?"

"At my own hand," Gregor began to drag his feet, to struggle, as the airlock chamber heaved into view, "not at the whim of a bunch of . . ." it took three guards to wrestle him now, "bloody *peasants!*"

Miles was getting seriously frantic. Screw the damn cover. "You know," he called out loudly, "you fellows are about to throw a fortune in ransom out the airlock!"

Two guards kept wrestling with Gregor, but the third paused. "How big a fortune?"

"Huge," Miles promised. "Buy your own fleet."

The lieutenant abandoned Gregor and closed on Miles, drawing a vibra-knife. The lieutenant was interpreting his orders with horrific literality, Miles realized when the man went for a grip on his tongue. He almost got it—the evil insect whine of the knife dopplered centimeters from Miles's nose—Miles bit the thick thrusting fingers, and twisted against the grip of the guard holding him. The tangle field binding Miles's arms to his torso whined and crackled, unbreakable. Miles jammed backward against the crotch of the man behind, who yipped at the field's bite. His grip slipped and Miles dropped, rolling and banging into the lieutenant's knees. It wasn't exactly a judo throw, the lieutenant more-or-less tripped over him.

Gregor's two opponents were distracted, as much by the bloody barbaric promise of the vibra-knife show as by Miles's ultimately futile struggles. They did not see the leather-faced man step out from a cross-corridor, aim his stunner, and spray. They arched convulsively as the buzzing charges struck their backs, and dropped heap-fashion to the deck. The man who'd been holding Miles, and was now trying to grab him again as he flopped around evasively as a fish, whirled just in time to intersect a beam square in the face.

Miles flung himself across the blond lieutenant's head, pinning him —only momentarily, alas—to the deck. Miles wriggled, to press the tangle-field into the man's face, then was heaved off with a curse. The lieutenant had one knee under himself, preparing to launch an attack and wobbling around in search of his target, when Gregor hopped over and kicked him in the jaw. A stunner charge hit the lieutenant in the back of the head and he went down.

"Damn fine soldiering," Miles panted to Sergeant Chodak in the sudden silence. "I don't think they even saw what hit them." *So, I*

*called him straight the first time. Haven't lost my touch after all.
Bless you, Sergeant.*

"You two aren't so bad yourselves, for men with both hands tied behind their backs." Chodak shook his head in harried amusement, and trod forward to release the tangle-fields.

"What a team," said Miles.

11

A quick ring of boots from further up the corridor drew Miles's eye. He exhaled, a long-held breath, and stood. *Elena.*

She wore a mercenary officer's undress uniform, grey-and-white pocketed jacket, trousers, ankle-topping boots gleaming on her long, long legs. Still tall, still slim, still with pale pure skin, ember-brown eyes, arched aristocratic nose and long sculptured jaw. *She's cut her hair,* Miles thought, stupid-stunned. Gone was the straight-shining black cascade to her waist. Now it was clipped out over her ears, only little dark points grace-noting her high cheekbones and forehead, a similar point echoed at the nape of her neck; severe, practical, very smart. Soldierly.

She strode up, eyes taking in Miles, Gregor, the four Oserans. "Good work, Chodak." She dropped to one knee beside the nearest body and probed its neck for a pulse. "Are they dead?"

"No, just stunned," Miles explained.

She regarded the open inner airlock door with some regret. "I don't suppose we can space them."

"They were going to space us, but no. But we probably ought to get them out of sight while we run," said Miles.

"Right." She rose and nodded to Chodak, who began helping Gregor drag the stunned bodies into the airlock. She frowned at the blond lieutenant, going past feet-first. "Not that spacing wouldn't *improve* some personalities."

"Can you give us a bolt-hole?"

"That's what we came for." She turned to the three soldiers who had followed her cautiously into view. A fourth stood guard at the nearest cross-corridor. "It seems we just got lucky," she told them. "Scout ahead and clear the aisles on our escape route—subtly. Then disappear. You weren't here and didn't see this."

They nodded and withdrew. Miles heard a retreating mutter. "Was that *him?*" "Yeah . . ."

Miles, Gregor, and Elena, with the bodies, piled cozily into the lock and closed the inner door temporarily. Chodak stood guard outside. Elena helped Gregor pull the boots from the Oseran nearest his size while Miles stripped off his blue prisoner's outfit and stood, revealing Victor Rotha's wrinkled clothing, much the worse for four days wear, sleep, and sweat. Miles wished for boots to replace the vulnerable sandals, but none here came close to his size.

Gregor and Elena exchanged looks, each warily amazed at the other, as Gregor yanked on grey-and-whites and plunged his feet into the boots.

"It's really you." Elena shook her head in dismay. "What are you doing here?"

"It was by mistake," said Gregor.

"No lie. Whose?"

"Mine, I'm afraid," said Miles. Somewhat to his annoyance, Gregor did not gainsay this.

A peculiar smile, her first, quirked Elena's lips. Miles decided not to ask her to explain it. This hurried practical exchange did not in the least resemble any of the dozens of conversations he had rehearsed in his head for this first, poignant meeting with her.

"The search will be up in minutes, when these guys don't report back," Miles jittered. He collected two stunners, the tangle-field, and the vibra-knife, and stuck them in his waistband. On second thought, he swiftly relieved the four Oserans of credit cards, pass chits, IDs, and odd cash, stuffing his pockets and Gregor's, and made sure Gregor ditched his prisoner's traceable ID. To his secret delight, he also found a half-eaten ration bar, and bit into it there and then. He chewed as Elena led the way back out the lock. He conscientiously offered a bite to Gregor, who shook his head. Gregor'd probably had dinner in that cafeteria.

Chodak hastily straightened Gregor's uniform, and they all marched off, Miles to the center, half-concealed, half-guarded. Before he could go half-paranoid at his conspicuousness they took to a drop-tube, emerged several decks down, and found themselves at a large cargo-lock, engaged to a shuttle. One of Elena's scout squad, leaning as if idle against the wall, nodded. With a half-salute to Elena, Chodak split off and they hurried away. Miles and Gregor followed Elena across the flex-seal of the shuttle hatch and into the empty cargo hold of one of the *Triumph*'s shuttles, stepping from the artificial gravity field of the mother ship abruptly into the vertigo of free fall. They floated forward to the pilot's compartment. Elena sealed the compartment hatch behind them, and anxiously gestured Gregor to the vacant seat at the engineering/comm station.

The pilot's and co-pilot's seats were filled. Arde Mayhew grinned cheerfully over his shoulder at Miles, and waved/saluted hello. Miles recognized the shaved bullet-head of the second man even before he turned.

"Hello, son." Ky Tung's smile was far more ironic than cheerful. "Welcome back. You took your sweet time." Tung, arms folded, did not salute.

"Hello, Ky," Miles nodded to the Eurasian. Tung had not changed, anyway. Still looked any age between forty and sixty. Still built like an ancient tank. Still seemed to see more than he spoke, most uncomfortable for the guilty of conscience.

Mayhew the pilot spoke into his comm. "Traffic control, I've traced that red light on my panel now. Defective pressure reading. All fixed. We're ready to break away."

"About time, C-2," a disembodied voice returned. "You're clear."

The pilot's swift hands activated hatch seal controls, aimed attitude jets. Some hissing and clanks, and the shuttle popped away from its mothership and started on its trajectory. Mayhew killed the comm and breathed a long sigh of relief. "Safe. For now."

Elena wedged herself across the aisle behind Miles, long legs locking. Miles hooked an arm around a handhold to anchor against Mayhew's current mild accelerations. "I hope you're right," said Miles, "but what makes you think so?"

"He means, safe to talk," said Elena. "Not safe in any cosmic sense. This is a routine scheduled run, except for us unlisted passengers. We know you haven't been missed yet, or traffic control would have stopped us. Oser will search the *Triumph* and the military station for you first. We may even be able to slip you back aboard the *Triumph* after the search has passed to wider areas."

"This is Plan B," Tung explained, swiveling around to half-face Miles. "Or maybe Plan C. Plan A, on the assumption that your rescue was going to be a lot noisier, was to flee at once to the *Ariel,* now on picket-station, and declare the revolution. I'm grateful for the chance to bring things off a little, er, less spontaneously."

Miles choked. "God! That would have been worse than the first time." Pitched into an interlocking chain of events he did not control, drafted gonfalonier to some mercenary military mutiny, thrust to the lead of its parade with all the free will of a head on a pike. . . . "No. No spontaneity, thanks. Definitely not."

"So," Tung steepled his thick fingers, "what *is* your plan?"

"My what?"

"Plan," Tung pronounced the word with sardonic care. "In other words, why are you here?"

"Oser asked me that same question," sighed Miles. "Would you believe, I'm here by accident? Oser wouldn't. You wouldn't happen to know *why* he wouldn't, would you?"

Tung pursed his lips. "Accident? Maybe. . . . Your 'accidents,' I once noticed, have ways of entangling your enemies that are the green envy of mature and careful strategists. Far too consistent for chance, I concluded it had to be unconscious will. If only you'd stuck with me, son, between us we could've . . . or maybe you are simply a supreme opportunist. In which case I direct your attention to the opportunity now before you to retake the Dendarii Mercenaries."

"You didn't answer my question," Miles noted.

"You didn't answer mine," Tung countered.

"I don't want the Dendarii Mercenaries."

"I do."

"Oh." Miles paused. "Why don't you split off with the personnel who are loyal to you and start your own, then? It's been done."

"Shall we swim through space?" Tung imitated fish fins with his waving fingers, and puffed his cheeks. "Oser controls the equipment. Including my ship. The *Triumph* is everything I've accumulated in a thirty-year career. Which I lost through your machinations. Somebody owes me another. If not Oser, then . . ." Tung glowered significantly at Miles.

"I tried to give you a fleet in trade," said Miles, harried. "How'd you lose control of it—old strategist?"

Tung tapped a finger to his left breast, to indicate a touché. "Things went well at first, for a year, year and a half after we departed Tau Verde. Got two sweet little contracts in a row out toward the East-net —small-scale commando operations, sure things. Well, not too sure— kept us on our toes. But we brought them off."

Miles glanced at Elena. "I'd heard about those, yes."

"On the third, we got into troubles. Baz Jesek had gotten more and more involved with equipment and maintenance—he is a good engineer, I'll give him that—I was tactical commander, and Oser—I thought by default, but now I think design—took up the administrative slack. Could have been good, each doing what he did best, if Oser'd been working with and not against us. In the same situation, I'd have sent assassins. Oser employed guerrilla accountants.

"We took a bit of a beating on that third contract. Baz was up to his ears in engineering and repairs, and by the time I got out of sickbay, Oser'd lined up one of his no-combat specials—wormhole guard duty work. Long-term contract. Seemed like a good idea at the time. But it gave him a wedge. With no actual combat going on, I . . ." Tung cleared his throat, "got bored, didn't pay attention. Oser'd outflanked me before I realized there was a war on. He sprang the financial reorganization on us—"

"I told you not to trust him, six months before that," Elena put in with a frown, "after he tried to seduce me."

Tung shrugged uncomfortably. "It seemed like an understandable temptation."

"To bang his commander's wife?" Elena's eyes sparked. "Anyone's wife? I knew then he wasn't level. If my oaths meant nothing to him, how little did his own?"

"He did take no for an answer, you said," Tung excused himself. "If he'd kept leaning on you, I'd have been willing to step in. I thought you ought to be flattered, ignore it, and go on."

"Overtures of that sort contain a judgment of my character that I find anything but flattering, thank you," Elena snapped.

Miles bit his knuckles, hard and secretly, remembering his own longings. "It might just have been an early move in his power-play," he put in. "Probing for weaknesses in his enemies' defenses. And in this case, not finding them."

"Hm." Elena seemed faintly comforted by this view. "Anyway, Ky was no help, and I got tired of playing Cassandra. Naturally, I couldn't tell Baz. But Oser's double-dealing didn't come as a complete surprise to *all* of us."

Tung frowned, frustrated. "Given the nucleus of his own surviving ships, all he had to do was swing the votes of half the other captain-owners. Auson voted with him. I could have strangled the bastard."

"You lost Auson yourself, with your moaning about the *Triumph,*" Elena put in, still acerb. "He thought you threatened his captaincy of it."

Tung shrugged. "As long as I was Chief-of-Staff/Tactical, in charge during actual combat, I didn't think he could really hurt my ship. I was content to let the *Triumph* ride along as if owned by the fleet corporation. I could wait—till *you* got back," his dark eyes glinted at Miles, "and we found out what was going on. And then you never came back."

"The king will return, eh?" murmured Gregor, who had been listening with fascination. He raised an eyebrow at Miles.

"Let it be a lesson to you," Miles murmured back through set teeth. Gregor subsided, less humorous.

Miles turned to Tung. "Surely Elena disabused you of any such immediate expectation."

"I tried," muttered Elena. "Although . . . I suppose, I couldn't help hoping a bit myself. Maybe you'd . . . quit your other project, come back to us."

If I flunked out of the Academy, eh? "It wasn't a project I could quit, short of death."

"I know that now."

"In five minutes, max," put in Arde Mayhew, "I've either got to lock into the transfer station traffic control for docking, or else cut for the *Ariel*. Which is it going to be, folks?"

"I can put over a hundred loyal officers and non-coms at your back at a word," said Tung to Miles. "Four ships."

"Why not at your own back?"

"If I could, I would have already. But I'm not going to tear the fleet apart unless I can be certain of putting it back together again. All of it. But with you as leader, with your reputation—which has grown in the retelling—"

"Leader? Or figurehead?" The image of that pike bobbed in Miles's mind's eye again.

Tung's hands opened noncommittally. "As you wish. The bulk of the officer cadre will go for the winning side. That means we must appear to be winning quickly, if we move at all. Oser has about another hundred personally loyal to himself, which we're going to have to physically overpower if he insists on holding out—which suggests to my mind that a well-timed assassination could save a lot of lives."

"Jolly. I think you and Oser have been working together too long, Ky. You're starting to think alike. Again. I did not come here to seize command of a mercenary fleet. I have other priorities." He schooled himself not to glance at Gregor.

"What higher priorities?"

"How about, preventing a planetary civil war? Maybe an interstellar one?"

"I have no professional interest in that." It almost succeeded in being a joke.

Indeed, what were Barrayar's agonies to Tung? "You do if you're on the doomed side. You only get paid for winning, and only get to spend your pay if you live, mercenary."

Tung's narrow eyes narrowed further. "What do you know that I don't? *Are* we on the doomed side?"

I am, if I don't get Gregor back. Miles shook his head. "Sorry. I can't talk about that. I've got to get to—" Pol closed to him, the Consortium station blocked, and now Aslund become even more dangerous, "Vervain." He glanced at Elena. "Get us both to Vervain."

"You working for the Vervani?" Tung asked.

"No."

"Who, then?" Tung's hands twitched, so tense with his curiosity they seemed to want to squeeze out information by main force.

Elena noticed the unconscious gesture too. "Ky, back off," she said sharply. "If Miles wants Vervain, Vervain he shall have."

Tung looked at Elena, at Mayhew. "Do you back him, or me?"

Elena's chin lifted. "We're both oath-sworn to Miles. Baz too."

"And you have to ask why I need you?" said Tung in exasperation to Miles, gesturing at the pair. "What is this larger game, that you all seem to know all about, and I, nothing?"

"I don't know anything," chirped Mayhew. "I'm just going by Elena."

"Is this a chain of command, or a chain of credulity?"

"There's a difference?" Miles grinned.

"You've exposed us, by coming here," Tung argued. "Think! We help you, you leave, we're left naked to Oser's wrath. There's too many witnesses already. There might be safety in victory, none in half-measure."

Miles looked with anguish at Elena, picturing her, quite vividly in light of his recent experiences, being shoved out an airlock by evil, witless goons. Tung noted with satisfaction the effect of his plea on Miles and sat smugly back. Elena glared at Tung.

Gregor stirred uneasily. "I think . . . should you become refugees on Our behalf," (Elena, Miles saw, heard that official capital O too, as Tung and Mayhew of course could not) "We can see that you do not suffer. Financially, at least."

Elena nodded understanding and acceptance. Tung leaned toward

Elena, jerking his thumb at Gregor. "All right, who is this guy?"
Elena shook her head mutely.

Tung vented a small hiss. "You've no means of support visible to
me, son. What if we become corpses on your behalf?"

Elena remarked, "We've risked becoming corpses for much less."

"Less than what?" snapped Tung.

Mayhew, his eyes going briefly distant, touched the communications plug in his ear. "Decision time, folks."

"Can this ship go across-system?" asked Miles.

"No. Not fueled up for it," Mayhew shrugged apology.

"Not fast enough or armored for it, either," said Tung.

"You'll have to smuggle us out on commercial transport, past Aslunder security," Miles said unhappily.

Tung stared around at his recalcitrant little committee, and sighed.
"Security's tighter for incoming than outgoing. I think it can be done.
Take us in, Arde."

After Mayhew had docked the cargo shuttle at its assigned loading
niche at the Aslunders' transfer station, Miles, Gregor, and Elena lay
low, locked in the pilot's compartment. Tung and Mayhew went off
"to see what we can do," as Tung put it, rather airily to Miles's mind.
Miles sat and nibbled his knuckles nervously, and tried not to jump
with each thump, clink, or hiss of the robotic loaders placing supplies
for the mercenaries on the other side of the bulkhead. Elena's steady
profile did not twitch at every little noise, Miles noticed enviously. *I
loved her once. Who is she now?*

Could one choose *not* to fall in love all over again with this new
person? A chance to choose. She seemed tougher, more willing to
speak her mind—this was good—yet her thoughts had a bitter tang.
Not good. That bitterness made him ache.

"Have you been all right?" he asked her hesitantly. "Apart from
this command structure mess, that is. Tung treating you right? He
was supposed to be your mentor. On-the-job, for you, the training I
was getting in the classroom . . ."

"Oh, he's a good mentor. He stuffs me with military information,
tactics, history . . . I can run every phase of a combat drop patrol
now, logistics, mapping, assault, withdrawal, even emergency shuttle
take-offs, and landings, if you don't mind a few bumps. I'm almost up
to really handling my fictional rank, at least on fleet equipment. He
likes teaching."

"It seemed to me you were a little . . . tense, with him."

She tossed her head. "Everything is tense, just now. It's not possible to be 'apart from' this command structure mess, thank you. Although . . . I suppose I haven't quite forgiven Tung for not being infallible about it. I thought he was, at first."

"Yeah, well, there's a lot of fallibility going around these days," Miles said uncomfortably. "Uh . . . how's Baz?" *Is your husband treating you right?* he wanted to demand, but didn't.

"He's well," she replied, not looking happy, "but discouraged. This power struggle was alien to him, repugnant, I think. He's a tech at heart, he sees a job that needs doing, he does it . . . Tung hints that if Baz hadn't buried himself in Engineering he might have foreseen —prevented—fought the takeover, but I think it was the other way around. He couldn't lower himself to fight on Oser's back-stabbing level, so he withdrew to where he could keep his own standards of honesty . . . for a little while longer. This schism's affected morale all up and down the line."

"I'm sorry," said Miles.

"You should be." Her voice cracked, steadied, harshened. "Baz felt he'd failed you, but you failed us first, when you never came back. You couldn't expect us to keep up the illusion forever."

"Illusion?" said Miles. "I knew . . . it would be difficult, but I thought you might . . . grow into your roles. Make the mercenaries your own."

"The mercenaries may be enough for Tung. I thought they might be for me, too, till we came to the killing. . . . I hate Barrayar, but better to serve Barrayar than nothing, or your own ego."

"What does Oser serve?" Gregor asked curiously, brows raised at this mixed declamation about their homeworld.

"Oser serves Oser. 'The fleet,' he says, but the fleet serves Oser, so it's just a short circuit," said Elena. "The fleet is no home-country. No building, no children . . . sterile. I don't mind helping out the Aslunders, though, they need it. A poor planet, and scared."

"You and Baz—and Arde—could have left, gone off on your own," began Miles.

"How?" said Elena. "You gave us the Dendarii in *charge.* Baz was a deserter once. Never again."

All my fault, right, thought Miles. *Great.*

Elena turned to Gregor, who had acquired a strange guarded expression on his face while listening to her charges of abandonment. "You still haven't said what you're doing here in the first place, besides putting your feet in things. Was this supposed to be some sort of secret diplomatic mission?"

"You explain it," said Miles to Gregor, trying not to grit his teeth. *Tell her about the balcony, eh?*

Gregor shrugged, eyes sliding aside from Elena's level look. "Like Baz, I deserted. Like Baz, I found it was not the improvement I'd hoped for."

"You can see why it's urgent to get Gregor back home as quickly as possible," Miles put in. "They think he's missing. Maybe kidnapped." Miles gave Elena a quick edited version of their chance meeting in Consortium Detention.

"God." Elena's lips pursed. "I see why it's urgent to you to get him off your hands, anyway. If anything happened to him in your company, fifteen factions would cry 'Treason plot!'"

"That thought has occurred to me, yes," growled Miles.

"Your father's Centrist coalition government would be the first thing to fall," Elena continued. "The military right would get behind Count Vorinnis, I suppose, and square off with the anti-centralization liberals. The French speakers would want Vorville, the Russian Vortugalov—or has he died yet?"

"The far-right blow-up-the-wormhole isolationist loonie faction would field Count Vortrifrani against the anti-Vor pro-galactic faction who want a written constitution," put in Miles glumly. "And I do mean field."

"Count Vortrifrani scares me," Elena shivered. "I've heard him speak."

"It's the suave way he mops the foam from his lips," said Miles. "The Greek minorists would seize the moment to attempt secession—"

"Stop it!" Gregor, who had propped his forehead on his hands, said from behind the barrier of his arms.

"I thought that was *your* job," said Elena tartly. At his bleak look, raising his head, she softened, her mouth twisting up. "Too bad I can't offer you a job with the fleet. We can always use formally-trained officers, to train the rest if nothing else."

"A mercenary?" said Gregor. "There's a thought. . . ."

"Oh, sure. A lot of our people are former regular military folk. Some are even legitimately discharged."

Fantasy lit Gregor's eye with brief amusement. He sighted down his grey-and-white jacket sleeve. "If only you were in charge here, aye, Miles?"

"No!" Miles cried in a suffused voice.

The light died. "It was a joke."

"Not funny." Miles breathed carefully, praying it would not occur to Gregor to make that an *order*. . . . "Anyway, we're now trying to make it to the Barrayaran Consul on Vervain Station. It's still there, I hope. I haven't heard news for days—what's going on with the Vervani?"

"As far as I know, it's business as usual, except for the heightened paranoia," said Elena. "Vervain's putting its resources into ships, not stations—"

"Makes sense, when you've got more than one wormlike to guard," Miles conceded.

"But it makes Aslund perceive the Vervani as potential aggressors. There's an Aslunder faction that's actually urging a first strike before the new Vervani fleet comes on-line. Fortunately, the defensive strategists have prevailed so far. Oser has set the price for a strike by us prohibitively high. He's not stupid. He knows the Aslunders couldn't back us up. Vervain hired a mercenary fleet as a stopgap too—in fact, that's what gave the Aslunders the idea to hire us. They're called Randall's Rangers, though I understand Randall is no more."

"We shall avoid them," Miles asserted fervently.

"I hear their new second officer is a Barrayaran. You might be able to swing some help, there."

Gregor's brows rose in speculation. "One of Illyan's plants? Sounds like his work."

Was that where Ungari had gone? "Approach with caution, anyway," Miles allowed.

"About time," Gregor commented under his breath.

"The Ranger's commander's name is Cavilo—"

"What?" yelped Miles.

Elena's winged brows rose. "Just Cavilo. Nobody seems to know if it's the given or surname—"

"Cavilo is the person who tried to buy me—or Victor Rotha—at the Consortium Station. For twenty thousand Betan dollars."

Elena's brows stayed up. "Why?"

"I don't know why." Miles rethought their goal. Pol, the Consortium, Aslund . . . no, it still came up Vervain. "But we definitely avoid the Vervani's mercs. We step off the ship and go straight to the Consul, go to ground, and don't even squeak till Illyan's men arrive to take us home, Momma. Right."

Gregor sighed. "Right."

No more playing secret agent. His best efforts had only served to get Gregor nearly murdered. It was time to try less hard, Miles decided.

"Strange," said Gregor, looking at Elena—at the new Elena, Miles guessed—"to think you've had more combat experience than either of us."

"Than both of you," Elena corrected dryly. "Yes, well . . . actual combat . . . is a lot stupider than I'd imagined. If two groups can cooperate to the incredible extent it takes to meet in battle, why not put in a tenth that effort to talk? That's not true of guerilla wars, though," Elena went on thoughtfully. "A guerilla is an enemy who won't play the game. Makes more sense to me. If you're going to be vile, why not be totally vile? That third contract—if I ever get involved in another guerilla war, I want to be on the side of the guerillas."

"Harder to make peace, between totally vile enemies," Miles reflected. "War is not its own end, except in some catastrophic slide into absolute damnation. It's peace that's wanted. Some better peace than the one you started with."

"Whoever can be the most vile longest, wins?" Gregor posited.

"Not . . . historically true, I don't think. If what you do during the war so degrades you that the next peace is worse. . . ." Human noises from the cargo bay froze Miles in midsentence, but it was Tung and Mayhew returning.

"Come on," Tung urged. "If Arde doesn't keep to schedule, he'll draw attention."

They filed into the cargo hold, where Mayhew held the control leash of a float pallet with a couple of plastic packing crates attached. "Your friend can pass as a fleet soldier," Tung told Miles. "For you, I found a box. It would have been classier to roll you up in a carpet, but since the freighter captain is male, I'm afraid the historical reference would be wasted."

Dubiously, Miles regarded the box. It seemed to lack air holes. "Where are you taking me?"

"We have a regular irregular arrangement, for getting fleet intelligence officers in and out quietly. Got this inner-system freighter captain, an independent owner—he's Vervani, but he's been on the payroll three times before. He'll take you across, get you through Vervani customs. After that you're on your own."

"How much danger is this arrangement to you all?" Miles worried.

"Not a lot," said Tung, "all things considered. He'll think he's delivering more mercenary agents, for a price, and naturally keep his mouth shut. It'll be days before he gets back to even be questioned. I arranged it all myself, Elena and Arde didn't appear, so he can't give them away."

"Thank you," Miles said quietly.

Tung nodded, and sighed. "If only you'd stayed on with us. What a soldier I could've made of you, these last three years."

"If you do find yourselves out of a job as a consequence of helping us," Gregor added, "Elena will know how to put you in touch."

Tung grimaced. "In touch with what, eh?"

"Better not to know," said Elena, helping Miles position himself in the packing crate.

"All right," grumbled Tung, "but . . . all right."

Miles found himself face to face with Elena, for the last time till—when? She hugged him, but then gave Gregor an identical, sisterly embrace. "Give my love to your mother," she told Miles. "I often think of her."

"Right. Uh . . . give my best to Baz. Tell him, it's all right. Your personal safety comes first, yours and his. The Dendarii are, are, were . . ." he could not quite bring himself to say, *not important,* or, a *naive dream,* or, *an illusion,* though that last came closest. "A good try," he finished lamely.

The look she gave him was cool, edged, indecipherable—no, readily decodable, he feared. *Idiot,* or stronger words to that effect. He sat down, his head to his knees, and let Mayhew affix the lid, feeling like a zoological specimen being crated for shipment to the lab.

The transfer went smoothly. Miles and Gregor found themselves installed in a small but decent cabin designed for the freighter's occasional super-cargo. The ship undocked, free of Aslund Station and danger of discovery, some three hours after they boarded. No Oseran search parties, no uproars . . . Tung, Miles had to admit, still did good work.

Miles was intensely grateful for a wash, a chance to clean his remaining clothes, a real meal, and sleep in safety. The ship's tiny crew seemed allergic to their corridor; he and Gregor were left strictly alone. Safe for three days, as he chugged across the Hegen Hub yet again, in yet another identity. Next stop, the Barrayaran consulate on Vervain Station.

Oh, God, he was going to have to write a report on all this when they got there. True confessions, in the approved ImpSec official style (dry as dust, judging from samples he'd read). Ungari, now, given the same tour, would have produced columns of concrete, objective data, all ready to be reanalyzed six different ways. What had Miles counted? *Nothing, I was in a box.* He had little to offer but gut feel based on a limited view snatched while dodging what seemed like every security goon in the system. Maybe he should center his report on the security forces, eh? One ensign's opinion. The general staff would be so impressed.

So what was his opinion, by now? Well, Pol didn't seem to be the source of the troubles in the Hegen Hub; they were reacting, not acting. The Consortium seemed supremely uninterested in military adventures, the only party weak enough for the eclectic Jacksonians to take on and beat was Aslund, and there would be little profit in conquering Aslund, a barely terraformed agricultural world. Aslund was paranoid enough to be dangerous, but only half-prepared, and shielded by a mercenary force waiting only the right spark to itself split into warring factions. No sustained threat there. The action, the energy for this destabilization, by elimination must be coming from or via Vervain. How could one find out . . . no. He'd sworn off secret agenting. Vervain was somebody else's problem.

Miles wondered wanly if he could persuade Gregor to give him an Imperial pardon from writing a report, and if Illyan would accept it. Probably not.

Gregor was very quiet. Miles, stretched out on his bunk, tucked his hands behind his head and smiled to conceal worry, as Gregor—somewhat regretfully, it seemed to Miles—put aside his stolen Dendarii uniform and donned civilian clothes contributed by Arde Mayhew. The shabby trousers, shirt, and jacket hung a little short and loose on Gregor's spare frame; so dressed he seemed a down-on-his-luck drifter, with hollow eyes. Miles secretly resolved to keep him away from high places.

Gregor regarded him back. "You were weird, as Admiral Naismith, you know? Almost like a different person."

Miles shrugged himself up onto one elbow. "I guess Naismith is me with no brakes. No constraints. He doesn't have to be a good little Vor, or any kind of a Vor. He doesn't have a problem with subordination, he isn't subordinate to anyone."

"I noticed." Gregor ordered the Dendarii uniform in Barrayaran regulation folds. "Do you regret having to duck out on the Dendarii?"

"Yes . . . no . . . I don't know." *Deeply.* The chain of command, it seemed, pulled both ways on a middle link. Pull hard enough, and that link must twist and snap. . . . "I trust you don't regret escaping contract slavery."

"No . . . it wasn't what I'd pictured. It was peculiar, that fight at the airlock, though. Total strangers wanting to kill me without even knowing who I was. Total strangers trying to kill the emperor of

Barrayar, I can understand. This . . . I'm going to have to think about this one."

Miles allowed himself a brief crooked grin. "Like being loved for yourself, only different."

Gregor gave him a sharp glance. "It was strange to see Elena again, too. Bothari's dutiful daughter . . . she's changed."

"I'd meant her to," Miles avowed.

"She seems quite attached to her deserter husband."

"Yes," Miles said shortly.

"Had you meant that too?"

"Not mine to choose. It . . . follows logically, from the integrity of her character. I might have foreseen it. Since her convictions about loyalty just saved both our lives, I can hardly . . . hardly regret them, eh?"

Gregor's brow rose, an oblique gloss.

Miles bit down irritation. "Anyway, I hope she'll be all right. Oser's proved himself dangerous. She and Baz seem to be protected only by Tung's admittedly eroding power base."

"I'm surprised you didn't take up Tung's offer." Gregor grinned as briefly as Miles had. "Instant admiralty. Skip all those tedious Barrayaran intervening steps."

"Tung's offer?" Miles snorted. "Didn't you hear him? I thought you said Dad made you read all those treaties. Tung didn't offer command, he offered a fight, at five to one odds against. He sought an ally, front-man, or cannon-fodder, not a boss."

"Oh. Hm." Gregor settled back on his bunk. "That's so. Yet I still wonder if you'd have chosen something other than this prudent retreat if I hadn't been along." His lids were hooded over a sharp glance.

Miles choked on visions. A sufficiently liberal interpretation of Illyan's vague "use Ensign Vorkosigan to clear the Dendarii Mercenaries from the Hub" might be stretched to include . . . no. "No. If I hadn't run into you, I'd be on my way to Escobar with Sergeant-nanny Overholt. You, I suppose, would still be installing lights." Depending, of course, on what the mysterious Cavilo—Commander Cavilo?—had planned for Miles once he'd caught up with him in Consortium Detention.

So where was Overholt, by now? Had he reported to HQ, tried to contact Ungari, been picked off by Cavilo? Or followed Miles? Too bad Miles couldn't have followed Overholt to Ungari—no, that was circular reasoning. It was all very weird, and they were well out of it.

"We're well out of it," Miles opined to Gregor.

Gregor rubbed the pale grey mark on his face, fading shadow of his shock-stick encounter. "Yeah, probably. I was getting good at the lights, though."

Almost over, Miles thought as he and Gregor followed the freighter captain through the hatch tube into the Vervain Station docking bay. Well, maybe not quite. The Vervani captain was nervous, obsequious, clearly tense. Still, if the man had managed this spy transfer three times before, he should know what he was doing by now.

The docking bay with its harsh lighting was the usual chilly echoing cavern, arranged to the rigid grid-pattern taste of robots, not human curves. It was in fact empty of humans, its machinery silent. Their path had been cleared before them, Miles supposed, though if he'd been doing it he'd have picked the busiest chaotic period of loading or unloading to slip something past.

The captain's eyes darted from corner to corner. Miles could not help following his glance. They stopped near a deserted control booth.

"We wait here," the freighter captain said. "There are some men coming who will take you the rest of the way." He leaned against the booth wall and kicked it gently with one heel in an idle compulsive rhythm for several minutes, then he stopped kicking and straightened, head turning.

Footsteps. Half a dozen men emerged from a nearby corridor. Miles stiffened. Uniformed men, with an officer, judging by their posture, but they weren't wearing the garb of either Vervani civil or military security. Unfamiliar short-sleeved tan fatigues with black tabs and trim, and short black boots. They carried stunners, drawn and ready. *But if it walks like an arrest squad, and talks like an arrest squad, and quacks like an arrest squad . . .*

"Miles," muttered Gregor doubtfully, talking in the same cues, "is this in the script?" The stunners were pointed their way, now.

"He's pulled this off three times," Miles offered in unfelt reassurance. "Why not a fourth?"

The freighter captain smiled thinly, and stepped away from the wall, out of the line of fire. "I pulled it off twice," he informed them. "The third time, I got caught."

Miles's hands twitched. He held them carefully away from his sides, biting back swear words. Slowly, Gregor raised his hands as well, face wonderfully blank. Score one for Gregor's self-control, as always, the one virtue his constrained life had surely inculcated.

Tung had set this up. All by himself. Had Tung known? Sold by

Tung? No . . . ! "Tung said you were reliable," Miles grated to the freighter captain.

"What's Tung to me?" the man snarled back. "I have a family, mister."

Under the stunners' aim, two—God, goons again!—soldiers stepped forward to lean Miles and Gregor hands to the wall, and shake them down, relieving them of all their hard-won Oseran weapons, equipment, and multiple IDs. The officer examined the cache. "Yeah, these are Oser's men, all right." He spoke into his wrist comm. "We have them."

"Carry on," a thin voice returned. "We'll be right down. Cavilo out."

Randall's Rangers, evidently, hence the unfamiliar uniforms. But why no Vervani in sight? "Pardon me," Miles said mildly to the officer, "but are you people acting under the misapprehension we are Aslunder agents?"

The officer stared down at him and snorted.

"I wonder if it might not be time to establish our real identity," Gregor murmured tentatively to Miles.

"Interesting dilemma," Miles returned out of the corner of his mouth. "We better find out if they shoot spies."

A brisk tapping of boots heralded a new arrival. The squad braced as the sound rounded the corner. Gregor came to attention too, in automatic military courtesy, his straightness looking very strange hung about with Arde Mayhew's clothes. Miles no doubt looked least military of all, with his mouth gaping open in shock. He closed it before something flew in, such as his foot.

Five feet tall and a bit added by black books with higher-than-regulation heels. Cropped blonde hair like a dandelion aureole on that sculptured head. Crisp tan-and-black rank-gilded uniform that fit her body language in perfect complement. *Livia Nu.*

The officer saluted. "Commander Cavilo, ma'am."

"Very good, Lieutenant. . . ." her blue eyes, falling on Miles, widened in unfeigned surprise, instantly covered. "Why, *Victor,* darling," her voice went syrupy with exaggerated amusement and delight, *"fancy* meeting you here. Still selling miracle suits to the unwitting?"

Miles spread his empty hands. "This is the totality of my luggage, ma'am. You should have bought when you could."

"I wonder." Her smile was tight and speculative. Miles found the glitter in her eyes disturbing. Gregor, silent, looked frantically bewildered.

So, your name wasn't Livia Nu, and you weren't a procurement agent. So why the devil was the commandant of Vervain's mercenary force meeting incognito on Pol Station with a representative of the most powerful House of the Jacksonian Consortium? *That was no mere arms deal, darling.*

Cavilo/Livia Nu raised her wrist comm to her lips. "Sickbay, *Kurin's Hand.* Cavilo here. I'm sending you up a couple of prisoners for questioning. I may sit in on this one myself." She keyed off.

The freighter captain stepped forward, half-fearful, half-pugnacious. "My wife and son. Now you prove they're safe."

Judiciously, she looked him over. "You may be good for another run. All right." She gestured to a soldier. "Take this man to the *Kurin's* brig and let him have a look on the monitors. Then bring him back to me. You're a fortunate traitor, captain. I have another job for you by which you may earn them—"

"Their freedom?" the freighter captain demanded.

She frowned slightly at the interruption. "Why should I inflate your salary? Another week of life."

He trailed off after the soldier, hands clenched angrily, teeth clenched prudently.

What the hell? Miles thought. He didn't know much about Vervain, but he was pretty sure not even their martial law made provisions for holding innocent relatives hostage against the good behavior of unconvicted traitors.

The freighter captain gone, Cavilo keyed her wristcom again. *"Kurin's Hand* Security? Ah, good. I'm sending you my pet double agent. Run the recording we made last week of Cell Six for his motivation, ai? Don't let him know it's not real-time . . . right. Cavilo out."

So, was the man's family free? Already dead? Being held elsewhere? What were they getting into here?

More boots rounded the corner, a heavy regulation tread. Cavilo smiled sourly, but smoothed the expression into something sweeter as she turned to greet the newcomer.

"Stanis, darling. Look what we netted this time. It's that little renegade Betan who was trying to deal stolen arms on Pol Station. It appears he isn't an independent after all."

The tan and black Rangers' uniform looked just fine on General Metzov, too, Miles noted crazily. Now would be a wonderful time to roll up his eyes and pass out, if only he had the trick of it.

General Metzov stood equally riveted, his iron-grey eyes ablaze with sudden unholy joy. "He's no Betan, Cavie."

12

"He's a Barrayaran. And not just any Barrayaran. We've got to get him out of sight, quickly," Metzov went on.

"Who sent him, then?" Cavilo stared anew at Miles, her lip in a dubious curl.

"God," Metzov avowed fervently. "God has delivered him into my hand." Metzov, that cheerful, was an unusual and alarming sight. Even Cavilo raised her brow.

Metzov glanced at Gregor for the first time. "We'll take him and his —bodyguard, I suppose . . ." Metzov slowed.

The pictures on the mark-notes didn't look much like Gregor, being several years out of date, but the emperor had appeared in enough vid-casts—not dressed like this, of course. . . . Miles could almost see Metzov thinking. *The face is familiar, I just can't place the name.* . . . Maybe he wouldn't recognize Gregor. Maybe he wouldn't *believe* it.

Gregor, drawn up in a dignity concealing dismay, spoke for the first time. "Is this yet another of your old friends, Miles?"

It was the measured, cultured voice that triggered the connection. Metzov's face, reddened with excitement, drained white. He looked around involuntarily—for Illyan, Miles guessed.

"Uh, this is General Stanis Metzov," Miles explained.

"The Kyril Island Metzov?"

"Yeah."

"Oh." Gregor maintained his closed reserve, nearly expressionless.

"Where is your security, sir?" Metzov demanded of Gregor, his voice harsh with unacknowledged fear.

You're looking at it, Miles mourned.

"Not far behind, I imagine," Gregor essayed, cool. "Let Us go Our way, and they will not trouble you."

"Who is this fellow?" Cavilo tapped a boot impatiently.

"What," Miles couldn't help asking Metzov, "what are you doing here?"

Metzov went grim. "How shall a man my age, stripped of his Imperial Pension—his life savings—live? Did you hope I would sit down and quietly starve? Not I."

Inopportune, to remind Metzov of his grudge, Miles realized. "This . . . looks like an improvement over Kyril Island," Miles suggested hopefully. His mind still boggled. Metzov, working under a woman? The internal dynamics of this command chain must be fascinating. Stanis *darling?*

Metzov did not look amused.

"Who are they?" Cavilo demanded again.

"Power. Money. Strategic leverage. More than you can imagine," Metzov answered.

"Trouble," Miles put in. "More than you can imagine."

"You are a separate matter, mutant," Metzov said.

"I beg to differ, General," said Gregor in his best Imperial tones. Feeling for footing in this floating conversation, though concealing his confusion well.

"We must take them to the *Kurin's Hand* at once. Out of sight," said Metzov to Cavilo. He glanced at the arrest squad. "Out of hearing. We'll continue this in private."

They marched off, escorted by the patrol. Metzov's gaze felt like a knife blade in Miles's back, prodding and probing. They passed through several deserted docking bays till they arrived at a major one actively servicing a ship. The command ship, judging by the number and formality of duty guards.

"Take them to Medical for questioning," Cavilo ordered the squad as they were saluted through a personnel hatch by the officer in charge.

"Hold on that," said Metzov. He stared around the cross-corridors, almost jittering. "Do you have a guard who's deaf and mute?"

"Hardly!" Cavilo stared indignantly at her mysteriously agitated subordinate. "To the brig, then."

"No," said Metzov sharply. Hesitating to throw the Emperor into a cell, Miles realized. Metzov turned to Gregor and said with perfect seriousness, "May I have your parole, sire—sir?"

"What?" cried Cavilo. "Have you stripped a gear, Stanis?"

"A parole," Gregor noted gravely, "is a promise given between honorable enemies. Your honor I am willing to assume. But are you thus declaring yourself Our enemy?"

Excellent bit of weaseling, Miles approved.

Metzov's eye fell on Miles. His lips thinned. "Perhaps not yours. But you have a poor choice of favorites. Not to mention advisors."

Gregor was now very hard to read. "Some acquaintances are imposed on me. Also some advisors."

"To my cabin," Metzov held up his hand as Cavilo opened her mouth to object, "for now. For our initial conversation. Without witnesses, or Security recordings. After that, we decide, Cavie."

Cavilo, eyes narrowing, closed her mouth. "All right, Stanis. Lead off." Her hand curved open ironically, and gestured them onward.

Metzov posted two guards outside his cabin door, and dismissed the rest. When the door had sealed behind them, he tied Miles with a tangle-cord and sat him on the floor. With helplessly ingrained deference, he then seated Gregor in the padded station chair at his comconsole desk, the best the spartan chamber had to offer.

Cavilo, seated cross-legged on the bed watching the play, objected to the logic of this. "Why tie up the little one and leave the big one loose?"

"Keep your stunner drawn, then, if he worries you," Metzov advised. Breathing heavily, he stood hands on hips and studied Gregor. He shook his head, as if still not believing his eyes.

"Why not your stunner?"

"I have not yet decided whether to draw a weapon in his presence."

"We're *alone* now, Stanis," Cavilo said in a sarcastic lilt. "Would you kindly explain this insanity? And it had better be good."

"Oh yes. That—" he pointed to Miles, "is Lord Miles Vorkosigan, the son of the Prime Minister of Barrayar. Admiral Aral Vorkosigan— I trust you've heard of *him.*"

Cavilo's brows lowered. "What was he doing on Pol Six in the guise of a Betan gunrunner, then?"

"I'm not sure. The last I'd heard he was under arrest by Imperial

Security, though of course no one believed they were serious about it."

"Detainment," Miles corrected. "Technically."

"And he—" Metzov swung to point to Gregor, "is the Emperor of Barrayar. Gregor Vorbarra. What *he's* doing here, I cannot imagine."

"Are you sure?" Even Cavilo was taken aback. At Metzov's stern nod, her eye lit with speculation. She looked at Gregor as if for the first time. *"Really. How interesting."*

"But where is his security? We must tread very cautiously, Cavie."

"What's he worth to them? Or for that matter, to the highest bidder?"

Gregor smiled at her. "I'm Vor, ma'am. In a sense, *the* Vor. Risk in service is the Vorish trade. I wouldn't assume my value was infinite, if I were you."

Gregor's complaint had some truth to it, Miles thought; when he wasn't being emperor he seemed hardly anyone at all. But he sure did the *role* well.

"An opportunity, yes," said Metzov, "but if we create an enemy we can't handle—"

"If we hold *him* hostage, we ought to be able to handle them with ease," Cavilo commented thoughtfully.

"An alternate and more prudent course," Miles interjected, "would be to help us swiftly and safely on our way, and collect a lucrative and honorable thank-you. An, as it were, win-win strategy."

"Honorable?" Metzov's eyes burned. He fell into a brooding silence, then muttered. "But what are they doing here? And where's the snake Illyan? I want the mutant, in any case. Damn! It must be played boldly, or not at all." He stared malignantly at Miles. "Vorkosigan . . . so. And what is Barrayar to me now, a Service that stabbed me in the back after thirty-five years. . . ." He straightened decisively, but still did not, Miles noticed, draw a weapon in the emperor's presence. "Yes, take them to the brig, Cavie."

"Not so fast," said Cavilo, looking newly pensive. "Send the little one to the brig, if you like. He's nothing, you say?"

The only son of the most powerful military leader on Barrayar kept his mouth shut for a change. If, if, if . . .

"By comparison," Metzov temporized, looking suddenly fearful of being cheated of his prey.

"Very well." Cavilo slid her stunner, which she had stopped aiming and started playing with some time back, soundlessly into her holster. She moved to unseal the door and beckon to the guards. "Put him," she gestured to Gregor, "in Cabin Nine, G Deck. Cut the outgoing comm, lock the door, and post a guard with a stunner. But supply him with any reasonable comfort he may request." She added aside to Gregor, "It's the most comfortable visiting officer's quarters the *Kurin's Hand* can supply, ah—"

"Call me Greg," Gregor sighed.

"Greg. Nice name. Cabin Nine is next to my own. We will continue this conversation shortly, after you, ah, freshen up. Perhaps over dinner. Oversee his arrival there, will you, Stanis?" She favored both men with an impartial, glittering smile, and wafted out, a neat trick in boots. She stuck her head back in and indicated Miles. "Bring *him* along to the brig."

Miles was removed by the second guard with a wave of a stunner and the prod of a blessedly inactivated shock-stick, to follow in her wake.

The *Kurin's Hand,* judging from his passing glimpses, was a much larger command ship than the *Triumph,* able to field bigger and punchier combat drop or boarding forces, but correspondingly sluggish in maneuver. Its brig was larger too, Miles discovered shortly, and more formidably secured. A single entrance opened onto an elaborate guard monitor station, from which led two dead-end cell bays.

The freighter captain was just leaving the guard station, under the watchful eye of the squadman detailed to escort him. He exchanged a hostile look with Cavilo.

"As you see, they remain in good health," Cavilo said to him. "My half of the bargain, Captain. See that you continue to complete your own part."

Let's see what happens. . . . "You saw a recording," Miles piped up. "Demand to see 'em in the flesh."

Cavilo's white teeth clenched rigidly, but her annoyed grimace melted seamlessly into a vulpine smile as the freighter captain jerked around. "What? You . . ." he planted himself mulishly. "All right, which of you is lying?"

"Captain, that's all the guarantee you get," said Cavilo, gesturing to the monitors. "You chose to gamble, gamble you shall."

"Then that—" he pointed to Miles, "is the last result you get."

A subtle hand motion down by her trouser seam brought the guards to the alert, stunners drawn. "Take him out," she ordered.

"No!"

"Very well," her eyes widened in exasperation, "take him to Cell Six. And lock him in."

As the freighter captain turned, torn between resistance and eagerness, Cavilo motioned the guard to open distance from his prisoner. He fell away, brows rising in question. Cavilo glanced at Miles and smiled very sourly, as if to say, *All right, Smartass, watch me.* In a cold smooth motion Cavilo flipped open her left side holster seal, brought up a nerve disruptor, took careful aim, and fried the back of the captain's head. He convulsed once and dropped, dead before he hit the deck.

She walked over and pensively prodded the body with the pointed toe of her boot, then glanced up at Miles, whose jaw was gaping open. "You *will* keep your mouth shut next time, won't you, little man?"

Miles's mouth shut with a snap. *You had to experiment. . . .* At least now he knew who'd killed Liga. The rabbity Polian's reported death seemed suddenly real and vivid. The exalted look flashing over Cavilo's face as she blew the freighter captain away fascinated even as it horrified Miles. *Who did you really see in your gunsights, darling?* "Yes, ma'am," he choked, trying to conceal his shakes, delayed reaction to this shocking turn. *Damn* his tongue. . . .

She stepped down to the security monitoring station and spoke to the tech at—frozen at—her post. "Unload the recording of General Metzov's cabin that includes the last half-hour, and give it to me. Start a fresh one. No, don't play it back!" She placed the disk in a breast pocket and carefully sealed the flap. "Put this one in Cell Fourteen," she nodded toward Miles. "Or, ah—if it's empty, make that Cell Thirteen." Her teeth bared briefly.

The guards re-searched Miles, and took ID scans. Cavilo blandly informed them that his name should be entered as Victor Rotha.

As he was pulled to his feet, two men with medical insignia arrived with a float-pallet to remove the body. Cavilo, watching without expression now, remarked tiredly to Miles, "You chose to damage my double-agent's utility. A vandal's prank. He had better uses than as an object-lesson for a fool. I do not warehouse non-useful items. I suggest you start thinking of how you can make yourself more useful to me than as merely General Metzov's catnip toy." She smiled faintly into some invisible distance. "Though he does jump for you, doesn't he? I shall have to explore that motivation."

"What is the use of Stanis-darling to you?" Miles dared, pig-headed-defiant in his wash of angry guilt. Metzov as her paramour? Revolting thought.

"He's an experienced ground combat commander."

"What's a fleet on all-space wormhole guard duty want with a ground commander?"

"Well, then," she smiled sweetly, "he amuses me."

That was supposed to have been the first answer. "No accounting for taste," Miles muttered inanely, careful not to be heard. Should he warn her about Metzov? On second thought, should he warn Metzov about *her?*

His head was still spinning with this new dilemma when the blank door of his solitary cell sealed him in.

It didn't take long for Miles to exhaust the novelties of his new quarters, a space a little larger than two by two meters, furnished only with two padded benches and a fold-out lavatory. No library viewer, no relief from the wheel of his thoughts mired in the quag of his self-recriminations.

A Ranger field-ration bar, inserted some time later through a force-shielded aperture in the door, proved even more repellent than the Barrayaran Imperial version, resembling a rawhide dog chew. Wetted with spit, it softened slightly, enough to tear off gummy shreds if your teeth were in good health. More than a temporary distraction, it promised to last till the next issue. Probably nutritious as hell. Miles wondered what Cavilo was serving Gregor for dinner. Was it as scientifically vitamin-balanced?

They'd been so close to their goal. Even now, the Barrayaran consulate was only a few locks and levels away, less than a kilometer. If only he could get there from here. If a chance came . . . On the other hand, how long would Cavilo hesitate to disregard diplomatic custom and violate the consulate, if she saw some utility in it? About as long as she'd hesitated to shoot the freighter captain in the back, Miles gauged. She would surely have ordered the consulate, and all known Barrayaran agents on Vervain Station, watched by now. Miles unstuck his teeth from a fragment of ration-leather, and hissed.

A beeping from the code-lock warned Miles he was about to have a visitor. Interrogation, so soon? He'd expected Cavilo to wine, dine, and evaluate Gregor first, then get back to him. Or was he to be a mere project for underlings? He swallowed, throat tight on a ration blob, and sat up, trying to look stern and not scared.

The door slid back to reveal General Metzov, still looking highly military and efficient in the tan and black Ranger fatigues.

"Sure you don't need me, sir?" the guard at his elbow asked as Metzov shouldered through the opening.

Metzov glanced contemptuously at Miles, looking low and unmilitary in Victor Rotha's now limp and grimy green silk shirt, baggy trousers, and bare feet—the processing guards had taken his sandals. "Hardly. *He's* not going to jump me."

Damn straight, Miles agreed with regret.

Metzov tapped his wrist comm. "I'll call you when I'm done."

"Very well, sir." The door sighed closed. The cell seemed suddenly very tiny indeed. Miles drew his legs up, sitting in a small defensive ball on his pallet. Metzov stood at ease, contemplating Miles for a long, satisfied moment, then settled himself comfortably on the bench opposite.

"Well, well," said Metzov, his mouth twisting. "What a turn of fate."

"I thought you'd be dining with the Emperor," said Miles.

"Commander Cavilo, being female, can get a little scattered under stress. When she calms down again, she'll see the need for my expertise in Barrayaran matters," said Metzov in measured tones.

In other words, you weren't invited. "You left the Emperor *alone* with her?" *Gregor, watch your step!*

"Gregor's no threat. I fear his upbringing has made him altogether weak."

Miles choked.

Metzov sat back, allowed his fingers to tap gently on his knee. "So tell me, Ensign Vorkosigan—if it is still Ensign Vorkosigan. There being no justice in the world, I suppose you've retained your rank and pay. What are you doing here? With *him?*"

Miles was tempted to confine himself to name, rank, and serial number, except Metzov knew all those already. Was Metzov an enemy, exactly? Of Barrayar, that is, not of Miles personally. Did Metzov divide the two in his own mind? "The Emperor became separated from his security. We hoped to regain contact with them via the Barrayaran consulate here." There, nothing in that that wasn't perfectly obvious.

"And where did you come from?"

"Aslund."

"Don't bother playing the idiot, Vorkosigan. I know Aslund. Who sent you there in the first place? And don't bother lying, I can cross-question the freighter captain."

"No, you can't. Cavilo killed him."

"Oh?" A flicker of surprise, suppressed. "Clever of her. He was the only witness to know where you went."

Had that been part of Cavilo's calculation, when she'd raised her nerve disruptor? Probably. And yet . . . the freighter captain was also the only corroborating witness who knew where they'd come *from.* Maybe Cavilo was not so formidable as she seemed at first glance.

"Again," Metzov said patiently—Miles could see he felt he had all the time in the world—"How did you come to be in the Emperor's company?"

"How do you think?" Miles countered, buying time.

"Some plot, of course," Metzov shrugged.

Miles groaned. "Oh, of course!" He uncurled in his indignation. "And what sane—or insane, for that matter—chain of conspiracy do you imagine accounts for our arrival here, alone, from Aslund? I mean, I know what it really was, I lived it, but what does it look like?" *To a professional paranoid, that is.* "I'd just love to hear it."

"Well . . ." Metzov was drawn out in spite of himself. "You have somehow separated the Emperor from his security. You must either be setting up an elaborate assassination, or planning to implement some form of personality-control."

"That's what just *springs* to mind, huh?" Miles thumped his back against the wall with a frustrated growl, and slumped.

"Or perhaps you're on some secret—and therefore dishonorable—diplomatic mission. Some sellout."

"If so, where's Gregor's security?" Miles sang. "Better watch out."

"So, my first hypothesis is proved."

"In that case, where's *my* security?" Miles snarled. Where, indeed?

"A Vorkosigan plot—no, perhaps not the Admiral's. He controls Gregor at home—"

"Thank you, I was about to point that out."

"A twisted plot from a twisted mind. Do you dream of making yourself emperor of Barrayar, mutant?"

"A nightmare, I assure you. Ask Gregor."

"It scarcely matters. The medical staff will squeeze out your secrets as soon as Cavilo gives the go-ahead. In a way, it's a shame fast-penta was ever invented. I'd enjoy breaking every bone in your body till you talked. Or screamed. You won't be able to hide behind your father's," he grinned briefly, "skirts, out here, Vorkosigan." He grew thoughtful. "Maybe I will anyway. One bone a day, for as long as they last."

206 bones in the human body. 206 days. Illyan ought to be able to catch up with us in 206 days. Miles smiled bleakly.

Metzov looked too comfortable to arise and initiate this plan immediately, though. This speculative conversation scarcely constituted a serious interrogation. But if not for interrogation, nor revenge-tortures, why was the man here?

His lover threw him out, he felt lonely and strange and wanted someone familiar to talk to. Even a familiar enemy. It was weirdly understandable. But for the Komarr invasion, Metzov had probably never set foot off Barrayar in his life. A life spent mostly in the constrained, ordered, predictable world-within-a-world of the Imperial military. Now the rigid man was adrift, and faced with more free-will choices than he'd ever imagined. *God. The maniac's homesick.* Chilling insight.

"I'm beginning to think I may have accidentally done you a good turn," Miles began. If Metzov was in a talking mood, why not encourage him? "Cavilo's certainly better-looking than your last commander."

"She is that."

"Is the pay higher?"

"Everyone pays more than the Imperial Service," Metzov snorted.

"Not boring, either. On Kyril Island, every day was like every other day. Here, you don't know what's going to happen next. Or does she confide in you?"

"I'm essential to her plans." Metzov practically smirked.

"As a bedroom warrior? Thought you were infantry. Switching specialties, at your age?"

Metzov merely smiled. "Now you're getting obvious, Vorkosigan."

Miles shrugged. *If so, I'm the only obvious thing here.* "As I recall, you didn't think much of women soldiers. Cavilo seems to have made you change your tune."

"Not at all." Metzov sat back smugly. "I expect to be in command of Randall's Rangers in six months."

"Isn't this cell monitored?" Miles asked, startled. Not that he cared how much trouble Metzov's mouth bought him, but still. . . .

"Not at present."

"Cavilo planning to retire, is she?"

"There are a number of ways her retirement might be expedited. The fatal accident Cavilo arranged for Randall might easily be repeated. Or I might even work out a way to charge her with it, since she was stupid enough to brag about murder in bed."

That was no boast, that was a warning, dunderhead. Miles's eyes nearly crossed, imagining pillowtalk between Metzov and Cavilo. "You two must have a lot in common. No wonder you get on so well."

Metzov's amusement thinned. "I have nothing in common with that mercenary slut. I was an Imperial officer." Metzov glowered. "Thirty-five years. And they wasted me. Well, they'll discover their mistake."

Metzov glanced at his chrono. "I still don't understand your presence here. Are you sure there isn't something else you want to say to me now, privately, before you say everything tomorrow to Cavilo under fast-penta?"

Cavilo and Metzov, Miles decided, had set up the old interrogation game of good-guy-bad-guy. Except they'd gotten their signals mixed, and both accidentally taken the part of bad-guy. "If you really want to be helpful, get Gregor to the Barrayaran Consul. Or even just get out a message that he's here."

"In good time, we may. Given suitable terms." Metzov's eyes were narrowed, studying Miles. As puzzled by Miles as Miles by him? After a stretched silence, Metzov called the guard on his wristcom, and withdrew, with no more violent parting threat than "See you tomorrow, Vorkosigan." Sinister enough.

I don't understand your presence here either, Miles thought as the door hissed closed and the lock beeped. Clearly, some kind of planetary ground-attack was in the planning stage. Were Randall's Rangers to spearhead a Vervani invasion force? Cavilo had met secretly with a high-ranking Jackson's Consortium representative. Why? To guarantee Consortium neutrality during the coming attack? That made excellent sense, but why hadn't the Vervani dealt directly? So they could disavow Cavilo's arrangements if the balloon went up too early?

And who, or what, was the target? Not the Consortium Station, obviously, nor its distant parent Jackson's Whole. That left Aslund and Pol. Aslund, a cul-de-sac, was not strategically tempting. Better to take Pol first, cut Aslund off from the Hub (with Consortium cooperation) and mop up the weak planet at leisure. But Pol had Barrayar behind it, who would like nothing better than an alliance with its nervous neighbor that would give the imperium a toehold in the Hegen Hub. An open attack must drive Pol into Barrayar's waiting arms. That left Aslund, but . . .

This makes no sense. It was almost more disturbing than the thought of Gregor supping unguarded with Cavilo, or the fear of the promised chemical interrogation. *I'm not seeing something. This makes no sense.*

The Hegen Hub turned in his head, in all its strategic complexity, all the light-dimmed night cycle. The Hub, and pictures of Gregor. Was Cavilo feeding him mind-altering drugs? Doggie chews, like Miles's? Steak and champagne? Was Gregor being tortured? Being seduced? Visions of Cavilo/Livia Nu's dramatic red evening-wear undulated in Miles's mind's eye. Was Gregor having a wonderful time? Miles thought Gregor'd had little more experience with women than he had, but he'd been out of touch with the Emperor these last few years; for all he knew Gregor was keeping a harem now. No, that couldn't be, or Ivan would have picked up the scent, and commented. At length. How susceptible was Gregor to a very old-fashioned form of mind-control?

The day-cycle crept by with Miles anticipating every moment being taken out for his very first experience of fast-penta interrogation from the wrong end of the hypospray. What would Cavilo and Metzov make of the bizarre truth of his and Gregor's odyssey? Three ration-chews arrived at interminable intervals, and the lights dimmed again, marking another ship-night. Three meals, and no interrogation. What was keeping them out there? No noises or subtle gravitic vibrations suggested the ship had left dock, they were still locked to Vervain Station. Miles tried to exercise himself weary, pacing, two steps, turn, two steps, turn, two steps . . . but merely succeeded in increasing his personal stink and making himself dizzy.

Another day writhed by, and another light-dimmed "night." Another breakfast chew fell through onto the floor. Were they artificially stretching or compressing time, confusing his biological clock to soften him up for interrogation? Why bother?

He bit his fingernails. He bit his toenails. He pulled tiny green threads from his shirt and tried flossing his teeth. Then he tried making little green designs with tiny, tiny knots. Then he hit on the idea of weaving messages. Could he macramé "Help, I am a prisoner . . ." and plant it on the back of someone's jacket by static charge? If someone ever came back, that is? He got as far as a delicate gossamer H, E, L, caught the thread on a hangnail while rubbing his stubbled chin, and reduced his plea to an illegible green wad. He pulled another thread and started over.

The lock twinkled and beeped. Miles snapped alert, realizing only then that he had fallen into an almost hypnotic fugue in his mumbling isolation. How much time had passed?

His visitor was Cavilo, crisp and businesslike in her Ranger's fatigues. A guard took up station just outside the cell door, which closed behind her. Another private chat, it seemed. Miles struggled to pull his thoughts together, to remember what he was about.

Cavilo settled herself opposite Miles in the same spot Metzov had chosen, in somewhat the same leisurely posture, leaning forward, hands clasped loosely on her knees, attentive, assured. Miles sat cross-legged, back to the wall, feeling distinctly at the disadvantage.

"Lord Vorkosigan, ah . . ." she cocked her head, interrupting herself aside, "you don't look at all well."

"Solitary confinement doesn't suit me." His disused voice came out raspy, and he had to stop and clear his throat. "Perhaps a library viewer," his brain grated into gear, "—or better, an exercise period." Which would get him out of this cell, and in contact with subornable humans. "My medical problems compel me to a self-disciplined lifestyle, if they're not to flare up and impede me. I definitely need an exercise period, or I'm going to get really sick."

"Hm. We'll see." She ran a hand through her short hair, and refocused. "So, Lord Vorkosigan. Tell me about your mother."

"Huh?" A most dizzying sharp left turn, for a military interrogation. "Why?"

She smiled ingratiatingly. "Greg's tales have interested me."

Greg's tales? Had the Emperor been fast-penta'd? "What . . . do you want to know?"

"Well . . . I understand Countess Vorkosigan is an off-worlder, a Betan who married into your aristocracy."

"The Vor are a military caste, but yes."

"How was she received, by the power-class—whatever they choose to call themselves? I'd thought Barrayarans were totally provincial, prejudiced against off-worlders."

"We are," Miles admitted cheerfully. "The first contact most Barrayarans—of all classes—had with off-worlders, after the end of the Time of Isolation when Barrayar was rediscovered, was with the Cetagandan invasion forces. They left a bad impression that lingers even now, three, four generations after we threw them off."

"Yet no one questioned your father's choice?"

Miles jerked up his chin in bafflement. "He was in his forties. And . . . and he was *Lord Vorkosigan.*" *So am I, now. Why doesn't it work for me like that?*

"Her background made no difference?"

"She was Betan. Is Betan. In the Astronomical Survey first, but then a combat officer. Beta Colony had just helped beat us soundly in that stupid attempt we made to invade Escobar."

"So despite being an enemy, her military background actually helped gain her respect and acceptance among the Vor?"

"I guess so. Plus, she established quite a local military reputation in the fighting of Vordarian's Pretendership, the year I was born twice. Led loyal troops, oh, several times, when my father couldn't be two places at once." And had been personally responsible for the five-year-old emperor-in-hiding's safety. More successfully than her son was doing so far for the twenty-five-year-old Gregor. *Total screw-up* was the phrase that sprang to mind, actually. "Nobody's messed with her since."

"Hm." Cavilo sat back, murmuring half to herself, "so, it has been done. Therefore, it can be done."

What, what can be done? Miles rubbed a hand over his face, trying to wake up and concentrate. "How is Gregor?"

"Quite amusing."

Gregor the Lugubrious, amusing? But then, if it matched the rest of her personality, Cavilo's sense of humor was probably vile. "I meant his health."

"Rather better than yours, from the look of you."

"I trust he's been better fed."

"What, a taste of real military life too strong for you, Lord Vorkosigan? You've been fed the same as my troops."

"Can't be." Miles held up a ragged half-gnawed breakfast chew. "They'd have mutinied by now."

"Oh, dear." She regarded the repellent morsel with a sympathetic frown. "Those. I thought they'd been condemned. How did they end up here? Someone must be economizing. Shall I order you a regular menu?"

"Yes, thank you," said Miles immediately, and paused. She had neatly misdirected his attention from Gregor to himself. He must keep his mind on the Emperor. How much *useful* information had Gregor spilled, by now?

"You realize," Miles said carefully, "you are creating a massive interplanetary incident between Vervain and Barrayar."

"Not at all," said Cavilo reasonably. "I'm Greg's friend. I've rescued him from falling into the hands of the Vervani secret police. He's now under my protection, until the opportunity arises to restore him to his rightful place."

Miles blinked. "Do the Vervani have a secret police, as such?"

"Close enough," Cavilo shrugged. "Barrayar, of course, definitely does. Stanis seems quite worried about them. They must be very embarrassed, back in ImpSec, to have so thoroughly mislaid their charge. I fear their reputation is exaggerated."

Not quite. I'm ImpSec, and I know where Gregor is. So technically, ImpSec is right on top of the situation. Miles wasn't sure whether to laugh or cry. *Or right under it.*

"If we're all such good friends," said Miles, "why am I locked in this cell?"

"For your protection too, of course. After all, General Metzov has openly threatened to, ah—what was it—break every bone in your body." She sighed. "I'm afraid dear Stanis is about to lose his utility."

Miles blanched, remembering what else Metzov had said in that conversation. "For . . . disloyalty?"

"Not at all. Disloyalty can be very useful at times, under proper management. But the overall strategic situation may be about to change drastically. Unimaginably. And after all the time I wasted cultivating him, too. I hope all Barrayarans are not so tedious as Stanis." She smiled briefly. "I very much hope it."

She leaned forward, growing more intent. "Is it true that Gregor, ah, ran away from home to evade pressure from his advisors to marry a woman he loathed?"

"He hadn't mentioned it to me," said Miles, startled. Wait—what was Gregor about, out there? He'd better be careful not to step on his lines. "Though there is . . . concern. If he were to die without an heir any time soon, many fear a factional struggle would follow."

"He has no heir?"

"The factions can't agree. Except on Gregor."

"So his advisors would be glad to see him marry."

"Overjoyed, I expect. Uh . . ." Miles's unease at this turn of the conversation bloomed into sudden light, like the flash before the shock-wave. "Commander Cavilo—you're *not* imagining you could make yourself Empress of Barrayar, are you?"

Her smile grew sharp. "Of course I couldn't. But Greg could." She straightened, evidently annoyed by Miles's stunned expression. "Why not? I'm the right sex. And, apparently, of the right military background."

"How old are you?"

"Lord Vorkosigan, really, what a rude question." Her blue eyes glinted. "If we were on the same side, we could work together."

"Commander Cavilo, I don't think you understand Barrayar. Or Barrayarans." Actually, there'd been eras in Barrayaran history where Cavilo's command style would have fit right in. Mad Emperor Yuri's reign of terror, for example. But they'd spent the last twenty years trying to get *away* from all that.

"I need your cooperation," Cavilo said. "Or at any rate, it could be very useful. To both of us. Your neutrality would be . . . tolerable. Your active opposition, however, would be a problem. For you. But we should avoid getting caught in negative attitude traps at this early stage, I think?"

"Whatever did happen to that freighter captain's wife and child? Widow and orphan, rather?" Miles inquired through his teeth.

Cavilo hesitated fractionally. "The man was a traitor. Of the worst sort. Sold out his planet for money. He was caught in an act of espionage. There is no moral difference between ordering an execution, and carrying it out."

"I agree. So do a lot of legal codes. How about a difference between execution and murder? Vervain is not at war. His actions may have been illegal, warranting arrest, trial, jail or sociopath therapy—where did the trial part drop out?"

"A Barrayaran, arguing legalities? How strange."

"And what happened to his family?"

She'd had a moment to think, blast it. "The tedious Vervani demanded their release. Naturally, I didn't want him to know they were out of my hands, or I'd lose my only hold on his actions at a distance."

Lie or truth? No way to tell. *But she backpedals from her mistake. She let establishing her dominance through terror rule her reactions, before she was sure of her ground. Because she was unsure of her ground. I know the look that was on her face. Homicidal paranoids are as familiar as breakfast, I had one for a bodyguard for seventeen years.* Cavilo, for a brief instant, seemed homey and routine, if no less dangerous. But he should strive to appear convinced, non-threatening, even if it made him gag.

"It's true," he conceded, "it's rank cowardice to give an order you're not willing to carry out yourself. And you're no coward, Commander, I'll grant you that." There, that was the right tone, persuadable but not changing his stance too suspiciously fast.

Her brow rose sardonically, as if to say, *Who are you to judge?* But her tension eased slightly. She glanced at her chrono and rose. "I'll leave you now, to think about the advantages of cooperation. You're theoretically familiar with the mathematics of the Prisoner's Dilemma, I hope. It will be an interesting test of your wits, to see if you can connect theory with practice."

Miles managed a weird return smile. Her beauty, her energy, even her flaring ego, did exert a real fascination. Had Gregor indeed been . . . activated, by Cavilo? Gregor, after all, hadn't watched her raise her nerve disruptor and . . . What weapon was a good ImpSec man to use, in the face of this personal assault on Gregor? Try and seduce her back? To sacrifice himself for the Emperor by flinging himself on Cavilo had about as much appeal as belly-smothering a live sonic grenade.

Besides, he doubted he could work it. The door slid closed, eclipsing her scimitar smile. Too late, he raised a hand to remind her of her promise to change his rations.

But she remembered anyway. Lunch arrived on a trolley, with an experienced, if expressionless, batman to serve it in five elegant courses with two wines and espresso coffee for an antidote. Miles didn't think Cavilo's troops ate like this, either. He envisioned a platoon of smiling, replete, obese gourmets strolling happily into battle . . . the dog chews would be much more effective for raising aggression levels.

A chance remark to his waiter brought a package along with the next meal-trolley, which proved to contain clean underwear, a set of insignialess Ranger fatigues cut down to his fit, and a pair of soft felt slippers; also a tube of depilatory and assorted toiletries. Miles was inspired to wash, by sections, in the fold-out lavatory basin, and shave before dressing. He felt almost human. Ah, the virtues of cooperation. Cavilo was not exactly subtle.

God, where had she come from? A mercenary veteran, she had to have been around for a while to have risen this far, even with short-cuts. Tung might know. *I think she must have lost bad at least once.* He wished Tung were here now. Hell, he wished *Illyan* were here now.

Her flamboyance, Miles increasingly felt, was an effective act, meant to be viewed at a distance like stage makeup, to dazzle her troops. At the right range, it might work rather well, like the popular Barrayaran general of his grandfather's generation who'd gained visibility by carrying a plasma rifle like a swagger stick. Usually uncharged, Miles had heard privately—the man wasn't stupid. Or a Vorish ensign who wore a certain antique dagger at every opportunity. A trademark, a banner. A calculated bit of mass psychology. Cavilo's public persona pushed the envelope of that strategy, surely. Was she scared inside, knowing herself for overextended? *You wish.*

Alas, after a dose of Cavilo, one thought of Cavilo, fogging one's tactical calculations. Focus, ensign. Had she forgotten Victor Rotha? Had Gregor concocted some bullshit explanation to account for their Pol Station encounter? Gregor seemed to be feeding Cavilo skewed facts—or were they? Maybe there really was a loathed proposed bride, and Gregor had not trusted Miles enough to mention it. Miles began to regret being quite so acerbic to Gregor.

His thoughts were still running like a hyped-up rat on an exercise wheel, spinning to nowhere, when the door code-lock beeped again.

Yes, he would fake cooperation, promise anything, if only she'd give him a chance to check on Gregor.

Cavilo appeared with a soldier in tow. The man looked vaguely familiar—one of the arresting goons? No. . . .

The man ducked his head through the cell door, stared at Miles a moment in bemusement, and turned to Cavilo.

"Yeah, that's him, all right. Admiral Naismith, of the Tau Verde Ring war. I'd recognize the little runt anywhere." He added aside to Miles, "What are you doing here, sir?"

Miles mentally transmuted the man's tan and blacks to grey and white. Yeah. There'd been several thousand mercenaries involved in the Tau Verde war. They all had to have gone somewhere.

"Thank you, that will be all, Sergeant." Cavilo took the man by the arm and firmly pulled him away. The non-com's fading advice drifted back down the cell bay, "You ought to try and hire him, ma'am, he's a military genius. . . ."

Cavilo reappeared after a moment, to stand in the aperture with her hands on her hips and her chin outthrust in exasperated disbelief. "How many people *are* you, anyway?"

Miles opened his hands and smiled weakly. Just as he'd been about to talk his way out of this hole . . .

"Huh." She spun on her heel, the closing door cutting off her sputter.

Now what? He'd slam his fist into the wall in frustration, but the wall was sure to slam back with greater devastation.

13

However, all three of his identities were granted an exercise period
that afternoon. A small on-board gymnasium was cleared for his
exclusive use. He studied the setup sharply for the hour as he tried
out various pieces of equipment, checking distances and trajectories
to guarded exits. He could see a couple of ways Ivan might succeed in
jumping a guard and making a break for it. Not fragile, short-legged
Miles. For a moment, he found himself actually wishing he had Ivan
along.

On the way back to Cell 13 with his escort, Miles passed another
prisoner being checked in at the guard station. He was a shambling,
wild-eyed man, his blond hair damped to brown with sweat. Miles's
shock of recognition was the greater for the changes it had to encom-
pass. *Oser's lieutenant.* The bland-faced killer was transformed.

He wore only grey trousers, his torso was bare. Livid shock-stick
marks dappled his skin. Recent hypospray injection points marched
like little pink paw prints up his arm. He mumbled continuously
through wet lips, shivered and giggled. Just coming back from interrogation, it seemed.

Miles was so startled he reached over to grasp the man's left hand,
to check—yes, there were his own scabbed-over teeth marks across

the knuckles, souvenir of last week's fight at the *Triumph*'s airlock, across the system. The silent lieutenant wasn't silent any more.

Miles's guards motioned him sternly along. Miles almost tripped, staring back over his shoulder till the door of Cell 13 sighed shut, imprisoning him once more.

What are you doing here? That had to be the most-asked, least-answered question in the Hegen Hub, Miles decided. Though he bet the Oseran lieutenant had answered it—Cavilo must command one of the sharpest counter-intelligence departments in the Hub. How fast had the Oseran mercenary traced Miles and Gregor here? How soon had Cavilo's people spotted him and picked him up? The marks on his body were not over a day old. . . .

Most important question of all, had the Oseran come to Vervain Station as part of a general, systematic sweep, or had he followed specific clues—was Tung compromised? Elena arrested? Miles shuddered, and paced frenetically, helplessly. *Have I just killed my friends?*

So, what Oser knew, Cavilo now knew, the whole silly mix of truth, lies, rumors and mistakes. So the identification of Miles as "Admiral Naismith" hadn't necessarily come from Gregor as Miles had first assumed. (The Tau Verde veteran had clearly been scrounged up as an unbiased cross-check.) If Gregor was systematically withholding information from her, Cavilo would now realize it. If he was withholding anything. Maybe he was in love by now. Miles's head throbbed, feeling on the verge of exploding.

The guards came for him in the middle of the night-cycle, and made him dress. Interrogation at last, eh? He thought of the drooling Oseran, and cringed. He insisted on washing up, and adjusted every burr-seam and cuff of his Ranger fatigues with slow deliberation, till the guards began to shift impatiently and tap fingers suggestively on shock sticks. He too would shortly be a drooling fool. On the other hand, what could he possibly say under fast-penta at this point that could make things worse? Cavilo had it all, as far as he could tell. He shrugged off the guards' grasps, and marched out of the brig between them with all the forlorn dignity he could muster.

They led him through the night-dimmed ship and exited a lift-tube at something marked "G-Deck." Miles snapped alert. Gregor was supposed to be around here somewhere. . . . They arrived at an otherwise-blank cabin door marked 10A, where the guards beeped the code-lock for permission to enter. The door slid aside.

Cavilo sat at a comconsole desk, a pool of light in the somber room

making her blond-white hair gleam and glow. They had arrived at
the Commander's personal office, apparently, adjoining her quarters.
Miles strained his eyes and ears for signs of the Emperor. Cavilo was
fully-dressed in her neat fatigues. At least Miles wasn't the only one
going short on sleep these days; he fancied optimistically that she
looked a little tired. She placed a stunner out on her desk, ominously
ready to her right hand, and dismissed the guards. Miles craned his
neck, looking for the hypospray. She stretched, and sat back. The
scent of her perfume, a greener, sharper, less musky scent than she'd
worn as Livia Nu, sublimated from her white skin and tickled Miles's
nose. He swallowed.

"Sit down, Lord Vorkosigan."

He took the indicated chair, and waited. She watched him with
calculating eyes. The insides of his nostrils began to itch abominably.
He kept his hands down, and still. The first question of this interview
would not catch him with his fingers shoved up his nose.

"Your Emperor is in terrible trouble, little Vor lord. To save him,
you must return to the Oseran Mercenaries, and retake them. When
you are back in command, we will communicate further instructions."

Miles boggled. "Danger from what?" he choked. "You?"

"Not at all! Greg is my best friend. The love of my life, at last. I'd do
anything for him. I'd even give up my career." She smirked piously.
Miles's lip curled in repelled response; she grinned. "If any other
course of action occurs to you besides following your instructions to
the letter, well . . . it could land Greg in unimaginable troubles. At
the hands of worse enemies."

Worse than you? Not possible . . . is it? "Why do you want me in
charge of the Dendarii Mercenaries?"

"I can't tell you." Her eyes widened, positively sparkling at her
private, ironic joke. "It's a surprise."

"What would you give me to support this enterprise?"

"Transportation to Aslund Station."

"What else? Troops, guns, ships, money?"

"I'm told you could do it with your wits alone. This I wish to see."

"Oser will kill me. He's already tried once."

"That's a chance I must take."

I really like that "I," lady. "You mean me to be killed," Miles
deduced. "What if I succeed instead?" His eyes were starting to
water; he sniffed. He would have to rub his madly-itching nose soon.

"The key of strategy, little Vor," she explained kindly, "is not to
choose *a* path to victory, but to choose so that *all* paths lead to a

victory. Ideally. Your death has one use; your success, another. I will emphasize that any premature attempt to contact the Barrayaran could be very counterproductive. Very."

A nice aphorism on strategy; he'd have to remember that one. "Let me hear my marching orders from my own supreme commander, then. Let me talk to Gregor."

"Ah. *That* will be your reward for success."

"The last guy who bought that line got shot in the back of his head for his credulity. What say we save steps, and you just shoot me now?" He blinked and sniffed, tears now running down the inside of his nose.

"*I* don't wish to shoot you." She actually batted her eyelashes at him, then straightened, frowning. "Really, Lord Vorkosigan, I hardly expected you to dissolve into tears."

He inhaled; his hands made a helpless pleading gesture. Startled, she tossed him a handkerchief from her breast pocket. A green-scented handkerchief. Without other recourse, he pressed it to his face.

"Stop crying, you cowar—" Her sharp order was interrupted by his first, mighty sneeze, followed by a rapid volley of repeats.

"I'm not crying, you bitch, I'm allergic to your goddamn perfume!" Miles managed to choke out between paroxysms.

She held her hand to her forehead and broke into giggles; real ones, not mannered ploys for a change. The real, spontaneous Cavilo at last; he'd been right, her sense of humor was vile. "Oh, dear," she gasped. "This gives me the most marvelous idea for a gas grenade. A pity I'll never . . . ah, well."

His sinuses throbbed like kettle drums. She shook her head helplessly, and tapped out something on her comconsole.

"I think I had best speed you on your way, before you explode," she told him.

Bent over in his seat wheezing, his water-clouded gaze fell on his brown felt slippers. "Can I at least have a pair of boots for this trip?"

She pursed her lips in a moment of thought. ". . . No," she decided. "It will be more interesting to see you carry on just as you are."

"In this uniform, on Aslund, I'll be like a cat in a dog suit," he protested. "Shot on sight by mistake."

"By mistake . . . on purpose . . . goodness, you're going to have an exciting time." She keyed the door lock open. He was still sneezing and gasping as the guards came in to take him away. Cavilo was still laughing.

*   *   *

The effects of her poisonous perfume took half an hour to wear off, by which time he was locked in a tiny cabin aboard an inner-system ship. They had boarded via a lock on the *Kurin's Hand;* he hadn't even set foot on Vervain Station again. Not a chance of a break for it.

He checked out the cabin. Its bed and lavatory arrangements were highly reminiscent of his last cell. Space duty, hah. The vast vistas of the wide universe, hah. The glory of the Imperial Service—un-hah. He'd lost Gregor. . . . *I may be small, but I screw up big because I'm standing on the shoulders of GIANTS.* He tried pounding on the door and screaming into the intercom. No one came.

It's a surprise.

He could surprise them all by hanging himself, a briefly attractive notion. But there was nothing up high to hook his belt on.

All right. This courier-type ship was swifter than the lumbering freighter in which he and Gregor had taken three days to cross the system last time, but it wasn't instantaneous. He had at least a day and a half to do some serious thinking, he and Admiral Naismith.

It's a surprise. God.

An officer and a guard came for him, very close to the time Miles estimated they would arrive back at Aslund Station's defense perimeter. *But we haven't docked yet. This seems premature.* His nervous exhaustion still responded to a shot of adrenalin; he inhaled, trying to clear his frenzy-fogged brain back to alertness again. Much more of this, though, and no amount of adrenalin would do him any good. The officer led him through the short corridors of the little ship to Nav and Com.

The Ranger captain was present, leaning over the communication console manned by his second officer. The pilot and flight engineer were busy at their stations.

"If they board, they'll arrest him, and he'll be automatically delivered as ordered," the second officer was saying.

"If they arrest him, they could arrest us too. She said to plant him, and she didn't care if it was head or feet first. She didn't order us to get ourselves interned," said the captain.

A voice from the comm; "This is the picket ship *Ariel,* Aslund Navy Contract Auxiliary, calling the *C6-WG* out of Vervain Hubside Station. Cease accelerating, and clear your portside lock for boarding for pre-docking inspection. Aslund Station reserves the right to deny you docking privileges if you fail to cooperate in pre-docking inspection." The voice took on a cheery tone, "I reserve the right to open fire if you don't stand and deliver in one minute. That's enough stalling, boys." The voice, once gone ironic, was suddenly intensely familiar. *Bel?*

"Cease accelerating," the captain ordered, and motioned the second to close the comm channel. "Hey you, Rotha," he called to Miles. "Come over here."

So I'm "Rotha" again. Miles mustered a smarmy smile, and sidled closer. He eyed the viewer, striving to conceal his hungry interest. The *Ariel?* Yes, there it was in the vid display, the sleek Illyrican-built cruiser . . . did Bel Thorne still command her? *How can I get myself onto that ship?*

"Don't throw me out there!" Miles protested urgently. "The Oserans are after my hide. I swear, I didn't know the plasma arcs were defective!"

"What plasma arcs?" asked the captain.

"I'm an arms dealer. I sold them some plasma arcs. Cheap. Turns out they had a tendency to lock on overload and blow their user's hand off. I didn't know, I got them wholesale."

The Ranger captain's right hand opened and closed in sympathetic identification. He rubbed his palm unconsciously on his trousers, back of his plasma arc holster. He studied Miles, frowning sourly. "Headfirst it is," he said after a moment. "Lieutenant, you and the corporal take this little mutant to the portside personnel lock, pack him in a bod-pod, and eject him. We're going home."

"No," said Miles weakly, as they each took an arm. *Yes!* He dragged his feet, careful not to offer enough resistance to risk his bones. "You're not going to space me . . . !" The *Ariel,* my God. . . .

"Oh, the Aslunder merc'll pick you up," said the captain. "Maybe. If they don't decide you're a bomb, and try to set you off in space with plasma fire from their ship or something." Smiling slightly at this vision, he turned back to the comm, and intoned in a bored traffic-control sing-song, "*Ariel,* ah, this is the *C6-WG.* We chose to, ah, change our filed flight plan and return to Vervain Station. We therefore have no need for pre-docking inspection. We are going to leave you a, ah, small parting gift, though. Quite small. What you choose to do with it is your problem. . . ."

The door to Nav and Com closed behind them. A few meters of corridor and a sharp turn brought Miles and his handlers to a personnel hatch. The corporal held Miles, who struggled; the lieutenant opened a locker and shook out a bod-pod.

The bod-pod was a cheap inflatable life-support unit designed to be entered in seconds by endangered passengers, suitable either for pressurization emergencies or abandoning ship. They were also

dubbed idiot-balloons. They required no knowledge to operate because they had no controls, merely a few hours of recyclable air and a
locator-beeper. Passive, foolproof, and not recommended for claus-
trophobes, they were very cost-effective in saving lives—when adequate pick-up ships arrived in time.

Miles emitted a realistic wail as he was stuffed into the bod-pod's
dank, plastic-smelling interior. A jerk of the rip cord, and it sealed
and inflated automatically. He had a brief, horrible flashback to the
mud-sunken bubble-shelter on Kyril Island, and choked back a real
scream. He was tumbled as his captors rolled the pod into the airlock.
A whoosh, a thump, a lurch, and he was free-falling in pitch darkness.

The spherical pod was little more than a meter in diameter. Miles,
half-doubled-up, felt around, his stomach and inner ear protesting
the spin imparted by the ejecting kick outward, till his shaking fingers found what he hoped was a cold-light tube. He squeezed it, and
was rewarded with a nauseous greenish glow.

The silence was profound, broken only by the tiny hiss of the air
recycler and his ragged breathing. *Well . . . it's better than the last
time somebody tried to shove me out an airlock.* He had several
minutes in which to imagine all the possible courses of action the
Ariel might take instead of picking him up. He had just discarded
skin-crawling anticipation of the ship opening fire on him in favor of
abandonment to cold dark asphyxiation, when he and his pod were
wrenched by a tractor beam.

The tractor beam's operator, clearly, had ham hands and palsy, but
after a few minutes of juggling the return of gravity and outside
sound reassured Miles he'd been safely stowed in a working airlock.
The swish of the inner door, garbled human voices. Another moment, and the idiot balloon began to roll. He yelped loudly, and
curled up into a protective ball to roll with the flow till the motion
stopped. He sat up, and took a deep breath, and tried to straighten his
uniform.

Muffled thumps against the bod-pod's fabric. "Somebody in
there?"

"Yeah!" Miles called back.

"Just a minute. . . ."

Squeaks, clinks, and a rending grind, as the seals were broken. The
bod-pod began to collapse as the air sighed out. Miles fought his way
clear of its folds, and stood, shakily, with all the gracelessness and
indignity of a newly-hatched chick.

He was in a small cargo bay. Three grey-and-white uniformed
soldiers stood in a circle around him, aiming stunners and nerve-

disruptors at his head. A slim officer with captain's insignia leaned with one foot on a canister, watching Miles emerge.

The officer's neat uniform and soft brown hair gave no clue whether one was looking at a delicate man or an unusually determined woman. This ambiguity was deliberately cultivated; Bel Thorne was a Betan hermaphrodite, minority descendant of a century-past social/genetic experiment that had not caught on. Thorne's expression melted from scepticism to astonishment as Miles rose into view.

Miles grinned back. "Hello, Pandora. The gods send you a gift. But there's a catch."

"Isn't there always?" Face lighting with delight, Thorne strode forward to grasp Miles's waist with bubbling enthusiasm. "Miles!" Thorne held Miles away again, and gazed avidly down into his face. "What are you doing here?"

"Somehow, I figured that might be your first question," Miles sighed.

"—and what are you doing in the Ranger-suit?"

"*Goodness,* I'm glad you're not of the shoot-first-and-ask-questions-later school." Miles kicked his slippered feet clear of the deflated bod-pod. The soldiers, somewhat uncertainly, held their aim. "Ah—" Miles gestured toward them.

"Stand down, men," Thorne ordered. "It's all right."

"I wish that were true," Miles said. "Bel, we've got to talk."

Thorne's cabin aboard the *Ariel* was the same wrenching mix of familiarity and change Miles had encountered in all the mercenary matters. The shapes, the sounds, the smells of the *Ariel's* interior triggered cascades of memory. The captain's cabin was now overlaid with Bel's personal possessions; vid library, weapons, campaign souvenirs including a half-melted space-armor helmet that had been slagged saving Thorne's life, now made into a lamp; a small cage housing an exotic pet from Earth Thorne called a *hamster.*

Between sips of a cup of Thorne's private stock of non-synthetic tea, Miles gave Thorne the Admiral-Naismith version of reality, closely related to the one he'd given Oser and Tung; the Hub evaluation assignment, the mystery employer, etc. Gregor, of course, was edited out, together with any mention of Barrayar; Miles Naismith spoke with a pure Betan accent. Otherwise Miles stuck as close as he could to the facts of his sojourn with Randall's Rangers.

"So Lieutenant Lake's been captured by our competitors," Thorne mused upon Miles's description of the blond lieutenant he'd passed in the *Kurin's Hand's* brig. "Couldn't happen to a nicer fellow, but— we'd better change our codes again."

"Quite." Miles set down his cup, and leaned forward. "I was autho- rized by my employer not only to observe but to prevent war in the Hegen Hub, if possible." Well, sort of. "I'm afraid it may no longer be possible. What does it look like from your end?"

Thorne frowned. "We were last in-dock five days ago. That's when the Aslunders concocted this pre-docking inspection routine. All the smaller ships were pressed into round-the-clock service on it. With their military station nearing completion, our employers are getting jumpier about sabotage—bombs, biologicals . . ."

"I won't argue with that. What about, ah, Fleet internal matters?"

"You mean rumors of your death, life, and/or resurrection? They're all over, fourteen garbled versions. I'd have discounted 'em —you've been sighted before, y'know—but then suddenly Oser ar- rested Tung."

"What?" Miles bit his lip. "Only Tung? Not Elena, Mayhew, Chodak?"

"Only Tung."

"That makes no sense. If he'd arrested Tung, he'd have fast-penta'd him, and he'd have to have spilled on Elena. Unless she's been left free as bait."

"Things got real tense, when Tung was taken. Ready to explode. I think if Oser'd moved on Elena and Baz it would have sparked the war right then. Yet he hasn't backed down and reinstated Tung. Very unstable. Oser's taking care to keep the old inner circle separated, that's why I've been out here for nearly a bloody week. But last time I saw Baz he was damn near edgy enough to commit to fight. And that was the last thing he'd wanted to do."

Miles exhaled slowly. "A fight . . . is exactly what Commander Cavilo wants. It's why she shipped me back gift-wrapped in that . . . undignified package. The Bod-pod of Discord. She doesn't care if I win or lose, as long as her enemy's forces are thrown into chaos just as she springs her *surprise.*"

"Have you figured out what her surprise is, yet?"

"No. The Rangers were setting up for some sort of ground-attack, at one point. Sending me here suggests they're aiming for Aslund, against all strategic logic. Or something else? The woman's mind is incredibly twisted. Gah!" He slapped his fist gently into his palm in nervous rhythm. "I've got to talk to Oser. And he's got to listen this time. I've thought it over. Cooperation between us may be the one and only course of action Cavilo doesn't expect, doesn't have a half-

sawn-through branch of her strategy-tree ready and waiting for me.
. . . Are you willing to put it all on the line for me, Bel?"

Thorne pursed lips judiciously. "From here, yeah. The *Ariel's* the
fleet's fastest ship. I can outrun retribution if I have to." Thorne
grinned.

Should we run to Barrayar? No—Cavilo still held Gregor. Better
appear to be following instructions. For a time yet.

Miles took a long breath, and settled himself firmly in the station
chair in the *Ariel's* Nav and Com room. He'd cleaned up, and borrowed a mercenary's grey-and-white uniform from the smallest
woman on the ship. The rolled-up pant cuffs were stuffed neatly out
of sight down boots that almost fit. A belt covered the fastener gaping
open at the too-narrow waistband. The loose jacket looked all right,
sitting down. Permanent alterations later. He nodded to Thorne. "All
right. Open your channel."

A buzz, a glitter, and Admiral Oser's hawk face materialized over
the vid plate. "Yes, what is it—you!" His teeth shut with a beak's snap;
his hand, a vague unfocused blur to the side, tapped on intercom keys
and vid controls.

He can't throw me out the airlock this time, but he can cut me off.
Time to talk fast.

Miles leaned forward and smiled. "Hello, Admiral Oser. I've completed my evaluation of Vervani forces in the Hegen Hub. And my
conclusion is, you are in deep trouble."

"How did you get on this secured channel?" snarled Oser. "Tight-
beam, double-encode—comm officer, trace this!"

"How, you will be able to determine in a few minutes. You'll have
to keep me on-line till you do," said Miles. "But your enemy is at
Vervain Station, not here. Not Pol, not Jackson's Whole. And most
certainly not me. Note I said Vervain Station, not Vervain. You know
Cavilo? Your opposite number, across-system?"

"I've encountered her once or twice." Oser's face was guarded
now, waiting for his scrambling tech team to report.

"Face like an angel, mind like a rabid mongoose?"

Oser's lips twitched very slightly. "You've met her."

"Oh, yes. She and I had several heart-to-heart talks. They were
. . . educational. Information is the most valuable trade-good in the
Hub right now. At any rate, mine is. I want to deal."

Oser held up his hand for a pause, and keyed off-line briefly. When
his face retuned, its expression was black. "Captain Thorne, this is
mutiny!"

Thorne leaned into the range of the vid pick-up, and said brightly, "No, sir, it's not. We are trying to save your ungrateful neck, if you will permit it. Listen to the man. He has lines we don't."

"He has lines, all right," and under his breath, "Damn Betans, sticking together. . . ."

"Whether you fight me, or I fight you, Admiral Oser, we both lose," said Miles rapidly.

"You can't win," said Oser. "You cannot take my fleet. Not with the *Ariel*."

"The *Ariel*'s just a starter-set, if it comes to that. But no, I probably can't win. What I can do is make an unholy mess. Divide your forces —screw you with your employer—every weapon-charge you expend, every piece of equipment that's damaged, every soldier hurt or killed is *pure loss* in an in-fight like this. Nobody wins but Cavilo, who expends nothing. Which is precisely what she sent me back here for. How much profit do you foresee in doing precisely what your enemy wishes you to, eh?"

Miles waited, breathless. Oser's jaw worked, chewing over this impassioned argument. "What's your profit?" he asked at last.

"Ah. I'm afraid I'm the dangerous variable in that calculation, Admiral. I'm not in it for profit." Miles grinned. "So I don't care what I wreck."

"Any information you had from Cavilo is worth shit," said Oser.

He begins to barter—he's hooked, he's hooked. . . . Miles tamped down exultation, cultivated a serious expression. "Anything Cavilo says must certainly be sifted with great care. But, ah . . . beauty is as beauty does. And I've found her vulnerable side."

"Cavilo has no vulnerable side."

"Yes, she does. Her passion for utility. Her self-interest."

"I fail to see how that makes her vulnerable."

"Precisely why you need to add *me* to your Staff at once. You need my vision."

"Hire you!" Oser recoiled in astonishment.

Well, he'd achieved surprise, anyway. A military objective of sorts. "I understand the post of Chief-of-Staff/Tactical is now empty."

Oser's expression flowed from astonished to stunned to a kind of amused fury. "You're insane."

"No, just in a tearing hurry. Admiral, there's nothing irrevocable gone wrong between us. Yet. You attacked me—not the other way around—and now you expect me to attack you back. But I'm not on holiday, and I don't have time to waste on personal amusements like revenge."

Oser's eyes narrowed. "What about Tung?"

Miles shrugged. "Keep him locked up, for now, if you insist. Unharmed, of course." *Just don't tell him I said so.*

"Suppose I hang him."

"Ah . . . *that* would be irrevocable." Miles paused. "I will point out, jailing Tung is like cutting off your right hand before heading into battle."

"What battle? With whom?"

"It's a surprise. Cavilo's surprise. Though I've developed an idea or two on the problem, that I'd be willing to share."

"Would you?" Oser had that same man-sucking-a-lemon expression Miles had now and then surprised on Illyan's face. It seemed almost homey.

Miles continued, "As an alternative to my becoming your employee, I'm willing to become your employer. I'm authorized to offer a bona fide contract, all the usual perqs, equipment replacement, insurance, from my . . . sponsor." *Illyan, hear my plea.* "Not in conflict with Aslund's interests. You can collect twice for the same fight, and you don't even have to switch sides. A mercenary's dream."

"What guarantees can you offer up front?"

"It seems to me that I'm the one who's owed a guarantee, sir. Let us begin with small steps. I won't start a mutiny; you stop trying to thrust me out airlocks. I will join you openly—everyone to know I've arrived—I will make my information available to you." How thin his "information" seemed, in the breeze of these airy promises. No numbers, no troop movements; all *intentions,* shifting mental topographies of loyalty, ambition, and betrayal. "We will confer. You may even have an angle I lack. Then we go on from there."

Oser thinned his lips, bemused, half-persuaded, deeply suspicious.

"The risk, I would point out," said Miles, "the personal risk, is more mine than yours."

"I think—"

Miles hung suspended on the mercenary's words.

"I think I'm going to regret this," Oser sighed.

The detailed negotiations just to bring the *Ariel* into dock took another half day. As the initial excitement wore off, Thorne became more thoughtful. As the *Ariel* actually maneuvered into its clamps, Thorne grew positively meditative.

"I'm still not exactly sure what's supposed to keep Oser from bringing us in, stunning us, and hanging us at leisure," Thorne said, buckling on a sidearm. Thorne kept the complaint to an undertone, in care for the tender ears of the escort squad kitting up nearby in the *Ariel's* shuttle hatch corridor.

"Curiosity," said Miles firmly.

"All right, stun, fast-penta, and hang, then."

"If he fast-penta's me, I'll tell him exactly the facts I was going to tell him anyway." *And a few more besides, alas.* "And he'll have fewer doubts. So much the better."

Miles was rescued from further hollow flummery by the clank and hiss of the flex-tubes sealing. Thorne's sergeant undogged the hatch without hesitation, though he was also careful not to stand silhouetted in the aperture, Miles noted.

"Squad, form up!" the sergeant ordered. His six people checked their stunners. Thorne and the sergeant in addition bore nerve disruptors, a nicely-calculated mix of weapons; stunners to allow for human error, the nerve disruptors to encourage the other side not to risk mistakes. Miles went unarmed. With a mental salute to Cavilo—well, a rude gesture, actually—he'd put his felt slippers back on. Thorne at his side, he took the lead of the little procession and marched through the flex tube into one of the Aslunder military station's almost-finished docking bays.

True to his word, Oser had a party of witnesses lined up and waiting. The squad of twenty or so bore a mix of weapons almost identical to the *Ariel's* group. "We're outnumbered," muttered Thorne.

"It's all in the mind," Miles muttered in return. "March like you had an empire at your back." *And don't look over your shoulder, they may be gaining on us. They'd better be gaining on us.* "The more people who see me, the better."

Oser himself stood waiting in parade rest, looking highly dyspeptic. Elena—*Elena!*— stood at his side, unarmed, face frozen. Her tight-lipped stare at Miles was tense with suspicion, not of his motives, perhaps, but certainly of his methods, *Now what foolishness?* her eyes asked. Miles gave her the briefest of ironic nods before saluting Oser.

Reluctantly, Oser returned the military courtesy. "Now—'Admiral'—let us return to the *Triumph* and get down to business," he grated.

"Indeed, yes. But let's have a little tour of this Station on the way, eh? The non-top-secured areas, of course. My last view was so . . . rudely cut short, after all. After you, Admiral?"

Oser gritted his teeth. "Oh, after you, Admiral."

It became a parade. Miles led them around for a good forty-five minutes, including a march through the cafeteria during the dinner rush with several noisy stops to greet by name the few old Dendarii he recognized, and favor the others with blinding smiles. He left babble in his wake, those in the dark demanding explanation from those in the know.

An Aslunder work crew was busy tearing out fiberboard paneling, and he paused to compliment them on their labors. Elena seized an opportunity of Oser's distraction to bend down and breathe fiercely in Miles's ear, *"Where's Gregor?"*

"Thereby hangs—me, if I fail to get him back," Miles whispered. "Too complicated, tell you later."

"Oh, God." She rolled her eyes.

When he had, judging from the admiral's darkening complexion, just about reached the limits of Oser's strained tolerance, Miles suffered himself to be led *Triumph*-ward again. There. Obedient to Cavilo's orders, Miles had made no attempt to contact Barrayar. But if Ungari couldn't find him after this, it was time to fire the man. A prairie bird thrumming out a mad mating dance could scarcely have put on a more conspicuous display.

Finishing touches on construction were still in progress around the *Triumph*'s docking bay as Miles marched his parade across it. A few Aslunder workers in tan, light blue, and green leaned over to goggle down from catwalks. Military techs in their dark blue uniforms paused in mid-installation to stare, then had to re-sort connections and realign bolts. Miles refrained from smiling and waving, lest Oser's set jaw crack. No more baiting, time to get serious. The thirty or so mercenaries could change from honor guard to prison guard with his next roll of the dice.

Thorne's tall sergeant, marching beside Miles, gazed around the bay, noting new construction. "The robotic loaders should be fully automated by this time tomorrow," he noted. "That'll be an improvement—*crap!*" His hand descended abruptly on Miles's head, shoving him downward. The sergeant half-spun, clawed hand arcing toward his holster, when the crackling blue bolt of a nerve disruptor charge struck him square in the chest at the level Miles's head had been. He spasmed, his breath stopping. The smell of ozone, hot plastic, and blistered meat slapped Miles's nose. Miles kept on diving, hitting the deck, rolling. A second bolt splattered on the deck, its outwashing field stinging like twenty wasps up Miles's outstretched arm. He jerked his hand back.

As the sergeant's corpse collapsed, Miles grabbed at the man's jacket and jerked himself underneath, burrowing his head and spine under where the meat was thickest, the sergeant's torso. He drew his arms and legs in as tight as he could. Another bolt crackled into the deck nearby, then two struck the body in close succession. Even with the absorbing mass between it was worse than the blow of a shock-stick on high power.

Miles's ringing ears heard screaming, thumping, yelling, running, chaos. The chirping buzz of stunner fire. A voice. "He's up there! Go get him!", and another voice, high and hoarse. "You spotted him— he's yours. *You* go get him!" Another bolt hit the decking.

The weight of the big man, the stench of his fatal injury, pressed into Miles's face. He wished the fellow'd massed another fifty kilos. No wonder Cavilo had been willing to front twenty thousand Betan dollars toward a line on a shield-suit. Of all the loathsome weapons Miles had ever faced, this had to be the most personally terrifying. A head injury that didn't quite kill him, but stole his humanity and left him animal or vegetable was the worst nightmare. His intellect was surely his sole justification for existence. Without it . . .

The crackle of a nerve disruptor *not* aimed his way penetrated his hearing. Miles turned his head to scream, cloth- and meat-muffled, "Stunners! Stunners! We want him alive for questioning!" *He's yours, you go get him.* . . . He should shove out from under this body and join the fight. But if he was the assassin's special target, and why else pump charges into a corpse . . . perhaps he ought to stay right here. He squirmed, trying to draw his hands and legs in tighter.

The shouting died down; the firing stopped. Someone kneeling beside him tried to roll the sergeant's body off Miles. It took Miles a moment to realize he had to unclutch the dead man's uniform jacket before he could be rescued. He straightened his fingers with difficulty.

Thorne's face wavered over him, white and breathing open-mouthed, urgent. "Are you all right, Admiral?"

"I think," Miles panted.

"He was aiming at you," Thorne reported. "Only."

"I noticed," Miles stuttered. "I'm only lightly fried." Thorne helped him sit up. He was shaking as badly as after the shock-stick beating. He regarded his spasming hands, lowered one to touch the corpse beside him in morbid wonder. *Every day of the rest of my life will be your gift. And I don't even know your name.* "Your sergeant— what was his name?"

"Collins."

"Collins. Thanks."

"Good man."

"I saw."

Oser came up, looking strained. "Admiral Naismith, this was *not* my doing."

"Oh?" Miles blinked. "Help me up, Bel. . . ." That might have been a mistake, Thorne then had to help him keep standing as his muscles twitched. He felt weak, washed-out as a sick man. *Elena— where? She had no weapon. . . .*

There she was, with another female mercenary. They were dragging a man in the dark blue uniform of an Aslunder ranker toward Miles and Oser. Each woman held a booted foot; the man's arms trailed nervelessly across the deck. Stunned? Dead? They dropped the feet with a thump beside Miles, with the matter-of-fact air of lionesses delivering prey to their cubs. Miles stared down at a very familiar face indeed. *General Metzov. What are you doing here?*

"Do you recognize this man?" Oser asked an Aslunder officer who had hurried up to join them. "Is he one of yours?"

"I don't know him—" The Aslunder knelt to check for IDs. "He had a valid pass. . . ."

"He could have had me, and gotten away," said Elena to Miles, "but he kept firing at you. You were bright to stay put."

A triumph of wit, or a failure of nerve? "Yes. Quite." Miles made another attempt to stand on his own, gave up, and leaned on Thorne. "I hope you didn't kill him."

"Just stunned," said Elena, holding up the weapon as evidence. Some intelligent person must have tossed it to her when the melee began. "He probably has a broken wrist."

"Who *is* he?" asked Oser. Quite sincerely, Miles judged.

"Why, Admiral," Miles bared his teeth, "I told you I was going to deliver you more intelligence data than your Section could collect in a month. May I present," rather like an entree at that—he made a gesture designed to evoke a waiter lifting a domed cover from a silver platter, but which probably looked like another muscle spasm, "General Stanis Metzov. Second-in-command, Randall's Rangers."

"Since when do senior staff officers undertake field assassinations?"

"Excuse me, second-in-command as of three days ago. That may have changed. He was up to his stringy neck in Cavilo's schemes. You, I, and he have an appointment with a hypospray."

Oser stared. "You planned this?"

"Why do you think I spent the last hour flitting around the Station, if not to smoke him out?" Miles said brightly. *He must have been stalking me this whole time. I think I'm going to throw up. Have I just claimed to be brilliant, or incredibly stupid?* Oser looked like he was trying in figure out the answer to that same question.

Miles stared down at Metzov's unconscious form, trying to think. Had Metzov been sent by Cavilo, or was this murder attempt entirely on his own time? If sent by Cavilo—had she planned him to fall alive into her enemies' hands? If not, was there a backup assassin around here somewhere, and if so was his target Metzov, if Metzov succeeded, or Miles, if Metzov failed? Or both? *I need to sit down and draw a flow-chart.*

Medical squads had arrived. "Yes, sickbay," said Miles faintly. "Till my old friend here wakes up."

"I'll agree to that," said Oser, shaking his head in something akin to dismay.

"Better put a protective as well as holding guard on our prisoner. I'm not sure if he was meant to survive capture."

"Right," Oser agreed bemusedly.

Thorne supporting one arm and Elena the other, Miles staggered home into the *Triumph's* hatchway.

14

Miles sat trembling on a bench in a glassed-in cubicle normally used for bio-isolation in the *Triumph*'s sickbay, and watched Elena tie General Metzov to a chair with a tangle-cord. It would have given Miles a smug sense of turn-about, if the interrogation upon which they were about to embark was not so fraught with dangerous complications. Elena was disarmed again. Two stunner-armed men stood guard beyond the soundproof transparent door, glancing in occasionally. It had taken all Miles's eloquence to keep the audience for this initial questioning limited to himself, Oser, and Elena.

"How hot can this man's information be?" Oser had inquired irritably. "They let him go out in the field."

"Hot enough that I think you should have a chance to think about it before broadcasting it to a committee," Miles had argued. "You'll still have the recording."

Metzov looked sick and silent, tight-mouthed and unresponsive. His right wrist was neatly bandaged. Awakening from stun accounted for the sick; the silence was futile, and everyone knew it. It was a kind of strange courtesy, not to badger him with questions before the fast-penta cut in.

Now Oser frowned at Miles. "Are you up to this yet?"

Miles glanced down at his still-shaking hands. "As long as no one asks me to do brain surgery, yes. Proceed. I have reason to suspect that time is of the essence."

Oser nodded to Elena, who held up a hypospray to calibrate the dose, and pressed it to Metzov's neck. Metzov's eyes shut briefly in despair. After a moment his clenched hands relaxed. The muscles of his face unlocked to sag into a loose, idiotic smile. The transformation was most unpleasant to watch. Without the tension his face looked aged.

Elena checked Metzov's pulse and pupils. "All right. He's all yours, gentlemen." She stepped back to lean against the doorframe with folded arms, her expression almost as closed as Metzov's had been.

Miles opened his hand. "After you, Admiral."

Oser's mouth twisted. "Thank you. Admiral." He walked over to stare speculatively into Metzov's face. "General Metzov. Is your name Stanis Metzov?"

Metzov grinned. "Yeah, that's me."

"Presently second-in-command, Randall's Rangers?"

"Yeah."

"Who sent you to assassinate Admiral Naismith?"

Metzov's face took on an expression of sunny bewilderment. "Who?"

"Call me Miles," Miles suggested. "He knows me under a . . . pseudonym." His chance of getting through this interview with his identity undisclosed equalled that of a snowball surviving a worm-hole jump to the center of a sun, but why rush the complications?

"Who sent you to kill Miles?"

"Cavie did. Of course. He escaped, you see. I was the only one she could trust . . . trust . . . the bitch. . . ."

Miles's brow twitched. "In fact, Cavilo shipped me back here herself," he informed Oser. "General Metzov was therefore set up. But to what end? My turn, now, I think."

Oser made the after-you gesture and stepped back. Miles tottered off his bench and into Metzov's line-of-sight. Metzov breathed rage even through the fast-penta euphoria, then grinned vilely.

Miles decided to start with the question that had driven him most nuts the longest. "Who—what target—was your ground-attack planned to be upon?"

"Vervain," said Metzov.

Even Oser's jaw dropped. The blood thudded in Miles's ears in the stunned silence.

"Vervain is your *employer*," Oser choked.

"God—God!—finally it adds up!" Miles almost capered; it came out a stagger, which Elena lurched away from the wall to catch. "Yes, yes, yes. . . ."

"It's *insane,*" said Oser. "So that's Cavilo's surprise."

"That's not the end of it, I'll bet. Cavilo's drop forces are bigger than ours by far, but no way are they big enough to take on a fully-settled planet like Vervain on the ground. They can only raid and run."

"Raid and run, right," smiled Metzov equably.

"What was your particular target, then?" asked Miles urgently.

"Banks . . . art museums . . . gene banks . . . hostages. . . ."

"That's a *pirate* raid," said Oser. "What the hell were you going to do with the loot?"

"Drop it off on Jackson's Whole, on the way out; they fence it."

"How did you figure to escape the irate Vervani Navy, then?" asked Miles.

"Hit them just before the new fleet comes on-line. Cetagandan invasion fleet'll catch 'em in orbital dock. Sitting targets. Easy."

The silence this time was utter.

"*That's* Cavilo's surprise," Miles whispered at last. "Yeah. That one's *worthy* of her."

"Cetagandan . . . invasion?" Oser unconsciously began to chew a fingernail.

"God, it fits, it fits." Miles began to pace the cubicle with uneven steps. "What's the only way to take a wormhole jump? From both sides at once. The Vervani aren't Cavilo's employers—the *Cetagandans* are." He turned to point at the slack-lipped, nodding general. "And now I see Metzov's place, clear as day."

"Pirate," shrugged Oser.

"No—goat."

"What?"

"This man—you apparently don't know—was cashiered from the Barrayaran Imperial Service for brutality."

Oser blinked. "From the Barrayaran Service? That must have taken some doing."

Miles bit down a twinge of irritation. "Well, yes. He, ah . . . took on the wrong victim. But anyway, don't you see it? The Cetagandan invasion fleet jumps through into Vervani local space on Cavilo's invitation—probably on Cavilo's signal. The Rangers raid, do a fast trash of Vervain. The Cetagandans, out of the kindness of their hearts, 'rescue' the planet from the treacherous mercenaries. The Rangers run. Metzov is left behind as goat—just like throwing the guy out of the troika to the wolves," oops, that wasn't a very Betan metaphor, "to be publicly hung by the Cetagandans to demonstrate their 'good faith.' See, this evil Barrayaran harmed you, you need our Imperial protection from the Barrayaran Imperial threat, and here we are.

"And Cavilo gets paid *three* times. Once by the Vervani, once by the Cetagandans, and the third time by Jackson's Whole when she fences her loot on the way out. Everybody profits. Except the Vervani, of course." He paused to catch his breath.

Oser was beginning to look convinced, and worried. "Do you think the Cetagandans plan to punch through into the Hub? Or will they stop at Vervain?"

"Of course they'll punch through. The Hub is the strategic target; Vervain is just a stepping stone to it. Hence the 'bad mercenary' setup. The Cetagandans want to expend as little energy as possible pacifying Vervani. They'll probably label them an 'allied satrapy,' hold the space routes, and barely touch down on the planet. Absorb them economically over a generation. The question is, will the Cetagandans stop at Pol? Will they try to take it on this one move, or leave it as a buffer between them and Barrayar? Conquest or wooing? If they can bait the Barrayarans into attacking through Pol without permission, it might even drive the Polians into a Cetagandan alliance—agh!" He paced again.

Oser looked like he'd bitten into something nasty. With half a worm in it. "I wasn't hired to take on the Cetagandan Empire. I expected to be fighting the Vervani's mercenaries, at most, if the whole thing didn't just fizzle out. If the Cetagandans arrive here, in force in the Hub, we'll be . . . trapped. Penned up with a cul-de-sac at our backs." And in a trailing mutter, "Maybe we ought to think about getting out while the getting's good. . . ."

"But Admiral Oser, don't you realize," Miles pointed to Metzov, *"she'd* never have let him out of her sight with all this in his head if it was still an active plan. She may have meant him to die trying to kill me, but there was always the chance he might not—that just this sort of interrogation might result. All this is the *old* plan. There must be a *new* plan." *And I think I know what it is.* "There is . . . another factor. A new X in the equation." *Gregor.* "Unless I miss my guess, the Cetagandan invasion is now a considerable embarrassment to Cavilo."

"Admiral Naismith, I would believe that Cavilo would double-cross anyone you care to name—except the Cetagandans. They'd spend a generation, pursuing their revenge. She couldn't run far enough. She wouldn't live to spend her profits. Incidentally, what conceivable profit outweighs triple pay?"

But if she expects to have the Barrayaran Empire to defend her from retribution—all our Security resources. . . . "I see one way she could expect to get away with it," said Miles. "If it works out like she wants, she'll have all the protection she wants. And all the profits."

It could work, it really could. If Gregor were indeed under her spell. And if two embarrassingly hostile character witnesses, Miles and General Metzov, conveniently killed each other. Abandoning her fleet, she could take Gregor and flee before the oncoming Cetagandans, presenting herself to Barrayar as Gregor's "rescuer" at great personal cost; if in addition a smitten Gregor urged her as his fiancee, worthy mother to a future scion of the military caste—the romantic appeal of the drama could swing popular support enough to overwhelm cooler advisors' judgments. God knew Miles's own mother had laid the groundwork for that scenario. *She could really bring this off. Empress Cavilo of Barrayar. It even scans.* And she could cap her career by betraying absolutely *everybody,* even her own forces. . . .

"Miles, the look on your face . . ." said Elena in worry.

"When?" said Oser. "When will the Cetagandans attack?" He got Metzov's wandering attention, and repeated the question.

"Only Cavie knows." Metzov snickered. "Cavie knows everything."

"It has to be imminent," Miles argued. "It may even be starting now. Guessing from Cavilo's timing of my return here. She meant the De—the Fleet to be paralyzed with our infighting right now."

"If that's true," murmured Oser, "what to do . . . ?"

"We're too far away. A day and a half from the action. Which will be at the Vervain Station wormhole. And beyond, in Vervani local space. We have to get closer. We have to move the Fleet across-system—pin Cavilo up against the Cetagandans. Blockade her—"

"Whoa! I'm not mounting a headlong attack against the Cetagandan Empire!" interrupted Oser sharply.

"You must. You'll have to fight them sooner or later. You pick the time, or they will. The only chance of stopping them is at the wormhole. Once they're through, it will be impossible."

"If I moved my fleet away from Aslund, the Vervani would think we were attacking them."

"And mobilize, go on the alert. Good. But in the wrong direction—not good. We would end up being a feint for Cavilo. Damn! No doubt another branch of her strategy-tree."

"Suppose—if the Cetagandans are now such an embarrassment to Cavilo as you claim—she doesn't send her code?"

"Oh, she still needs them. But for a different purpose. She needs them to flee from. And to mass-murder her witnesses for her. But she doesn't need them to succeed. In fact, she now needs their invasion to bog down. If she's really thinking as long-term as she should be, in her new plan."

Oser shook his head, as if to clear it. "Why?"

"Our only hope—Aslund's only hope—is to capture Cavilo, and fight the Cetagandans to a standstill at the Vervain Station wormhole. No, wait—we have to hold both sides of the Hub-Vervain jump. Until reinforcements arrive."

"What reinforcements?"

"Aslund, Pol—once the Cetagandans actually materialize in force, they'll see their threat. And if Pol comes in on Barrayar's side instead of Cetaganda's, Barrayar can pour forces through via them. The Cetagandans can be stopped, if everything occurs in the right order." But could Gregor be rescued alive? Not a path to victory, but all paths. . . .

"Would the Barrayarans come in?"

"Oh, I think so. Your counter-intelligence must keep track of these things—haven't they noticed a sudden increase in Barrayaran Intelligence activity here in the Hub the last few days?"

"Now that you mention it, yes. Their coded traffic has quadrupled."

Thank God. Maybe relief was closer than he'd dared hope. "Have you broken any of their codes?" Miles asked brightly, while he was at it.

"Only the least sensitive one, so far."

"Ah. Good. That is, too bad."

Oser stood with his arms folded, gnawing at his lip, intensely inward for a full minute. It reminded Miles uncomfortably of the meditative expression the admiral'd had just before ordering him shoved out the nearest airlock, barely more than a week back. "No," Oser said at last. "Thanks for the information. In return, I suppose I will spare your life. But we're pulling out. It's not a fight we can possibly win. Only some propaganda-blinded planetary force, with a planet's resources behind it, can afford that sort of insane self-sacrifice. I designed my fleet to be a fine tactical tool, not a, a damn doorstop made of dead bodies. I'm not a—as you say—goat."

"Not a goat, a spearhead."

"Your 'spearhead' has no spear behind it. No."

"Is that your last word, sir?" asked Miles in a thin voice.

"Yes." Oser reached to key his wristcom, to call in the waiting guards. "Corporal, this party's going to the brig. Call down and notify them."

The guard saluted through the glass as Oser keyed off.

"But sir," Elena approached him, her arms raised in pleading. With a snake-strike sideways flick of her wrist, she jabbed the hypospray against the side of Oser's neck. His eyes widened, his pulse beat once, twice, three times, as his lips drew back in rage. He tensed to strike her. His blow sagged in mid-arc.

The guards beyond the glass snapped alert at Oser's sudden movement, drawing their stunners. Elena caught Oser's hand and kissed it, smiling gratefully. The guards relaxed; one nudged the other and said something pretty nasty, judging from their grins, but Miles's wits were too momentarily scattered to try and read lips.

Oser swayed and panted, fighting the drug. Elena sidled up the captured arm and slipped a hand cozily around his waist, half-turning him so they stood with their backs to the door. The sterotypical stupid fast-penta smile slipped across and receded from Oser's face, then fixed itself at last.

"He acted like I was unarmed." Elena shook her head in exasperation, and slipped the hypospray into her jacket pocket.

"Now what?" Miles hissed frantically as the guard-corporal bent over the door's code-lock.

"We all go to the brig, I guess. Tung's there," said Elena.

"Ah . . ." Oh-hell-we'll-never-bring-this-off. Had to try. Miles smiled cheerily at the entering guards, and helped them release Metzov, largely getting in their way and keeping their attention off the peculiarly happy-looking Oser. At a moment when their eyes were elsewhere, he tripped Metzov, who staggered.

"You'd better each take one of his arms, he's not too steady," Miles told the guards. He was none too steady himself, but he managed to block the doorway so the guards and Metzov led the way, himself second, and Elena, arm-in-arm with Oser, followed last. "Come, love, come," he heard Elena intone behind him, like a woman coaxing a cat to her lap.

It was the longest short walk he'd ever taken. He dropped back to growl out of the corner of his mouth to Elena. "All right, we get to the brig, it will be stocked with Oser's finest. What then?"

She bit her lip. "Don't know."

"That's what I was afraid of. Turn right here." They swung around the next corner.

A guard looked back over his shoulder. "Sir?"

"Carry on, boys," Miles called. "When you've got that spy locked up, report back to us at the Admiral's cabin."

"Very good, sir."

"Keep walking," breathed Miles. "Keep smiling. . . ."

The guards' footsteps faded. "Where now?" asked Elena. Oser stumbled. "This is untenable."

"Admiral's cabin, why not?" Miles decided. His grin was fixed and fey. Elena's inspired mutinous gesture had given him the best break of the day. He had the momentum now. He wouldn't stop till he was brought down bodily. His head spun with the unutterable relief of at last getting the shifting, writhing, chittering *might-be-might-be-might-be* nailed to a fixed *is*. *This time is now. The word is go.*

Maybe. If.

They passed a few Oseran techs. Oser was sort of nodding, Miles hoped it would pass as casual acknowledgment of their salutes. Nobody turned and cried Hey!, anyway. Two levels and another turn brought them to the well-remembered corridors of officer's country. They passed the Captain's cabin (God, he'd have to deal with Auson, and soon); Oser's palm, pressed by Elena against the lock, admitted them to the quarters Oser had made his flag office. When the door slipped shut behind them Miles realized he'd been holding his breath.

"We're in it now," said Elena, sagging for a moment with her back to the door. "You going to run out on us again?"

"Not this time," Miles replied grimly. "You may have noticed one item I didn't bring up for discussion, down in sickbay."

"Gregor."

"Just so. Cavilo holds him hostage aboard her flagship right now."

Elena's neck bent in dismay. "She means to sell him to the Cetagandans for a bonus, then?"

"No. Weirder than that. She means to marry him."

Elena's lip curled in astonishment. "What? Miles, there's no way she could have got such an impossible notion in her head, unless—"

"Unless Gregor planted it. Which, I believe, he did. Watered and fertilized it, too. What I don't know is whether he was serious, or playing for time. She was very careful to keep us separated. You knew Gregor almost as well as I do. What do you think?"

"It's hard to imagine Gregor love-struck to idiocy. He was always . . . rather quiet. Almost, well, undersexed. Compared to, say, Ivan."

"I'm not sure that's a fair comparison."

"No, you're right. Well, compared to you, then."

Miles wondered just how to take that. "Gregor never had much in the way of opportunities, when we were younger. I mean, no privacy. Security always in his back pocket. That . . . that can inhibit a man, unless he's a bit of an exhibitionist."

Her hand turned, as if measuring out Gregor's smooth gripless surface. "He was not that."

"Certainly Cavilo must be taking care to present only her most attractive side."

Elena licked her lips in thought. "Is she pretty?"

"Yeah, if you happen to like blonde power-mad homicidal maniacs, I suppose she could be quite overwhelming." His hand closed, the texture of Cavilo's pelted hair remembered like an itch on his palm. He rubbed it on his trouser seam.

Elena brightened slightly. "Ah. You don't like her."

Miles gazed up at Elena's Valkyrie face. "She's too short for my taste."

Elena grinned. "That, I believe." She guided the shambling Oser to a chair and sat him down. "We're going to have to tie him up soon. Or something."

The comm buzzed. Miles went to Oser's desk console to answer it. "Yes?" he said in his calmest bored voice.

"Corporal Meddis here, sir. We've put the Vervani agent in Cell Nine."

"Thank you, Corporal. Ah . . ." It was worth a try, "We still have some fast-penta left. Would you two please bring Captain Tung up here for questioning?"

Beyond range of the vid pick-up, Elena's dark brows rose in hope.

"Tung, sir?" The guard's voice was doubtful. "Uh, may I add a couple of reinforcements to my squad, then?"

"Sure . . . see if Sergeant Chodak's around, he may have some people up for extra duties. In fact, isn't he on the extra-duty roster himself?" He glanced up to see Elena hold up her thumb and forefinger in an O.

"I think so, sir."

"Fine, whatever. Carry on. Naismith out." He keyed off the comm and stared at it, as if it had transmuted into Aladdin's lamp. "I don't think I'm destined to die today. I must be being saved for day after tomorrow."

"You think?"

"Oh, yes. I'll have a much bigger, more public and spectacular chance to blow it all away then. Be able to take thousands more lives down with me."

"Don't you fall into one of your stupid funks now, you haven't got time for it." She rapped the hypospray smartly across his knuckles. "You've got to think us out of this hole."

"Yes, ma'am," Miles said meekly, rubbing his hand. *Whatever happened to "my lord"? No respect, none. . . .* But he was strangely comforted. "By the way, when Oser arrested Tung for arranging my getaway, why didn't he go on to take you and Arde and Chodak, and the rest of your cadre?"

"He didn't arrest Tung for that. At least, I don't think so. He was baiting Tung, which is his habit, they were both on the bridge at the same time—that was unusual—and Tung finally lost his temper and tried to deck him. Did deck him, I heard, and was part way to strangling him when security pulled him off."

"It had nothing to do with us, then?" That was a relief.

"I'm . . . not sure. I wasn't there. It might have been an emergency diversion, to get Oser's attention away from making just that connection." Elena nodded to the still-blandly-smiling Oser. "And now?"

"Leave him loose, till Tung is delivered. We're all just happy allies here." Miles grimaced. "But for the love of God don't let anybody try to talk to him."

The door comm buzzed. Elena went to stand behind Oser's chair with one hand on his shoulder, trying to look as allied as possible. Miles went to the door and keyed the lock. The door slid open.

Six nervous squadmen surrounded a hostile-looking Ky Tung. Tung wore prisoner's bright yellow pajamas, and radiated malice like a small pre-nova sun. His teeth clenched in utter confusion when he saw Miles.

"Ah, thank you, Corporal," said Miles. "We will be having a little informal staff conference after this interrogation. I'd appreciate it if you and your squad would stand guard out here. And in case Captain Tung gets violent again, we'd better have—oh, Sergeant Chodak and a couple of your people inside." He emphasized the *your* with no change of voice, but only a direct look into Chodak's eyes.

Chodak made the catch. "Yes, sir. You, Private, come with me."

I'm promoting you to lieutenant, Miles thought, and stood aside to let the sergeant and his chosen man guide Tung within. Oser, looking cheerful, was quite clearly visible to the squad for a moment before the door hissed closed again.

Oser was clearly visible to Tung, too. Tung shrugged off his guards and stalked toward the admiral. "What now, you son-of-a-bitch, do you think you—" Tung paused, as Oser continued to smile dimly up at him. "What's wrong with him?"

"Nothing," shrugged Elena. "I think that dose of fast-penta made a real improvement in his personality. Too bad it's only temporary."

Tung threw back his head and barked a laugh, and whirled to shake Miles by the shoulders. "You did it, you little—you came back! We're in business!"

Chodak's man twitched, as if uncertain which way, or whom, to jump. Chodak caught him by the arm, shook his head silently, and indicated the wall by the door. Chodak holstered his stunner and leaned against the doorframe with his arms folded; after a startled moment, his man followed suit, flanking the other side. "Fly on the wall," Chodak grinned out of the corner of his mouth to him. "Consider it a gift."

"It wasn't exactly voluntary," said Miles through his teeth to Tung, only in part to keep from biting his tongue in the blast of the Eurasian's enthusiasm. "And we're not in business yet." *Sorry, Ky. I can't be your front man this time. You've got to follow me.* Miles kept his face stern, and removed Tung's hands from his shoulders with icy deliberation. "That Vervani freighter captain you found delivered me straight to Commander Cavilo. And I've been wondering ever since if it was an accident."

"Ah!" Tung fell back, looking as if Miles had just hit him in the stomach.

Miles felt like he had. No, Tung was no traitor. But Miles dared not give up the only edge he had. "Betrayal, or botchery, Ky?" *And have you stopped beating your wife?*

"Botchery," whispered Tung, gone sallow-pale. "Dammit, I'm going to kill the triple-crossing—"

"That's already been done," said Miles coldly. Tung's brows rose in surprised respect.

"I came to the Hegen Hub on a contract," continued Miles, "which is now in disarray almost beyond repair. I haven't come back here to put you in operational combat command of the Dendarii—" a beat, as Tung's worried features attempted to settle on an expression, "unless you are prepared to serve *my* ends. Priorities and targets are to be my choice. Only the *how* is yours." And just who was going to put whom in command of the Dendarii? As long as that question didn't occur to Tung.

"As my ally," began Tung.

"Not ally. Your commander. Or nothing," said Miles.

Tung stood stockily, his brows struggling to find their level. In a mild tone he finally said, "Daddy Ky's little boy is growing up, it seems."

"That's not the half of it. Are you in, or out?"

"The other half of this is something I've got to hear." Tung sucked on his lower lip. "In."

Miles stuck out his hand. "Done."

Tung took it. "Done." His grip was determined.

Miles let out a long breath. "All right. I gave you some half-truths, last time. Here's what's really going on." He began to pace, his shaking not all from the nerve disruptor nimbus. "I do have a contract with an interested outsider, but it wasn't for 'military evaluation,' which is the smoke screen I gave Oser. The part I told you about preventing a planetary civil war was not smoke. I was hired by the Barrayarans."

"They don't normally hire mercenaries," said Tung.

"I'm not a normal mercenary. I'm being paid by Barrayaran Imperial Security," God, at least one whole-truth, "to find and rescue a hostage. On the side I hope to stop a now-imminent Cetagandan invasion fleet from taking over the Hub. Our second strategic priority will be to hold both sides of the Vervain wormhole jump and as much else as we can till Barrayaran reinforcements arrive."

Tung cleared his throat. "Second priority? What if they don't arrive? There's Pol to cross. . . . And, ah, hostage-rescue does not normally take precedence over fleetwide strat-tac ops, eh?"

"Given the identity of this hostage, I guarantee their arrival. The Barrayaran emperor, Gregor Vorbarra, was kidnapped. I found him, lost him, and now I've got to get him back. As you can imagine, I expect the reward for his safe return to be substantial."

Tung's face was a study in appalled enlightenment. "That skinny neurasthenic git you had in tow before—that wasn't *him*, was it?"

"Yes, it was. And between us, you and I managed to deliver him straight to Commander Cavilo."

"Oh. Shit." Tung rubbed his burr-haired skull. "She'll sell him straight to the Cetagandans."

"No. She means to collect her reward from Barrayar."

Tung opened his mouth, closed it, held up a finger. "Wait a minute. . . ."

"It's *complicated*, ' Miles conceded helplessly. "That's why I'm going to delegate the simple part, holding the wormhole, to you. The hostage-rescue part will be my responsibility."

"Simple. The Dendarii mercenaries. All five thousand of us. Single-handed. Against the Cetagandan Empire. Have you forgotten how to count in the last four years?"

"Think of the glory. Think of your reputation. Think how great it'll look on your next resume."

"On my cenotaph, you mean. Nobody will be able to collect enough of my scattered atoms to bury. You going to cover my funeral expenses, son?"

"Splendidly. Banners, dancing girls, and enough beer to float your coffin to Valhalla."

Tung sighed. "Make it plum wine to float the boat, eh? Drink the beer. Well." He stood silent a moment, rubbing his lips. "The first step is to put the fleet on one-hour-alert status instead of twenty-four."

"They're not already?" Miles frowned.

"We were defensive. We figured we had at least thirty-six hours to study anything coming at us across the Hub. Or, so Oser figured it. It'll take about six hours to bring us up to one-hour readiness."

"Right . . . that's the second step, then. Your first step will be to kiss and make up with Captain Auson."

"Kiss my ass!" cried Tung. "That vacuumhead—"

"Is needed to command the *Triumph* while you run Fleet Tac. You can't do both. I can't reorganize the fleet this close to the action. If I had a week to weed out—well, I don't. Oser's people must be persuaded to stay on their jobs. If I have Auson," Miles's upheld hand closed cage-like, "I can run the rest. One way or another."

Tung growled frustrated acquiescence. "All right." His glower faded to a slow grin. "I'd pay money to watch you make him kiss Thorne, though."

"One miracle at a time."

Captain Auson, a big man four years ago, had put on a little more weight but seemed otherwise unchanged. He stepped into Oser's cabin, took in the stunners aimed his way, and stood, hands clenching. When he saw Miles, sitting on the edge of Oser's comconsole desk (a psychological ploy to put his head level with everyone else's; in the station chair Miles feared he looked like a child in need of a booster seat at the dinner table), Auson's expression melted from anger to horror. "Oh, hell! Not you again!"

"But of course," shrugged Miles. The stunner-armed flies on the wall, Chodak and his man, suppressed grins of happy anticipation. "The action's about to start."

"You can't take this—" Auson broke off to peer at Oser. "What did you do to him?"

"Let's just say, we adjusted his attitude. As for the fleet, it's already mine." Well, he was working on it, anyway. "The question is, will you choose to be on the winning side? Pocket a combat bonus? Or shall I give command of the *Triumph* to—"

Auson bared his teeth to Tung in a silent snarl.

"—Bel Thorne?"

"What?" Auson yelped. Tung flinched, wincing. "You can't—"

Miles cut over him. "Do you happen to recall how you graduated from command of the *Ariel* to command of the *Triumph?* Yes?"

Auson pointed to Tung. "What about him?"

"My contractor will contribute value equal to the *Triumph,* which will become Tung's vested share in the fleet corporation. In return Commodore Tung will relinquish all claim on the ship itself. I will confirm Tung's rank as Chief of Staff/Tactical, and yours as captain of the flagship *Triumph.* Your original contribution, equal to the value of the *Ariel* less liens, will be confirmed as your vested share in the fleet corporation. Both ships will be listed as owned by the fleet."

"Do you go along with this?" Auson demanded of Tung.

Miles prodded Tung with a steely look. "Yeah," said Tung grudgingly.

Auson frowned over this. "It isn't just the money . . ." He paused, brow wrinkling. "What combat bonus? What combat?"

He who hesitates, is had. "Are you in or out?"

Auson's moon face took on a cunning look. "I'm in—if he apologizes."

"What? This meatmind thinks—"

"Apologize to the man, Tung dear," Miles sang through his teeth, "and let's get on. Or the *Triumph* gets a captain who can be its own first mate. Who, among other manifold virtues, doesn't *argue* with me."

"Of course not, the little Betan flipsider's in love," snapped Auson. "I've never been able to figure out if it wants to get screwed or bugger you—"

Miles smiled and held up a restraining hand. "Now, now." He nodded toward Elena, who had holstered her stunner in favor of a nerve disruptor. Pointed steadily at Auson's head.

Her smile reminded Miles unsettlingly of one of Sergeant Bothari's. Or worse, of Cavilo's. "Have I ever mentioned, Auson, how much the sound of your voice *irritates* me?" she inquired.

"You wouldn't fire," said Auson uncertainly.

"I wouldn't stop her," Miles lied. "I need your ship. It would be convenient—but not necessary—if you would command her for me." His gaze flicked like a knife toward his putative Chief of Staff/Tac. *"Tung?"*

With ill-grace, Tung mouthed a nobly-worded, if vague, apology to Auson for past slurs on his character, intelligence, ancestry, appearance—as Auson's face darkened Miles stopped Tung's catalogue in mid-list and made him start over. "Keep it simpler."

Tung took a breath. "Auson, you can be a real shithead sometimes, but dammit, you can fight when you have to. I've seen you. In the tight and the bad and the crazy, I'll take you at my back before any other captain in the fleet."

One side of Auson's mouth curled up. "Now, *that's* sincere. Thank you so much. I really appreciate your concern for my safety. How tight and bad and crazy do you think this is going to get?"

Tung, Miles decided, had a most unsavory chuckle.

The captain-owners were brought in one by one, to be persuaded, bribed, blackmailed and bedazzled till Miles's mouth was dry, throat raw, voice hoarse. Only the *Peregrine*'s captain tried to physically fight. He was stunned and bound, and his second-in-command given the immediate choice between brevet promotion and a long walk out a short airlock. He chose promotion, though his eyes said, *Another day.* As long as that other day came after the Cetagandans, Miles was satisfied.

They moved to the larger conference chamber across from the Tactics Room for the strangest Staff conference Miles had ever attended. Oser was fortified with a booster shot of fast-penta and propped up at the head of the table like a stuffed and smiling corpse. At least two others were tied to their chairs gagged. Tung traded his yellow pajamas for undress greys, commodore's insignia pinned hastily over his captain's tags. The reaction of the audience to Tung's initial tactical presentation ranged from dubious to appalled, overcome (almost) by the pelting headlong pace of the actions demanded of them. Tung's most compelling argument was the sinister suggestion that if they didn't set themselves up as the wormhole's defenders, they might be required to attack through it later against a prepared Cetagandan defense, a vision that generated shudders all around the table. *It could be worse* was always an unassailable assertion.

Partway through, Miles massaged his temples and leaned over to whisper to Elena, "Was it always this bad, or have I just forgotten?"

She pursed her lips thoughtfully and murmured back, "No, the insults were better in the old days."

Miles muffled a grin.

Miles made a hundred unauthorized claims and unsupported promises, and at last things broke up, each to their duty stations. Oser and the *Peregrine*'s captain were marched away under guard to the brig. Tung paused only to frown down at the brown felt slippers. "If you're going to command my outfit, son, would you please do an old soldier a favor and get a pair of regulation boots?" At last only Elena remained.

"I want you to re-interrogate General Metzov," Miles told her. "Pull out all the Ranger tactical disposition data you can—codes, ships on-line, off-line, last known positions, personnel oddities, plus whatever he may know about the Vervani. Edit out any unfortunate references he may make to my real identity, and pass it on to Ops, with the warning that not everything Metzov thinks is true, necessarily is. It may help."

"Right."

Miles sighed, slumping wearily on his elbows at the empty conference table. "You know, the planetary patriots like the Barrayarans— us Barrayarans—have it wrong. Our officer cadre thinks that mercenaries have no honor, because they can be bought and sold. But honor is a luxury only a free man can afford. A good Imperial officer like me isn't honor-bound, he's just *bound*. How many of these honest people have I just lied to their deaths? It's a strange game."

"Would you change anything, today?"

"Everything. Nothing. I'd have lied twice as fast if I'd had to."

"You do talk faster in your Betan accent," she allowed.

"You understand. Am I doing the right thing? If I can bring it off. Failure being automatically wrong." *Not a path to disaster, but all paths. . . .*

Her brows rose. "Certainly."

His lips twisted up. "So you," *whom I love,* "my Barrayaran lady who hates Barrayar, are the only person in the Hub I can honestly sacrifice."

She tilted her head in consideration of this. "Thank you, my lord." She touched her hand to the top of his head, passing out of the chamber.

Miles shivered.

15

Miles returned to Oser's cabin for a fast perusal of the admiral's comconsole files, trying to get a handle on all the changes in equipment and personnel that had occurred since he'd last commanded, and to assimilate the Dendarii/Aslunder intelligence picture of events in the Hub. Somebody brought him a sandwich and coffee, which he consumed without tasting. The coffee was no longer working to keep him alert, though he was still keyed to an almost unbearable tension.

As soon as we undock, I'll crash in Oser's bed. He'd better spend at least some of the thirty-six hours transit time sleeping, or he'd be more liability than asset upon arrival. When he would have to deal with Cavilo, who made him feel like the proverbial unarmed man in the battle of wits even when he was at his best.

Not to mention the Cetagandans. Miles considered the historical three-legged-race between weapons development and tactics.

Projectile weapons for ship-to-ship combat in space had early been made obsolete by mass shielding and laser weapons. Mass shielding, designed to protect moving ships from space debris encountered at normal-space speeds up to half-cee, shrugged off missiles without even trying. Laser weapons in turn had been rendered useless by the arrival of the Sword-swallower, a Betan-developed defense that actu-

ally used the enemy fire as its own power source; a similar principle
in the plasma mirror, developed in Miles's parents' generation,
promised to do the same to the shorter-range plasma weapons. Another decade might see plasma all phased out.

The up-and-coming weapon for ship-to-ship fighting in the last
couple of years seemed to be the gravitic imploder lance, a modifica-
tion of tractor-beam technology; variously-designed artificial-gravity
shields were still lagging behind in protection from it. The imploder
beam made ugly twisty wreckage where it hit mass. What it did to a
human body was a horror.

But the energy-sucking imploder lance's range was insanely short,
in terms of space speeds and distances, barely a dozen kilometers.
Now, ships had to cooperate to grapple, to slow and close up to
maneuver. Given also the small scale of wormhole volumes, fighting
looked like it might suddenly become tight and intimate once again,
except that too-tight formations invited "sun wall" attacks of massed
nuclears. Round and round. It was hinted that ramming and boarding could actually become practical popular tactics once again. Till
the next surprise arrived from the devil's workshops, anyway. Miles
longed briefly for the good old days of his grandfather's generation,
when people could kill each other from a clean fifty thousand kilometers. Just bright sparks.

The effect of the new imploders on concentration of firepower
promised to be curious, especially where a wormhole was involved. It
was now possible that a small force in a small area could apply as
much power per cubic whatever as a large force, which could not
squeeze its largeness down to the effective range; although the difference in reserves still held good, of course. A large force willing to
make sacrifices could keep beating away till sheer numbers over-
came the smaller concentration. The Cetagandan ghem-lords were
not allergic to sacrifice, though generally preferring to start with
subordinates, or better still, allies. Miles rubbed his knotted neck
muscles.

The cabin buzzer blatted; Miles reached across the comconsole
desk to key the door open.

A lean, dark-haired man in his early thirties wearing mercenary
grey-and-whites with tech insignia stood uncertainly in the aperture.
"My lord?" he said in a soft voice.

Baz Jesek, Fleet Engineering Officer. Once, Barrayaran Imperial
Service deserter on the run; subsequently liege-sworn as a private
Armsman to Miles in his identity as Lord Vorkosigan. And finally,
husband to the woman Miles loved. Once loved. Still loved. Baz.

Damn. Miles cleared his throat uncomfortably. "Come in, Commodore Jesek."

Baz trod soundlessly across the deck matting, looking defensive and guilty. "I just got in off the repairs tender, and heard the word that you were back." His Barrayaran accent was polished thin and smooth by his years of galactic exile, significantly less pronounced than four years ago.

"Temporarily, anyway."

"I'm . . . sorry you didn't find things as you'd left them, my lord. I feel like I've squandered Elena's dowry that you bestowed. I didn't realize the implications of Oser's economic maneuvers until . . . well . . . no excuses."

"The man finessed Tung, too," Miles pointed out. He cringed inwardly, to hear Baz apologize to him. "I gather it wasn't exactly a fair fight."

"It wasn't a fight at all, my lord," Baz said slowly. "That was the problem." Baz stood to parade rest. "I've come to offer you my resignation, my lord."

"Offer rejected," said Miles promptly. "In the first place, liege-sworn Armsmen can't resign, in the second place, where am I going to get a competent fleet engineer on," he glanced at his chrono, "two hours' notice, and in the third place, in the third place . . . I need a witness to clear my name if things go wrong. Wronger. You've got to fill me in on Fleet equipment capabilities, then help get it all in motion. And I've got to fill you in on what's really going on. You're the only one besides Elena I can trust with the secret half of this."

With difficulty, Miles persuaded the hesitant engineer to sit down. Miles poured out a speed-edited precis of his adventures in the Hegen Hub, leaving out only mention of Gregor's half-hearted suicide attempt; that was Gregor's private shame. Miles was not altogether surprised to learn Elena had not confided his earlier, brief and ignominious return, rescue, and departure from the Dendarii; Baz seemed to think the presence of the incognito Emperor obvious and sufficient reason for her silence. By the time Miles finished, Baz's inner guilt was quite thoroughly displaced by outer alarm.

"If the Emperor is killed—if he doesn't return—the mess at home could go on for years," Baz said. "Maybe you should let Cavilo rescue him, rather than risk—"

"Up to a point, that's just what I intend to do," said Miles. "If only I knew Gregor's *mind.*" He paused. "If we lose both Gregor and the wormhole battle, the Cetagandans will arrive on our doorstep just at the point we will be in maximum internal disarray. What a temptation to them—what a lure—they've always wanted Komarr—we could be looking down the throat of the second Cetagandan invasion, almost as much a surprise to them as to us. They may prefer deep-laid plans, but they're not above a little opportunism—not an opportunity this overwhelming—"

Determinedly, driven by this vision, they turned to the tech specs, Miles reminding himself about the ancient saying about the want of a nail. They had nearly completed an overview when the comm officer on duty paged Miles through his comconsole.

"Admiral Naismith, sir?" The comm officer stared with interest at Miles's face, then went on, "There's a man in the docking bay who wants to see you. He claims to have important information."

Miles bethought himself of the theorized backup assassin. "What's his ID?"

"He says to tell you his name's Ungari. That's all he'll say."

Miles caught his breath. The cavalry at last! Or a clever ploy to gain admittance. "Can you give me a look at him, without letting him know he's being scanned?"

"Right, sir." The comm officer's face was replaced on the vid by a view of the *Triumph*'s docking bay. The vid zoomed down to focus on a pair of men in Aslunder tech coveralls. Miles melted with relief. Captain Ungari. And blessed Sergeant Overholt.

"Thank you, comm officer. Have a squad escort the two men to my cabin." He glanced at Baz. "In, uh, about ten minutes." He keyed off and explained, "It's my ImpSec boss. Thank God! But—I'm not sure I'd be able to explain to him the peculiar status of your desertion charges. I mean, he's ImpSec, not Service Security, and I don't imagine your old arrest order is exactly at the top of his list of concerns right now, but it might be . . . simpler, if you avoid him, eh?"

"Mm." Baz grimaced in agreement. "I believe I have duties to attend to?"

"No lie. Baz . . ." for a wild moment he longed to tell Baz to take Elena and run, safe away from the coming danger, "It's going to get real crazy soon."

"With Mad Miles back in charge, how could it be otherwise?" Baz shrugged, smiling. He started for the door.

"I'm not as crazy as Tung—Good God, nobody calls me that, do they?"

"Ah—it's an old joke. Only among a few old Dendarii." Baz's step quickened.

And there are very few old Dendarii. That, unfortunately, was not a funny joke. The door hissed closed behind the engineer.

Ungari. Ungari. Somebody in charge at last. *If only I had Gregor with me, I could be done right now. But at least I can find out what Our Side has been up to all this time.* Exhausted, he laid his head down on his arms on Oser's comconsole desk, and smiled. Help. Finally.

Some wriggling dream was fogging his mind; he snatched himself back from too-long-delayed sleep as the cabin buzzer blatted again. He rubbed his numb face and hit the lock control on the desk. "Enter." He glanced at the chrono; he'd lost only four minutes, on that downward slide of consciousness. It was definitely time for a break.

Chodak and two Dendarii guards escorted Captain Ungari and Sergeant Overholt into the room. Ungari and Overholt were both dressed in tan Aslunder supervisor's coveralls, no doubt with IDs and passes to match. Miles smiled happily at them.

"Sergeant Chodak, you and your men wait outside." Chodak looked sadly disappointed at this exclusion. "And if she's finished with her current task, ask Commander Elena Bothari-Jesek to attend on us here. Thanks."

Ungari waited impatiently till the door had hissed closed behind Chodak to stride forward. Miles stood up and saluted him smartly. "Glad to see y—"

To Miles's surprise, Ungari did not return the salute; instead his hands clenched on Miles's uniform jacket and lifted. Miles sensed that it was only with the greatest restraint that Ungari's grip had closed on his lapels and not his neck. "Vorkosigan, you idiot! What the hell kind of game have you been up to?"

"I found Gregor, sir. I—" don't say *lost him.* "I'm mounting an expedition to recover him right now. I'm so glad you made contact with me, another hour and you'd have missed the boat. If we pool our information and resources—"

Ungari's clutch did not loosen, nor did his peeled-back lips relax. "We know you found the Emperor, we traced you both here from Consortium Detention. Then you both vanished utterly."

"Didn't you ask Elena? I thought you would—look sir, sit down, please," *and put me down, dammit*—Ungari seemed not to notice that Miles's toes were stretched to the floor, "and tell me what all this looked like from your point of view. It's very important."

Ungari, breathing heavily, released Miles and sat in the indicated station chair, or at least on its edge. At a hand signal, Overholt took up a pose of parade rest at his shoulder. Miles gazed with some relief at Overholt, whom he'd last seen face-down unconscious on the

Consortium Station concourse; the sergeant appeared fully recovered, if tired and strained.

Ungari said, "When he finally woke up, Sergeant Overholt followed you to Consortium Detention, but by then you'd disappeared. He thought *they'd* done it, they thought *he'd* done it. He spent bribe-money like water, finally got the story from the contract-slave you'd beaten up—a day later, when the man could finally talk—"

"He lived, then," said Miles. "Good, Gre—we were worried about that."

"Yes, but Overholt didn't recognize the emperor at first, in the contract-slave records—the sergeant hadn't been on the need-to-know list about his disappearance."

A faint irate look passed over the sergeant's face, as if in memory of great injustices.

"—it wasn't until he'd made contact with me here, we dead-ended, and we retraced all the steps in hopes of finding some clue about you we'd overlooked, that I identified the missing contract-slave as Emperor Gregor. *Days* lost."

"I was sure you'd make contact with Elena Bothari-Jesek, sir. She knew where we'd gone. You knew she was my sworn liegewoman, it's in my files."

Ungari shot him a flat-lipped glare, but did not otherwise offer explanation for this gaffe. "When the first wave of Barrayaran agents hit the Hub, we finally had enough reinforcements to mount a serious search—"

"Good! So they know Gregor's in the Hub, back home. I was afraid Illyan would still be squandering all his resources on Komarr, or worse, towards Escobar."

Ungari's fingers clenched again. "Vorkosigan, *what did you do with the emperor?*"

"He's safe, but in great danger." Miles thought that one over a second. "That is, he's all right for the moment, I think, but that will change with the tactical—"

"We know *where* he is, he was spotted three days ago by an agent in Randall's Rangers."

"Must have been just after I left," Miles calculated. "Not that he could have spotted me, I was in the brig—what are we doing about it?"

"Rescue forces are being scrambled; I don't know how large a fleet."

"What about permission to cross Pol?"

"I doubt they'll wait for it."

"We've got to alert them, not to offend Pol! The—"

"Ensign, Vervain holds the emperor!" Ungari snarled in exasperation. "I'm not going to tell the—"

"Vervain doesn't hold Gregor, Commander Cavilo does," Miles interrupted urgently. "It's strictly nonpolitical, a plot for her personal gain. I think—in fact, I'm dead certain—the Vervani government doesn't know the first thing about her 'guest.' Our rescue forces must be warned to commit no hostile act until the Cetagandan invasion shows up."

"The what?"

Miles faltered, and said in a smaller voice, "You mean you don't know anything about the Cetagandan invasion?" He paused. "Well, just because you don't have the word yet, doesn't mean Illyan hasn't figured it out. Even if we haven't spotted where they're massing, inside the Empire, as soon as ImpSec adds up how many Cetagandan warships have disappeared from their home bases, they'll realize something must be up. Somebody must still be keeping track of such things, even in the current flap over Gregor." Ungari was still sitting there looking stunned, so Miles kept explaining. "I expect a Cetagandan force to invade Vervani local space and continue on to secure the Hegen Hub, with Commander Cavilo's connivance. Very shortly. I plan to take the Dendarii fleet across-system and fight them at the Vervani wormhole, hold it till Gregor's rescue fleet arrives. I hope they're sending more than a diplomatic negotiation team. . . . By the way, do you still have that blank mercenary contract credit chit Illyan gave you? I need it."

"You, mister," Ungari began when he had mastered his voice again, "are going *nowhere* but to our safe-house on Aslund Station. Where you will wait quietly—very quietly—until Illyan's reinforcements arrive to take you *off my hands.*"

Miles politely ignored this impractical outburst. "You have to have been collecting data for your report to Illyan. Got anything I can use?"

"I have a complete report on Aslund Station, it's naval and mercenary dispositions and strengths, but—"

"*I* have all that, now." Miles tapped his fingers impatiently on Oser's comconsole. "Damn. I wish you'd spent the last two weeks on Vervain Station instead."

Ungari gritted, "Vorkosigan, you will stand up now, and come with Sergeant Overholt and me. Or so help me I will have Overholt carry you bodily."

Overholt was eyeing him with cool calculation, Miles realized.

"That could be a serious mistake, sir. Worse than your failure to contact Elena. If you will just let me explain the over-all strategic situation—"

Goaded beyond endurance, Ungari snapped, "Overholt, grab him."

Miles hit the alarm on his comconsole desk as Overholt swooped down on him. He dodged around his station chair, knocking it loose from its clamps, as Overholt missed his first grab. The cabin door hissed open. Chodak and his two guards pelted through, followed by Elena. Overholt, chasing Miles around the end of the comconsole desk, skidded straight into Chodak's stunner fire. Overholt dropped with a massive thud; Miles winced. Ungari lurched to his feet and stopped, bracketed by the aim of four Dendarii stunners. Miles felt like bursting into tears, or possibly cackles. Neither would be useful. He got control of his breath and voice.

"Sergeant Chodak, take these two men to the *Triumph*'s brig. Put them . . . put them next to Metzov and Oser, I guess."

"Yes, Admiral."

Ungari went bravely silent, as befit a captured spy, and suffered himself to be led out, though the veins in his neck pulsed with suppressed fury as he glared back at Miles.

And I can't even fast-penta him, Miles thought mournfully. An agent of Ungari's level was certain to have been implanted with an induced allergic reaction to fast-penta; not euphoria, but anaphylactic shock and death, would result from such a dose. In a moment two more Dendarii appeared with a float pallet and removed the inert Overholt.

As the door closed behind them, Elena asked, "All right, what was all that about?"

Miles sighed deeply. "That, unfortunately, was my ImpSec superior, Captain Ungari. He was not in a listening mood."

Elena's eye lit with a skewed enthusiasm. "Dear God, Miles. Metzov—Oser—Ungari—all in a row—you sure are hard on your commanding officers. What are you going to do when the time comes to let them all out?"

Miles shook his head mutely. "I don't know."

The fleet disengaged from Aslund Station within the hour, maintaining strict comm silence; the Aslunders, naturally, were thrown into a panic. Miles sat in the *Triumph*'s comm center and monitored their frantic queries, resolved not to interfere with the natural course of events unless the Aslunders opened fire. Until he again laid hands on Gregor, he must at all costs present the correct profile to Cavilo. Let her think she was getting what she wanted, or at least what she'd asked for.

In fact, the natural course of events promised to deliver more of the results Miles wanted than he could have gained through planning and persuasion. The Aslunders had three main theories, Miles deduced from their comm chatter; the mercenaries were fleeing from the Hub altogether at secret word of some impending attack, the mercenaries were off to join one or more of Aslund's enemies, or worst of all, the mercenaries were opening an unprovoked attack on said enemies, with subsequent retribution to recoil on the Aslunder's heads. Aslunder forces went to maximum alert status. Reinforcements were called for, mobile forces shifted into the Hub, reserves brought on-line as the sudden departure of their faithless mercenaries stripped them of assumed defenses.

Miles breathed relief as the last of the Dendarii fleet cleared the Aslunders' region and headed into open space. Delayed by the confusion, no Aslunder naval pursuit force could catch them now till they decelerated near the Vervain wormhole. Where, with the arrival of the Cetagandans, it should not be hard to persuade the Aslunders to reclassify themselves as Dendarii reserves.

Timing was, if not everything, a lot. Suppose Cavilo hadn't already transmitted her go-code to the Cetagandans. The sudden movement of the Dendarii fleet might well spook her into aborting the plot. Fine, Miles decided. In that case he would have stopped the Cetagandan invasion without a shot being fired. A perfect war of maneuver, by Admiral Aral Vorkosigan's own definition. *Of course, I'll have political egg on my face and a lynch mob after me from three sides, but Dad will understand. I hope.* That would leave staying alive and rescuing Gregor as his only tactical goals, which in present contrast seemed absurdly, delightfully simple. Unless, of course, Gregor didn't want to be rescued. . . .

Further, finer branches of the strategy-tree must await events. Miles decided blearily. He staggered off to Oser's cabin to fall into bed and sleep for twelve solid, sodden hours.

The *Triumph* 's comm officer woke Miles, paging him on the vid. Miles, in his underwear, padded across to the comconsole and slung himself into the station chair. "Yes?"

"You asked to be apprised of messages from Vervain Station, sir."

"Yes, thank you." Miles rubbed amber grains of sleep from his eyes, and checked the time. Twelve hours flight-time left till their arrival at target. "Any signs of abnormal activity levels at Vervain Station or their wormhole yet?"

"Not yet, sir."

"All right. Continue to monitor, record, and track any outbound traffic. What's the transmission time lag from us to them at present?"

"Thirty-six minutes, sir."

"Mm. Very well. Pipe the message down here." Yawning, he leaned his elbows on Oser's comconsole and studied the vid. A high-ranking Vervani officer appeared over the plate, and demanded explanation for the Oseran/Dendarii Fleet's movements. He sounded a lot like the Aslunders. No sign of Cavilo. Miles keyed the comm officer. "Transmit back that their important message was hopelessly garbled by static and a malfunction in our de-scrambler. Urgently request a repeat, with amplification."

"Yes, sir."

In the ensuing seventy minutes Miles took a leisurely shower, dressed in a properly fitting uniform (and boots) that had been provided while he slept, and ate a balanced breakfast. He strolled into the *Triumph*'s Nav and Com just in time for the second transmission. This time, Commander Cavilo stood, arms crossed, at the Vervani officer's shoulder. The Vervani repeated himself, literally with amplification, his voice was louder and sharper this time around. Cavilo added, "Explain yourselves at once, or we will regard you as a hostile force and respond accordingly."

That was the amplification he'd wanted. Miles settled himself in the comm station chair and adjusted his Dendarii uniform as neatly as possible. He made sure the admiral's rank insignia was clearly visible in the vid. "Ready to transmit," he nodded to the comm officer. He smoothed his features into as straight-faced and dead-serious an expression as he could manage.

"Admiral Miles Naismith, Commanding, Dendarii Free Mercenary Fleet, speaking. To Commander Cavilo, Randall's Rangers, eyes only. Ma'am. I have accomplished my mission precisely as you ordered. I remind you of the reward you promised me for my success. What are your next instructions? Naismith out."

The comm officer logged the recording into the tight-beam scrambler. "Sir," she said uncertainly, "if that's for Commander Cavilo's eyes only, should we be sending it on the Vervain command channel? The Vervani will have to de-process it before sending it on. It will be seen by a lot of eyes besides hers."

"Just so, Lieutenant," said Miles. "Go ahead and transmit."

"Oh. And when—if—they respond, what do you want me to do?"

Miles checked his chrono. "By the time of their next response, our line of travel should take us behind the twin suns' interference corona. We should be out of communications for a good, oh, three hours."

"I can boost the gain, sir, and cut through—"

"No, no, Lieutenant. The interference is going to be something terrible. In fact, if you can stretch that to four hours, so much the better. But make it look real. Until we're in range for a tight-beam conference between myself and Cavilo in near-real-time, I want you to think of yourself as a non-communications officer."

"Yes, sir," she grinned. "Now I understand."

"Carry on. Remember, I want maximum inefficiency, incompetence, and error. On the Vervani channels, that is. You've worked with trainees, surely. Be creative."

"Yes, *sir.*"

Miles went off to find Tung.

He and Tung were deeply engrossed in the tactical computer display in the *Triumph*'s tactics room, running projected wormhole scenarios, when the comm officer paged again.

"Changes at Vervain Station, sir. All outgoing commercial ship traffic has been halted. Incoming are being denied permission to dock. Encoded transmissions on all military channels have just about tripled. And four large warships just jumped."

"Into the Hub, or out to Vervain?"

"Out to Vervain, sir."

Tung leaned forward. "Dump data into the tactics display as you confirm it, Lieutenant."

"Yes, sir."

"Thank you," said Miles. "Continue to keep us advised. And monitor civilian clear-code messages, too, any you can pick up. I want to keep tabs on the rumors as they start to fly."

"Right, sir. Out."

Tung keyed up what was laughingly called the "real-time" tactics display, a colorful schematic, as the comm officer shunted the new data. He studied the identity of the four departing warships. "It's starting," he said grimly. "You called it."

"You don't think it's something we're causing?"

"Not those four ships. They wouldn't have moved off-station if they weren't badly wanted elsewhere. Better get your ass over to—that is, transfer your flag to the *Ariel*, son."

* * *

Miles rubbed his lips nervously, and eyed what he'd mentally dubbed his "Little Fleet" in the schematic display in the *Ariel*'s tactics room. The equipment was now displaying the *Ariel* itself plus the two next-fastest ships in the Dendarii forces. His own personal attack-group; fast, maneuverable, amenable to violent course-changes, requiring less turning-room than any other possible combination. Admittedly, they were low in firepower. But if things went as Miles projected, firing was not going to be a desirable option anyway.

The *Ariel*'s tac room was manned now by a mere skeleton crew; Miles, Elena as his personal communications officer, Arde Mayhew for all other systems. Inner Circle all, in anticipation of this next most-private conversation. If it came to actual combat, he'd turn the chamber over to Thorne, presently exiled to Nav and Com. And then, perhaps, retire to his cabin and slit his belly open.

"Let's see Vervain Station now," he told Elena in her comm station chair. The main holovid display in the center of the room whirled dizzyingly at her touch on the controls. The schematic representation of their target area seemed to boil with shifting lines and colors, representing ship movements, power shunts to various weapons systems and shieldings, and communications transmissions. The Dendarii were now barely a million kilometers out, a little more than three light-seconds. The rate of closure was slowing as the Little Fleet, fully two hours ahead of the slower ships of the main Dendarii fleet, decelerated.

"They're sure stirred up now," Elena commented. Her hand went to her ear-bug. "They're reiterating their demands that we communicate."

"But still not launching a counter-attack," Miles observed, studying the schematic. "I'm glad they realize where the true danger lies. All right. Tell them that we've got our comm problems straightened out—finally—but say again that I will speak first only to Commander Cavilo."

"They—ah—I think they're finally putting her through. I've got a tight-beam coming in on the dedicated channel."

"Trace it." Miles hung over her shoulder as she coaxed this information from the comm net.

"The source is moving. . . ."

Miles closed his eyes in prayer, snapped them open again at Elena's triumphant, "Got it! There. That little ship."

"Give me its course and energy profile. Is she heading toward the wormhole?"

"No, away."

"Ha!"

"It's a fast ship—small—it's a *Falcon*-class courier," Elena reported. "If her goal is Pol—and Barrayar—she must intersect our triangle."

Miles exhaled. "Right. Right. She waited to speak on a line her Vervani bosses couldn't monitor. I thought she might. Wonder what lies she's told them? She's past the point of no return, does she know it?" He opened his arms to the new short vector line in the schematic. "Come, love. Come to me."

Elena raised her brow sardonically at him. "Coming through. Your sweetheart is about to appear on Monitor Three."

Miles swung into the indicated Station chair, settling himself before the holovid plate, which began to sparkle. Now was the time to muster every bit of self-control he'd ever owned. He smoothed his face to an expression of cool ironic interest, as Cavilo's fine features formed before him. Out of range of the vid pick-up, he rubbed his sweating palms on his trouser knees.

Cavilo's blue eyes were alight with triumph, constrained by her tight mouth and tense brows as if in echo of Miles's ships constraining her flight-path. "Lord Vorkosigan. What are you doing here?"

"Following your orders, ma'am. You told me to go get the Dendarii. And I've transmitted nothing to Barrayar."

A six-second time-lag, as the tight-beam flew from ship to ship and returned her answer. Alas that it gave her as much time to think as it did him.

"I didn't order you to cross the Hub."

Miles wrinkled his brow in puzzlement. "But where else would you need my fleet except at the point of action? I'm not dense."

Cavilo's pause this time was longer than accounted for by the transmission lag. "You mean you didn't get Metzov's message?" she asked.

Damn near. What a fabulous array of double meanings there. "Why, did you send him as a courier?"

Lag. "Yes!"

A palpable lie for a palpable lie. "I never saw him. Maybe he deserted. He must have realized he'd lost your love to another. Perhaps he's holed up in some spaceport bar right now, drowning his sorrows." Miles sighed deeply at this sad scenario.

Cavilo's concerned attentive expression melted to rage when this one arrived. "Idiot! I know you took him prisoner!"

"Yes, and I've been wondering ever since why you allowed that to happen. If that accident was undesired, you should have taken precautions against it."

Cavilo's eyes narrowed; she shifted her ground. "I feared Stanis's emotions made him unreliable. I wanted to give him one more chance to prove himself. I gave my backup man orders to kill him if he tried to kill you, but when Metzov missed, the dolt waited."

Substitute *as soon as/succeeded* for that *if/tried,* and the statement was probably near-truth. Miles wished he had a recording of that Ranger agent's field report, and Cavilo's blistering reply. "There, you see? You *do* want subordinates who can think for themselves. Like me."

Cavilo's head jerked back. "You, for a subordinate? I'd sooner sleep with a snake!"

Interesting image, that. "You'd better get used to me. You're seeking entry into a world strange to you, familiar to me. The Vorkosigans are an integral part of Barrayar's power-class. You could use a native guide."

Lag. "Exactly. I'm trying—I must—get your emperor to safety. You're blocking his flight path. Out of my way!"

Miles spared a glance for the tactics display. Yes, just so. *Good, come to me.* "Commander Cavilo, I feel certain you are missing an important datum in your calculations about me."

Lag. "Let me clarify my position, little Barrayaran. I hold your emperor. I control him absolutely."

"Fine, let me hear those orders from him, then."

Lag . . . fractionally briefer, yes. "I can have his throat cut before your eyes. Let me pass!"

"Go ahead," Miles shrugged. "It'll make an awful mess on your deck, though."

She grinned sourly, after the lag. "You bluff badly."

"I bluff not at all. Gregor is far more valuable alive to you than to me. You can do nothing, where you're going, except through him. He's your meal ticket. But has anyone mentioned to you yet that if Gregor dies, I could become the next emperor of Barrayar?" Well, arguably, but this was hardly time to go into the finer details of the six competing Barrayaran succession theories.

Cavilo's face froze. "He said . . . he had no heir. You said so too."

"None *named.* Because my father refuses to be named, not because he lacks the bloodlines. But ignoring the bloodlines doesn't erase them. And I am my father's only child. And he can't live forever. Ergo . . . So, resist my boarding parties, by all means. Threaten away. Carry out your threats. Give me the Imperium. I shall thank you prettily, before I have you summarily executed. Emperor Miles the First. How does it sound? As good as Empress

Cavilo?" Miles gave it an intense beat, *"Or,* we could work together. The Vorkosigans have traditionally felt that the substance was better than the name. The power behind the throne, as my father before me—who has held just that power, as Gregor has doubtless told you, for far too long—you're not going to dislodge *him* by batting your eyelashes. He's immune to women. But I know his every weakness. I've thought it through. This could be my big chance, one way or another. By the way—milady—do you care which emperor you wed?"

The time lag allowed him to fully savor her changes of expression, as his plausible calumnies thudded home. Alarm; revulsion; finally, reluctant respect.

"I underestimated you, it seems. Very well . . . Your ships may escort us to safety. Where—clearly—we must confer further."

"I will *transport* you to safety, aboard the *Ariel.* Where we will confer immediately."

Cavilo straightened, nostrils flaring. "No way."

"All right, let's compromise. I will abide by Gregor's orders, and Gregor's orders only. As I said, milady, you'd better get used to this. No Barrayaran will take orders from you directly at first, till you've established yourself. If that's the game you're choosing to play, you'd better start practicing. It only gets more complicated after this. Or, you can choose to resist, in which case I get it all." *Play for time, Cavilo! Bite!*

"I'll get Gregor." The vid went to the grey haze of a holding-signal.

Miles flung himself back in his station chair, rubbed his neck and rolled his head, trying to relieve his screaming nerves. He was shaking. Mayhew was staring at him in alarm.

"Damn," said Elena in a hushed voice. "If I didn't know you, I'd think you were Mad Yuri's understudy. The look on your face . . . am I reading too much into all that innuendo, or did you in fact just connive to assassinate Gregor in one breath, offer to cuckold him in the next, accuse your father of homosexuality, suggest a patricidal plot against him, and league yourself with Cavilo—what are you going to do for an encore?"

"Depends on the straight lines. I can hardly wait to find out," Miles panted. "Was I convincing?"

"You were *scary.*"

"Good." He wiped his palms on his trousers again. "It's mind-to-mind, between Cavilo and me, before it ever becomes ship-to-ship . . . She's a compulsive plotter. If I can smoke her, wind her in with words, with what-ifs, with all the bifurcations of her strategy-tree, just long enough to get her eye off the one real *now . . .*"

"Signal," Elena warned.

Miles straightened, waited. The next face to form over the vid plate was Gregor's. Gregor, alive and well. Gregor's eyes widened, then his face went very still.

Cavilo hovered behind his shoulder, just slightly out of focus. "Tell him what we want, love."

Miles bowed sitting down, as profoundly as physically possible. "Sire. I present you with the Emperor's Own Dendarii Free Mercenary Fleet. Do with us as You will."

Gregor glanced aside, evidently as some tactical readout analogous to the *Ariel*'s own. "By God, you've even got them *with* you. Miles, you are supernatural." The flash of humor was instantly muffled in sere formality. "Thank you, Lord Vorkosigan. I accept your vassal-offering of troops."

"If you would care to step aboard the *Ariel*, sire, you can take personal command of your forces."

Cavilo leaned forward, interrupting. "And *now* his treachery is made plain. Let me play a portion of his last words for you, Greg." Cavilo reached past Gregor to touch a control, and Miles was treated to an instant replay of his breathless sedition, beginning with—naturally—the flim-flam about the named heir, and ending with his offer of himself as a substitute Imperial groom. Very nicely selected, clearly unedited.

Gregor listened with his head in a thoughtful tilt, his face perfectly controlled, as the Miles-image stammered to its damning conclusion. "But does this surprise you, Cavie?" asked Gregor in an innocent tone, taking her hand and looking over his shoulder at her. From the expression on her face, *something* was surprising her. "Lord Vorkosigan's mutations have driven him mad, everyone knows that! He's been sulking around muttering like that for years. Of course, I trust him no further than I can throw him—"

Thanks, Gregor. I'll remember that line.

"—but as long as he feels he can further his interests by furthering ours, he'll be a valuable ally. House Vorkosigan has always been powerful in Barrayaran affairs. His grandfather Count Piotr put my grandfather Emperor Ezar on the throne. They'd make an equally powerful enemy. I should prefer us to rule Barrayar with their cooperation."

"Their extermination would do as well, surely," Cavilo glared at Miles.

"Time is on our side, love. His father is an old man. He, is a mutant. His bloodline-threat is empty, Barrayar would never accept a mutant as emperor, as Count Aral well knows and as even Miles realizes in his saner moments. But he can trouble us, if he chooses. An interesting balance of power, eh, Lord Vorkosigan?"

Miles bowed again. "I think much on it." *So have you, apparently.* He spared a quelling glance at Elena, who had fallen off her station chair somewhere around Gregor's word-picture of Miles's mad soliloquies, aside at state banquets no doubt, and was now sitting on the floor with her sleeve jammed in her mouth to muffle the shrieks of laughter. Her eyes blazed, over the grey cloth. She got control of her stifled giggles and scrambled back into her seat. *Close your mouth, Arde.*

"Then, Cavie, let's join my would-be Grand Vizier. At that point, I will control his ships. And your wish," he turned his head to kiss her hand, still resting in his grasp on his shoulder, "will be my command."

"Do you really think it's safe? If he's as psycho as you say."

"Brilliant—nervous—skittish—but he's all right as long as his medications are adjusted properly, I promise you. I expect his dose is a little off at the moment, due to our irregular travels."

The transmission time-lag was much reduced, now. "Twenty minutes to rendezvous, sir," Elena reported, off-sides.

"Will you transfer in your shuttle, or ours, sire?" Miles inquired politely.

Gregor shrugged carelessly. "Commander Cavilo's choice."

"Ours," said Cavilo immediately.

"I will be waiting." *And ready.*

Cavilo broke transmission.

16

Miles watched through the vid link as the first space-armored Ranger stepped into the *Ariel*'s shuttle hatch corridor. The wary point-man was followed immediately by four more, who scanned the empty passageway, converted into a chamber by the closed blast doors sealing each end. No enemies, no targets, not even automatic weapons threatened them. An utterly deserted chamber. Bewildered, the Rangers took up a defensive stance around the shuttle hatch.

Gregor stepped through. Miles was unsurprised to see that Cavilo had not provided the Emperor with space armor. Gregor wore a neatly-pressed set of Ranger fatigues, minus insignia; his only protection was his boots. Even they would be quite inadequate, if one of those heavy-armored monsters stepped on his toe. Battle armor was lovely stuff, proof against stunners and nerve disruptors, most poisons and biologicals; resistant (to a degree) to plasma fire and radioactivity, stuffed with clever built-in weaponry, tac comps, and telemetry. Very suitable for a boarding expedition. Though in fact, Miles had once captured the *Ariel* himself with fewer personnel, less formidably armed and totally unarmored. He'd had surprise on his side, then.

Cavilo came through behind Gregor. She wore space armor, though for the moment she carried her helmet tucked under her arm like a decapitated head. She stared around the empty corridor, and frowned. "All right, what's the trick?" she demanded loudly.

To answer your question. . . . Miles pressed the button on the remote-control box in his hand.

A muffled explosion made the corridor reverberate. The flex-tube tore violently away from the shuttle hatch. The automatic doors, sensing the pressure drop, clapped shut instantly. A bare breath of air escaped. Good system. Miles had made the techs make sure it was working properly, before they'd inserted the directional mines in the shuttle clamps. He checked his monitors. Cavilo's combat shuttle was tumbling away from the side of the *Ariel* now, thrusters and sensors damaged in the same blast that propelled it outward, its weapons and reserve Rangers useless until the no-doubt-frantic pilot regained attitude control. If he could.

"Keep an eye on him, Bel, I don't want him coming back to haunt us," Miles spoke into his comm link to Thorne, on deck in the *Ariel's* tactics room.

"I can blow him up now, if you like."

"Wait a little. We're a long way from sorted out, down here." *God help us now.*

Cavilo was snapping her helmet on, her startled troops in defensive formation around her. All dressed up, and nothing to shoot. Let them settle down for just a moment, enough to prevent spinal-reflexive fusilades, but not enough to think. . . .

Miles glanced around at his own space-armored troops, six in number, and closed his own helmet. Not that numbers mattered. A million troops with nuclears, one guy with a club; either would suffice when the target was one unarmed hostage. Miniaturizing the situation, Miles realized sadly, had made no qualitative difference. He could still screw up just as big. The main difference was his plasma cannon, sighted down the corridor. He nodded to Elena, manning the big weapon. Not normally an indoor toy, it would stop charging space armor. And blow out the hull beyond. Miles figured that, theoretically, they could blow away, oh, one out of Cavilo's five at this range, if they came on at a dead run, before all became hand-to-hand, or glove-to-glove.

"Here we go," Miles warned through his command channel. "Remember the drill." He pressed another control; the blast doors between his group and Cavilo's began to draw back. Slowly, not suddenly, at a rate carefully calculated to inspire dread without startling.

Full broadcast on all channels plus loudspeaker. It was absolutely essential to Miles's plan that he get in the first word.

"Cavilo!" he shouted. "Deactivate your weapons and freeze, or I'll blow Gregor to atoms!"

Body language was a wonderful thing. It was amazing, how much expression could come through the blank shining surface of space armor. The littlest armored figure stood openhanded, stunned. Bereft of words; bereft, for precious seconds, of reactions. Because, of course, Miles had just stolen her opening line. *Now what do you have to say for yourself, love?* It was a desperate ploy. Miles had judged the hostage-problem logically insoluble; therefore, clearly the only thing to do was make it Cavilo's problem instead of his own.

Well, he'd obtained as much as the *freeze* part, anyway. But he dared not let the standoff stand. "Drop it, Cavilo! It only takes one nervous twitch to convert you from Imperial fiancée to no one of importance at all. And then to no one at all. And you're making me *real tense.*"

"You said he was safe," Cavilo hissed to Gregor.

"His meds must be further off-dose than I thought," Gregor replied, looking anxious. "No, watch—he's bluffing. I'll prove it."

Hands held out open to his sides, Gregor walked straight toward the plasma cannon. Miles's jaw fell open, behind his faceplate. *Gregor, Gregor, Gregor . . . !*

Gregor gazed steadily into Elena's faceplate. His step never quickened or faltered. He stopped only when his chest touched the beaded tip of the cannon. It was an enormously dramatic and arresting moment. Miles was so lost in appreciation, it took him that long to move his finger an imperceptible few centimeters and hit the button on his control box that closed the blast doors.

The shield hadn't been programmed for slow-closure; it banged shut faster than the eye could follow. Brief noises, from the other side, of plasma fire, shouts; Cavilo screaming at one of her men just in time to stop him from the fatal error of firing a mine at the wall of a closed chamber he himself occupied. Then silence.

Miles dropped his plasma rifle, tore off his helmet. "God almighty, I wasn't expecting *that.* Gregor, you're a genius."

Gently, Gregor raised a finger and moved the tip of the plasma cannon aside.

"Don't worry," said Miles. "None of our weapons are charged. I didn't want to risk any accidents."

"I was almost certain that was the case," Gregor murmured. He stared back over his shoulder at the blast doors. "What would you have done if I'd been asleep on my feet?"

"Kept talking. Tried for various compromises. I had a trick or two yet . . . behind the other blast door, there's a squad with live weapons. In the end, if she didn't bite, I was prepared to surrender."

"That's what I was afraid of."

Some peculiar muffled noises penetrated the blast doors.

"Elena, take over," said Miles. "Mop up. Take Cavilo alive if possible, but I don't want any Dendarii to die trying. Take no chances, trust nothing she says."

"I have the picture." Elena waved a salute, and motioned to her squad, which broke up to insert weapons-charges. Elena began to confer over the command-channel headset with the leader of the twin squad waiting on Cavilo's other side and with the commander of the *Ariel's* combat shuttle, closing in from space.

Miles motioned Gregor along the corridor, removing him as swiftly as possible from the region of potential messiness. "To the tactics room, and I'll fill you in. You have some decisions to make."

They entered a lift-tube, and rose. Miles breathed easier with every meter he increased the range between Gregor and Cavilo.

"My biggest worry," Miles said, "till we spoke face-to-face, was that Cavilo really had done what she thought she had, fogged your mind. I didn't see where she could be getting her ideas except from you. Wasn't sure what I could do in that case, except play along till I could hand you over to higher experts on Barrayar. If I survived. I didn't know how fast you'd see through her."

"Oh, at once," shrugged Gregor. "She had the same hungry smile Vordrozda used to get. And a dozen lesser cannibals, since. I can smell a power-hungry flatterer at a thousand meters, now."

"I yield to my master in strategy," Miles's armored hand made a genuflecting motion. "Do you know you rescued yourself? She'd have taken you all the way home, even if I hadn't come along."

"It was easy." Gregor frowned. "All that was required was that I have no personal honor at all." Gregor's eyes, Miles realized, were deathly, devoid of triumph.

"You can't cheat an honest man," said Miles uncertainly. "Or woman. What would you have done, if she'd got you home?"

"Depends." Gregor stared into the middle distance. "If she'd managed to get you killed, I suppose I'd have had her executed." Gregor glanced back, as they stepped out of the tube. "This is better. Maybe . . . maybe there's some way to give her a fair chance."

Miles blinked. "I'd be very careful about giving Cavilo any kind of a chance at all, if I were you. Even with tongs. Does she deserve it? Do you realize what's going on, how many she's betrayed?"

"In part. And yet . . ."

"Yet, what?"

Gregor's tone was so low as to be nearly inaudible. "I wish she had been real."

". . . and that's the present tactical situation in the Hub and Vervain local space, as far as my information goes," Miles concluded his presentation to Gregor. They had the *Ariel's* briefing room all to themselves; Arde Mayhew stood guard in the corridor. Miles had begun his speed-precis as soon as Elena reported that the hostile boarders had been successfully secured. He'd paused only to peel out of his ill-fitting armor and back into his Dendarii greys. The armor had been hastily borrowed from the same female soldier who'd lent him kit before, and the plumbing perforce left unconnected.

Miles froze the holovid display in the center of the table. Would that he could freeze real time and events the same way, at the touch of a keypad, that he might halt their terrible rush. "You'll notice our biggest intelligence holes are in precise information about the Cetagandan forces. I'm hoping the Vervani will plug some of those gaps, if we can persuade them we're their allies, and the Rangers may yield more. One way or another.

"Now—sire—the decision lands on you. Fight or flight? I can detach the *Ariel* from the Dendarii right now, to run you home, with little loss to this hot and dirty wormhole fight. Firepower and armor, not speed, are going to be at a premium there. There's not much doubt which course my father and Illyan would vote for."

"No." Gregor stirred. "On the other hand, they aren't here."

"True. Alternately, going to the opposite extreme, do you wish to be commander-in-chief of this mess? In fact, as well as name?"

Gregor smiled softly. "What a temptation. But don't you think there's a certain . . . hubris, in undertaking field leadership without a prior apprenticing in field followership?"

Miles reddened slightly. "I—hem!—face a similar dilemma. You've met the solution, his name's Ky Tung. We'll be conferring with him when we transfer back to the *Triumph,* later." Miles paused. "There are a couple of other things you might do for us. If you choose. Real things."

Gregor rubbed his chin, watching Miles as he might a play. "Trot them out, Lord Vorkosigan."

"Legitimatize the Dendarii. Present them to the Vervani as the Barrayaran pickup force. I can only bluff. Your breath is law. You can conclude a legally binding defensive treaty between Barrayar and Vervain—Aslund too, if we can bring them in. Your greatest value is

—sorry—diplomatic, not military. Go to Vervain Station, and deal with these people. And I do mean deal."

"Safely behind the lines," Gregor noted dryly.

"Only if we win, on the other side of the jump. If we lose, the lines will come to you."

"I would I could be a soldier. Some lowly lieutenant, with only a handful of men to care for."

"There's no moral difference between one and ten thousand, I assure you. You're just as thoroughly damned however many you get killed."

"I want to be in on the fight. Probably the only chance I'll have in my life for real risk."

"What, the risk you run every day from lunatic assassins isn't enough thrill for you? You want more?"

"Active. Not passive. Real service."

"If—in your judgment—the best and most vital service you can give everyone else risking their lives here is as a minor field officer, I will of course support you to the best of my ability," said Miles bleakly.

"Ouch," murmured Gregor. "You can turn a phrase like a knife, you know?" He paused. "Treaties, eh?"

"If you would be so kind, sire."

"Oh, stop it," Gregor sighed. "I will play my assigned part. As always."

"Thank you." Miles thought of offering some apology, some solace, then thought better of it. "The other wild card is Randall's Rangers. Who are now, unless I miss my guess, in considerable disarray. Their second-in-command has vanished, their commander has deserted at the start of the action—how was it the Vervani let her make an exit, by the way?"

"She told them she was going out to confer with you—implied she'd somehow added you to her forces. She was going to jump her fast courier to the hot side immediately thereafter, supposedly."

"Hm. She may have inadvertently paved our way—is she denying involvement with the Cetagandans?"

"I don't think the Vervani have caught on yet about the Rangers opening the door to the Cetagandans. At the time we left Vervain Station they were still putting the Rangers' failures to defend the Cetagandan-side jump down to incompetence."

"Probably with considerable supporting evidence. I doubt the bulk of the Rangers knew about the betrayal, or it couldn't have stayed secret this long. And whatever inner cadre that was working with the

Cetas, were left in the dark when Cavilo took off on her Imperial tangent. You realize, Gregor, you did this? Sabotaged the Cetagandan invasion single-handedly?"

"Oh," breathed Gregor, "it took both hands."

Miles decided not to touch that one. "Anyway—if we can—we need to lock the Rangers down. Get them under control, or at least out from behind everyone's backs."

"Very well."

"I suggest a round of good-guy-bad-guy. I'll be happy to take the part of bad guy."

Cavilo was brought in between two men with hand tractors. She still wore her space armor, now marred and scarred. Her helmet was gone. The armor's weapons packs had been removed, control systems disconnected, and joints locked, turning it into a hundred-kilo prison, tight as a sarcophagus. The two Dendarii soldiers set her upright near the end of the conference table and stepped back with a flourish. A statue with a live head, some Pygmalion-like metamorphosis interrupted and horribly incomplete.

"Thank you, gentlemen, dismissed," said Miles. "Commander Bothari-Jesek, please stay."

Cavilo rolled her short-cropped blonde head in futile resistance, the limit of physically possible motion. She glared furiously at Gregor as the soldiers exited. "You snake," she snarled. "You *bastard.*"

Gregor sat with his elbows on the conference table, chin resting in his hands. He raised his head to say tiredly, "Commander Cavilo, both my parents died violently in political intrigue before I was six years old. A fact you might have researched. Did you think you were dealing with an *amateur?*"

"You were out of your league from the beginning, Cavilo," said Miles, walking slowly around her as if inspecting his prize. Her head turned to follow him, then had to swivel to pick up his orbit on the other side. "You should have stuck to your original contract. Or your second plan. Or your third. You should, in fact, have stuck to *something.* Anything. Your total self-interest didn't make you strong, it made you a rag in the wind, anybody's to pick up. Now, Gregor—though not I—thinks you should be given a chance to earn your worthless life."

"You haven't got the balls to shove me out the airlock." Her eyes were slitted with her rage.

"I wasn't planning to." Since it clearly made her skin crawl, Miles circled her again. "No. Looking ahead—when this is over—I thought

I might give you to the Cetagandans. A treaty tidbit that will cost us nothing, and help turn them up sweet. I imagine they'll be looking for you, don't you?" He fetched up before her and smiled.

Her face drained. The tendons stood out on her slender neck.

Gregor spoke. "But if you do as we ask, I will grant you safe passage out of the Hegen Hub, via Barrayar, when this is over. Together with any surviving remnant of your forces that will still follow you. It will give you a two-month head start on the Cetagandan vengeance for this debacle."

"In fact," put in Miles, "if you play your part, you could even come out of this a heroine. What fun!"

Gregor's glower at him was not entirely feigned.

"I'll get you," Cavilo breathed to Miles.

"It's the best deal you'll get today. Life. Salvage. A new start, far from here—very far from here. That, Simon Illyan will assure. Far away, but not unwatched."

Calculation began to edge out the rage in her eyes. "What do you want me to do?"

"Not much. Yield up what control you still have of your forces to an officer of our choice. Probably a Vervani liaison, they're paying for you, after all. You will introduce your replacement to your chain of command, and retire to the safety of the *Triumph*'s brig for the duration."

"There won't be any surviving remnant of the Rangers when this is done!"

"There is that chance," Miles conceded. "You were going to throw them all away. Note, please, I'm not offering a choice between this and some better deal. It's this or the Cetagandans. Whose approval of treason is strictly limited to those who deal in their favor."

Cavilo looked like she wanted to spit, but said, "Very well. I yield. You have your deal."

"Thank you."

"But you . . ." her eyes were chips of blue ice, her voice low and venomous, "you will learn, little man. You're riding high today, but time will bring you down. I'd say, just wait twenty years, but I doubt you're going to live that long. Time will teach you how much *nothing* your loyalties will buy you. The day they finally grind you up and spit you out, I'm just sorry I won't be there to watch, 'cause you're gonna be *hamburger*."

Miles called the soldiers back in. "Take her away." It was almost a plea. As the door closed behind the prisoner and her porters, he turned to find Elena's eyes upon him.

"God, that woman makes me cold," he shivered.

"Ah?" Gregor remarked, elbows still planted. "Yet in a weird way, you seem to get along with each other. You think alike."

"Gregor!" Miles protested. "Elena?" he called for a counter-vote.

"You're both very twisty," said Elena doubtfully. "And, er, short." At Miles's tight-lipped look of outrage she explained, "It's more a matter of pattern than content. If you were power-crazy, instead of, of . . ."

"Some other kind of crazy, yes, go on."

"—you could plot like that. You seemed to kind of enjoy figuring her out."

"Thank-you-I-think." He hunched his shoulders. Was it true? Could that be himself in twenty years? Sick with cynicism and unvented rage, a shelled self thrilled only by mastery, power games, control, armor-plate with a wounded beast inside?

"Let's get back to the *Triumph,*" he said shortly. "We've all got work to do."

Miles paced impatiently across the short breadth of Admiral Oser's cabin aboard *Triumph.* Gregor leaned hip-slung on the edge of the comconsole desk, watching him oscillate.

". . . naturally the Vervani will be suspicious, but with the Cetagandans breathing down their necks they'll have a real will to believe. And deal. You'll want to make it as attractive as possible, to close things up quickly, but of course don't give away any more than you have to—"

Gregor said dryly, "Perhaps you'd like to come along and operate my holoprompter?"

Miles stopped, cleared his throat. "Sorry. I know you know more about treaties than I do. I . . . babble when I'm nervous, sometimes."

"Yes, I know."

Miles managed to keep his mouth shut, though not his feet still, until the cabin buzzer blatted.

"Prisoners as ordered, sir," came Sergeant Chodak's voice over the intercom.

"Thank you, enter." Miles leaned across the desk and hit the door control.

Chodak and a squad marched Captain Ungari and Sergeant Overholt into the cabin. The prisoners were indeed just as Miles had ordered; washed, shaved, combed, and provided with fresh pressed

Dendarii greys with equivalent rank insignia. They also looked palpa-
bly surly and hostile about it.

"Thank you, Sergeant, you and your squad are dismissed."

"Dismissed?" Chodak's eyebrows questioned the wisdom of this.
"Sure you don't want us to at least stand-to in the corridor, sir?
Remember the last time."

"It won't be necessary this time."

Ungari's glare denied that airy assertion. Chodak withdrew doubtfully, keeping his stunner-aim steady on the pair until the doors
closed across his view.

Ungari inhaled deeply. "Vorkosigan! You mutinous little mutant,
I'm going to have you court-martialed, skinned, stuffed, and
mounted for this—"

They had not yet noticed quiet Gregor, still leaning on the comconsole and also wearing courtesy Dendarii greys, though without
insignia, there being no Dendarii equivalent for emperor.

"Uh, sir—" Miles motioned the dark-faced captain's eye toward
Gregor.

"Those are such widely shared sentiments, Captain Ungari, that
I'm afraid you might have to stand in line and wait your turn,"
Gregor remarked, smiling slightly.

The remaining air went out of Ungari unvoiced. He braced to
attention; to his credit, the uppermost of the wildly mixed emotions
on his face was profound relief. *"Sire."*

"My apologies, Captain," said Miles, "for my high-handed treatment of you and Sergeant Overholt, but I judged my plan for retrieving Gregor too, uh, delicate for, for—" *your nerves,* "I thought I'd
better take personal responsibility." *You were happier not watching,
really. And I was happier not having my elbow jogged.*

"Ensigns don't have personal responsibility for operations of this
magnitude, their commanders do," Ungari snarled. "As Simon Illyan
would have been the first to point out to me if your plan—however
delicate—had failed. . . ."

"Well, then congratulations, sir; you have just rescued the emperor," snapped Miles. "Who, as your commander-in-chief, has a few
orders for you, if you will permit him to get a word in edgewise."

Ungari's teeth closed. With visible effort, he dismissed Miles from
his attention and focused on Gregor. "Sire?"

Gregor spoke. "As the only members of ImpSec within a couple
million kilometers—except for Ensign Vorkosigan, who has other
chores—I'm attaching you and Sergeant Overholt to my person, until
we make contact with our reinforcements. I may also require courier

duties of you. Before we leave the *Triumph,* please share any pertinent intelligence you may possess with Dendarii Ops; they're now my Imperial, uh . . ."

"Most obedient servants," suggested Miles under his breath.

"Forces," Gregor concluded. "Consider that grey suit," (Ungari glanced down at his with loathing) "regulation wear, and respect it accordingly. You'll doubtless get your greens back when I get mine."

Miles put in, "I'll be detaching the Dendarii light cruiser *Ariel* and the faster of our two fast couriers to Gregor's personal service, when you depart for Vervain Station. If you have to split off on courier duties, I suggest you take the smaller ship and leave the *Ariel* with Gregor. Its captain, Bel Thorne, is my most trusted Dendarii shipmaster."

"Still thinking about my line of retreat, eh, Miles?" Gregor raised a brow at him.

Miles bowed slightly. "If things go very wrong, someone must live to avenge us. Not to mention to make damn sure the Dendarii survivors get paid. We owe them that much, I think."

"Yes," Gregor agreed softly.

"I also have my personal report on recent events for you to deliver to Simon Illyan," Miles went on, "in case I—in case you see him before I do." Miles handed Ungari a data disk.

Ungari looked dizzy at this rapid reordering of his priorities. "Vervain Station? Pol Six is where your safety lies, surely, sire."

"Vervain Station is where my duty lies, Captain, and perforce yours. Come along, I'll explain it all as we go."

"Are you leaving Vorkosigan loose?" Ungari frowned at Miles. "With these mercenaries? I have a problem with that, sire."

"I'm sorry, sir," said Miles to Ungari, "that I cannot, cannot . . ." *obey you,* but Miles left that unsaid. "I have a deeper problem with arranging a battle for these mercenaries and then not showing up for it. A difference between myself and . . . the Rangers' former commander. There must be some difference between us, maybe that's it. Gre—the Emperor understands."

"Hm," said Gregor. "Yes. Captain Ungari, I officially detach Ensign Vorkosigan as Our Dendarii liaison. On my personal responsibility. Which should be sufficient even for you."

"It's not me that it has to be sufficient for, sire!"

Gregor hesitated fractionally. "For Barrayar's best interests, then. A sufficient argument even for Simon. Let us go, Captain."

"Sergeant Overholt," Miles added, "you will be the Emperor's personal bodyguard and batman, until relieved."

Overholt looked anything but relieved at this abrupt field promotion. "Sir," he whispered aside to Miles, "I haven't had the advanced course!"

He referred to Simon Illyan's mandatory, personally-conducted ImpSec course for the palace guard, that gave Gregor's usual crew that hard-polished edge.

"We all have a similar problem here, Sergeant, believe me," Miles murmured back. "Do your best."

The *Triumph*'s tactics room was alive with activity, every station chair occupied, every holovid display bright with the flow of ship and fleet tactical changes. Miles stood at Tung's elbow and felt doubly redundant. He bethought of the jape back at the Academy. *Rule 1: Only overrule the tactical computer if you know something it doesn't. Rule 2: The tac comp always knows more than you do.*

This was combat? This muffled chamber, swirl of lights, these padded chairs? Maybe the detachment was a good thing, for commanders. His heart hammered even now. A tac room of this caliber could cause information overload and mind-lock, if you let it. The trick was to pick out what was important, and never, ever to forget that the map was not the territory.

His job here, Miles reminded himself, was not to command. It was to watch Tung command, and learn how he did it, his alternate modes of thinking to Barrayaran Academy Standard. Miles's only legitimate point of overrule might come if some external political/strategic need took precedence over internal tactical logic. Miles prayed that event would not arise, because a shorter and uglier name for it was *betraying your troops.*

Miles's attention sharpened as a little jumpscout winked into existence at the throat of the wormhole. On the tactics display it was a pink point of light in a slowly moving whirlpool of darkness. On a telescreen, it was a slim ship against fixed and distant stars. From its own wired-in pilot's point of view, it was some strange extension of his own body. In yet another vid display, it was a collection of telemetry readouts, numerology, some Platonic ideal. *What is truth? All. None.*

"Sharkbait One reporting to Fleet One," the pilot's voice came over Tung's console. "You have ten minutes clearance. Stand by for tight-beam burst."

Tung spoke into his comm. "Fleet commence Jump, tight by the numbers."

The first Dendarii ship waiting by the wormhole jockeyed into place, glowed brightly in the tac display (though it appeared to do nothing in the televid), and vanished. A second ship followed in thirty seconds, pushing the safety limit of time margins between jumps. Two ships trying to rematerialize in the same place at the same time would result in no ships and a very large explosion.

As the Sharkbait's tightbeam telemetry was digested by the tac comp, the image rotated so that the dark vortex representing (but in no way picturing) the wormhole was suddenly mirrored by an exit vortex. Beyond that exit vortex an array of dots and specks and lines represented ships in flight, maneuvering, firing, fleeing; the hardened Homeside battle station of the Vervani, twin to the Hubside station where Miles had left Gregor; the Cetagandan attackers. A view of their destination at last. All lies, of course, it was minutes out of date.

"Yech," Tung commented. "What a mess. Here we go . . ."

The jump klaxon sounded. It was the *Triumph*'s turn. Miles gripped the back of Tung's chair, though intellectually he knew the feeling of motion was illusory. A whirl of dreams seemed to cloud his mind, for a moment, for an hour; it was unmeasurable. The wrench in his stomach and the godawful wave of nausea that followed were anything but dreamlike. Jump over. A moment of silence throughout the room, as others struggled to overcome their disorientation. Then the murmur picked up where it had left off. *Welcome to Vervain. Take a wormhole jump to hell.*

The tac display spun and shifted, shunting in new data, recentering its little universe. Their wormhole was presently guarded by its beleaguered Station and a thin and battered string of Vervani Navy and Vervani-commanded Ranger ships. The Cetagandans had hit it once already, been driven off, and now hovered out of range awaiting reinforcements for the next strike. Cetagandan re-supply was streaming across the Vervain system from the other wormhole.

The other wormhole had fallen fast, the only way to fly from the attacker's viewpoint. Even with complete surprise on the Cetagandans' side for their massive first strike, the Vervani might have stopped them had not three Ranger ships apparently misunderstood their orders and broken off when they should have counterattacked. But the Cetagandans had secured their bridgehead and begun to pour through.

The second wormhole, Miles's wormhole, had been better equipped for defense—until the panicked Vervani had pulled everything that could be spared back to guard the high orbitals of the homeworld. Miles could scarcely blame them; it was a hard strategic choice either way. But now the Cetagandans boiled across the system practically unimpeded, hopscotching the heavily guarded planet, in a bold attempt to take the Hegen wormhole, if not by surprise, at least at speed.

The first method of choice for attacking a wormhole was by subterfuge, subornment, and infiltration, i.e., to cheat. The second, also preferring subterfuge in its execution, was by an end-run, sending forces around by another route (if there was one) into the contested local space. The third was to open the attack with a sacrifice ship laying down a "sun wall," a massive blanket of nuclear missilettes deployed as a unit, creating a planar wave that cleared near-space of everything including, frequently, the attack ship; but sun walls were costly, rapidly dissipated, and only locally effective. The Cetagandans had attempted to combine all three methods, as the Rangers' disarray and the filthy radioactive fog still outgassing from the vicinity of their first conquest testified.

The fourth approved approach for the problem of frontally attacking a guarded wormhole was to shoot the officer who suggested it. Miles trusted the Cetagandans would work around to that one too, by the time he was done.

Time passed. Miles hooked a station chair into clamps and studied the central display till his eyes watered and his mind threatened to fall into a hypnotic fugue, then rose and shook himself and circulated among the duty stations, kibbitzing.

The Cetagandans maneuvered. The sudden and unexpected arrival of the Dendarii force during the lull had thrown them into temporary confusion; their planned final attack on the strained Vervani must needs be converted on the fly into yet another softening-up round of hit-and-run. Expensive. At this point the Cetagandans had few ways of concealing their numbers or movements. The defending Dendarii had the implication of hidden reserves (who knew how unlimited? Not Miles, certainly) concealed on the other side of the jump. A brief hope flared in Miles that this threat alone might be enough to make the Cetagandans break off the attack.

"Naw," sighed Tung when Miles confided this optimistic thought. "They're too far into it now. The butcher's bill's too high already for them to pretend they were only fooling. Even to themselves. A Cetagandan commander who packed it in now would go home to a court martial. They'll keep going long after it's hopeless, as their brass tries desperately to cover their bleeding asses with a flag of victory."

"That is . . . vile."

"That is the system, son, and not just for the Cetagandans. One of the system's several built-in defects. And besides," Tung grinned briefly, "it's not as hopeless as all that yet. A fact we will try to conceal from them."

The Cetagandan forces began to move, their directions and accelerations telegraphing their intention for a pounding pass. The trick was to try for local concentrations of force, three or four ships ganging up on one, overwhelming the defender's plasma mirrors. The Dendarii and Vervani would attempt an identical strategy against Cetagandan stragglers, but for a few bravura captains on both sides equipped with the new imploder lances playing an insane game of chicken, trying to put a target within the weapon's short range. Miles also tried to keep one eye on the Rangers' dispositions. Not every Ranger ship had Vervani advisors aboard, and battle arrays that put the Rangers in front of the Cetagandans were much to be preferred to ones that put Rangers behind Dendarii backs.

The quiet murmur of techs and computers within the tactics room scarcely changed pace. There ought to be a flourish of drums, bagpipes, something to herald this dance with death. But if reality broke in at all to this upholstered bubble, it would be sudden, absolute, and over.

A vid-comm message interrupted, intra-ship—yes, there was still a real ship encasing them—a breathless officer reporting to Tung. "Brig, sir. Watch yourselves up there. We've had a break-out. Admiral Oser's escaped, and he let all the other prisoners out too."

"Dammit," said Tung, glared at Miles, and pointed to the comm. "*Handle* that. Jack up Auson." He turned his attention back to his tactics display, muttering. "This wouldn't have happened in *my* day."

Miles slipped into the comm chair, and paged the *Triumph*'s bridge. "Auson! Did you get the word on Oser?"

Auson's irritated face appeared, "Yeah, we're working on it."

"Order extra commando guards to the tactics room, engineering, and your own bridge. This is a real bad time for interruptions down here."

"Tell me. We can see the Ceta bastards coming." Auson punched off.

Miles began monitoring internal security channels, pausing only to note the arrival of well-armed guards in the corridor. Oser had clearly had help in his escape, some loyal Oseran officer or officers, which made Miles wonder in turn about the security of the security guards. And would Oser try to combine with Metzov and Cavilo? A couple of Dendarii imprisoned for disciplinary infractions were found wandering the corridors and returned to the brig; another came back on his own. A suspected spy was cornered in a storeroom. No sign yet of the truly dangerous . . .

"There he goes!"

Miles keyed in the channel. A cargo shuttle was breaking out of its clamps, away from the side of the *Triumph* and into space.

Miles overrode channels, found fire control. "Don't, repeat, *Do not* open fire on that shuttle!"

"Uh . . ." came the reply. "Yes, sir. Do not open fire."

Why did Miles get the subliminal impression that tech hadn't been planning to open fire in the first place? Clearly a well-coordinated escape. The witch-hunt later was going to be nasty. "Patch me through to that shuttle!" Miles demanded of the comm officer. *And, oh yes, send a guard to the shuttle hatch corridors* . . . too late.

"I'll try, sir, but they're not answering."

"How many aboard?"

"Several, but we're not sure exactly—"

"Patch me through. They've got to listen, even if they won't reply."

"I have a channel, sir, but I have no idea if they're listening."

"I'll try it." Miles took a breath. "Admiral Oser! Turn your shuttle around and come back to the *Triumph.* It's too dangerous out there, you're running headlong into a fire zone. Return, and I will personally guarantee your safety—"

Tung was looking down over Miles's shoulder. "He's trying to make it to the *Peregrine.* Dammit, if that ship pulls out, our defensive array will collapse."

Miles glanced back at the tac comp. "Surely not. I thought we put the *Peregrine* in the reserve area precisely because we doubted its reliability."

"Yes, but if the *Peregrine* pulls out I can name three other captain-owners who will follow it. And if four ships pull out—"

"The Rangers will break despite their Vervani commander, and we'll be cooked, right, I see." Miles glanced again at the tac comp. "I don't think he's going to make it—Admiral Oser! Can you read me?"

"Yike!" Tung returned to his seat, absorbed in the Cetagandans once again. Four Cetagandan ships were combining against the edge of the Dendarii formation, while another attempted to penetrate the center, clearly trying to close the range for a lance attack. Casually, in passing, a Cetagandan plasma gunner from it picked off the stray shuttle. Just bright sparks.

"He didn't know the Cetagandans were making their attack run till his stolen shuttle cleared the *Triumph*," Miles whispered. "Good plan, rotten timing. . . . He could have turned around, he chose to try and run for it. . . ." Oser chose his death? Was that the comforting argument?

The Cetagandans did not so much break off their attack run as complete it, in depressingly good order. The score was slightly in the Dendarii's favor. A number of Cetagandan ships had been badly chewed, and one blown up entirely. Dendarii and Ranger damage control channels were frantic. The Dendarii had not lost ships yet, but had lost fire-power, engines, flight control, life support, shielding. The next attack run would be more devastating.

They can afford to lose three to our one. If they keep coming, keep nibbling, they must inevitably win, Miles reflected coldly. *Unless we are reinforced.*

Hours passed, while the Cetagandans formed up again. Miles took short breaks in the wardroom provided for that purpose off the tactics room, but was too keyed up to emulate Tung's amazing fifteen-minute instant naps. Miles knew Tung wasn't faking relaxation for morale effect; nobody could simulate such a disgusting snore.

It was possible to watch the Cetagandan reinforcements coming on across the Vervain system in the televid. That was the time trade-off, the risk. The longer the Cetas waited, the better-equipped they could be, but the longer they waited, the better the chance that their enemies would recover too. There was doubtless a tac comp aboard the Cetagandan command ship that had generated a probability curve marking the optimum intersection of Us and Them. If only the damned Vervani would be more aggressive in attacking that supply stream from their planetary base. . . .

And here they came on again. Tung watched his displays, his hands unconsciously clenching and unclenching in his lap between jerky, thick-fingered dances on his control panel, sending orders, correcting, anticipating. Miles's fingers twitched in tiny echoes, his mind trying to get around Tung's thought, to absorb everything. Their picture of reality was getting lacy with hidden holes, as data points dropped out due to damaged sensors or senders on various ships. The Cetagandans flew through the Dendarii formation, pounding . . . a Dendarii ship blew apart, another, weapons dead, tried to scramble out of range, three Ranger ships broke away as a unit . . . it looked bad. . . .

"*Sharkbait Three* reporting," an abrupt voice overrode all other comm channels, making Miles jump in his seat. "Hold this wormhole *clear.* Help coming."

"Not *now,"* snarled Tung, but began to attempt a rapid re-deployment to cover the tiny volume of space, keep it clear of debris, missiles, enemy fire, and most of all enemy ships with imploder lances. Those Cetagandan ships that were in position to respond seemed almost to prick their ears, hesitating as Dendarii ship movements telegraphed *changes coming.* The Dendarii might be in retreat . . . some exploitable opportunity might be about to open up. . . .

"Whatinhell's *that?"* Tung said, as something huge and temporarily indecipherable appeared in the throat of the wormhole and began instantly to accelerate. He punched up readouts. "It's too big to be that fast. It's too fast to be that *big."*

Miles recognized the energy profile even before the televiewer yielded up a visual. *What a shakedown cruise they're having.* "It's the *Prince Serg.* Our Barrayaran Imperial reinforcements have just arrived." He took a dizzy breath. "Did I not promise you . . ."

Tung swore horribly, in pure aesthetic admiration. Other ships followed, Aslunder, Polian Navy, spreading out rapidly into attack—not defensive—formation.

The ripple in the Cetagandan formations was like a silent cry of dismay. An imploder-armed Cetagandan ship dove bravely at the *Prince Serg,* and was sliced in half discovering that the *Serg's* imploder lances had been improved to triple the Cetagandans' range. That was the first mortal blow.

The second came over the commlink, a call to the Cetagandan aggressors to surrender or be destroyed—in the name of the Hegen Alliance Navy, Emperor Gregor Vorbarra and Admiral Count Aral Vorkosigan, Joint Commanders.

For a moment, Miles thought Tung was about to faint. Tung inhaled alarmingly, and bellowed with delight, "Aral Vorkosigan! Here? Hot damn!" And in an only slightly more private whisper, "How'd they lure him out of retirement? Maybe I'll get to meet him!"

Tung the military history nut was one of Miles's father's most fanatical fans, Miles recalled, and until and unless firmly suppressed could rattle off every public detail of the Barrayaran admiral's early campaigns. "I'll see what I can arrange," Miles promised.

"If you can arrange *that,* son. . . ." With an effort, Tung pulled his mind away from his beloved hobby of studying military history and back to his (admittedly, closely related) job of making it.

The Cetagandan ships were breaking, first in panicked singles and then in more coordinated groups, trying to organize a properly covered retreat. The *Prince Serg* and its support group did not waste a millisecond, but followed up instantly, attacking and disordering attempted self-covering arrays of enemy ships, worrying the resulting stragglers. In the ensuing hours the retreat became a true rout when the Vervani ships protecting their high planetary orbitals, encouraged, at last broke orbit and joined the attack. The Vervani reserve was merciless, in the terror for their homes the Cetagandans had instilled in them.

The mopping-up detail, the appalling damage control problems, the personnel rescues, were so absorbing that it took Miles those several hours to gradually realize the war was over for the Dendarii fleet. They had done their job.

17

Before departing the tactics room, Miles prudently checked with the *Triumph*'s security to determine how their roundup of escaped prisoners was progressing. Missing and still unaccounted for remained Oser, the *Peregrine*'s captain and two other loyal Oseran officers, Commander Cavilo, and General Metzov.

Miles was fairly certain he had witnessed Oser and his officers converted to radioactive ash in his monitors. Had Metzov and Cavilo been aboard that fleeing shuttle too? Fine irony, for Cavilo to die at the hands of the Cetagandans after all. Though—admittedly—it would have been equally ironic had she died at the hands of the Vervani, Randall's Rangers, the Aslunders, the Barrayarans, or anyone else she'd double-crossed in her brief, cometary career in the Hegen Hub. Her end was neat and convenient if true, but—he didn't like to think that her last, savage remarks to him had now acquired the prophetic weight of a dying curse. He ought to fear Metzov more than Cavilo. He ought to, but he didn't. He shuddered, and borrowed a commando guard for the walk back to his cabin.

On the way, he encountered a shuttle-load of wounded being transferred to the *Triumph*'s sickbay. The *Triumph*, in the reserve group (such as it was) had taken no hits its shields couldn't handle, but other ships had not been so fortunate. Space battle casualty lists usually had the proportions reversed from planetary, the dead out-numbering the wounded, yet in lucky circumstances where the artificial environment was preserved, soldiers might survive their injuries. Uncertainly, Miles changed course and followed the procession along. What good could he do in sickbay?

The triage people had not sent minor cases to the *Triumph.* Three hideous burns and a massive head injury went to the head of the line, and were whisked off by the anxiously waiting staff. A few soldiers were conscious, quietly waiting their turns, immobilized with air bag braces on their float pallets, eyes cloudy with pain and pain-killers.

Miles tried to say a few words to each. Some stared uncomprehendingly, some seemed to appreciate it; he lingered a little longer with these, giving what encouragement he could. He then withdrew and stood dumbly by the door for several minutes, awash in the familiar, terrifying odors of a sickbay after a battle, disinfectants and blood, burnt meat, urine, and electronics, until he realized exhaustion was making him thoroughly stupid and useless, shaky and near-tears. He pushed off from the wall and stumped out. Bed. If anyone really wanted his command presence, they could come find him.

He hit the code lock on Oser's cabin. Now that he'd inherited it, he supposed he ought to change the numbers. He sighed and entered. As he stepped inside he became conscious of two unfortunate facts. First, although he had dismissed his commando guard upon entering sickbay, he had forgotten to call him back, and second, he was not alone. The door closed behind him before he could recoil into the corridor, and he banged into it backing up.

The dusky red hue of General Metzov's face was even more arresting to the eye than the silver gleam of the nerve disruptor parabola in his hand, aim centered on Miles's head.

Metzov had somehow acquired a set of Dendarii greys, a little small for him. Commando Cavilo, standing behind Metzov, had acquired a similar set, a little large for her. Metzov looked huge and furious. Cavilo looked . . . strange. Bitter, ironic, weirdly amused. Bruises marred her neck. She bore no weapon.

"Got you," Metzov whispered triumphantly. "At last." With a rictus smile, he advanced stepwise on Miles till he could pin him to the wall by his neck with one big hand. He dropped the nerve disruptor with a clatter and wrapped the other hand around Miles's neck, not to break but to squeeze it.

"You'll never survive—" was all Miles managed to choke out before his air pinched off. He could feel his trachea begin to crunch, crumpling, his head felt on the verge of dark explosion as his blood supply was cut off. No talking Metzov out of *this* murder. . . .

Cavilo slipped forward, crouching, soundless and unnoticed as a cat, to take up the dropped nerve disruptor, then step back, around to Miles's left.

"Stanis, darling," she cooed. Metzov, obsessed with Miles's lingering strangulation, did not turn his head. Cavilo, clearly imitating Metzov's cadences, recited. " 'Open your legs to me, you bitch, or I'll blow your brains out.' "

Metzov's head twisted round then, his eyes widening. She blew his brains out. The crackling blue bolt hit him square between the eyes. He almost snapped Miles's neck, plastic-reinforced though those bones were, in his last convulsion, before he dropped to the deck. The blistering electrochemical smell of nerve-disruptor death slapped Miles in the face.

Miles sagged frozen against the wall, not daring to move. He raised his eyes from the corpse to Cavilo. Her lips were curved in a smile of immense satisfaction, satiated. Had Cavilo's line been a direct and recent quote? What had they been doing, all the long hours they must have been waiting in the hunter's blind of Oser's cabin? The silence lengthened.

"Not," Miles swallowed, trying to clear his bruised throat, and croaked, "not that I'm complaining, mind you, but why aren't you going ahead and shooting me too?"

Cavilo smirked. "A quick revenge is better than none. A slow and lingering one is better still, but to savor it fully I must survive it. Another day, kid." She tilted the nerve disruptor up as if to flourish it into a holster, then let it hang pointed down by her side in her relaxed hand. "You've sworn you'll see me safe out of the Hegen Hub, Vor lord. And I've come to believe you are actually stupid enough to keep your word. Not that I'm complaining, mind you. Now, if Oser had issued more than one weapon between us, or if he'd given the nerve disruptor to me and the code to his cabin to Stanis and not the other way around, or if Oser'd taken us with him as I begged . . . things might have worked out differently."

Very differently. Very slowly, and very, very carefully, Miles inched over to the comconsole and called security. Cavilo watched him thoughtfully. After a few moments, coming up on the time they might expect the reinforcements to storm in, she strolled over to his side. "I underestimated you, you know."

"I never underestimated you."

"I know. I'm not used to that . . . thank you." Contemptuously, she tossed the nerve disruptor onto Metzov's body. Then, with a sudden baring of her teeth, she wheeled, wrapped an arm around Miles's neck, and kissed him vigorously. Her timing was perfect; Security, Elena and Sergeant Chodak in the lead, burst through the door just before Miles managed to fight her off.

Miles stepped from the *Triumph's* shuttle through the short flex tube and on board the *Prince Serg.* He stared around enviously at the clean, spacious, beautifully-lit corridor, at the row of smart and gleaming honor guards snapping to attention, at the polished officers waiting in their Barrayaran Imperial dress greens. He stole an anxious glance down at his own Dendarii grey-and-whites. The *Triumph,* key and pride of the Dendarii fleet, seemed to shrink into something small and gritty and battered and used.

Yeah, but you guys would not look so pretty now if we had not used ourselves so hard, Miles consoled himself.

Tung, Elena, and Chodak were all goggling like tourists too. Miles called them firmly to attention to receive and return the crisp welcoming salutes of their hosts.

"I'm Commander Natochini, executive officer of the *Prince Serg,*" the senior Barrayaran introduced himself. "Lieutenant Yegorov, here, will escort you and Commander Bothari-Jesek to Admiral Vorkosigan for your meeting, Admiral Naismith. Commodore Tung, I will be personally conducting your tour of the *Prince Serg,* and will be pleased to answer any of your questions. If the answers aren't classified, of course."

"Of course." Tung's broad face looked immensely pleased. In fact, if Tung grew any smugger he might implode.

"We will join Admiral Vorkosigan for lunch in the senior officers' mess, after your meeting and our tour," Commander Natochini continued to Miles. "Our last dinner guest there was the President of Pol and his entourage, twelve days ago."

Certain that the mercenaries understood the magnitude of the privilege they were being granted, the Barrayaran exec led the happy Tung and Chodak off down the corridor. Miles heard Tung chuckle under his breath, "Lunch with Admiral Vorkosigan, heh, heh. . . ."

Lieutenant Yegorov motioned Miles and Elena in the opposite direction. "You are Barrayaran, ma'am?" he inquired of Elena.

"My father was liege-sworn Armsman to the late Count Piotr for eighteen years," Elena stated. "He died in the Count's service."

"I see," said the lieutenant respectfully. "You are acquainted with the family, then." *That explains you,* Miles could almost see him thinking.

"Ah, yes."

The lieutenant glanced down a little more dubiously at "Admiral Naismith." "And, uh, I understand you are Betan, sir?"

"Originally," said Miles, in his flattest Betan accent.

"You . . . may find the way we Barrayarans do things to be a little more formal than what you're used to," the lieutenant warned. "The Count, you understand, is accustomed to the respect and deference due his rank."

Miles watched, delighted, as the earnest officer sought a polite way of saying, *Call him sir, don't wipe your nose on your sleeve, and none of your damned Betan egalitarian backchat, either.* "You may find him rather formidable," Yegorov concluded.

"A real stuffed shirt, eh?"

The lieutenant frowned. "He is a great man."

"Aw, I bet if we pour enough wine into him at lunch, he'll loosen up and tell dirty stories with the best of 'em."

Yegorov's polite smile became fixed. Elena, eyes dancing, leaned down and whispered forcefully, "Admiral, behave!"

"Oh, all right," Miles sighed regretfully.

The lieutenant glanced gratefully at Elena, over Miles's head.

Miles admired the spit and polish, in passing. Besides just being new, the *Prince Serg* had been designed with diplomacy as well as war in mind, a ship fit to carry the emperor on state visits without loss of military efficiency. He saw a young ensign, down a cross-corridor that had a wall panel apart, directing some tech crew on minor repairs—no, by God, it was original installation. The *Prince Serg* had broken orbit with work crews still aboard, Miles had heard. He glanced back over his shoulder. *There but for the grace of God and General Metzov go I.* If he'd kept his nose clean on Kyril Island for just six months . . . he felt an illogical twinge of envy for that busy ensign.

They entered officers' country. Lieutenant Yegorov led them through an antechamber and into a spartanly-appointed flag office twice the size of anything Miles had seen on a Barrayaran ship before. Admiral Count Aral Vorkosigan looked up from his comconsole desk as the doors slid silently back.

Miles stepped through, his belly suddenly shaking inside. To conceal and control his emotion he tossed off, "Hey, you Imperial snails are going to go all fat and soft, lolling around in this kind of luxury, y'know?"

"Ha!" Admiral Vorkosigan stumbled out of his chair and banged around the corner of his desk in his haste. *Well, no wonder, how can he see with all that water standing in his eyes?* He enfolded Miles in a hard embrace. Miles grinned and blinked and swallowed, face smashed against that cool green sleeve, and almost had control of his features again when Count Vorkosigan held him out at arm's length for an anxious, searching inspection. "You all right, boy?"

"Just fine. How'd you like your wormhole jump?"

"Just fine," breathed Count Vorkosigan back. "Mind you, there were moments when certain of my advisors wanted to have you shot. And there were moments when I agreed with 'em."

Lieutenant Yegorov, cut off in mid-announcement of their arrival (Miles hadn't heard him speaking, and he doubted his father had either), was standing with his mouth still open, looking perfectly stunned. Lieutenant Jole, suppressing a grin himself, arose from the other side of the comconsole desk and guided Yegorov gently and mercifully back out the door. "Thank you, Lieutenant. The Admiral appreciates your services, that will be all. . . ." Jole glanced back over his shoulder, quirked a pensive brow, and followed Yegorov out. Miles just glimpsed the blond lieutenant drape himself across a chair in the antechamber, head back in the relaxed posture of a man anticipating a long wait, before the door slid closed. Jole could be supernaturally courteous at times.

"Elena." With an effort, Count Vorkosigan broke away from Miles to take both Elena's hands in a firm brief grip. "You are well?"

"Yes, sir."

"That pleases me . . . more than I can say. Cordelia sends her love and her best hopes. If I saw you, I was to remind you, ah—I must get the phrase exact, it was one of her Betan cracks—'Home is where, when you have to go there, they have to take you in.'"

"I can hear her voice," smiled Elena. "Tell her thank you. Tell her . . . I will remember."

"Good." Count Vorkosigan pressed her no further. "Sit, sit," he waved them at chairs, which he snugged up closed to the comconsole desk,and sat himself. For an instant, changing gears, his features relaxed, then concentrated with attention once again. *God, he looks tired,* Miles realized; for a split second, almost ghastly. *Gregor, you have much to answer for.* But Gregor knew that.

"What's the latest word on the cease-fire?" Miles asked.

"Still holding nicely, thank you. The only Cetagandan ships that haven't jumped back where they came from, had damaged Necklin rods or control systems or injured pilots. Or all three. We're letting them repair two of them and jump them out with skeleton crews, the rest are not salvageable. I estimate controlled commercial travel could resume in six weeks."

Miles shook his head. "So ends the Five-Day War. I never once saw a Cetagandan face-to-face. All that effort and bloodshed, just to return to the status quo ante."

"Not quite for everyone. A number of Cetagandan senior officers have been recalled to their capital, to explain their 'unauthorized adventure' to their emperor. Their apologies are expected to be fatal."

Miles snorted. "Expiate their failure, rather. 'Unauthorized adventure.' Does anyone believe that? Why do they even bother?"

"Finesse, boy. A retreating enemy should be offered all the face he can carry off. Just don't let him carry off anything else."

"I understand you finessed the Polians. All this time, I expected it would be Simon Illyan to show up in person to haul us lost boys home."

"He longed to come, but there was no way we could both leave home at the same time. The wobbly cover we'd put over Gregor's absence could have collapsed at any moment."

"How did you pull that one off, by the way?"

"Picked out a young officer who looked a lot like Gregor, told him there was an assassination plot afoot against the Emperor and that he was to be the bait. Bless him, he volunteered at once. He—and his Security, who had the same tale told them—spent the next several weeks leading a life of ease down at Vorkosigan Surleau, eating off the best plates—but with indigestion. We finally sent him off on a rustic camping trip, as inquiries from the capital were getting pressing. People will twig soon, I'm sure, if they haven't already, but now we've got Gregor back we can explain it away any way we like. Any way *he* likes." Count Vorkosigan frowned an odd brief frown, odd because not wholly displeased.

"I was surprised," said Miles, "though very happy, that you got your forces past Pol so fast. I was afraid they wouldn't let you through till the Cetagandans were in the Hub. And then it would be too late."

"Yes, well, that's the other reason you got me instead of Simon. As Prime Minister and former Regent, it was perfectly reasonable for me to make a state visit to Pol. We came up with a quick list of the top five diplomatic concessions they've been wanting from us for years, and suggested it for an agenda.

"It being all formal and official and aboveboard, it was then perfectly reasonable for us to combine my visit with the *Prince Serg*'s shakedown cruise. We were in orbit at Pol, shuttling up and down to official receptions and parties," (his hand unconsciously rubbed his abdomen in a pain-warding motion) "with me still trying desperately to talk our way into the Hub without shooting anybody, when word of the Cetagandan surprise attack on Vervain broke. At that point, getting permission to proceed was suddenly expedited. And we were only days, not weeks, away from the action. Getting the Aslunders to lie down with the Polians was a trickier matter. Gregor astonished me, handling that. The Vervani were no problem, they were highly motivated to seek allies by then."

"I hear Gregor is now quite popular on Vervain."

"He's being feted in their capital even as we speak, I believe." Count Vorkosigan glanced at his chrono. "They've gone wild over him. Letting him ride shotgun in the *Prince Serg*'s tac room may have been a better idea that I thought. Purely from a diplomatic stand-point." Count Vorkosigan looked rather abstracted.

"It . . . astonished me, that you permitted him to jump with you into the fire zone. I hadn't expected that."

"Well, when you came down to it, the *Prince Serg*'s fleet tac room had to have been among the most tightly defended few cubic meters anywhere in Vervain local space. It was, it was . . ."

Miles watched with fascination as his father tried to spit out the words *perfectly safe,* and gagged on them instead. Light dawned. "It wasn't your idea, was it? Gregor ordered himself aboard!"

"He had several good arguments to support his position," Count Vorkosigan said. "The propaganda angle certainly seems to be bear-ing fruit."

"I thought you'd be too . . . prudent. To permit him the risk."

Count Vorkosigan studied his own square hands. "I was not in love with the idea, no. But I once swore an oath to serve an emperor. The most morally dangerous moment for a guardian is when the tempta-tion to become a puppet-master seems most rational. I always knew the moment must . . . no. I knew that if the moment *never* came, I should have failed my oath most profoundly." He paused. "It was still a shock to the system, though. The letting-go."

Gregor faced you down? Oh, to have been a fly on the wall of *that* chamber.

"Even with you to practice on, all these years," Count Vorkosigan added meditatively.

"Ah . . . how's your ulcers?"

Count Vorkosigan grimaced. "Don't ask." He brightened slightly.

"Better, the last three days. I may actually demand food for lunch, instead of that miserable medical mush."

Miles cleared his throat. "How's Captain Ungari?"

Count Vorkosigan twitched a lip. "He's not overly pleased with you."

"I . . . cannot apologize. I made a lot of mistakes, but disobeying his order to wait on Aslund Station wasn't one of them."

"Apparently not." Count Vorkosigan frowned at the far wall. "And yet . . . I'm more than ever convinced the regular Service is not the place for you. It's like trying to fit a square peg—no, worse than that. Like trying to fit a tesseract into a round hole."

Miles suppressed a twinge of panic. "I won't be discharged, will I?"

Elena regarded her fingernails and put in, "If you were, you could get a job as a mercenary. Just like General Metzov. I understand Commander Cavilo is looking for a few good men." Miles nearly meowed at her; she traded a smirk for his exasperated look.

"I was almost sorry to learn that Metzov was killed," remarked Count Vorkosigan. "We'd been planning to try and extradite him, before things went crazy with Gregor's disappearance."

"Ah! Did you finally decide the death of that Komarran prisoner way back when during their revolt was murder? I thought it might be—"

Count Vorkosigan held up two fingers. "Two murders."

Miles paused. "My God, he didn't try and track down poor Ahn before he left, did he?" He'd almost forgotten Ahn.

"No, but we tracked him down. Though not, alas, before Metzov had left Barrayar. And yes, the Komarran rebel had been tortured to death. Not wholly intentionally, he apparently had had some hidden medical weakness. But it was not, as the original investigator had suspected, in revenge for the death of the guard. It was the other way around. The Barrayaran guard corporal, who had participated in or at least acquiesced to the torture, though over some feeble protest, according to Ahn—the corporal suffered a revulsion of feeling, and threatened to turn Metzov in.

"Metzov murdered him in one of his panic-rages, then made Ahn help him cook up and vouch for the cover story about the escape. So Ahn was twice tainted with the thing. Metzov kept Ahn in terror, yet was equally in Ahn's power if the facts ever came out, a kind of strange lock on each other . . . which Ahn at last escaped. Ahn seemed almost relieved, and volunteered to be fast-penta'd, when Illyan's agents came for him."

Miles thought of the weatherman with regret. "Will anything bad happen to Ahn now?"

"We'd planned to make him testify, at Metzov's trial . . . Illyan thought we might even turn it to our favor, with respect to the Komarrans. Present that poor idiot guard corporal to them as an unsung hero. Hang Metzov as proof of the emperor's good faith and commitment to justice for Barrayarans and Komarrans alike . . . nice scenario." Count Vorkosigan frowned bitterly. "I think we will quietly drop it now. Again."

Miles puffed out his breath. "Metzov. A goat to the end. Must be some bad karma, clinging to him . . . not that he didn't earn it."

"Beware of wishing for justice. You might get it."

"I've already learned that, sir."

"Already?" Count Vorkosigan cocked an eyebrow at him. "Hm."

"Speaking of justice," Miles seized the opening. "I'm concerned over the matter of Dendarii pay. They took a lot of damage, more than a mercenary fleet will usually tolerate. Their only contract was my breath and voice. If . . . if the Imperium does not back me, I will be forsworn."

Count Vorkosigan smiled slightly. "We have already considered the matter."

"Will Illyan's covert ops budget stretch, to cover this?"

"Illyan's budget would burst trying to cover this. But you, ah, seem to have a friend in a high place. We will draw you an emergency credit chit from ImpSec, this fleet's fund, and the Emperor's privy purse, and hope to recoup it all later from a special appropriation rammed through the Council of Ministers and the Council of Counts. Submit a bill."

Miles fished a data disk from his pocket. "Here, sir. From the Dendarii fleet accountant. She was up all night. Some damage estimates are still preliminary." He set it on the comconsole desk.

One corner of Count Vorkosigan's mouth twisted up. "You're learning, boy. . . ." He inserted the disk in his desk for a fast scan. "I'll have a credit chit prepared over lunch. You can take it with you when you depart."

"Thank you, sir."

"Sir," Elena put in, leaning forward earnestly, "what will happen to the Dendarii fleet now?"

"Whatever it chooses, I presume. Though they cannot linger, this close to Barrayar."

"Are we to be abandoned again?" asked Elena.

"Abandoned?"

"You made us an Imperial force, once. I thought. Baz thought. Then Miles left us, and then . . . nothing."

"Just like Kyril Island," Miles remarked. "Out of sight, out of mind." He shrugged dolefully. "I gather they suffered a similar deterioration of morale."

Count Vorkosigan gave him a sharp look. "The fate of the Dendarii —like your future military career, Miles—is a matter still under discussion."

"Do I get to be in on that discussion? Do they?"

"We'll let you know." Count Vorkosigan planted his hands on his desktop, and rose. "That's all I can say now, even to you. Lunch, officers?"

Miles and Elena perforce rose too. "Commodore Tung knows nothing of our real relationship yet," Miles cautioned. "If you wish to keep that covert, I'm going to have to play Admiral Naismith when we rejoin him."

Count Vorkosigan's smile turned peculiar. "Illyan and Captain Ungari must certainly favor not breaking a potentially useful cover identity. By all means. Should be fascinating."

"I should warn you, Admiral Naismith is not very deferential."

Elena and Count Vorkosigan looked at each other, and both broke into laughter. Miles waited, wrapped in what dignity he could muster, till they subsided. Finally.

Admiral Naismith was painfully polite during lunch. Even Lieutenant Yegorov could have found no fault.

The Vervani government courier handed the credit chit across the homeside station commandant's comconsole desk. Miles testified receipt of it with thumbprint, retina scan, and Admiral Naismith's flourishing illegible scrawl, nothing at all like Ensign Vorkosigan's careful signature. "It's a pleasure doing business with you honorable gentlemen," Miles said, pocketing the chit with satisfaction and carefully sealing the pocket.

"It's the least we can do," said the jumppoint station commandant. "I cannot tell you my emotions, knowing that the next pass the Cetagandans made was going to be their last, nerving to fight to the end, when the Dendarii materialized to reinforce us."

"The Dendarii couldn't have done it alone," said Miles modestly. "All we did was help you hold the bridgehead till the real big guns arrived."

"And if it had not been held, the Hegen Alliance forces—the big guns, as you say—could not have jumped into Vervani local space."

"Not without great cost, certainly," Miles conceded.

The station commandant glanced at his chrono. "Well, my planet will be expressing its opinion of that in more tangible form quite shortly. May I escort you to the ceremony, Admiral? It's time."

"Thank you." Miles rose, and preceded him out of his office, his hand rechecking the tangible thanks in his pocket. *Medals, huh. Medals buy no fleet repairs.*

He paused at a transparent portal, caught half by the vista from the jump station and half by his own reflection. Oseran/Dendarii dress greys were all right, he decided; soft grey velvet tunic set off with blinding white trim and silver buttons on the shoulders, matching trousers and grey synthasuede boots. He fancied the outfit made him look taller. Perhaps he would keep the design.

Beyond the portal floated a scattering of ships, Dendarii, Ranger, Vervani and Alliance. The *Prince Serg* was not among them, being now in orbit above the Vervani homeworld while high-level—literally—talks continued, hammering out the details of the permanent treaty of friendship, commerce, tariff reduction, mutual defense pact, &etc, among Barrayar, Vervain, Aslund and Pol. Gregor, Miles had heard, was being quite luminous in both the public relations and the actual nuts and bolts part of the business. *Better you than me, boy.* The Vervani jumppoint station was letting its own repairs schedule slacken to lend aid to the Dendarii; Baz was working around the clock. Miles tore himself away from the vista and followed the station commandant.

They paused in the corridor outside the large briefing room where the ceremony was to take place, waiting for the attendees to settle. The Vervani apparently wished the principals to make a grand entrance. The commandant went in to prepare. The audience was not large—too much vital work going on—but the Vervani had scraped up enough warm bodies to make it look respectable, and Miles had contributed a platoon of convalescent Dendarii to fluff up the crowd. He would accept on their behalf, in his speech, he decided.

As Miles waited, he saw Commander Cavilo arrive with her Barrayaran honor guard. As far as he knew, the Vervani were not yet aware that the honor-guard's weapons were lethally charged and they had orders to shoot to kill if their prisoner attempted escape. Two hard-faced women in Barrayaran auxiliary uniforms made sure Cavilo was watched both night and day. Cavilo did a good job of ignoring their presence.

The Ranger dress uniform was a neater version of their fatigues, in tan, black, and white, subliminally reminding Miles of a guard dog's fur. *This bitch bites,* he reminded himself. Cavilo smiled and drifted up to Miles. She reeked of her poisonous green-scented perfume; she must have bathed in it.

Miles tilted his head in salute, reached into a pocket, and took out two nose filters. He thrust one up each nostril, where they expanded softly to create a seal, and inhaled deeply to test them. Working fine. They would filter out much smaller molecules than the vile organics of that damned perfume. Miles breathed out through his mouth.

Cavilo watched this performance with an expression of thwarted fury. *"Damn* you," she muttered.

Miles shrugged, palms out, as if to say, *What would you have of me?* "Are you and your survivors about ready to move out?"

"Right after this idiot charade. I have to abandon six ships, too damaged to jump."

"Sensible of you. If the Vervani don't catch on to you soon, the Cetagandans, when they realize they can't get at you themselves, will probably tell them the ugly truth. You shouldn't linger in these parts."

"I don't intend to. If I never see this place again it will be too soon. That goes double for you, mutant. If not for you . . ." she shook her head bitterly.

"By the way," Miles added, "the Dendarii have now been paid three times for this operation. Once by our original contractors the Aslunders, once by the Barrayarans, and once by the grateful Vervani. Each agreed to cover all our expenses in full. Leaves a very tidy profit."

She actually hissed. "You better *pray* we never meet again."

"Goodbye, then."

They entered the chamber to collect their honors. Would Cavilo have the iron nerve to accept hers on behalf of the Rangers her twisted plots had destroyed? Yes, it turned out. Miles gagged quietly.

The first medal I ever won, Miles thought as the station commandant pinned his on him with embarrassingly fulsome praise, *and I can't even wear it at home.* The medal, the uniform, and Admiral Naismith himself must soon return to the closet. Forever? The life of Ensign Vorkosigan was not too attractive, by comparison. And yet . . . the mechanics of soldiering was the same, from side to side. If there was any difference between himself and Cavilo, it must be in what they chose to serve. And how they chose to serve it. *Not all paths, but one path. . . .*

* * *

When Miles arrived back on Barrayar for home leave, a few weeks later, Gregor invited him for lunch at the Imperial Residence. They sat at a wrought-iron table in the North Gardens, which were famous for having been designed by Emperor Ezar, Gregor's grandfather. In summer the spot would be deeply shaded; now it was laced with light filtering through young leaves, rippling in the soft airs of spring. The guards did their guarding out of sight, and servants waited out of earshot unless Gregor touched his pager. Replete with the first three courses, Miles sipped scalding coffee and plotted an assault on a second pastry, which cowered across the table linen under a thick camouflage of cream. Or would that overmatch his forces? This had it all over the contract slave rations they'd once divided, not to mention Cavilo's doggie chews.

Even Gregor seemed to be seeing it all with new eyes. "Space stations are really boring, y'know? All those corridors," he commented, staring out past a fountain, eye following a curving brick path that dove into a riot of flowers. "I stopped seeing how beautiful Barrayar was, looking at it every day. Had to forget to remember. Strange."

"There were moments I couldn't remember which space station I was on," Miles agreed around a mouthful of pastry and cream. "The luxury trade's another matter, but the Hegen Hub stations did tend to the utilitarian." He grimaced at the association of that last word.

The conversation wandered over the recent events in the Hegen Hub. Gregor brightened upon learning that Miles had never issued an actual battle order in the *Triumph*'s fleet tac room either, except to handle the internal security crisis as delegated by Tung.

"Most officers have finished their jobs when the action begins, because the battle transpires too rapidly for the officers to affect it," Miles assured him. "Once you set up a good tac comp—and, if you're lucky, a man with a magic nose—it's better to keep your hands in your pockets. I had Tung, you had . . . ahem."

"And nice deep pockets," said Gregor. "I'm still thinking about it. It seemed almost unreal, till I visited sickbay afterwards. And realized, such-and-such a point of light meant this man's arm lost, that man's lungs frozen. . . ."

"Gotta watch out for those little lights. They tell such soothing lies," Miles agreed. "If you let them." He chased another gooey bite with coffee, paused, and remarked, "You didn't tell Illyan the truth about your topple off the balcony, did you." It was observation, not question.

"I told him I was drunk, and climbed down." Gregor watched the flowers. ". . . how did you know?"

"He doesn't talk about you with secret terror in his eyes."

"I've just got him . . . giving a little. I don't want to screw it up now. You didn't tell him either—for that I thank you."

"You're welcome." Miles drank more coffee. "Do me a favor in return. Talk to someone."

"Who? Not Illyan. Not your father."

"How about my mother?"

"Hm." Gregor bit into his torte, upon which he had been making furrows with his fork, for the first time.

"She could be the only person on Barrayar to automatically put Gregor the man before Gregor the emperor. All our ranks look like optical illusions to her, I think. And you know she can keep her own counsel."

"I'll think about it."

"I don't want to be the only one who . . . the only one. I know when I'm out of my depth."

"You do?" Gregor raised his brows, one corner of his mouth crooking up.

"Oh, yes. I just don't normally let on."

"All right. I will," said Gregor.

Miles waited.

"My word," Gregor added.

Miles relaxed, immeasurably relieved. "Thank you." He eyed a third pastry. The portions were sort of dainty. "Are you feeling better, these days?"

"Much, thank you." Gregor went back to plowing furrows in his cream.

"Really?"

Crosshatches. "I don't know. Unlike that poor sod they had parading around playing me while I was gone, I didn't exactly volunteer for this."

"All Vor are draftees, in that sense."

"Any other Vor could run away and not be missed."

"Wouldn't you miss me a little?" said Miles plaintively. Gregor snickered. Miles glanced around the garden. "It doesn't look like such a tough post, compared to Kyril Island."

"Try it alone in bed at midnight, wondering when your genes are going to start generating monsters in your mind. Like Great Uncle Mad Yuri. Or Prince Serg." His glance at Miles was secretly sharp.

"I . . . know about Prince Serg's, uh, problems," said Miles carefully.

"Everyone seems to have known. Except me."

So that *had* been the trigger of depressive Gregor's first real suicide attempt. Key and lock, click! Miles tried not to look triumphant at this sudden feat of insight. "When did you find out?"

"During the Komarr conference. I'd run across hints, before . . . put them down to enemy propaganda."

Then, the ballet on the balcony had been an immediate response to the shock. Gregor'd had no one to vent it to. . . .

"Was it true, that he really got off torturing—"

"Not everything rumored about Crown Prince Serg is true," Miles cut hastily across this. "Though the true core is . . . bad enough. Mother knows. She was eyewitness to crazy things even *I* don't know, about the Escobar invasion. But she'll tell you. Ask her straight, she'll tell you straight back."

"That seems to run in the family," Gregor allowed. "Too."

"She'll tell you how different you are from him—nothing wrong with your mother's blood, that I ever heard—anyway, I probably carry almost as many of Mad Yuri's genes as you do, through one line of descent or another."

Gregor actually grinned. "Is that supposed to be reassuring?"

"Mm, more on the theory that misery loves company."

"I'm afraid of power . . ." Gregor's voice went low, contemplative.

"You aren't afraid of power, you're afraid of hurting people. If you wield that power," Miles deduced suddenly.

"Huh. Close guess."

"Not dead-on?"

"I'm afraid I might enjoy it. The hurting. Like *him.*"

Prince Serg, he meant. His father.

"Rubbish," said Miles. "I watched my grandfather try and get you to enjoy hunting for years. You got good, I suppose because you thought it was your Vorish duty, but you damn near threw up every time you half-missed and we had to chase down some wounded beastie. You may harbor some other perversion, but not sadism."

"What I've read . . . and heard," said Gregor, "is so horribly fascinating. I can't help thinking about it. Can't put it out of my mind."

"Your head is full of horrors because the *world* is full of horrors. Look at the horrors Cavilo caused in the Hegen Hub."

"If I'd strangled her while she slept—which I had a chance to do—none of those horrors would have come to pass."

"If none of those horrors had come to pass, she wouldn't have deserved to be strangled. Some kind of time-travel paradox, I'm afraid. The arrow of justice flies one way. Only. You can't regret not strangling her first. Though I suppose you can regret not strangling her after. . . ."

"No . . . no . . . I'll leave that to the Cetagandans, if they can catch her now that she has her head start."

"Gregor, I'm sorry, but I just don't think Mad Emperor Gregor is in the cards. It's your *advisors* who are going to go crazy."

Gregor stared at the pastry tray, and sighed. "I suppose it would disturb the guards if I tried to shove a cream torte up your nose."

"Deeply. You should have done it when we were eight and twelve, you could have gotten away with it then. The cream pie of justice flies one way," Miles snickered.

Several unnatural and sophomoric things to do with a tray full of pastry were then suggested by both principals, which left them laughing. Gregor needed a good cream pie fight, Miles judged, even if only verbal and imaginary. When the laughter finally died down, and the coffee was cooling, Miles said, "I know flattery sends you straight up a wall, but dammit, you're actually good at your job. You have to know that, on some level inside, after the Vervain talks. Stay on it, huh?"

"I think I will." Gregor's fork dove more forcefully into his last bite of dessert. "You're going to stay on yours, too, right?"

"Whatever it may be. I am to meet with Simon Illyan on just that topic later this afternoon," said Miles. He decided to forgo that third pastry after all.

"You don't sound exactly excited about it."

"I don't suppose he can demote me, there is no rank below ensign."

"He's pleased with you, what else?"

"He didn't look pleased, when I gave him my debriefing report. He looked dyspeptic. Didn't say much." He glanced at Gregor in sudden suspicion. "You know, don't you? Give!"

"Mustn't interfere in the chain of command," said Gregor sententiously. "Maybe you'll move up it. I hear the command at Kyril Island is open."

Miles shuddered.

Spring in the Barrayaran capital city of Vorbarr Sultana was as beautiful as the autumn, Miles decided. He paused a moment before turning in to the front entrance to the big blocky building that was

ImpSec HQ. The Earth maple still stood, down the street and around
the corner, its tender leaves backlit to a delicate green glow by the
afternoon sun. Barrayaran native vegetation ran to dull reds and
browns, mostly. Would he ever visit Earth? Maybe.

Miles produced proper passes for the door guards. Their faces were
familiar, they were the same crew he'd helped supervise for that
interminable period last winter—only a few months ago? It seemed
longer. He could still rattle off their pay-rates. They exchanged pleas-
antries, but being good ImpSec men they did not ask the question
alight in their eyes, *Where have you been sir?* Miles was not issued a
security escort to Illyan's office, a good sign. It wasn't like he didn't
know the way, by now.

He followed the familiar turns into the labyrinth, up the lift tubes.
The captain in Illyan's outer office merely waved him through, barely
glancing up from his comconsole. The inner office was unchanged,
Illyan's oversized comconsole desk was unchanged, Illyan himself
was . . . rather tireder-looking, paler. He ought to get out and catch
some of that spring sun, eh? At least his hair hadn't all turned white, it
was still about the same brown-grey mix. His taste in clothes was still
bland to the point of camouflage.

Illyan pointed to a seat—another good sign, Miles took it promptly
—finished whatever had been absorbing him, and at last looked up.
He leaned forward to put his elbows on the comconsole and lace his
fingers together, and regarded Miles with a kind of clinical disapproval, as if he were a data point that messed up the curve, and Illyan
was deciding if he could still save the theory by re-classifying him as
experimental error.

"Ensign Vorkosigan," Illyan sighed. "It seems you still have a little
problem with subordination."

"I know, sir. I'm sorry."

"Do you ever intend to do anything about it besides feel sorry?"

"I can't help it, sir, if people give me the wrong orders."

"If you can't obey my orders, I don't want you in my Section."

"Well . . . I thought I had. You wanted a military evaluation of the
Hegen Hub. I made one. You wanted to know where the destabilization was coming from. I found out. You wanted the Dendarii Mercenaries out of the Hub. They'll be leaving in about three more weeks, I
understand. You asked for results. You got them."

"Lots of them," Illyan murmured.

"I admit, I didn't have a direct order to rescue Gregor, I just
assumed you'd want it done. Sir."

Illyan searched him for irony, lips thinning as he apparently found it. Miles tried to keep his face bland, though out-blanding Illyan was a major effort. "As I recall," said Illyan (and Illyan's memory was eiditic, thanks to an Illyrican bio-chip) "I gave those orders to Captain Ungari. I gave you just one order. Can you remember what it was?" This inquiry was in the same encouraging tone one might use on a six-year-old just learning to tie his shoes. Trying to out-irony Illyan was as dangerous as trying to out-bland him.

"Obey Captain Ungari's orders," Miles recalled reluctantly.

"Just so." Illyan leaned back. "Ungari was a good, reliable operative. If you'd botched it, you'd have taken him down with you. The man is now half-ruined."

Miles made little negative motions with his hands. "He made the correct decisions, for his level. You can't fault him. It's just . . . things got too important for me to go on playing ensign when the man who was needed was Lord Vorkosigan." *Or Admiral Naismith.*

"Hm," Illyan said. "And yet . . . who shall I assign you to now? Which loyal officer gets his career destroyed next?"

Miles thought this over. "Why don't you assign me directly to yourself, sir?"

"Thanks," said Illyan dryly.

"I didn't mean—" Miles began to sputter protest, stopped, detecting the oblique gleam of humor in Illyan's brown eyes. *Roasting me for your sport, are you?*

"In fact, just that proposal has been floated. Not, needless to say, by me. But a galactic operative must function with a high degree of independence. We're considering making a virtue of necessity—" a light on Illyan's comconsole distracted him. He checked something, and touched a control. The door on the wall to the right of his desk slid open, and Gregor stepped through. The emperor shed one guard who stayed in the passageway, the other trod silently through the office to take up station beyond the antechamber. All doors slid shut. Illyan rose to pull up a chair for the emperor, and gave him a nod, a sort of vestigial bow, before reseating himself. Miles, who had also risen, sketched a salute and sat too.

"Did you tell him about the Dendarii yet?" Gregor asked Illyan.

"I was working around to it," said Illyan.

Gradually. "What about the Dendarii?" Miles asked, unable to keep the eagerness out of his voice, try though he might for a junior version of Illyan's impassive surface.

"We've decided to put them on a permanent retainer," said Illyan. "You, in your cover identity as Admiral Naismith, will be our liaison officer."

"Consulting mercenaries?" Miles blinked. *Naismith lives!*

Gregor grinned. "The Emperor's Own. We owe them, I think something more than just their base pay for their services to us—and to Us—in the Hegen Hub. And they have certainly demonstrated the, er, utility of being able to reach places cut off to our regular forces by political barriers."

Miles interpreted the expression on Illyan's face as deep mourning for his Section budget, rather than disapproval as such.

"Simon shall be alert for, and pursue, opportunities to use them actively," Gregor went on. "We'll need to justify that retainer, after all."

"I see them as more use in espionage than covert ops," Illyan put in hastily. "This isn't a license to go adventuring, or worse, some kind of letter of marque and reprisal. In fact, the first thing I want you to do is beef up your intelligence department. I know you're in funds for it. I'll lend you a couple of my experts."

"Not bodyguard-puppeteers again, sir?" Miles asked nervously.

"Shall I ask Captain Ungari if he wants to volunteer?" inquired Illyan with a repressed ripple of his lips. "No. You will operate independently. God help us. After all, if I don't send you someplace else, you'll be right here. So the scheme has that much merit even if the Dendarii never do anything."

"I fear it is primarily your youth, which is the cause of Simon's lack of confidence," murmured twenty-five-year-old Gregor. "*We* feel it is time he gave up that prejudice."

Yes, that had been an Imperial We, Miles's Barrayaran-tuned ears did not deceive him. Illyan had heard it as clearly. The chief leaner, leaned upon. Illyan's irony this time was tinged with underlying . . . approval? "Aral and I have labored twenty years to put ourselves out of work. We may live long enough to retire after all." He paused. "That's called 'success' in my business, boys. I wouldn't object." And under his breath ". . . get this hellish chip taken out of my head at last. . . ."

"Mm, don't go scouting surfside retirement cottages just yet," said Gregor. Not caving or backpedaling or submission, merely an expression of confidence in Illyan. No more, no less. Gregor glanced at Miles's . . . neck? The deep bruises from Metzov's grip were almost gone by now, surely. "Were you still working around to the other thing, too?" he asked Illyan.

Illyan opened a hand. "Be my guest." He rummaged in a drawer underneath his comconsole.

"We—and We—thought we owed you something more, too, Miles," said Gregor.

Miles hesitated between a *shucks-t'weren't-nothin'* speech and a *what-did-you-bring-me?!* and settled on an expression of alert inquiry.

Illyan reemerged, and tossed Miles something small that flashed red in the air. "Here. You're a lieutenant. Whatever that means to you."

Miles caught them between his hands, the plastic collar rectangles of his new rank. He was so surprised he said the first thing that came into his head, which was, "Well, that's a start on the subordination problem."

Illyan favored him with a driven glower. "Don't get carried away. About ten percent of ensigns are promoted after their first year of service. Your Vorish social circle will think it's all nepotism anyway."

"I know," said Miles bleakly. But he opened his collar and began switching tabs on the spot.

Illyan softened slightly. "Your father will know better, though. And Gregor. And, er . . . myself."

Miles looked up, to catch his eye direct for almost the first time this interview. "Thank you."

"You earned it. You won't get anything from me you don't earn. That includes the dressing-downs."

"I'll look forward to them, sir."

MILES VORKOSIGAN/NAISMITH
HIS UNIVERSE AND TIMES

CHRONOLOGY	EVENTS	CHRONICLE
Approx. 200 years before Miles's birth	Quaddies are created by genetic engineering.	*Falling Free*
During Beta-Barrayaran War	Cordelia Naismith meets Lord Aral Vorkosigan while on opposite sides of a war. Despite difficulties, they fall in love and are married.	*Shards of Honor*
	While Cordelia is pregnant, an attempt to assassinate Aral by poison gas fails, but Cordelia is affected; Miles Vorkosigan is born with bones that will always be brittle and other medical problems. His growth will be stunted.	
Miles is 17	Miles fails to pass physical test to get into the Service Academy. On trip, necessities force him to improvise the Free Dendarii Mercenaries into existence; he has unintended but unavoidable adventures for four months. Leaves the Dendarii in Ky Tung's competent hands and takes Elli Quinn to Beta for rebuilding of her damaged face; returns to Barrayar to thwart plot against his father. Emperor pulls strings to get Miles into the Academy.	*The Warrior's Apprentice*
Miles is 20	Ensign Miles graduates and immediately has to take on one of the duties of the Barrayaran nobility and act as detective and judge in a murder case. Shortly afterward, his first military assignment ends with his ar-	"The Mountains of Mourning" in *Borders of Infinity*

The Vor Game |

rest. Miles has to rejoin the Dendarii to rescue the young Barrayaran emperor. Emperor accepts Dendarii as his personal secret service force.

Miles is 22

Miles sends Commander Elli Quinn, who's been given a new face on Beta, on a solo mission to Kline Station.

Ethan of Athos

Miles is 23

Now a Barrayaran Lieutenant, Miles goes with the Dendarii to smuggle a scientist out of Jackson's Whole. Miles's fragile leg bones have been replaced by synthetics.

"Labyrinth" in *Borders of Infinity*

Miles is 24

Miles plots from within a Cetagandan prison camp on Dagoola IV to free the prisoners. The Dendarii fleet is pursued by the Cetagandans and finally reaches Earth for repairs. Miles has to juggle both his identities at once, raise money for repairs, and defeat a plot to replace him with a double. Ky Tung stays on Earth. Commander Elli Quinn is now Miles's right hand officer. Miles and the Dendarii depart for Sector IV on a rescue mission.

"The Borders of Infinity" in *Borders of Infinity*

Brothers in Arms

Miles is 25

Hospitalized after previous mission, Miles's broken arms are replaced by synthetic bones. With Simon Illyan, Miles undoes yet another plot against his father while flat on his back.

Borders of Infinity

BORDERS OF INFINITY

For John

1

"You have a visitor, Lieutenant Vorkosigan." A little glassy panic twitched in the normally matter-of-fact corpsman's face. He stepped aside to let the man he escorted enter Miles's hospital room. Miles caught a glimpse of the corpsman retreating hastily even before the door hissed shut behind the visitor.

Snub nose, bright eyes, and an open, mild expression gave the man a false air of youth, though his brown hair was greying at the temples. He was slight of body, wore civilian clothes, and radiated no aura of menace, despite the corpsman's reaction. In fact, he had scarcely an aura at all. Work as a covert agent in his early days had given Simon Illyan, Chief of Barrayar's Imperial Security, a life-long habit of being inconspicuous.

"Hi, boss," said Miles.

"You look like hell," Illyan noted agreeably. "Don't bother saluting."

Miles snorted a laugh, which hurt. Everything seemed to hurt except his arms, bandaged and immobilized from shoulderblades to fingertips; they were still numb from the surgical stunners. He wriggled his hospital-gowned body further into his bedclothes, futilely seeking comfort.

"How was your bone-replacement surgery?" asked Illyan.

"About what I expected, from having my legs done before. The ugliest part was opening my right arm and hand up to pick out all the bone fragments. Tedious. The left went a lot faster, the pieces were bigger. Now I get to sit around for a while to see if the marrow transplants are going to take in their synthetic matrix. I'll be a bit anemic for a while."

"I hope you are not going to make a habit of returning from your mission assignments on a stretcher."

"Now, now, this is only the second time that's happened. Besides, eventually I'll run out of unreplaced bones. By the time I'm thirty I could be entirely plastic." Glumly, Miles considered this possibility. If more than half of him became spare parts, could he be declared legally dead? Would he ever walk into a prosthetics manufacturing plant and cry, "Mother!"? Were the medical sedatives making him just a little spacey . . . ?

"About your missions," said Illyan firmly.

Ah. So this visit wasn't just an expression of personal concern, if Illyan had ever owned any personal concern. It was sometimes hard to tell. "You have my reports," said Miles warily.

"Your reports, as usual, are masterpieces of understatement and misdirection," said Illyan. He sounded perfectly serene about it.

"Well . . . anybody might read 'em. You can't tell."

"Hardly 'anyone,'" said Illyan. "But just so."

"So what's the problem?"

"Money. Specifically, accountability for same."

Maybe it was the drugs he was stuffed with, but Miles could make no sense of this. "Don't you like my work?" he said rather plaintively.

"Apart from your injuries, the results of your latest mission are highly satisfactory," began Illyan.

"They'd by-God better be," Miles muttered grimly.

"—and your late, er, adventures on Earth, just prior to it, are still fully classified. We will discuss them later."

"I've got to report to a couple of higher authorities first," Miles put in urgently.

Illyan waved this aside. "So I understand. No. These charges date to the Dagoola affair, and before."

"Charges?" Miles muttered in bewilderment.

Illyan studied him thoughtfully. "I consider what the emperor spends to keep up your connection to the Dendarii Free Mercenaries to be worth it purely from an internal security standpoint. Were you to be permanently posted at, say, Imperial HQ here at the capital, you'd be a damned plot-magnet all the time. Not just for favor- and office-seekers, but for anyone who wants to touch your father through you. As now."

Miles squinted, as though focusing his eyes could focus his thoughts. "Ah?"

"In brief, certain parties in Imperial Accounting are going over your reports from your mercenary fleet's covert ops with a microscope. They would like to know in more detail where certain large packets of cash have gone. Some of your equipment-replacement chits have been outrageous. More than once. Even from my point of view. They would very much like to prove an on-going pattern of peculation. A court-martial charging you with lining your own pockets at the emperor's expense would be gloriously embarrassing just now, for your father and his whole Centrist coalition."

Miles exhaled, stunned. "Has it gone so far—?"

"Not yet. I fully intend to quash it before it gets off the ground. But to do so I need more details. So as not to get blindsided, as I have sometimes been in your more tangled affairs—*I* still remember, if you do not, spending a month in my own prison because of you . . ." Illyan glowered into the past.

"That was part of a plot against Dad," Miles protested.

"So is this, if I'm picking up the early signals correctly. But Count Vorvolk in Accounting is their front-man, and he is depressingly loyal, in addition to having the emperor's personal, er, support. Untouchable. But manipulatable, I fear. He's been primed. He thinks he's being a watch-dog. The more he's given a run-around the more tenacious he'll become. He must be handled with utmost care, whether he's mistaken or not."

"Not . . . ?" breathed Miles. The full import of the timing of Illyan's visit now dawned on him. Not anxiety for an injured subordinate after all. But to put his questions to Miles just post-surgery, when Miles was weak, hurting, drugged, maybe confused. . . . "Why don't you just fast-penta me and get it over with?" Miles snarled.

"Because I have the report about your idiosyncratic reaction to truth drugs," said Illyan equably. "Unfortunate, that."

"You could twist my arm." There was a bitter taste in Miles's mouth.

Illyan's expression was dry and grim. "I thought about it. Then I decided to let the surgeons do it for me."

"You can be a real sonofabitch some days, Simon, do you know?"

"Yes." Illyan sat unmoved and unmoving. Waiting. Watching. "Your father cannot afford a scandal in his government this month. Not during this appropriations fight. This plot must be quashed regardless of its truth. What is said in this room will remain—must remain—between you and me alone. But I must know."

"Are you offering me an amnesty?" Miles's voice was low, dangerous. He could feel his heart begin to pound.

"If necessary." Illyan's voice was perfectly flat.

Miles couldn't clench or even feel his fists, but his toes curled. He found himself gulping for air in the pulsing waves of his rage; the room seemed to waver. "You . . . vile . . . *bastard!* You dare call me a thief. . . ." He rocked in the bed, kicking off tangling strangling covers. His medical monitor began to bleep alarms. His arms were useless weights hanging from his shoulders, flopping nervelessly. "As if I would steal from *Barrayar.* As if I would steal from my *own dead . . .*" He swung his feet out, pulled himself upright with a mighty wrench of abdominal muscles. Dizzied, half-blacking-out, he toppled forward precipitously with no hands to catch himself.

Illyan leapt to grab him before he smashed face-first on the matting. "What the hell do you think you're *doing,* boy?" Miles wasn't sure himself.

"What are you doing to my patient?" the white-faced military doctor cried, plunging through the door. "This man just had major surgery!"

The doctor was frightened and furious; the corpsman, in his wake, merely frightened. He tried to impede his superior, plucking at his arm and hissing, "Sir, that's Security Chief *Illyan!*"

"I know who he is. I don't care if he's Emperor Dorca's ghost. I will not have him carrying on his . . . *business,* here." The doctor glared courageously at Illyan. "Your interrogation, or whatever, can take place in your own damned headquarters. I will not have that kind of thing going on in my hospital. This patient is not released to anybody yet!"

Illyan looked at first baffled, then outraged. "I was *not . . .*"

Miles considered, briefly, clutching artistically at certain nerve junctions in his body and screaming, except that he wasn't equipped to clutch at anything just at present. "Appearances can be so damning," he purred in Illyan's ear, sinking in Illyan's arms. He grinned evilly through clenched teeth. His body shook, shocky, the sheen of cold sweat on his forehead quite unfeigned.

Illyan frowned at him, but put him back to bed very carefully.

"It's all right," Miles wheezed to the doctor. "It's all right. I was merely . . . merely . . ." *Upset* didn't quite seem to cover it; he'd felt for a moment as if the top of his head had been about to blow off. "Never mind." He felt horribly unbalanced. To think that Illyan, whom he'd known all his life, whom he'd assumed trusted him implicitly or why else send him on a series of such distant, independent missions . . . He'd been proud to be so trusted, while still a young officer, with so little direct supervision in his covert ops . . . Could his whole career to date have been, not desperately needed Service to the Imperium, but just a ploy to get a dangerously clumsy Vor puppy out from underfoot? Toy soldiers . . . no, that made no sense. A peculator. Ugly word. What a profound slur upon his honor, and his wit; as if he did not know where Imperial funds came from, or at what cost.

The black anger sagged into a black depression. His heart hurt. He felt smeared. Could Illyan—Illyan!—really think, even for one hypothetical moment. . . . Yes, Illyan could. Illyan would not be here, not doing this, if he were not genuinely worried the charge could be proved true. To his dismay, Miles found himself silently crying. *Damn* the drugs.

Illyan was staring at him in considerable disquiet. "One way or another, Miles, I must defend your expenditures—which are my department's expenditures—tomorrow."

"I'd rather be court-martialed."

Illyan's lips thinned. "I'll come back later. When you've had a chance to sleep. Perhaps you'll be more coherent."

The doctor fussed over him, zapped him with yet another damned drug, and left. Leadenly, Miles turned his face to the wall; not to sleep, but to remember.

The Mountains of Mourning

Miles heard the woman weeping as he was climbing the hill from the long lake. He hadn't dried himself after his swim, as the morning already promised shimmering heat. Lake water trickled cool from his hair onto his naked chest and back, more annoyingly down his legs from his ragged shorts. His leg braces chafed on his damp skin as he pistoned up the faint trail through the scrub, military double-time. His feet squished in his old wet shoes. He slowed curiously as he became conscious of the voices.

The woman's voice grated with grief and exhaustion. "Please, lord, please. All I want is m'justice . . ."

The front gate guard's voice was irritated and embarrassed. "I'm no lord. C'mon, get *up*, woman. Go back to the village and report it at the district magistrate's office."

"I tell you, I just came from there!" The woman did not move from her knees as Miles emerged from the bushes and paused to take in the tableau across the paved road. "The magistrate's not to return for weeks, weeks. I walked four days to get here. I only have a little money. . . ." A desperate hope rose in her voice, and her spine bent and straightened as she scrabbled in her skirt pocket and held out her cupped hands to the guard. "A mark and twenty pence, it's all I have, but—"

The exasperated guard's eye fell on Miles, and he straightened abruptly, as if afraid Miles might suspect him of being tempted by so pitiful a bribe. "Be off, woman!" he snapped.

Miles quirked an eyebrow, and limped across the road to the main gate. "What's all this about, Corporal?" he inquired easily.

The guard corporal was on loan from Imperial Security, and wore the high-necked dress greens of the Barrayaran Service. He was sweating and uncomfortable in the bright morning light of this southern district, but Miles fancied he'd be boiled before he'd undo his collar on this post. His accent was not local, he was a city man from the capital, where a more-or-less efficient bureaucracy absorbed such problems as the one on her knees before him.

The woman, now, was local and more than local—she had backcountry written all over her. She was younger than her strained voice had at first suggested. Tall, fever-red from her weeping, with stringy blonde hair hanging down across a ferret-thin face and protuberant grey eyes. If she were cleaned up, fed, rested, happy and confident, she might achieve a near-prettiness, but she was far from that now, despite her remarkable figure. Lean but full-breasted—no, Miles revised himself as he crossed the road and came up to the gate. Her bodice was all blotched with dried milk leaks, though there was no baby in sight. Only temporarily full-breasted. Her worn dress was factory-woven cloth, but hand-sewn, crude and simple. Her feet were bare, thickly-callused, cracked and sore.

"No problem," the guard assured Miles. "Go *away,*" he hissed to the woman.

She lurched off her knees and sat stonily.

"I'll call my sergeant," the guard eyed her warily, "and have her removed."

"Wait a moment," said Miles.

She stared up at Miles from her cross-legged position, clearly not knowing whether to identify him as hope or not. His clothing, what there was of it, offered her no clue as to what he might be. The rest of him was all too plainly displayed. He jerked up his chin and smiled thinly. Too-large head, too-short neck, back thickened with its crooked spine, crooked legs with their brittle bones too-often broken, drawing the eye in their gleaming chromium braces. Were the hill woman standing, the top of his head would barely be even with the top of her shoulder. He waited in boredom for her hand to make the back-country hex sign against evil mutations, but it only jerked and clenched into a fist.

"I must see my lord Count," she said to an uncertain point halfway between Miles and the guard. "It's my right. My daddy, he died in the Service. It's my right."

"Prime Minister Count Vorkosigan," said the guard stiffly, "is on his country estate to rest. If he were working, he'd be back in Vorbarr Sultana." The guard looked like he wished *he* were back in Vorbarr Sultana.

The woman seized the pause. "You're only a city man. He's *my* count. My right."

"What do you want to see Count Vorkosigan for?" asked Miles patiently.

"Murder," growled the girl/woman. The security guard spasmed slightly. "I want to report a murder."

"Shouldn't you report to your village speaker first?" inquired Miles, with a hand-down gesture to calm the twitching guard.

"I did. He'll do *nothing.*" Rage and frustration cracked her voice. "He says it's over and done. He won't write down my accusation, says it's nonsense. It would only make trouble for everybody, he says. I don't care! I want my justice!"

Miles frowned thoughtfully, looking the woman over. The details checked, corroborated her claimed identity, added up to a solid if subliminal sense of authentic truth which perhaps escaped the professionally paranoid security man. "It's true, Corporal," Miles said. "She has a right to appeal, first to the district magistrate, then to the count's court. And the district magistrate won't be back for two weeks."

This sector of Count Vorkosigan's native district had only one overworked district magistrate, who rode a circuit that included the lakeside village of Vorkosigan Surleau but one day a month. Since the region of the Prime Minister's country estate was crawling with Imperial Security when the great lord was in residence, and closely monitored even when he was not, prudent troublemakers took their troubles elsewhere.

"Scan her, and let her in," said Miles. "On my authority."

The guard was one of Imperial Security's best, trained to look for assassins in his own shadow. He now looked scandalized, and lowered his voice to Miles. "Sir, if I let every country lunatic wander the estate at will—"

"I'll take her up. I'm going that way."

The guard shrugged helplessly, but stopped short of saluting; Miles was decidedly not in uniform. The gate guard pulled a scanner from his belt and made a great show of going over the woman. Miles wondered if he'd have been inspired to harass her with a strip-search without Miles's inhibiting presence. When the guard finished demonstrating how alert, conscientious, and loyal he was, he palmed open the gate's lock, entered the transaction, including the woman's retina scan, into the computer monitor, and stood aside in a pose of rather pointed parade rest. Miles grinned at the silent editorial, and steered the bedraggled woman by the elbow through the gates and up the winding drive.

She twitched away from his touch at the earliest opportunity, yet still refrained from superstitious gestures, eyeing him with a strange and hungry curiosity. Time was, such openly repelled fascination with the peculiarities of his body had driven Miles to grind his teeth; now he could take it with a serene amusement only slightly tinged with acid. They would learn, all of them. They would learn.

"Do you serve Count Vorkosigan, little man?" she asked cautiously.

Miles thought about that one a moment. "Yes," he answered finally. The answer was, after all, true on every level of meaning but the one she'd asked it. He quelled the temptation to tell her he was the court jester. From the look of her, this one's troubles were much worse than his own.

She had apparently not quite believed in her own rightful destiny, despite her mulish determination at the gate, for as they climbed unimpeded toward her goal a nascent panic made her face even more drawn and pale, almost ill. "How—how do I talk to him?" she choked. "Should I curtsey . . . ?" She glanced down at herself as if conscious for the first time of her own dirt and sweat and squalor.

Miles suppressed a facetious set-up starting with, *Kneel and knock your forehead three times on the floor before speaking, that's what the General Staff does,* and said instead, "Just stand up straight and speak the truth. Try to be clear. He'll take it from there. He does not, after all," Miles's lips twitched, "lack experience."

She swallowed.

A hundred years ago, the Vorkosigans' summer retreat had been a guard barracks, part of the outlying fortifications of the great castle on the bluff above the village of Vorkosigan Surleau. The castle was now a burnt-out ruin, and the barracks transformed into a comfortable low stone residence, modernized and re-modernized, artistically landscaped and bright with flowers. The arrow slits had been widened into big glass windows overlooking the lake, and comm link antennae bristled from the roof. There was a new guard barracks concealed in the trees downslope, but it had no arrow slits.

A man in the brown-and-silver livery of the Count's personal retainers exited the residence's front door as Miles approached with the strange woman in tow. It was the new man, what was his name? Pym, that was it.

"Where's m'lord Count?" Miles asked him.

"In the upper pavilion, taking breakfast with m'lady." Pym glanced at the woman, waited on Miles in a posture of polite inquiry.

"Ah. Well, this woman has walked four days to lay an appeal before the district magistrate's court. The court's not here, but the Count is, so she now proposes to skip the middlemen and go straight to the top. I like her style. Take her up, will you?"

"During *breakfast?*" said Pym.

Miles cocked his head at the woman. "Have you had breakfast?" She shook her head mutely.

"I thought not." Miles turned his hands palm-out, dumping her, symbolically, on the retainer. "Now, yes."

"My daddy, he died in the Service," the woman repeated faintly. "It's my right." The phrase seemed as much to convince herself as anyone else, now.

Pym was, if not a hill man, district-born. "So it is," he sighed, and gestured her to follow him without further ado. Her eyes widened, as she trailed him around the house, and she glanced back nervously over her shoulder at Miles. "Little man . . . ?"

"Just stand straight," he called to her. He watched her round the corner, grinned, and took the steps two at a time into the residence's main entrance.

After a shave and cold shower, Miles dressed in his own room overlooking the long lake. He dressed with great care, as great as he'd expended on the Service Academy ceremonies and Imperial Review two days ago. Clean underwear, long-sleeved cream shirt, dark green trousers with the side piping. High-collared green tunic tailor-cut to his own difficult fit. New pale blue plastic ensign's rectangles aligned precisely on the collar and poking most uncomfortably into his jaw. He dispensed with the leg braces and pulled on mirror-polished boots to the knee, and swiped a bit of dust from them with his pajama pants, ready-to-hand on the floor where he'd dropped them before going swimming.

He straightened and checked himself in the mirror. His dark hair hadn't even begun to recover from that last cut before the graduation ceremonies. A pale, sharp-featured face, not too much dissipated bag under the grey eyes, nor too bloodshot—alas, the limits of his body compelled him to stop celebrating well before he could hurt himself.

Echoes of the late celebration still boiled up silently in his head, crooking his mouth into a grin. He was on his way now, had his hand clamped firmly around the lowest rung of the highest ladder on Barrayar, Imperial Service itself. There were no give-aways in the Service even for sons of the old Vor. You got what you earned. His brother-officers could be relied on to know that, even if outsiders wondered. He was in position at last to prove himself to all doubters. Up and away and never look down, never look back.

One last look back. As carefully as he'd dressed, Miles gathered up the necessary objects for his task. The white cloth rectangles of his former Academy cadet's rank. The hand-calligraphed second copy, purchased for this purpose, of his new officer's commission in the Barrayaran Imperial Service. A copy of his Academy three-year scholastic transcript on paper, with all its commendations (and demerits). No point in anything but honesty in this next transaction. In a cupboard downstairs he found the brass brazier and tripod, wrapped in its polishing cloth, and a plastic bag of very dry juniper bark. Chemical firesticks.

Out the back door and up the hill. The landscaped path split, right going up to the pavilion overlooking it all, left forking sideways to a garden-like area surrounded by a low fieldstone wall. Miles let himself in by the gate. "Good morning, crazy ancestors," he called, then quelled his humor. It might be true, but lacked the respect due the occasion.

He strolled over and around the graves until he came to the one he sought, knelt, and set up the brazier and tripod, humming. The stone was simple, *General Count Piotr Pierre Vorkosigan,* and the dates. If they'd tried to list all the accumulated honors and accomplishments, they'd have had to go to microprint.

He piled in the bark, the very expensive papers, the cloth bits, a clipped mat of dark hair from that last cut. He set it alight and rocked back on his heels to watch it burn. He'd played a hundred versions of this moment over in his head, over the years, ranging from solemn public orations with musicians in the background, to dancing naked on the old man's grave. He'd settled on this private and traditional ceremony, played straight. Just between the two of them.

"So, Grandfather," he purred at last. "And here we are after all. Satisfied now?"

All the chaos of the graduation ceremonies behind, all the mad efforts of the last three years, all the pain, came to this point; but the grave did not speak, did not say, *Well done; you can stop now.* The ashes spelled out no messages, there were no visions to be had in the rising smoke. The brazier burned down all too quickly. Not enough stuff in it, perhaps.

He stood, and dusted his knees, in the silence and the sunlight. So what had he expected? Applause? Why was he here, in the final analysis? Dancing out a dead man's dreams—who did his Service really serve? Grandfather? Himself? Pale Emperor Gregor? Who cared?

"Well, old man," he whispered, then shouted: "ARE YOU SATIS-FIED YET?" The echoes rang from the stones.

A throat cleared behind him, and Miles whirled like a scalded cat, heart pounding.

"Uh . . . my lord?" said Pym carefully. "Pardon me, I did not mean to interrupt . . . anything. But the Count your father requires you to attend on him in the upper pavilion."

Pym's expression was perfectly bland. Miles swallowed, and waited for the scarlet heat he could feel in his face to recede. "Quite," he shrugged. "The fire's almost out. I'll clean it up later. Don't . . . let anybody else touch it."

He marched past Pym and didn't look back.

The pavilion was a simple structure of weathered silver wood, open on all four sides to catch the breeze, this morning a few faint puffs from the west. Good sailing on the lake this afternoon, maybe. Only ten days precious home leave left, and much Miles wanted to do, including the trip to Vorbarr Sultana with his cousin Ivan to pick out his new lightflyer. And then his first assignment would be coming through—ship duty, Miles prayed. He'd had to overcome a major temptation, not to ask his father to make sure it was ship duty. He would take whatever assignment fate dealt him, that was the first rule of the game. And win with the hand he was dealt.

The interior of the pavilion was shady and cool after the glare outside. It was furnished with comfortable old chairs and tables, one of which bore the remains of a noble breakfast—Miles mentally marked two lonely-looking oil cakes on a crumb-scattered tray as his own. Miles's mother, lingering over her cup, smiled across the table at him.

Miles's father, casually dressed in an open-throated shirt and shorts, sat in a worn armchair. Aral Vorkosigan was a thick-set, grey-haired man, heavy-jawed, heavy-browed, scarred. A face that lent itself to savage caricature—Miles had seen some, in Opposition press, in the histories of Barrayar's enemies. They had only to draw one lie, to render dull those sharp penetrating eyes, to create everyone's parody of a military dictator.

And how much is he haunted by Grandfather? Miles wondered. He doesn't show it much. But then, he doesn't have to. Admiral Aral Vorkosigan, space master strategist, conqueror of Komarr, hero of Escobar, for sixteen years Imperial Regent, supreme power on Barrayar in all but name. And then he'd capped it, confounded history and all self-sure witnesses and heaped up honor and glory beyond all that had gone before by voluntarily stepping *down* and transferring command smoothly to Emperor Gregor upon his majority. Not that the Prime Ministership hadn't made a dandy retirement from the Regency, and he was showing no signs yet of stepping down from *that*.

And so Admiral Aral's life took General Piotr's like an overpowering hand of cards, and where did that leave Ensign Miles? Holding two deuces and the joker. He must surely either concede or start bluffing like crazy. . . .

The hill woman sat on a hassock, a half-eaten oil cake clutched in her hands, staring open-mouthed at Miles in all his power and polish. As he caught and returned her gaze her lips pressed closed and her eyes lit. Her expression was strange—anger? Exhilaration? Embarrassment? Glee? Some bizarre mixture of all? *And what did you think I was, woman?*

Being in uniform (showing off his uniform?), Miles came to attention before his father. "Sir?"

Count Vorkosigan spoke to the woman. "That is my son. If I send him as my Voice, would that satisfy you?"

"Oh," she breathed, her wide mouth drawing back in a weird, fierce grin, the most expression Miles had yet seen on her face, *"yes, my lord."*

"Very well. It will be done."

What will be done? Miles wondered warily. The Count was leaning back in his chair, looking satisfied himself, but with a dangerous tension around his eyes hinting that something had aroused his true anger. Not anger at the woman, clearly they were in some sort of agreement, and—Miles searched his conscience quickly—not at Miles himself. He cleared his throat gently, cocking his head and baring his teeth in an inquiring smile.

The Count steepled his hands and spoke to Miles at last. "A most interesting case. I can see why you sent her up."

"Ah . . ." said Miles. What had he got hold of? He'd only greased the woman's way through Security on a quixotic impulse, for God's sake, and to tweak his father at breakfast. ". . . ah?" he continued noncommittally.

Count Vorkosigan's brows rose. "Did you not know?"

"She spoke of a murder, and a marked lack of cooperation from her local authorities about it. Figured you'd give her a lift on to the district magistrate."

The Count settled back still further, and rubbed his hand thoughtfully across his scarred chin. "It's an infanticide case."

Miles's belly went cold. *I don't want anything to do with this.* Well, that explained why there was no baby to go with the breasts. "Unusual . . . for it to be reported."

"We've fought the old customs for twenty years and more," said the Count. "Promulgated, propagandized . . . In the cities, we've made good progress."

"In the cities," murmured the Countess, "people have access to alternatives."

"But in the backcountry—well—little has changed. We all know what's going on, but without a report, a complaint—and with the family invariably drawing together to protect its own—it's hard to get leverage."

"What," Miles cleared his throat, nodded at the woman, "what was your baby's mutation?"

"The cat's mouth," the woman dabbed at her upper lip to demonstrate. "She had the hole inside her mouth, too, and was a weak sucker, she choked and cried, but she was getting enough, she *was.* . . ."

"Hare-lip," the Count's off-worlder wife murmured half to herself, translating the Barrayaran term to the galactic standard, "and a cleft palate, sounds like. Harra, that's not even a mutation. They had that back on Old Earth. A . . . a normal birth defect, if that's not a contradiction in terms. Not a punishment for your Barrayaran ancestors' pilgrimage through the Fire. A simple operation could have corrected—" Countess Vorkosigan cut herself off. The hill woman was looking anguished.

"I'd heard," the woman said. "My lord had made a hospital to be built at Hassadar. I meant to take her there, when I was a little stronger, though I had no money. Her arms and legs were sound, her head was well-shaped, anybody could see—surely they would have—" her hands clenched and twisted, her voice went ragged, "but Lem killed her first."

A seven-day walk, Miles calculated, from the deep Dendarii Mountains to the lowland town of Hassadar. Reasonable, that a woman newly risen from childbed might delay that hike a few days. An hour's ride in an aircar. . . .

"So one is reported as a murder at last," said Count Vorkosigan, "and we will treat it as exactly that. This is a chance to send a message to the farthest corners of my own district. You, Miles, will be my Voice, to reach where it has not reached before. You will dispense Count's justice upon this man—and not quietly, either. It's time for the practices that brand us as barbarians in galactic eyes to end."

Miles gulped. "Wouldn't the district magistrate be better qualified . . . ?"

The Count smiled slightly. "For this case, I can think of no one better qualified than yourself."

The messenger and the message all in one; *Times have changed.* Indeed. Miles wished himself elsewhere, anywhere—back sweating blood over his final examinations, for instance. He stifled an unworthy wail, *My home leave . . . !*

Miles rubbed the back of his neck. "Who, ah . . . who is it killed your little girl?" *Meaning, who is it I'm expected to drag out, put up against a wall, and shoot?*

"My husband," she said tonelessly, looking at—through—the polished silvery floorboards.

I knew this was going to be messy. . . .

"She cried and cried," the woman went on, "and wouldn't go to sleep, not nursing well—he shouted at me to shut her up—"

"Then?" Miles prompted, sick to his stomach.

"He swore at me, and went to go sleep at his mother's. He said at least a working man could sleep there. I hadn't slept either. . . ."

This guy sounds like a real winner. Miles had an instant picture of him, a bull of a man with a bullying manner—nevertheless, there was something missing in the climax of the woman's story.

The Count had picked up on it too. He was listening with total attention, his strategy-session look, a slit-eyed intensity of thought you could mistake for sleepiness. That would be a grave mistake. "Were you an eyewitness?" he asked in a deceptively mild tone that put Miles on full alert. "Did you actually see him kill her?"

"I found her dead in the midmorning, lord."

"You went into the bedroom—" Count Vorkosigan led her on.

"We've only got one room." She shot him a look as if doubtful for the first time of his total omniscience. "She had slept, slept at last. I went out to get some brillberries, up the ravine a way. And when I came back . . . I should have taken her with me, but I was so glad she slept at last, didn't want to risk waking her—" tears leaked from the woman's tightly-closed eyes. "I let her sleep when I came back, I was glad to eat and rest, but I began to get full," her hand touched a breast, "and I went to wake her . . ."

"What, were there no marks on her? Not a cut throat?" asked the Count. That was the usual method for these backcountry infanticides, quick and clean compared to, say, exposure.

The woman shook her head. "Smothered, I think, lord. It was cruel, something cruel. The village Speaker said I must have overlain her, and wouldn't take my plea against Lem. I did not, I did not! She had her own cradle, Lem made it with his own hands when she was still in my belly. . . ." She was close to breaking down.

The Count exchanged a glance with his wife, and a small tilt of his head. Countess Vorkosigan rose smoothly.

"Come, Harra, down to the house. You must wash and rest before Miles takes you home."

The hill woman looked taken aback. "Oh, not in your house, lady!"

"Sorry, it's the only one I've got handy. Besides the guard barracks. The guards are good boys, but you'd make 'em uncomfortable . . ." The Countess eased her out.

"It is clear," said Count Vorkosigan as soon as the women were out of earshot, "that you will have to check out the medical facts before, er, popping off. And I trust you will also have noticed the little problem with a positive identification of the accused. This could be the ideal public-demonstration case we want, but not if there's any ambiguity about it. No bloody mysteries."

"I'm not a coroner," Miles pointed out immediately. If he could wriggle off this hook. . . .

"Quite. You will take Dr. Dea with you."

Lieutenant Dea was the Prime Minister's physician's assistant. Miles had seen him around—an ambitious young military doctor, in a constant state of frustration because his superior would never let him touch his most important patient—oh, he was going to be thrilled with this assignment, Miles predicted morosely.

"He can take his osteo kit with him, too," the Count went on, brightening slightly, "in case of accidents."

"How economical," said Miles, rolling his eyes. "Look, uh—suppose her story checks out and we nail this guy. Do I have to, personally . . . ?"

"One of the liveried men will be your bodyguard. And—if the story checks—the executioner."

That was only slightly better. "Couldn't we wait for the district magistrate?"

"Every judgment the district magistrate makes, he makes in my place. Every sentence his office carries out, is carried out in my name. Someday, it will be done in your name. It's time you gained a clear understanding of the process. Historically, the Vor may be a military caste, but a Vor lord's duties were never only military ones."

No escape. Damn, damn, damn. Miles sighed. "Right. Well . . . we could take the aircar, I suppose, and be up there in a couple of hours. Allow some time to find the right hole. Drop out of the sky on 'em, make the message loud and clear . . . be back before bedtime." Get it over with quickly.

The Count had that slit-eyed look again. "No . . ." he said slowly, "not the aircar, I don't think."

"No roads for a groundcar, up that far. Just trails." He added uneasily—surely his father could not be thinking of—"I don't think I'd cut a very impressive figure of central Imperial authority on foot, sir."

His father glanced up at his crisp dress uniform and smiled slightly. "Oh, you don't do so badly."

"But picture this after three or four days of beating through the bushes," Miles protested. "You didn't see us in Basic. Or smell us."

"I've been there," said the Admiral dryly. "But no, you're quite right. Not on foot. I have a better idea."

My own cavalry troop, thought Miles ironically, turning in his saddle, *just like Grandfather.* Actually, he was pretty sure the old man would have had some acerbic comments about the riders now strung out behind Miles on the wooded trail, once he'd got done rolling on the ground laughing at the equitation being displayed. The Vorkosigan stables had shrunk sadly since the old man was no longer around to take an interest, the polo string sold off, the few remaining ancient and ill-tempered ex-cavalry beasts put permanently out to pasture. The handful of riding horses left were retained for their sure-footedness and good manners, not their exotic bloodlines, and kept exercised and gentle for the occasional guest by a gaggle of girls from the village.

Miles gathered his reins, tensed one calf, and shifted his weight slightly, and Fat Ninny responded with a neat half turn and two precise back steps. The thickset roan gelding could not have been mistaken by the most ignorant urbanite for a fiery steed, but Miles adored him, for his dark and liquid eye, his wide velvet nose, his phlegmatic disposition equally unappalled by rushing streams or screaming aircars, but most of all for his exquisite dressage-trained responsiveness. Brains before beauty. Just being around him made Miles calmer, the beast was an emotional blotter, like a purring cat. Miles patted Fat Ninny on the neck. "If anybody asks," he murmured, "I'll tell them your name is Chieftan." Fat Ninny waggled one fuzzy ear, and heaved a wooshing, barrel-chested sigh.

Grandfather had a great deal to do with the unlikely parade Miles now led. The great guerilla general had poured out his youth in these mountains, fighting the Cetagandan invaders to a standstill and then reversing their tide. Anti-flyer heatless seeker-strikers smuggled in at bloody cost from off-planet had a lot more to do with the final victory than cavalry horses, which, according to Grandfather, had saved his forces through the worst winter of that campaign mainly by being edible. But through retroactive romance, the horse had become the symbol of that struggle.

Miles thought his father was being overly optimistic, if he thought Miles was going to cash in thusly on the old man's residual glory. The guerilla caches and camps were shapeless lumps of rust and *trees,* dammit, not just weeds and scrub anymore—they had passed some, earlier in today's ride—the men who had fought that war had long since gone to ground for the last time, just like Grandfather. What was he doing here? It was Jump ship duty he wanted, taking him high, high above all this. The future, not the past, held his destiny.

Miles's meditations were interrupted by Dr. Dea's horse, which, taking exception to a branch lying across the logging trail, planted all four feet in an abrupt stop and snorted loudly. Dr. Dea toppled off with a faint cry.

"Hang onto the *reins,*" Miles called, and pressed Fat Ninny back down the trail.

Dr. Dea was getting rather better at falling off, he'd landed more-or-less on his feet this time. He made a lunge at the dangling reins, but his sorrel mare shied away from his grab. Dea jumped back as she swung on her haunches and then, realizing her freedom, bounced back down the trail, tail bannering, horse body-language for *Nyah, nyah, ya can't catch me!* Dr. Dea, red and furious, ran swearing in pursuit. She broke into a canter.

"No, no, don't run after her!" called Miles.

"How the hell am I supposed to catch her if I don't run after her?" snarled Dea. The space surgeon was not a happy man. "My medkit's on that bloody beast!"

"How do you think you can catch her if you do?" asked Miles. "She can fun faster than you can."

At the end of the little column, Pym turned his horse sideways, blocking the trail. "Just wait, Harra," Miles advised the anxious hill woman in passing. "Hold your horse still. Nothing starts a horse running faster than another running horse."

The other two riders were doing rather better. The woman Harra Csurik sat her horse wearily, allowing it to plod along without interference, but at least riding on balance instead of trying to use the reins as a handle like the unfortunate Dea. Pym, bringing up the rear, was competent if not comfortable.

Miles slowed Fat Ninny to a walk, reins loose, and wandered after the mare, radiating an air of calm relaxation. *Who, me? I don't want to catch you. We're just enjoying the scenery, right. That's it, stop for a bite.* The sorrel mare paused to nibble at a weed, but kept a wary eye on Miles's approach.

At a distance just short of starting the mare bolting off again, Miles stopped Fat Ninny and slid off. He made no move toward the mare, but instead stood still and made a great show of fishing in his pockets. Fat Ninny butted his head against Miles eagerly, and Miles cooed and fed him a bit of sugar. The mare cocked her ears with interest. Fat Ninny smacked his lips and nudged for more. The mare snuffled up for her share. She lipped a cube from Miles's palm as he slid his other arm quietly through the loop of her reins.

"Here you go, Dr. Dea. One horse. No running."

"No fair," wheezed Dea, trudging up. "You had sugar in your pockets."

"Of course I had sugar in my pockets. It's called foresight and planning. The trick of handling horses isn't to be faster than the horse, or stronger than the horse. That pits your weakness against his strengths. The trick is to be smarter than the horse. That pits your strength against his weakness, eh?"

Dea took his reins. "It's snickering at me," he said suspiciously.

"That's nickering, not snickering," Miles grinned. He tapped Fat Ninny behind his left foreleg, and the horse obediently grunted down onto one knee. Miles clambered up readily to his conveniently-lowered stirrup.

"Does mine do that?" asked Dr. Dea, watching with fascination.

"Sorry, no."

Dea glowered at his horse. "This animal is an idiot. I shall lead it for a while."

As Fat Ninny lurched back to his four feet Miles suppressed a riding-instructorly comment gleaned from his Grandfather's store such as, *Be smarter than the horse, Dea.* Though Dr. Dea was officially sworn to Lord Vorkosigan for the duration of this investigation, Space Surgeon Lieutenant Dea certainly outranked Ensign Vorkosigan. To command older men who outranked one called for a certain measure of tact.

The logging road widened out here, and Miles dropped back beside Harra Csurik. Her fierceness and determination of yesterday morning at the gate seemed to be fading even as the trail rose toward her home. Or perhaps it was simply exhaustion catching up with her. She'd said little all morning, been sunk in silence all afternoon. If she was going to drag Miles all the way up to the back of beyond and then wimp out on him . . .

"What, ah, branch of the Service was your father in, Harra?" Miles began conversationally.

She raked her fingers through her hair in a combing gesture more nervousness than vanity. Her eyes looked out at him through the straw-colored wisps like skittish creatures in the protection of a hedge.

"District Militia, m'lord. I don't really remember him, he died when I was real little."

"In combat?"

She nodded. "In the fighting around Vorbarr Sultana, during Vordarian's Pretendership."

Miles refrained from asking which side he had been swept up on—most footsoldiers had had little choice, and the amnesty had included the dead as well as the living.

"Ah . . . do you have any sibs?"

"No, lord. Just me and my mother left."

A little anticipatory tension eased in Miles's neck. If this judgment indeed drove all the way through to an execution, one misstep could trigger a blood feud among the in-laws. *Not* the legacy of justice the Count intended him to leave behind. So the fewer in-laws involved, the better. "What about your husband's family?"

"He's got seven. Four brothers and three sisters."

"Hm." Miles had a mental flash of an entire team of huge, menacing hill hulks. He glanced back at Pym, feeling a trifle understaffed for his task. He had pointed out this factor to the Count, when they'd been planning this expedition last night.

"The village Speaker and his deputies will be your back-up," the Count had said, "just as for the district magistrate on court circuit."

"What if they don't want to cooperate?" Miles had asked nervously.

"An officer who expects to command Imperial troops," the Count had glinted, "should be able to figure out how to extract cooperation from a backcountry headman."

In other words, his father had decided this was a test, and wasn't going to give him any more clues. Thanks, Dad.

"You have no sibs, lord?" said Harra, snapping him back to the present.

"No. But surely that's known, even in the back-beyond."

"They *say* a lot of things about you," Harra shrugged.

Miles bit down on the morbid question in his mouth like a wedge of raw lemon. He would not ask it, he would not . . . he couldn't help himself. "Like what?" forced out past his stiff lips.

"Everyone knows the Count's son is a mutant." Her eyes flicked defiant-wide. "Some said it came from the off-worlder woman he married. Some said it was from radiation from the wars, or a disease from, um, corrupt practices in his youth among his brother-officers—"

That last was a new one to Miles. His brow lifted.

"—but most say he was poisoned by his enemies."

"I'm glad most have it right. It was an assassination attempt using soltoxin gas, when my mother was pregnant with me. But it's not—" *a mutation,* his thought hiccoughed through the well-worn grooves —how many times had he explained this?—*it's teratogenic, not genetic, I'm not a mutant, not. . . .* What the hell did a fine point of biochemistry matter to this ignorant, bereaved woman? For all practical purposes—for her purposes—he might as well be a mutant. "—important," he finished.

She eyed him sideways, swaying gently in the clop-a-clop rhythm of her mount. "Some said you were born with no legs, and lived all the time in a float chair in Vorkosigan House. Some said you were born with no bones—"

"—and kept in a jar in the basement, no doubt," Miles muttered.

"But Karal said he'd seen you with your grandfather at Hassadar Fair, and you were only sickly and undersized. Some said your father had got you into the Service, but others said no, you'd gone off-planet to your mother's home and had your brain turned into a computer and your body fed with tubes, floating in a liquid—"

"I knew there'd be a jar turn up in this story somewhere," Miles grimaced. *You knew you'd be sorry you asked, too, but you went and did it anyway.* She was baiting him, Miles realized suddenly. How *dare* she . . . but there was no humor in her, only a sharp-edged watchfulness.

She had gone out, way out on a limb to lay this murder charge, in defiance of family and local authorities alike, in defiance of established custom. And what had her Count given her for a shield and support, going back to face the wrath of all her nearest and dearest? Miles. Could he handle this? She must be wondering indeed. Or would he botch it, cave and cut and run, leaving her to face the whirlwind of rage and revenge alone?

He wished he'd left her weeping at the gate.

The woodland, fruit of many generations of terraforming forestry, opened out suddenly on a vale of brown native scrub. Down the middle of it, through some accident of soil chemistry, ran a half-kilometer-wide swathe of green and pink—feral roses, Miles realized with astonishment as they rode nearer. Earth roses. The track dove into the fragrant mass of them and vanished.

He took turns with Pym, hacking their way through with their Service bush knives. The roses were vigorous and studded with thick thorns, and hacked back with a vicious elastic recoil. Fat Ninny did his part by swinging his big head back and forth and nipping off blooms and chomping them down happily. Miles wasn't sure just how many he ought to let the big roan eat—just because the species wasn't native to Barrayar didn't mean it wasn't poisonous to horses. Miles sucked at his wounds and reflected upon Barrayar's shattered ecological history.

The fifty thousand Firsters from Earth had only meant to be the spearhead of Barrayar's colonization. Then, through a gravitational anomoly, the worm-hole jump through which the colonists had come shifted closed, irrevocably and without warning. The terraforming which had begun, so careful and controlled in the beginning, collapsed along with everything else. Imported Earth plant and animal species had escaped everywhere to run wild, as the humans turned their attention to the most urgent problems of survival. Biologists still mourned the mass extinctions of native species that had followed, the erosions and droughts and floods, but really, Miles thought, over the centuries of the Time of Isolation the fittest of both worlds had fought it out to a perfectly good new balance. If it was alive and covered the ground who cared where it came from?

We are all here by accident. Like the roses.

They camped that night high in the hills, and pushed on in the morning to the flanks of the true mountains. They were now out of the region Miles was personally familiar with from his childhood, and he checked Harra's directions frequently on his orbital survey map. They stopped only a few hours short of their goal at sunset of the second day. Harra insisted she could lead them on in the dusk from here, but Miles did not care to arrive after nightfall, unannounced, in a strange place of uncertain welcome.

He bathed the next morning in a stream, and unpacked and dressed carefully in his new officer's Imperial dress greens. Pym wore the Vorkosigan brown-and-silver livery, and pulled the Count's standard on a telescoping aluminum pole from the recesses of his saddlebag and mounted it on his left stirrup. *Dressed to kill,* thought Miles joylessly. Dr. Dea wore ordinary black fatigues and looked uncomfortable. If they constituted a message, Miles was damned if he knew what it was.

They pulled the horses up at midmorning before a two-room cabin set on the edge of a vast grove of sugar maples, planted who-knew-how-many centuries ago but now raggedly marching up the vale by self-seeding. The mountain air was cool and pure and bright. A few chickens stalked and bobbed in the weeds. An algae-choked wooden pipe from the woods dribbled water into a trough, which overflowed into a squishy green streamlet and away.

Harra slid down and smoothed her skirt and climbed the porch. "Karal?" she called. Miles waited high on horseback for the initial contact. Never give up a psychological advantage.

"Harra? Is that you?" came a man's voice from within. He banged open the door and rushed out. "Where have you been, girl? We've been beating the bushes for you! Thought you'd broke your neck in the scrub somewhere—" he stopped short before the three silent men on horseback.

"You wouldn't write down my charges, Karal," said Harra rather breathlessly. Her hands kneaded her skirt. "So I walked to the district magistrate at Vorkosigan Surleau to Speak them myself."

"Oh, girl," Karal breathed regretfully, "that was a *stupid* thing to do . . ." His head lowered and swayed, as he stared uneasily at the riders. He was a balding man of maybe sixty, leathery and worn, and his left arm ended in a stump. Another veteran.

"Speaker Serg Karal?" began Miles sternly. "I am the Voice of Count Vorkosigan. I am charged to investigate the crime Spoken by Harra Csurik before the Count's court, namely the murder of her infant daughter Raina. As Speaker of Silvy Vale, you are requested and required to assist me in all matters pertaining to the Count's justice."

At this point Miles ran out of prescribed formalities, and was on his own. That hadn't taken long. He waited. Fat Ninny snuffled. The silver-on-brown cloth of the standard made a few soft snapping sounds, lifted by a vagrant breeze.

"The district magistrate wasn't there," put in Harra, "but the Count was."

Karal was grey-faced, staring. He pulled himself together with an effort, came to a species of attention, and essayed a creaking half-bow. "Who—who are you, sir?"

"Lord Miles Vorkosigan."

Karal's lips moved silently. Miles was no lip reader, but he was pretty sure it came to a dismayed variant of *Oh, shit.* "This is my liveried man Sergeant Pym, and my medical examiner, Lieutenant Dea of the Imperial Service."

"You are my lord Count's son?" Karal croaked.

"The one and only." Miles was suddenly sick of the posing. Surely that was a sufficient first impression. He swung down off Ninny, landing lightly on the balls of his feet. Karal's gaze followed him down, and down. *Yeah, so I'm short. But wait'll you see me dance.* "All right if we water our horses in your trough here?" Miles looped Ninny's reins through his arm and stepped toward it.

"Uh, that's for the people, m'lord," said Karal. "Just a minute and I'll fetch a bucket." He hitched up his baggy trousers and trotted off around the side of the cabin. A minute's uncomfortable silence, then Karal's voice floating faintly, "Where'd you put the goat bucket, Zed?"

Another voice, light and young, "Behind the woodstack, Da." The voices fell to a muffled undertone. Karal came trotting back with a battered aluminum bucket, which he placed beside the trough. He knocked out a wooden plug in the side and a bright stream arced out to splash and fill. Fat Ninny flickered his ears and snuffled and rubbed his big head against Miles, smearing his tunic with red and white horsehairs and nearly knocking him off his feet. Karal glanced up and smiled at the horse, though his smile fell away as his gaze passed on to the horse's owner. As Fat Ninny gulped his drink Miles caught a glimpse of the owner of the second voice, a boy of around twelve who flitted off into the woods behind the cabin.

Karal fell to, assisting Miles and Harra and Pym in securing the horses. Miles left Pym to unsaddle and feed, and followed Karal into his house. Harra stuck to Miles like glue, and Dr. Dea unpacked his medical kit and trailed along. Miles's boots rang loud and unevenly on the wooden floorboards.

"My wife, she'll be back in the nooning," said Karal, moving uncertainly around the room as Miles and Dea settled themselves on a bench and Harra curled up with her arms around her knees on the floor beside the fieldstone hearth. "I'll . . . I'll make some tea, m'lord." He skittered back out the door to fill a kettle at the trough before Miles could say, *No, thank you.* No, let him ease his nerves in ordinary movements. Then maybe Miles could begin to tease out how much of this static was social nervousness and how much was— perhaps—guilty conscience. By the time Karal had the kettle on the coals he was noticeably better controlled, so Miles began.

"I'd prefer to commence this investigation immediately, Speaker. It need not take long."

"It need not . . . take place at all, m'lord. The baby's death was natural—there were no marks on her. She was weakly, she had the cat's mouth, who knows what else was wrong with her? She died in her sleep, or by some accident."

"It is remarkable," said Miles dryly, "how often such accidents happen in this district. My father the Count himself has . . . remarked on it."

"There was no call to drag you up here." Karal looked in exasperation at Harra. She sat silent, unmoved by his persuasion.

"It was no problem," said Miles blandly.

"Truly, m'lord," Karal lowered his voice, "I believe the child might have been overlain. 'S no wonder, in her grief, that her mind rejected it. Lem Csurik, he's a good boy, a good provider. She really doesn't want to do this, her reason is just temporarily overset by her troubles."

Harra's eyes, looking out from her hair-thatch, were poisonously cold.

"I begin to see," Miles's voice was mild, encouraging.

Karal brightened slightly. "It all could still be all right. If she will just be patient. Get over her sorrow. Talk to poor Lem. I'm sure he didn't kill the babe. Not rush to something she'll regret."

"I begin to see," Miles let his tone go ice cool, "why Harra Csurik found it necessary to walk four days to get an unbiased hearing. 'You think.' 'You believe.' 'Who knows what?' Not you, it appears. I hear speculation—accusation—innuendo—assertion. I came for *facts*, Speaker Karal. The Count's justice doesn't turn on guesses. It doesn't have to. This isn't the Time of Isolation. Not even the backbeyond.

"My investigation of the facts will begin now. No judgment will be —rushed into, before the facts are complete. Confirmation of Lem Csurik's guilt or innocence will come from his own mouth, under fast-penta, administered by Dr. Dea before two witnesses—yourself and a deputy of your choice. Simple, clean, and quick." *And maybe I can be on my way out of this benighted hole before sundown.* "I require you, Speaker, to go now and bring Lem Csurik for questioning. Sergeant Pym will assist you."

Karal killed another moment pouring the boiling water into a big brown pot before speaking. "I'm a travelled man, lord. A twenty-year Service man. But most folks here have never been out of Silvy Vale. Interrogation chemistry might as well be magic to them. They might say it was a false confession, got that way."

"Then you and your deputy can say otherwise. This isn't exactly like the good old days, when confessions were extracted under torture, Karal. Besides, if he's as innocent as you *guess*—he'll clear himself, no?"

Reluctantly, Karal went into the adjoining room. He came back shrugging on a faded Imperial Service uniform jacket with a corporal's rank marked on the collar, the buttons of which did not quite meet across his middle anymore. Preserved, evidently, for such official functions. Even as in Barrayaran custom one saluted the uniform, and not the man in it, so might the wrath engendered by an unpopular duty fall on the office and not the individual who carried it out. Miles appreciated the nuance.

Karal paused at the door. Harra still sat wrapped in silence by the hearth, rocking slightly.

"M'lord," said Karal. "I've been Speaker of Silvy Vale for sixteen years now. In all that time nobody has had to go to the district magistrate for a Speaking, not for water rights or stolen animals or swiving or even the time Neva accused Bors of tree piracy over the maple sap. We've not had a blood feud in all that time."

"I have no intention of starting a blood feud, Karal. I just want the facts."

"That's the thing, m'lord. I'm not so in love with facts as I used to be. Sometimes, they bite." Karal's eyes were urgent.

Really, the man was doing everything but stand on his head and juggle cats—one-handed—to divert Miles. How overt was his obstruction likely to get?

"Silvy Vale cannot be permitted to have its own little Time of Isolation," said Miles warningly. "The Count's justice is for everyone, now. Even if they're small. And weakly. And have something wrong with them. And cannot even speak for themselves—*Speaker.*"

Karal flinched, white about the lips—point taken, evidently. He trudged away up the trail, Pym following watchfully, one hand loosening the stunner in his holster.

They drank the tea while they waited, and Miles pottered about the cabin, looking but not touching. The hearth was the sole source of heat for cooking and washwater. There was a beaten metal sink for washing up, filled by hand from a covered bucket but emptied through a drainpipe under the porch to join the streamlet running down out of the trough. The second room was a bedroom, with a double bed and chests for storage. A loft held three more pallets; the boy around back had brothers, apparently. The place was cramped, but swept, things put away and hung up.

On a side table sat a government-issue audio receiver, and a second and older military model, opened up, apparently in the process of getting minor repairs and a new power pack. Exploration revealed a drawer full of old parts, nothing more complex than for simple audio sets, unfortunately. Speaker Karal must double as Silvy Vale's comm link specialist. How appropriate. They must pick up broadcasts from the station in Hassadar, maybe the high-power government channels from the capital as well.

No other electricity, of course. Powersat receptors were expensive pieces of precision technology. They would come even here, in time; some communities almost as small, but with strong economic co-ops, already had them. Silvy Vale was obviously still stuck in subsistence-level, and must needs wait till there was enough surplus in the district to gift them, if the surplus was not grabbed off first by some competing want. If only the city of Vorkosigan Vashnoi had not been obliterated by Cetagandan atomics, the whole district could be years ahead, economically. . . .

Miles walked out on the porch and leaned on the rail. Karal's son had returned. Down at the end of the cleared yard Fat Ninny was standing tethered, hip-shot, ears aflop, grunting with pleasure as the grinning boy scratched him vigorously under his halter. The boy looked up to catch Miles watching him, and scooted off fearfully to vanish again in the scrub downslope. "Huh," muttered Miles.

Dr. Dea joined him. "They've been gone a long time. About time to break out the fast-penta?"

"No, your autopsy kit, I should say. I fancy that's what we'll be doing next."

Dea glanced at him sharply. "I thought you sent Pym along to enforce the arrest."

"You can't arrest a man who's not there. Are you a wagering man, Doctor? I'll bet you a mark they don't come back with Csurik. No, hold it—maybe I'm wrong. I hope I'm wrong. Here are three coming back. . . ."

Karal, Pym, and another were marching down the trail. The third was a hulking young man, big-handed, heavy-browed, thick-necked, surly. "Harra," Miles called, "is this your husband?" He looked the part, by God, just what Miles had pictured. And four brothers just like him—only bigger, no doubt. . . .

Harra appeared by Miles's shoulder, and let out her breath. "No, m'lord. That's Alex, the Speaker's deputy."

"Oh." Miles's lips compressed in silent frustration. *Well, I had to give it a chance to be simple.*

Karal stopped beneath him and began a wandering explanation of his empty-handed state. Miles cut him off with a lift of his eyebrows. "Pym?"

"Bolted, m'lord," said Pym laconically. "Almost certainly warned."

"I agree." He frowned down at Karal, who prudently stood silent. Facts first. Decisions, such as how much deadly force to pursue the fugitive with, second. "Harra. How far is it to your burying place?"

"Down by the stream, lord, at the bottom of the valley. About two kilometers."

"Get your kit, Doctor, we're taking a walk. Karal, fetch a shovel."

"M'lord, surely it isn't needful to disturb the peace of the dead," began Karal.

"It is entirely needful. There's a place for the autopsy report right in the Procedural I got from the district magistrate's office. Where I will file my completed report upon this case when we return to Vorkosigan Surleau. I have permission from the next-of-kin—do I not, Harra?"

She nodded numbly.

"I have the two requisite witnesses, yourself and your," *gorilla,* "deputy, we have the doctor and the daylight—if you don't stand there arguing till sundown. All we need is the shovel. Unless you're volunteering to dig with your hand, Karal." Miles's voice was flat and grating and getting dangerous.

Karal's balding head bobbed in his distress. "The—the father is the legal next-of-kin, while he lives, and you don't have his—"

"Karal," said Miles.

"M'lord?"

"Take care the grave you dig is not your own. You've got one foot in it already."

Karal's hand opened in despair. "I'll . . . get the shovel, m'lord."

*   *   *

The mid-afternoon was warm, the air golden and summer-sleepy. The shovel bit with a steady *scrunch-scrunch* through the soil at the hands of Karal's deputy. Downslope, a bright stream burbled away over clean rounded stones. Harra hunkered watching, silent and grim.

When big Alex levered out the little crate—so little!—Sergeant Pym went off for a patrol of the wooded perimeter. Miles didn't blame him. He hoped the soil at that depth had been cool, these last eight days. Alex pried open the box, and Dr. Dea waved him away and took over. The deputy too went off to find something to examine at the far end of the graveyard.

Dea looked the cloth-wrapped bundle over carefully, lifted it out and set it on his tarp laid out on the ground in the bright sun. The instruments of his investigation were arrayed upon the plastic in precise order. He unwrapped the brightly-patterned cloths in their special folds, and Harra crept up to retrieve them, straighten and fold them ready for re-use, then crept back.

Miles fingered the handkerchief in his pocket, ready to hold over his mouth and nose, and went to watch over Dea's shoulder. Bad, but not too bad. He'd seen and smelled worse. Dea, filter-masked, spoke procedurals into his recorder, hovering in the air by his shoulder, and made his examination first by eye and gloved touch, then by scanner.

"Here, my lord," said Dea, and motioned Miles closer. "Almost certainly the cause of death, though I'll run the toxin tests in a moment. Her neck was broken. See here on the scanner where the spinal cord was severed, then the bones twisted back into alignment."

"Karal, Alex," Miles motioned them up to witness; they came reluctantly.

"Could this have been accidental?" said Miles.

"Very remotely possible. The re-alignment had to be deliberate, though."

"Would it have taken long?"

"Seconds only. Death was immediate."

"How much physical strength was required? A big man's or . . ."

"Oh, not much at all. Any adult could have done it, easily."

"Any sufficiently motivated adult." Miles's stomach churned at the mental picture Dea's words conjured up. The little fuzzy head would easily fit under a man's hand. The twist, the muffled cartilagenous crack—if there was one thing Miles knew by heart, it was the exact tactile sensation of breaking bone, oh yes.

"Motivation," said Dea, "is not my department." He paused. "I might note, a careful external examination could have found this. Mine did. An experienced layman—" his eye fell cool on Karal, "paying attention to what he was doing, should not have missed it."

Miles too stared at Karal, waiting.

"Overlain," hissed Harra. Her voice was ragged with scorn.

"M'lord," said Karal carefully, "it's true I suspected the possibility—"

Suspected, hell. You knew.

"But I felt—and still feel, strongly," his eye flashed a wary defiance, "that only more grief would come from a fuss. There was nothing I could do to help the baby at that point. My duties are to the living."

"So are mine, Speaker Karal. As, for example, my duty to the next small Imperial subject in mortal danger from those who should be his or her protectors, for the grave fault of being," Miles flashed an edged smile, "physically different. In Count Vorkosigan's view this is not just a case. This is a test case, fulcrum of a thousand cases. Fuss . . ." he hissed the sibilant; Harra rocked to the rhythm of his voice, "you haven't begun to see *fuss* yet."

Karal subsided as if folded.

There followed an hour of messiness yielding mainly negative data; no other bones were broken, the infant's lungs were clear, her gut and bloodstream free of toxins except those of natural decomposition. Her brain held no secret tumors. The defect for which she had died did not extend to spina bifida, Dea reported. Fairly simple plastic surgery would indeed have corrected the cat's mouth, could she somehow have won access to it. Miles wondered what comfort this confirmation was to Harra; cold, at best.

Dea put his puzzle back together, and Harra re-wrapped the tiny body in intricate, meaningful folds. Dea cleaned his tools and placed them in their cases and washed his hands and arms and face thoroughly in the stream, for rather a longer time than needed for just hygiene Miles thought, while the gorilla re-buried the box.

Harra made a little bowl in the dirt atop the grave and piled in some twigs and bark scraps and a sawed-off strand of her lank hair.

Miles, caught short, felt in his pockets. "I have no offering on me that will burn," he said apologetically. Harra glanced up, surprised at even the implied offer. "No matter, m'lord." Her little pile of scraps flared briefly and went out, like her infant Raina's life.

But it does matter, thought Miles.

Peace to you, small lady, after our rude invasions. I will give you a better sacrifice, I swear by my word as Vorkosigan. And the smoke of that burning will rise and be seen from one end of these mountains to the other.

Miles charged Karal and Alex straightly with producing Lem Csurik, and gave Harra Csurik a ride home up behind him on Fat Ninny. Pym accompanied them.

They passed a few scattered cabins on the way. At one a couple of grubby children playing in the yard loped alongside the horses, giggling and making hex signs at Miles, egging each other on to bolder displays, until their mother spotted them and ran out and hustled them indoors with a fearful look over her shoulder. In a weird way it was almost relaxing to Miles, the welcome he'd expected, not like Karal's and Alex's strained, self-conscious, careful not-noticing. Raina's life would not have been an easy one.

Harra's cabin was at the head of a long draw, just before it narrowed into a ravine. It seemed very quiet and isolated, in the dappled shade.

"Are you sure you wouldn't rather go stay with your mother?" asked Miles dubiously.

Harra shook her head. She slid down off Ninny, and Miles and Pym dismounted and followed her in.

The cabin was of standard design, a single room with a fieldstone fireplace and a wide roofed front porch. Water apparently came from the rivulet in the ravine. Pym held up a hand and entered first behind Harra, his hand on his stunner. If Lem Csurik had run, might he have run home first? Pym had been making scanner checks of perfectly innocent clumps of bushes all the way here.

The cabin was deserted. Although not long deserted; it did not have the lingering, dusty silence one would expect of eight days mournful disoccupation. The remains of a few hasty meals sat on the sinkboard. The bed was slept-in, rumpled and unmade. A few man's garments were scattered about. Automatically Harra began to move about the room, straightening it up, reasserting her presence, her existence, her worth. If she could not control the events of her life, at least she might control one small room.

The one untouched item was a cradle that sat beside the bed, little blankets neatly folded. Harra had fled for Vorkosigan Surleau just a few hours after the burial.

Miles wandered about the room, checking the view from the windows. "Will you show me where you went to get your brillberries, Harra?"

She led them up the ravine; Miles timed the hike. Pym divided his attention unhappily between the brush and Miles, alert to catch any bone-breaking stumble. After flinching away from about three aborted protective grabs Miles was ready to tell him to go climb a tree. Still, there was a certain understandable self-interest at work here, if Miles broke a leg it would be Pym who'd be stuck with carrying him out.

The brillberry patch was nearly a kilometer up the ravine. Miles plucked a few seedy red berries and ate them absently, looking around, while Harra and Pym waited respectfully. Afternoon sun slanted through green and brown leaves, but the bottom of the ravine was already grey and cool with premature twilight. The brillberry vines clung to the rocks and hung down invitingly, luring one to risk one's neck reaching. Miles resisted their weedy temptations, not being all that fond of brillberries. "If someone called out from your cabin, you couldn't hear them up here, could you?" remarked Miles.

"No, m'lord."

"About how long did you spend picking?"

"About," Harra shrugged, "a basketful."

The woman didn't own a chrono. "An hour, say. And a twenty-minute climb each way. About a two hour time window, that morning. Your cabin was not locked?"

"Just a latch, m'lord."

"Hm."

Method, motive, and opportunity, the district magistrate's Procedural had emphasized. Damn. The method was established, and almost anybody could have used it. The opportunity angle, it appeared, was just as bad. Anyone at all could have walked up to that cabin, done the deed, and departed, unseen and unheard. It was much too late for an aura detector to be of use, tracing the shining ghosts of movements in and out of that room, even if Miles had brought one.

Facts, hah. They were back to motive, the murky workings of men's minds. Anybody's guess.

Miles had, as per the instructions in the district magistrate's Procedural, been striving to keep an open mind about the accused, but it was getting harder and harder to resist Harra's assertions. She'd been proved right about everything so far.

They left Harra re-installed in her little home, going through the motions of order and the normal routine of life as if they could somehow re-create it, like an act of sympathetic magic.

"Are you sure you'll be all right?" Miles asked, gathering Fat Ninny's reins and settling himself in the saddle. "I can't help but think that if your husband's in the area, he could show up here. You say nothing's been taken, so it's unlikely he's been here and gone before we arrived. Do you want someone to stay with you?"

"No, m'lord." She hugged her broom, on the porch. "I'd . . . I'd like to be alone for a while."

"Well . . . all right. I'll, ah, send you a message if anything important happens."

"Thank you, m'lord." Her tone was unpressing; she really did want to be left alone. Miles took the hint.

At a wide place in the trail back to Speaker Karal's, Pym and Miles rode stirrup to stirrup. Pym was still painfully on the alert for boogies in the bushes.

"My lord, may I suggest that your next logical step be to draft all the able-bodied men in the community for a hunt for this Csurik? Beyond doubt, you've established that the infanticide was a murder."

Interesting turn of phrase, Miles thought dryly. *Even Pym doesn't find it redundant. Oh, my poor Barrayar.* "It seems reasonable at first glance, Sergeant Pym, but has it occurred to you that half the able-bodied men in this community are probably relatives of Lem Csurik's?"

"It might have a psychological effect. Create enough disruption, and perhaps someone would turn him in just to get it over with."

"Hm, possibly. Assuming he hasn't already left the area. He could have been halfway to the coast before we were done at the autopsy."

"Only if he had access to transport." Pym glanced at the empty sky.

"For all we know one of his sub-cousins had a rickety lightflyer in a shed somewhere. But . . . he's never been out of Silvy Vale. I'm not sure he'd know how to run, where to go. Well, if he has left the district it's a problem for Imperial Civil Security, and I'm off the hook." Happy thought. "But—one of the things that bothers me, a lot, are the inconsistencies in the picture I'm getting of our chief suspect. Have you noticed them?"

"Can't say as I have, m'lord."

"Hm. Where did Karal take you, by the way, to arrest this guy?"

"To a wild area, rough scrub and gullies. Half a dozen men were out searching for Harra. They'd just called off their search and were on their way back when we met up with them. By which I concluded our arrival was no surprise."

"Had Csurik actually been there, and fled, or was Karal just ring-leading you in a circle?"

"I think he'd actually been there, m'lord. The men claimed not, but as you point out they were relatives, and besides, they did not, ah, lie well. They were tense. Karal may begrudge you his cooperation, but I don't think he'll quite dare disobey your direct orders. He is a twenty-year man, after all."

Like Pym himself, Miles thought. Count Vorkosigan's personal guard was legally limited to a ceremonial twenty men, but given his political position their function included very practical security. Pym was typical of their number, a decorated veteran of the Imperial Service who had retired to this elite private force. It was not Pym's fault that when he had joined he had stepped into a dead man's shoes, replacing the late Sergeant Bothari. Did anyone in the universe besides himself miss the deadly and difficult Bothari? Miles wondered sadly.

"I'd like to question *Karal* under fast-penta," said Miles morosely. "He displays every sign of being a man who knows where the body's buried."

"Why don't you, then?" asked Pym logically.

"I may come to that. There is, however, a certain unavoidable degradation in a fast-penta interrogation. If the man's loyal it may not be in our best long-range interest to shame him publicly."

"It wouldn't be in public."

"No, but he would remember being turned into a drooling idiot. I need . . . more information."

Pym glanced back over his shoulder. "I thought you had all the information, by now."

"I have facts. Physical facts. A great big pile of—meaningless, useless facts." Miles brooded. "If I have to fast-penta every backbeyonder in Silvy Vale to get to the bottom of this, I will. But it's not an elegant solution."

"It's not an elegant problem, m'lord," said Pym dryly.

They returned to find Speaker Karal's wife back and in full possession of her home. She was running in frantic circles, chopping, beating, kneading, stoking, and flying upstairs to change the bedding on the three pallets, driving her three sons before her to fetch and run and carry. Dr. Dea, bemused, was following her about trying to slow her down, explaining that they had brought their own tent and food, thank you, and that her hospitality was not required. This produced a most indignant response from Ma Karal.

"My lord's own son come to my house, and I to turn him out in the fields like his horse! I'd be ashamed!" And she returned to her work.

"She seems rather distraught," said Dea, looking over his shoulder.

Miles took him by the elbow and propelled him out onto the porch. "Just get out of her way, Doctor. We're doomed to be Entertained. It's an obligation on both sides. The polite thing to do is sort of pretend we're not here till she's ready for us."

Dea lowered his voice. "It might be better, in light of the circumstances, if we were to eat only our packaged food."

The chatter of a chopping knife, and a scent of herbs and onions, wafted enticingly through the open window. "Oh, I would imagine anything out of the common pot would be all right, wouldn't you?" said Miles. "If anything really worries you, you can wisk it off and check it, I suppose, but—discreetly, eh? We don't want to insult anyone."

They settled themselves in the homemade wooden chairs, and were promptly served tea again by a boy draftee of ten, Karal's youngest. He had apparently already received private instructions in manners from one or the other of his parents, for his response to Miles's deformities was the same flickering covert not-noticing as the adults, not quite as smoothly carried off.

"Will you be sleeping in my bed, m'lord?" he asked. "Ma says we got to sleep on the porch."

"Well, whatever your Ma says, goes," said Miles. "Ah . . . do you like sleeping on the porch?"

"Naw. Last time, Zed kicked me and I rolled off in the dark."

"Oh. Well, perhaps, if we're to displace you, you would care to sleep in our tent by way of trade."

The boy's eyes widened. "Really?"

"Certainly. Why not?"

"Wait'll I tell Zed!" He danced down the steps and shot away around the side of the house. "Zed, hey, Zed . . . !"

"I suppose," said Dea, "we can fumigate it, later. . . ."

Miles's lips twitched. "They're no grubbier than you were at the same age, surely. Or than I was. When I was permitted." The late afternoon was warm. Miles took off his green tunic and hung it on the back of his chair, and unbuttoned the round collar of his cream shirt.

Dea's brows rose. "Are we keeping shopman's hours, then, m'lord, on this investigation? Calling it quits for the day?"

"Not exactly." Miles sipped tea thoughtfully, gazing out across the yard. The trees and treetops fell away down to the bottom of this feeder valley. Mixed scrub climbed the other side of the slope. A crested fold, then the long flanks of a backbone mountain, beyond, rose high and harsh to a summit still flecked with dwindling dirty patches of snow.

"There's still a murderer loose out there somewhere," Dea pointed out helpfully.

"You sound like Pym." Pym, Miles noted, had finished with their horses and was taking his scanner for another walk. "I'm waiting."

"What for?"

"Not sure. The piece of information that will make sense of all this. Look, there's only two possibilities. Csurik's either innocent or he's guilty. If he's guilty, he's not going to turn himself in. He'll certainly involve his relations, hiding and helping him. I can call in reinforcements by comm link from Imperial Civil Security in Hassadar, if I want to. Any time. Twenty men, plus equipment, here by aircar in a couple of hours. Create a circus. Brutal, ugly, disruptive, exciting—could be quite popular. A manhunt, with blood at the end.

"Of course, there's also the possibility that Csurik's innocent, but scared. In which case . . ."

"Yes?"

"In which case, there's still a murderer out there." Miles drank more tea. "I merely note, if you want to catch something, running after it isn't always the best way."

Dea cleared his throat, and drank his tea too.

"In the meantime, I have another duty to carry out. I'm here to be seen. If your scientific spirit is yearning for something to do to wile away the hours, try keeping count of the number of Vor-watchers that turn up tonight."

Miles's predicted parade began almost immediately. It was mainly women, at first, bearing gifts as to a funeral. In the absence of a comm link system Miles wasn't sure by what telepathy they managed to communicate with each other, but they brought covered dishes of food, flowers, extra bedding, and offers of assistance. They were all introduced to Miles with nervous curtseys, but seldom lingered to chat; apparently a look was all their curiosity desired. Ma Karal was polite, but made it clear that she had the situation well in hand, and set their culinary offerings well back of her own.

Some of the women had children in tow. Most of these were sent to play in the woods in back, but a small party of whispering boys sneaked back around the cabin to peek up over the rim of the porch at Miles. Miles had obligingly remained on the porch with Dea, remarking that it was a better view, without saying for whom. For a few moments Miles pretended not to notice his audience, restraining

Pym with a hand signal from running them off. *Yes, look well, look your fill,* thought Miles. *What you see is what you're going to get, for the rest of your lives or at any rate mine. Get used to it.* . . . Then he caught Zed Karal's whisper, as self-appointed tour guide to his cohort —"That big one's the one that's come to kill Lem Csurik!"

"Zed," said Miles.

There was an abrupt frozen silence from under the edge of the porch. Even the animal rustlings stopped.

"Come here," said Miles.

To a muted background of dismayed whispers and nervous giggles, Karal's middle boy slouched warily up on to the porch.

"You three—" Miles's pointing finger caught them in mid-flight, "wait there." Pym added his frown for emphasis, and Zed's friends stood paralyzed, eyes wide, heads lined up at the level of the porch floor as if stuck up on some ancient battlement as a warning to kindred malefactors.

"What did you just say to your friends, Zed?" asked Miles quietly. "Repeat it."

Zed licked his lips. "I jus' said you'd come to kill Lem Csurik, lord." Zed was clearly now wondering if Miles's murderous intent included obnoxious and disrespectful boys as well.

"That is not true, Zed. That is a dangerous lie."

Zed looked bewildered. "But Da—said it."

"What is true, is that I've come to catch the person who killed Lem Csurik's baby daughter. That may be Lem. But it may not. Do you understand the difference?"

"But Harra said Lem did it, and she ought to know, he's her husband and all."

"The baby's neck was broken by someone. Harra thinks Lem, but she didn't see it happen. What you and your friends here have to understand is that I won't make a mistake. I *can't* condemn the wrong person. My own truth drugs won't let me. Lem Csurik has only to come here and tell me the truth to clear himself, if he didn't do it.

"But suppose he did. What should I do with a man who would kill a baby, Zed?"

Zed shuffled. "Well, she was only a mutie . . ." then shut his mouth and reddened, not-looking at Miles.

It was, perhaps, a bit much to ask a twelve-year-old boy to take an interest in any baby, let alone a mutie one . . . *no,* dammit. It wasn't too much. But how to get a hook into that prickly defensive surface? And if Miles couldn't even convince one surly twelve-year-old, how was he to magically transmute a whole District of adults? A rush of despair made him suddenly want to rage. These people were so bloody *impossible.* He checked his temper firmly.

"Your Da was a twenty-year man, Zed. Are you proud that he served the Emperor?"

"Yes, lord." Zed's eyes sought escape, trapped by these terrible adults.

Miles forged on. "Well, these practices—mutie-killing—shame the Emperor, when he stands for Barrayar before the galaxy. I've been out there. I know. They call us all savages, for the crimes of a few. It shames the Count my father before his peers, and Silvy Vale before the District. A soldier gets honor by killing an armed enemy, not a baby. This matter touches my honor as a Vorkosigan, Zed. Besides," Miles's lips drew back on a mirthless grin, and he leaned forward intently in his chair—Zed recoiled as much as he dared—"you will all be astonished at what *only a mutie* can do. *That* I have sworn on my grandfather's grave."

Zed looked more suppressed than enlightened, his slouch now almost a crouch. Miles slumped back in his chair and released him with a weary wave of his hand. "Go play, boy."

Zed needed no urging. He and his companions shot away around the house as though released from springs.

Miles drummed his fingers on the chair arm, frowning into the silence that neither Pym nor Dea dared break.

"These hill-folk are ignorant, lord," offered Pym after a moment.

"These hill-folk are *mine*, Pym. Their ignorance is . . . a shame upon my house." Miles brooded. How had this whole mess become his anyway? He hadn't created it. Historically, he'd only just got here himself. "Their continued ignorance, anyway," he amended in fairness. It still made a burden like a mountain. "Is the message so complex? So difficult? 'You don't have to kill your children anymore.' It's not like we're asking them all to learn—5-Space navigational math." That had been the plague of Miles's last Academy semester.

"It's not easy for them," shrugged Dea. "It's easy for the central authorities to make the rules, but these people have to live every minute of the consequences. They have so little, and the new rules force them to give their margin to marginal people who can't pay back. The old ways were wise, in the old days. Even now you have to wonder how many premature reforms we can afford, trying to ape the galactics."

And what's your definition of a marginal person, Dea? "But the margin is growing," Miles said aloud. "Places like this aren't up against famine every winter any more. They're not isolated in their disasters, relief can get from one district to another under the Imperial seal . . . we're all getting more connected, just as fast as we can. Besides," Miles paused, and added rather weakly, "perhaps you underestimate them."

Dea's brows rose ironically. Pym strolled the length of the porch, running his scanner in yet another pass over the surrounding scrubland. Miles, turning in his chair to pursue his cooling teacup, caught a slight movement, a flash of eyes, behind the casement-hung front window swung open to the summer air—Ma Karal, standing frozen, listening. For how long? Since he'd called her boy Zed, Miles guessed, arresting her attention. She raised her chin as his eyes met hers, sniffed, and shook out the cloth she'd been holding with a snap. They exchanged a nod. She turned back to her work before Dea, watching Pym, noticed her.

Karal and Alex returned, understandably, around suppertime. "I have six men out searching," Karal reported cautiously to Miles on the porch, now well on its way to becoming Miles's official HQ. Clearly, Karal had covered ground since midafternoon. His face was sweaty, lined with physical as well as the underlying emotional strain. "But I think Lem's gone into the scrub. It could take days to smoke him out. There's hundreds of places to lie low out there."

Karal ought to know. "You don't think he's gone to some relatives?" asked Miles. "Surely, if he intends to evade us for long, he has to take a chance on re-supply, on information. Will they turn him in when he surfaces?"

"It's hard to say." Karal turned his hand palm-out. "It's . . . a hard problem for 'em, m'lord."

"Hm."

How long would Lem Csurik hang around out there in the scrub, anyway? His whole life—his blown-to-bits life—was all here in Silvy Vale. Miles considered the contrast. A few weeks ago, Csurik had been a young man with everything going for him; a home, a wife, a family on the way, happiness; by Silvy Vale standards, comfort and security. His cabin, Miles had not failed to note, though simple, had been kept with love and energy, and so redeemed from the potential squalor of its poverty. Grimmer in the winter, to be sure. Now Csurik was a hunted fugitive, all the little he had torn away in the twinkling of an eye. With nothing to hold him, would he run away and keep running? With nothing to run to, would he linger near the ruins of his life?

The police force available to Miles a few hours way in Hassadar was an itch in his mind. Was it not time to call them in, before he fumbled this into a worse mess? But . . . if he were meant to solve this by a show of force, why hadn't the Count let him come by aircar on the first day? Miles regretted that two-and-a-half-day ride. It had sapped his forward momentum, slowed him down to Silvy Vale's walking pace, tangled him with time to doubt. Had the Count foreseen it? What did he know that Miles didn't? What *could* he know? Dammit, this test didn't need to be made harder by artificial stumbling blocks, it was bad enough all on its own. *He wants me to be clever,* Miles thought morosely. *Worse, he wants me to be seen to be clever, by everyone here.* He prayed he was not about to be spectacularly stupid instead.

"Very well, Speaker Karal. You've done all you can for today. Knock off for the night. Call your men off too. You're not likely to find anything in the dark."

Pym held up his scanner, clearly about to volunteer its use, but Miles waved him down. Pym's brows rose, editorially. Miles shook his head slightly.

Karal needed no further urging. He dispatched Alex to call off the night search with torches. He remained wary of Miles. Perhaps Miles puzzled him as much as he puzzled Miles? Dourly, Miles hoped so.

Miles was not sure at what point the long summer evening segued into a party. After supper the men began to drift in, Karal's cronies, Silvy Vale's elders. Some were apparently regulars who shared the evening government news broadcasts on Karal's audio set. Too many names, and Miles daren't forget a one. A group of amateur musicians arrived with their homemade mountain instruments, rather breathless, obviously the band tapped for all the major weddings and wakes in Silvy Vale; this all seemed more like a funeral to Miles every minute.

The musicians stood in the middle of the yard and played. Miles's porch-HQ now became his aristocratic box seat. It was hard to get involved with the music when the audience was all so intently watching him. Some songs were serious, some—rather carefully at first— funny. Miles's spontaneity was frequently frozen in mid-laugh by a faint sigh of relief from those around him; his stiffening froze them in turn, self-stymied like two people trying to dodge each other in a corridor.

But one song was so hauntingly beautiful—a lament for lost love— that Miles was struck to the heart. *Elena. . . .* In that moment, old pain transformed to melancholy, sweet and distant; a sort of healing, or at least the realization that a healing had taken place, unwatched. He almost had the singers stop there, while they were perfect, but feared they might think him displeased. But he remained quiet and inward for a time afterward, scarcely hearing their next offering in the gathering twilight.

At least the piles of food that had arrived all afternoon were thus accounted for. Miles had been afraid Ma Karal and her cronies had expected him to get around that culinary mountain all by himself.

At one point Miles leaned on the rail and glanced down the yard to see Fat Ninny at tether, making more friends. A whole flock of pubescent girls were clustered around him, petting him, brushing his fetlocks, braiding flowers and ribbons in his mane and tail, feeding him tidbits, or just resting their cheeks against his warm silky side. Ninny's eyes were half-closed in smug content.

God, thought Miles jealously, *if I had half the sex-appeal of that bloody horse I'd have more girlfriends than my cousin Ivan.* Miles considered, very briefly, the pros and cons of making a play for some unattached female. The striding lords of old and all that . . . no. There were some kinds of stupid he didn't have to be, and that was definitely one of them. The service he had already sworn to one small lady of Silvy Vale was surely all he could bear without breaking; he could feel the strain of it all around him now, like a dangerous pressure in his bones.

He turned to find Speaker Karal presenting a woman to him, far from pubescent; she was perhaps fifty, lean and little, work-worn. She was carefully clothed in an aging best-dress, her greying hair combed back and bound at the nape of her neck. She bit at her lips and cheeks in quick tense motions, half-suppressed in her self-consciousness.

" 'S Ma Csurik, m'lord. Lem's mother." Speaker Karal ducked his head and backed away, abandoning Miles without aid or mercy—*Come back, you coward!*

"Ma'am," Miles said. His throat was dry. Karal had set him up, dammit, a public play—no, the other guests were retreating out of earshot too, most of them.

"M'lord," said Ma Csurik. She managed a nervous curtsey.

"Uh . . . do sit down." With a ruthless jerk of his chin Miles evicted Dr. Dea from his chair and motioned the hill woman into it. He turned his own chair to face hers. Pym stood behind them, silent as a statue, tight as a wire. Did he imagine the old woman was about to whip a needler-pistol from her skirts? No—it was Pym's job to imagine things like that for Miles, so that Miles might free his whole mind for the problem at hand. Pym was almost as much an object of study as Miles himself. Wisely, he'd been holding himself apart, and would doubtless continue to do so till the dirty work was over.

"M'lord," said Ma Csurik again, and stumbled again to silence. Miles could only wait. He prayed she wasn't about to come unglued and weep on his knees or some damn thing. This was excruciating. *Stay strong, woman,* he urged silently.

"Lem, he . . ." she swallowed, "I'm sure he didn't kill the babe. There's never been any of that in our family, I swear it! He says he didn't, and I believe him."

"Good," said Miles affably. "Let him come say the same thing to me under fast-penta, and I'll believe him too."

"Come away, Ma," urged a lean young man who had accompanied her and now stood waiting by the steps, as if ready to bolt into the dark at a motion. "It's no good, can't you see." He glowered at Miles.

She shot the boy a quelling frown—another of her five sons?—and turned back more urgently to Miles, groping for words. "My Lem. He's only twenty, lord."

"*I'm* only twenty, Ma Csurik," Miles felt compelled to point out. There was another brief impasse.

"Look, I'll say it again," Miles burst out impatiently. "And again, and again, till the message penetrates all the way back to its intended recipient. I *cannot* condemn an innocent person. My truth drugs won't let me. Lem can clear himself. He has only to come in. Tell him, will you? Please?"

She went stony, guarded. "I . . . haven't seen him, m'lord."

"But you might."

She tossed her head. "So? I might not." Her eyes shifted to Pym and away, as if the sight of him burned. The silver Vorkosigan logos embroidered on Pym's collar gleamed in the twilight like animal eyes, moving only with his breathing. Karal was now bringing lighted lamps onto the porch, but keeping his distance still.

"Ma'am," said Miles tightly. "The Count my father has ordered me to investigate the murder of your granddaughter. If your son means so much to you, how can his child mean so little? Was she . . . your first grandchild?"

Her face was sere. "No, lord. Lem's older sister, she has two. *They're* all right," she added with emphasis.

Miles sighed. "If you truly believe your son is innocent of this crime, you must help me prove it. Or—do you doubt?"

She shifted uneasily. There was doubt in her eyes—she didn't know, blast it. Fast-penta would be useless on her, for sure. As Miles's magic wonder drug, much counted-upon, fast-penta seemed to be having wonderfully little utility in this case so far.

"Come away, Ma," the young man urged again. "It's no good. The mutie lord came up here for a killing. They have to have one. It's a show."

Damn straight, thought Miles acidly. He was a perceptive young lunk, that one.

Ma Csurik let herself be persuaded away by her angry and embarrassed son plucking at her arm. She paused on the steps, though, and shot bitterly over her shoulder, "It's all so easy for you, isn't it?"

My head hurts, thought Miles.

There was worse to come before the evening ended.

The new woman's voice was grating, low and angry. "Don't you talk down to me, Serg Karal. I got a right for one good look at this mutie lord."

She was tall and stringy and tough. *Like her daughter,* Miles thought. She had made no attempt to freshen up. A faint reek of summer sweat hung about her working dress. And how far had she walked? Her grey hair hung in a switch down her back, a few strands escaping the tie. If Ma Csurik's bitterness had been a stabbing pain behind the eyes, this one's rage was a wringing knot in the gut.

She shook off Karal's attempted restraint and stalked up to Miles in the lamplight. "So."

"Uh . . . this is Ma Mattulich, m'lord," Karal introduced her. "Harra's mother."

Miles rose to his feet, managed a short formal nod. "How do you do, madam." He was very conscious of being a head shorter. She had once been of a height with Harra, Miles estimated, but her aging bones were beginning to pull her down.

She merely stared. She was a gum-leaf chewer, by the faint blackish stains around her mouth. Her jaw worked now on some small bit, tiny chomps, grinding too hard. She studied him openly, without subterfuge or the least hint of apology, taking in his head, his neck, his back, his short and crooked legs. Miles had the unpleasant illusion that she saw right through to all the healed cracks in his brittle bones as well. Miles's chin jerked up twice in the twitchy, nervous-involuntary tic that he was sure made him look spastic, before he controlled it with an effort.

"All right," said Karal roughly, "you've seen. Now come away, for God's sake, Mara." His hand opened in apology to Miles. "Mara, she's been pretty distraught over all this, m'lord. Forgive her."

"Your only grandchild," said Miles to her, in an effort to be kind, though her peculiar anguish repelled kindness with a scraped and bleeding scorn. "I understand your distress, ma'am. But there will be justice for little Raina. That I have sworn."

"How can there be justice *now?*" she raged, thick and low. "It's too late—a world too late—for justice, mutie lordling. What use do I have for your damned justice *now?*"

"Enough, Mara!" Karal insisted. His brows drew down and his lips thinned, and he forced her away and escorted her firmly off his porch.

The last lingering remnant of visitors parted for her with an air of respectful mercy, except for two lean teenagers hanging on the fringes who drew away as if avoiding poison. Miles was forced to revise his mental image of the Brothers Csurik. If those two were another sample, there was no team of huge menacing hill hulks after all. They were a team of little skinny menacing hill squirts instead. Not really an improvement, they looked like they could move as fast as striking ferrets if they had to. Miles's lips curled in frustration.

The evening's entertainments ended finally, thank God, close to midnight. Karal's last cronies marched off into the woods by lantern light. The repaired and re-powered audio set was carried off by its owner with many thanks to Karal. Fortunately it had been a mature and sober crowd, even somber, no drunken brawls or anything. Pym got the Karal boys settled in the tent, took a last patrol around the cabin, and joined Miles and Dea in the loft. The pallets' stuffing had been spiked with fresh scented native herbs, to which Miles hoped devoutly he was not allergic. Ma Karal had wanted to turn her own bedroom over to Miles's exclusive lordly use, exiling herself and her husband to the porch too, but fortunately Pym had been able to persuade her that putting Miles in the loft, flanked by Dea and himself, was to be preferred from a security standpoint.

Dea and Pym were soon snoring, but sleep eluded Miles. He tossed on his pallet as he turned his ploys of the day, such as they had been, over and over in his mind. Was he being too slow, too careful, too conservative? This wasn't exactly good assault tactics, surprise with a superior force. The view he'd gained of the terrain from Karal's porch tonight had been ambiguous at best.

On the other hand, it did no good to charge off across a swamp, as his fellow cadet and cousin Ivan Vorpatril had demonstrated so memorably once on summer maneuvers. It had taken a heavy hovercab with a crane to crank the six big, strong, healthy, fully field-equipped young men of Ivan's patrol out of the chest-high, gooey black mud.

Ivan had got his revenge simultaneously, though, when the cadet "sniper" they had been attacking fell out of his tree and broke his arm while laughing hysterically as they sank slowly and beautifully into the ooze. Ooze that a little guy, with his laser rifle wrapped in his loincloth, could swim across like a frog. The war games umpire had ruled it a draw. Miles rubbed his forearm and grinned in memory, and faded out at last.

Miles awoke abruptly and without transition deep in the night with a sense of something wrong. A faint orange glow shimmered in the blue darkness of the loft. Quietly, so as not to disturb his sleeping companions, he rose on his pallet and peered over the edge into the main room. The glow was coming through the front window.

Miles swung onto the ladder and padded downstairs for a look out doors. "Pym," he called softly.

Pym shot awake with a snort. "M'lord?" he said, alarmed.

"Come down here. Quietly. Bring your stunner."

Pym was by his side in seconds. He slept in his trousers with his stunner holster and boots by his pillow. "What the hell—?" Pym muttered, looking out too.

The glow was from fire. A pitchy torch, flung to the top of Miles's tent set up in the yard, was burning quietly. Pym lurched toward the door, then controlled his movements as the same realization came to him as had to Miles. Theirs was a Service-issue tent, and its combat-rated synthetic fabric would neither melt nor burn.

Miles wondered if the person who'd heaved the torch had known that. Was this some arcane warning, or a singularly inept attack? If the tent had been ordinary fabric, and Miles in it, the intended result might not have been trivial. Worse with Karal's boys in it—a bursting blossom of flame—Miles shuddered.

Pym loosened his stunner in his holster and stood poised by the front door. "How long?"

"I'm not sure. Could have been burning like that for ten minutes before it woke me."

Pym shook his head, took a slight breath, raised his scanner, and vaulted into the fire-gilded darkness.

"Trouble, m'lord?" Speaker Karal's anxious voice came from his bedroom door.

"Maybe. Wait—" Miles halted him as he plunged for the door. "Pym's running a patrol with a scanner and a stunner. Wait'll he calls the all-clear, I think. Your boys may be safer inside the tent."

Karal came up to the window, caught his breath, and swore.

Pym returned in a few minutes. "There's no one within a kilometer, now," he reported shortly. He helped Karal take the goat bucket and douse the torch. The boys, who had slept through the fire, woke at its quenching.

"I think maybe it was a bad idea to lend them my tent," said Miles from the porch in a choked voice. "I am profoundly sorry, Speaker Karal. I didn't think."

"This should never . . ." Karal was spluttering with anger and delayed fright, "this should *never* have happened, m'lord. I apologize for . . . for Silvy Vale." He turned helplessly, peering into the darkness. The night sky, star-flecked, lovely, was threatening now.

The boys, once the facts penetrated their sleepiness, thought it was all just great, and wanted to return to the tent and lie in wait for the next assassin. Ma Karal, shrill and firm, herded them indoors instead and made them bed down in the main room. It was an hour before they stopped complaining at the injustice of it and went back to sleep.

Miles, keyed up nearly to the point of gibbering, did not sleep at all. He lay stiffly on his pallet, listening to Dea, who slept breathing heavily, and Pym, feigning sleep for courtesy and scarcely seeming to breathe at all.

Miles was about to suggest to Pym that they give up and go out on the porch for the rest of the night when the silence was shattered by a shrill squeal, enormously loud, pain-edged, from outside.

"The horses!" Miles spasmed to his feet, heart racing, and beat Pym to the ladder. Pym cut ahead of him by dropping straight over the side of the loft into an elastic crouch, and beat him to the door. There, Pym's trained bodyguard's reflexes compelled him to try and thrust Miles back inside. Miles almost bit him. "Go, dammit! I've got a weapon!"

Pym, good intentions frustrated, swung out the cabin door with Miles on his heels. Halfway down the yard they split to each side as a massive snorting shape loomed out of the darkness and nearly ran them down; the sorrel mare, loose again. Another squeal pierced the night from the lines where the horses were tethered.

"Ninny?" Miles called, panicked. It was Ninny's voice making those noises, the like of which Miles had not heard since the night a shed had burned down at Vorkosigan Surleau with a horse trapped inside. "Ninny!"

Another grunting squeal, and a thunk like someone splitting a watermelon with a mallet. Pym staggered back, inhaling with difficulty, a resonant deep stutter, and tripped to the ground where he lay curled up around himself. Not killed outright, apparently, because between gasps he was managing to swear lividly. Miles dropped to the ground beside him, checked his skull—no, thank God it had been Pym's chest Ninny's hoof had hit with that alarming sound. The bodyguard only had the wind knocked out of him, maybe a cracked rib. Miles more sensibly ran around to the *front* of the horse lines. "Ninny!"

Fat Ninny was jerking his head against his rope, attempting to rear. He squealed again, his white-rimmed eyes gleaming in the darkness. Miles ran to his head. "Ninny, boy! What is it?" His left hand slid up the rope to Ninny's halter, his right stretched to stroke Ninny's shoulder soothingly. Fat Ninny flinched, but stopped trying to rear, and stood trembling. The horse shook his head. Miles's face and chest were suddenly spattered with something hot and dark and sticky.

"Dea!" Miles yelled. *"Dea!"*

Nobody slept through this uproar. Six people tumbled off the porch and down the yard, and not one of them thought to bring a light . . . no, the brilliant flare of a cold light sprang from between Dr. Dea's fingers, and Ma Karal was struggling even now to light a lantern. "Dea, get that damn light over here!" Miles demanded, and stopped to choke his voice back down an octave to its usual carefully-cultivated deeper register.

Dea galloped up and thrust the light toward Miles, then gasped, his face draining. "My lord! Are you shot?" In the flare the dark liquid soaking Miles's shirt glowed suddenly scarlet.

"Not me," Miles said, looking down at his chest in horror. A flash of memory turned his stomach over, cold at the vision of another blood-soaked death, that of the late Sergeant Bothari whom Pym had replaced. Would never replace.

Dea spun. "Pym?"

"He's all right," said Miles. A long inhaling wheeze rose from the grass a few meters off, the exhalation punctuated with obscenities. "But he got kicked by the horse. Get your medkit!" Miles peeled Dea's fingers off the cold light, and Dea dashed back to the cabin.

Miles held the light up to Ninny, and swore in a sick whisper. A huge cut, a third of a meter long and of unknown depth, scored Ninny's glossy neck. Blood soaked his coat and runneled down his foreleg. Miles's fingers touched the wound fearfully; his hands spread on either side, trying to push it closed, but the horse's skin was elastic and it pulled apart and bled profusely as Fat Ninny shook his head in pain. Miles grabbed the horse's nose—"Hold still, boy!" Somebody had been going for Ninny's jugular. And had almost made it; Ninny—

tame, petted, friendly, trusting Ninny—would not have moved from the touch until the knife bit deep.

Karal was helping Pym to his feet as Dr. Dea returned. Miles waited while Dea checked Pym over, then called, "Here, Dea!"

Zed, looking quite as horrified as Miles, helped to hold Ninny's head as Dea made inspection of the cut. "I took tests," Dea complained *sotto voce* as he worked. "I beat out twenty-six other applicants, for the honor of becoming the Prime Minister's personal physician. I have practiced the procedures of seventy separate possible medical emergencies, from coronary thrombosis to attempted assassination. Nobody—*nobody*—told me my duties would include sewing up a damned horse's neck in the middle of the night in the middle of a howling wilderness. . . ." But he kept working as he complained, so Miles didn't quash him, but kept gently petting Ninny's nose, and hypnotically rubbing the hidden pattern of his muscles, to soothe and still him. At last Ninny relaxed enough to rest his slobbery chin on Miles's shoulder.

"Do horses get anesthetics?" asked Dea plaintively, holding his medical stunner as if not sure just what to do with it.

"This one does," said Miles stoutly. "You treat him just like a person, Dea. This is the last animal that the Count my grandfather personally trained. He named him. I watched him get born. We trained him together. Grandfather had me pick him up and hold him every day for a week after he was foaled, till he got too big. Horses are creatures of habit, Grandfather said, and take first impressions to heart. Forever after Ninny thought I was bigger than he was."

Dea sighed and made busy with anesthetic stun, cleansing solution, antibiotics, muscle relaxants, and biotic glue. With a surgeon's touch he shaved the edges of the cut and placed the reinforcing net. Zed held the light anxiously.

"The cut is clean," said Dea, "but it will undergo a lot of flexing—I don't suppose it can very well be immobilized, in this position? No, hardly. This should do. If he were a human, I'd tell him to rest at this point."

"He'll be rested," Miles promised firmly. "Will he be all right now?"

"I suppose so. How the devil should I know?" Dea looked highly aggrieved, but his hand sneaked out to re-check his repairs.

"General Piotr," Miles assured him, "would have been very pleased with your work." Miles could hear him in his head now, snorting, *Damned technocrats. Nothing but horse doctors with a more expensive set of toys.* Grandfather would have loved being proved right. "You, ah . . . never met my grandfather, did you?"

"Before my time, my lord," said Dea. "I've studied his life and campaigns, of course."

"Of course."

Pym had a hand-light now, and was limping with Karal in a slow spiral around the horse lines, inspecting the ground. Karal's eldest boy had recaptured the sorrel mare and brought her back and re-tethered her. Her tether had been torn loose, not cut; had the myste-rious attacker's choice of equine victim been random, or calculated? How calculated? Was Ninny attacked as a mere symbol of his master, or had the person known how passionately Miles loved the animal? Was this vandalism, a political statement, or an act of precisely-directed, subtle cruelty?

What have I ever done to you? Miles's thought howled silently to the surrounding darkness.

"They got away, whoever it was," Pym reported. "Out of scanner range before I could breathe again. My apologies, m'lord. They don't seem to have dropped anything on the ground."

There had to have been a knife, at least. A knife, its haft gory with horse blood in a pattern of perfect fingerprints, would have been extremely convenient just now. Miles sighed.

Ma Karal drifted up and eyed Dea's medkit, as he cleaned and re-packed it. "All that," she muttered under her breath, "for a horse. . . ."

Miles refrained, barely, from leaping to a hot defense of the value of this particular horse. How many people in Silvy Vale had Ma Karal seen suffer and die, in her lifetime, for lack of no more medical technology than what Dea was carrying under his arm just now?

Guarding his horse, Miles watched from the porch as dawn crept over the landscape. He had changed his shirt and washed off. Pym was inside getting his ribs taped. Miles sat with his back to the wall and a stunner on his lap as the night mists slowly grew grey. The valley was a grey blur, fog-shrouded, the hills darker rolls of fog beyond. Directly overhead, grey thinned to a paling blue. The day would be fine and hot once the fog burned away.

It was surely time now to call out the troops from Hassadar. This was getting just too weird. His bodyguard was half out of commission —true, it was Miles's horse that had rendered him so, not the mystery attacker. But just because the attacks hadn't been fatal didn't mean they hadn't been intended so. Perhaps a third attack would be brought off more expertly. Practice makes perfect.

Miles felt unstrung with nervous exhaustion. How had he let a mere horse become such a handle on his emotions? Bad, that, almost unbalanced—yet Ninny's was surely one of the truly innocent pure souls Miles had ever known. Miles remembered the other innocent in the case then, and shivered in the damp. *It was cruel, lord, something cruel. . . .* Pym was right, the bushes could be crawling with Csurik assassins right now.

Dammit, the bushes *were* crawling—over there, a movement, a damping wave of branch lashing in recoil from—what? Miles's heart lurched in his chest. He adjusted his stunner to full power, slipped silently off the porch, and began his stalk, crouching low, taking advantage of cover wherever the long grasses of the yard had not been trampled flat by the activities of the last day, and night. Miles froze like a predatory cat as a shape seemed to coalesce out of the mist.

A lean young man, not too tall, dressed in the baggy trousers that seemed to be standard here, stood wearily by the horse lines, staring up the yard at Karal's cabin. He stood so for a full two minutes without moving. Miles held a bead on him with his stunner. If he dared make one move toward Ninny. . . .

The young man walked back and forth uncertainly, then crouched on his heels, still gazing up the yard. He pulled something from the pocket of his loose jacket—Miles's finger tightened on the trigger—but he only put it to his mouth and bit. An apple. The crunch carried clearly in the damp air, and the faint perfume of its juices. He ate about half, then stopped, seeming to have trouble swallowing. Miles checked the knife at his belt, made sure it was loose in its sheath. Ninny's nostrils widened, and he nickered hopefully, drawing the young man's attention. He rose and walked over to the horse.

The blood pulsed in Miles's ears, louder than any other sound. His grip on the stunner was damp and white-knuckled. The young man fed Ninny his apple. The horse chomped it down, big jaw rippling under his skin, then cocked his hip, dangled one hind hoof, and sighed hugely. If he hadn't seen the man eat off the fruit first Miles might have shot him on the spot. It couldn't be poisoned. . . . The man made to pet Ninny's neck, then his hand drew back in startlement as he encountered Dea's dressing. Ninny shook his head uneasily. Miles rose slowly and stood waiting. The man scratched Ninny's ears instead, looked up one last time at the cabin, took a deep breath, stepped forward, saw Miles, and stood stock still.

"Lem Csurik?" said Miles.

A pause, a frozen nod. "Lord Vorkosigan?" said the young man. Miles nodded in turn.

Csurik swallowed. "Vor lord," he quavered, "do you keep your word?"

What a bizarre opening. Miles's brows climbed. Hell, go with it. "Yes. Are you coming in?"

"Yes and no, m'lord."

"Which?"

"A bargain, lord. I must have a bargain, and your word on it."

"If you killed Raina . . ."

"No, lord. I swear it. I didn't."

"Then you have nothing to fear from me."

Lem Csurik's lips thinned. What the devil could this hill man find ironic? How dare he find irony in Miles's confusion? Irony, but no amusement.

"Oh, lord," breathed Csurik, "I wish that were so. But I have to prove it to Harra. Harra must believe me—you have to make her believe me, lord!"

"You have to make me believe you first. Fortunately, that isn't hard. You come up to the cabin and make that same statement under fast-penta, and I will rule you cleared."

Csurik was shaking his head.

"Why not?" said Miles patiently. That Csurik had turned up at all was strong circumstantial indication of his innocence. Unless he somehow imagined he could beat the drug. Miles would be patient for, oh, three or four seconds at least. Then, by God, he'd stun him, drag him inside, tie him up till he came round, and get to the bottom of this before breakfast.

"The drug—they say you can't hold anything back."

"It would be pretty useless if you could."

Csurik stood silent a moment.

"Are you trying to conceal some lesser crime on your conscience? Is that the bargain you wish to strike? An amnesty? It . . . might be possible. If it's short of another murder, that is."

"No, lord. I've never killed anybody!"

"Then maybe we can deal. Because if you're innocent, I need to know as soon as possible. Because it means my work isn't finished here."

"That's . . . that's the trouble, m'lord." Csurik shuffled, then seemed to come to some internal decision and stood sturdily. "I'll come in and risk your drug. And I'll answer anything about me you want to ask. But you have to promise—swear!—you won't ask me about . . . about anything else. Anybody else."

"Do you know who killed your daughter?"

"Not for sure." Csurik threw his head back defiantly. "I didn't see it. I have guesses."

"I have guesses too."

"That's as may be, lord. Just so's they don't come from my mouth. That's all I ask."

Miles holstered his stunner, and rubbed his chin. "Hm." A very slight smile turned one corner of his lip. "I admit, it would be more—elegant—to solve this case by reason and deduction than brute force. Even so tender a force as fast-penta."

Csurik's head lowered. "I don't know elegant, lord. But I don't want it to be from my mouth."

Decision bubbled up in Miles, straightening his spine. Yes. He *knew*, now. He had only to run through the proofs, step by chained step. Just like 5-Space math. "Very well. I swear by my word as Vorkosigan, I shall confine my questions to the facts to which you were an eyewitness. I will not ask you for conjectures about persons or events for which you were not present. There, will that do?"

Csurik bit his lip. "Yes, lord. If you keep your word."

"Try me," suggested Miles. His lips wrinkled back on a vulpine smile, absorbing the implied insult without comment.

Csurik climbed the yard beside Miles as if to an executioner's block. Their entrance created a tableau of astonishment among Karal and his family, clustered around their wooden table where Dea was treating Pym. Pym and Dea looked rather blanker, till Miles made introduction: "Dr. Dea, get out your fast-penta. Here's Lem Csurik come to talk with us."

Miles steered Lem to a chair. The hill man sat with his hands clenched. Pym, a red and purpling bruise showing at the edges of the white tape circling his chest, took up his stunner and stepped back.

Dr. Dea muttered under his breath to Miles as he got out the hypospray. "How'd you *do* that?"

Miles's hand brushed his pocket. He pulled out a sugar cube and held it up, and grinned through the C of his thumb and finger. Dea snorted, but pursed his lips with reluctant respect.

Lem flinched as the hypospray hissed on his arm, as if he expected it to hurt.

"Count backwards from ten," Dea instructed. By the time Lem reached three, he had relaxed; at zero, he giggled.

"Karal, Ma Karal, Pym, gather round," said Miles. "You are my witnesses. Boys, stay back and stay quiet. No interruptions, please."

Miles ran through the preliminaries, half a dozen questions designed to set up a rhythm and kill time while the fast-penta took full effect. Lem Csurik grinned foolishly, lolling in his chair, and answered them all with sunny good will. Fast-penta interrogation had been part of Miles's military intelligence course at the Service Academy. The drug seemed to be working exactly as advertised, oddly enough.

"Did you return to your cabin that morning, after you spent the night at your parents'?"

"Yes, m'lord," Lem smiled.

"About what time?"

"Midmorning."

Nobody here had a chrono, that was probably as precise an answer as Miles was likely to get. "What did you do when you got there?"

"Called for Harra. She was gone, though. It frightened me that she was gone. Thought she might've run out on me." Lem hiccoughed. "I want my Harra."

"Later. Was the baby asleep?"

"She was. She woke up when I called for Harra. Started crying again. It goes right up your spine."

"What did you do then?"

Lem's eyes widened. "I got no milk. She wanted Harra. There's nothing I could do for her."

"Did you pick her up?"

"No, lord, I let her lay. There was nothing I could do for her. Harra, she'd hardly let me touch her, she was that nervous about her. Told me I'd drop her or something."

"You didn't shake her, to stop her screaming?"

"No, lord, I let her lay. I left to look down the path for Harra."

"Then where did you go?"

Lem blinked. "My sister's. I'd promised to help haul wood for a new cabin. Bella—m'other sister—is getting married, y'see, and—"

He was beginning to wander, as was normal for this drug. "Stop," said Miles. Lem fell silent obediently, swaying slightly in his chair. Miles considered his next question carefully. He was approaching the fine line, here. "Did you meet anyone on the path? Answer yes or no."

"Yes."

Dea was getting excited. "Who? Ask him who!"

Miles held up his hand. "You can administer the antagonist now, Dr. Dea."

"Aren't you going to ask him? It could be vital!"

"I can't. I gave my word. Administer the antagonist now, doctor!"

Fortunately, the confusion of two interrogators stopped Lem's mumbled willing reply to Dea's question. Dea, bewildered, pressed his hypospray against Lem's arm. Lem's eyes, half-closed, snapped open within seconds. He sat up straight and rubbed his arm, and his face.

"Who did you meet on the path?" Dea asked him directly.

Lem's lips pressed tight; he looked for rescue to Miles.

Dea looked too. "Why won't you ask him?"

"Because I don't need to," said Miles. "I know precisely who Lem met on the path, and why he went on and not back. It was Raina's murderer. As I shall shortly prove. And—witness this, Karal, Ma Karal—that information did not come from Lem's mouth. Confirm!"

Karal nodded slowly. "I . . . see, m'lord. That was . . . very good of you."

Miles gave him a direct stare, his mouth set in a tight smile. "And when is a mystery no mystery at all?"

Karal reddened, not replying for a moment. Then he said, "You may as well keep on like you're going, m'lord. There's no stopping you now, I suppose."

"No."

Miles sent runners to collect the witnesses, Ma Karal in one direction, Zed in a second, Speaker Karal and his eldest in a third. He had Lem wait with Pym, Dea, and himself. Having the shortest distance to cover, Ma Karal arrived back first, with Ma Csurik and two of her sons in tow.

His mother fell on Lem, embracing him and then looking fearfully over her shoulder at Miles. The younger brothers hung back, but Pym had already moved between them and the door.

"It's all right, Ma," Lem patted her on the back. "Or . . . anyway, I'm all right. I'm clear. Lord Vorkosigan believes me."

She glowered at Miles, still holding Lem's arm. "You didn't let the mutie lord give you that poison drug, did you?"

"Not poison," Miles denied. "In fact, the drug may have saved his life. That damn near makes it a medicine, I'd say. However," he turned toward Lem's two younger brothers, and folded his arms sternly, "I would like to know which of you young morons threw the torch on my tent last night?"

The younger one whitened; the elder, hotly indignant, noticed his brother's expression and cut his denial off in mid-syllable. "You didn't!" he hissed in horror.

"Nobody," said the white one. "Nobody did."

Miles raised his eyebrows. There followed a short, choked silence.

"Well, *nobody* can make his apologies to Speaker and Ma Karal, then," said Miles, "since it was their sons who were sleeping in the tent last night. I and my men were in the loft."

The boy's mouth opened in dismay. The youngest Karal stared at the pale Csurik brother, his agemate, and whispered importantly, "You, Dono! You idiot, didn't ya know that tent wouldn't burn? It's real Imperial Service issue!"

Miles clasped his hands behind his back, and fixed the Csuriks with a cold eye. "Rather more to the point, it was attempted assassination upon your Count's heir, which carries the same capital charge of treason as an attempt upon the Count himself. Or perhaps Dono didn't think of that?"

Dono was thrown into flummoxed confusion. No need for fast-penta here, the kid couldn't carry off a lie worth a damn. Ma Csurik now had hold of Dono's arm too, without letting go of Lem's; she looked as frantic as a hen with too many chicks, trying to shelter them from a storm.

"I wasn't trying to kill you, lord!" cried Dono.

"What were you trying to do, then?"

"You'd come to kill Lem. I wanted to . . . make you go away. Frighten you away. I didn't think anyone would really get hurt—I mean, it was only a tent!"

"You've never seen anything burn down, I take it. Have you, Ma Csurik?"

Lem's mother nodded, lips tight, clearly torn between a desire to protect her son from Miles, and a desire to beat Dono till he bled for his potentially lethal stupidity.

"Well, but for a chance, you could have killed or horribly injured three of your friends. Think on that, please. In the meantime, in view of your youth and ah, apparent mental defectiveness, I shall hold the treason charge. In return, Speaker Karal and your parents shall be responsible for your good behavior in future, and decide what punishment is appropriate."

Ma Csurik melted with relief and gratitude. Dono looked like he'd rather have been shot. His brother poked him, and whispered, "Mental defective!" Ma Csurik slapped the taunter on the side of his head, suppressing him effectively.

"What about your horse, m'lord?" asked Pym.

"I . . . do not suspect them of the business with the horse," Miles replied slowly. "The attempt to fire the tent was plain stupidity. The other was . . . a different order of calculation altogether."

Zed, who had been permitted to take Pym's horse, returned then with Harra up behind him. Harra entered Speaker Karal's cabin, saw Lem, and stopped with a bitter glare. Lem stood openhanded, his eyes wounded, before her.

"So, lord," Harra said. "You caught him." Her jaw was clenched in joyless triumph.

"Not exactly," said Miles. "He came here and turned himself in. He's made his statement under fast-penta, and cleared himself. Lem did not kill Raina."

Harra turned from side to side. "But I saw he'd been there! He'd left his jacket, and took his good saw and wood planer away with him. I knew he'd been back while I was out! There must be something wrong with your drug!"

Miles shook his head. "The drug worked fine. Your deduction was correct as far as it went. Lem did visit the cabin while you were out. But when he left, Raina was still alive, crying vigorously. It wasn't Lem."

She swayed. "Who, then?"

"I think you know. I think you've been working very hard to deny that knowledge, hence your excessive focus on Lem. As long as you were sure it was Lem, you didn't have to think about the other possibilities."

"But who else would care?" Harra cried. "Who else would bother?"

"Who, indeed?" sighed Miles. He walked to the front window and glanced down the yard. The fog was clearing in the full light of morning. The horses were moving uneasily. "Dr. Dea, would you please get a second dose of fast-penta ready?" Miles turned, paced back to stand before the fireplace, its coals still banked for the night. The faint heat was pleasant on his back.

Dea was staring around, the hypospray in his hand, clearly wondering to whom to administer it. "My lord?" he queried, brows lowering in demand for explanation.

"Isn't it obvious to you, Doctor?" Miles asked lightly.

"*No,* my lord." His tone was slightly indignant.

"Nor to you, Pym?"

"Not . . . entirely, m'lord." Pym's glance, and stunner aim, wavered uncertainly to Harra.

"I suppose it's because neither of you ever met my grandfather," Miles decided. "He died just about a year before you entered my father's service, Pym. He was born at the very end of the Time of Isolation, and lived through every wrenching change this century has dealt to Barrayar. He was called the last of the Old Vor, but really, he was the first of the new. He changed with the times, from the tactics of horse cavalry to that of flyer squadrons, from swords to atomics, and he changed *successfully.* Our present freedom from the Cetagandan occupation is a measure of how fiercely he could adapt, then throw it all away and adapt again. At the end of his life he was called a conservative, only because so much of Barrayar had streamed past him in the direction he had led, prodded, pushed, and pointed all his life.

"He changed, and adapted, and bent with the wind of the times. Then, in his age—for my father was his youngest and sole surviving son, and did not himself marry till middle-age—in his age, he was hit with me. And he had to change again. And he couldn't.

"He begged for my mother to have an abortion, after they knew more or less what the fetal damage would be. He and my parents were estranged for five years after I was born. They didn't see each other or speak or communicate. Everyone thought my father moved us to the Imperial Residence when he became Regent because he was angling for the throne, but in fact it was because the Count my grandfather denied him the use of Vorkosigan House. Aren't family squabbles jolly fun? Bleeding ulcers run in my family, we give them to each other." Miles strolled back to the window and looked out. Ah, yes. Here it came.

"The reconciliation was gradual, when it became quite clear there would be no other son," Miles went on. "No dramatic denouement. It helped when the medics got me walking. It was essential that I tested out bright. Most important of all, I never let him see me give up."

Nobody had dared interrupt this lordly monologue, but it was clear from several expressions that the point of it was escaping them. Since half the point was to kill time, Miles was not greatly disturbed by their failure to track. Footsteps sounded on the wooden porch outside. Pym moved quietly to cover the door with an unobscured angle of fire.

"Dr. Dea," said Miles, sighting through the window, "would you be so kind as to administer that fast-penta to the first person through the door, as they step in?"

"You're not waiting for a volunteer, my lord?"

"Not this time."

The door swung inward, and Dea stepped forward, raising his hand. The hypospray hissed. Ma Mattulich wheeled to face Dea, the skirts of her work dress swirling around her veined calves, hissing in return—"You dare!" Her arm drew back as if to strike him, but slowed in mid-swing and failed to connect as Dea ducked out of her way. This unbalanced her, and she staggered. Speaker Karal, coming in behind, caught her by the arm and steadied her. "You dare!" she wailed again, then turned to see not only Dea but all the other witnesses waiting; Ma Csurik, Ma Karal, Lem, Harra, Pym. Her shoulders sagged, and then the drug cut in and she just stood, a silly smile fighting with anguish for possession of her harsh face.

The smile made Miles ill, but it was the smile he needed. "Sit her down, Dea, Speaker Karal."

They guided her to the chair lately vacated by Lem Csurik. She was fighting the drug desperately, flashes of resistance melting into flaccid docility. Gradually the docility became ascendant, and she sat draped in the chair, grinning helplessly. Miles sneaked a peek at Harra. She stood white and silent, utterly closed.

For several years after the reconciliation Miles had never been left with his grandfather without his personal bodyguard. Sergeant Bothari had worn the Count's livery, but been loyal to Miles alone, the one man dangerous enough—some said, crazy enough—to stand up to the great General himself. There was no need, Miles decided, to spell out to these fascinated people just what interrupted incident had made his parents think Sergeant Bothari a necessary precaution. Let General Piotr's untarnished reputation serve—Miles, now. As *he* willed. Miles's eyes glinted.

Lem lowered his head. "If I had known—if I had guessed—I wouldn't have left them alone together, m'lord. I thought—Harra's mother would take care of her. I couldn't have—I didn't know *how*—"

Harra did not look at him. Harra did not look at anything.

"Let us conclude this," Miles sighed. Again, he requested formal witness from the crowd in the room, and cautioned against interruptions, which tended to unduly confuse a drugged subject. He moistened his lips and turned to Ma Mattulich.

Again, he began with the standard neutral questions, name, birthdate, parents' names, checkable biographical facts. Ma Mattulich was harder to lull than the cooperative Lem had been, her responses scattered and staccato. Miles controlled his impatience with difficulty. For all its deceptive ease, fast-penta interrogation required skill, skill and patience. He'd got too far to risk a stumble now. He worked his questions up gradually to the first critical ones.

"Were you there, when Raina was born?"

Her voice was low and drifting, dreamy. "The birth came in the night. Lem, he went for Jean the midwife. The midwife's son was supposed to go for me but he fell back to sleep. I didn't get there till morning, and then it was too late. They'd all seen."

"Seen what?"

"The cat's mouth, the dirty mutation. Monsters in us. Cut them out. Ugly little man." This last, Miles realized, was an aside upon himself. Her attention had hung up on him, hypnotically. "Muties make more muties, they breed faster, overrun . . . I saw you watching the girls. You want to make mutie babies on clean women, poison us all . . ."

Time to steer her back to the main issue. "Were you ever alone with the baby after that?"

"No, Jean she hung around. Jean knows me, she knew what I wanted. None of her damn business. And Harra was always there. Harra must not know. Harra must not . . . why should she get off so soft? The poison must be in her. Must have come from her Da, I lay only with her Da and they were all wrong but the one."

Miles blinked. "What were all wrong?" Across the room Miles saw Speaker Karal's mouth tighten. The headman caught Miles's glance and stared down at his own feet, absenting himself from the proceedings. Lem, his lips parted in absorption, and the rest of the boys were listening with alarm. Harra hadn't moved.

"All my babies," Ma Mattulich said.

Harra looked up sharply at that, her eyes widening.

"Was Harra not your only child?" Miles asked. It was an effort to keep his voice cool, calm; he wanted to shout. He wanted to be gone from here. . . .

"No, of course not. She was my only clean child, I thought. I thought, but the poison must have been hidden in her. I fell on my knees and thanked God when she was born clean, a clean one at last, after so many, so much pain. . . . I thought I had finally been punished enough. She was such a pretty baby, I thought it was over at last. But she must have been mutie after all, hidden, tricksy, sly. . . ."

"How many," Miles choked, "babies did you have?"

"Four, besides Harra my last."

"And you killed all four of them?" Speaker Karal, Miles saw, gave a slow nod to his feet.

"No!" said Ma Mattulich. Indignation broke through the fast-penta wooze briefly. "Two were born dead already, the first one, and the twisted-up one. The one with too many fingers and toes, and the one with the bulgy head, those I cut. Cut out. My mother, she watched over me to see I did it right. Harra, I made it soft for Harra. I did it for her."

"So you have in fact murdered not one infant, but three?" said Miles frozenly. The younger witnesses in the room, Karal's boys and the Csurik brothers, looked horrified. The older ones, Ma Mattulich's contemporaries, who must have lived through the events with her, looked mortified, sharing her shame. Yes, they all must have known.

"Murdered?" said Ma Mattulich. "No! I cut them out. I had to. I had to do the right thing." Her chin lifted proudly, then drooped. "Killed my babies, to please, to please . . . I don't know who. And now you call me a murderer? Damn you! What use is your justice to me *now?* I needed it then—where were you *then?*" Suddenly, shockingly, she burst into tears, which wavered almost instantly into rage. "If mine must die then so must hers! Why should she get off so soft? Spoiled her . . . I tried my best, I did my best, it's not fair . . ."

The fast-penta was not keeping up with this . . . no, it was working, Miles decided, but her emotions were too overwhelming. Upping the dose might level her emotional surges, at some risk of respiratory arrest, but it would not elicit any more complete a confession. Miles's belly was trembling, a reaction he trusted he concealed. It had to be completed now.

"Why did you break Raina's neck, instead of cutting her throat?"

"Harra, she must not know," said Ma Mattulich. "Poor baby. It would look like she just died. . . ."

Miles eyed Lem, Speaker Karal. "It seems a number of others shared your opinion that Harra should not know."

"I didn't want it to be from my mouth," repeated Lem sturdily.

"I wanted to save her double grief, m'lord," said Karal. "She'd had so much. . . ."

Miles met Harra's eyes at that. "I think you all underestimate her. Your excessive tenderness insults both her intelligence and will. She comes from a tough line, that one."

Harra inhaled, controlling her own trembling. She gave Miles a short nod, as if to say *Thank you, little man.* He returned her a slight inclination of the head, *Yes, I understand.*

"I'm not sure yet where justice lies in this case," said Miles, "but this I swear to you, the days of cooperative concealment are over. No more secret crimes in the night. Daylight's here. And speaking of crimes in the night," he turned back to Ma Mattulich, *"was* it you who tried to cut my horse's throat last night?"

"I tried," said Ma Mattulich, calmer now in a wave of fast-penta mellowness, "but it kept rearing up on me."

"Why my *horse?*" Miles could not keep exasperation from his voice, though a calm, even tone was enjoined upon fast-penta interrogators by the training manual.

"I couldn't get at you," said Ma Mattulich simply.

Miles rubbed his forehead. "Retroactive infanticide by proxy?" he muttered.

"You," said Ma Mattulich, and her loathing came through even the nauseating fast-penta cheer, *"you* are the worst. All I went through, all I did, all the grief, and you come along at the end. A mutie made lord over us all, and all the rules changed, betrayed at the end by an off-worlder woman's weakness. You make it all for *nothing.* Hate you. Dirty mutie . . ." her voice trailed off in a drugged mumble.

Miles took a deep breath, and looked around the room. The stillness was profound, and no one dared break it.

"I believe," he said, "that concludes my investigation into the facts of this case."

The mystery of Raina's death was solved.

The problem of justice, unfortunately, remained.

Miles took a walk.

The graveyard, though little more than a crude clearing in the woodland, was a place of peace and beauty in the morning light. The stream burbled endlessly, shifting green shadows and blinding brilliant reflections. The faint breeze that had shredded away the last of the night fog whispered in the trees, and the tiny, short-lived creatures that everyone on Barrayar but biologists called bugs sang and twittered in the patches of native scrub.

"Well, Raina," Miles sighed, "and what do I do now?" Pym lingered by the borders of the clearing, giving Miles room. "It's all right," Miles assured the tiny grave, "Pym's caught me talking to dead people before. He may think I'm crazy, but he's far too well-trained to say so."

Pym in fact did not look happy, nor altogether well. Miles felt rather guilty for dragging him out; by rights the man should be resting in bed, but Miles had desperately needed this time alone. Pym wasn't just suffering the residual effect of having been kicked by Ninny. He had been silent ever since Miles had extracted the confession from Ma Mattulich. Miles was unsurprised. Pym had steeled himself to play executioner to their imagined hill bully; the substitution of a mad grandmother as his victim had clearly given him pause. He would obey whatever order Miles gave him, though, Miles had no doubt of that.

Miles considered the peculiarities of Barrayaran law, as he wandered about the clearing, watching the stream and the light, turning over an occasional rock with the toe of his boot. The fundamental principle was clear; the spirit was to be preferred over the letter, truth over technicalities. Precedent was held subordinate to the judgment of the man on the spot. Alas, the man on the spot was himself. There was no refuge for him in automated rules, no hiding behind *the law says* as if the law were some living overlord with a real Voice. The only voice here was his own.

And who would be served by the death of that half-crazed old woman? Harra? The relationship between mother and daughter had been wounded unto death by this, Miles had seen that in their eyes, yet still Harra had no stomach for matricide. Miles rather preferred it that way, having her standing by his ear crying for bloody revenge would have been enormously distracting just now. The obvious justice made a damn poor reward for Harra's courage in reporting the crime. Raina? Ah. That was more difficult.

"I'd like to lay the old gargoyle right there at your feet, small lady," Miles muttered to her. "Is it your desire? Does it serve you? What *would* serve you?" Was this the great burning he had promised her?

What judgment would reverberate along the entire Dendarii mountain range? Should he indeed sacrifice these people to some larger political statement, regardless of their wants? Or should he forget all that, make his judgment serve only those directly involved? He scooped up a stone and flung it full force into the stream. It vanished invisibly in the rocky bed.

He turned to find Speaker Karal waiting by the edge of the graveyard. Karal ducked his head in greeting and approached cautiously.

"So, m'lord," said Karal.

"Just so," said Miles.

"Have you come to any conclusion?"

"Not really." Miles gazed around. "Anything less than Ma Mattulich's death seems . . . inadequate justice, and yet . . . I cannot see who her death would serve."

"Neither could I. That's why I took the position I did in the first place."

"No . . ." said Miles slowly, "no, you were wrong in that. For one thing, it very nearly got Lem Csurik killed. I was getting ready to pursue him with deadly force at one point. It almost destroyed him with Harra. Truth is better. Slightly better. At least it isn't a fatal error. Surely I can do . . . something with it."

"I didn't know what to expect of you, at first," admitted Karal.

Miles shook his head. "I meant to make changes. A difference. Now . . . I don't know."

Speaker Karal's balding forehead wrinkled. "But we are changing."

"Not enough. Not fast enough."

"You're young yet, that's why you don't see how much, how fast. Look at the difference between Harra and her mother. God—look at the difference between Ma Mattulich and *her* mother. *There* was a harridan." Speaker Karal shuddered. "I remember her, all right. And yet, she was not so unusual, in her day. So far from having to make change, I don't think you could stop it if you tried. The minute we finally get a powersat receptor up here, and get on the comm net, the past will be done and over. As soon as the kids see the future—their future—they'll be mad after it. They're already lost to the old ones like Ma Mattulich. The old ones know it, too, don't believe they don't know it. Why d'you think we haven't been able to get at least a small unit up here yet? Not just the cost. The old ones are fighting it. They call it off planet corruption, but it's really the future they fear."

"There's so much still to be done."

"Oh, yes. We are a desperate people, no lie. But we have hope. I don't think you realize how much you've done, just by coming up here."

"I've done nothing," said Miles bitterly. "Sat around, mostly. And now, I swear, I'm going to end up doing more nothing. And then go home. Hell!"

Speaker Karal pursed his lips, looked at his feet, at the high hills. "You are doing something for us every minute. Mutie lord. Do you think you are invisible?"

Miles grinned wolfishly. "Oh, Karal, I'm a one-man band, I am. I'm a parade."

"As you say, just so. Ordinary people need extraordinary examples. So they can say to themselves, well, if he can do *that*, I can surely do *this*. No excuses."

"No quarter, yes, I know that game. Been playing it all my life."

"I think," said Karal, "Barrayar needs you. To go on being just what you are."

"Barrayar will eat me, if it can."

"Yes," said Karal, his eyes on the horizon, "so it will." His gaze fell to the graves at his feet. "But it swallows us all in the end, doesn't it? You will outlive the old ones."

"Or in the beginning." Miles pointed down. "Don't tell *me* who I'm going to outlive. Tell Raina."

Karal's shoulders slumped. "True. S'truth. Make your judgment, lord. I'll back you."

Miles assembled them all in Karal's yard for his Speaking, the porch now having become his podium. The interior of the cabin would have been impossibly hot and close for this crowd, suffocating with the afternoon sun beating on the roof, though outdoors the light made them squint. They were all here, everyone they could round up, Speaker Karal, Ma Karal, their boys, all the Csuriks, most of the cronies who had attended last night's funereal festivities, men, women, and children. Harra sat apart. Lem kept trying to hold her hand, though from the way she flinched it was clear she didn't want to be touched. Ma Mattulich sat displayed by Miles's side, silent and surly, flanked by Pym and an uncomfortable-looking Deputy Alex.

Miles jerked up his chin, settling his head on the high collar of his dress greens, as polished and formal as Pym's batman's expertise could make him. The Imperial Service uniform that Miles had earned. Did these people know he had earned it, or did they all imagine it a mere gift from his father, nepotism at work? Damn what they thought. He knew. He stood before his people, and gripped the porch rail.

"I have concluded the investigation of the charges laid before the Count's Court by Harra Csurik of the murder of her daughter Raina. By evidence, witness, and her own admission, I find Mara Mattulich guilty of this murder, she having twisted the infant's neck until it broke, and then attempted to conceal that crime. Even when that concealment placed her son-in-law Lem Csurik in mortal danger from false charges. In light of the helplessness of the victim, the cruelty of the method, and the cowardly selfishness of the attempted concealment, I can find no mitigating excuse for the crime.

"In addition, Mara Mattulich by her own admission testifies to two previous infanticides, some twenty years ago, of her own children. These facts shall be announced by Speaker Karal in every corner of Silvy Vale, until every subject has been informed."

He could feel Ma Mattulich's glare boring into his back. *Yes, go on and hate me, old woman. I will bury you yet, and you know it.* He swallowed, and continued, the formality of the language a sort of shield before him.

"For this unmitigated crime, the only proper sentence is death. And I so sentence Mara Mattulich. But in light of her age and close relation to the next-most-injured party in the case, Harra Csurik, I choose to hold the actual execution of that sentence. Indefinitely." Out of the corner of his eye Miles saw Pym let out, very carefully and covertly, a sigh of relief. Harra combed at her straw-colored bangs with her fingers and listened intently.

"But she shall be as dead before the law. All her property, even to the clothes on her back, now belongs to her daughter Harra, to dispose of as she wills. Mara Mattulich may not own property, enter contracts, sue for injuries, nor exert her will after death in any testament. She shall not leave Silvy Vale without Harra's permission. Harra shall be given power over her as a parent over a child, or as in senility. In Harra's absence Speaker Karal will be her deputy. Mara Mattulich shall be watched to see she harms no other child.

"Further. She shall die without sacrifice. No one, not Harra nor any other, shall make a burning for her when she goes into the ground at last. As she murdered her future, so her future shall return only death to her spirit. She will die as the childless do, without remembrance."

A low sigh swept the older members of the crowd before Miles. For the first time, Mara Mattulich bent her stiff neck.

Some, Miles knew, would find this only spiritually symbolic. Others would see it as literally lethal, according to the strength of their beliefs. The literal-minded, such as those who saw mutation as a sin to be violently expiated. But even the less superstitious, Miles saw in their faces, found the meaning clear. So.

Miles turned to Ma Mattulich, and lowered his voice. "Every breath you take from this moment on is by my mercy. Every bite of food you eat, by Harra's charity. By charity and mercy—such as you did not give—you shall live. Dead woman."

"Some mercy. Mutie lord." Her growl was low, weary, beaten.

"You get the point," he said through his teeth. He swept her a bow, infinitely ironic, and turned his back on her. "I am the Voice of Count Vorkosigan. This concludes my Speaking."

Miles met Harra and Lem afterwards, in Speaker Karal's cabin.

"I have a proposition for you." Miles controlled his nervous pacing and stood before them. "You're free to turn it down, or think about it for a while. I know you're very tired right now." *As are we all.* Had he really been in Silvy Vale only a day and a half? It seemed like a century. His head ached with fatigue. Harra was red-eyed too. "First of all, can you read and write?"

"Some," Harra admitted. "Speaker Karal taught us some, and Ma Lannier."

"Well, good enough. You wouldn't be starting completely blind. Look. A few years back Hassadar started a teacher's college. It's not very big yet, but it's begun. There are some scholarships. I can swing one your way, if you will agree to live in Hassadar for three years of intense study."

"Me!" said Harra. "I couldn't go to a college! I barely know . . . any of that stuff."

"Knowledge is what you're supposed to have coming out, not going in. Look, they know what they're dealing with in this district. They have a lot of remedial courses. It's true, you'd have to work harder, to catch up with the town-bred and the lowlanders. But I know you have courage, and I know you have will. The rest is just picking yourself up and ramming into the wall again and again until it falls down. You get a bloody forehead, so what? You can do it, I swear you can."

Lem, sitting beside her, looked worried. He captured her hand again. "Three years?" he said in a small voice. "Gone away?"

"The school stipend isn't that much," said Miles. "But Lem, I understand you have carpenter's skills. There's a building boom going on in Hassadar right now. Hassadar's going to be the next Vorkosigan Vashnoi, I think. I'm certain you could get a job. Between you, you could live."

Lem looked at first relieved, then extremely worried. "But they all use power tools—computers—robots. . . ."

"By no means. And they weren't all born knowing how to use that stuff either. If they can learn it, you can. Besides, the rich pay well for hand-work, unique one-off items, if the quality's good. I can see you get a start, which is usually the toughest moment. After that you should be able to figure it out all right."

"To leave Silvy Vale . . ." said Harra in a dismayed tone.

"Only in order to return. That's the other half of the bargain. I can send a comm unit up here, a small one with a portable power pack that lasts a year. Somebody'd have to hump down to Vorkosigan Surleau to replace it annually, no big problem. The whole set up wouldn't cost much more than oh, a new lightflyer." Such as the shiny red one Miles had coveted in a dealer's showroom in Vorbarr Sultana, very suitable for a graduation present, he had pointed out to his parents. The credit chit was sitting in the top drawer of his dresser in the lake house at Vorkosigan Surleau right now. "It's not a massive project like installing a powersat receptor for the whole of Silvy Vale or anything. The holovid would pick up the educational satellite broadcasts from the capital; set it up in some central cabin, add a couple of dozen lap-links for the kids, and you've got an instant school. All the children would be required to attend, with Speaker Karal to enforce it, though once they'd discovered the holovid you'd probably have to beat them to make them go home. I, ah," Miles cleared his throat, "thought you might name it the Raina Csurik Primary School."

"Oh," said Harra, and began to cry for the first time that grueling day. Lem patted her clumsily. She returned the grip of his hand at last.

"I can send a lowlander up here to teach," said Miles. "I'll get one to take a short-term contract, till you're ready to come back. But he or she won't understand Silvy Vale like you do. Wouldn't understand *why*. You—you already know. You know what they can't teach in any lowland college."

Harra scrubbed her eyes, and looked up—not very far up—at him. "You went to the Imperial Academy."

"I did." His chin jerked up.

"Then I," she said shakily, "can manage . . . Hassadar Teacher's College." The name was awkward in her mouth. At first. "At any rate —I'll try, m'lord."

"I'll bet on you," Miles agreed. "Both of you. Just, ah," a smile sped across his mouth and vanished, "stand up straight and speak the truth, eh?"

Harra blinked understanding. An answering half-smile lit her tired face, equally briefly. "I will. Little man."

Fat Ninny rode home by air the next morning, in a horse van, along with Pym. Dr. Dea went along with his two patients, and his nemesis the sorrel mare. A replacement bodyguard had been sent with the groom who flew the van from Vorkosigan Surleau, who stayed with Miles to help him ride the remaining two horses back down. Well, Miles thought, he'd been considering a camping trip in the mountains with his cousin Ivan as part of his home leave anyway. The liveried man was the laconic veteran Esterhazy, whom Miles had known most of his life; excellent company for a man who didn't want to talk about it, unlike Ivan you could almost forget he was there. Miles wondered if Esterhazy's assignment had been random chance, or a mercy of the Count's. Esterhazy was good with horses.

They camped overnight by the river of roses. Miles walked up the vale in the evening light, desultorily looking for the spring of it;

indeed, the floral barrier did seem to peter out a couple of kilometers upstream, merging into slightly less impassable scrub. Miles plucked a rose, checked to make sure that Esterhazy was nowhere in sight, and bit into it curiously. Clearly, he was not a horse. A cut bunch would probably not survive the trip back as a treat for Ninny. Ninny could settle for oats.

Miles watched the evening shadows flowing up along the backbone of the Dendarii range, high and massive in the distance. How small those mountains looked from space! Little wrinkles on the skin of a globe he could cover with his hand, all their crushing mass made invisible. Which was illusory, distance or nearness? Distance, Miles decided. Distance was a damned lie. Had his father known this? Miles suspected so.

He contemplated his urge to throw all his money, not just a lightflyer's worth, at those mountains; to quit it all and go teach children to read and write, to set up a free clinic, a powersat net, or all of these at once. But Silvy Vale was only one of hundreds of such communities buried in these mountains, one of thousands across the whole of Barrayar. Taxes squeezed from this very district helped maintain the very elite military school he'd just spent—how much of their resources in? How much would he have to give back just to make it even, now? He was himself a planetary resource, his training had made him so, and his feet were set on their path.

What God means you to do, Miles's theist mother claimed, could be deduced from the talents He gave you. The academic honors, Miles had amassed by sheer brute work. But the war games, outwitting his opponents, staying one step ahead—a necessity, true, he had no margin for error—the war games had been an unholy joy. War had been no game here once, not so long ago. It might be so again. What you did best, that was what was wanted from you. God seemed to be lined up with the Emperor on that point, at least, if no other.

Miles had sworn his officer's oath to the Emperor less than two weeks ago, puffed with pride at his achievement. In his secret mind he had imagined himself keeping that oath through blazing battle, enemy torture, what-have-you, even while sharing cynical cracks afterwards with Ivan about archaic dress swords and the sort of people who insisted on wearing them.

But in the dark of subtler temptations, those which hurt without heroism for consolation, he foresaw, the Emperor would no longer be the symbol of Barrayar in his heart.

Peace to you, small lady, he thought to Raina. *You've won a twisted poor modern knight, to wear your favor on his sleeve. But it's a twisted poor world we were both born into, that rejects us without mercy and ejects us without consultation. At least I won't just tilt at windmills for you. I'll send in sappers to mine the twirling suckers, and blast them into the sky. . . .*

He knew who he served now. And why he could not quit. And why he must not fail.

2

"Are you feeling better?" said Illyan cautiously.

"Somewhat," Miles replied carefully, and waited. He could outwait Illyan now, oh yes.

The security chief pulled up a chair and settled himself by Miles's bedside, regarded Miles, and pursed his lips. "My . . . apologies, Lord Vorkosigan, for doubting your word."

"You owe me that," Miles agreed.

"Yes. Nevertheless," Illyan frowned into the middle distance. "I wonder, Miles, if you've ever realized the extent that, in your position as your father's son, it is not only necessary to be honest, but to appear so."

"As my father's son—no," said Miles flatly.

Illyan snorted involuntarily. "Ha. Perhaps not." His fingers drummed. "Be that as it may, Count Vorvolk has seized on two discrepancies in your mercenary covert ops reports. Wild cost over-runs in what should have been the simplest of tasks, personnel pick-ups. I realize Dagoola blew up on you, but what about the first time?"

"The first time what?"

"They're looking again at the pick-up you made from Jackson's Whole. Their theory being that your successfully-concealed initial peculation there tempted you to larger efforts at Dagoola."

"That was almost two years ago!" Miles protested.

"They're reaching," Illyan agreed. "They're looking hard. They want to nail you to the wall in public if they possibly can. I am, as it were, trying to confiscate the hammer. Dammit," he added irritably, "don't look at me like that. There's nothing personal in it. If you were anyone else's son the matter would not have arisen—you know it, I know it, and they know it. Financial oversight audits by untouchable Vor bores are not my idea of an amusement. My one hope is to tire him out and make him go away. So give."

Miles sighed. "Sir, I am at your disposal, as always. What d'you want to know?"

"Explain the equipment bill for the Jackson's Whole pick up."

"It was all accounted for in my report at the time, I thought." Miles tried to remember.

"Accounted for, yes. Explained, no."

"We left half a cargo of high-class weaponry on the dock at Fell Station. If we hadn't, you might have been out a scientist, a ship, and a subordinate."

"Yes?" said Illyan. He templed his fingers and leaned back in his chair. "Why?"

"Ah . . . it's a long story. Complicated, y'know." Despite himself, Miles smiled in memory. "Can this still be just between you and me?"

Illyan tilted his head. "All right. . . ."

Labyrinth

Miles contemplated the image of the globe glowing above the vid plate, crossed his arms, and stifled queasiness. The planet of Jackson's Whole, glittering, wealthy, corrupt. . . . Jacksonians claimed their corruption was entirely imported—if the galaxy were willing to pay for virtue what it paid for vice, the place would be a pilgrimage shrine. In Miles's view this seemed rather like debating which was superior, maggots or the rotten meat they fed off. Still, if Jackson's Whole didn't exist, the galaxy would probably have had to invent it. Its neighbors might feign horror, but they wouldn't permit the place to exist if they didn't find it a secretly useful interface with the sub-economy.

The planet possessed a certain liveliness, anyway. Not as lively as a century or two back, to be sure, in its hijacker-base days. But its cutthroat criminal gangs had senesced into Syndicate monopolies, almost as structured and staid as little governments. An aristocracy, of sorts. Naturally. Miles wondered how much longer the major Houses would be able to fight off the creeping tide of integrity.

House Dyne, detergent banking—launder your money on Jackson's Whole. House Fell, weapons deals with no questions asked. House Bharaputra, illegal genetics. Worse, House Ryoval, whose motto was "Dreams Made Flesh," surely the damndest—Miles used the adjective precisely—procurer in history. House Hargraves, the galactic fence, prim-faced middlemen for ransom deals—you had to give them credit, hostages exchanged through their good offices came back alive, mostly. And a dozen smaller syndicates, variously and shiftingly allied.

Even we find you useful. Miles touched the control and the vid image vanished. His lip curled in suppressed loathing, and he called up his ordnance inventory for one final check of his shopping list. A subtle shift in the vibrations of the ship around him told him they were matching orbits—the fast cruiser *Ariel* would be docking at Fell Station within the hour.

His console was just extruding the completed data disk of weapons orders when his cabin door chimed, followed by an alto voice over its comm, "Admiral Naismith?"

"Enter." He plucked off the disk and leaned back in his station chair.

Captain Thorne sauntered in with a friendly salute. "We'll be docking in about thirty minutes, sir."

"Thank you, Bel."

Bel Thorne, the *Ariel*'s commander, was a Betan hermaphrodite, man/woman descendant of a centuries-past genetic-social experiment every bit as bizarre, in Miles's private opinion, as anything rumored to be done for money by House Ryoval's ethics-free surgeons. A fringe effort of Betan egalitarianism run amok, hermaphroditism had not caught on, and the original idealists' hapless descendants remained a minority on hyper-tolerant Beta Colony. Except for a few stray wanderers like Bel. As a mercenary officer Thorne was conscientious, loyal, and aggressive, and Miles liked him/her/it—Betan custom used the neuter pronoun—a lot. *However. . . .*

Miles could smell Bel's floral perfume from her. Bel was emphasizing the female side today. And had been, increasingly, for the five days of this voyage. Normally Bel chose to come on ambiguous-to-male, soft short brown hair and chiselled, beardless facial features counteracted by the grey-and-white Dendarii military uniform, assertive gestures, and wicked humor. It worried Miles exceedingly to sense Bel soften in his presence.

Turning to his computer console's holovid plate, Miles again called up the image of the planet they were approaching. Jackson's Whole looked demure enough from a distance, mountainous, rather cold— the populated equator was only temperate—ringed in the vid by a lacy schematic net of colored satellite tracks, orbital transfer stations, and authorized approach vectors. "Have you ever been here before, Bel?"

"Once, when I was a lieutenant in Admiral Oser's fleet," said the mercenary. "House Fell has a new baron since then. Their weaponry still has a good reputation, as long as you know what you're buying. Stay away from the sale on neutron hand grenades."

"Heh. For those with strong throwing arms. Fear not, neutron hand grenades aren't on the list." He handed the data disk to Bel.

Bel sidled up and leaned over the back of Miles's station chair to take it. "Shall I grant leaves to the crew while we're waiting for the baron's minions to load cargo? How about yourself? There used to be a hostel near the docks with all the amenities, pool, sauna, great food . . ." Bel's voice lowered. "I could book a room for two."

"I'd only figured to grant day passes." Necessarily, Miles cleared his throat.

"I *am* a woman, too," Bel pointed out in a murmur.

"Among other things."

"You're so hopelessly monosexual, Miles."

"Sorry." Awkwardly, he patted the hand that had somehow come to rest on his shoulder.

Bel sighed and straightened. "So many are."

Miles sighed too. Perhaps he ought to make his rejection more emphatic—this was only about the seventh time he'd been round with Bel on this subject. It was almost ritualized by now, almost, but not quite, a joke. You had to give the Betan credit for either optimism or obtuseness . . . or, Miles's honesty added, genuine feeling. If he turned round now, he knew, he might surprise an essential loneliness in the hermaphrodite's eyes, never permitted on the lips. He did not turn round.

And who was he to judge another, Miles reflected ruefully, whose own body brought him so little joy? What did Bel, straight and healthy and of normal height, if unusual genital arrangements, find so attractive in a little half-crippled part-time crazy man? He glanced down at the grey Dendarii officer's uniform he wore. The uniform he had won. *If you can't be seven feet tall, be seven feet smart.* His reason had so far failed to present him with a solution to the problem of Thorne, though.

"Have you ever thought of going back to Beta Colony, and seeking one of your own?" Miles asked seriously.

Thorne shrugged. "Too boring. That's why I left. It's so very safe, so very narrow. . . ."

"Mind you, a great place to raise kids." One corner of Miles's mouth twisted up.

Thorne grinned. "You got it. You're an almost perfect Betan, y'know? Almost. You have the accent, the in-jokes . . ."

Miles went a little still. "Where do I fail?"

Thorne touched Miles's cheek; Miles flinched.

"Reflexes," said Thorne.

"Ah."

"I won't give you away."

"I know."

Bel was leaning in again. "I could polish that last edge . . ."

"Never mind," said Miles, slightly flushed. "We have a mission."

"Inventory," said Thorne scornfully.

"That's not a mission," said Miles, "that's a cover."

"Ah ha." Thorne straightened up. "At last."

"At last?"

"It doesn't take a genius. We came to purchase ordnance, but instead of taking the ship with the biggest cargo capacity, you chose the *Ariel*—the fleet's fastest. There's no deader dull routine than inventory, but instead of sending a perfectly competent quartermaster, you're overseeing it personally."

"I do want to make contact with the new Baron Fell," said Miles mildly. "House Fell is the biggest arms supplier this side of Beta Colony, and a lot less picky about who its customers are. If I like the quality of the initial purchase, they could become a regular supplier."

"A quarter of Fell's arms are Betan manufacture, marked up," said Thorne. "Again, ha."

"And while we're here," Miles went on, "a certain middle-aged man is going to present himself and sign on to the Dendarii Mercenaries as a medtech. At that point all Station passes are cancelled, we finish loading cargo as quickly as possible, and we leave."

Thorne grinned in satisfaction. "A pick-up. Very good. I assume we're being well-paid?"

"Very. If he arrives at his destination alive. The man happens to be the top research geneticist of House Bharaputra's Laboratories. He's been offered asylum by a planetary government capable of protecting him from the long arms of Baron Luigi Bharaputra's enforcers. His soon-to-be-former employer is expected to be highly irate at the lack of a month's notice. We are being paid to deliver him to his new masters alive and not, ah, forcibly debriefed of all his trade secrets.

"Since House Bharaputra could probably buy and sell the whole Dendarii Free Mercenary Fleet twice over out of petty cash, I would prefer we not have to deal with Baron Luigi's enforcers either. So we shall be innocent suckers. All we did was hire a bloody medtech, sir. And we shall be irate ourselves when he deserts after we arrive at fleet rendezvous off Escobar."

"Sounds good to me," conceded Thorne. "Simple."

"So I trust," Miles sighed hopefully. Why, after all, shouldn't things run to plan, just this once?

The purchasing offices and display areas for House Fell's lethal wares were situated not far from the docks, and most of House Fell's smaller customers never penetrated further into Fell Station. But shortly after Miles and Thorne placed their order—about as long as needed to verify a credit chit—an obsequious person in the green silk of House Fell's uniform appeared, and pressed an invitation into Admiral Naismith's hand to a reception in the Baron's personal quarters.

Four hours later, giving up the pass cube to Baron Fell's major domo at the sealed entrance to the station's private sector, Miles checked Thorne and himself over for their general effect. Dendarii dress uniform was a grey velvet tunic with silver buttons on the shoulders and white edging, matching grey trousers with white side piping, and grey synthasuede boots—perhaps just a trifle effete? Well, he hadn't designed it, he'd just inherited it. Live with it.

The interface to the private sector was highly interesting. Miles's eye took in the details while the major domo scanned them for weapons. Life-support—in fact, all systems—appeared to be run separately from the rest of the station. The area was not only sealable, it was detachable. In effect, not Station but Ship—engines and armament around here somewhere, Miles bet, though it could be lethal to go looking for them unescorted. The major domo ushered them through, pausing to announce them on his wrist comm: "Admiral Miles Naismith, commanding, Dendarii Free Mercenary Fleet. Captain Bel Thorne, commanding the fast cruiser *Ariel,* Dendarii Free Mercenary Fleet." Miles wondered who was on the other end of the comm.

The reception chamber was large and gracefully appointed, with iridescent floating staircases and levels creating private spaces without destroying the illusions of openness. Every exit (Miles counted six) had a large green-garbed guard by it trying to look like a servant and not succeeding very well. One whole wall was a vertigo-inducing transparent viewport overlooking Fell Station's busy docks and the bright curve of Jackson's Whole bisecting the star-spattered horizon beyond. A crew of elegant women in green silk saris rustled among the guests offering food and drink.

Grey velvet, Miles decided after one glance at the other guests, was a positively demure choice of garb. He and Bel would blend right into the walls. The thin scattering of fellow privileged customers wore a wide array of planetary fashions. But they were a wary bunch, little groups sticking together, no mingling. Guerrillas, it appeared, did not speak to mercenaries, nor smugglers to revolutionaries; the Gnostic Saints, of course, spoke only to the One True God, and perhaps to Baron Fell.

"Some party," commented Bel. "I went to a pet show with an atmosphere like this once. The high point was when somebody's Tau Cetan beaded lizard got loose and ate the Best-In-Show from the canine division."

"Hush," Miles grinned out of the corner of his mouth. "This is business."

A green-sari'd woman bowed silently before them, offering a tray. Thorne raised a brow at Miles—*do we . . . ?*

"Why not?" Miles murmured. "We're paying for it, in the long run. I doubt the baron poisons his customers, it's bad for business. Business is emperor, here. Laissez-faire capitalism gone completely over the edge." He selected a pink tid-bit in the shape of a lotus and a mysterious cloudy drink. Thorne followed suit. The pink lotus, alas, turned out to be some sort of raw fish. It squeaked against his teeth. Miles, committed, swallowed it anyway. The drink was potently alcoholic, and after a sip to wash down the lotus he regretfully abandoned it on the first level surface he could find. His dwarfish body refused to handle alcohol, and he had no desire to meet Baron Fell while either semi-comatose or giggling uncontrollably. The more metabolically fortunate Thorne kept beverage in hand.

A most extraordinary music began from somewhere, a racing rich complexity of harmonics. Miles could not identify the instrument—instruments, surely. He and Thorne exchanged a glance, and by mutual accord drifted toward the sound. Around a spiraling staircase, backed by the panoply of station, planet, and stars, they found the musician. Miles's eyes widened. *House Ryoval's surgeons have surely gone too far this time. . . .*

Little decorative colored sparkles defined the spherical field of a large null-gee bubble. Floating within it was a woman. Her ivory arms flashed against her green silk clothes as she played. All *four* of her ivory arms. . . . She wore a flowing, kimono-like belted jacket and matching shorts, from which the second set of arms emerged where her legs should have been. Her hair was short and soft and ebony black. Her eyes were closed, and her rose-tinted face bore the repose of an angel, high and distant and terrifying.

Her strange instrument was fixed in air before her, a flat polished wooden frame strung across both top and bottom with a bewildering array of tight gleaming wires, soundboard between. She struck the wires with four felted hammers with blinding speed, both sides at once, her upper hands moving at counterpoint to her lowers. Music poured forth in a cascade.

"Good God," said Thorne, "it's a quaddie."

"It's a what?"

"A quaddie. She's a long way from home."

"She's—not a local product?"

"By no means."

"I'm relieved. I think. Where the devil does she come from, then?"

"About two hundred years ago—about the time hermaphrodites were being invented," a peculiar wryness flashed across Thorne's face, "there was this rush of genetic experimentation on humans, in the wake of the development of the practical uterine replicator. Followed shortly by a rush of laws restricting such, but meanwhile, somebody thought they'd make a race of free fall dwellers. Then artificial gravity came in and blew them out of business. The quaddies fled—their descendants ended up on the far side of nowhere, way beyond Earth from us in the Nexus. They're rumored to keep to themselves, mostly. Very unusual, to see one this side of Earth. H'sh." Lips parted, Thorne tracked the music.

As unusual as finding a Betan hermaphrodite in a free mercenary fleet, Miles thought. But the music deserved undivided attention, though few in this paranoid crowd seemed to even be noticing it. A shame. Miles was no musician, but even he could sense an intensity of passion in the playing that went beyond talent, reaching for genius. An evanescent genius, sounds woven with time and, like time, forever receding beyond one's futile grasp into memory alone.

The outpouring of music dropped to a haunting echo, then silence. The four-armed musician's blue eyes opened, and her face came back from the ethereal to the merely human, tense and sad.

"Ah," breathed Thorne, stuck its empty glass under its arm, raised hands to clap, then paused, hesitant to become conspicuous in this indifferent chamber.

Miles was all for being inconspicuous. "Perhaps you can speak to her," he suggested by way of an alternative.

"You think?" Brightening, Thorne tripped forward, swinging

down to abandon the glass on the nearest handy floor and raising splayed hands against the sparkling bubble. The hermaphrodite mustered an entranced, ingratiating smile. "Uh . . ." Thorne's chest rose and fell.

Good God, Bel, tongue-tied? Never thought I'd see it. "Ask her what she calls that thing she plays," Miles supplied helpfully.

The four-armed woman tilted her head curiously, and starfished gracefully over her boxy instrument to hover politely before Thorne on the other side of the glittering barrier. "Yes?"

"What do you call that extraordinary instrument?" Thorne asked.

"It's a double-sided hammer dulcimer, ma'am—sir . . ." her servant-to-guest dull tone faltered a moment, fearing to give insult, "Officer."

"Captain Bel Thorne," Bel supplied instantly, beginning to recover accustomed smooth equilibrium. "Commanding the Dendarii fast cruiser *Ariel.* At your service. How ever did you come to be here?"

"I had worked my way to Earth. I was seeking employment, and Baron Fell hired me." She tossed her head, as if to deflect some implied criticism, though Bel had offered none.

"You are a true quaddie?"

"You've heard of my people?" Her dark brows rose in surprise. "Most people I encounter here think I am a *manufactured* freak." A little sardonic bitterness edged her voice.

Thorne cleared its throat. "I'm Betan, myself. I've followed the history of the early genetics explosion with a rather more personal interest." Thorne cleared its throat again, "Betan hermaphrodite, you see," and waited anxiously for the reaction.

Damn. Bel never waited for reactions, Bel sailed on and let the chips fall anyhow. *I wouldn't interfere with this for all the world.* Miles faded back slightly, rubbing his lips to wipe off a twitching grin as all Thorne's most masculine mannerisms reasserted themselves from spine to fingertips and outward into the aether.

Her head tilted in interest. One upper hand rose to rest on the sparkling barrier not far from Bel's. *"Are* you? You're a genetic too, then."

"Oh, yes. And tell me, what's your name?"

"Nicol."

"Nicol. Is that all? I mean, it's lovely."

"My people don't use surnames."

"Ah. And, uh, what are you doing after the party?"

At this point, alas, interference found them. "Heads up, *Captain,*"

Miles murmured. Thorne drew up instantly, cool and correct, and followed Miles's gaze. The quaddie floated back from the force barrier and bowed her head over her hands held palm-to-palm and palm-to-palm as a man approached. Miles too came to a polite species of attention.

Georish Stauber, Baron Fell, was a surprisingly old man to have succeeded so recently to his position, Miles thought. In the flesh he looked older than the holovid Miles had viewed of him at his own mission briefing. The baron was balding, with a white fringe of hair around his shiny pate, jovial and fat. He looked like somebody's grandfather. Not Miles's; Miles's grandfather had been lean and predatory even in his great age. And the old Count's title had been as real as such things got, not the courtesy-nobility of a Syndicate survivor. Jolly red cheeks or no, Miles reminded himself, Baron Fell had climbed a pile of bodies to attain this high place.

"Admiral Naismith. Captain Thorne. Welcome to Fell Station," rumbled the baron, smiling.

Miles swept him an aristocratic bow. Thorne somewhat awkwardly followed suit. Ah. He must copy that awkwardness next time. Of such little details were cover identities made. And blown.

"Have my people been taking care of your needs?"

"Thank you, yes." So far the proper businessmen.

"So glad to meet you at last," the baron rumbled on. "We've heard a great deal about you here."

"Have you," said Miles encouragingly. The baron's eyes were strangely avid. *Quite a glad-hand for a little tin-pot mercenary, eh?* This was a little more stroke than was reasonable even for a high-ticket customer. Miles banished all hint of wariness from his return smile. *Patience. Let the challenge emerge, don't rush to meet what you cannot yet see.* "Good things, I hope."

"Remarkable things. Your rise has been as rapid as your origins are mysterious."

Hell, hell, what kind of bait was this? Was the baron hinting that he actually knew "Admiral Naismith's" real identity? This could be sudden and serious trouble. No—fear outran its cause. Wait. Forget that such a person as Lieutenant Lord Vorkosigan, Barrayaran Imperial Security, ever existed in this body. *It's not big enough for the two of us anyway, boy.* Yet why was this fat shark smiling so ingratiatingly? Miles cocked his head, neutrally.

"The story of your fleet's success at Vervain reached us even here. So unfortunate about its former commander."

Miles stiffened. "I regret Admiral Oser's death."

The baron shrugged philosophically. "Such things happen in the business. Only one can command."

"He could have been an outstanding subordinate."

"Pride is so dangerous," smiled the baron.

Indeed. Miles bit his tongue. *So he thinks I "arranged" Oser's death. So let him.* That there was one less mercenary than there appeared in this room, that the Dendarii were now through Miles an arm of the Barrayaran Imperial Service so covert most of them didn't even know it themselves . . . it would be a dull Syndicate baron who couldn't find profit in those secrets somewhere. Miles matched the baron's smile and added nothing.

"You interest me exceedingly," continued the baron. "For example, there's the puzzle of your apparent age. And your prior military career."

If Miles had kept his drink, he'd have knocked it back in one gulp right then. He clasped his hands convulsively behind his back instead. Dammit, the pain lines just didn't age his face enough. If the baron was indeed seeing right through the pseudo-mercenary to the twenty-three-year-old Security lieutenant—and yet, he usually carried it off—

The baron lowered his voice. "Do the rumors run equally true about your Betan rejuvenation treatment?"

So *that's* what he was on about. Miles felt faint with relief. "What interest could you have in such treatments, my lord?" he gibbered lightly. "I thought Jackson's Whole was the home of practical immortality. It's said there are some here on their third cloned body."

"I am not one of them," said the baron rather regretfully.

Miles's brows rose in genuine surprise. Surely this man didn't spurn the process as murder. "Some unfortunate medical impediment?" he said, injecting polite sympathy into his voice. "My regrets, sir."

"In a manner of speaking." The baron's smile revealed a sharp edge. "The brain transplant operation itself kills a certain irreducible percentage of patients—"

Yeah, thought Miles, *starting with 100% of the clones, whose brains are flushed to make room. . . .*

"—another percentage suffer varying sorts of permanent damage. Those are the risks anyone must take for the reward."

"But the reward is so great."

"But then there are a certain number of patients, indistinguishable from the first group, who do not die on the operating table by accident. If their enemies have the subtlety and clout to arrange it. I have a number of enemies, Admiral Naismith."

Miles made a little who-would-think-it gesture, flipping up one hand, and continued to cultivate an air of deep interest.

"I calculate my present chances of surviving a brain transplant to be rather worse than the average," the baron went on. "So I've an interest in alternatives." He paused expectantly.

"Oh," said Miles. Oh, indeed. He regarded his fingernails and thought fast. "It's true, I once participated in an . . . unauthorized experiment. A premature one, as it happens, pushed too eagerly from animal to human subjects. It was not successful."

"No?" said the baron. "You appear in good health."

Miles shrugged. "Yes, there was some benefit to muscles, skin tone, hair. But my bones are the bones of an old man, fragile." *True.* "Subject to acute osteo-inflammatory attacks—there are days when I can't walk without medication." *Also true, dammit.* A recent and unsettling medical development. "My life expectancy is not considered good." *For example, if certain parties here ever figure out who "Admiral Naismith" really is, it could go down to as little as fifteen minutes.* "So unless you're extremely fond of pain and think you would enjoy being crippled, I fear I must dis-recommend the procedure."

The baron looked him up and down. Disappointment pulled down his mouth. "I see."

Bel Thorne, who knew quite well there was no such thing as the fabled "Betan rejuvenation treatment," was listening with well-concealed enjoyment and doing an excellent job of keeping the smirk off its face. Bless its little black heart.

"Still," said the baron, "your . . . scientific acquaintance may have made some progress in the intervening years."

"I fear not," said Miles. "He died." He spread his hands helplessly. "Old age."

"Oh." The baron's shoulders sagged slightly.

"Ah, there you are, Fell," a new voice cut across them. The baron straightened and turned.

The man who had hailed him was as conservatively dressed as Fell, and flanked by a silent servant with "bodyguard" written all over him. The bodyguard wore a uniform, a high-necked red silk tunic and loose black trousers, and was unarmed. Everyone on Fell Station went unarmed except Fell's men; the place had the most strictly-enforced weapons regs Miles had ever encountered. But the pattern of calluses on the lean bodyguard's hands suggested he might not need weapons. His eyes flickered and his hands shook just slightly, a hyper-alertness induced by artificial aids—if ordered, he could strike with blinding speed and adrenalin-insane strength. He would also retire young, metabolically crippled for the rest of his short life.

The man he guarded was also young—some great lord's son? Miles wondered. He had long shining black hair dressed in an elaborate braid, smooth dark olive skin, and a high-bridged nose. He couldn't be older than Miles's real age, yet he moved with a mature assurance.

"Ryoval," Baron Fell nodded in return, as a man to an equal, not a junior. Still playing the genial host, Fell added, "Officers, may I introduce Baron Ryoval of House Ryoval. Admiral Naismith, Captain Thorne. They belong to the Illyrican-built mercenary fast cruiser in dock, Ry, that you may have noticed."

"Haven't got your eye for hardware, I'm afraid, Georish." Baron Ryoval bestowed a nod upon them, of a man being polite to his social inferiors for the principle of it. Miles bowed clumsily in return.

Dropping Miles from his attention with an almost audible thump, Ryoval stood back with his hands on his hips and regarded the null-gee bubble's inhabitant. "My agent didn't exaggerate her charms."

Fell smiled sourly. Nicol had withdrawn—recoiled—when Ryoval first approached, and now floated behind her instrument, fussing with its tuning. Pretending to be fussing with its tuning. Her eyes glanced warily at Ryoval, then returned to her dulcimer as if it might put some magic wall between them.

"Can you have her play—" Ryoval began, and was interrupted by a chime from his wrist comm. "Excuse me, Georish." Looking slightly annoyed, he turned half-away from them and spoke into it. "Ryoval. And this had better be important."

"Yes, m'lord," a thin voice responded. "This is Manager Deem in Sales and Demonstrations. We have a problem. That creature House Bharaputra sold us has savaged a customer."

Ryoval's Greek-statue lips rippled in a silent snarl. "I told you to chain it with duralloy."

"We did, my lord. The chains held, but it tore the bolts right out of the wall."

"Stun it."

"We have."

"Then punish it suitably when it awakes. A sufficiently long period without food should dull its aggression—its metabolism is unbelievable."

"What about the customer?"

"Give him whatever comforts he asks for. On the House."

"I . . . don't think he'll be in shape to appreciate them for quite some time. He's in the clinic now. Still unconscious."

Ryoval hissed. "Put my personal physician on his case. I'll take care of the rest when I get back downside, in about six hours. Ryoval out." He snapped the link closed. "Morons," he growled. He took a controlled, meditative breath, and recalled his social manner as if booting it up out of some stored memory bank. "Pardon the interruption, please, Georish."

Fell waved an understanding hand, as if to say, *Business.*

"As I was saying, can you have her play something?" Ryoval nodded to the quaddie.

Fell clasped his hands behind his back, his eyes glinting in a falsely benign smile. "Play something, Nicol."

She gave him an acknowledging nod, positioned herself, and closed her eyes. The frozen worry tensing her face gradually gave way to an inner stillness, and she began to play, a slow, sweet theme that established itself, rolled over, and began to quicken.

"Enough!" Ryoval flung up a hand. "She's precisely as described."

Nicol stumbled to a halt in mid-phrase. She inhaled through pinched nostrils, clearly disturbed by her inability to drive the piece through to its destined finish, the frustration of artistic incompletion. She stuck her hammers into their holders on the side of the instrument with short, savage jerks, and crossed her upper and lower arms both. Thorne's mouth tightened, and it crossed its arms in unconscious echo. Miles bit his lip uneasily.

"My agent conveyed the truth," Ryoval went on.

"Then perhaps your agent also conveyed my regrets," said Fell dryly.

"He did. But he wasn't authorized to offer more than a certain standard ceiling. For something so unique, there's no substitute for direct contact."

"I happen to be enjoying her skills where they are," said Fell. "At my age, enjoyment is much harder to obtain than money."

"So true. Yet other enjoyments might be substituted. I could arrange something quite special. Not in the catalog."

"Her *musical* skills, Ryoval. Which are more than special. They are unique. Genuine. Not artificially augmented in any way. Not to be duplicated in your laboratories."

"My laboratories can duplicate anything sir." Ryoval smiled at the implied challenge.

"Except originality. By definition."

Ryoval spread his hands in polite acknowledgment of the philosophical point. Fell, Miles gathered, was not just enjoying the quaddie's musical talent, he was vastly enjoying the possession of something his rival keenly wanted to buy, that he had absolutely no need to sell. One-upsmanship was a powerful pleasure. It seemed even the famous Ryoval was having a tough time coming up with a better—and yet, if Ryoval could find Fell's price, what force on Jackson's Whole could save Nicol? Miles suddenly realized he knew what Fell's price could be. Would Ryoval figure it out too?

Ryoval pursed his lips. "Let's discuss a tissue sample, then. It would do her no damage, and you could continue to enjoy her unique services uninterrupted."

"It would damage her uniqueness. Circulating counterfeits always brings down the value of the real thing, you know that, Ry," grinned Baron Fell.

"Not for some time," Ryoval pointed out. "The lead time for a mature clone is at least ten years—ah, but you know that." He reddened and made a little apologetic bow, as if he realized he'd just committed some faux pas.

By the thinning of Fell's lips, he had. "Indeed," said Fell coldly.

At this point Bel Thorne, tracking the interplay, interrupted in hot horror, "You can't sell her tissues! You don't own them. She's not some Jackson's Whole construct, she's a freeborn galactic citizen!"

Both barons turned to Bel as if the mercenary were a piece of furniture that had suddenly spoken. Out of turn. Miles winced.

"He can sell her contract," said Ryoval, mustering a glassy tolerance. "Which is what we are discussing. A *private* discussion."

Bel ignored the hint. "On Jackson's Whole, what practical difference does it make if you call it a contract or call it flesh?"

Ryoval smiled a little cool smile. "None whatsoever. Possession is rather more than nine points of the law, here."

"It's totally illegal!"

"Legal, my dear—ah—you are Betan, aren't you? That explains it," said Ryoval. "And illegal, is whatever the planet you are on chooses to call so and is able to enforce. I don't see any Betan enforcers around here to impose their peculiar version of morality on us all, do you, Fell?"

Fell was listening with raised brows, caught between amusement and annoyance.

Bel twitched. "So if I were to pull out a weapon and blow your head off, it would be perfectly legal?"

The bodyguard tensed, balance and center-of-gravity flowing into launch position.

"Quash it, Bel," Miles muttered under his breath.

But Ryoval was beginning to enjoy baiting his Betan interrupter. "You have no weapon. But legality aside, my subordinates have instructions to avenge me. It is, as it were, a natural or virtual law. In effect you'd find such an ill-advised impulse to be illegal indeed."

Baron Fell caught Miles's eye and tilted his head just slightly. Time to intervene. "Time to move on, Captain," Miles said. "We aren't the baron's only guests here."

"Try the hot buffet," suggested Fell affably.

Ryoval pointedly dropped Bel from his attention and turned to Miles. "Do stop by my establishment if you get downside, Admiral. Even a Betan could stand to expand the horizons of his experience. I'm sure my staff could find something of interest in your price range."

"Not any more," said Miles. "Baron Fell already has our credit chit."

"Ah, too bad. Your next trip, perhaps." Ryoval turned away in easy dismissal.

Bel didn't budge. "You can't sell a galactic citizen down there," gesturing jerkily to the curve of the planet beyond the viewport. The quaddie Nicol, watching from behind her dulcimer, had no expression at all upon her face, but her intense blue eyes blazed.

Ryoval turned back, feigning sudden surprise. "Why, Captain, I just realized. Betan—you must be a genuine genetic hermaphrodite. You possess a marketable rarity yourself. I can offer you an eye-opening employment experience at easily twice your current rate of pay. And you wouldn't even have to get shot at. I guarantee you'd be extremely popular. Group rates."

Miles swore he could see Thorne's blood pressure skyrocketing as the meaning of what Ryoval had just said sunk in. The hermaphrodite's face darkened, and it drew breath. Miles reached up and grasped Bel by the shoulder, hard. The breath held.

"No?" said Ryoval, cocking his head. "Oh, well. But seriously, I would pay well for a tissue sample, for my files."

Bel's breath exploded. "My clone-siblings, to be—be—some sort of sex-slaves into the next century! Over my dead body—or yours—you—"

Bel was so mad it was stuttering, a phenomenon Miles had never seen in seven years' acquaintance including combat.

"So Betan," smirked Ryoval.

"Stop it, Ry," growled Fell.

Ryoval sighed. "Oh, very well. But it's so easy."

"We can't win, Bel," hissed Miles. "It's time to withdraw." The bodyguard was quivering.

Fell gave Miles an approving nod.

"Thank you for your hospitality, Baron Fell," Miles said formally. "Good day, Baron Ryoval."

"Good day, Admiral," said Ryoval, regretfully giving up what was obviously the best sport he'd had all day. "You seem a cosmopolitan sort, for a Betan. Perhaps you can visit us sometime without your moral friend, here."

A war of words should be won with words. "I don't think so," Miles murmured, racking his brain for some stunning insult to withdraw on.

"What a shame," said Ryoval. "We have a dog-and-dwarf act I'm sure you'd find *fascinating.*"

There was a moment's absolute silence.

"Fry 'em from orbit," Bel suggested tightly.

Miles grinned through clenched teeth, bowed, and backed off, Bel's sleeve clutched firmly in his hand. As he turned he could hear Ryoval laughing.

Fell's major domo appeared at their elbows within moments. "This way to the exit, please, officers," he smiled. Miles had never before been thrown out of any place with such exquisite politeness.

Back aboard the *Ariel* in dock, Thorne paced the wardroom while Miles sat and sipped coffee as hot and black as his own thoughts.

"Sorry I lost my temper with that squirt Ryoval," Bel apologized gruffly.

"Squirt, hell," said Miles. "The brain in that body has got to be at least a hundred years old. He played you like a violin. No. We couldn't expect to count coup on him. I admit, it would have been nice if you'd had the sense to shut up." He sucked air to cool his scalded tongue.

Bel made a disturbed gesture of acknowledgment and paced on. "And that poor girl, trapped in that bubble—I had one chance to talk to her, and I blew it—I *blithered. . . .*"

She really had brought out the male in Thorne, Miles reflected wryly. "Happens to the best of us," he murmured. He smiled into his coffee, then frowned. No. Better not to encourage Thorne's interest in the quaddie after all. She was clearly much more than just one of Fell's house servants. They had one ship here, a crew of twenty; even if he had the whole Dendarii fleet to back him he'd want to think twice about offending Baron Fell in Fell's own territory. They had a mission. Speaking of which, where was their blasted pick-up? Why hadn't he yet contacted them as arranged?

The intercom in the wall bleeped.

Thorne strode to it. "Thorne here."

"This is Corporal Nout at the portside docking hatch. There's a . . . woman here who's asking to see you."

Thorne and Miles exchanged a raised-brows glance. "What's her name?" asked Thorne.

An off-side mumble, then, "She says it's Nicol."

Thorne grunted in surprise. "Very well. Have her escorted to the wardroom."

"Yes, Captain." The corporal failed to kill his intercom before turning away, and his voice drifted back, ". . . stay in this outfit long enough, you see one of *everything.*"

Nicol appeared in the doorway balanced in a float chair, a hovering tubular cup that seemed to be looking for its saucer, enameled in a blue that precisely matched her eyes. She slipped it through the doorway as easily as a woman twitching her hips, zipped to a halt near Miles's table, and adjusted the height to that of a person sitting. The controls, run by her lower hands, left her uppers entirely free. The lower body support must have been custom-designed just for her. Miles watched her maneuver with great interest. He hadn't been sure she could even live outside her null-gee bubble. He'd expected her to be weak. She didn't look weak. She looked determined. She looked at Thorne.

Thorne looked all cheered up. "Nicol. How nice to see you again."

She nodded shortly. "Captain Thorne. Admiral Naismith." She glanced back and forth between them, and fastened on Thorne. Miles thought he could see why. He sipped coffee and waited for developments.

"Captain Thorne. You are a mercenary, are you not?"

"Yes. . . ."

"And . . . pardon me if I misunderstood, but it seemed to me you had a certain . . . empathy, for my situation. An understanding of my position."

Thorne rendered her a slightly idiotic bow. "I understand you are dangling over a pit."

Her lips tightened, and she nodded mutely.

"She got herself into it," Miles pointed out.

Her chin lifted. "And I intend to get myself out of it."

Miles turned a hand palm-out, and sipped again.

She readjusted her float chair, a nervous gesture ending at about the same altitude it began.

"It seems to me," said Miles, "that Baron Fell is a formidable protector. I'm not sure you have anything to fear from Ryoval's, er, carnal interest in you as long as Fell's in charge."

"Baron Fell is dying." She tossed her head. "Or at any rate, he thinks he is."

"So I gathered. Why doesn't he have a clone made?"

"He did. It was all set up with House Bharaputra. The clone was fourteen years old, full-sized. Then a couple of months ago, somebody assassinated the clone. The baron still hasn't found out for sure who did it, though he has a little list. Headed by his half-brother."

"Thus trapping him in his aging body. What a . . . fascinating tactical maneuver," Miles mused. "What's this unknown enemy going to do next, I wonder? Just wait?"

"I don't know," said Nicol. "The Baron's had another clone started, but it's not even out of the replicator yet. Even with growth accelerators it'd be years before it would be mature enough to transplant. And . . . it has occurred to me that there are a number of ways the baron could die besides ill health between now and then."

"An unstable situation," Miles agreed.

"I want out. I want to buy passage out."

"Then why, he asked," said Miles dryly, "don't you just go plunk your money down at the offices of one of the three galactic commercial passenger lines that dock here, and buy a ticket?"

"It's my contract," said Nicol. "When I signed it back on Earth, I didn't realize what it would mean once I got to Jackson's Whole. I can't even buy my way out of it, unless the baron chooses to let me. And somehow . . . it seems to cost more and more just to live here. I ran a calculation . . . it gets much worse before my time is up."

"How much time?" asked Thorne.

"Five more years."

"Ouch," said Thorne sympathetically.

"So you, ah, want us to help you jump a Syndicate contract," said Miles, making little wet coffee rings on the table with the bottom of his mug. "Smuggle you out in secret, I suppose."

"I can pay. I can pay more right now than I'll be able to next year. This wasn't the gig I expected, when I came here. There was talk of recording a vid demo . . . it never happened. I don't think it's ever going to happen. I have to be able to reach a wider audience, if I'm ever to pay my way back home. Back to my people. I want . . . *out* of here, before I fall down that gravity well." She jerked an upper thumb in the general direction of the planet they orbited. "People go downside here, who never come up again." She paused. "Are you *afraid* of Baron Fell?"

"No!" said Thorne, as Miles said, "Yes." They exchanged a sardonic look.

"We are inclined to be careful of Baron Fell," Miles suggested. Thorne shrugged agreement.

She frowned, and maneuvered to the table. She drew a wad of assorted planetary currencies out of her green silk jacket and laid it in front of Miles. "Would this bolster your nerve?"

Thorne fingered the stack, flipped through it. At least a couple thousand Betan dollars worth, at conservative estimate, mostly in middle denominations, though a Betan single topped the pile, camouflaging its value to a casual glance. "Well," said Thorne, glancing at Miles, "and what do we mercenaries think of that?"

Miles leaned back thoughtfully in his chair. The kept secret of Miles's identity wasn't the only favor Thorne could call in if it chose. Miles remembered the day Thorne had helped capture an asteroid mining station and the pocket dreadnought *Triumph* for him with nothing but sixteen troops in combat armor and a hell of a lot of nerve. "I encourage creative financing on the part of my commanders," he said at last. "Negotiate away, Captain."

Thorne smiled, and pulled the Betan dollar off the stack. "You have the right idea," Thorne said to the musician, "but the amount is wrong."

Her hand went uncertainly to her jacket and paused, as Thorne pushed the rest of the stack of currency, minus the single, back to her. "What?"

Thorne picked up the single and snapped it a few times. "This is the right amount. Makes it an official contract, you see." Bel extended a hand to her; after a bewildered moment, she shook it. "Deal," said Thorne happily.

"Hero," said Miles, holding up a warning finger, "beware, I'll call in my veto if you can't come up with a way to bring this off in dead secret. That's my cut of the price."

"Yes, *sir,*" said Thorne.

Several hours later, Miles snapped awake in his cabin aboard the *Ariel* to an urgent bleeping from his comconsole. Whatever he had been dreaming was gone in the instant, though he had the vague idea it had been something unpleasant. Biological and unpleasant. "Naismith here."

"This is the duty officer in Nav and Com, sir. You have a call originating from the downside commercial comm net. He says to tell you it's Vaughn."

Vaughn was the agreed-upon code name of their pick-up. His real name was Dr. Canaba. Miles grabbed his uniform jacket and shrugged it on over his black T-shirt, passed his hands futilely through his hair, and slid into his console station chair. "Put him through."

The face of a man on the high side of middle age materialized above Miles's vid plate. Tan-skinned, racially indeterminate features, short wavy hair greying at the temples; more arresting was the intelligence that suffused those features and quickened the brown eyes. *Yep, that's my man,* thought Miles with satisfaction. *Here we go.* But Canaba looked more than tense. He looked distraught.

"Admiral Naismith?"

"Yes. Vaughn?"

Canaba nodded.

"Where are you?" asked Miles.

"Downside."

"You were to meet us up here."

"I know. Something's come up. A problem."

"What sort of problem? Ah—is this channel secure?"

Canaba laughed bitterly. "On this planet, nothing is secure. But I don't think I'm being traced. But I can't come up yet. I need . . . help."

"Vaughn, we aren't equipped to break you out against superior forces—if you've become a prisoner—"

He shook his head. "No, it's not that. I've . . . lost something. I need help to get it back."

"I'd understood you were to leave everything. You would be compensated later."

"It's not a personal possession. It's something your employer wants very badly. Certain . . . samples, have been removed from my . . . power. They won't take me without them."

Dr. Canaba took Miles for a mercenary hireling, entrusted with minimum classified information by Barrayaran Security. So. "All I was asked to transport was you and your skills."

"They didn't tell you everything."

The hell they didn't. Barrayar would take you stark naked, and be grateful. What was this?

Canaba met Miles's frown with a mouth set like iron. "I *won't* leave without them. Or the deal's off. And you can whistle for your pay, mercenary."

He meant it. Damn. Miles's eyes narrowed. "This is all a bit mysterious."

Canaba shrugged acknowledgment. "I'm sorry. But I *must* . . . Meet with me, and I'll tell you the rest. Or go, I don't care which. But a certain thing must be accomplished, must be . . . expiated." He trailed off in agitation.

Miles took a deep breath. "Very well. But every complication you add increases your risk. And mine. This had better be worth it."

"Oh, Admiral," breathed Canaba sadly, "it is to me. It is to me."

Snow sifted through the little park where Canaba met them, giving Miles something new to swear at if only he hadn't run out of invective hours ago. He was shivering even in his Dendarii-issue parka by the time Canaba walked past the dingy kiosk where Miles and Bel roosted. They fell in behind him without a word.

Bharaputra Laboratories were headquartered in a downside town Miles frankly found worrisome; guarded shuttleport, guarded syndicate buildings, guarded municipal buildings, guarded walled residential compounds; in between, a crazy disorder of neglected aging structures that didn't seem to be guarded by anyone, occupied by people who *slunk*. It made Miles wonder if the two Dendarii troopers he'd detailed to shadow them were quite enough. But the slithery people gave them a wide berth; they evidently understood what guards meant. At least during daylight.

Canaba led them into one of the nearby buildings. Its lift tubes were out-of-order, its corridors unheated. A darkly-dressed maybe-female person scurried out of their way in the shadows, reminding Miles uncomfortably of a rat. They followed Canaba dubiously up the safety ladder set in the side of a dead lift tube, down another corridor, and through a door with a broken palm-lock into an empty dirty room, greyly lit by an unpolarized but intact window. At least they were out of the wind.

"I think we can talk safely here," said Canaba, turning and pulling off his gloves.

"Bel?" said Miles.

Thorne pulled an assortment of anti-surveillance detectors from its parka and ran a scan, as the two guards prowled the perimeters. One stationed himself in the corridor, the second near the window.

"It scans clean," said Bel at last, as if reluctant to believe its own instruments. "For now." Rather pointedly, Bel walked around

Canaba and scanned him too. Canaba waited with bowed head, as if he felt he deserved no better. Bel set up the sonic baffler.

Miles shrugged back his hood and opened his parka, the better to reach his concealed weapons in the event of a trap. He was finding Canaba extraordinarily hard to read. What were the man's motivations anyway? There was no doubt House Bharaputra had assured his comfort—his coat, the rich cut of his clothing beneath it, spoke of that —and though his standard of living surely would not drop when he transferred his allegiance to the Barrayaran Imperial Science Institute, he would not have nearly the opportunities to amass wealth on the side that he had here. So, he wasn't in it for the money. Miles could understand that. But why work for a place like House Bharaputra in the first place unless greed overwhelmed integrity?

"You puzzle me, Dr. Canaba," said Miles lightly. "Why this mid-career switch? I'm pretty well acquainted with your new employers, and frankly, I don't see how they could out-bid House Bharaputra." There, that was a properly mercenary way to put it.

"They offered me protection from House Bharaputra. Although, if *you're* it . . ." he looked doubtfully down at Miles.

Ha. And, hell. The man really was ready to bolt. Leaving Miles to explain the failure of his mission to Chief of Imperial Security Illyan in person. "They bought our services," said Miles, "and therefore you command our services. They want you safe and happy. But we can't begin to protect you when you depart from a plan designed to maximize your safety, throw in random factors, and ask us to operate in the dark. I need full knowledge of what's going on if I'm to take full responsibility for the results."

"No one is asking you to take responsibility."

"I beg your pardon, doctor, but they surely have."

"Oh," said Canaba. "I . . . see." He paced to the window, back. "But will you do what I ask?"

"I will do what I can."

"Happy," Canaba snorted. "God . . ." he shook his head wearily, inhaled decisively. "I never came here for the money. I came here because I could do research I couldn't do anywhere else. Not hedged round with outdated legal restrictions. I dreamed of breakthroughs . . . but it became a nightmare. The freedom became slavery. The things they wanted me to do . . . ! Constantly interrupting the things I wanted to do. Oh, you can always find someone to do anything for money, but they're second-raters. These labs are full of second-raters. The very best can't be bought. I've done things, unique things, that Bharaputra won't develop because the profit would be too small, never mind how many people it would benefit—I get no credit, no standing for my work—every year, I see in the literature of my field galactic honors going to lesser men, because I cannot publish my results . . ." He stopped, lowered his head. "I doubtless sound like a megalomaniac to you."

"Ah . . ." said Miles, "you sound quite frustrated."

"The frustration," said Canaba, "woke me from a long sleep. Wounded ego—it was only wounded ego. But in my pride, I redis-covered shame. And the weight of it stunned me, stunned me where I stood. *Do* you understand? Does it matter if you understand? Ah!" He paced away to the wall, and stood facing it, his back rigid.

"Uh," Miles scratched the back of his head ruefully, "yeah. I'd be glad to spend many fascinating hours listening to you explain it to me —on my ship. Outbound."

Canaba turned with a crooked smile. "You are a practical man, I perceive. A soldier. Well, God knows I need a soldier now."

"Things are that screwed up, eh?"

"It . . . happened suddenly. I thought I had it under control."

"Go on," sighed Miles.

"There were seven synthesized gene-complexes. One of them is a cure for a certain obscure enzyme disorder. One of them will in-crease oxygen-generation in space station algae twenty-fold. One of them came from outside Bharaputra Labs, brought in by a man—we never found out who he really was, but death followed him. Several of my colleagues who had worked on his project were murdered all in one night, by the commandos who pursued him—their records destroyed—I never told anyone I'd borrowed an unauthorized tissue sample to study. I've not unravelled it fully yet, but I can tell you, it's absolutely unique."

Miles recognized that one, and almost choked, reflecting upon the bizarre chain of circumstances that had placed an identical tissue sample in the hands of Dendarii Intelligence a year ago. Terrence See's telepathy complex—and the main reason *why* His Imperial Majesty suddenly wanted a top geneticist. Dr. Canaba was in for a little surprise when he arrived at his new Barrayaran laboratory. But if the other six complexes came anywhere near matching the value of the known one, Security Chief Illyan would peel Miles with a dull knife for letting them slip through his fingers. Miles's attention to Canaba abruptly intensified. This side-trip might not be as trivial as he'd feared.

"Together, these seven complexes represent tens of thousands of hours of research time, mostly mine, some of others—my life's work.

I'd planned from the beginning to take them with me. I bundled them up in a viral insert and placed them, bound and dormant, in a live . . ." Canaba faltered, "organism, for storage. An organism, I thought, that no one would think to look at for such a thing."

"Why didn't you just store them in your own tissue?" Miles asked irritably. "Then you couldn't lose 'em."

Canaba's mouth opened. "I . . . never thought of that. How elegant. Why didn't I think of that?" His hand touched his forehead wonderingly, as if probing for systems failure. His lips tightened again. "But it would have made no difference. I would still need to . . ." he fell silent. "It's about the organism," he said at last. "The . . . creature." Another long silence.

"Of all the things I did," Canaba continued lowly, "of all the interruptions this vile place imposed on me, there is one I regret the most. You understand, this was years ago. I was younger, I thought I still had a future here to protect. And it wasn't all my doing—guilt by committee, eh? Spread it around, make it easy, say it was *his* fault, *her* doing . . . well, it's mine now."

You mean it's *mine* now, thought Miles grimly. "Doctor, the more time we spend here, the greater the chance of compromising this operation. Please get to the point."

"Yes . . . yes. Well, a number of years ago, House Bharaputra Laboratories took on a contract to manufacture a . . . new species. Made to order."

"I thought it was House Ryoval that was famous for making people, or whatever, to order," said Miles.

"They make slaves, one-off. They are very specialized. And small—their customer base is surprisingly small. There are many rich men, and there are, I suppose, many depraved men, but a House Ryoval customer has to be a member of both sets, and the overlap isn't as large as you'd think. Anyway, our contract was supposed to lead to a major production run, far beyond Ryoval's capabilities. A certain subplanetary government, hard-pressed by its neighbors, wanted us to engineer a race of super-soldiers for them."

"What, again?" said Miles. "I thought that had been tried. More than once."

"This time, we thought we could do it. Or at least, the Bharaputran hierarchy was willing to take their money. But the project suffered from too much input. The client, our own higher-ups, the genetics project members, everybody had ideas they were pushing. I swear it was doomed before it ever got out of the design committee."

"A super-soldier. Designed by a committee. Ye gods. The mind boggles." Miles's eyes were wide in fascination. "So then what happened?"

"It seemed to . . . several of us, that the physical limits of the merely human had already been reached. Once a, say, muscle system has been brought to perfect health, stimulated with maximum hormones, exercised to a certain limit, that's all you can do. So we turned to other species for special improvements. I, for instance, became fascinated by the aerobic and anaerobic metabolism in the muscles of the thoroughbred horse—"

"What?" said Thorne, shocked.

"There were other ideas. Too many. I swear, they weren't all mine."

"You mixed human and animal genes?" breathed Miles.

"Why not? Human genes have been spliced into animals from the crude beginnings—it was almost the first thing tried. Human insulin from bacteria and the like. But till now, no one dared do it in reverse. I broke the barrier, cracked the codes . . . It looked good at first. It was only when the first ones reached puberty that all the errors became fully apparent. Well, it was only the initial trial. They were meant to be formidable. But they ended up monstrous."

"Tell me," Miles choked, "were there any actual combat-experienced soldiers on the committee?"

"I assume the client had them. They supplied the parameters," said Canaba.

Said Thorne in a suffused voice, "*I* see. They were trying to reinvent the *enlisted* man."

Miles shot Thorne a quelling glower, and tapped his chrono. "Don't let us interrupt, doctor."

There was a short silence. Canaba began again. "We ran off ten prototypes. Then the client . . . went out of business. They lost their war—"

"Why am I not surprised?" Miles muttered under his breath.

"—funding was cut off, the project was dropped before we could apply what we had learned from our mistakes. Of the ten prototypes, nine have since died. There was one left. We were keeping it at the labs due to . . . difficulties, in boarding it out. I placed my gene complexes in it. They are there still. The last thing I meant to do before I left was kill it. A mercy . . . a responsibility. My expiation, if you will."

"And then?" prodded Miles.

"A few days ago, it was suddenly sold to House Ryoval. As a novelty, apparently. Baron Ryoval collects oddities of all sorts, for his tissue banks—"

Miles and Bel exchanged a look.

"—I had no idea it was to be sold. I came in in the morning and it was gone. I don't think Ryoval has any idea of its real value. It's there now, as far as I know, at Ryoval's facilities."

Miles decided he was getting a sinus headache. From the cold, no doubt. "And what, pray, d'you want us soldiers to do about it?"

"Get in there, somehow. Kill it. Collect a tissue sample. Only then will I go with you."

And stomach twinges. "What, both ears and the tail?"

Canaba gave Miles a cold look. "The left gastrocnemius muscle. That's where I injected my complexes. These storage viruses aren't virulent, they won't have migrated far. The greatest concentration should still be there."

"I see." Miles rubbed his temples, and pressed his eyes. "All right. We'll take care of it. This personal contact between us is very dangerous, and I'd rather not repeat it. Plan to report to my ship in forty-eight hours. Will we have any trouble recognizing your critter?"

"I don't think so. This particular specimen topped out at just over eight feet. I . . . want you to know, the fangs were *not* my idea."

"I . . . see."

"It can move very fast, if it's still in good health. Is there any help I can give you? I have access to painless poisons . . ."

"You've done enough, thank you. Please leave it to us professionals, eh?"

"It would be best if its body can be destroyed entirely. No cells remaining. If you can."

"That's why plasma arcs were invented. You'd best be on your way."

"Yes." Canaba hesitated. "Admiral Naismith?"

"Yes. . . ."

"I . . . it might also be best if my future employer didn't learn about this. They have intense military interests. It might excite them unduly."

"Oh," said Miles/Admiral Naismith/Lieutenant Lord Vorkosigan of the Barrayaran Imperial Service, "I don't think you have to worry about that."

"Is forty-eight hours enough for your commando raid?" Canaba worried. "You understand, if you don't get the tissue, I'll go right back downside. I will not be trapped aboard your ship."

"You will be happy. It's in my contract," said Miles. "Now you'd better get gone."

"I must rely on you, sir." Canaba nodded in suppressed anguish, and withdrew.

They waited a few minutes in the cold room, to let Canaba put some distance between them. The building creaked in the wind; from an upper corridor echoed an odd shriek, and later, a laugh abruptly cut off. The guard shadowing Canaba returned. "He made it to his ground car all right, sir."

"Well," said Thorne, "I suppose we'll need to get hold of a plan of Ryoval's facilities, first—"

"I think not," said Miles.

"If we're to raid—"

"Raid, hell. I'm not risking my men on anything so idiotic. I said I'd slay his sin for him. I didn't say how."

The commercial comconsole net at the downside shuttleport seemed as convenient as anything. Miles slid into the booth and fed the machine his credit card while Thorne lurked just outside the viewing angle and the guards, outside, guarded. He encoded the call.

In a moment, the vid plate produced the image of a sweet-faced receptionist with dimples and a white fur crest instead of hair. "House Ryoval, Customer Services. How may I help you, sir?"

"I'd like to speak to Manager Deem, in Sales and Demonstrations," said Miles smoothly, "about a possible purchase for my organization."

"Who may I say is calling?"

"Admiral Miles Naismith, Dendarii Free Mercenary Fleet."

"One moment, sir."

"You really think they'll just sell it?" Bel muttered from the side as the girl's face was replaced by a flowing pattern of colored lights and some syrupy music.

"Remember what we overheard yesterday?" said Miles. "I'm betting it's *on* sale. Cheap." He must try not to look too interested.

In a remarkably short time, the colored glop gave way to the face of an astonishingly beautiful young man, a blue-eyed albino in a red silk shirt. He had a huge livid bruise up one side of his white face. "This is Manager Deem. May I help you, Admiral?"

Miles cleared his throat carefully. "A rumor has been brought to my attention that House Ryoval may have recently acquired from House Bharaputra an article of some professional interest to me. Supposedly, it was the prototype of some sort of new improved fighting man. Do you know anything about it?"

Deem's hand stole to his bruise and palpated it gently, then twitched away. "Indeed, sir, we do have such an article."

"Is it for sale?"

"Oh, *ye*—I mean, I think some arrangement is pending. But it may still be possible to bid on it."

"Would it be possible for me to inspect it?"

"Of course," said Deem with suppressed eagerness. "How soon?"

There was a burst of static, and the vid image split, Deem's face abruptly shrinking to one side. The new face was only too familiar. Bel hissed under its breath.

"I'll take this call, Deem," said Baron Ryoval.

"Yes, my lord," Deem's eyes widened in surprise, and he cut out. Ryoval's image swelled to occupy the space available.

"So, Betan," Ryoval smiled, "it appears I have something you want after all."

Miles shrugged. "Maybe," he said neutrally. "If it's in my price range."

"I thought you gave all your money to Fell."

Miles spread his hands. "A good commander always has hidden reserves. However, the actual value of the item hasn't yet been established. In fact, its existence hasn't even been established."

"Oh, it exists, all right. And it is . . . impressive. Adding it to my collection was a unique pleasure. I'd hate to give it up. But for you," Ryoval smiled more broadly, "it may be possible to arrange a special cut rate." He chuckled, as at some secret pun that escaped Miles.

A special cut throat is more like it. "Oh?"

"I propose a simple trade," said Ryoval. "Flesh for flesh."

"You may overestimate my interest, Baron."

Ryoval's eyes glinted. "I don't think so."

He knows I wouldn't touch him with a stick if it weren't something pretty compelling. So. "Name your proposal, then."

"I'll trade you even, Bharaputra's pet monster—ah, you should see it, Admiral!—for three tissue samples. Three tissue samples that will, if you are clever about it, cost you nothing." Ryoval held up one finger. "One from your Betan hermaphrodite," a second finger, "one from yourself," a third finger, making a W, "and one from Baron Fell's quaddie musician."

Over in the corner, Bel Thorne appeared to be suppressing an apopleptic fit. Quietly, fortunately.

"That third could prove extremely difficult to obtain," said Miles, buying time to think.

"Less difficult for you than me," said Ryoval. "Fell knows my agents. My overtures have put him on guard. You represent a unique opportunity to get in under that guard. Given sufficient motivation, I'm certain it's not beyond you, mercenary."

"Given sufficient motivation, very little is beyond me, Baron," said Miles semi-randomly.

"Well, then. I shall expect to hear from you within—say—twenty-four hours. After that time my offer will be withdrawn." Ryoval nodded cheerfully. "Good day, Admiral." The vid blanked.

"Well, then," echoed Miles.

"Well what?" said Thorne with suspicion. "You're not actually seriously considering that—vile proposal, are you?"

"What does he want my tissue sample for, for God's sake?" Miles wondered aloud.

"For his dog and dwarf act, no doubt," said Thorne nastily.

'Now, now. He'd be dreadfully disappointed when my clone turned out to be six feet tall, I'm afraid." Miles cleared his throat. "It wouldn't actually hurt anyone, I suppose. To take a small tissue sample. Whereas a commando raid risks lives."

Bel leaned back against the wall and crossed its arms. "Not true. You'd have to fight me for mine. And *hers.*"

Miles grinned sourly. "So."

"So?"

"So let's go find a map of Ryoval's flesh pit. It seems we're going hunting."

House Ryoval's palatial main biologicals facility wasn't a proper fortress, just some guarded buildings. Some bloody big guarded buildings. Miles stood on the roof of the lift-van and studied the layout through his night-glasses. Fog droplets beaded in his hair. The cold damp wind searched for chinks in his jacket much as he searched for chinks in Ryoval's security.

The white complex loomed against the dark forested mountainside, its front gardens floodlit and fairy-like in the fog and frost. The utility entrances on the near side looked more promising. Miles nodded slowly to himself and climbed down off the rented lift-van, artistically broke-down on the little mountain side-trail overlooking Ryoval's. He swung into the back, out of the piercing wind.

"All right, people, listen up." His squad hunkered around as he set up the holovid map in the middle. The colored lights of the display sheened their faces, tall Ensign Murka, Thorne's second-in-command, and two big troopers. Sergeant Laureen Anderson was the van driver, assigned to outside back-up along with Trooper Sandy Hereld and Captain Thorne. Miles harbored a secret Barrayaran prejudice against taking female troops inside Ryoval's, that he trusted he concealed. It went double for Bel Thorne. Not that one's sex would necessarily make any difference to the adventures that might follow in the event of capture, if even a tenth of the bizarre rumors he'd heard were true. Nevertheless . . . Laureen claimed to be able to fly any vehicle made by man through the eye of a needle, not that Miles figured she'd ever done anything so domestic as thread a needle in her life. She would not question her assignment.

"Our main problem remains, that we still don't know where exactly in this facility Bharaputra's creature is being kept. So first we penetrate the fence, the outer courts, and the main building, here and here." A red thread of light traced their projected route at Miles's touch on the control board. "Then we quietly pick up an inside employee and fast-penta him. From that point on we're racing time, since we must assume he'll be promptly missed.

"The key word is quietly. We didn't come here to kill *people,* and we are not at war with Ryoval's employees. You carry your stunners, and keep those plasma arcs and the rest of the toys packed till we locate our quarry. We dispatch it fast and quietly, I get my sample," his hand touched his jacket, beneath which rested the collection case that would keep the tissue alive till they got back to the *Ariel.* "Then we fly. If anything goes wrong before I get that very expensive cut of meat, we don't bother to fight our way out. Not worth it. They have peculiar summary ways of dealing with murder charges here, and I don't see the need for any of us to end up as spare parts in Ryoval's tissue banks. We wait for Captain Thorne to arrange a ransom, and then try something else. We hold a lever or two on Ryoval in case of emergencies."

"Dire emergencies," Bel muttered.

"If anything goes wrong after the butcher-mission is accomplished, it's back to combat rules. That sample will then be irreplaceable, and must be got back to Captain Thorne at all costs. Laureen, you sure of our emergency pickup spot?"

"Yes, sir." She pointed on the vid display.

"Everybody else got that? Any questions? Suggestions? Last-minute observations? Communications check, then, Captain Thorne."

Their wrist comms all appeared to be in good working order. Ensign Murka shrugged on the weapons pack. Miles carefully pocketed the blueprint map cube, that cost them a near-ransom from a certain pliable construction company just a few hours ago. The four members of the penetration team slipped from the van and merged with the frosty darkness.

They slunk off through the woods. The frozen crunchy layer of plant detritus tended to slide underfoot, exposing a layer of slick mud. Murka spotted a spy eye before it spotted them, and blinded it with a brief burst of microwave static while they scurried past. The useful big guys made short work of boosting Miles over the wall. Miles tried not to think about the ancient pub sport of dwarf tossing. The inner court was stark and utilitarian, loading docks with big locked doors, rubbish collection bays, and a few parked vehicles.

Footsteps echoed, and they ducked down in a rubbish bay. A red-clad guard passed, slowly waving an infra-red scanner. They crouched and hid their faces in their infra-red blank ponchos, looking like so many bags of garbage no doubt. Then it was tiptoe up to the loading docks.

Ducts. The key to Ryoval's facility had turned out to be ducts, for heating, for access to power-optics cables, for the comm system. Narrow ducts. Quite impassable to a big guy. Miles slipped out of his poncho and gave it to a trooper to fold and pack.

Miles balanced on Murka's shoulders and cut his way through the first ductlet, a ventilation grille high on the wall above the loading dock doors. Miles handed the grille down silently, and after a quick visual scan for unwanted company, slithered through. It was a tight fit even for him. He let himself down gently to the concrete floor, found the door control box, shorted the alarm, and raised the door about a meter. His team rolled through, and he let the door back down as quietly as he could. So far so good; they hadn't yet had to exchange a word.

They made it to cover on the far side of the receiving bay just before a red-coveralled employee wandered through, driving an electric cart loaded with cleaning robots. Murka touched Miles's sleeve, and looked his inquiry—*This one?* Miles shook his head, *Not yet.* A maintenance man seemed less likely than an employee from the inner sanctum to know where their quarry was kept, and they didn't have time to litter the place with the unconscious bodies of false trials. They found the tunnel to the main building, just as the map cube promised. The door at the end was locked as expected.

It was up on Murka's shoulders again. A quick zizz of Miles's cutters loosened a panel in the ceiling, and he crawled through—the frail supporting framework would surely not have held a man of greater weight—and found the power cables running to the door lock. He was just looking over the problem and pulling tools out of his pocketed uniform jacket when Murka's hand reached up to thrust the weapons pack beside him and quietly pull the panel back into place. Miles flung himself to his belly and pressed his eye to the crack as a voice from down the corridor bellowed, "Freeze!"

Swear words screamed through Miles's head. He clamped his jaw on them. He looked down on the tops of his troopers' heads. In a moment, they were surrounded by half-a-dozen red-clad black-trousered armed guards. "What are you doing here?" snarled the guard sergeant.

"Oh, shit!" cried Murka. *"Please,* mister, don't tell my CO you caught us in here. He'd bust me back to private!"

"Huh?" said the guard sergeant. He prodded Murka with his weapon, a lethal nerve disruptor. "Hands up! Who are you?"

"M'name's Murka. We came in on a mercenary ship to Fell Station, but the captain wouldn't grant us downside passes. Think of it—we come all the way to Jackson's Whole, and the sonofabitch wouldn't let us go downside! Bloody pure-dick wouldn't let us see Ryoval's!"

The red-tunic'd guards were doing a fast scan-and-search, none too gently, and finding only stunners and the portion of security-penetration devices that Murka had carried.

"I made a bet we could get in even if we couldn't afford the front door." Murka's mouth turned down in great discouragement. "Looks like I lost."

"Looks like you did," growled the guard sergeant, drawing back. One of his men held up the thin collection of baubles they'd stripped off the Dendarii. "They're not equipped like an assassination team," he observed.

Murka drew himself up, looking wonderfully offended. "We aren't!"

The guard sergeant turned over a stunner. "AWOL, are you?"

"Not if we make it back before midnight." Murka's tone went wheedling. "Look, m' CO's a right bastard. Suppose there's any way you could see your way clear that he doesn't find out about this?" One of Murka's hands drifted suggestively past his wallet pocket.

The guard sergeant looked him up and down, smirking. "Maybe."

Miles listened with open-mouthed delight. *Murka, if this works I'm promoting you. . . .*

Murka paused. "Any chance of seeing inside first? Not the girls even, just the place? So I could say that I'd seen it."

"This isn't a whorehouse, soldier boy!" snapped the guard sergeant.

Murka looked stunned. "What?"

"This is the *biologicals* facility."

"Oh," said Murka.

"You *idiot,*" one of the troopers put in on cue. Miles sprinkled silent blessings down upon his head. None of the three so much as flicked an eyeball upward.

"But the man in town told me—" began Murka.

"What man?" said the guard sergeant.

"The man who took m'money," said Murka.

A couple of red-tunic'd guards were beginning to grin. The guard sergeant prodded Murka with his nerve disruptor. "Get going, soldier boy. Back that way. This is your lucky day."

"You mean we get to see inside?" said Murka hopefully.

"No," said the guard sergeant, "I mean we aren't going to break both your legs before we throw you out on your ass." He paused and added more kindly, "There's a whorehouse back in town." He slipped Murka's wallet out of his pocket, checked the name on the credit card and put it back, and removed all the loose currency. The guards did the same to the outraged-looking troopers, dividing the assorted cash up among them. "They take credit cards, and you've still got till midnight. Now move!"

And so Miles's squad was chivvied, ignominiously but intact, down the tunnel. Miles waited till the whole mob was well out of earshot before keying his wrist comm. "Bel?"

"Yes," came back the instant reply.

"Trouble. Murka and the troops were just picked up by Ryoval's security. I believe the boy genius has just managed to bullshit them into throwing them out the back door, instead of rendering them down for parts. I'll follow as soon as I can, we'll rendezvous and regroup for another try." Miles paused. This was a total bust, they were now worse off than when they'd started. Ryoval's security would be stirred up for the rest of the long Jacksonian night. He added to the comm, "I'm going to see if I can't at least find out the location of the critter before I withdraw. Should improve our chances of success next round."

Bel swore in a heartfelt tone. "Be careful."

"You bet. Watch for Murka and the boys. Naismith out."

Once he'd identified the right cables it was the work of a moment to make the door slide open. He then had an interesting dangle by his fingertips while coaxing the ceiling panel to fall back into place before he dropped from maximum downward extension, fearful for his bones. Nothing broke. He slipped across the portal to the main building and took to the ducts as soon as possible, the corridors having been proved dangerous. He lay on his back in the narrow tube and balanced the blueprint holocube on his belly, picking out a new and safer route not necessarily passable to a couple of husky troopers. And where did one look for a monster? A closet?

It was at about the third turn, inching his way through the system dragging the weapon pack, that he became aware that the territory no longer matched the map. Hell and damnation. Were these changes in the system since its construction, or a subtly sabotaged map? Well, no matter, he wasn't really lost, he could still retrace his route.

He crawled along for about thirty minutes, discovering and disarming two alarm sensors before they discovered him. The time factor was getting seriously pressing. Soon he would have to—ah, there! He peered through a vent grille into a dim room filled with holovid and communications equipment. *Small Repairs,* the map cube named it. It didn't look like a repairs shop. Another change since Ryoval had moved in? But a man sat alone with his back to Miles's wall. Perfect, too good to pass up.

Breathing silently, moving slowly, Miles eased his dart-gun out of the pack and made sure he loaded it with the right cartridge, fast-penta spiked with a paralyzer, a lovely cocktail blended for the purpose by the *Ariel's* medtech. He sighted through the grille, aimed the needle-nose of the dart gun with tense precision, and fired. Bullseye. The man slapped the back of his neck once and sat still, hand falling nervelessly to his side. Miles grinned briefly, cut his way through the grille, and lowered himself to the floor.

The man was well-dressed in civilian-type clothes—one of the scientists, perhaps? He lolled in his chair, a little smile playing around his lips, and stared with unalarmed interest at Miles. He started to fall over.

Miles caught him and propped him back upright. "Sit up now, that's right, you can't talk with your face in the carpet now, can you?"

"Nooo . . ." The man bobbled his head and smiled agreeably.

"Do you know anything about a genetic construct, a monstrous creature, just recently bought from House Bharaputra and brought to this facility?"

The man blinked and smiled. "Yes."

Fast-penta subjects did tend to be literal, Miles reminded himself. "Where is it being kept?"

"Downstairs."

"Where exactly downstairs?"

"In the sub-basement. The crawl-space around the foundations.

We were hoping it would catch some of the rats, you see." The man giggled. "Do cats eat rats? Do rats eat cats . . . ?"

Miles checked his map-cube. Yes. That looked good, in terms of the penetration team getting in and out, though it was still a large search area, broken up into a maze by structural elements running down into the bedrock, and specially-set low-vibration support columns running up into the laboratories. At the lower edge, where the mountainside sloped away, the space ran high-ceilinged and very near the surface, a possible break-out point. The space thinned to head-cracking narrowness and then to bedrock at the back where the building wedged into the slope. All right. Miles opened his dart case to find something that would lay his victim out cold and nonquestionable for the rest of the night. The man pawed at him and his sleeve slipped back to reveal a wrist-comm almost as thick and complex as Miles's own. A light blinked on it. Miles looked at the device, suddenly uneasy. This room . . . "By the way, who are you?"

"Moglia, Chief of Security, Ryoval Biologicals," the man recited happily. "At your service, sir."

"Oh, indeed you are." Miles's suddenly-thick fingers scrabbled faster in his dart case. Damn, damn, *damn.*

The door burst open. "Freeze, mister!"

Miles hit the tight-beam alarm/self-destruct on his own wrist comm and flung his hands up, and the wrist comm off, in one swift motion. Not by chance, Moglia sat between Miles and the door, inhibiting the trigger reflexes of the entering guards. The comm melted as it arced through the air—no chance of Ryoval security tracing the outside squad through it now, and Bel would at least know something had gone wrong.

The security chief chuckled to himself, temporarily fascinated by the task of counting his own fingers. The red-clad guard sergeant, backed by his squad, thundered into what was now screamingly obvious to Miles as the Security Operations Room, to jerk Miles around, slam him face-first into the wall, and begin frisking him with vicious efficiency. Within moments he had separated Miles from a clanking pile of incriminating equipment, his jacket, boots, and belt. Miles clutched the wall and shivered with the pain of several expertly-applied nerve jabs and the swift reversal of his fortune.

The security chief, when un-penta'd at last, was not at all pleased with the guard sergeant's confession about the three uniformed men he had let go with a fine earlier in the evening. He put the whole guard shift on full alert, and sent an armed squad out to try and trace the escaped Dendarii. Then, with an apprehensive expression on his face very like the guard-sergeant's during his mortified admission—compounded with sour satisfaction, contemplating Miles, and drug-induced nausea—he made a vid call.

"My lord?" said the security chief carefully.

"What is it, Moglia?" Baron Ryoval's face was sleepy and irritated.

"Sorry to disturb you sir, but I thought you might like to know about the intruder we just caught here. Not an ordinary thief, judging from his clothes and equipment. Strange-looking fellow, sort of a tall dwarf. He squeezed in through the ducts." Moglia held up tissue-collection kit, chip-driven alarm-disarming tools, and Miles's weapons, by way of evidence. The guard sergeant bundled Miles, stumbling, into range of the vid's pick-up. "He was asking a lot of questions about Bharaputra's monster."

Ryoval's lips parted. Then his eyes lit, and he threw back his head and laughed. "I should have guessed. Stealing when you should be buying, Admiral?" he chortled. "Oh, very good, Moglia!"

The security chief looked fractionally less nervous. "Do you know this little mutant, my lord?"

"Yes, indeed. He calls himself Miles Naismith. A mercenary—bills himself as an admiral. Self-promoted, no doubt. Excellent work, Moglia. Hold him, and I'll be there in the morning and deal with him personally."

"Hold him how, sir?"

Ryoval shrugged. "Amuse yourselves. Freely."

When Ryoval's image faded, Miles found himself pinned between the speculative glowers of both the security chief and the guard sergeant.

Just to relieve feelings, a burly guard held Miles while the security chief delivered a blow to his belly. But the chief was still too ill to really enjoy this as he should. "Came to see Bharaputra's toy soldier, did you?" he gasped, rubbing his own stomach.

The guard sergeant caught his chief's eye. "You know, I think we should give him his wish."

The security chief smothered a belch, and smiled as at a beatific vision. "Yes . . ."

Miles, praying they wouldn't break his arms, found himself being frog-marched down a complex of corridors and lift tubes by the burly guard, followed by the sergeant and the chief. They took a last lift-tube to the very bottom, a dusty basement crowded with stored and discarded equipment and supplies. They made their way to a locked hatch set in the floor. It swung open on a metal ladder descending into obscurity.

"The last thing we threw down there was a rat," the guard sergeant informed Miles cordially. "Nine bit its head right off. Nine gets very hungry. Got a metabolism like an ore furnace."

The guard forced Miles onto the ladder and down it a meter or so by the simple expedient of striking at his clinging hands with a truncheon. Miles hung just out of range of the stick, eyeing the dimly lit stone below. The rest was pillars and shadows and a cold dankness.

"Nine!" called the guard sergeant into the echoing darkness. "Nine! Dinner! Come and catch it!"

The security chief laughed mockingly, then clutched his head and groaned under his breath.

Ryoval had said he'd deal with Miles personally in the morning, surely the guards understood their boss wanted a live prisoner. Didn't they? Didn't he? "Is this the dungeon?" Miles spat blood and peered around.

"No, no, just a basement," the guard sergeant assured him cheerily. "The dungeon is for the *paying* customers. Heh, heh, heh." Still chortling at his own humor, he kicked the hatch closed. The chink of the locking mechanism rained down; then silence.

The bars of the ladder bit chill through Miles's socks. He hooked an arm around an upright and tucked one hand into the armpit of his black T-shirt to warm it briefly. His grey trousers had been emptied of everything but a ration bar, his handkerchief, and his legs.

He clung there for a long time. Going up was futile; going down, singularly uninviting. Eventually the startling ganglial pain began to dull, and the shaking physical shock to wear off. Still he clung. Cold.

It could have been worse, Miles reflected. The sergeant and his squad could have decided they wanted to play Lawrence of Arabia and the Six Turks. Commodore Tung, Miles's Dendarii chief of staff and a certified military history nut, had been plying Miles with a series of classic military memoirs lately. How had Colonel Lawrence escaped an analogous tight spot? Ah, yes, played dumb and persuaded his captors to throw him out in the mud. Tung must have pressed that book-fax on Murka, too.

The darkness, Miles discovered as his eyes adjusted, was only relative. Faint luminescent panels in the ceiling here and there shed a sickly yellow glow. He descended the last two meters to stand on solid rock.

He pictured the newsfax, back home on Barrayar—*Body of Imperial Officer Found in Flesh-Czar's Dream Palace. Death From Ex-*

haustion? Dammit, this wasn't the glorious sacrifice in the Emperor's service he'd once vowed to risk, this was just embarrassing. Maybe Bharaputra's creature would eat the evidence.

With this morose comfort in mind, he began to limp from pillar to pillar, pausing, listening, looking around. Maybe there was another ladder somewhere. Maybe there was a hatch someone had forgotten to lock. Maybe there was still hope.

Maybe there was something moving in the shadows just beyond that pillar. . . .

Miles's breath froze, then eased again, as the movement materialized into a fat albino rat the size of an armadillo. It shied as it saw him and waddled rapidly away, its claws clicking on the rock. Only an escaped lab rat. A bloody big rat, but still, only a rat.

The huge rippling shadow struck out of nowhere, at incredible speed. It grabbed the rat by its tail and swung it squealing against a pillar, dashing out its brains with a crunch. A flash of a thick claw-like fingernail, and the white furry body was ripped open from sternum to tail. Frantic fingers peeled the skin away from the rat's body as blood splattered. Miles first saw the fangs as they bit and tore and buried themselves in the rat's tissues.

They were functional fangs, not just decorative, set in a protruding jaw, with long lips and a wide mouth; yet the total effect was lupine rather than simian. A flat nose, ridged, powerful brows, high cheekbones. Hair a dark matted mess. And yes, fully eight feet tall, a rangy, tense-muscled body.

Climbing back up the ladder would do no good, the creature could pluck him right off and swing him just like the rat. Levitate up the side of a pillar? Oh, for suction-cup fingers and toes, something the bioengineering committee had missed somehow. Freeze and play invisible? Miles settled on this last defense by default—he was paralyzed with terror.

The big feet, bare on the cold rock, also had claw-like toenails. But the creature was dressed, in clothes made of green lab-cloth, a belted kimono-like coat and loose trousers. And one other thing.

They didn't tell me it was female.

She was almost finished with the rat when she looked up and saw Miles. Bloody-faced, bloody-handed, she froze as still as he.

In a spastic motion, Miles whipped the squashed ration bar from his trouser thigh-pocket and extended it toward her in his outstretched hand. "Dessert?" he smiled hysterically.

Dropping the rat's stripped carcass, she snatched the bar out of his hand, ripped off the cover, and devoured it in four bites. Then she stepped forward, grabbed him by an arm and his black T-shirt, and lifted him up to her face. The clawed fingers bit into his skin, and his feet dangled in air. Her breath was about what he would have guessed. Her eyes were raw and burning. "Water!" she croaked.

They didn't tell me she talked.

"Um, um—water," squeaked Miles. "Quite. There ought to be water around here—look, up at the ceiling, all those pipes. If you'll, um, put me down, good girl, I'll try and spot a water pipe or something. . . ."

Slowly, she lowered him back to his feet and released him. He backed carefully away, his hands held out open at his sides. He cleared his throat, and tried to bring his voice back down to a low, soothing tone. "Let's try over here. The ceiling gets lower, or rather, the bedrock rises . . . over near that light panel, there, that thin composite plastic tube—white's the usual color-code for water. We don't want grey, that's sewage, or red, that's the power-optics . . ." No telling what she understood, tone was everything with creatures. "If you, uh, could hold me up on your shoulders like Ensign Murka, I could have a go at loosening that joint there . . ." He made pantomime gestures, uncertain if anything was getting through to whatever intelligence lay behind those terrible eyes.

The bloody hands, easily twice the size of his own, grabbed him abruptly by the hips and boosted him upward. He clutched the white pipe, inched along it to a screw-joint. Her thick shoulders beneath his feet moved along under him. Her muscles trembled, it wasn't all his own shaking. The joint was tight—he needed tools—he turned with all his strength, in danger of snapping his fragile finger bones. Suddenly the joint squeaked and slid. It gave, the plastic collar was moving, water began to spray between his fingers. One more turn and it sheared apart, and water arced in a bright stream down onto the rock beneath.

She almost dropped him in her haste. She put her mouth under the stream, wide open, let the water splash straight in and all over her face, coughing and guzzling even more frantically than she'd gone at the rat. She drank, and drank, and drank. She let it run over her hands, her face and head, washing away the blood, and then drank some more. Miles began to think she'd never quit, but at last she backed away and pushed her wet hair out of her eyes, and stared down at him. She stared at him for what seemed like a full minute, then suddenly roared, "Cold!"

Miles jumped. "Ah . . . cold . . . right. Me too, my socks are wet. Heat, you want heat. Lessee. Uh, let's try back this way, where the ceiling's lower. No point here, the heat would all collect up there out of reach, no good . . ." She followed him with all the intensity of a cat tracking a . . . well . . . rat, as he skittered around pillars to where the crawl space's floor rose to genuine crawl-height, about four feet. There, that one, that was the lowest pipe he could find. "If we could get this open," he pointed to a plastic pipe about as big around as his waist, "it's full of hot air being pumped along under pressure. No handy joints though, this time." He stared at his puzzle, trying to think. This composite plastic was extremely strong.

She crouched and pulled, then lay on her back and kicked up at it, then looked at him quite woefully.

"Try this." Nervously, he took her hand and guided it to the pipe, and traced long scratches around the circumference with her hard nails. She scratched and scratched, then looked at him again as if to say, *This isn't working!*

"Try kicking and pulling again now," he suggested.

She must have weighed three hundred pounds, and she put it all behind the next effort, kicking then grabbing the pipe, planting her feet on the ceiling and arching with all her strength. The pipe split along the scratches. She fell with it to the floor, and hot air began to hiss out. She held her hands, her face to it, nearly wrapped herself around it, sat on her knees and let it blow across her. Miles crouched down and stripped off his socks and flopped them over the warm pipe to dry. Now would be a good opportunity to run, if only there were anywhere to run to. But he was reluctant to let his prey out of his sight. His prey? He considered the incalculable value of her left calf muscle, as she sat on the rock and buried her face in her knees.

They didn't tell me she wept.

He pulled out his regulation handkerchief, an archaic square of cloth. He'd never understood the rationale for the idiotic handkerchief, except, perhaps, that where soldiers went there would be weeping. He handed it to her. "Here. Mop your eyes with this."

She took it, and blew her big flat nose in it, and made to hand it back.

"Keep it," Miles said. "Uh . . . what do they call you, I wonder?"

"Nine," she growled. Not hostile, it was just the way her strained voice came out of that big throat. ". . . What do they call you?"

Good God, a complete sentence. Miles blinked. "Admiral Miles Naismith." He arranged himself cross-legged.

She looked up, transfixed. "A soldier? A *real* officer?" And then more doubtfully, as if seeing him in detail for the first time, "You?"

Miles cleared his throat firmly. "Quite real. A bit down on my luck just at the moment," he admitted.

"Me too," she said glumly, and sniffled. "I don't know how long I've been in this basement, but that was my first drink."

"Three days, I think," said Miles. "Have they not, ah, given you any food, either?"

"No." She frowned; the effect, with the fangs, was quite overpowering. "This is worse than anything they did to me in the lab, and I thought that was bad."

It's not what you don't know that'll hurt you, the old saying went. *It's what you do know that isn't so.* Miles thought of his map cube; Miles looked at Nine. Miles pictured himself taking this entire mission's carefully-worked-out strategy plan delicately between thumb and forefinger and flushing it down a waste-disposal unit. The ductwork in the ceiling niggled at his imagination. Nine would never fit through it. . . .

She clawed her wild hair away from her face and stared at him with renewed fierceness. Her eyes were a strange light hazel, adding to the wolfish effect. "What are you *really* doing here? Is this another test?"

"No, this is real life." Miles's lips twitched. "I, ah, made a mistake."

"Guess I did too," she said, lowering her head.

Miles pulled at his lip and studied her through narrowed eyes. "What sort of life have you had, I wonder?" he mused, half to himself.

She answered literally. "I lived with hired fosterers till I was eight. Like the clones do. Then I started to get big and clumsy and break things—they brought me to live at the lab after that. It was all right, I was warm and had plenty to eat."

"They can't have simplified you too much if they seriously intended you to be a soldier. I wonder what your IQ is?" he speculated.

"A hundred and thirty-five."

Miles fought off stunned paralysis. "I . . . see. Did you ever get . . . any training?"

She shrugged. "I took a lot of tests. They were . . . OK. Except for the aggression experiments. I don't like electric shocks." She brooded a moment. "I don't like experimental psychologists, either. They lie a lot." Her shoulders slumped. "Anyway, I failed. We all failed."

"How can they know if you failed if you never had any proper training?" Miles said scornfully. "Soldiering entails some of the most complex, cooperative learned behavior ever invented—I've been studying strategy and tactics for years, and I don't know half yet. It's all up *here."* He pressed his hands urgently to his head.

She looked across at him sharply. "If that's so," she turned her huge clawed hands over, staring at them, "then why did they do *this* to me?"

Miles stopped short. His throat was strangely dry. *So, admirals lie too. Sometimes, even to themselves.* After an unsettled pause he asked, "Did you never think of breaking open a water pipe?"

"You're punished, for breaking things. Or I was. Maybe not you, you're human."

"Did you ever think of escaping, breaking out? It's a soldier's duty, when captured by the enemy, to escape. Survive, escape, sabotage, in that order."

"Enemy?" She looked upward at the whole weight of House Ryoval pressing overhead. "Who are my friends?"

"Ah. Yes. There is that . . . point." And where would an eight-foot-tall genetic cocktail with fangs run to? He took a deep breath. No question what his next move must be. Duty, expediency, survival, all compelled it. "Your friends are closer than you think. Why do you think I came here?" *Why, indeed?*

She shot him a silent, puzzled frown.

"I came for you. I'd heard of you. I'm . . . recruiting. Or I was. Things went wrong, and now I'm escaping. But if you came with me, you could join the Dendarii Mercenaries. A top outfit—always looking for a few good men, or whatever. I have this master-sergeant who . . . who *needs* a recruit like you." Too true. Sergeant Dyeb was infamous for his sour attitude about women soldiers, insisting that they were too soft. Any female recruit who survived his course came out with her aggression highly developed. Miles pictured Dyeb being dangled by his toes from a height of about eight feet. . . . He controlled his runaway imagination in favor of concentration on the present crisis. Nine was looking . . . unimpressed.

"Very funny," she said coldly, making Miles wonder for a wild moment if she'd been equipped with the telepathy gene complex—no, she pre-dated that—"but I'm not even human. Or hadn't you heard?"

Miles shrugged carefully. "Human is as human does." He forced himself to reach out and touch her damp cheek. "Animals don't weep, Nine."

She jerked, as from an electric shock. "Animals don't lie. Humans do. All the time."

"Not *all* the time." He hoped the light was too dim for her to see the flush in his face. She was watching his face intently.

"Prove it." She tilted her head as she sat cross-legged. Her pale gold eyes were suddenly burning, speculative.

"Uh . . . sure. How?"

"Take off your clothes."

". . . what?"

"Take off your clothes, and lie down with me as *humans* do. Men and women." Her hand reached out to touch his throat.

The pressing claws made little wells in his flesh. "Blrp?" choked Miles. His eyes felt wide as saucers. A little more pressure, and those wells would spring forth red fountains. *I am about to die. . . .*

She stared into his face with a strange, frightening, bottomless hunger. Then abruptly, she released him. He sprang up and cracked his head on the low ceiling, and dropped back down, the stars in his eyes unrelated to love at first sight.

Her lips wrinkled back on a fanged groan of despair. "Ugly," she wailed. Her clawed nails raked across her cheeks leaving red furrows. "Too *ugly* . . . animal . . . you *don't* think I'm human—" She seemed to swell with some destructive resolve.

"No, no, no!" gibbered Miles, lurching to his knees and grabbing her hands and pulling them down. "It's not that. It's just, uh—how old are you, anyway?"

"Sixteen."

Sixteen. God. He remembered sixteen. Sex-obsessed and dying inside every minute. A horrible age to be trapped in a twisted, fragile, abnormal body. God only knew how he had survived his own self-hatred then. No—he remembered how. *He'd* been saved by one who loved him. "Aren't you a little young for this?" he tried hopefully.

"How old were you?"

"Fifteen," he admitted, before thinking to lie. "But . . . it was traumatic. Didn't work out at all in the long run."

Her claws turned toward her face again.

"Don't *do* that!" he cried, hanging on. It reminded him entirely too much of the episode of Sergeant Bothari and the knife. The Sergeant had taken Miles's knife away from him by superior force. Not an option open to Miles here. "Will you *calm down?*" he yelled at her.

She hesitated.

"It's just that, uh, an officer and gentleman doesn't just fling himself onto his lady on the bare ground. One . . . one sits down. Gets comfortable. Has a little conversation, drinks a little wine, plays a little music . . . slows down. You're hardly warm yet. Here, sit over here where it's warmest." He positioned her nearer the broken duct, got up on his knees behind her, tried rubbing her neck and shoulders. Her muscles were tense, they felt like rocks under his thumbs. Any attempt on his part to strangle her would clearly be futile.

I can't believe this. Trapped in Ryoval's basement with a sex-starved teenage werewolf. There was nothing about this in any of my Imperial training manuals. . . . He remembered his mission, which was to get her left calf muscle back to the *Ariel* alive. *Dr. Canaba, if I survive you and I are going to have a little talk about this. . . .*

Her voice was muffled with grief and the odd shape of her mouth. "You think I'm too tall."

"Not at all." He was getting hold of himself a bit, he could lie faster. "I adore tall women, ask anyone who knows me. Besides, I made the happy discovery some time back that height difference only matters when we're standing up. When we're lying down it's, ah, less of a problem. . . ." A rapid mental review of everything he'd ever learned by trial and error, mostly error, about women was streaming uninvited through his mind. It was harrowing. What did women *want?*

He shifted around and took her hand, earnestly. She stared back equally earnestly, waiting for . . . *instruction.* At this point the realization came over Miles that he was facing his first virgin. He smiled at her in total paralysis for several seconds. "Nine . . . you've never done this before, have you?"

"I've seen vids." She frowned introspectively. "They usually start with kisses, but . . ." a vague gesture toward her misshapen mouth, "maybe you don't want to."

Miles tried not to think about the late rat. She'd been systematically starved, after all. "Vids can be very misleading. For women—especially the first time—it takes practice to learn your own body responses, woman friends have told me. I'm afraid I might hurt you." *And then you'll disembowel me.*

She gazed into his eyes. "That's all right. I have a very high pain threshold."

But I don't.

This was mad. She was mad. *He* was mad. Yet he could feel a creeping fascination for the—proposition—rising from his belly to his brain like a fey fog. No doubt about it, she was the tallest female thing he was ever likely to meet. More than one woman of his acquaintance had accused him of wanting to go mountain-climbing. He could get that out of his system once for all. . . .

Damn, I do believe she'd clean up good. She was not without a

certain . . . charm was *not* the word—whatever beauty there was
to be found in the strong, the swift, the leanly athletic, the function-
ing form. Once you got used to the *scale* of it. She radiated a smooth
heat he could feel from here—*animal magnetism?* the suppressed
observer in the back of his brain supplied. Power? Whatever else it
was, it would certainly be *astonishing.*

One of his mother's favorite aphorisms drifted through his head.
Anything worth doing, she always said, *is worth doing well.*

Dizzy as a drunkard, he abandoned the crutch of logic for the
wings of inspiration. "Well then, doctor," he heard himself muttering
insanely, "let us experiment."

Kissing a woman with fangs was indeed a novel sensation. Being
kissed back—she was clearly a fast learner—was even more novel.
Her arms circled him ecstatically, and from that point on he lost
control of the situation, somehow. Though some time later, coming
up for air, he did look up to ask, "Nine, have you ever heard of the
black widow spider?"

"No . . . what is it?"

"Never mind," he said airily.

It was all very awkward and clumsy, but sincere, and when he was
done the water in her eyes was from joy, not pain. She seemed
enormously (how else?) pleased with him. He was so unstrung he
actually fell asleep for a few minutes, pillowed on her body.

He woke up laughing.

"You really do have the most elegant cheekbones," he told her,
tracing their line with one finger. She leaned into his touch, cuddled
up equally to him and the heat pipe. "There's a woman on my ship
who wears her hair in a sort of woven braid in the back—it would
look just great on you. Maybe she could teach you how."

She pulled a wad of her hair forward and looked cross-eyed at it, as
if trying to see past the coarse tangles and filth. She touched his face
in turn. "You are very handsome, Admiral."

"Huh? Me?" He ran a hand over the night's beard stubble, sharp
features, the old pain lines . . . *she must be blinded by my putative
rank, eh?*

"Your face is very . . . alive. And your eyes see what they're looking at."

"Nine . . ." he cleared his throat, paused. "Dammit, that's not a
name, that's a number. What happened to Ten?"

"He died." *Maybe I will too,* her strange-colored eyes added silently, before her lids shuttered them.

"Is Nine all they ever called you?"

"There's a long biocomputer code-string that's my actual designation."

"Well, we all have serial numbers," Miles had two, now that he thought of it, "but this is absurd. I can't call you Nine, like some robot. You need a proper name, a name that fits you." He leaned back onto her warm bare shoulder—she was like a furnace, they had spoken truly about her metabolism—and his lips drew back on a slow grin. "Taura."

"Taura?" Her long mouth gave it a skewed and lilting accent. ". . . it's too beautiful for me!"

"Taura," he repeated firmly. "Beautiful but strong. Full of secret meaning. Perfect. Ah, speaking of secrets . . ." Was now the time to tell her about what Dr. Canaba had planted in her left calf? Or would she be hurt, as someone falsely courted for her money—or his title— Miles faltered. "I think, now that we know each other better, that it's time for us to blow out of this place."

She stared around, into the grim dimness. "How?"

"Well, that's what we have to figure out, eh? I confess, ducts rather spring to my mind." Not the heat pipe, obviously. He'd have to go anorexic for months to fit in it, besides, he'd cook. He shook out and pulled on his black T-shirt—he'd put on his trousers immediately after he'd woke, that stone floor sucked heat remorselessly from any flesh that touched it—and creaked to his feet. God. He was getting too old for this sort of thing already. The sixteen-year-old, clearly, possessed the physical resilience of a minor goddess. What was it he'd gotten into at sixteen? Sand, that was it. He winced in memory of what it had done to certain sensitive body folds and crevices. Maybe cold stone wasn't so bad after all.

She pulled her pale green coat and trousers out from under herself, dressed, and followed him in a crouch until the space was sufficient for her to stand upright.

They quartered and re-quartered the underground chamber. There were four ladders with hatches, all locked. There was a locked vehicle exit to the outside on the downslope side. A direct breakout might be simplest, but if he couldn't make immediate contact with Thorne it was a twenty-seven-kilometer hike to the nearest town. In the snow, in his sock feet—her bare feet. And if they got there, he wouldn't be able to use the vidnet anyway because his credit card was still locked in the Security Ops office upstairs. Asking for charity in Ryoval's town was a dubious proposition. So, break straight out and be sorry later, or linger and try to equip themselves, risking recapture, and be sorry sooner? Tactical decisions were such fun.

Ducts won. Miles pointed upward to the most likely one. "Think you can break that open and boost me in?" he asked Taura.

She studied it, nodded slowly, the expression closing on her face. She stretched up and moved along to a soft metal clad joint, slipped her claw-hard fingernails under the strip, and yanked it off. She worked her fingers into the exposed slot and hung on it as if chinning herself. The duct bent open under her weight. "There you go," she said.

She lifted him up as easily as a child, and he squirmed into the duct. This one was a particularly close fit, though it was the largest he had spotted as accessible in this ceiling. He inched along it on his back. He had to stop twice to suppress a residual, hysteria-tinged laughing fit. The duct curved upward, and he slithered around the curve in the darkness only to find that it split here into a Y, each branch half-sized. He cursed and backed out.

Taura had her face turned up to him, an unusual angle of view.

"No good that way," he gasped, reversing direction gymnastically at the gap. He headed the other way. This too curved up, but within moments he found a grille. A tightly-fitted, unbudgable, unbreakable, and with his bare hands uncuttable grille. Taura might have the strength to rip it out of the wall, but Taura couldn't fit through the duct to reach it. He contemplated it a few moments. "Right," he muttered, and backed out again.

"So much for ducts," he reported to Taura. "Uh . . . could you help me down?" She lowered him to the floor, and he dusted himself futilely. "Let's look around some more."

She followed him docilely enough, though something in her expression hinted she might be losing faith in his admiralness. A bit of detailing on a column caught his eye, and he went to take a closer look in the dim light.

It was one of the low-vibration support columns. Two meters in diameter, set deep in the bedrock in a well of fluid, it ran straight up to one of the labs, no doubt, to provide an ultra-stable base for certain kinds of crystal generation projects and the like. Miles rapped on the side of the column. It rang hollow. *Ah yes, makes sense, concrete doesn't float too well, eh?* A groove in the side outlined . . . an access port? He ran his fingers around it, probing. There was a concealed . . . something. He stretched his arms and found a twin spot on the opposite side. The spots yielded slowly to the hard pressure of his thumbs. There was a sudden pop and hiss, and the whole panel came away. He staggered, and barely kept from dropping it down the hole. He turned it sideways and drew it out.

"Well, well," Miles grinned. He stuck his head through the port, looked down and up. Black as pitch. Rather gingerly, he reached his arm in and felt around. There was a ladder running up the damp inside, for access for cleaning and repairs; the whole column could apparently be filled with fluid of whatever density at need. Filled, it would have been self-pressure-sealed and unopenable. Carefully, he examined the inner edge of the hatch. Openable from either side, by God. "Let's go see if there's any more of these, further up."

It was slow going, feeling for more grooves as they ascended in the blackness. Miles tried not to think about the fall, should he slip from the slimy ladder. Taura's deep breathing, below him, was actually rather comforting. They had gone up perhaps three stories when Miles's chilled and numbing fingers found another groove. He'd almost missed it, it was on the opposite side of the ladder from the first. He then discovered, the hard way, that he didn't have nearly the reach to keep one arm hooked around the ladder and press both release catches at the same time. After a terrifying slip, trying, he clung spasmodically to the ladder till his heart stopped pounding. "Taura?" he croaked. "I'll move up, and you try it." Not much up was left, the column ended a meter or so above his head.

Her extra arm length was all that was needed—the catches surrendered to her big hands with a squeak of protest.

"What do you see?" Miles whispered.

"Big dark room. Maybe a lab."

"Makes sense. Climb back down and put that lower panel back on, no sense advertising where we went."

Miles slipped through the hatch into the darkened laboratory while Taura accomplished her chore. He dared not switch on a light in the windowless room, but a few instrument readouts on the benches and walls gave enough ghostly glow for his dark-adapted eyes that at least he didn't trip over anything. One glass door led to a hallway. A heavily electronically-monitored hallway. With his nose pressed to the glass Miles saw a red shape flit past a cross-corridor; guards here. What did they guard?

Taura oozed out of the access hatch to the column—with difficulty —and sat down heavily on the floor, her face in her hands. Concerned, Miles nipped back to her. "You all right?"

She shook her head. "No. Hungry."

"What, already? That was supposed to be a twenty-four hour rat—

er, ration bar." Not to mention the two or three kilos of meat she'd had for an appetizer.

"For you, maybe," she wheezed. She was shaking.

Miles began to see why Canaba had dubbed his project a failure. Imagine trying to feed a whole army of such appetites. Napoleon would quail. Maybe the raw-boned kid was still growing. Daunting thought.

There was a refrigerator at the back of the lab. If he knew lab techs . . . ah, ha. Indeed, in among the test tubes was a package with half a sandwich and a large, if bruised, pear. He handed them to Taura. She looked vastly impressed, as if he'd conjured them from his sleeve by magic, and devoured them at once, and grew less pale.

Miles foraged further for his troop. Alas, the only other organics in the fridge were little covered dishes of gelatinous stuff with unpleasant multi-colored fuzz growing in them. But there were three big shiny walk-in wall freezers lined up in a row. Miles peered through a glass square in one thick door, and risked pressing the wall pad that turned on the light inside. Within were row on row on row of labelled drawers, full of clear plastic trays. Frozen samples of some kind. Thousands—Miles looked again, and calculated more carefully— hundreds of thousands. He glanced at the lighted control panel by the freezer drawer. The temperature inside was that of liquid nitrogen. Three freezers . . . *Millions* of. . . . Miles sat down abruptly on the floor himself. "Taura, do you know where we *are?*" he whispered intensely.

"Sorry, no," she whispered back, creeping over.

"That was a rhetorical question. *I* know where we are."

"Where?"

"Ryoval's treasure chamber."

"What?"

"That," Miles jerked his thumb at the freezer, "is the baron's hundred-year-old tissue collection. My God. Its value is almost incalculable. Every unique, irreplaceable, mutant bizarre bit he's begged, bought, borrowed or stolen for the last three-fourths of a century, all lined up in neat little rows, waiting to be thawed and cultured and cooked up into some poor new slave. This is the living heart of his whole human biologicals operation." Miles sprang to his feet and pored over the control panels. His heart raced, and he breathed open-mouthed, laughing silently, feeling almost like he was about to pass out. "Oh, shit. Oh, God." He stopped, swallowed. Could it be done?

These freezers had to have an alarm system, monitors surely, piped up to Security Ops at the very least. Yes, there was a complex device for opening the door—that was fine, he didn't want to open the door. He left it untouched. It was systems readout he was after. If he could bugger up just one sensor. . . . Was the thing broadcast-output to several outside monitor locations, or did they run an optic thread to just one? The lab benches supplied him with a small hand light, and drawers and drawers of assorted tools and supplies. Taura watched him in puzzlement as he darted here, there, taking inventory.

The freezer monitor *was* broadcast-output, inaccessible; could he hit it on the input side? He levered off a smoke-dark plastic cover as silently as he could. There, *there,* the optic thread came out of the wall, pumping continuous information about the freezer's interior environment. It fit into a simple standard receiver plug on the more daunting black box that controlled the door alarm. There'd been a whole drawer full of assorted optic threads with various ends and Y-adaptors. . . . Out of the spaghetti-tangle he drew what he needed, discarding several with broken ends or other damage. There were three optical data recorders in the drawer. Two didn't work. The third did.

A quick festoon of optic thread, a swift unplugging and plugging, and he had one freezer talking to two control boxes. He set the freed thread to talking to the datacorder. He simply had to chance the blip during transfer. If anyone checked they'd find all seemed well again. He gave the datacorder several minutes to develop a nice continuous replay loop, crouching very still with even the tiny hand light extinguished. Taura waited with the patience of a predator, making no noise.

One, two, three, and he set the datacorder to talking to all three control boxes. The real thread plugs hung forlornly loose. Would it work? There were no alarms going off, no thundering herd of irate security troops. . . .

"Taura, come here."

She loomed beside him, baffled.

"Have you ever met Baron Ryoval?" asked Miles.

"Yes, once . . . when he came to buy me."

"Did you like him?"

She gave him an are-you-out-of-your-mind? look.

"Yeah, I didn't much care for him either." Restrained murder, in point of fact. He was now meltingly grateful for that restraint. "Would you like to rip his lungs out, if you could?"

Her clawed hands clenched. "Try me!"

"Good!" He smiled cheerily. "I want to give you your first lesson in tactics." He pointed. "See that control? The temperature in these freezers can be raised to almost 200 degrees centigrade, for heat sterilization during cleaning. Give me your finger. One finger. Gently. More gently than that." He guided her hand. "The least possible pressure you can apply to the dial, and still move . . . Now the next," he pulled her to the next panel, "and the last." He exhaled, still not quite able to believe it.

"And the lesson is," he breathed, "it's not how much force you use. It's where you apply it."

He resisted the urge to scrawl something like *The Dwarf Strikes Back* across the front of the freezer with a flow pen. The longer the baron in his mortal rage took to figure out who to pursue, the better. It would take several hours to bring all that mass in there from liquid nitrogen temperature up to *well-done,* but if no one came in till morning shift, the destruction would be absolute.

Miles glanced at the time on the wall digital. Dear God, he'd spent a lot of time in that basement. Well-spent, but still . . . "Now," he said to Taura, who was still meditating on the dial, and her hand, with her gold eyes glowing, "we have to get out of here. Now we *really* have to get out of here." Lest her next tactics lesson turn out to be, Don't blow up the bridge you're standing on, Miles allowed nervously.

Contemplating the door-locking mechanism more closely, plus what lay beyond—among other things, the sound-activated wall-mounted monitors in the halls featured automatic laser fire—Miles almost went to turn the freezer temperatures back down. His chip-driven Dendarii tools, now locked in the Security Ops office, might barely have handled the complex circuitry in the pried-open control box. But of course, he couldn't get at his tools without his tools . . . a nice paradox. It shouldn't surprise Miles, that Ryoval saved his most sophisticated alarm system for this lab's one and only door. But it made the room a much worse trap than even the sub-basement.

He made another tour of the lab with the filched hand light, checking drawers again. No computer-keys came to hand, but he did find a big, crude pair of cutters in a drawer full of rings and clamps, and bethought him of the duct grille that had lately defeated him in the basement. So. The passage up to this lab had merely been the illusion of progress toward escape.

"There's no shame in a strategic retreat to a better position," he whispered to Taura when she balked at re-entering the support column's dark tube. "This is a dead-end, here. Maybe literally." The doubt in her tawny eyes was strangely unsettling, a weight in his heart. *Still don't trust me, eh? Well, maybe those who have been greatly betrayed need great proof.* "Stick with me, kid," he muttered under his breath, swinging into the tube. "We're going places." Her doubt was merely masked under lowered eyelids, but she followed him, sealing the hatch behind them.

With the hand light, the descent was slightly less nasty than the ascent into the unknown had been. There were no other exits to be found, and shortly they stood on the stone they had started from. Miles checked the progress of their ceiling waterspout, while Taura drank again. The splattering water ran off in a flat greasy trickle downslope; given the vast size of the chamber, it would be some days before the pool collecting slowly against the lower wall offered any useful strategic possibilities, though there was always the hope it might do a bit to undermine the foundations.

Taura boosted him back into the duct. "Wish me luck," he murmured over his shoulder, muffled by the close confines.

"Goodbye," she said. He could not see the expression on her face; there was none in her voice.

"See you later," he corrected firmly.

A few minutes of vigorous wriggling brought him back to his grille. It opened onto a dark room stacked with stuff, part of the basement proper, quiet and unoccupied. The snip of his cutters, biting through the grille, seemed loud enough to bring down Ryoval's entire security force, but none appeared. Maybe the security chief was sleeping off his drug hangover. A scrabbling noise, not of Miles's own making, echoed thinly through the duct and Miles froze. He flashed his light down a side-branching tube. Twin red jewels flashed back, the eyes of a huge rat. He briefly considered trying to clout it and haul it back to Taura. No. When they got back to the *Ariel*, he'd give her a steak dinner. Two steak dinners. The rat saved itself by turning and scampering away.

The grille parted at last, and he squeezed into the storage room. What time was it, anyway? Late, very late. The room gave onto a corridor, and on the floor at the end, one of the access hatches gleamed dully. Miles's heart rose in serious hope. Once he'd got Taura, they must next try to reach a vehicle. . . .

This hatch, like the first, was manual, no sophisticated electronics to disarm. It re-locked automatically upon closing, however. Miles jammed it with his clippers before descending the ladder. He aimed his light around—"Taura!" he whispered. "Where are you?"

No immediate answer; no glowing gold eyes flashing in the forest of pillars. He was reluctant to shout. He slapped down the rungs and began a silent fast trot through the chamber, the cold stone draining the heat through his socks and making him long for his lost boots.

He came upon her sitting silently at the base of a pillar, her head turned sideways resting on her knees. Her face was pensive, sad. Really, it didn't take long at all to begin reading the subtleties of feeling in her wolfish features.

"Time to march, soldier girl," Miles said.

Her head lifted. "You came back!"

"What did you think I was going to do? Of course I came back. You're my recruit, aren't you?"

She scrubbed her face with the back of a big paw—hand, Miles corrected himself severely—and stood up, and up. "Guess I must be." Her outslung mouth smiled slightly. If you didn't have a clue what the expression was, it could look quite alarming.

"I've got a hatch open. We've got to try to get out of this main building, back to the utility bay. I saw several vehicles parked there earlier. What's a little theft, after—"

With a sudden whine, the outside vehicle entrance, downslope to their right, began to slide upward. A rush of cold dry air swept through the dankness, and a thin shaft of yellow dawn light made the shadows blue. They shielded their eyes in the unexpected glare. Out of the bright squinting haze coalesced half-a-dozen red-clad forms, double-timing it, weapons at the ready.

Taura's hand was tight on Miles's. *Run,* he started to cry, and bit back the shout; no way could they outrun a nerve disruptor beam, a weapon which at least two of the guards now carried. Miles's breath hissed out through his teeth. He was too infuriated even to swear. They'd been so *close.* . . .

Security Chief Moglia sauntered up. "What, still in one piece, Naismith?" he smirked unpleasantly. "Nine must have finally realized it's time to start cooperating, eh, Nine?"

Miles squeezed her hand hard, hoping the message would be properly understood as, *Wait.*

She lifted her chin. "Guess so," she said coldly.

"It's about time," said Moglia. "Be a good girl, and we'll take you upstairs and feed you breakfast after this."

Good, Miles's hand signalled. She was watching him closely for cues, now.

Moglia prodded Miles with his truncheon. "Time to go, dwarf. Your friends have actually made ransom. Surprised me."

Miles was surprised himself. He moved toward the exit, still towing Taura. He didn't look at her, did as little as possible to draw unwanted attention to their, er, togetherness, while still maintaining it. He let go of her hand as soon as their momentum was established.

What the hell . . . ? Miles thought as they emerged into the blinking dawn, up the ramp and onto a circle of tarmac slick with glittering rime. A most peculiar tableau was arranged there.

Bel Thorne and one Dendarii trooper, armed with stunners, shifted uneasily—not prisoners? Half a dozen armed men in the green uniform of House Fell stood at the ready. A float truck emblazoned with Fell's logo was parked at the tarmac's edge. And Nicol the quaddie, wrapped in white fur against the frost, hovered in her float chair at the stunner-point of a big green-clad guard. The light was grey and gold and chilly as the sun, lifting over the dark mountains in the distance, broke through the clouds.

"Is that the man you want?" the green-uniformed guard captain asked Bel Thorne.

"That's him." Thorne's face was white with an odd mixture of relief and distress. "Admiral, are you all right?" Thorne called urgently. Its eyes widened, taking in Miles's tall companion. "What the hell's *that?*"

"*She* is recruit-trainee Taura," Miles said firmly, hoping 1) Bel would unravel the several meanings packed in that sentence and 2) Ryoval's guards wouldn't. Bel looked stunned, so evidently Miles had got at least partly through; Security Chief Moglia looked suspicious, but baffled. Miles was clearly a problem Moglia thought he was about to get rid of, however, and he thrust his bafflement aside to deal with the more important person of Fell's guard captain.

"What *is* this?" Miles hissed at Bel, sidling closer until a red-clad guard lifted his nerve disruptor and shook his head. Moglia and Fell's captain were exchanging electronic data on a report panel, heads bent together, evidently the official documentation.

"When we lost you last night, I was in a panic," Bel pitched its voice low toward Miles. "A frontal assault was out of the question. So I ran to Baron Fell to ask for help. But the help I got wasn't quite what I expected. Fell and Ryoval cooked up a deal between them to exchange Nicol for you. I swear, I only found out the details an hour ago!" Bel protested at Nicol's thin-lipped glower in its direction.

"I . . . see." Miles paused. "Are we planning to refund her dollar?"

"*Sir,*" Bel's voice was anguished, "we had *no idea* what was happening to you in there. We were expecting Ryoval to start beaming up a holocast of obscene and ingenious tortures, starring you, at any minute. Like Commodore Tung says, on hemmed-in ground, use subterfuge."

Miles recognized one of Tung's favorite Sun Tzu aphorisms. On bad days Tung had a habit of quoting the 4000-year-dead general in the original Chinese; when Tung was feeling benign they got a translation. Miles glanced around, adding up weapons, men, equipment. Most of the green guards carried stunners. Thirteen to . . . three? Four? He glanced at Nicol. Maybe five? *On desperate ground,* Sun Tzu advised, *fight.* Could it get much more desperate than this?

"Ah . . ." said Miles. "Just what the devil did we offer Baron Fell in exchange for this extraordinary charity? Or is he doing it out of the goodness of his heart?"

Bel shot him an exasperated look, then cleared its throat. "I promised you'd tell him the real truth about the Betan rejuvenation treatment."

"Bel . . ."

Thorne shrugged unhappily. "I thought, once we'd got you back, we'd figure something out. But I never thought he'd offer Nicol to Ryoval, I swear!"

Down in the long valley, Miles could see a bead moving on the thin gleam of monorail. The morning shift of bioengineers and technicians, janitors and office clerks and cafeteria cooks, was due to arrive soon. Miles glanced at the white building looming above, pictured the scene to come in that third floor lab as the guards deactivated the alarms and let them in to work, as the first one through the door sniffed and wrinkled his nose and said plaintively, "What's that awful *smell?*"

"Has 'Medtech Vaughn' signed aboard the *Ariel* yet?" Miles asked.

"Within the hour."

"Yeah, well . . . it turns out we didn't need to kill his fatted calf after all. It comes with the package." Miles nodded toward Taura.

Bel lowered its voice still further. *"That's* coming with us?"

"You'd better believe it. Vaughn didn't tell us everything. To put it mildly. I'll explain later," Miles added as the two guard captains broke up their tete-a-tete. Moglia swung his truncheon jauntily, heading toward Miles. "Meantime, you made a slight miscalculation. This isn't hemmed-in ground. This is *desperate* ground. Nicol, I want you to know, the Dendarii don't give refunds."

Nicol frowned in bewilderment. Bel's eyes widened, as it checked out the odds—calculating them thirteen to three, Miles could tell.

"Truly?" Bel choked. A subtle hand signal, down by its trouser seam, brought the trooper to full alert.

"Truly desperate," Miles reiterated. He inhaled deeply. "Now! Taura, attack!"

Miles launched himself toward Moglia, not so much actually expecting to wrestle his truncheon from him as hoping to maneuver Moglia's body between himself and the fellows with the nerve disruptors. The Dendarii trooper, who had been paying attention to details, dropped one of the nerve disruptor wielders with his first stunner shot, then rolled away from the second's return fire. Bel dropped the second nerve disruptor man and leapt aside. Two red guards, aiming their stunners at the running hermaphrodite, were lifted abruptly by their necks. Taura cracked their heads together, unscientifically but hard; they fell to hands and knees, groping blindly for their lost weapons.

Fell's green guards hesitated, not certain just whom to shoot, until Nicol, her angel's face alight, suddenly shot skyward in her float chair and dropped straight down again on the head of her guard, who was distracted by the fight. He fell like an ox. Nicol flipped her floater sideways as green-guard stunner fire found her, shielding herself from its flare, and shot upwards again. Taura picked up a red guard and threw him at a green one; they both went down in a tangle of arms and legs.

The Dendarii trooper closed on a green guard hand-to-hand, to shield himself from stunner blast. Fell's captain wouldn't buy the maneuver, and ruthlessly stunned them both, a sound tactic with the numbers on his side. Moglia got his truncheon up against Miles's windpipe and started to press, meanwhile yelling into his wrist comm, calling for back-up from Security Ops. A green guard screamed as Taura yanked his arm out of its shoulder socket and swung him into the air by the dislocated joint at another one aiming his stunner at her.

Colored lights danced before Miles's eyes. Fell's captain, focusing on Taura as the biggest threat, dropped to stunner fire from Bel Thorne as Nicol whammed her float chair into the back of the last green guard left standing.

"The float truck!" Miles croaked. "Go for the float truck!" Bel cast him a desperate look and sprinted toward it. Miles fought like an eel until Moglia got a hand down to his boot, drew a sharp, thin knife, and pressed it to Miles's neck.

"Hold still!" snarled Moglia. "That's better . . ." He straightened in the sudden silence, realizing he'd just pulled domination from disaster. "*Everybody* hold still." Bel froze with its hand on the float-truck's door pad. A couple of the men splayed on the tarmac twitched and moaned.

"Now stand away from—glk," said Moglia.

Taura's voice whispered past Moglia's ear, a soft, soft growl. "Drop the knife. Or I'll rip your throat out with my bare hands."

Miles's eyes wrenched sideways, trying to see around his own clamped head, as the sharp edge sang against his skin.

"I can kill him, before you do," croaked Moglia.

"The little man is mine," Taura crooned. "You gave him to me yourself. He came *back* for me. Hurt him one little bit, and I'll tear your head off and then I'll drink your blood."

Miles felt Moglia being lifted off his feet. The knife clattered to the pavement. Miles sprang away, staggering. Taura held Moglia by his neck, her claws biting deep. "I still want to rip his head off," she growled petulantly, remembrance of abuse sparking in her eyes.

"Leave him," gasped Miles. "Believe me, in a few hours he's going to be suffering a more artistic vengeance than anything we can dream up."

Bel galloped back to stun the security chief at can't miss range while Taura held him out like a wet cat. Miles had Taura throw the unconscious Dendarii over her shoulder while he ran around to the back of the float truck and released the doors for Nicol, who zipped her chair inside. They tumbled within, dropped the doors, and Bel at the controls shot them into the air. A siren was going off somewhere in Ryoval's.

"Wrist comm, wrist comm," Miles babbled, stripping his unconscious trooper of the device. "Bel, where is our drop shuttle parked?"

"We came in at a little commercial shuttleport just outside Ryoval's town, about forty kilometers from here."

"Anybody left manning it?"

"Anderson and Nout."

"What's their scrambled comm channel?"

"Twenty-three."

Miles slid into the seat beside Bel and opened the channel. It took a small eternity for Sergeant Anderson to answer, fully thirty or forty seconds, while the float truck streaked above the treetops and over the nearest ridge.

"Laureen, I want you to get your shuttle into the air. We need an emergency pick-up, soonest. We're in a House Fell float truck, heading—" Miles thrust his wrist under Bel's nose.

"North from Ryoval Biologicals," Bel recited. "At about two hundred sixty kilometers per hour, which is all the faster this crate will go."

"Home in on our screamer," Miles set the wrist comm emergency signal. "Don't wait for clearance from Ryoval's shuttleport traffic control, 'cause you won't get it. Have Nout patch my comm through to the *Ariel.*"

"You got it, sir," Anderson's thin voice came cheerily back over his comm.

Static, and another few seconds excruciating delay. Then an excited voice, "Murka here. I thought you were coming out right behind us last night! You all right, sir?"

"Temporarily. Is 'Medtech Vaughn' aboard?"

"Yes, sir."

"All right. Don't let him off. Assure him I have his tissue sample with me."

"Really! How'd you—"

"Never mind how. Get all the troops back aboard and break from the station into free orbit. Plan to make a flying pick-up of the drop shuttle, and tell the pilot-officer to plot a course for the Escobar wormhole jump at max acceleration as soon as we're clamped on. Don't wait for clearance."

"We're still loading cargo. . . ."

"Abandon any that's still unloaded."

"Are we in serious shit, sir?"

"Mortal, Murka."

"Right, sir. Murka out."

"I thought we were all supposed to be as quiet as mice here on Jackson's Whole," Bel complained. "Isn't this all a bit splashy?"

"The situation's changed. There'd be no negotiating with Ryoval for Nicol, or for Taura either, after what we did last night. I struck a blow for truth and justice back there that I may live to regret, briefly. Tell you about it later. Anyway, do you really want to stick around while I explain to Baron Fell the real truth about the Betan rejuvenation treatment?"

"Oh," Thorne's eyes were alight, as it concentrated on its flying, "I'd pay money to watch that, sir."

"Ha. No. For one last moment back there, all the pieces were in our hands. Potentially, anyway." Miles began exploring the readouts on the float-truck's simple control panel. "We'd never get everybody together again, never. One maneuvers to the limit, but the golden moment demands action. If you miss it, the gods damn you forever. And vice versa. . . . Speaking of action, did you see Taura take out *seven* of those guys?" Miles chortled in memory. "What's she going to be like after basic training?"

Bel glanced uneasily over its shoulder, to where Nicol had her float chair lodged and Taura hunkered in the back along with the body of the unconscious trooper. "I was too busy to keep count."

Miles swung out of his seat, and made his way into the back to check on their precious live cargo.

"Nicol, you were great," he told her. "You fought like a falcon. I may have to give you a discount on that dollar."

Nicol was still breathless, ivory cheeks flushed. An upper hand shoved a strand of black hair out of her sparkling eyes. "I was afraid they'd break my dulcimer." A lower hand stroked a big box-shaped case jammed into the float-chair's cup beside her. "Then I was afraid they'd break Bel. . . ."

Taura sat leaning against the truck wall, a bit green.

Miles knelt beside her. "Taura dear, are you all right?" He gently lifted one clawed hand to check her pulse, which was bounding. Nicol gave him a rather strange look at his tender gesture, her float chair was wedged as far from Taura as it could get.

"Hungry," Taura gasped.

"Again? But of course, all that energy expenditure. Anybody got a ration bar?" A quick check found an only-slightly-nibbled rat bar in the stunned trooper's thigh pocket, which Miles immediately liberated. Miles smiled benignly at Taura as she wolfed it down; she smiled back as best she could with her mouth full. *No more rats for you after this,* Miles promised silently. *Three steak dinners when we get back to the* Ariel, *and a couple of chocolate cakes for dessert. . . .*

The float-truck jinked. Taura, reviving somewhat, extended her feet to hold Nicol's dented cup in place against the far wall and keep it from bouncing around. "Thank you," said Nicol warily. Taura nodded.

"Company," Bel Thorne called over its shoulder. Miles hastened forward.

Two aircars were coming up fast behind them. Ryoval's security. Doubtless beefed up tougher than the average civilian police car—yes. Bel jinked again as a plasma bolt boiled past, leaving bright green streaks across Miles's retinas. Quasi-military and seriously annoyed, their pursuers were.

"This is one of Fell's trucks, we ought to have *something* to fling back at them." There was nothing in front of Miles that looked like any kind of weapons-control.

A *whoomp,* a scream from Nicol, and the float truck staggered in air, righted itself under Bel's hands. A roar of air and vibration—Miles cranked his head around frantically—one top back corner of the truck's cargo area was blown away. The rear door was fused shut on one side, whanging loose along the opposite edge. Taura still braced the float chair, Nicol now had her upper hands wrapped around Taura's ankles. "Ah," said Thorne. "No armor."

"What did they think this was going to be, a peaceful mission?" Miles checked his wrist comm. "Laureen, are you in the air yet?"

"Coming, sir."

"Well, if you've ever itched to red-line it, now's your chance. Nobody's going to complain about your abusing the equipment this time."

"*Thank* you, sir," she responded happily.

They were losing speed and altitude. "Hang on!" Bel yelled over its shoulder, and suddenly reversed thrust. Their closing pursuers shot past them, but immediately began climbing turns. Bel accelerated again; another scream from the back as their live cargo was thus shifted toward the now-dubious rear doors.

The Dendarii hand stunners were of no use at all. Miles clambered into the back again, looking for some sort of luggage compartment, gun rack, anything—surely Fell's people did not rely only on the fearsome reputation of their House for protection. . . .

The padded benches along each side of the cargo compartment, upon which Fell's guard squad had presumably sat, swung up on storage space. The first was empty, the second contained personal luggage—Miles had a brief flash of strangling an enemy with someone's pajama pants, flinging underwear into thruster air-intakes—the third compartment was also empty. The fourth was locked.

The float truck rocked under another blast, part of the top peeled away in the wind, Miles grabbed for Taura, and the truck plummeted downward. Miles's stomach, and the rest of him, seemed to float upward. They were all flattened to the floor again as Bel pulled up. The float truck shivered and lurched, and all, Miles and Taura, the unconscious trooper, Nicol in her float chair, were flung forward in a tangle as the truck plowed to a tilted stop in a copse of frost-blackened scrub.

Bel, blood streaming down its face, clambered back to them crying "Out, out, out!" Miles stretched for the new opening in the roof, jerked his hand back at the burning touch of hot slagged metal and plastics. Taura, standing up, stuck her head out through the hole, then crouched back down to boost Miles through. He slithered to the ground, looked around. They were in an unpeopled valley of native

vegetation, flanked by ropy, ridgy hills. Flying up the slot toward
them came the two pursuing aircars, swelling, slowing—coming in
for a capture, or just taking careful aim?

The *Ariel*'s combat drop shuttle roared up over the ridge and
descended like the black hand of God. The pursuing aircars looked
suddenly *much* smaller. One veered off and fled, the second was
smashed to the ground not by plasma fire but by a swift swat from a
tractor beam. Not even a trickle of smoke marked where it went
down. The drop shuttle settled demurely beside them in a deafening
crackling crush of shrubbery. Its hatch extended and unfolded itself
in a sort of suave, self-satisfied salute.

"Show-off," Miles muttered. He pulled the woozy Thorne's arm
over his shoulder, Taura carried the stunned man, Nicol's battered
cup stuttered through the air, and they all staggered gratefully to
their rescue.

Subtle noises of protest emanated from the ship around him as
Miles stepped into the *Ariel*'s shuttle hatch corridor. His stomach
twitched queasily from an artificial gravity not quite in synch with
over-loaded engines. They were on their way, breaking orbit already.
Miles wanted to get to Nav and Com as quickly as possible, though
the evidence so far suggested that Murka was carrying on quite
competently. Anderson and Nout hauled in the downed trooper,
now moaning his way to consciousness, and turned him over to the
medtech waiting with a float pallet. Thorne, who had acquired a
temporary plas dressing for the forehead cut during the shuttle flight,
sent Nicol in her damaged float chair after them and whisked off
toward Nav and Com. Miles turned to encounter the man he least
wanted to see. Dr. Canaba hovered anxiously in the corridor, his
tanned face strained.

"You," said Miles to Canaba, in a voice dark with rage. Canaba
stepped back involuntarily. Miles wanted, but was too short, to pin
Canaba to the wall by his neck, and regretfully dismissed the idea of
ordering Trooper Nout to do it for him. Miles pinned Canaba with a
glare instead. "You cold-blooded double-dealing son-of-a-bitch. You
set me up to murder a sixteen-year-old girl!"

Canaba raised his hands in protest. "You don't understand—"

Taura ducked through the shuttle hatch. Her tawny eyes widened
in a surprise only exceeded by Canaba's. "Why, Dr. Canaba! What
are you doing here?"

Miles pointed to Canaba. "You, stay there," he ordered thickly. He
tampered his anger down and turned to the shuttle pilot. "Laureen?"

"Yes, sir?"

Miles took Taura by the hand and led her to Sergeant Anderson. "Laureen, I want you to take Recruit-trainee Taura here in tow and get her a square meal. All she can eat, and I do mean all. Then help her get a bath, a uniform, and orient her to the ship."

Anderson eyed the towering Taura warily. "Er . . . yes, sir."

"She's had a hell of a time," Miles felt compelled to explain, then paused and added, "Do us proud. It's important."

"Yes, sir," said Anderson sturdily, and led off, Taura following with an uncertain backward glance to Miles and Canaba.

Miles rubbed his stubbled chin, conscious of his stains and stink, fear-driven weariness stretching his nerves taut. He turned to the stunned geneticist. "All right, doctor," he snarled, "make me understand. Try real hard."

"I couldn't leave her in Ryoval's hands!" said Canaba in agitation. "To be made a victim, or worse, an agent of his, his merchandized depravities . . ."

"Didn't you ever think of asking us to rescue her?"

"But," said Canaba, confused, "why should you? It wasn't in your contract—a mercenary—"

"Doctor, you've been living on Jackson's Whole too damn long."

"I knew that back when I was throwing up every morning before going to work." Canaba drew himself up with a dry dignity. "But Admiral, you don't understand." He glanced down the corridor in the direction Taura had gone. "I couldn't leave her in Ryoval's hands. But I can't possibly take her to Barrayar. They kill mutants there!"

"Er . . ." said Miles, given pause. "They're attempting to reform those prejudices. Or so I understand. But you're quite right. Barrayar is not the place for her."

"I had hoped, when you came along, not to have to do it, to kill her myself. Not an easy task. I've known her . . . too long. But to leave her down there would have been the most vile condemnation . . ."

"That's no lie. Well, she's out of there now. Same as you." *If we can keep so. . . .* Miles was frantic to get to Nav and Com and find out what was happening. Had Ryoval launched pursuit yet? Had Fell? Would the space station guarding the distant wormhole exit be ordered to block their escape?

"I didn't want to just abandon her," dithered Canaba, "but I couldn't take her with me!"

"I should hope not. You're totally unfit to have charge of her. I'm going to urge her to join the Dendarii Mercenaries. It would seem to be her genetic destiny. Unless you know some reason why not?"

"But she's going to die!"

Miles stopped short. "And you and I are not?" he said softly after a moment, then more loudly, "Why? How soon?"

"It's her metabolism. Another mistake, or concatenation of mistakes. I don't know when, exactly. She could go another year, or two, or five. Or ten."

"Or fifteen?"

"Or fifteen, yes, though not likely. But early, still."

"And yet you wanted to take from her what little she had? Why?"

"To spare her. The final debilitation is rapid, but very painful, to judge from what some of the other . . . prototypes, went through. The females were more complex than the males, I'm not certain . . . But it's a ghastly death. Especially ghastly as Ryoval's slave."

"I don't recall encountering a lovely death yet. And I've seen a variety. As for duration, I tell you we could all go in the next fifteen minutes, and where is your tender mercy then?" He *had* to get to Nav and Com. "I declare your interest in her forfeit, doctor. Meanwhile, let her grab what life she can."

"But she was my project—I must answer for her—"

"No. She's a free woman now. She must answer for herself."

"How free can she ever be, in that body, driven by that metabolism, that face—a freak's life—better to die painlessly, than to have all that suffering inflicted on her—"

Miles spoke through his teeth. With emphasis. "No. It's. Not."

Canaba stared at him, shaken out of the rutted circle of his unhappy reasoning at last.

That's right, doctor, Miles's thought glittered. *Get your head out of your ass and look at me. Finally.*

"Why should . . . you care?" asked Canaba.

"I like her. Rather better than I like you, I might add." Miles paused, daunted by the thought of having to explain to Taura about the gene complexes in her calf. And sooner or later they'd have to retrieve them. Unless he could fake it, pretend the biopsy was some sort of medical standard operating procedure for Dendarii induction —no. She deserved more honesty than that.

Miles was highly annoyed at Canaba for putting this false note between himself and Taura and yet—without the gene complexes, would he have indeed gone in after her as his boast implied? Extended and endangered his assigned mission just out of the goodness of his heart, yeah? Devotion to duty, or pragmatic ruthlessness, which was which? He would never know, now. His anger receded, and exhaustion washed in, the familiar post-mission down—too soon, the mission was far from over, Miles reminded himself sternly. He inhaled. "You can't save her from being alive, Dr. Canaba. Too late. Let her go. Let *go.*"

Canaba's lips were unhappily tight, but, head bowing, he turned his hands palm-out.

"Page the Admiral," Miles heard Thorne say as he entered Nav and Com, then "Belay that," as heads swivelled toward the swish of the doors and they saw Miles. "Good timing, sir."

"What's up?" Miles swung into the com station chair Thorne indicated. Ensign Murka was monitoring ship's shielding and weapons systems, while their Jump pilot sat at the ready beneath the strange crown of his headset with its chemical cannulae and wires. Pilot Padget's expression was inward, controlled and meditative; his consciousness fully engaged, even merged, with the *Ariel.* Good man.

"Baron Ryoval is on the com for you," said Thorne. "Personally."

"I wonder if he's checked his freezers yet?" Miles settled in before the vid link. "How long have I kept him waiting?"

"Less than a minute," said the com officer.

"Hm. Let him wait a little longer, then. What's been launched in pursuit of us?"

"Nothing, so far," reported Murka.

Miles's brows rose at this unexpected news. He took a moment to compose himself, wishing he'd had time to clean up, shave, and put on a fresh uniform before this interview, just for the psychological edge. He scratched his itching chin and ran his hands through his hair, and wriggled his damp sock toes against the deck matting, which they barely reached. He lowered his station chair slightly, straightened his spine as much as he could, and brought his breathing under control. "All right, bring him up."

The rather blurred background to the face that formed over the vid plate seemed faintly familiar—ah yes, the Security Ops room at Ryoval Biologicals. Baron Ryoval had arrived personally on that scene as promised. It took only one glance at the dusky, contorted expression on Ryoval's youthful face to fill in the rest of the scenario. Miles folded his hands and smiled innocently. "Good morning, Baron. What can I do for you?"

"*Die,* you little mutant!" Ryoval spat. "You! There isn't going to be a bunker deep enough for you to burrow in. I'll put a price on your head that will have every bounty hunter in the galaxy all over you like a second skin—you'll not eat or sleep—I'll have you—"

Yes, the baron had seen his freezers all right. Recently. Gone entirely was the suave contemptuous dismissal of their first encounter. Yet Miles was puzzled by the drift of his threats. It seemed the baron expected them to escape Jacksonian local space. True, House Ryoval owned no space fleet, but why not rent a dreadnought from Baron Fell and attack now? That was the ploy Miles had most expected and feared, that Ryoval and Fell, and maybe Bharaputra too, would combine against him as he attempted to carry off their prizes.

"Can you afford to hire bounty hunters now?" asked Miles mildly. "I thought your assets were somewhat reduced. Though you still have your surgical specialists, I suppose."

Ryoval, breathing heavily, wiped spittle from his mouth. "Did my dear little brother put you up to this?"

"Who?" said Miles, genuinely startled. Yet another player in the game . . . ?

"Baron Fell."

"I was . . . not aware you were related," said Miles. "*Little* brother?"

"You lie badly," sneered Ryoval. "I knew he had to be behind this."

"You'll have to ask him," Miles shot at random, his head spinning as the new datum rearranged all his estimates. *Damn* his mission briefing, which had never mentioned this connection, concentrating in detail only on House Bharaputra. Half-brothers only, surely—yes, hadn't Nicol mentioned something about "Fell's half-brother"?

"I'll have your head for this," foamed Ryoval. "Shipped back frozen in a box. I'll have it encased in plastic and hang it over my—no, better. Double the money for the man who brings you in alive. You will die slowly, after infinite degradation—"

In all, Miles was glad the distance between them was widening at high acceleration.

Ryoval interrupted his own tirade, dark brows snapping down in sudden suspicion. "Or was it Bharaputra who hired you? Trying to block me from cutting in on their biologicals monopoly at the last, not merging as they promised?"

"Why, now," drawled Miles, "would Bharaputra really mount a plot against the head of another House? Do you have personal evidence that they do that sort of thing? Or—who did kill your, ah, brother's clone?" The connections were locking into place at last. Ye gods. It seemed Miles and his mission had blundered into the middle of an on-going power struggle of byzantine complexity. Nicol had testified that Fell had never pinned down the killer of his young duplicate. . . . "Shall I guess?"

"You know bloody well," snapped Ryoval. "But which of them hired you? Fell, or Bharaputra? *Which?*"

Ryoval, Miles realized, knew absolutely nothing yet of the real Dendarii mission against House Bharaputra. And with the atmosphere among the Houses being what it apparently was, it could be quite a long time before they got around to comparing notes. The longer the better, from Miles's point of view. He began to suppress, then deliberately released, a small smile. "What, can't you believe it was just my personal blow against the genetic slave trade? A deed in honor of my lady?"

This reference to Taura went straight over Ryoval's head; he had his idea-fixee now, and its ramifications and his rage were an effective block against incoming data. Really, it should not be at all hard to convince a man who had been conspiring deeply against his rivals, that those rivals were conspiring against him in turn.

"Fell, or Bharaputra?" Ryoval reiterated furiously. "Did you think to conceal a theft for Bharaputra with that wanton destruction?"

Theft? Miles wondered intently. Not of Taura, surely—of some tissue sample Bharaputra had been dealing for, perhaps? Oh *ho*. . . .

"Isn't it obvious?" said Miles sweetly. "You gave your brother the motive, in your sabotage of his plans to extend his life. And you wanted too much from Bharaputra, so they supplied the method, placing their super-soldier inside your facility where I could rendezvous with her. They even made you pay for the privilege of having your security screwed! You played right into our hands. The master plan, of course," Miles buffed his fingernails on his T-shirt, "was mine."

Miles glanced up through his eyelashes. Ryoval seemed to be having trouble breathing. The baron cut the vid connection with an abrupt swat of his shaking hand. Blackout.

Humming thoughtfully, Miles went to get a shower.

He was back in Nav and Com in fresh grey-and-whites, full of salicylates for his aches and contusions and with a mug of hot black coffee in his hands as antidote to his squinting red eyes, when the next call came in.

So far from breaking into a tirade like his half-brother, Baron Fell sat silent a moment in the vid, just staring at Miles. Miles, burning under his gaze, felt extremely glad he'd had the chance to clean up. So, had Baron Fell missed his quaddie at last? Had Ryoval communicated to him yet any part of the smouldering paranoid misconceptions Miles had so lately fanned to flame? No pursuit had yet been launched from Fell Station—it must come soon, or not at all, or any craft light enough to match the *Ariel's* acceleration would be too light to match its firepower. Unless Fell planned to call in favors from the consortium of Houses that ran the Jumppoint Station. . . . One more minute of this heavy silence, Miles felt, and he would break into uncontrollable blither. Fortunately, Fell spoke at last.

"You seem, Admiral Naismith," Baron Fell rumbled, "whether accidentally or on purpose, to be carrying off something that does not belong to you."

Quite a few somethings, Miles reflected, but Fell referred only to Nicol if Miles read him right. "We were compelled to leave in rather a hurry," he said in an apologetic tone.

"So I'm told." Fell inclined his head ironically. He must have had a report from his hapless squad commander. "But you may yet save yourself some trouble. There was an agreed-upon price for my musician. It's of no great difference to me, if I give her up to you or to Ryoval, as long as I get that price."

Captain Thorne, working the *Ariel's* monitors, flinched under Miles's glance.

"The price you refer to, I take it, is the secret of the Betan rejuvenation technique," said Miles.

"Quite."

"Ah . . . hum." Miles moistened his lips. "Baron, I cannot."

Fell turned his head. "Station commander, launch pursuit ships—"

"Wait!" Miles cried.

Fell raised his brows. "You reconsider? Good."

"It's not that I *will* not tell you," said Miles desperately, "it's just that the truth would be of no use to you. None whatsoever. Still, I agree you deserve some compensation. I have another piece of information I could trade you, more immediately valuable."

"Oh?" said Fell. His voice was neutral but his expression was black.

"You suspected your half-brother Ryoval in the murder of your clone, but could not chain any evidence to him, am I right?"

Fell looked fractionally more interested. "All my agents and Bharaputra's could not turn up a connection. We tried."

"I'm not surprised. Because it was Bharaputra's agents who did the deed." Well, it was possible, anyway.

Fell's eyes narrowed. "Killed their own product?" he said slowly.

"I believe Ryoval struck a deal with House Bharaputra to betray you," said Miles rapidly. "I believe it involved the trade of some unique biological samples in Ryoval's possession; I don't think cash alone would have been worth their risk. The deal was done on the highest levels, obviously. I don't know how they figured to divide the spoils of House Fell after your eventual death—maybe they didn't mean to divide it at all. They seem to have had some ultimate plan of combining their operations for some larger monopoly of biologicals on Jackson's Whole. A corporate merger of sorts." Miles paused to let this sink in. "May I suggest you may wish to reserve your forces and favors against enemies more, er, intimate and immediate than myself? Besides, you have all our credit chit but we have only half our cargo. Will you call it even?"

Fell glowered at him for a full minute, the face of a man thinking in three different directions at once. Miles knew the feeling. He then turned his head, and grated out of the corner of his mouth, "Hold pursuit ships."

Miles breathed again.

"I thank you for this information, Admiral," said Fell coldly, "but not very much. I shall not impede your swift exit. But if you or any of your ships appear in Jacksonian space again—"

"Oh, Baron," said Miles sincerely, "staying far, far away from here is fast becoming one of my dearest ambitions."

"You're wise," Fell growled, and moved to cut the link.

"Baron Fell," Miles added impulsively. Fell paused. "For your future information—is this link secured?"

"Yes."

"The true secret of the Betan rejuvenation technique—is that there is none. Don't be taken in again. I look the age I do, because it is the age I am. Make of it what you will."

Fell said absolutely nothing. After a moment a faint, wintry smile moved his lips. He shook his head and cut the com.

Just in case, Miles lingered on in sort of a glassy puddle in one corner of Nav and Com until the Comm Officer reported their final clearance from Jumppoint Station traffic control. But Miles calculated Houses Fell, Ryoval, and Bharaputra were going to be too busy with each other to concern themselves with him, at least for a while. His late transfer of information both true and false among the combatants—to each according to his measure—had the feel of throwing one bone to three starving, rabid dogs. He almost regretted not being able to stick around and see the results. Almost.

Hours after the Jump he woke in his cabin, fully dressed but with his boots set neatly by his bed, with no memory of how he'd got there. He rather fancied Murka must have escorted him. If he'd fallen asleep while walking alone he'd surely have left the boots on.

* * *

Miles first checked with the duty officer as to the *Ariel*'s situation and status. It was refreshingly dull. They were crossing a blue star system between Jump points on the route to Escobar, unpeopled and empty of everything but a smattering of routine commercial traffic. Nothing pursued them from the direction of Jackson's Whole. Miles had a light meal, not sure if it was breakfast, lunch, or dinner, his bio-rhythm being thoroughly askew from shiptime after his downside adventures. He then sought out Thorne and Nicol. He found them in Engineering. A tech was just polishing out the last dent in Nicol's float chair.

Nicol, now wearing a white tunic and shorts trimmed with pink piping, lay sprawled on her belly on a bench watching the repairs. It gave Miles an odd sensation to see her out of her cup, it was like looking at a hermit crab out of its shell, or a seal on the shore. She looked strangely vulnerable in one-gee, yet in null gee she'd looked so right, so clearly at ease, he'd stopped noticing the oddness of the extra arms very quickly. Thorne helped the tech fit the float cup's blue shell over its reconditioned antigrav mechanism, and turned to greet Miles as the tech proceeded to lock it in place.

Miles sat down-bench from Nicol. "From the looks of things," he told her, "you should be free of pursuit from Baron Fell. He and his half-brother are going to be fully occupied avenging themselves on each other for a while. Makes me glad I'm an only child."

"Hm," she said pensively.

"You should be safe," Thorne offered encouragingly.

"Oh—no, it's not that," Nicol said. "I was just thinking about my sisters. Time was I couldn't wait to get away from them. Now I can't wait to see them again."

"What are you plans now?" Miles asked.

"I'll stop at Escobar, first," she replied. "It's a good nexus crossing, from there I should be able to work my way back to Earth. From Earth I can get to Orient IV, and from there I'm sure I can get home."

"Is home your goal now?"

"There's a lot more galaxy to be seen out this way," Thorne pointed out. "I'm not sure if Dendarii rosters can be stretched to include a ship's musician, but—"

She was shaking her head. "Home," she said firmly. "I'm tired of fighting one-gee all the time. I'm tired of being alone. I'm starting to have nightmares about growing legs."

Thorne sighed faintly.

"We do have a little colony of downsiders living among us now," she added suggestively to Thorne. "They've fitted out their own asteroid with artificial gravity—quite like the real thing downside, only not as drafty."

Miles was faintly alarmed—to lose a ship commander of proven loyalty—

"Ah," said Thorne in a pensive tone to match Nicol's. "A long way from my home, your asteroid belt."

"Will you return to Beta Colony, then, someday?" she asked. "Or are the Dendarii Mercenaries your home and family?"

"Not quite that passionate, for me," said Thorne. "I mainly stick around due to an overwhelming curiosity to see what happens next." Thorne favored Miles with a peculiar smile.

Thorne helped load Nicol back into her blue cup. After a brief systems check she was hovering upright again, as mobile—more mobile—than her legged companions. She rocked and regarded Thorne brightly.

"It's only three more days to Escobar orbit," said Thorne to Nicol rather regretfully. "Still—seventy-two hours. 4,320 minutes. How much can you do in 4,320 minutes?"

Or how often, thought Miles dryly. *Especially if you don't sleep.* Sleep, per se, was not what Bel had in mind, if Miles recognized the signs. Good luck—to both of them.

"Meanwhile," Thorne maneuvered Nicol into the corridor, "let me show you around the ship. Illyrican-built—that's out your way a bit, I understand. It's quite a story, how the *Ariel* first fell into Dendarii hands—we were the Oseran Mercenaries, back then—"

Nicol made encouraging noises. Miles suppressed an envious grin, and turned the other way up the corridor, to search out Dr. Canaba and arrange the discharge of his last unpleasant duty.

Bemusedly, Miles set aside the hypospray he'd been turning over in his hands as the door to sickbay sighed open. He swivelled in the medtech's station chair and glanced up as Taura and Sergeant Anderson entered. "My *word,*" he murmured.

Anderson sketched a salute. "Reporting as ordered, sir." Taura's hand twitched, uncertain whether to attempt to mimic this military greeting or not. Miles gazed up at Taura and his lips parted with involuntary delight. Taura's transformation was all he'd dreamed of and more.

He didn't know how Anderson had persuaded the stores computer to so exceed its normal parameters, but somehow she'd made it disgorge a complete Dendarii undress kit in Taura's size: crisp grey-

and-white pocketed jacket, grey trousers, polished ankle-topping boots. Taura's face and hair were clean enough to outshine her boots. Her dark hair was now drawn back in a thick, neat, and rather mysterious braid coiling up the back of her head—Miles could not make out where the ends went—and glinting with unexpected mahogany highlights.

She looked, if not exactly well-fed, at least less rawly starving, her eyes bright and interested, not the haunted yellow flickers in bony caverns he'd first seen. Even from this distance he could tell that rehydration and the chance to brush her teeth and fangs had cured the ketone-laced breath that several days in Ryoval's sub-basement on a diet of raw rats and nothing had produced. The dirt-encrusted scale was smoothed away from her huge hands, and—inspired touch—her clawed nails had been, not blunted, but neatened and sharpened, and then enamelled with an iridescent pearl-white polish that complemented her grey-and-whites like a flash of jewelry. The polish had to have been shared out of some personal stock of the sergeant's.

"Outstanding, Anderson," said Miles in admiration.

Anderson smirked proudly. "That about what you had in mind, sir?"

"Yes, it was." Taura's face reflected his delight straight back at him. "What did you think of your first wormhole jump?" he asked her.

Her long lips rippled, what happened when she tried to purse them, Miles guessed. "I was afraid I was getting sick, I was so dizzy all of a sudden, till Sergeant Anderson explained what it was."

"No little hallucinations, or odd time-stretching effects?"

"No, but it wasn't—well, it was quick, anyway."

"Hm. It doesn't sound like you're one of the fortunates—or unfortunates—to be screened for Jump pilot aptitudes. From the talents you demonstrated on Ryoval's landing pad yesterday morning, Tactics should be loathe to lose you to Nav and Com." Miles paused. "Thank you, Laureen. What did my page interrupt?"

"Routine systems checks on the drop shuttles, putting them to bed. I was having Taura look over my shoulder while I worked."

"Right, carry on. I'll send Taura back to you when she's done here."

Anderson exited reluctantly, clearly curious. Miles waited till the doors swished closed to speak again. "Sit down, Taura. So your first twenty-four hours with the Dendarii have been satisfactory?"

She grinned, settling herself carefully in a station chair, which creaked. "Just fine."

"Ah." He hesitated. "You understand, when we reach Escobar, you do have the option to go your own way. You're not compelled to join us. I could see you got some kind of start, downside there."

"What?" Her eyes widened in dismay. "No! I mean . . . do I eat too much?"

"Not at all! You fight like four men, we can bloody well afford to feed you like three. But . . . I need to set a few things straight, before you make your trainee's oath." He cleared his throat. "I didn't come to Ryoval's to recruit you. A few weeks before Bharaputra sold you, do you remember Dr. Canaba injecting something into your leg? With a needle, not a hypospray."

"Oh, yes." She rubbed her calf half-consciously. "It made a knot."

"What, ah, did he tell you it was?"

"An immunization."

She'd been right, Miles reflected, when they'd first met. Humans did lie a lot. "Well, it wasn't an immunization. Canaba was using you as a live repository for some engineered biological material. Molecularly bound, dormant material," he added hastily as she twisted around and looked at her leg in disquiet. "It can't activate spontaneously, he assures me. My original mission was only to pick up Dr. Canaba. But he wouldn't leave without his gene complexes."

"He planned to take me with him?" she said in thrilled surprise. "So I should thank *him* for sending you to me!"

Miles wished he could see the look on Canaba's face if she did. "Yes and no. Specifically, no." He rushed roughly on before his nerve failed him. "You have nothing to thank him for, nor me either. He meant to take only your tissue sample, and sent me to get it."

"Would you rather have left me at—is that why Escobar—" she was still bewildered.

"It was your good luck," Miles plunged on, "that I'd lost my men and was disarmed when we finally met. Canaba lied to me, too. In his defense, he seems to have had some dim idea of saving you from a brutal life as Ryoval's slave. He sent me to kill you, Taura. He sent me to slay a monster, when he should have been begging me to rescue a princess in disguise. I'm not too pleased with Dr. Canaba. Nor with myself. I lied through my teeth to you down in Ryoval's basement, because I thought I had to, to survive and win."

Her face was confused, congealing, the light in her eyes fading. "Then you didn't . . . really think I was human—"

"On the contrary. Your choice of test was an excellent one. It's much harder to lie with your body than with your mouth. When I, er, demonstrated my belief, it had to be real." Looking at her, he still felt a twinge of lurching, lunatic joy, somatic residual from that adven-

ture-of-the-body. He supposed he always would feel something—
male conditioning, no doubt. "Would you like me to demonstrate it
again?" he asked half-hopefully, then bit his tongue. "No," he answered his own question. "If I am to be your commander—we have
these non-fraternization rules. Mainly to protect those of lower rank
from exploitation, though it can work both—ahem!" He was di-
gressing dreadfully. He picked up the hypospray, fiddled with it
nervously, and put it back down.

"Anyway, Dr. Canaba has asked me to lie to you again. He wanted
me to sneak up on you with a general anesthetic, so he could biopsy
back his sample. He's a coward, you may have noticed. He's outside
now, shaking in his shoes for fear you'll find out what he intended for
you. I think a local zap with a medical stunner would suffice. I'd sure
want to be conscious and watching if he were working on *me*, anyway." He flicked the hypospray contemptuously with one finger.

She sat silent, her strange wolfish face—though Miles was getting
used to it—unreadable. "You want me to let him . . . cut into my
leg?" she said at last.

"Yes."

"Then what?"

"Then nothing. That will be the last of Dr. Canaba for you, and
Jackson's Whole and all the rest of it. That, I promise. Though if
you're doubtful of my promises, I can understand why."

"The last . . ." she breathed. Her face lowered, then rose, and her
shoulders straightened. "Then let's get it over with." There was no
smile to her long mouth now.

Canaba, as Miles expected, was not happy to be presented with a
conscious subject. Miles truly didn't care how unhappy Canaba was
about it, and after one look at his cold face, Canaba didn't argue.
Canaba took his sample wordlessly, packaged it carefully in the bio-
tainer, and fled with it back to the safety and privacy of his own cabin
as soon as he decently could.

Miles sat with Taura in sickbay till the medical stun wore off
enough for her to walk without stumbling. She sat without speaking
for a long time. He watched her still features, wishing beyond measure he knew how to re-light those gold eyes.

"When I first saw you," she said softly, "it was like a miracle.
Something magic. Everything I'd wished for, longed for. Food. Wa-
ter. Heat. Revenge. Escape." She gazed down at her polished claws,
"Friends . . ." and glanced up at him, ". . . touching."

"What else do you wish for, Taura?" Miles asked earnestly.

Slowly she replied. "I wish I were normal."

Miles was silent too. "I can't give you what I don't possess myself," he said at length. The words seemed to lie in inadequate lumps between them. He roused himself to a better effort. "No. Don't wish that. I have a better idea. Wish to be yourself. To the hilt. Find out what you're best at, and develop it. Hopscotch your weaknesses. There isn't time for them. Look at Nicol—"

"So beautiful," sighed Taura.

"Or look at Captain Thorne, and tell me what 'normal' is, and why I should give a damn for it. Look at me, if you will. Should I kill myself trying to overcome men twice my weight and reach in unarmed combat, or should I shift the ground to where their muscle is useless, 'cause it never gets close enough to apply its strength? I haven't got *time* to lose, and neither have you."

"Do you know how little time?" demanded Taura suddenly.

"Ah . . ." said Miles cautiously, "do you?"

"I am the last survivor of my creche mates. How could I not know?" Her chin lifted defiantly.

"Then don't wish to be normal," said Miles passionately, rising to pace. "You'll only waste your precious time in futile frustration. Wish to be great! That at least you have a fighting chance for. Great at whatever you are. A great trooper, a great sergeant. A great quartermaster, for God's sake, if that's what comes with ease. A great musician like Nicol—only think how horrible if she were wasting her talents trying to be merely normal." Miles paused self-consciously in his pep talk, thinking, *Easier to preach than practice. . . .*

Taura studied her polished claws, and sighed. "I suppose it's useless for me to wish to be beautiful, like Sergeant Anderson."

"It is useless for you to try to be beautiful *like* anyone but yourself," said Miles. "Be beautiful like Taura, ah, that you can do. Superbly well." He found himself gripping her hands, and ran one finger across an iridescent claw, "Though Laureen seems to have grasped the principle, you might be guided by her taste."

"Admiral," said Taura slowly, not releasing his hands, "are you actually my commander yet? Sergeant Anderson said something about orientation, and induction tests, and an oath. . . ."

"Yes, all that will come when we make fleet rendezvous. Till then, technically, you're our guest."

A certain sparkle was beginning to return to her gold eyes. "Then —till then—it wouldn't break any Dendarii rules, would it, if you showed me again how human I am? One more time?"

It must be, Miles thought, akin to the same drive that used to propel men to climb sheer rock faces without an antigrav belt, or jump out of ancient aircraft with nothing to stop them going splat but a wad of silk cloth. He felt the fascination rising in him, the death-defying laugh. "Slowly?" he said in a strangled voice. "Do it right this time? Have a little conversation, drink a little wine, play a little music? Without Ryoval's guard squad lurking overhead, or ice cold rock under my . . ."

Her eyes were huge and gold and molten. "You did say you liked to practice what you were great at."

Miles had never realized how susceptible he was to flattery from tall women. A weakness he must guard against. Sometime.

They retired to his cabin and practiced assiduously till halfway to Escobar.

3

"Whatever happened to the wolf girl?" inquired Illyan after a long, fascinated silence.

"Ah. She's doing well, I'm glad to say. She made sergeant not long ago. My Dendarii fleet surgeon has her on some meds to slow her metabolism down a bit. Somewhat experimental."

"Will they increase her life-span, then?"

Miles shrugged. "I wish we knew. Maybe. We're hoping."

"Well." Illyan shifted. "That leaves Dagoola, about which, I might remind you, the only report I had from you before the other operatives took over was that, er, excessively succinct one you filed from Mahata Solaris."

"That was only meant to be preliminary. I thought I'd be reporting home sooner than this."

"That's not a problem—or at any rate, not a problem for Count Vorvolk. Dagoola, Miles. Cough it up, and then you can get some sleep."

Miles frowned wearily. "It started out so simply. Almost as simple as the Jackson's Whole job. Then things went wrong. Then things went very wrong. . . ."

"So begin at the beginning."

"The beginning. God. Well . . ."

"The Borders of Infinity"

How could I have died and gone to hell without noticing the transition?

The opalescent force dome capped a surreal and alien landscape, frozen for a moment by Miles's disorientation and dismay. The dome defined a perfect circle, half a kilometer in diameter. Miles stood just inside its edge, where the glowing concave surface dove into the hard-packed dirt and disappeared. His imagination followed the arc buried beneath his feet to the far side, where it erupted again to complete the sphere. It was like being trapped inside an eggshell. An unbreakable eggshell.

Within was a scene from an ancient limbo. Dispirited men and women sat, or stood, or mostly lay down, singly or in scattered irregular groups, across the breadth of the arena. Miles's eye searched anxiously for some remnant of order or military grouping, but the inhabitants seemed splashed randomly as a liquid across the ground.

Perhaps he had been killed just now, just entering this prison camp. Perhaps his captors had betrayed him to his death, like those ancient Earth soldiers who had lured their victims sheeplike into poisoned showers, diverting and soothing their suspicions with stone soap, until their final enlightenment burst upon them in a choking cloud. Perhaps the annihilation of his body had been so swift, his neurons had not had time to carry the information to his brain. Why else did so many antique myths agree that hell was a circular place?

Dagoola IV Top Security Prison Camp #3. This was it? This naked . . . dinner plate? Miles had vaguely visioned barracks, marching guards, daily head counts, secret tunnels, escape committees.

It was the dome that made it all so simple, Miles realized. What need for barracks to shelter prisoners from the elements? The dome did it. What need for guards? The dome was generated from without. Nothing inside could breach it. No need for guards, or head counts. Tunnels were a futility, escape committees an absurdity. The dome did it all.

The only structures were what appeared to be big grey plastic mushrooms evenly placed about every hundred meters around the perimeter of the dome. What little activity there was seemed clustered around them. Latrines, Miles recognized.

Miles and his three fellow prisoners had entered through a temporary portal, which had closed behind them before the brief bulge of force dome containing their entry vanished in front of them. The nearest inhabitant of the dome, a man, lay a few meters away upon a sleeping mat identical to the one Miles now clutched. He turned his head slightly to stare at the little party of newcomers, smiled sourly, and rolled over on his side with his back to them. Nobody else nearby even bothered to look up.

"Holy shit," muttered one of Miles's companions. He and his two buddies drew together unconsciously. The three had been from the same unit once, they'd said. Miles had met them bare minutes ago, in their final stages of processing, where they had all been issued their total supply of worldly goods for life in Dagoola #3.

A single pair of loose grey trousers. A matching short-sleeved grey tunic. A rectangular sleeping mat, rolled up. A plastic cup. That was all. That, and the new numbers encoded upon their skins. It bothered Miles intensely that their captors had chosen to locate the numbers in the middle of their backs, where they couldn't see them. He resisted a futile urge to twist and crane his neck anyway, though his hand snaked up under his shirt to scratch a purely psychosomatic itch. You couldn't feel the encode either.

Some motion appeared in the tableau. A group of four or five men approaching. The welcoming committee at last? Miles was desperate for information. Where among all these countless grey men and women—no, not countless, Miles told himself firmly. They were all accounted for here.

The battered remnants of the 3rd and 4th Armored All-Terrain

Rangers. The ingenious and tenacious civilian defenders of Garson Transfer Station. Winoweh's 2nd Battalion had been captured almost intact. And the 14th Commandos, survivors of the high-tech fortress at Fallow Core. Particularly the survivors of Fallow Core. Ten thousand, two hundred fourteen exactly. The plant Marilac's finest. Ten thousand, two hundred fifteen, counting himself. Ought he to count himself?

The welcoming committee drew up in a ragged bunch a few meters away. They looked tough and tall and muscular and not noticeably friendly. Dull, sullen eyes, full of a deadly boredom that even their present calculation did not lighten.

The two groups, the five and the three, sized each other up. The three turned, and started walking stiffly and prudently away. Miles realized belatedly that he, not a part of either group, was thus left alone.

Alone and immensely conspicuous. Self-consciousness, body-consciousness, normally held at bay by the simple fact that he didn't have time to waste on it, returned to him with a rush. Too short, too odd-looking—his legs were even in length now, after the last operation, but surely not long enough to outrun these five. And where did one run to, in this place? He crossed off flight as an option.

Fight? Get serious.

This isn't going to work, he realized sadly, even as he started walking toward them. But it was more dignified than being chased down with the same result.

He tried to make his smile austere rather than foolish. No telling whether he succeeded. "Hi, there. Can you tell me where to find Colonel Guy Tremont's 14th Commando Division?"

One of the five snorted sardonically. Two moved behind Miles.

Well, a snort was almost speech. Expression, anyway. A start, a toehold. Miles focused on that one. "What's your name and rank and company, soldier?"

"No ranks in here, mutant. No companies. No soldiers. No nothing."

Miles glanced around. Surrounded, of course. Naturally. "You got some friends, anyway."

The talker almost smiled. "You don't."

Miles wondered if perhaps he had been premature in crossing off flight as an option. "I wouldn't count on that if I were—*unh!*" The kick to his kidneys, from behind, cut him off—he damn near bit his tongue—he fell, dropping bedroll and cup and landing in a tangle. A barefoot kick, no combat boots this time, thank God—by the rules of

Newtonian physics, his attackers' foot ought to hurt just as much as his back. Fine. Jolly. Maybe they'd bruise their knuckles, punching him out. . . ."

One of the gang gathered up Miles's late wealth, cup and bedroll. "Want his clothes? They're too little for me."

"Naw."

"Yeah," said the talker. "Take 'em anyway. Maybe bribe one of the women."

The tunic was jerked off over Miles's head, the pants over his feet. Miles was too busy protecting his head from random kicks to fight much for his clothes, trying obliquely to take as many hits as possible on his belly or ribcage, not arms or legs or jaw. A cracked rib was surely the most injury he could afford right now, here, at the beginning. A broken jaw would be the worst.

His assailants desisted only a little before they discovered by experimentation the secret weakness of his bones.

"*That's* how it is in here, mutant," said the talker, slightly winded.

"I was born naked," Miles panted from the dirt. "Didn't stop me."

"Cocky little shit," said the talker.

"Slow learner," remarked another.

The second beating was worse than the first. Two cracked ribs at least—his jaw barely escaped being smashed, at the cost of something painfully wrong in his left wrist, flung up as a shield. This time Miles resisted the impulse to offer any verbal parting shots. He lay in the dirt and wished he could pass out.

He lay a long time, cradled in pain. He was not sure how long. The illumination from the force dome was even and shadowless, unchanging. Timeless, like eternity. Hell was eternal, was it not? This place had too damn many congruencies with hell, that was certain.

And here came another demon. . . . Miles blinked the approaching figure into focus. A man, as bruised and naked as Miles himself, gaunt-ribbed, starveling, knelt in the dirt a few meters away. His face was bony, aged by stress—he might have been forty, or fifty—or twenty-five.

His eyes were unnaturally prominent, due to the shrinking of his flesh. Their whites seemed to gleam feverishly against the dirt darkening his skin. Dirt, not beard stubble—every prisoner in here, male and female, had their hair cut short and the air follicles stunned to prevent re-growth. Perpetually clean-shaven and crew-cut. Miles had undergone the same process bare hours ago. But whoever had processed this fellow must have been in a hurry. The hair stunner had missed a line of his cheek and a few dozen hairs grew there like a stripe on a badly-mown lawn. Even curled as they were, Miles could see they were several centimeters long, draggling down past the man's jaw. If only he knew how fast hair grew, he could calculate how long this fellow had been here. *Too long, whatever the numbers,* Miles thought with an inward sigh.

The man had the broken-off bottom half of a plastic cup, which he pushed cautiously toward Miles. His breath whistled raggedly past his yellowish teeth, from exertion or excitement or disease—probably not disease, they were all well immunized here. Escape, even through death, was not that easy. Miles rolled over and propped himself stiffly on his elbow, regarding his visitor through the thinning haze of his aches and pains.

The man scrabbled back slightly, smiled nervously. He nodded toward the cup. "Water. Better drink. The cup's cracked, and it all leaks out if you wait too long."

"Thanks," croaked Miles. A week ago, or in a previous lifetime, depending on how you counted time, Miles had dawdled over a selection of wines, dissatisfied with this or that nuance of flavor. His lips cracked as he grinned in memory. He drank. It was perfectly ordinary water, lukewarm, faintly redolent of chlorine and sulfur. *A refined body, but the bouquet is a bit presumptuous. . . .*

The man squatted in studied politeness until Miles finished drinking, then leaned forward on his knuckles in restrained urgency. "Are you the One?"

Miles blinked. "Am I the what?"

"The One. The *other* one, I should say. The scripture says there has to be two."

"Uh," Miles hesitated cautiously, "what exactly does the scripture say?"

The man's right hand wrapped over his knobby left wrist, around which was tied a rag screwed into a sort of rope. He closed his eyes; his lips moved a moment, and then he recited aloud, ". . . but the pilgrims went up that hill with ease, because they had these two men to lead them by the arms; also they had left their garments behind them, for though they went in with them, they came out without them." His eyes popped back open to stare hopefully at Miles.

So, now we begin to see why this guy seems to be all by himself. . . . "Are you, perchance, the other One?" Miles shot at a venture.

The man nodded, shyly.

"I see. Um . . ." How was it that he always attracted the nut cases? He licked the last drops of water from his lips. The fellow might have some screws loose, but he was certainly an improvement over the last lot, always presuming he didn't have another personality or two of the homicidal loonie variety tucked away in his head. No, in that case he'd be introducing himself as the Chosen Two, and not be looking for outside assistance. "Um . . . what's your name?"

"Suegar."

"Suegar. Right, all right. My name is Miles, by the way."

"Huh." Suegar grimaced in a sort of pleased irony. "Your name means 'soldier,' did you know?"

"Uh, yeah, so I've been told."

"But you're not a soldier . . . ?"

No subtle expensive trick of clothing line or uniform style here to hide from himself, if no one else, the peculiarities of his body. Miles flushed. "They were taking anything, toward the end. They made me a recruiting clerk. I never did get to fire my gun. Listen, Suegar— how did you come to know you were the One, or at any rate one of the Ones? Is it something you've always known?"

"It came on me gradually," confessed Suegar, shifting to sit cross-legged. "I'm the only one in here with the words, y'see." He caressed his rag rope again. "I've hunted all up and down the camp, but they only mock me. It was a kind of process of elimination, y'see, when they all gave up but me."

"Ah." Miles too sat up, only gasping a little in pain. Those ribs were going to be murder for the next few days. He nodded toward the rope bracelet. "Is that where you keep your scripture? Can I see it?" And how the hell had Suegar ever gotten a plastic flimsy, or loose piece of paper or whatever, in here?

Suegar clutched his arms protectively to his chest and shook his head. "They've been trying to take them from me for months, y'see. I can't be too careful. Until you prove you're the One. The devil can quote scripture, y'know."

Yes, that was rather what I had in mind. . . . Who knew what opportunities Suegar's "scripture" might contain? Well, maybe later. For now, keep dancing. "Are there any other signs?" asked Miles. "You see, I don't know that I'm your One, but on the other hand I don't know I'm not, either. I just got here, after all."

Suegar shook his head again. "It's only five or six sentences, y'see. You have to interpolate a lot."

I'll bet. Miles did not voice the comment aloud. "However did you come by it? Or get it in here?"

"It was at Port Lisma, y'see, just before we were captured," said Suegar. "House-to-house fighting. One of my boot heels had come a bit loose, and it clicked when I walked. Funny, with all that barrage coming down around our ears, how a little thing like that can get under your skin. There was this bookcase with a glass front, real antique books made of paper—I smashed it open with my gun butt and tore out part of a page from one, and folded it up to stick in my boot heel, to make a sort of shim, y'see, and stop the clicking. Didn't look at the book. Didn't even know it was scripture till later. At least, I think it's scripture. It sounds like scripture, anyway. It must be scripture."

Suegar twisted his beard hairs nervously around his finger. "When we were waiting to be processed, I'd pulled it out of my boot, just idle-like, y'know. I had it in my hand—the processing guard saw it, but he just didn't take it away from me. Probably thought it was just a harmless piece of paper. Didn't know it was scripture. I still had it in my hand when we were dumped in here. D'you know, it's the only piece of writing in this whole camp?" he added rather proudly. "It must be scripture."

"Well . . . you take good care of it, then," advised Miles kindly. "If you've preserved it this long, it was obviously meant to be your job."

"Yeah . . ." Suegar blinked. Tears? "I'm the only one in here with a job, aren't I? So I must be one of the Ones."

"Sounds good to me," said Miles agreeably. "Say, ah," he glanced around the vast featureless dome, "how do you find your way around in here, anyway?" The place was decidedly undersupplied with landmarks. It reminded Miles of nothing so much as a penguin rookery. Yet penguins seemed able to find their rocky nests. He was going to have to start thinking like a penguin—or get a penguin to direct him. He studied his guide bird, who had gone absent and was doodling in the dirt. Circles, naturally.

"Where's the mess hall?" Miles asked more loudly. "Where did you get that water?"

"Water taps are on the outside of the latrines," said Suegar, "but they only work part of the time. No mess hall. We just get rat bars. Sometimes."

"Sometimes?" said Miles angrily. He could count Suegar's ribs. "Dammit, the Cetagandans are claiming loudly to be treating their POW's by Interstellar Judiciary Commission rules. So many square meters of space per person, 3,000 calories a day, at least fifty grams of protein, two liters of drinking water—you should be getting at least two IJC standard ration bars a day. Are they starving you?"

"After a while," Suegar sighed, "you don't really care if you get yours or not." The animation that his interest in Miles as a new and hopeful object in his world had lent Suegar seemed to be falling away. His breathing had slowed, his posture slumped. He seemed about to lie down in the dirt. Miles wondered if Suegar's sleeping mat had suffered the same fate as his own. Quite some time ago, probably.

"Look, Suegar—I think I may have a relative in this camp somewhere. A cousin of my mother's. D'you think you could help me find him?"

"It might be good for you, to have a relative," Suegar agreed. "It's not good to be by yourself, here."

"Yeah, I found that out. But how can you find anyone? It doesn't look too organized."

"Oh, there's—there's groups and groups. Everyone pretty much stays in the same place after a while."

"He was in the 14th Commandos. Where are they?"

"None of the *old* groups are left, much."

"He was Colonel Tremont. Colonel Guy Tremont."

"Oh, an officer." Suegar's forehead wrinkled in worry. "That makes it harder. You weren't an officer, were you? Better not let on, if you were—"

"I was a clerk," repeated Miles.

"—because there's groups here who don't like officers. A clerk. You're probably OK, then."

"Were you an officer, Suegar?" asked Miles curiously.

Suegar frowned at him, twisted his beard hairs. "Marilac Army's gone. If there's no army, it can't have officers, can it?"

Miles wondered briefly if he might get farther faster by just walking away from Suegar and trying to strike up a conversation with the next random prisoner he came across. Groups and groups. And, presumably, groups, like the five burly surly brothers. He decided to stick with Suegar for a while longer. For one thing, he wouldn't feel quite so naked if he wasn't naked by himself.

"Can you take me to anybody who used to be in the 14th?" Miles urged Suegar anew. "Anybody, who might know Tremont by sight."

"You don't know him?"

"We'd never met in person. I've seen vids of him. But I'm afraid his appearance may be . . . changed, by now."

Suegar touched his own face pensively. "Yeah, probably."

Miles clambered painfully to his feet. The temperature in the dome was just a little cool, without clothes. A voiceless draft raised the hairs on his arms. If he could just get one garment back, would he prefer his pants, to cover his genitals, or his shirt, to disguise his crooked back? Screw it. No time. He held out a hand to help Suegar up. "Come on."

Suegar glanced up at him. "You can always tell a newcomer. You're still in a hurry. In here, you slow down. Your brain slows down. . . ."

"Your scripture got anything to say on that?" inquired Miles impatiently.

"'. . . they therefore went up here with much agility and speed, through the foundation of the city . . .'" Twin verticals appeared between Suegar's eyebrows, as he frowned speculatively at Miles.

Thank you, thought Miles. *I'll take it.* He pulled Suegar up. "Come on, then."

Neither agility nor speed, but at least progress. Suegar led him on a shambling walk across a quarter of the camp, through some groups, in wide arcs around others. Miles saw the surly brothers again at a distance, sitting on their collection of mats. Miles upped his estimation of the size of the tribe from five to about fifteen. Some men sat in twos or threes or sixes, a few sat alone, as far as possible from any others, which still wasn't very far.

The largest group by far consisted entirely of women. Miles studied them with electric interest as soon as his eyes picked up the size of their unmarked boundary. There were several hundred of them at least. None were matless, although some shared. Their perimeter was actually patrolled, by groups of half a dozen or so strolling slowly about. They apparently defended two latrines for their exclusive use.

"Tell me about the girls, Suegar," Miles urged his companion, with a nod toward their group.

"Forget the girls." Suegar's grin actually had a sardonic edge. "They do not put out."

"What, not at all? None of them? I mean, here we all are, with nothing to do but entertain each other. I'd think at least some of them would be interested." Miles's reason raced ahead of Suegar's answer, mired in unpleasantness. How unpleasant did it get in here?

For answer, Suegar pointed upward to the dome. "You know we're all monitored in here. They can see everything, pick up every word if they want. That is, if there's still anybody out there. They may have all gone away, and just forgotten to turn the dome off. I have dreams about that, sometimes. I dream that I'm here, in this dome, forever. Then I wake up, and I'm here, in this dome. . . . Sometimes I'm not sure if I'm awake or asleep. Except that the food is still coming, and once in a while—not so often, anymore—somebody new, like you. The food could be automated, though, I suppose. You could be a dream. . . ."

"They're still out there," said Miles grimly.

Suegar sighed. "You know, in a way, I'm almost glad."

Monitored, yes. Miles knew all about the monitoring. He put down an urge to wave and call *Hi, Mom!* Monitoring must be a stultifying job for the goons out there. He wished they might be bored to death. "But what's that got to do with the girls, Suegar?"

"Well, at first everybody was pretty inhibited by that—" he pointed skywards again. "Then after a while we discovered that they didn't interfere with anything we did. At all. There were some rapes. . . . Since then things have been—deteriorating."

"Hm. Then I suppose the idea of starting a riot, and breaching the dome when they bring troops inside to restore order, is a no-go?"

"That was tried once, a long time ago. Don't know how long." Suegar twisted his hairs. "They don't have to come inside to stop a riot. They can reduce the dome's diameter—they reduced it to about a hundred meters, that time. Nothing to stop them reducing it down to one meter, with all of us still inside, if they choose. It stopped the riot, anyway. Or they can reduce the gas permeability of the dome to zilch and just let us breathe ourselves into a coma. That's happened twice."

"I see," said Miles. It made his neck crawl.

A bare hundred or so meters away, the side of the dome began to bulge inward like an aneurysm. Miles touched Suegar's arm. "What's happening there? More new prisoners being delivered?"

Suegar glanced around. "Uh oh. We're not in a real good position, here." He hovered a moment, as if uncertain whether to go forward or back.

A wave of movement rippled through the camp from the bulge outward, of people getting to their feet. Faces turned magnetically toward the side of the dome. Little knots of men came together; a few sprinters began running. Some people didn't get up at all. Miles glanced back towards the women's group. About half of them were forming rapidly into a sort of phalanx.

"We're so close—what the hell, maybe we've got a chance," said Suegar. "Come on!" He started toward the bulge at his most rapid pace, a jog. Miles perforce jogged too, trying to jar his ribs as little as possible. But he was quickly winded, and his rapid breathing added an excruciating torque to his torso.

"What are we doing?" Miles started to pant to Suegar, before the dome's extruding bulge dissolved with a fading twinkle, and he saw what they were doing, saw it all.

Before the force dome's shimmering barrier now sat a dark brown pile, roughly a meter high, two meters deep, three meters wide. IJC standard ration bars, Miles recognized. Rat bars, apocryphally named after their supposed principal ingredient. Fifteen hundred calories each. Twenty-five grams of protein, fifty percent of the human MDR for vitamins A, B, C, and the rest of the alphabet—tasted like a shingle sprinkled with sugar and would sustain life and health forever or for as long as you could stand to keep eating them.

Shall we have a contest, children, to guess how many rat bars are in that pile? Miles thought. *No contest. I don't even have to measure the height and divide by three centimeters. It has to be 10,215 exactly. How ingenious.*

The Cetagandan Psy Ops corps must contain some remarkable minds. If they ever fell into his hands, Miles wondered, should he recruit them—or exterminate them? This brief fantasy was overwhelmed by the need to keep to his feet in the present reality, as 10,000 or so people, minus the wholly despairing and those too weak to move, all tried to descend on the same six square meters of the camp at once.

The first sprinters reached the pile, grabbed up armloads of rat bars, and started to sprint off. Some made it to the protection of friends, divided their spoils, and started to move away from the center of the growing human maelstrom. Others failed to dodge clots of operators like the burly surly brothers, and were violently relieved of their prizes. The second wave of sprinters, who didn't get away in time, were pinned up against the side of the dome by the incoming bodies.

Miles and Suegar, unfortunately, were in this second category. Miles's view was reduced to a sweating, heaving, stinking, swearing mass of elbows and chests and backs.

"Eat, eat!" Suegar urged around stuffed cheeks as he and Miles were separated by the pack. But the bar Miles had grabbed was twisted out of his hands before he had gathered his wits enough to follow Suegar's advice. Anyway, his hunger was nothing to his terror of being crushed, or worse, falling underfoot. His own feet pummeled over something soft, but he was unable to push back with enough strength to give the person—man, woman, who knew?—a chance to get up again.

In time the press lessened, and Miles found the edge of the crowd and broke free again. He staggered a little way off and fell to the dirt to sit, shaken and shaking, pale and cold. His breath rasped unevenly in his throat. It took him a long time to get hold of himself again.

Sheer chance, that this had hit his rawest nerve, his darkest fears, threatened his most dangerous weakness. *I could die here,* he realized, *without ever seeing the enemy's face.* But there seemed to be no new bones broken, except possibly in his left foot. He was not too sure about his left foot. The elephant who had trod on it was surely getting more than his fair share of rat bars.

All right, Miles thought at last. *That's enough time spent on R&R. On your feet, soldier.* It was time to go find Colonel Tremont.

Guy Tremont. The real hero of the siege of Fallow Core. The defiant one, the one who'd held, and held, and held, after General Xian fled, after Baneri was killed.

Xian had sworn to return, but then Xian had run into that meat grinder at Vassily Station. HQ had promised re-supply, but then HQ and its vital shuttleport had been taken by the Cetagandans.

But by this time Tremont and his troops had lost communication. So they held, waiting, and hoping. Eventually resources were reduced to hope and rocks. Rocks were versatile, they could either be boiled for soup or thrown at the enemy. At last Fallow Core was taken. Not surrendered. Taken.

Guy Tremont. Miles wanted very much to meet Guy Tremont.

On his feet and looking around, Miles spotted a distant shambling scarecrow being pelted off from a group with clods of dirt. Suegar paused out of range of their missiles, still pointing to the rag on his wrist and talking. The three or four men he was haranguing turned their backs to him by way of a broad hint.

Miles sighed and started trudging toward him. "Hey, Suegar!" he called and waved when he got closer.

"Oh, there you are." Suegar turned and brightened, and joined him. "I lost you." Suegar rubbed dirt out of his eyebrows. "Nobody wants to listen, y'know?"

"Yeah, well, most of them have heard you at least once by now, right?"

"Pro'bly twenty times. I keep thinking I might have missed one, y'see. Maybe the very One, the other One."

"Well, I'd be glad to listen to you, but I've really got to find Colonel Tremont first. You said you knew somebody . . . ?"

"Oh, right. This way." Suegar led off again.

"Thanks. Say, is every chow call like that last one?"

"Pretty much."

"What's to keep some—group—from just taking over that arc of the dome?"

"It's never issued at the same place twice. They move it all around

the perimeter. There was a lot of strategy debated at one time, as to
whether it was better to be at the center, so's you're never more than
half a diameter away, or near the edge, so's to be up front at least part
of the time. Some guys had even worked out the mathematics of it,
probabilities and all that."

"Which do you favor?"

"Oh, I don't have a spot, I move around and take my chances." His
right hand touched his rag. "It's not the most important thing, anyway. Still, it was good to eat—today. Whatever day this is."

"Today is November 2, '97, Earth Common Era."

"Oh? Is that all?" Suegar pulled his beard strands out straight and
rolled his eyes, attempting to look across his face at them. "Thought
I'd been here longer than that. Why, it hasn't even been three years.
Huh." He added apologetically, "In here it's always today."

"Mm," said Miles. "So the rat bars are always delivered in a pile
like that, eh?"

"Yeah."

"Damned ingenious."

"Yeah," Suegar sighed. Rage, barely breathed, was camouflaged in
that sigh, in the twitch of Suegar's hands. *So, my madman is not so
simple. . . .*

"Here we are," Suegar added. They paused before a group defined
by half a dozen sleeping mats in a rough circle. One man looked up
and glowered.

"Go away, Suegar. I ain't in the mood for a sermon."

"That the colonel?" whispered Miles.

"Naw, his name's Oliver. I knew him—a long time ago. He was at
Fallow Core, though," Suegar whispered back. "He can take you to
him."

Suegar bundled Miles forward. "This is Miles. He's new. Wants to
talk to you." Suegar himself backed away. Helpfully, Miles realized.
Suegar was aware of his unpopularity, it seemed.

Miles studied the next link in his chain. Oliver had managed to
retain his grey pajamas, sleeping mat, and cup intact, which reminded Miles again of his own nakedness. On the other hand, Oliver
did not seem to be in possession of any ill-gotten duplicates. Oliver
might be as burly as the surly brothers, but was not otherwise related.
That was good. Not that Miles in his present state need have any
more worries about thievery.

Oliver stared at Miles without favor, then seemed to relent. "What
d'you want?" he growled.

Miles opened his hands. "I'm looking for Colonel Guy Tremont."

"Ain't no colonels in here, boy."

"He was a cousin of my mother's. Nobody in the family—nobody in the outside world—has heard anything from or about him since Fallow Core fell. I—I'm not from any of the other units or pieces of units that are in here. Colonel Tremont is the only person I know anything about at all." Miles clasped his hands together and tried to look waif-like. Real doubt shook him, drew down his brows. "Is he still alive, even?"

Oliver frowned. "Relative, eh?" He scratched the side of his nose with a thick finger. "I suppose you got a right. But it won't do you any good, boy, if that's what you're thinking."

"I . . ." Miles shook his head. "At this point, I just want to *know.*"

"Come on, then." Oliver levered himself to his feet with a grunt and lumbered off without looking over his shoulder.

Miles limped in his wake. "Are you taking me to him?"

Oliver made no answer until they'd finished their journey, only a few dozen meters, among and between sleeping mats. One man swore, one spat; most ignored them.

One mat lay at the edge of a group, almost far enough away to look alone. A figure lay curled up on his side with his back to them. Oliver stood silent, big fists on hips, and regarded it.

"Is that the colonel?" Miles whispered urgently.

"No, boy." Oliver sucked on his lower lip. "Only his remains."

Miles, alarmed, knelt down. Oliver was speaking poetically. Miles realized with relief. The man breathed. "Colonel Tremont? Sir?"

Miles's heart sank again, as he saw that breathing was about all that Tremont did. He lay inert, his eyes open but fixed on nothing. They did not even flick toward Miles and dismiss him with contempt. He was thin, thinner than Suegar even. Miles traced the angle of his jaw, the shape of his ear, from the holovids he'd studied. The remains of a face, like the ruined fortress of Fallow Core. It took nearly an archeologist's insight to recognize the connections between past and present.

He was dressed, his cup sat upright by his head, but the dirt around his mat was churned to acrid, stinking mud. From urine, Miles realized. Tremont's elbows were marked with lesions, the beginning of decubiti, bedsores. A damp patch on the grey fabric of his trousers over his body hips hinted at more advanced and horrible sores beneath.

Yet somebody must be tending him, Miles thought, *or he wouldn't be looking even this good.*

Oliver knelt beside Miles, bare toes squishing in the mud, and pulled a hunk of rat bar from beneath the elastic waistband of his trousers. He crumbled a bit between his thick fingers and pushed it between Tremont's lips. "Eat," he whispered. The lips almost moved; the crumbs dribbled to the mat. Oliver tried again, seemed to become conscious of Miles's eyes upon him, and stuffed the rest of the rat bar back into his pants with an unintelligible grumble.

"Was—was he injured when Fallow Core was overrun?" asked Miles. "Head injury?"

Oliver shook his head. "Fallow Core wasn't stormed, boy."

"But it fell on October 6th, it was reported, and—"

"It fell on October 5th. Fallow Core was betrayed." Oliver turned and walked away before his stiffened face could betray any emotion.

Miles knelt in the mud and let his breath trickle out slowly.

So. And so.

Was this the end of his quest, then?

He wanted to pace and think, but walking still hurt too much. He hobbled a little way off, trying not to accidentally infringe upon the territory of any sizeable group, and sat, then lay in the dirt with his hands behind his head, staring up at the pearly glow of the dome sealed like a lid over them all.

He considered his options, one, two, three. He considered them carefully. It didn't take long.

I thought you didn't believe in good guys and bad guys? He had cauterized his emotions, he'd thought, coming in here, for his own protection, but he could feel his carefully cultivated impartiality slipping. He was beginning to hate that dome in a really intimate, personal way. Aesthetically elegant, form united with function as perfectly as an eggshell, a marvel of physics—perverted into an instrument of torture.

Subtle torture . . . Miles reviewed the Interstellar Judiciary Commission's rules for the treatment of POW's, to which Cetaganda was a signatory. So many square meters of space per person, yes, they were certainly supplied with that. No prisoner to be solitarily confined for a period exceeding twenty-four hours—right, no solitude in here except by withdrawal into madness. No dark periods longer than twelve hours, that was easy, no dark periods at all, the perpetual glare of noon instead. No beatings—indeed, the guards could say with truth that they never laid a hand on their prisoners. They just watched, while the prisoners beat each other up instead. Rapes, even more strictly forbidden, doubtless handled the same way.

Miles had seen what they could do with their issue of two IJC standard ration bars per person per day. The rat bar riot was a particularly neat touch, he thought. No one could fail to participate (he rubbed his growling stomach). The enemy might have seeded the initial breakdown by sending in a short pile. But maybe not—the first person who snatched two instead of one left another foodless. Maybe next time that one took three, to make up for it, and so it quickly snowballed. Breaking down any hope of order, pitting group against group, person against person in a scrambling dogfight, a twice-a-day reminder of their powerlessness and degradation. None could afford for long to hold themselves aloof unless they wished to embrace slow starvation.

No forced labor—hah, check. That would require the imposition of order. Access to medical personnel—right, the various units' own medics must be mixed in out there somewhere. He re-ran the wording of that paragraph through his memory again—by God, it *did* say "personnel," didn't it? No medicine, just medical personnel. Empty-handed, naked doctors and medtechs. His lips drew back in a mirthless grin. Accurate lists of prisoners taken had been duly dispatched, as required. But no other communication . . .

Communication. This lack of word from the outside world might drive even him crazy shortly. It was as bad as prayer, talking to a God who never talked back. No wonder they all seemed touched with a sort of solipsistic schizophrenia here. Their doubts infected him. *Was* anybody still out there? Could his voice be heard and understood?

Ah, blind faith. The leap of faith. His right hand clenched, as if crushing an eggshell. "This," he enunciated clearly, "calls for a major change of plans."

He drove himself to his feet to go find Suegar again.

Miles found him not far off, hunkered in the dirt doodling. Suegar looked up with a brief smile. "Did Oliver take you to—to your cousin?"

"Yes, but I came too late. He's dying."

"Yeah . . . I was afraid that might be the case. Sorry."

"Me too." Miles was momentarily distracted from his purpose by a practical curiosity. "Suegar, what do they do with dead bodies here?"

"There's a rubbish pile of sorts, over against one side of the dome. The dome sort of extrudes and laps it up every once in a while, same way as food and new prisoners are introduced. Usually by the time a body swells and starts to stink, somebody'll drag it over there. I take 'em sometimes."

"No chance of anybody sneaking out in the rubbish pile, I suppose?"

"They microwave-incinerate it all before the portal's opened."

"Ah." Miles took a deep breath, and launched himself. "Suegar, it's come to me. I *am* the other One."

Suegar nodded serenely, unsurprised. "I'd had it figured."

Miles paused, nonplussed. Was that all the response . . . ? He had expected something more energetic, either pro or con. "It came to me in a vision," he declared dramatically, following his script anyway.

"Oh, yeah?" Suegar's attention sharpened gratifyingly. "I've never gotten a vision," he added with envy. "Had to figure it all out, y'know, from context. What's it like? A trance?"

Shit, and here I thought this guy talked with elves and angels. . . . Miles backed down slightly. "No, it's like a thought, only more compelling. It storms your will—burns like lust, only not so easy to satisfy. Not like a trance, because it drives you outward, not inward." He hesitated, unsettled, having spoken more truth than he'd intended.

Suegar looked vastly encouraged. "Oh, good. I was afraid for a second you might be one of those guys who start talking to people nobody else can see."

Miles glanced upward involuntarily, returned his gaze straightly to Suegar.

"—so that's a vision. Why, I've felt like that." His eyes seemed to focus and intensify.

"Didn't you recognize it in yourself?" asked Miles blandly.

"Not by name . . . it's not a comfortable thing, to be chosen so. I tried to evade it for a long time, but God finds ways of dealing with draft dodgers."

"You're too modest, Suegar. You've believed in your scripture, but not in yourself. Don't you know that when you're given a task, you're given the power to accomplish it as well?"

Suegar sighed in joyous satisfaction. "I knew it was a job for two. It's just like the scripture said."

"Uh, right. So now we are two. But we must be more. I guess we'd better start with your friends."

"That won't take much time," said Suegar wryly. "You got a step two in mind, I hope?"

"Then we'll start with your enemies. Or your nodding acquaintances. We'll start with the first bleeding body that crosses our path. It doesn't matter where we start, because I mean to have them all, in the end. All, to the last and least." A particularly apt quote shot across his memory, and he declaimed vigorously, " 'Those who have ears, let them hear.' All." Miles sent a prayer up from his heart with that one.

"All right," Miles pulled Suegar to his feet, "let's go preach to the unconverted."

Suegar laughed suddenly. "I had a top kick once who used to say, 'Let's go kick some ass,' in just that tone of voice."

"That, too," Miles grimaced. "You understand, universal membership in this congregation won't come all voluntary. But you leave the recruiting to me, hear?"

Suegar stroked his beard hairs, regarded Miles from beneath raised brows. "A clerk, eh?"

"Right."

"Yes, sir."

They started with Oliver.

Miles gestured. "May we step into your office?"

Oliver rubbed his nose with the back of his hand and sniffed. "Let me give you a piece of advice, boy. You ain't gonna make it in here as a stand-up comic. Every joke that can possibly be made has been run into the ground. Even the sick ones."

"Very well." Miles sat cross-legged, near Oliver's mat, but not too near. Suegar hunkered down behind Miles's shoulder, not so welded to the ground, as if ready to skip backwards if necessary. "I'll lay it out straight, then. I don't like the way things are run around here."

Oliver's mouth twisted sardonically; he did not comment aloud. He didn't need to.

"I'm going to change them," Miles added.

"Shit," said Oliver, and rolled back over.

"Starting here and now."

After a moment's silence Oliver added, "Go away or I'll pound you."

Suegar started to get up; Miles irritably motioned him back down.

"He was a commando," Suegar whispered worriedly. "He can break you in half."

"Nine-tenths of the people in this camp can break me in half, including the girls," Miles whispered back. "It's not a significant consideration."

Miles leaned forward, grasped Oliver's chin, and twisted his face back toward him. Suegar sucked his breath through his teeth with a whistle at this dangerous tactic.

"Now, there's this about cynicism, Sergeant. It's the universe's most supine moral position. Real comfortable. If nothing can be done, then you're not some kind of shit for not doing it, and you can lie there and stink to yourself in perfect peace."

Oliver batted Miles's hand down, but did not turn away again. Rage flared in his eyes. "Suegar tell you I was a sergeant?" he hissed.

"No, it's written on your forehead in letters of fire. Listen up, Oliver—"

Oliver rolled over and up as far as supporting his upper body with his knuckles on his sleeping mat. Suegar flinched, but did not flee.

"You listen up, mutant," Oliver snarled. "We've done it all already. We've done drill, and games, and clean living, exercise, and cold showers, except there ain't no cold showers. We've done group sings and floor shows. We've done it by the numbers, by the book, by candlelight. We've done it by force, and made real war on each other. After that we did sin and sex and sadism till we were ready to puke. We've done it all at least ten times. You think you're the first reformer to come through here?"

"No, Oliver," Miles leaned into his face, his eyes boring into Oliver's burning eyes unscorched. His voice fell to a whisper. "I think I'm the last."

Oliver was silent a moment, then barked a laugh. "By God, Suegar has found his soul-mate at last. Two loonies together, just like his scripture says."

Miles paused thoughtfully, sat up as straight as his spine would allow. "Read me your scripture, again, Suegar. The full text." He closed his eyes for total concentration, also to discourage interruptions from Oliver.

Suegar rustled around and cleared his throat nervously. "'For those that shall be the heirs of salvation,'" he began. "'Thus they went along toward the gate. Now you must note that the city stood upon a mighty hill, but the pilgrims went up that hill with ease, because they had these two men to lead them by the arms; also they had left their mortal garments behind them in the river, for though they went in with them, they came out without them. They therefore went up here with much agility and speed, through the foundation upon which the city was framed higher than the clouds. They therefore went up through the regions of the air . . .'" He added apologetically, "It breaks off there. That's where I tore the page. Not sure what that signifies."

"Probably means that after that you're supposed to improvise for yourself," Miles suggested, opening his eyes again. So, that was the raw material he was building on. He had to admit the last line in particular gave him a turn, a chill like a bellyfull of cold worms. So be it. Forward.

"There you are, Oliver. That's what I'm offering. The only hope worth breathing for. Salvation itself."

"Very uplifting," sneered Oliver.

" 'Uplifted' is just what I intend you all to be. You've got to understand, Oliver, I'm a fundamentalist. I take my scriptures *very* literally."

Oliver opened his mouth, then closed it with a snap. Miles had his utter attention.

Communication at last, Miles breathed inwardly. *We have connected.*

"It would take a miracle," said Oliver at last, "to uplift this whole place."

"Mine is not a theology of the elect. I intend to preach to the masses. Even," he was definitely getting into the swing of this, "the sinners. Heaven is for everyone.

"But miracles, by their very nature, must break in from outside. We don't carry them in our pockets—"

"You don't, that's for sure," muttered Oliver with a glance at Miles's undress.

"—we can only pray, and prepare ourselves for a better world. But miracles come only to the prepared. Are you prepared, Oliver?" Miles leaned forward, his voice vibrating with energy.

"Sh· ." Oliver's voice trailed off. He glanced for confirmation, oddly enough, at Suegar. "Is this guy for real?"

"He thinks he's faking it," said Suegar blandly, "but he's not. He's the One, all right and tight."

The cold worms writhed again. Dealing with Suegar, Miles decided, was like fencing in a hall of mirrors. Your target, though real, was never quite where it looked like it should be.

Oliver inhaled. Hope and fear, belief and doubt, intermingled in his face. "How shall we be saved, Rev'rend?"

"Ah—call me Brother Miles, I think. Yes. Tell me—how many converts can you deliver on your own naked, unsupported authority?"

Oliver looked extremely thoughtful. "Just let them see *that* light, and they'll follow it anywhere."

"Well . . . well . . . salvation is for all, to be sure, but there may be certain temporary practical advantages to maintaining a priesthood. I mean, blessed also are they who do not see, and yet believe."

"It's true," agreed Oliver, "that if your religion failed to deliver a miracle, that a human sacrifice would certainly follow."

"Ah . . . quite," Miles gulped. "You are a man of acute insight."

"That's not an insight," said Oliver. "That's a personal guarantee."

"Yes, well . . . to return to my question. How many followers can you raise? I'm talking bodies here, not souls."

Oliver frowned, cautious still. "Maybe twenty."

"Can any of them bring in others? Branch out, hook in more?"

"Maybe."

"Make them your corporals, then. I think we had better disregard any previous ranks here. Call it, ah, the Army of the Reborn. No. The Reformation Army. That scans better. We shall be re-formed. The body has disintegrated like the caterpillar in its chrysalis, into nasty green gook, but we shall re-form into the butterfly and fly away."

Oliver sniffed again. "Just what reforms you planning?"

"Just one, I think. The food."

Oliver gave him a disbelieving stare. "You sure this isn't just a scam to get yourself a free meal?"

"True, I *am* getting hungry . . ." Miles backed off from the joke as Oliver remained icily unimpressed. "But so are a lot of other people. By tomorrow, we can have them all eating out of our hands."

"When would you want these twenty guys?"

"By the next chow call." Good, he'd startled the man.

"That soon?"

"You understand, Oliver, the belief that you have all the time in the world is an illusion this place fosters on purpose. Resist it."

"You're sure in a hurry."

"So, you got a dental appointment? I think not. Besides, I'm only half your mass. I gotta move twice as fast just to keep up the momentum. Twenty, plus. By next chow call."

"What the hell do you think you're gonna be able to do with twenty guys?"

"We're going to take the food pile."

Oliver's lips tightened in disgust. "Not with twenty guys, you're not. No go. Besides, it's been done. I told you we'd made real war in here. It'd be a quick massacre."

"—and then, after we've taken it—we re-distribute it. Fair and square, one rat bar per customer, all controlled and quartermasterly. To sinners and all. By the next chow call everybody who's ever been shorted will be coming over to us. And then we'll be in a position to deal with the hard cases."

"You're nuts. You can't do it. Not with twenty guys."

"Did I say we were only going to have twenty guys? Suegar, did I say that?"

Suegar, listening in rapt fascination, shook his head.

"Well, I ain't sticking my neck out to get pounded unless you can produce some visible means of support," said Oliver. "This could get us killed."

"Can do," Miles promised recklessly. One had to start lifting somewhere; his imaginary bootstraps would do well enough. "I will deliver 500 troops to the sacred cause by chow call."

"You do that, and I'll walk the perimeter of this camp naked on my hands," retorted Oliver.

Miles grinned. "I may hold you to that, Sergeant. Twenty plus. By chow call." Miles stood. "Come on, Suegar."

Oliver waved them off irritably. They retreated in good order. When Miles looked back over his shoulder, Oliver had arisen, and was walking toward a group of occupied mats tangential to his own, waving down an apparent acquaintance.

"So where do we get 500 troops before next chow call?" Suegar asked. "I better warn you, Oliver was the best thing I had. The next is bound to be tougher."

"What," said Miles, "is your faith wavering so soon?"

"I believe," said Suegar, "I just don't see. Maybe that makes me blessed, I dunno."

"I'm surprised. I thought it was pretty obvious. There." Miles pointed across the camp toward the unmarked border of the women's group.

"Oh." Suegar stopped short. "Oh, oh. I don't think so, Miles."

"Yes. Let's go."

"You won't get in there without a change-of-sex operation."

"What, as God-driven as you are, haven't you tried to preach your scripture to them?"

"I tried. Got pounded. Tried elsewhere after that."

Miles paused, and pursed his lips, studying Suegar. "It wasn't defeat, or you wouldn't have hung on long enough to meet me. Was it— ah, shame, that drained your usual resolve? You got something to work off in that quarter?"

Suegar shook his head. "Not personally. Except maybe, sins of omission. I just didn't have the heart to harass 'em any more."

"This whole place is suffering from sins of omission." A relief, that Suegar wasn't some sort of self-confessed rapist. Miles's eyes swept the scene, teasing out the pattern from the limited cues of position, grouping, activity. "Yes . . . predator pressure produces herd behavior. Social—fragmentation here being what it is, the pressure must be pretty high, to hold a group of that size together. But I hadn't noticed any incidents since I got here. . . ."

"It comes and goes," said Suegar. "Phases of the moon or something."

Phases of the moon, right. Miles sent up a prayer of thanks in his heart to whatever gods might be—to Whom it may concern—that the Cetagandans appeared to have implanted some standard time-release anti-ovulant in all their female prisoners, along with their other immunizations. Bless the forgotten individual who'd put *that* clause in the IJC rules, forcing he Cetagandans into more subtle forms of legal torture. And yet, would the presence of pregnancies, infants, and children among the prisoners have been another destabilizing stress—or a stabilizing force deeper and stronger than all the previous loyalties the Cetagandans seemed to have so successfully broken down? From a purely logistical viewpoint, Miles was elated that the question was theoretical.

"Well . . ." Miles took a deep breath, and pulled an imaginary hat down over his eyes at an aggressive angle. "I'm new here, and so temporarily unembarrassed. Let he who is without sin cast the first lure. Besides, I have an advantage for this sort of negotiation. I'm clearly not a threat." He marched forward.

"I'll wait for you here," called Suegar helpfully, and hunkered down where he was.

Miles timed his forward march to intersect a patrol of six women strolling down their perimeter. He arranged himself in front of them and swept off his imaginary hat to hold strategically over his crotch. "Good afternoon, ladies. Allow me to apologize for m'beh—"

His opening line was interrupted by a mouthful of dirt abruptly acquired as his legs were swept backward and his shoulders forward by the four women who had parted around him, dumping him neatly on his face. He had not even managed to spit it out when he found himself plucked up and whirled dizzily through the air, still face-down, by hands grasping his arms and legs. A muttered count of three, and he was soaring in a short forlorn arc, to land in a heap not far from Suegar. The patrollers walked on without another word.

"See what I mean?" said Suegar.

Miles turned his head to look at him. "You had that trajectory calculated to the centimeter, didn't you?" he said smearily.

"Just about," agreed Suegar. "I figured they could heave you quite a bit farther than usual, on account of your size."

Miles scrambled back up to a sitting position, still trying to get his wind. Damn the ribs, which had grown almost bearable, but which now wrung his chest with electric agony at every breath. In a few minutes he got up and brushed himself off. As an afterthought, he picked up his invisible hat, too. Dizzied, he had to brace his hands on his knees a moment.

"All right," he muttered, "back we go."

"Miles—"

"It's gotta be done, Suegar. No other choice. Anyway, I can't quit, once I've started. I've been told I'm pathologically persistent. I *can't* quit."

Suegar opened his mouth to object, then swallowed his protest. "Right," he said. He settled down cross-legged, his right hand unconsciously caressing his rag rope library. "I'll wait till you call me in." He seemed to fall into a reverie, or meditation—or maybe a doze.

Miles's second foray ended precisely like the first, except that his trajectory was perhaps a little wider and a little higher. The third attempt went the same way, but his flight was much shorter.

"Good," he muttered to himself. "Must be tiring 'em out."

This time he skipped in parallel to the patrol, out of reach but well within hearing. "Look," he panted, "you don't have to do this piecemeal. Let me make it easy for you. I have this teratogenic bone disorder—I'm not a mutant, you understand, my genes are normal, it's just their expression got distorted, from my mother being exposed to a certain poison while she was pregnant—it was a one-shot thing, won't affect any children *I* might have—I always felt it was easier to get dates when that was clearly understood, *not* a mutant—anyway, my bones are brittle, in fact any one of you could probably break every one in my body. You may wonder why I'm telling you all this— in fact, I usually prefer not to advertise it—you have to stop and listen to me. I'm not a threat—do I look like a threat?—a challenge, maybe, not a threat—are you going to make me run all around this camp after you? Slow down, for God's sake—" He would be out of wind, and therefore verbal ammunition, very shortly at this rate. He hopped around in front of them and planted himself, arms outstretched.

"—so if you *are* planning to break every bone in my body, please do it now and get it over with, because I'm going to keep coming back here until you do."

At a brief hand signal from their leader the patrol stopped, facing him.

"Take him at his word," suggested a tall redhead. Her short brush of electric copper hair fascinated Miles to distraction; he pictured missing masses of it having fallen to the floor at the clippers of the ruthless Cetagandan prison processors. "I'll break the left arm if you'll break the right, Conr," she continued.

"If that's what it takes to get you to stop and listen to me for five minutes, so be it," Miles responded, not retreating. The redhead stepped forward and braced herself, locking his left elbow in an arm bar, putting on the pressure.

"Five minutes, right?" Miles added desperately as the pressure mounted. Her stare scorched his profile. He licked his lips, closed his eyes, held his breath, and waited. The pressure reached critical—he rose on his toes . . .

She released him abruptly, so that he staggered. "Men," she commented disgustedly. "Always gotta make everything a peeing contest."

"Biology is Destiny," gasped Miles, popping his eyes back open.

"—or are you some kind of pervert—do you get off on being beaten up by women?"

God, I hope not. He remained unbetrayed by unauthorized salutes from his nether parts, just barely. If he was going to be around that redhead much he was definitely going to have to get his pants back somehow. "If I said yes, would you refrain, just to punish me?" he offered.

"Shit, no."

"It was just a thought—"

"Cut the crap, Beatrice," said the patrol leader. At a jerk of her head the redhead stepped back into formation. "All right, runt, you've got your five minutes. Maybe."

"Thank you, ma'am." Miles took a breath, and reordered himself as best he could with no uniform to adjust. "First, let me apologize for intruding upon your privacy in this undress. Practically the first persons I met upon entering this camp were a self-help group—they helped themselves to my clothes, among other things—"

"I saw that," confirmed Beatrice-the-redhead unexpectedly. "Pitt's bunch."

Miles pulled off his hat and swept her a bow with it. "Yes, thank you."

"You moon people behind you when you do that," she commented dispassionately.

"That's their look-out," responded Miles. "For myself, I want to talk to your leader, or leaders. I have a serious plan for improving the tone of this place with which I wish to invite your group to collaborate. Bluntly, you are the largest remaining pocket of civilization, not to mention military order, in here. I'd like to see you expand your borders."

"It takes everything we've got to keep our borders from being overrun, son," replied the leader. "No can do. So take yourself off."

"Jack yourself off, too," suggested Beatrice. "You ain't gettin' any in here."

Miles sighed, and turned his hat around in his hands by its wide brim. He spun it for a moment on one finger, and locked eyes with the redhead. "Note my hat. It was the one garment I managed to keep from the ravages of the burly surly brothers—Pitt's bunch, you say."

She snorted at the turn of phrase. "Those jerks . . . why just a hat? Why not pants? Why not a full-dress uniform while you're at it?" she added sarcastically.

"A hat is a more useful object for communicating. You can make broad gestures," he did so, "denote sincerity," he held it over his heart, "or indicate embarrassment," over his genitals, with a hang-dog crouch, "or rage—" he flung it to earth as if he might drive it into the ground, then picked it up and brushed it off carefully, "or determination—" he jammed it on his head and yanked the brim down over his eyes, "or make courtesies." He swept it off again in salute to her. "Do you see the hat?"

She was beginning to be amused. "Yes . . ."

"Do you see the feathers on the hat?"

"Yes . . ."

"Describe them."

"Oh—plumey things."

"How many?"

"Two. Bunched together."

"Do you see the color of the feathers?"

She drew back, suddenly self-conscious again, with a sidewise glance at her companions. "No."

"When you can see the color of the feathers," said Miles softly, "you'll also understand how you can expand your borders to infinity."

She was silent, her face closed and locked. But the patrol leader muttered, "Maybe this little runt better talk to Tris. Just this once."

The woman in charge had clearly been a front line trooper once, not a tech like the majority of the females. She had certainly not acquired the muscles that flowed like braided leather cords beneath her skin from crouching by the hour in front of a holovid display in some rear-echelon underground post. She had toted the real weapons that spat real death, and sometimes broke down; had rammed against the limits of what could really be done by flesh and bone and metal, and been marked by that deforming press. Illusion had been burned out of her like an infection, leaving a cauterized scar. Rage burned permanently in her eyes like a fire in a coal seam, underground and unquenchable. She might be thirty-five, or forty.

God, I'm in love, thought Miles. *Brother Miles wants YOU for the Reformation Army* . . . then got hold of his thoughts. Here, now, was the make-or-break point for his scheme, and all the persiflage, verbal misdirection, charm, chutzpah, and bullshit he could muster weren't going to be enough, not even tied up with a big blue bow.

The wounded want power, nothing else; they think it will keep them from being hurt again. This one will not be interested in Suegar's strange message—at least, not yet. . . . Miles took a deep breath.

"Ma'am, I'm here to offer you command of this camp."

She stared at him as if he were something she'd found growing on the walls in a dark corner of the latrine. Her eyes raked over his nudity; Miles could feel the claw marks glowing from his chin to his toes.

"Which you store in your duffel bag, no doubt," she growled. "Command of this camp doesn't exist, mutant. So it's not yours to give. Deliver him to our perimeter in pieces, Beatrice."

He ducked the redhead. He would pursue correction of the mutant business later. "Command of this camp is mine to *create,*" he asserted. "Note, please, that what I offer is power, not revenge. Revenge is too expensive a luxury. Commanders can't afford it."

Tris uncoiled from her sleeping mat to her full height, then had to bend her knees to bring her face level to his, hissing. "Too bad, little turd. You almost interest me. Because I *want* revenge. On every man in this camp."

"Then the Cetagandans have succeeded; you've forgotten who your real enemy is."

"Say, rather, that I've discovered who my real enemy is. Do you want to know the things they've done to us—our own guys—"

"The Cetagandans want you to believe this," a wave of his hand embraced the camp, "is something you're doing to each other. So fighting each other, you become their puppets. They watch you all the time, you know, voyeurs of your humiliation."

Her glance flicked upward, infinitesimally; good. It was almost a disease among these people, that they would look in any direction at all in preference to up at the dome.

"Power is better than revenge," suggested Miles, not flinching before her snake-cold, set face, her hot coal eyes. "Power is a live thing, by which you reach out to grasp the future. Revenge is a dead thing, reaching out from the past to grasp you."

"—and you're a bullshit artist," she interrupted, "reaching out to grasp whatever's going down. I've got you pegged now. *This* is power." She flexed her arm under his nose, muscles coiling and loosing. "This is the only power that exists in here. You haven't got it, and you're looking for some to cover your ass. But you've come to the wrong store."

"No," Miles denied, and tapped his forehead. *"This* is power. And I own the store. This controls that," he slapped his bunched fist. "Men may move mountains, but ideas move men. Minds can be reached through bodies—what else is the point of all this," he waved at the camp, "but to reach your minds through your bodies. But that power flows both ways, and the outflow is the stronger tide.

"When you have allowed the Cetagandans to reduce your power to *that* alone," he squeezed her bicep for emphasis—it was like squeezing a rock covered in velvet, and she tensed, enraged at the liberty, "then you have allowed them to reduce you to your weakest part. And they win."

"They win anyway," she snapped, shrugging him off. He breathed relief that she hadn't chosen to break his arm. "Nothing that we do within this circle will result in any net change. We're still prisoners, whatever we do. They can cut off the food, or the damn air, or squeeze us to mush. And time's on their side. If we spill our guts restoring order—if that's what you're trying to work up to—all they have to do is wait for it to break down again. We're *beaten*. We're *taken*. There's nobody left *out there.* We're here forever. And you'd better start getting used to the idea."

"I've heard that song before," said Miles. "Use your head. If they meant to keep you forever, they could have incinerated you at the start, and saved the considerable expense of operating this camp. No. It's your minds they want. You are all here because you were Marilac's best and brightest, the hardest fighters, the strongest, baddest, most dangerous. The ones any potential resisters to the occupation would look to for leadership. It's the Cetagandans' plan to break you, and then return you to your world like little innoculated infections, counseling surrender to your people.

"When this is killed," he touched her forehead, oh so lightly, "then the Cetagandans have nothing more to fear from this," one finger on her bicep, "and you will all go free. To a world whose horizon will encircle you just like this dome, and just as inescapably. The war's not over. You are *here* because the Cetagandans are still waiting for the surrender of Fallow Core."

He thought for a moment she might murder him, strangle him on the spot. She must certainly prefer ripping him apart to letting him see her weep.

She regained her protective bitter tension with a toss of her head, a gulp of air. "If that's true, then following you puts us farther from freedom, not closer."

Damn, a logician to boot. She didn't have to pound him, she could parse him to death if he didn't scramble. He scrambled. "There is a subtle difference between being a prisoner and being a slave. I don't mistake either for being free. Neither do you."

She fell silent, staring at him through slitted eyes, pulling unconsciously on her lower lip. "You're an odd one," she said at last. "Why do you say 'you' and not 'we'?"

Miles shrugged casually. Blast—he rapidly reviewed his pitch—she was right, he had. A little too close to the edge, there. He might yet make an opportunity of the mistake, though. "Do I look like the flower of Marilac's military might? I'm an outsider, trapped in a world I never made. A traveller—a pilgrim—just passing through. Ask Suegar."

She snorted. "That loonie."

She'd missed the catch. Rats, as Elli would say. He missed Elli. Try again later. "Don't discount Suegar. He has a message for you. I found it fascinating."

"I've heard it. I find it irritating. . . . So, what do you want out of this? And don't tell me 'nothing,' 'cause I won't believe you. Frankly, I think you're after command of the camp yourself, and I'm not volunteering to be your stepping stone in some empire-building scheme."

She was thinking at speed now, and constructively, actually following out trains of thought besides that of having him removed to her border in bits. He was getting warmer. . . .

"I only wish to be your spiritual advisor. I do not want—indeed, can't use—command. Just an advisor."

It must have been something about the term "advisor" that clicked, some old association of hers. Her eyes flicked fully open suddenly. He was close enough to see her pupils dilate. She leaned forward, and her index finger traced the faint indentations on his face beside his nose caused by certain control leads in a space armor helmet. She straightened again, and her first two fingers in a V caressed the deeper marks permanently flanking her own nose. "What did you say you were, before?"

"A clerk. Recruiting office," Miles replied sturdily.

"I . . . see."

And if what she saw was the absurdity of someone claiming to be a rear-echelon clerk having worn combat armor often and long enough to have picked up its stigmata, he was in. Maybe.

She coiled herself back on her sleeping mat, and gestured toward its other end. "Sit down, chaplain. And keep talking."

Suegar was genuinely asleep when Miles found him again, sitting up cross-legged and snoring. Miles tapped him on the shoulder.

"Wake up, Suegar, we're home."

He snorted to consciousness. "God, I miss coffee. Huh?" He blinked at Miles. "You're still in one piece?"

"It was a near thing. Look, this garments-in-the-river bit—now that we've found each other, do we have to go *on* being naked? Or is the prophecy sufficiently fulfilled?"

"Huh?"

"Can we get dressed now?" Miles repeated patiently.

"Why—I don't know. I suppose, if we were meant to have clothes, they'd be given to us—"

Miles prodded and pointed. "There. They're given to us."

Beatrice stood a few meters away in a hip-shot pose of bored exasperation, a bundle of grey cloth under her arm. "You two loonies want this stuff or not? I'm going back."

"You got them to give you clothes?" Suegar whispered in amazement.

"Us, Suegar, us." Miles motioned to Beatrice. "I think it's all right."

She fired the bundle at him, sniffed, and stalked away.

"Thanks," Miles called. He shook out the fabric. Two sets of grey pajamas, one small, one large. Miles had only to turn up the bottoms of the pants legs one fold to keep them from catching under his heels. They were stained and stiff with old sweat and dirt, and had probably been peeled off a corpse, Miles reflected. Suegar crawled into his and stood fingering the grey fabric in wonder.

"They gave us clothes. *Gave* us," he muttered. "How'd you do that?"

"They gave us everything, Suegar. Come on, I've got to talk to Oliver again." Miles dragged Suegar off determinedly. "I wonder how much time we've actually got before the next chow call? Two in each twenty-four-hour cycle, to be sure, but I wouldn't be surprised if it's irregular, to increase your temporal disorientation—after all, it's the only clock in here . . ."

Movement caught Miles's eye, a man running. It wasn't the occasional flurry of someone outrunning a hostile group; this one just ran, head down, flat out, bare feet thumping the dirt in frantic rhythm. He followed the perimeter generally, except for a detour around the border of the women's group. As he ran, he wept.

"What's this?" Miles asked Suegar, with a nod at the approaching figure.

Suegar shrugged. "It takes you like that sometimes. When you can't stand sitting in here any more. I saw a guy run till he died, once. Around and around and around . . ."

"Well," Miles decided, "this one's running to us."

"He's gonna be running away from us in a second . . ."

"Then help me catch him."

Miles hit him low and Suegar high. Suegar sat on his chest. Miles sat on his right arm, halving his effective resistance. He must have been a very young soldier when he was captured—maybe he had lied about his age at induction—for even now he had a boy's face, ravaged by tears and his personal eternity inside this hollow pearl. He inhaled in sobbing gasps and exhaled in garbled obscenities. After a time he quieted.

Miles leaned into his face and grinned wolfishly. "You a party animal, boy?"

"Yeah . . ." his white-rimmed eyes rolled, right and left, but no rescue approached.

"How 'bout your friends? They party animals too?"

"The best," the boy asserted, perhaps secretly shaken by the suspicion that he'd fallen into the hands of someone even crazier than himself. "You better clear off me, mutant, or they'll take you apart."

"I want to invite you and your friends to a *major* party," Miles chanted. "We gonna have a party tonight that's an his-tor-i-cal event. You know where to find Sergeant Oliver, late of the 14th Commandos?"

"Yeah . . ." the boy admitted cautiously.

"Well, you go get your friends and report to him. You better reserve your seat aboard his ve-hic-le now, 'cause if you're not on it, you gonna be *under* it. The Reformation Army is moving out. You copy?"

"Copy," he gasped, as Suegar pressed his fist into the boy's solar plexus for emphasis.

"Tell him Brother Miles sent you," Miles called as the boy staggered off, glancing nervously over his shoulder. "You can't hide in here. If you don't show, I'll send the Cosmic Commandos to find you."

Suegar shook out his cramped limbs, his new used clothes. "Think he'll come?"

Miles grinned. "Fight or flight. That one'll be all right." He stretched himself, recaptured his original orientation. "Oliver."

In the end they had not twenty, but 200. Oliver had picked up forty-six. The running boy brought in eighteen. The signs of order and activity in the area brought in the curious—a drifter at the edge of the group had only to ask, "What's going on?" to be inducted and promoted to corporal on the spot. Interest among the spectators was aroused to a fever when Oliver's troops marched up to the women's border—and were admitted within. They picked up another seventy-five volunteers instantly.

"Do you know what's going on?" Miles asked one such, as he fed them through a short gauntlet of inspection and sent them off to one of the fourteen command groups he had devised.

"No," the man admitted. He waved an arm eagerly toward the center of the women's group. "But I wanta go where *they're* going . . ."

Miles cut the admissions off at 200 total in deference to Tris's growing nervousness at this infiltration of her borders, and promptly turned the courtesy into a card in his own hand in their still-continuing strategy debate. Tris wanted to divide her group in the usual way, half for the attack, half to maintain home base and keep the borders from collapsing. Miles was insisting on an all-out effort.

"If we win, you won't need guards anymore."

"What if we lose?"

Miles lowered his voice. "We don't dare lose. This is the only time we'll have surprise on our side. Yes, we can fall back—re-group—try again—I for one am prepared—no, compelled—to keep trying till it kills me. But after this, what we're trying to do will be fully apparent to any counter-group, and they'll have time to plan counter-strategies of their own. I have a particular aversion to stalemates. I prefer winning wars to prolonging them."

She sighed, momentarily drained, tired, old. "I've been at war a long time, y'know? After a while even losing a war can start to look preferable to prolonging it."

He could feel his own resolve slip, sucked into the vortex of that same black doubt. He pointed upwards, dropping his voice to a rasping whisper. "But not, surely, to *those* bastards."

She glanced upwards. Her shoulders straightened. "No. Not to those . . ." She took a deep breath. "All right, chaplain. You'll get your all-out effort. Just once . . ."

Oliver returned from a circuit of the command groups and squatted beside them. "They've got their orders. How many's Tris contributing to each group?"

"Commandant Tris," Miles quickly corrected for her as her brows beetled. "It's gonna be an all-out shot. You'll get every walking body in here."

Oliver made a quick calculation in the dirt with his finger for a stylus. "That'll put about fifty in each group—ought to be enough . . . matter of fact, what say we set up twenty groups? It'll speed distribution when we get the lines set up. Could make the difference between bringing this off, and not."

"No," Miles cut in quickly as Tris began to nod agreement. "It has to be fourteen. Fourteen battle groups make fourteen lines for fourteen piles. Fourteen is—is a theologically significant number," he added as they stared doubtfully at him.

"Why?" asked Tris.

"For the fourteen apostles," Miles intoned, tenting his hands piously.

Tris shrugged. Suegar scratched his head, started to speak—Miles speared him with a baleful glance, and he stilled.

Oliver eyed him narrowly. "Huh." But he did not argue further.

Then came the waiting. Miles stopped worrying about his uppermost fear—that their captors would introduce the next food pile early, before his plans were in place—and started worrying about his second greatest fear, that the food pile would come so late he'd lose control of his troops and they would start to wander off, bored and discouraged. Getting them all assembled had made Miles feel like a man pulling on a goat with a rope made of water. Never had the insubstantial nature of the Idea seemed more self-apparent.

Oliver tapped him on the shoulder and pointed. "Here we go . . ."

A side of the dome about a third of the way around the edge from them began to bulge inward.

The timing was perfect. His troops were at the peak of readiness. Too perfect . . . the Centagandans had been watching all this, surely they wouldn't miss an opportunity to make life more difficult

for their prisoners. If the food pile wasn't early, it had to be late.
Or . . .

Miles bounded to his feet, screaming. "Wait! Wait! Wait for my
order!"

His sprint groups wavered, drawn toward the anticipated goal. But
Oliver had chosen his group commanders well—they held, and held
their groups, and looked to Oliver. They *had* been soldiers once.
Oliver looked to Tris, flanked by her lieutenant Beatrice, and Tris
looked to Miles, angrily.

"What is it now? We're gonna lose our advantage . . ." she began,
as the general stampede throughout the camp started toward the
bulge.

"If I'm wrong," Miles moaned, "I'm going to kill myself—wait,
dammit! On my order. I can't see—Suegar, give me a boost—" He
clambered up on the thin man's shoulders and stared toward the
bulge. The force wall had only half twinkled out when the first
distant cries of disappointment met his straining ears. Miles's head
swivelled frantically. How many wheels within wheels—if the Cetagandans knew, and he knew they knew, and they knew he knew they
knew, and . . . He cut off his internal gibber as a second bulge
began, on the opposite side of the camp from the first.

Miles's arm flung out, pointing toward it like a man rolling dice.
"There! There! Go, go go!"

Tris caught on then, whistling and shooting him a look of startled
respect, before whirling and dashing off to double-time the main
body of their troops after the sprint groups. Miles slithered off Suegar
and started limping after.

He glanced back over his shoulder, as the rolling grey mass of
humanity crashed up against the opposite side of the dome and
reversed itself. He felt suddenly like a man trying to outrun a tidal
wave. He indulged himself with one brief anticipatory whimper, and
limped faster.

One more chance to be mortally wrong—no. His sprint groups had
reached the pile, and the pile was really there. Already they were
starting to break it down. The support troops surrounded them with
a wall of bodies as they began to spread out along the perimeter of
the dome. The Cetagandans had outfoxed themselves. This time.

Miles was reduced from the commander's eagle overview to the
grunt's worm's-eye as the tidal wave overtook him. Someone shoved
him from behind, and his face hit the dirt. He thought he recognized
the back of the surly Pitt, vaulting over him, but he wasn't certain—
surly Pitt would have stepped on, not over him. Suegar yanked him

up by the left arm, and Miles bit back a scream of pain. There was enough howling already.

Miles recognized the running boy, squaring off with another tough. Miles shoved past him with a shouted reminder—"You're supposed to be yelling *Get in line!*, NOT *Get fucked!* . . . The signal always gets degraded in combat," he muttered to himself. "Always . . ."

Beatrice materialized beside him. Miles clung to her instantly. Beatrice had personal space, her own private perimeter, maintained even as Miles watched, by a casual elbow to somebody's jaw with a quite sickening crack. If he tried that, Miles reflected enviously, not only would he smash his own elbow, but his opponent's nipple would probably be quite undamaged. Speaking of nipples, he found himself face to—well, not face—confronting the redhead. He resisted the urge to cuddle into the soft grey fabric covering home base with a contented sigh on the grounds that it would certainly get both his arms broken. He uncrossed his eyes and looked up into her face.

"C'mon," she said, and dragged him off through the mob. Was the noise level dropping? The human wall of his own troops parted just enough to let them squeeze through.

They were near the exit point of the chow line. It was working, by God it was working. The fourteen command groups, still bunched rather too closely along the dome wall—but that could be improved next run—were admitting the hungry supplicants one at a time. The expediters kept the lines moving at top speed, and channeled the already-supplied along the perimeter behind the human shield wall in a steady stream, to flow back out into the larger camp at the edge of the mob. Oliver had put his toughest-looking bravos to work in pairs, patrolling the outflow and making sure no one's rat bar was taken by force.

It was a long time since anyone here had had a chance to be a hero. Not a few of the newly-appointed policemen were approaching their work with great enthusiasm—maybe some personal grudges being worked off there—Miles recognized one of the burly surlys prone beneath a pair of patrollers, apparently getting his face beaten in. Miles, remembering what he was about, tried not to find music in the meaty thunks of fist on flesh.

Miles and Beatrice and Suegar bucked the stream of rat bar-clutching prisoners back toward the distribution piles. With a slightly regretful sigh, Miles sought out Oliver and dispatched him to the exit to restore order among his order-keepers.

Tris had the distribution piles and their immediate lines under tight control. Miles congratulated himself on having the women hand out the food. He had definitely tuned into a deep emotional resonance there. Not a few of the prisoners even muttered a sheepish "thank you" as their rat bars were shoved into their hands, and so did the ones in line behind them, when their turns came.

Nyah! Miles thought upward to the bland and silent dome. *You don't have the monopoly on psychological warfare any more, you bastards. We're gonna reverse your peristalsis, and I hope you barf your bowels out—*

An altercation at one of the food piles interrupted his meditations. Miles's lip curled with annoyance as he saw Pitt in the middle of it. He limped hastily toward it.

Pitt, it appeared, had repaid his rat bar not with a "thank you" but with a leer, a jeer, and a filthy remark. At least three of the women within hearing were trying to rip him apart, without success; he was big and beefy and had no inhibitions about fighting back. One of the females, not much taller than Miles himself, was knocked back in a heap and didn't get up again. In the meantime, the line was jammed, and the smooth civilized flow of would-be diners totally disrupted. Miles cursed under his breath.

"You, you, you, and—you," Miles tapped shoulders, "grab that guy. Get him out of here—back to the dome wall—"

Miles's draftees were not terribly pleased with their assignment, but by this time Tris and Beatrice had run up and led the attack with rather more science. Pitt was seized and pulled away, behind the lines. Miles made sure the rat bar distribution pile was running again before turning his attention to the savage, foul-mouthed Pitt. Oliver and Suegar had joined him by this time.

"I'm gonna rip the bastard's balls off," Tris was saying. "I command—"

"A military command," Miles interrupted. "If this one is accused of disorderly conduct, you should court martial him."

"He is a rapist and a murderer," she replied icily. "Execution's too good for him. He's got to die *slowly*."

Miles pulled Suegar aside. "It's tempting, but I feel real uneasy about handing him over to her just now. And yet . . . real uneasy. Why is that?"

Suegar eyed him respectfully. "I think you're right. You see, there's —there's too many guilty."

Pitt, now in a foaming fury, spotted Miles. "You! You little cunt-licking wimp—you think *they* can protect you?" He jerked his head toward Tris and Beatrice. "They ain't got the muscle. We've run 'em over before and we'll run 'em over again. We wouldn'ta lost the damn war if we'd had real soldiers—like the Barrayarans. They didn't fill their army with cunts and cunt-lickers. And they ran the Cetagandans right off their planet—"

"Somehow," Miles growled, drawn in, "I doubt you're an expert in the Barrayarans' defense of their homeworld in the First Cetagandan War. Or you might have learned something—"

"Did Tris make you an honorary girl, mutant?" jeered Pitt in return. "It wouldn't take much—"

Why am I standing here bandying words with this low-life crazy? Miles asked himself as Pitt raved on. *No time. Let's finish it.*

Miles stepped back and folded his arms. "Has it occurred to any of you yet that this man is clearly a Cetagandan agent?"

Even Pitt was shocked to silence.

"The evidence is plain," Miles went on forcefully, raising his voice so all bystanders could hear. "He is a ringleader in your disruption. By example and guile he has corrupted the honest soldiers around him, set them one against another. You were Marilac's best. The Cetagandans could not count on your fall. So they planted a seed of evil among you. Just to make sure. And it worked—wonderfully well. You never suspected—"

Oliver grabbed Miles's ear and muttered, "Brother Miles—I know this guy. He's no Cetagandan agent. He's just one of a whole lot of—"

"Oliver," Miles hissed back through clenched teeth, *"shut up."* And continued in his clearest parade-ground bellow, "Of course he's a Cetagandan spy. A mole. And all this time you thought this was something you were doing to *yourselves.*"

And where the devil does not exist, Miles thought to himself, *it may become expedient to invent him.* His stomach churned, but he kept his face set in righteous rage. He glanced at the faces around him. Not a few were as white as his must be, though for a different reason. A low mutter rose among them, partly bewildered, partly ominous.

"Pull off his shirt," Miles ordered, "and lay him down on his face. Suegar, give me your cup."

Suegar's plastic cup had a jagged point along its broken edge. Miles sat on Pitt's buttocks, and using the point as a stylus scratched the words

CETA

SPY

across Pitt's back in large print. He dug deep and ruthlessly, and the blood welled. Pitt screamed and swore and bucked.

Miles scrambled to his feet, shaking and breathless from more than just the physical exertion.

"Now," he ordered, "give him his rat bar and escort him to the exit."

Tris's teeth opened in objection, clicked back down. Her eyes burned into Pitt's back as he was hustled off. Her gaze turned rather more doubtfully to Miles, as she stood on one side of him and Oliver on the other.

"Do you really think he was a Cetagandan?" she asked Miles lowly.

"No way," scoffed Oliver. "What the hell's the charade all about, Brother Miles?"

"I don't doubt Tris's accusation of his other crimes," said Miles tightly. "You must know. But he couldn't be punished for them without dividing the camp, and so undermining Tris's authority. This way, Tris and the women have their revenge without half the men being set against them. The commandant's hands are clean, yet justice is done on a criminal, and a hard case who would doubtless be stockade bait outside is removed from under our feet. Furthermore, any like-minded souls are handed a warning they can't ignore. It works on every level."

Oliver's face had grown expressionless. After a silent moment he remarked, "You fight dirty, Brother Miles."

"I can't afford to lose." Miles shot him a black look from beneath his own lowered brows. "Can you?"

Oliver's lips tightened. "No."

Tris made no comment at all.

Miles personally oversaw the delivery of rat bars to all those prisoners too sick or weak or beaten to have attempted the chow line.

Colonel Tremont lay too still upon his mat, curled up, staring blankly. Oliver knelt and closed the drying, fixed eyes. The colonel might have died anytime in the last few hours.

"I'm sorry," said Miles sincerely. "Sorry I came so late."

"Well . . ." said Oliver, "well . . ." He stood, chewing on his lip, shook his head, and said no more. Miles and Suegar, Tris and Beatrice, helped Oliver carry the body, mat, clothes, cup and all, to the rubbish pile. Oliver shoved the rat bar he had reserved under the dead man's arm. No one attempted to strip the corpse after they had turned away, although another one stiffening there had already been so robbed, lying naked and tumbled.

They stumbled across Pitt's body shortly thereafter. The cause of death was most probably strangulation, but the face was so battered that its empurpling was not a certain clue.

Tris, squatting beside it, looked up at Miles in slow re-estimation. "I think you may be right about power after all, little man."

"And revenge?"

"I thought I could never get my fill of it," she sighed, contemplating the thing beside her. "Yeah . . . that too."

"Thank you." Miles prodded the body with his toe. "Make no mistake, *that* is a loss for our side."

Miles made Suegar let somebody else drag it to the rubbish pile.

Miles held a council of war immediately after chow call. Tremont's pallbearers, whom Miles had begun to think of as his general staff, and the fourteen group leaders gathered around him at a spot near the borders of the women's group. Miles paced back and forth before them, gesturing energetically.

"I commend the group leaders for an excellent job, and Sergeant Oliver for choosing them. By bringing this off, we have bought not only the allegiance of the greater part of the camp, but time as well. Each chow call after this should run a little easier, a little smoother, each become a real-life practice drill for the next.

"And make no mistake, this is a military exercise. We're at war again. We've already suckered the Cetagandans into breaking their carefully calculated routine and making a counter-move. We acted. They reacted. Strange as it may all seem to you, *we* had the offensive advantage.

"Now we start planning our next strategies. I want your thinking on what the next Cetagandan challenge will be." *Actually, I want you thinking, period.* "So much for the sermon—Commandant Tris, take over." Miles forced himself to sit down cross-legged, yielding the floor to his chosen one whether she wanted it or not. He reminded himself that Tris had been a field officer, not a staff officer; she needed the practice more than he did.

"Of course, they can send in short piles again, like they did before," she began after clearing her throat. "It's been suggested that's how this mess got started in the first place." Her glance crossed Miles's, who nodded encouragingly. "This means we're going to have to start keeping head counts, and work out a strict rotation schedule in advance of people to divide their rations with the short-changed. Each group leader must choose a quartermaster and a couple of accountants to double-check his count."

"An equally disruptive move the Cetagandans may try," Miles couldn't help putting in, "is to send in an overstock, giving us the interesting problem of how to equitably divide the extras. I'd provide for that, too, if I were you." He smiled blandly up at Tris.

She raised an eyebrow at him, and continued. "They may also try dividing the chow pile, complicating our problem of capturing it so as to strictly control its re-distribution. Are there any other really dirty tricks any of you can anticipate?" She couldn't help glancing at Miles.

One of the group leaders raised his hand hesitantly. "Ma'am—they're listening to all this. Aren't we doing their thinking for them?"

Miles rose to answer that one, loud and clear. "Of course they're listening. We've doubtless got their quivering attention." He made a rude gesture domewards. "Let them. Every move they make is a message from outside, a shadow marking their shape, information about them. We'll take it."

"Suppose," said another group leader even more hesitantly, "they cut off our air again? Permanently?"

"Then," said Miles smoothly, "they lose their hard-won position one-up on the IJC, which they've gone to enormous trouble to gain. It's a propaganda coup they've been making much of lately, particularly since our side, in the stress of the way things are going back home, hasn't been able to maintain its own troops in style, let alone any captured Cetagandans. The Cetagandans, whose published view is that they're sharing their Imperial government with us out of cultural generosity, are claiming this as a demonstration of their superior civilization and good manners—"

Some jeers and catcalls marked the prisoners' view of this assertion, and Miles smiled and went on. "The death rate reported for this camp is so extraordinary, it's caught the IJC's attention. The Cetagandans have managed to account for it so far, through three separate IJC inspections, but 100% would be a bit extreme even for them to justify." A shiver of agreement, compressed rage, ran through his rapt listeners.

Miles sat again. Oliver leaned over to him to whisper, "How the hell did you come by all that information?"

Miles smirked. "Did it sound convincing? Good."

Oliver sat back, looking unnerved. "You don't have any inhibitions at all, do you?"

"Not in combat."

Tris and her group leaders spent the next two hours laying out chow call scenario flow charts, and their tactical responses at each branching. They broke up to let the group leaders pass it on to their

chosen subordinates, and Oliver to his crew of supplementary Enforcers.

Tris paused before Miles, who had succumbed to gravity sometime
during the second hour and now lay in the dirt staring somewhat
blankly at the dome, blinking in an effort to keep his blurring eyes
open. He had not slept in the day and a half before entering this
place. He was not sure how much time had passed since then.

"I thought of one more scenario," Tris remarked. "What do we do
if they do nothing at all? Do nothing, change nothing."

Miles smiled sleepily. "It seems most probable. That attempted
double-cross on the last chow call was a slip on their part, I think."

"But in the absence of an enemy, how long can we go on pretending we're an army?" she persisted. "You scraped us up off the bottom
for this. When it runs down at last, what then?"

Miles curled up on his side, drowning in weird and shapeless
thoughts, and enticed by the hint of an erotic dream about a tall
aggressive redhead. His yawn cracked his face. "Then we pray for a
miracle. Remind me to discuss miracles with you . . . later. . . ."

He half-woke once when somebody shoved a sleeping mat under
him. He gave Beatrice a sleepy bedroom smile.

"Crazy mutant," she snarled at him, and rolled him roughly onto
the pad. "Don't you go thinking this was my idea."

"Why Suegar," Miles muttered, "I think she *likes* me." He cuddled
back into the entwining limbs of the dream-Beatrice in fleeting
peace.

To Miles's secret dismay, his analysis proved right. The Cetagandans returned to their original rat bar routine, unresponsive
again to their prisoners' internal permutations. Miles was not sure he
liked that. True, it gave him ample opportunity to fine-tune his distribution scheme. But some harassment from the dome would have
directed the prisoners' attention outward, given them a foe again,
above all broken the paralyzing boredom of their lives. In the long
run, Tris must prove right.

"I hate an enemy who doesn't make mistakes," Miles muttered
irritably, and flung his efforts into events he could control.

He found a phlegmatic prisoner with a steady heartbeat to lie in
the dirt and count his own pulse, and began timing distribution, and
then working on reducing timing.

"It's a spiritual exercise," he announced when he had his fourteen
quartermasters start issuing the rat bars 200 at a time, with thirty-
minute breaks between groups.

"It's a change of pace," he explained in an aside to Tris. "If we can't induce the Cetagandans to provide some variety, we'll just have to do it ourselves." He also finally got an accurate head count of the surviving prisoners. Miles was everywhere, exhorting, producing, pushing, restraining.

"If you really want it to go faster, make more bleeding piles," Oliver protested.

"Don't blaspheme," said Miles, and went to work inducing his groups to cart their rat bars away to distribution piles spaced evenly around the perimeter.

At the end of the nineteenth chow call since he had entered the camp, Miles judged his distribution system complete and theologically correct. Calling every two chow calls a "day," he had been there nine days.

"I'm all done," he realized with a groan, "and it's *too early.*"

"Weeping because you have no more worlds to conquer?" inquired Tris with a sarcastic grin.

By the thirty-second chow call, the system was still running smoothly, but Miles was getting frayed.

"Welcome to the long haul," said Beatrice dryly. "You better start pacing yourself, Brother Miles. If what Tris says is true, we're going to be in here even longer because of you. I must remember to thank you for that properly sometime." She treated him to a threatening smirk, and Miles prudently remembered an errand on the opposite side of the camp.

She was right, Miles thought, depressed. Most prisoners here counted their captivity not in days and weeks, but months and years. He himself was likely to be gibbering nuts in a space of time that most of them would regard as a mere breath. He wondered glumly what form his madness would take, Manic, inspired by the glittering delusion that he was—say—the Conquerer of Komarr? Or depressive, like Tremont, curling up in himself until he was no one at all, a sort of human black hole?

Miracles. There had been leaders throughout history who had been wrong in their timing for armageddon, leading their shorn flocks up the mountain to await an apotheosis that never came. Their later lives were usually marked by obscurity and drinking problems. Nothing to drink in here. Miles wanted about six doubles, right now.

Now. Now. Now.

Miles took to walking the dome perimeter after each chow call, partly to make or at least pretend to inspection, partly to burn off a little of his uncomfortably accumulating nervous energy. It was getting harder and harder to sleep. There had been a period of quiet in the camp after the chow calls were successfully regulated, as if their ordering had been a crystal dropped in a supersaturated solution. But in the last few days the number of fistfights broken up by the Enforcers had risen. The Enforcers themselves were getting quicker to violence, acquiring a potentially unsavory swagger. Phases of the moon. Who could outrace the moon?

"Slow down, Miles," complained Suegar, ambling along beside him.

"Sorry." Miles restrained his stride and broke his self-absorption to look around. The glowing dome rose on his left hand, seeming to pulse to an unsettling hum just out of the range of his hearing. Quiet spread out on his right, groups of people mostly sitting. Not that much visible change since his first day in here. Maybe a little less tension, maybe a little more concerted care being taken of the injured or ill. Phases of the moon. He shook off his unease and smiled cheerfully at Suegar.

"You getting any more positive responses to your sermons these days?" Miles asked.

"Well—nobody tries to beat me up anymore," said Suegar. "But then, I haven't been preaching so often, being busy with the chow calls and all. And then, there are the Enforcers now. It's hard to say."

"You going to keep trying?"

"Oh, yes." Suegar paused. "I've seen worse places than this, y'know. I was at a mining camp once, when I was scarcely more than a kid. A fire gem strike. For a change, instead of one big company or the government muscling in, it had gotten divided up into hundreds and hundreds of little claims, usually about two meters square. Guys dug out there by hand, with trowels and whisk brooms—big fire gems are delicate, y'know, they'll shatter at a careless blow—they dug under the broiling sun, day after day. A lot of these guys had less clothes than us now. A lot of 'em didn't eat as good, or as regular. Working their butts off. More accidents, more disease than here. There were fights, too, in plenty.

"But they lived for the future. Performed the most incredible feats of physical endurance for hope, all voluntary. They were obsessed. They were—well, you remind me a lot of them. They wouldn't quit for *nothing*. They turned a mountain into a chasm in a year, with hand trowels. It was nuts. I loved it.

"This place," Suegar glanced around, "just makes me scared shitless." His right hand touched his rag rope bracelet. "It'll suck up your future, swallow you down—it's like death is just a formality, after that. Zombie town, suicide city. The day I stop trying, this place'll eat me."

"Mm," agreed Miles. They were nearing what Miles thought of as the farthest point of their circuit, across the camp from the women's group at whose now-permeable borders Miles and Suegar kept their sleeping mats.

A couple of men walking the perimeter from the opposite direction coalesced with another grey-pajama'd pair. As if casually and spontaneously, three more arose from their mats on Miles's right. He could not be sure without turning his head, but Miles thought he caught more peripheral motion closing in behind him.

The approaching four stopped a few meters in front of them. Miles and Suegar hesitated. Grey-clad men, all variously larger than Miles —who wasn't?—frowning, full of a fierce tension that arced to Miles and scree'd down his nerves. Miles recognized only one of them, an ex-surly brother he'd seen in Pitt's company. Miles didn't bother taking his eyes off Pitt's lieutenant to look around for Enforcers. For one thing, he was pretty sure one of the men in the company facing them *was* an Enforcer.

And the worst of it was, getting cornered—if you could call it that in here—was his own fault, for letting his movements fall into a predictable daily routine. A stupid, basic, beginner's mistake, that; inexcusable.

Pitt's lieutenant stepped forward, chewing on his lip, staring at Miles with hollowed eyes. *He's psyching himself up,* Miles realized. *If all he wanted was to beat me to a pulp, he could do it in his sleep.* The man slid a carefully-braided rag rope through his fingers. A strangling cord . . . no, it wasn't going to be another beating. This time, it was going to be premeditated murder.

"You," said Pitt's lieutenant hoarsely. "I couldn't figure you out at first. You're not one of us. You could never have been one of us. Mutant . . . You gave me the clue yourself. Pitt wasn't a Ceta-gandan spy. *You* are!" And lunged forward.

Miles dodged, overwhelmed by onslaught and insight. Damn, he'd known there must be a good reason scragging Pitt that way had felt so much like a mistake despite its efficiency. The false accusation was two-edged, as dangerous to its wielder as its victim—Pitt's lieutenant might even believe *his* accusation true—Miles had started a witch-hunt. Poetic justice, that he be its first victim, but where would it end? No wonder their captors hadn't interfered lately. Their silent Cetagandan watchers must be falling off their station chairs laughing right now—mistake piled on mistake, culminating here by dying stupidly like vermin at the hands of vermin in this verminous hole. . . .

Hands grabbed him; he contorted spasmodically, kicking out, but only half-broke their hold. Beside him Suegar whirled, kicked, struck, shouted with demonic energy. He had reach, but lacked mass. Miles lacked both reach and mass. Still Suegar managed to break an assailant's hold on Miles for a moment.

Suegar's left arm, lashing out for a backhand blow, was caught and locked. Miles winced in sympathetic anticipation of the familiar muffled crack of breaking bones, but instead the man stripped off the rag rope bracelet from Suegar's wrist.

"Hey, Suegar!" the man taunted, dancing backward. "Look what I got!"

Suegar's head swivelled, his attention wrenched from his determined defense of Miles. The man peeled the wrinkled, tattered piece of paper from its cloth covering and waved it in the air. Suegar cried out in dismay and started to plunge toward him, but found himself blocked by two other bodies. The man tore the paper in half twice, then paused, as if momentarily puzzled how to dispose of it—then, with a sudden grin, stuffed the pieces in his mouth and started chewing. Suegar screamed.

"Dammit," cried Miles furiously, "it was me you wanted! You didn't have to do that—" He jammed his fist with all his strength into the smirking face of the nearest attacker, whose attention had been temporarily distracted by Suegar's show.

He could feel his bones shatter all the way back through his wrist. He was so damn *tired* of the bones, tired of being hurt again and again. . . .

Suegar was screaming and sobbing and trying to gain on the paper chewer, who stood and chewed on through his grin. Suegar had lost all science in his attack, flailing like a windmill. Miles saw him go down, then had no attention left for anything but the anaconda coil of the strangling cord, settling over his own neck. He managed to get one hand between the cord and his throat, but it was the broken one. Cables of pain shuddered up his arm, seeming to burrow under his skin all the way to his shoulder. The pressure in his head mounted to bursting, closing down his vision. Dark purple and yellow moire-patterned clouds boiled up in his eyes like thunder heads. A flashing brush of red hair sizzled past his tunneling vision. . . .

He was on the ground then, with blood, wonderful blood, thudding back into his oxygen-starved brain. It hurt good, hot and pulsing. He lay for a moment not caring about anything else. It would be so good not to have to get up again. . . .

The damn dome, cold and white and featureless, mocked his returning vision. Miles jerked onto his knees, staring around wildly. Beatrice, some Enforcers, and some of Oliver's commando buddies were chasing Miles's would-be assassins across the camp. Miles had probably only passed out for a few seconds. Suegar lay on the ground a couple of meters off.

Miles crawled over to Suegar. The thin man lay curled up around his stomach, his face pale green and clammy, involuntary shivers coursing through his body. Not good. Shocky. Keep patient warm and administer synergine. No synergine. Miles peeled clumsily out of his tunic and laid it over Suegar. "Suegar? You all right? Beatrice chased the barbarians off . . ."

Suegar looked up and smiled briefly, but the smile was reabsorbed almost immediately by distancing pain.

Beatrice came back eventually, mussed and breathing heavily. "You loonies," she greeted them dispassionately. "You don't need a bodyguard, you need a bloody keeper." She flopped onto her knees beside Miles to stare at Suegar. Her lips thinned to a white slit. She glanced at Miles, her eyes darkening, the creases between her brows deepening.

I've changed my mind, Miles thought. *Don't start caring for me, Beatrice, don't start caring for anybody. You'll only get hurt. Over and over and over . . .*

"You better come back to my group," said Beatrice.

"I don't think Suegar can walk."

Beatrice rounded up some muscle, and the thin man was rolled onto a sleeping mat and carried, too much like Colonel Tremont's corpse for Miles's taste, back to their now-usual sleeping place.

"Find a doctor for him," Miles demanded.

Beatrice came back, strong-arming an angry, older woman.

"He's probably got a busted belly," snarled the doctor. "If I had a diagnostic viewer, I could tell you just what was busted. You got a diagnostic viewer? He needs synergine and plasma. You got any? I could cut him, and glue him back together, and speed his healing with electra-stim, if I had an operating theatre. Put him back on his feet in three days, no sweat. You got an operating theatre? I thought not.

"Stop looking at me like that. I used to think I was a healer. It took this place to teach me I was nothing but an interface between the technology, and the patient. Now the technology is gone, and I'm just nothing."

"But what can we do?" asked Miles.

"Cover him up. In a few days he'll either get better or die, depending on what got busted. That's all." She paused, standing with folded arms and regarding Suegar with rancor, as if his injury was a personal affront. And so it was, for her: another load of grief and failure, grinding her hard-won healer's pride into the dirt. "I think he's going to die," she added.

"I think so too," said Miles.

"Then what did you want me for?" She stomped off.

Later she came back with a sleeping mat and a couple of extra rags, and helped put them around and over Suegar for added insulation, then stomped off again.

Tris reported to Miles. "We got those guys who tried to kill you rounded up. What do you want done with 'em?"

"Let them go," said Miles wearily. "They're not the enemy."

"The hell they're not!"

"They're not my enemies, anyway. It was just a case of mistaken identity. I'm just a hapless traveller, passing through."

"Wake up, little man. I don't happen to share Oliver's belief in your 'miracle.' You're not passing through here. This is the last stop."

Miles sighed. "I'm beginning to think you're right." He glanced at Suegar, breathing shallowly and too fast, beside whom he crouched in watch. "You're almost certainly right, by this time. Nevertheless— let them go."

"Why?" she wailed, outraged.

"Because I said to. Because I asked you to. Would you have me beg for them?"

"Aargh! No. All right!" She wheeled away, running he hands through her clipped hair and muttering under her breath.

A timeless time passed. Suegar lay on his side not speaking, though his eyes flicked open now and then to stare unseeing. Miles moistened his lips with water periodically. A chow call came and went without incident or Miles's participation; Beatrice passed by and dropped two rat bars beside them, stared at them with a carefully-hardened gaze of general disapproval, and stalked off.

Miles cradled his injured hand and sat cross-legged, mentally reviewing the catalogue of errors that had brought him to this pass. He contemplated his seeming genius for getting his friends killed. He had a sick premonition that Suegar's death was going to be almost as bad as Sergeant Bothari's, six years ago, and he had known Suegar only weeks, not years. Repeated pain, as he had reason to know, made one more afraid of injury, not less, a growing, gut-wrenching dread. Not again, never again . . .

He lay back and stared at the dome, the white, unblinking eye of a dead god. And had more friends than he knew already been killed by this megalomanic escapade? It would be just like the Cetagandans, to leave him in here all unknowing, and let the growing doubt and fear gradually drive him crazy.

Swiftly drive him crazy—the god's eye blinked.

Miles blinked in sympathetic nervous recoil, opened his eyes wide, stared at the dome as if his eyes could bore right through it. Had it blinked? Had the flicker been hallucinatory? Was he losing it?

It flickered again. Miles shot to his feet, inhaling, inhaling, inhaling.

The dome blinked out. For a brief instant, planetary night swept in, fog and drizzle and the kiss of a cold wet wind. This planet's unfiltered air smelled like rotten eggs. The unaccustomed dark was blinding.

"CHOW CALL!" Miles screamed at the top of his lungs.

Then limbo transmuted to chaos in the brilliant flash of a smart bomb going off beyond a cluster of buildings. Red light glared off the underside of an enormous billowing cloud of debris, blasting upward. A racketing string of similar hits encircled the camp, peeled back the night, deafened the unprotected. Miles, still screaming, could not hear his own voice. A returning fire from the ground clawed the clouds with lines of colored light.

Tris, her eyes stunned, rocketed past him. Miles grabbed her by the arm with his good hand and dug in his heels to brake her, yanking her down so he could scream in her ear.

"This is it! Get the fourteen group leaders organized, make 'em get their first blocks of 200 lined up and waiting all around the perimeter. Find Oliver, we've *got* to get the Enforcers moving to get the rest waiting their turn under control. If this goes exactly as we drilled it, we'll all get off." *I hope.* "But if they mob the shuttles like they used to mob the rat bar pile, none of us will. You copy?"

"I never believed—I didn't think—*shuttles?*"

"You don't have to think. We've drilled this fifty times. Just follow the chow drill. The *drill!*"

"You *sneaky* little sonofabitch!" The acknowledging wave of her arm, as she dashed off, was very like a salute.

A string of flares erupted in the sky above the camp, as if a white strobe of lightning went on and on, casting a ghastly illumination on the scene below. The camp seethed like a termite mound kicked over. Men and women were running every which way in shouting confusion. Not exactly the orderly vision Miles had had in mind— why, for example, had his people chosen a night drop and not a daytime one?—he would grill his staff later on that point, after he got done kissing their feet—

"Beatrice!" Miles waved her down. "Start passing the word! We're doing the chow call drill. But instead of a rat bar, each person gets a shuttle seat. Make 'em understand that—don't let anybody go haring off into the night or they'll miss their flight. Then come back here and stay by Suegar. I don't want him getting lost or trampled on. *Guard,* you copy?"

"I'm not a damn dog. What shuttles?"

The sound Miles's ears had been straining for penetrated the din at last, a high-pitched, multi-faceted whine that grew louder and louder. They loomed down out of the boiling scarlet-tinged clouds like monstrous beetles, carapaced and winged, feet extending even as they watched. Fully armored combat drop shuttles, two, three, six . . . seven, eight . . . Miles's lips moved as he counted. Thirteen, fourteen, by God. They *had* managed to get #B-7 out of the shop in time.

Miles pointed. *"My* shuttles."

Beatrice stood with her mouth open, staring upward. "My God. They're beautiful." He could almost see her mind start to ratchet forward. "But they're not *ours.* Not Cetagandan either. Who the hell . . . ?"

Miles bowed. "This is a paid political rescue."

"Mercenaries?"

"We're not something wriggling with too many legs that you found in your sleeping bag. The proper tone of voice is *Mercenaries!*—with a glad cry."

"But—but—but—"

"Go, dammit. Argue *later."*

She flung up her hands and ran.

Miles himself started tackling every person within reach, passing on the order of the day. He captured one of Oliver's tall commando buddies and demanded a boost on his shoulders. A quick look around showed fourteen coagulating knots of people in the mob scattered around the perimeter in nearly the right positions. The shuttles hovered, engines howling, then thumped to the ground one by one all around the camp.

"It'll have to do," Miles muttered to himself. He slapped the commando's shoulder. "Down."

He forced himself to walk to the nearest shuttle, a run on the shuttles being just the scenario he had poured out blood and bone and pride these last—three, four?—weeks to avoid.

A quartet of fully-armed and half-armored troops were the first down the shuttle ramp, taking up guard positions. Good. They even had their weapons pointed in the right direction, toward the prisoners they were here to rescue. A larger patrol, fully armored, followed to gallop off double time, leapfrogging their own covering-fire range into the dark toward the Cetagandan installations surrounding the dome circle. Hard to judge which direction held the most danger—from the continuing fireworks, his fighter shuttles were providing plenty of external distraction for the Cetagandans.

At last came the man Miles most wanted to see, the shuttle's comm officer.

"Lieutenant, uh," he connected face and name, "Murka! Over here!"

Murka spotted him. He fumbled excitedly with his equipment and called into his audio pick-up, "Commodore Tung! He's *here*, I *got* him!"

Miles peeled the comm set ruthlessly from the lieutenant's head, who obligingly ducked down to permit the theft, and jammed it on his own head left-handed in time to hear Tung's voice reply tinnily, "Well, for God's sake don't lose him again, Murka. Sit on him if you have to."

"I want my staff," called Miles into the pick-up. "Have you retrieved Elli and Elena yet? How much time have we got for this?"

"Yes, sir, no, and about two hours—if we're lucky," Tung's voice snapped back. "Good to have you back aboard, Admiral Naismith."

"You're telling me . . . Get Elena and Elli. Priority One."

"Working. Tung out."

Miles turned to find that the rat bar group leader in this section had actually succeeded in marshalling his first group of 200, and was engaged in making the second 200 sit back down in a block to wait their turns. Excellent. The prisoners were being channeled up the ramp one at a time through a strange gauntlet. A mercenary slit the back of each grey tunic with a swift slice from a vibra-knife. A second mercenary slapped each prisoner across the back with a medical stunner. A third made a pass with a surgical hand-tractor, roughly ripping out the Cetagandan serial numbers encoded beneath the skin. He didn't bother to waste time on bandaging after. "Go to the front and sit five across, go to the front and sit five across, go to the front . . ." he chanted, droning in time to his hypnotically moving device.

Miles's sometime-adjutant Captain Thorne appeared, hurrying out of the glare and black shadows, flanked by one of the fleet's ship's surgeons and—praise be—a soldier carrying some of Miles's clothes, and boots. Miles dove for the boots, but was captured instead by the surgeon.

She ran a med stunner between his bare uneven shoulderblades, and zipped a hand-tractor across in its path.

"Ow!" Miles yelped. "Couldn't you wait one bleeding second for the stun to cut in?" The pain faded rapidly to numbness as Miles's left hand patted for the damage. "What's this all about?"

"Sorry, sir," said the surgeon insincerely. "Stop that, your fingers are dirty." She applied a plastic bandage. Rank hath its privileges. "Captain Bothari-Jesek and Commander Quinn learned something from their fellow Cetagandan prison monitors that we hadn't known before you went in. These encodes are permeated with drug beads, whose lipid membranes are kept aligned by a low-power magnetic field the Cetagandans were generating in the dome. An hour out of the dome, and the membranes start to break down, releasing a poison. About four hours later the subject dies—very unpleasantly. A little insurance against escapes, I guess."

Miles shuddered, and said faintly, "I see." He cleared his throat, and added more loudly, "Captain Thorne, mark a commendation—with *highest* honors—to Commander Elli Quinn and Captain Elena Bothari-Jesek. The, ah, our employer's intelligence service didn't even have that one. In fact, our employer's intelligence data lacked on a truly vast number of points. I shall have to speak to them—sharply—when I present the bill for this expanded operation. Before you put that away, doctor, numb my hand, please." Miles stuck out his right hand for the surgeon's inspection.

"Did it again, did you?" muttered the surgeon. "I'd think you'd learn . . ." A pass with the medical stunner, and Miles's swollen hand disappeared from his senses entirely, nothing left from the wrist down. Only his eyes assured him it was still attached to his arm.

"Yes, but will they pay for the expanded operation?" asked Captain Thorne anxiously. "This started out as a one-shot lightning strike to hook out one guy, just the sort of thing little outfits like us specialize in—now it's straining the whole Dendarii fleet. These damn prisoners outnumber *us* two to one. This wasn't in the original contract. What if our perennial mystery employer decides to stiff us?"

"They won't," said Miles. "My word. But—there's no doubt I'll have to deliver the bill in person."

"God help them, then," muttered the surgeon, and took herself off to continue pulling encodes from the waiting prisoners.

Commodore Ky Tung, a squat, middle-aged Eurasian in half-armor and a command channel headset, turned up at Miles's elbow as the first shuttles loaded with prisoners clapped their locks shut and screamed up into the black fog. They took off in first-come first-served positions, no waiting. Knowing Tung's passion for tight formations, Miles judged time must be their most dangerous limiting factor.

"What are we loading these guys onto, upstairs?" Miles asked Tung.

"We gutted a couple of used freighters. We can cram about 5,000 in the holds of each. The ride out is going to be fast and nasty. They'll all have to lie down and breathe as little as possible."

"What are the Cetagandans scrambling to catch us?"

"Right now, barely more than some police shuttles. Most of their local space military contingent just happens to be on the other side of their sun just now, which is why we just happened to pick this moment to drop by . . . we had to wait for their practice maneuvers again, in case you were starting to wonder what was keeping us. In other words, the same scenario as our original plan to pull Colonel Tremont."

"Except expanded by a factor of 10,000. And we've got to get in— what, four lifts? instead of one," said Miles.

"Yeah, but get this," grinned Tung. "They sited these prison camps on this miserable outpost planet so's they wouldn't have to expend troops and equipment guarding them—counted on distance from Marilac, and the downgearing of the war there, to discourage rescue attempts. But in the period since you went in, half of their original guard complement has been pulled to other hot spots. Half!"

"They were relying on the dome." Miles eyed him. "And for the bad news?" he murmured.

Tung's smile soured. "This round, our total time window is only two hours."

"Ouch. Half their local space fleet is still too many. And they'll be back in two hours?"

"One hour, forty minutes, now." A sidewise flick of Tung's eyes betrayed the location of his ops clock, holovid-projected by his command headset into the air at a corner of his vision.

Miles did a calculation in his head, and lowered his voice. "Are we going to be able to lift the last load?"

"Depends on how fast we can lift the first three," said Tung. His ordinarily stoic face was more unreadable than ever, betraying neither hope nor fear.

Which depends in turn on how effectively I managed to drill them all . . . What was done was done; what was coming was not yet. Miles wrenched his attention to the immediate now.

"Have you found Elli and Elena yet?"

"I have three patrols out searching."

He hadn't found them yet. Miles's guts tightened. "I wouldn't have even attempted to expand this operation in midstream if I hadn't known they were monitoring me, and could translate all those oblique hints back into orders."

"Did they get 'em all right?" asked Tung. "We argued over some of their interpretations of your double-talk on the vids."

Miles glanced around. "They got 'em right . . . you got vids of all this?" A startled wave of Miles's hand took in the circle of the camp.

"Of you, anyway. Right off the Cetagandan monitors. They burst-transmitted them all daily. Very—er—entertaining, sir," Tung added blandly.

Some people would find entertainment in watching someone swallow slugs, Miles reflected. "Very dangerous . . . when was your last communication with them?"

"Yesterday." Tung's hand clamped on Miles's arm, restraining an involuntary leap. "You can't do better than my three patrols, sir, and I haven't any to spare to go looking for *you.*"

"Yah, yah." Miles slapped his right fist into his left palm in frustration before remembering that was a bad idea. His two co-agents, his vital link between the dome and the Dendarii, missing. The Cetagandans shot spies with depressing consistency. After, usually, a series of interrogations that rendered death a welcome release. . . . He tried to reassure himself with logic. If they'd blown their covers as Cetagandan monitor techs, and been interrogated, Tung would have run into a meat grinder here. He hadn't, ergo, they hadn't. Of course, they might have been killed by friendly fire, just now. . . . Friends. He had too many friends to stay sane in this crazy business.

"You," Miles retrieved his clothes from the still-waiting soldier, "go over there," he pointed, "and find a redhaired lady named Beatrice and an injured man named Suegar. Bring them to me. Carry him carefully, he has internal injuries."

The soldier saluted and marched off. Ah, the pleasure again of being able to give a command without having to follow it up with a supporting theological argument. Miles sighed. Exhaustion waited to swallow him, lurking at the edge of his adrenalin-spurred bubble of hyperconsciousness. All the factors—shuttles, timing, the approaching enemy, distance to the get-away jump point, formed and reformed in all their possible permutations in his mind. Small variations in timing in particular multiplied into major troubles. But he'd known it would be like this back when he'd started. A miracle they'd got this far. No—he glanced at Tung, at Thorne—not a miracle, but the extraordinary initiative and devotion of his people. *Well done, oh, well done. . . .*

Thorne helped him as he fumbled to dress himself one-handed. "Where the hell is my command headset?" Miles asked.

"We were told you were injured, sir, and in a state of exhaustion. You were scheduled for immediate evacuation."

"Damn presumptuous of somebody . . ." Miles bit back ire. No place in this schedule for running errands topside. Besides, if he had his headset, he'd be tempted to start giving orders, and he wasn't yet sufficiently briefed on the internal complexities of the operation from the Dendarii fleet's point of view. Miles swallowed his observer status without further comment. It did free him for rear guard.

Miles's batman reappeared, with Beatrice and four drafted prisoners, carrying Suegar on his mat to lay at Miles's feet.

"Get my surgeon," Miles said. His soldier obediently trotted off and found her. She knelt beside the semi-conscious Suegar and pulled the encode from his back. A knot of tension unwound in Miles's neck at the reassuring hiss of a hypospray of synergine.

"How bad?" Miles demanded.

"Not good," the surgeon admitted, checking her diagnostic viewer. "Burst spleen, oozing hemorrhage in the stomach—this one had better go direct to surgery on the command ship. Medtech—" she motioned to a Dendarii waiting with the guards for the return of the shuttle, and gave triage instructions. The medtech swathed Suegar in a thin foil heat wrap.

"I'll make sure he gets there," promised Miles. He shivered, envying the heat wrap a little as the drizzly acid fog beaded in his hair and coiled into his bones.

Tung's expression and attention were abruptly absorbed by a message from his comm set. Miles, who had yielded Lieutenant Murka's headset back to him so that he might continue his duties, shifted from foot to foot in agony for news. *Elena, Elli, if I've killed you . . .*

Tung spoke into his pick-up. "Good. Well done. Report to the A7

drop site." A jerk of his chin switched channels. "Sim, Nout, fall back
with your patrols to your shuttle drop site perimeters. They've been
found."

Miles found himself bent over with his hand supported on gelid
knees, waiting for his head to clear, his heart lurching in huge slow
gulps. "Elli and Elena? Are they all right?"

"They didn't call for a medtech . . . you sure you don't need one
yourself? You're green."

"I'm all right." Miles's heart steadied, and he straightened up, to
meet Beatrice's questing eyes. "Beatrice, would you please go get
Tris and Oliver for me? I need to talk to them before the next shuttle
relay goes up."

She shook her head helplessly and wheeled away. She did not
salute. On the other hand, she didn't argue, either. Miles was insensibly cheered.

The booming racket around the dome circle had died down to the
occasional whine of small-arms fire, human cry, or blurred amplified
voice. Fires burned in the distance, red-orange glows in the muffling
fog. Not a surgically clean operation . . . the Cetagandans were going to be extremely pissed when they'd counted their casualties,
Miles judged. Time to be gone, and long gone. He tried to keep the
poisoned encodes in mind, as anodyne to the vision of Cetagandan
clerks and techs crushed in the rubble of their burning buildings, but
the two nightmares seemed to amplify instead of cancelling each
other out.

Here came Tris and Oliver, both looking a little wild-eyed. Beatrice took up station at Tris's right shoulder.

"Congratulations," Miles began, before they could speak. He had a
lot of ground to cover and not much time left. "You have achieved an
army." A wave of his arm swept the orderly array of prisoners—ex-
prisoners—spread across the camp in their shuttle groups. They
waited quietly, most seated on the ground. Or was it the Cetagandans who had ingrained such patience in them? Whatever.

"Temporarily," said Tris. "This is the lull, I believe. If things hot up,
if you lose one or more shuttles, if somebody panics and it spreads—"

"You can tell anybody who's inclined to panic they can ride up with
me if it'll make them feel better. Ah—better also mention that I'm
going up in the *last* load," said Miles.

Tung, dividing his attention between this confab and his headset,
grimaced in exasperation at this news.

"That'll settle 'em," grinned Oliver.

"Give them something to think about, anyway," conceded Tris.

"Now I'm going to give you something to think about. The new Marilac resistance. You're it," said Miles. "My employer originally engaged me to rescue Colonel Tremont, that he might raise a new army and carry on the fight. When I found him . . . as he was, dying, I had to decide whether to follow the letter of my contract, and deliver a catatonic or a corpse, or the spirit—and deliver an army. I chose this, and I chose you two. *You* must carry on Colonel Tremont's work."

"I was only a field lieutenant," began Tris in horror, in chorus with Oliver's, "I'm a grunt, not a staff officer. Colonel Tremont was a genius—"

"You are his heirs now. *I* say so. Look around you. Do I make mistakes in choosing my subordinates?"

After a moment's silence Tris muttered, "Apparently not."

"Build yourselves a staff. Find your tactics geniuses, your technical wizards, and put 'em to work for you. But the drive, and the decisions, and the direction, must be yours, forged in this pit. It is you two who will remember this place, and so remember what it is you are doing, and why, always."

Oliver spoke quietly. "And when do we muster out of this army, Brother Miles? My time was up during the siege of Fallow Core. If I'd been anywhere else, I could have gone home."

"Until the Cetagandan army of occupation rolled down your street."

"Even then. The odds aren't good."

"The odds were worse for Barrayar, in its day, and they ran the Cetagandans right off. It took twenty years, and more blood than either of you have seen in your lives combined, but they did it," asserted Miles.

Oliver seemed more struck by this historical precedent than Tris, who said skeptically, "Barrayar had those crazy Vor warriors. Nuts who rushed into battle, who *liked* to die. Marilac just doesn't have that sort of cultural tradition. We're civilized—or we were, once. . . ."

"Let me tell you about the Barrayaran Vor," cut in Miles. "The loonies who sought a glorious death in battle found it very early on. This rapidly cleared the chain of command of the accumulated fools. The survivors were those who learned to fight dirty, and live, and fight another day, and win, and win, and win, and for whom nothing, not comfort or security, not family or friends or their immortal souls, was more important than winning. Dead men are losers by definition. Survival and victory. They weren't supermen, or immune to pain. They sweated in confusion and darkness. And with not one-half the physical resources Marilac possessed even now, they won. When you're Vor," Miles ran down a little, "there is no mustering out."

After a silence Tris said, "Even a volunteer patriotic army must eat. And we won't beat the Cetagandans by firing spitballs at them."

"There will be financial and military aid forthcoming through a covert channel other than myself. If there is a Resistance command to deliver it to."

Tris measured Oliver by eye. The fire in her burned closer to the surface than Miles had ever seen it, coursing down those corded muscles. The whine of the first returning shuttles pierced the fog. She spoke quite softly. "And here I thought I was the atheist, Sergeant, and you were the believer. Are you coming with me—or mustering out?"

Oliver's shoulders bowed. With the weight of history, Miles realized, not defeat, for the heat in his eyes matched Tris's. "Coming," he grunted.

Miles caught Tung's eyes. "How we doing?"

Tung shook his head, held up fingers. "About six minutes slow, unloading upstairs."

"Right." Miles turned back to Tris and Oliver. "I want you both to go up on this wave, in separate shuttles, one to each troopship. When you get there, start expediting the off-loading of your people. Lieutenant Murka will give you your shuttle assignment—" he motioned Murka over, and packed them off.

Beatrice lingered. "I'm inclined to panic," she informed Miles in a distant tone. Her bare toe smudged whorls in the dampening dirt.

"I don't need a bodyguard anymore," Miles said. He grinned. "A keeper, maybe . . ."

A smile lighted her eyes that did not yet reach her mouth. Later, Miles promised himself. Later, he would make that mouth laugh.

The second wave of shuttles began to lift, even as the remnants of the returning first wave were still landing. Miles prayed everyone's sensors were operating properly, passing each other in this fog. Their timing could only get more ragged from now on. The fog itself was coagulating into a cold rain, silver needles pelting down.

The focus of the operation was narrowing rapidly now, more of machines and numbers and timing, less of loyalties and souls and fearsome obligations. An emotionally pathological mind, devoid of love and fear, might even call it fun, Miles thought. He began jotting scores left-handed in the dirt, numbers up, down, in transit, remaining, but the dirt was turning to gluey black mud and did not retain the impressions.

"Shit," Tung hissed suddenly through clenched teeth. The air before his face blurred in a flurry of vid-projected incoming information, his eyes flicking through it with practiced rapidity. His right hand bunched and twitched, as if tempted to wrench off his headset and stamp it into the mud in frustration and disgust. "That tears it. We just lost two shuttles out of the second wave."

Which two? Miles's mind screamed. *Oliver, Tris* . . . He forced his first question to be, "How?" *I swear, if they crashed into each other, I'm going to go find a wall and beat my head on it till I go numb. . . .*

"Cetagandan fighter broke through our cordon. He was going for the troop freighters, but we nailed him in time. Almost in time."

"You got identifications on which two shuttles? And were they loaded or returning?"

Tung's lips moved in subvocalization. "A-4, fully loaded. B-7, returning empty. Loss total, no survivors. Fighter shuttle 5 from the *Triumph* is disabled by enemy fire; pilot recovery now in progress."

He hadn't lost his commanders. His hand-picked and carefully nurtured successors to Colonel Tremont were safe. He opened his eyes, squeezed shut in pain, to find Beatrice, to whom the shuttle IDs meant nothing, waiting anxiously for interpretation.

"Two hundred dead?" she whispered.

"Two hundred six," Miles corrected. The faces, names, voices of the six familiar Dendarii fluttered through his memory. The 200 ciphers must have had faces too. He blocked them out, as too crushing an overload.

"These things happen," Beatrice muttered numbly.

"You all right?"

"Of course I'm all right. These things happen. Inevitable. I am not a weepy wimp who folds under fire." She blinked rapidly, lifting her chin. "Give me . . . something to do. Anything."

Quickly, Miles added for her. *Right.* He pointed across the camp. "Got to Pel and Liant. Divide their remaining shuttle groups into blocks of thirty-three, and add them to each of the remaining third-wave shuttle groups. We'll have to send the third wave up overloaded. Then report back to me. Go quick, the rest will be back in minutes."

"Yessir," she saluted. For her sake, not his; for order, structure, rationality, a lifeline. He returned the salute gravely.

"They were already overloaded," objected Tung as soon as she was out of earshot. "They're going to fly like bricks with 233 squeezed on board. And they'll take longer to load on here and unload topside."

"Yes. God." Miles gave up scratching figures in the useless mud. "Run the numbers through the computer for me, Ky. I don't trust myself to add two and two just now. How far behind will we be by the time the main body of the Cetagandans comes in range? Come close as you can, no fudge factors, please."

Tung mumbled into his headset, reeled off numbers, margins, timing. Miles tracked every detail with predatory intensity. Tung concluded bluntly. "At the end of the last wave, five shuttles are still going to be waiting to unload when the Cetagandan fire fries us."

A thousand men and women . . .

"May I respectfully suggest, sir, that the time has come to start cutting our losses?" added Tung.

"You may, Commodore."

"Option One, maximally efficient; only drop seven shuttles in the last wave. Leave the last five shuttle loads of prisoners on the ground. They'll be re-taken, but at least they'll be alive." Tung's voice grew persuasive on this last line.

"Only one problem, Ky. *I* don't want to stay here."

"You can still be on the last shuttle up, just like you said. By the way, sir, have I expressed myself yet, sir, on what a genuinely dumb-shit piece of grandstanding that is?"

"Eloquently, with your eyebrows, a while ago. And while I'm inclined to agree with you, have you noticed yet how closely the remaining prisoners keep watching me? Have you ever watched a cat sneaking up on a horned hopper?"

Tung stirred uneasily, eyes taking in the phenomenon Miles described.

"I don't fancy gunning down the last thousand in order to get my shuttle into the air."

"Skewed as we are, they might not realize there were no more shuttles coming till after you were in the air."

"So we just leave them standing there, waiting for us?" *The sheep look up, but are not fed . . .*

"Right."

"You like that option, Ky?"

"Makes me want to puke, but—consider the 9,000 others. And the Dendarii fleet. The idea of dropping them all down the rat hole in a pre-doomed effort to pack up all these—miserable sinners of yours, makes me want to puke a lot more. Nine-tenths of a loaf is *much* better than none."

"Point taken. Let us go on to option two, please. The flight out of orbit is calculated on the speed of the slowest ship, which is . . . ?"

"The freighters."

"And the *Triumph* remains the swiftest?"

"Betcher ass." Tung had captained the *Triumph* once.

"And the best armored."

"Yo. So?" Tung saw perfectly well where he was being driven. His obtuseness was but a form of oblique balking.

"So. The first seven shuttles up on the last wave lock onto the troop freighters and boost on schedule. We call back five of the *Triumph*'s fighter pilots and dump and destroy their craft. One's damaged already, right? The last five of these drop shuttles clamp to the *Triumph* in their place, protected from the now-arriving fire of the Cetagandan ships by the *Triumph*'s full shielding. Pack the prisoners into the *Triumph*'s corridors, lock shuttle hatches, boost like hell."

"The added mass of a thousand people—"

"Would be less than that of a couple of the drop shuttles. Dump and blow them too, if you have to, to fit the mass/acceleration window."

"—would overload life support—"

"The emergency oxygen will take us to the wormhole jump point. After Jump the prisoners can be distributed among the other ships at our leisure."

Tung's voice grew anguished. "Those combat drop shuttles are *brand new*. And my fighters—*five* of them—do you realize how hard it will be to recoup the funds to replace 'em? It comes to—"

"I asked you to calculate the time, Ky, not the price tag," said Miles through his teeth. He added more quietly, "I'll tack them on to our bill for services rendered."

"You ever hear the term *cost overrun*, boy? You will. . . ." Tung switched his attention back to his headset, itself but an extension of the tactics room aboard the *Triumph*. Calculations were made, new orders entered and executed.

"It flies," sighed Tung. "Buys a damned expensive fifteen minutes. If nothing else goes wrong . . ." he trailed off in a frustrated mumble, as impatient as Miles himself with his inability to be three places at once.

"There comes my shuttle back," Tung noted aloud. He glanced at Miles, plainly unwilling to leave his admiral to his own devices, as plainly itching to be out of the acid rain and dark and mud and closer to the nerve center of operations.

"Get gone," said Miles. "You can't ride up with me anyway, it's against procedure."

"Procedure, hah," said Tung blackly.

With the lift-off of the third wave, there were barely 2,000 prisoners left on the ground. Things were thinning out, winding down; the armored combat patrols were falling back now from their penetration of the surrounding Cetagandan installations, back toward their assigned shuttle landing sites. A dangerous turning of the tide, should some surviving Cetagandan officer recover enough organization to harry their retreat.

"See you aboard the *Triumph*," Tung emphasized. He paused to brace Lieutenant Murka, out of Miles's earshot. Miles grinned in sympathy for the overworked lieutenant, in no doubt about the orders Tung was now laying on him. If Murka didn't come back with Miles in tow, he'd probably be wisest not to come back at all.

Nothing left now but a little last waiting. Hurry up and wait. Waiting, Miles realized, was very bad for him. It allowed his self-generated adrenalin to wear off, allowed him to feel how tired and hurt he really was. The illuminating flares were dying to a red glow.

There was really very little time between the fading of the labored thunder of the last third wave shuttle to depart, and the screaming whine of the first fourth-wave shuttle plunging back. Alas that this had more to do with being skewed than being swift. The Marilacans still waited in their rat bar blocks, discipline still holding. Of course, nobody'd told them about the little problem in timing they faced. But the nervous Dendarii patrols, chivvying them up the ramps, kept things moving at a pace to Miles's taste. Rear guard was never a popular position to draw, even among the lunatic fringe who defaced their weapons with notches and giggled among themselves while speculating upon newer and more grotesque methods of blowing away their enemies.

Miles saw the semi-conscious Suegar carried up the ramp first. Suegar would actually reach the *Triumph*'s sickbay faster in his company, Miles calculated, on this direct flight, than had he been sent on an earlier shuttle to one of the troop freighters and had to await a safe moment to transfer.

The arena they were leaving had grown silent and dark, sodden and sad, ghostly. *I will break the doors of hell, and bring up the dead* . . . there was something not quite right about the half-remembered quote. No matter.

This shuttle's armored patrol, the last, drew back out of the fog and darkness, electronically whistled in like a pack of sheepdogs by their master Murka, who stood at the foot of the ramp as liaison between the ground patrol and the shuttle pilot, who was expressing her anxiety to be gone with little whining revs on the engines.

Then from the darkness—plasma fire, sizzling through the rain-sodden, saturated air. Some Cetagandan hero—officer, troop, tech, who knew?—had crawled up out of the rubble and found a weapon—and an enemy to fire it at. Splintered afterimages, red and green, danced in Miles's eyes. A Dendarii patroller rolled out of the dark, a glowing line across the back of his armor smoking and sparking until quenched in the black mud. His armor legs seized up, and he lay wriggling like a frantic fish in an effort to peel out of it. A second plasma burst, ill-aimed, spent itself turning a few kilometers of fog and rain to superheated steam on a straight line to some unknown infinity.

Just what they needed, to be pinned down by sniper fire *now*. . . . A pair of Dendarii rear guards started back into the fog. An excited prisoner—ye gods, it was Pitt's lieutenant again—grabbed up the armor-paralyzed soldier's weapon and made to join them.

"No! Come back later and fight on your own time, you jerk!" Miles sloshed toward Murka. "Fall back, load up, get in the air! Don't stop to fight! No time!"

Some of the last of the prisoners had fallen flat to the ground, burrowing like mudpuppies, a sound sensible reflex in any other context. Miles dashed among them, slapping rumps. "Get *aboard,* up the *ramp,* go, go, go!" Beatrice popped up out of the mud and mimicked him, shakily driving her fellows before her.

Miles skidded to a stop beside his fallen Dendarii and snapped the armor clamps open left-handed. The soldier kicked off his fatal carapace, rolled to his feet, and limped for the safety of the shuttle. Miles ran close behind him.

Murka and one patrolman waited at the foot of the ramp.

"Get ready to pull in the ramp and lift on my mark," Murka began to the shuttle pilot. "R—" his words were lost in an explosive pop as the plasma beam sliced across his neck. Miles could feel the searing heat from it pass centimeters above his head as he stood next to his lieutenant. Murka's body crumpled.

Miles dodged, paused to yank off Murka's comm headset. The head came too. Miles had to brace it with his numb hand to pull the headset free. The weight of the head, its density and roundness, hammered into his senses. The precise memory of it would surely be with him until his dying day. He let it fall by Murka's body.

He staggered up the ramp, a last armored Dendarii pulling on his arm. He could feel the ramp sag peculiarly under their feet, glanced down to see a half-melted seam across it where the plasma arc that had killed Murka had passed on.

He fell through the hatchway, clutching the headset and yelling into it. "Lift, lift! Mark, now! Go!"

"Who is this?" came the shuttle pilot's voice back.

"Naismith."

"Yes, *sir.*"

The shuttle heaved off the ground, engines roaring, even before the ramp had withdrawn. The ramp mechanism labored, metal and plastic complaining—then jammed on the twisted distortion of the melt.

"Get that hatch sealed back there!" the shuttle pilot's voice yowled over the headset.

"Ramp's jammed," Miles yowled back. "Jettison it!"

The ramp mechanism skreeled and shrieked, reversing itself. The ramp shuddered, jammed again. Hands reached out to thump on it urgently. "You'll never get it that way!" Beatrice, across the hatch from Miles, yelled fiercely, and twisted around to kick at it with her bare feet. The wind of their flight screamed over the open hatchway, buffeting and vibrating the shuttle like a giant blowing across the top of a bottle.

To a chorus of shouting, thumping, and swearing, the shuttle lurched abruptly onto its side. Men, women, and loose equipment tangled across the tilting deck. Beatrice kicked bloodily at a final buggered bolt. The ramp tore loose at last. Beatrice, sliding, fell with it.

Miles dove at her, lunging across the hatchway. If he connected, he never knew, for his right hand was a senseless blob. He saw her face only as a white blur as she whipped away into the blackness.

It was like a silence, a great silence, in his head. Although the roar of wind and engines, screaming and swearing and yelling, went on as before, it was lost somewhere between his ears and his brain, and went unregistered. He saw only a white blur, smearing into the darkness, repeated again and again, replaying like a looping vid.

He found himself crouched on his hands and knees, the shuttle's acceleration sucking him to the deck. They'd gotten the hatch closed. The merely human babble within seemed muffled and thin, now that the roaring voices of the gods were silenced. He looked up into the pale face of Pitt's lieutenant, crouched beside him still clutching the unfired Dendarii weapon he'd grabbed up in that other lifetime.

"You'd better kill a whole lot of Cetagandans for Marilac, boy,"

Miles rasped to him at last. "You better be worth something to *some-body*, 'cause I've sure paid too much for you."

The Marilacan's face twitched uncertainly, too cowed even to try to look apologetic. Miles wondered what his own face must look like. From the reflection in that mirror, strange, very strange.

Miles began to crawl forward, looking for something, somebody. . . . Formless flashes made yellow streaks in the corners of his vision. An armored Dendarii, her helmet off, pulled him to his feet.

"Sir? Hadn't you better come forward to the pilot's compartment, sir?"

"Yes, all right . . ."

She got an arm around him, under his arm, so he didn't fall down again. They picked their way forward in the crowded shuttle, through Marilacans and Dendarii mixed. Faces were drawn to him, marked him fearfully, but none dared an expression of any kind. Miles's eye was caught by a silver cocoon, as they neared the forward end.

"Wait . . ."

He fell to his knees beside Suegar. A hit of hope . . . "Suegar. Hey, Suegar!"

Suegar opened his eyes to slits. No telling how much of this he was taking in, through the pain and the shock and the drugs.

"You're on your way now. We made it, made the timing. With all ease. With agility and speed. Up through the regions of the air, higher than the clouds. You had the scripture right, you did."

Suegar's lips moved. Miles bent his head closer.

". . . wasn't really a scripture," Suegar whispered. "I knew it . . . you knew it . . . don't shit me . . ."

Miles paused, cold-stoned. Then he leaned forward again. "No, brother," he whispered. "For though we went in clothed, we have surely come out naked."

Suegar's lips puffed on a dry laugh.

Miles didn't weep until after they'd made the wormhole jump.

4

Illyan sat silent.

Miles lay back, pale and exhausted, a stupid trembling concealed in his belly making his voice shake. "Sorry. Thought I'd got over it. So much craziness has happened since then, no time to think, digest. . . ."

"Combat fatigue," Illyan suggested.

"The combat only lasted a couple of hours."

"Ah? I'd reckon it at six weeks, by that account."

"Whatever. But if your Count Vorvolk wants to argue that I should have traded lives for equipment, well . . . I had maybe five minutes to make a decision, under enemy fire. If I'd had a month to study it, I'd have come to the same conclusion. And I'll stand behind it now, in a court martial or any goddamn arena he wants to fight me in."

"Calm down," Illyan advised. "*I* will deal with Vorvolk, and his shadow-advisors. I think . . . no, I *guarantee* their little plot will not intrude further on your recovery, Lieutenant Vorkosigan." His eyes glinted. Illyan had served thirty years in Imperial Security, Miles reminded himself. Aral Vorkosigan's Dog still had teeth.

"I'm sorry my . . . carelessness shook your confidence in me, sir," said Miles. It was an odd wound that doubt had dealt him; Miles could feel it still, an invisible ache in his chest, slow to heal. So, trust was more of a feedback loop than he had ever realized. Was Illyan right, should he pay more attention to appearances? "I'll try to be more intelligent in future."

Illyan gave him an indecipherable look, his mouth set, neck oddly flushed. "So shall I, Lieutenant."

The swish of the door, the sweep of skirts. Countess Vorkosigan was a tall woman, hair gone red-roan, with a stride that had never quite accommodated itself to Barrayaran female fashions. She wore the long rich skirts of a Vor-class matron as cheerfully as a child playing dress-up, and about as convincingly.

"M'lady," Illyan nodded, rising.

"Hello, Simon. Goodbye, Simon," she grinned back. "That doctor you spooked begs me to use my superior firepower to throw you out. I know you officers and gentlemen have business, but it's time to wrap it up. Or so the medical monitors indicate." She glanced at Miles. A frown flickered across her easy-going features, a hint of steel.

Illyan caught it too, and bowed. "We're quite finished, m'lady. No problem."

"So I trust." Chin lifted, she watched him out.

Miles, studying that steady profile, realized with a sudden lurch just why the death of a certain tall aggressive redhead might still be wringing his gut, long after his reconciliation to other casualties for which he was surely no less responsible. *Ha. How late we come to our insights. And how uselessly.* Still, a tightness eased in his throat as Countess Vorkosigan turned back to him.

"You look like a defrosted corpse, love." Her lips brushed his forehead warmly.

"Thank you, Mother," Miles chirped.

"That nice Commander Quinn who brought you in says you haven't been eating properly. As usual."

"Ah." Miles brightened. "Where is Quinn? Can I see her?"

"Not here. She is excluded from classified areas, to wit this Imperial Military Hospital, on the grounds of her being foreign military personnel. Barrayarans!" That was Captain Cordelia Naismith's (Betan Astronomical Survey, retired) favorite swear word, delivered with a multitude of inflections as the occasion demanded; this time with exasperation. "I took her to Vorkosigan House to wait."

"Thank you. I . . . owe a lot to Quinn."

"So I gather." She smiled at him. "You can be at the long lake three hours after you delude that doctor into releasing you from this dismal place. I've invited Commander Quinn along—there, I thought that might motivate you to pay more serious attention to recovery."

"Yes, *ma'am.*" Miles eased down into his covers. Sensation was beginning to return to his arms. Unfortunately, the sensation in question was pain. He smiled whitely. It was better than no sensation at all, oh yes.

"We will take turns, feeding and spoiling you," she envisioned. "And . . . you can tell me all about Earth."

"Ah . . . yes. I have a great deal to tell you about Earth."

"Rest, then." Another kiss, and she was gone.